To my wife, Edna

ACKNOWLEDGEMENTS

With special thanks to Stephen, for his continuing and untiring assistance and expertise. Also to Mrs Nel Mason, for her specialist knowledge and help.

Harry Bowling was born in Bermondsey, London, and left school at fourteen to supplement the family income as an office boy in a riverside provisions' merchant. Called up for National Service in the 1950s, he has since been variously employed as lorry driver, milkman, meat cutter, carpenter and decorator, and community worker. He now writes full time. He is the author of five previous novels, *Gaslight in Page Street*, *Paragon Place*, *Ironmonger's Daughter*, *Tuppence to Tooley Street* and *Conner Street's War*. He is married and lives with his family, dividing his time between Lancashire and Deptford.

Also by Harry Bowling

Gaslight in Page Street
Paragon Place
Ironmonger's Daughter
Tuppence to Tooley Street
Conner Street's War

The Girl from Cotton Lane

Harry Bowling

HEADLINE

First published in 1992
by HEADLINE BOOK PUBLISHING PLC

First published in paperback in 1992
by HEADLINE BOOK PUBLISHING PLC

10 9 8 7 6 5 4 3 2 1

ISBN 0 7472 3869 3

Phototypeset by Intype, London

Printed and bound in Great Britain by
HarperCollins Manufacturing, Glasgow

HEADLINE BOOK PUBLISHING PLC
Headline House
79 Great Titchfield Street
London W1P 7FN

1920

Chapter One

Fifteen months had passed since the end of the Great War, and now the docks and wharves of London were filling up with produce and commodities of all kinds. Along London's fast-flowing River Thames freighters and trampers were steaming in on every tide, and the jetties and berths echoed all day long with the sounds of wheeling cranes, dockers' shouts and curses, and the chugging of busy tugs. The dirty, oily waters of the river were lifeblood to the capital, and the steady throb of activity along its shores was as the living heart of London.

Cotton Lane in dockland Bermondsey was one of the many small cobbled streets which served the wharves, and it differed very little from other riverside throughways. It smelt of clay mud, petrol fumes and horse-dung, and it was narrow and grimy. It had got its name from the bales of jute which were once landed at its high wharves. A few low hovels that had once been homes to river people were now derelict, and an empty building which was once a sailmaker's and then a barge-builder's premises now stood empty after its last owner, a steam-traction engineer, foundered in the changing times. The cobbled lane boasted a pub, the Bargee, which the rivermen used, but it saw very few customers once the wharf gates clanged shut. Cotton Lane had a corner shop which was a favourite

3

eating-place of the rivermen and horse and motor drivers. The premises had recently been painted in a garish olive green and over the shopfront large gilt lettering announced it as 'Bradley's Dining Rooms'.

All day long the murky weather had held over the River Thames and as night closed in the February fog swirled out into the narrow cobbled lanes and backstreets of Bermondsey. It was more than an hour since the last of the horsecarts had clattered through Cotton Lane and now the fog was thickening. The sound of heavy boots in the street below faded and Carrie Bradley stretched out her stockinged feet towards the coke fire and yawned. It had been a hard day. The Danish butter freighter was in dock, and along the river wall laden barges were moored and waiting for daylight. For the next week or two there would be work enough for the rivermen, and they would shoulder their way into the dining rooms during the coming days for mugs of steaming tea and coffee, thick bacon sandwiches and thick slices of new bread liberally coated with dripping. It was how it had been for the past two weeks and the young woman tried to ignore her protesting muscles and her aching back as she stared into the hearth and watched the tiny flames flickering in and out of the carefully banked-up grate.

Down in the shuttered shop below Fred Bradley finished scrubbing the cutting-board and stood it on its end against the wall to dry. It was the last of his nightly chores and he looked around once more to make certain that he had not forgotten anything before going up to the room where his young wife was resting. Fred was in his mid-forties, a heavily built man with thick, dark hair that was streaked with grey above his ears. His wide-spaced eyes were dark and brooding, but there was a softness in them which mirrored his nature and which his wife Carrie found to be comforting and

4

reassuring. It was his soft eyes that had put her at ease the first time she met him, when she timidly knocked at his door just a few years ago, the evening when Fred employed a helper and found his future wife.

Carrie eased her position in the cushioned chair and stretched again. She could hear Fred's footsteps on the stairs and knew that her short reverie was over. There was the evening meal to prepare and Rachel to wash, feed and settle down for the night. Fred would offer to cook the meal and even wash the baby but Carrie always declined with a smile and a determined shake of her head. Her husband would have spent the whole day cooking for the steady stream of customers in the small, steamy back kitchen below and she felt that he needed a break. At first she had let him wash their three-month-old child but Fred's face had become red and perspiration stood out on his forehead as he held the mite as though she were made of china. His large, gnarled hands had very gently stroked the soft flannel over the protesting muddle of arms and legs on his towelled lap, and when he held one leg by the ankle and it slipped from his grasp as the baby kicked, his sudden exclamation of horror had started a loud wail and reduced Carrie to a fit of laughter at her husband's awkwardness. After that particular evening he had often volunteered to try again with the bathing, if half-heartedly, but seemed happy to be refused, though he was more confident about cooking the evening meal.

Fred's smile was brief as he entered the small sitting-room above the street on that February evening, and he turned and entered the back room where the baby lay in her cot. Carrie could hear his cooing to the child and the answering wail of discomfort and her face became serious for a moment or two. Normally her husband would make himself comfortable beside the fire, sometimes holding their child in his arms, and

5

make small talk as she peeled the potatoes and washed the greens, but tonight Carrie knew it would be different. He had seen Tommy Allen sitting in the dining rooms that morning and noticed the young man exchange a few words with her before he left. It was all so innocent but Fred's face had darkened and he had become quiet as he went about his work, the occasional grunt of irritation replacing the tuneless whistling and humming that usually emanated from the kitchen. But she had made Fred aware of her involvement with Tommy Allen from the start. It was a long time ago now. He had been her lover, her first love, and now he was married. It was the first time for a long while that Tommy had come into the dining rooms for his morning break and Carrie had spotted him from the window as he pulled up outside and climbed down wearily from his horsecart. She had been more than a little taken aback by his unexpected appearance in the area and also somewhat intrigued, though she had heard from one of the carmen who frequented the cafe that the young man had recently married.

Fred came into the room and picked up the evening paper then settled himself in his usual chair. 'Rachel needs changing,' he said tersely.

Carrie had already gathered up the baby's toiletries in her arms and she left the room without answering him. She felt suddenly irritable as she bent over the cot and lifted the child to her breast. Fred was a lovely man, he was warm and tender towards her, and she knew that he loved her dearly, but he had become very possessive since Rachel was born. She had never given him any reason to feel suspicious, and she certainly never encouraged any impropriety with the carmen and dockers who came regularly into the dining rooms. There was the usual bawdy banter, of course, and it had been that way ever since she first put on her white

6

apron and began serving behind the counter. Carrie remembered those early days clearly, how Fred had praised her cheerfulness and efficiency, and had been quick to point out that the upturn in trade was largely due to her. She had soon seen the potential of his drab and neglected establishment, and now they were married the business was doing very well. It was largely due to her that Fred had been able to secure the leasehold of the cafe and build up trade by extending the seating arrangement and brightening up the fare on offer. Even when the docks and wharves were quiet the local carmen often made detours so they could eat at Bradley's Dining Rooms. Carrie remembered with a smile how Fred had reacted when she suggested renovating the back store room and putting a few tables in there. He had been apprehensive but had gone along with her idea all the same and now the small room was a regular haunt of the local foremen and managers, as well as a meeting-place for the trade union officials who held impromptu meetings over mugs of steaming hot tea and bacon sandwiches.

Carrie sighed to herself as she threw the soiled towelling napkin in an enamel bucket at her feet and placed the clean and folded napkin under the baby's bottom. The tiny child's pale blue eyes stared up at her appealingly and she could not help feeling guilty. She had married Fred Bradley without being in love with the kind and considerate man who was employing her. She had entered into the union for her own reasons and she had taken her marriage vows with no thoughts other than to be a dutiful wife to him and to give him the happiness he deserved. From the beginning she had never tried to pretend that she was in love, although she was very fond of him, and Fred had told her he was happy that she cared enough for him to become his wife. He had hoped that in time she would have his

7

children and one day she might come to love him.

Carrie cooed softly as she fixed the large safety pin to the napkin and wrapped the child in a small flannelette sheet, tucking the edges under her chin as she cuddled the soft, sweet-smelling bundle to her. Fred was a good husband to her and the difference in their ages did not matter to Carrie. Her mother had pointed out to her that being married to an older man had its advantages. She had said there was less chance of being burdened down with a large brood and less risk of losing the husband to another woman. Her father, himself ten years older than her mother, seemed more concerned about his daughter marrying a man who was seventeen years older than her, and had felt that she was entering into the marriage largely because of the misfortune that had afflicted her family. He was right of course, Carrie thought, and as she nestled the child to her and placed the teat of the bottle against the child's searching mouth she bit on her lip and tried to suppress the anger which welled up inside her.

In the warm and cosy sitting-room Fred Bradley put down the evening paper and stared moodily into the bright fire. He had begun to feel that Carrie was really growing to love him, and having borne him his first child the future had seemed so promising, but now today he had been reminded that everything he had hoped and prayed for could so easily crumble into dust. Perhaps he was making too much of it. Tommy Allen was married now and it was not unnatural that he should have a conversation with Carrie, but the nagging feeling would not go away. Fred knew that his young wife and Tommy were once lovers and Carrie had been very upset when they parted. Perhaps she still yearned for him, he thought with a pang of anxiety. Maybe she wished it was still the young man who shared her bed instead of a man who was almost old enough to be her father. Maybe the young man was unhappy in his marriage and had made his feelings known to her. Maybe he and Carrie had discussed her marriage and she had told him things, secret things that were intimate to the marriage bed. They might have joked about his shortcomings as a husband and lover, he thought with anger and frustration building up inside him. True, he had struggled at first to satisfy his beautiful young bride; he had been too long a bachelor and too set in his ways. He had worked in his father's cafe on the riverside almost from leaving school and was never allowed to make his own way in life. He had never been allowed to mix properly with women and his few lady friends were discouraged by his mother and not made welcome in the Bradley home. Only after his ageing parents had died and he was left to manage the dining rooms did he begin to look around for a wife, and Fred smiled bitterly at the memory. He had been pathetically shy and awkward, and one particularly painful experience had sent him back to his lonely flat with the firm belief that he would die a bachelor. The woman had taunted him for his lack of passion and forthrightness and she had walked off with one of the young dockers. If she had given him time he would have been able to show her passion, he knew, but it was hard for him to relax and act confidently after years of being cowed in a stern loveless household. Carrie had changed his life and he would somehow make her love him. He would also fight tooth and nail to keep her from the likes of Tommy Allen.

The hot cinder falling from the grate jerked Fred from his thoughts and he licked his fingers and quickly tossed it back on to the fire.

Carrie walked into the room and sat down heavily in

her chair. 'I've put the veg on an' the chops are doin' nicely,' she announced flatly, waiting for the inevitable question.

Fred merely nodded and picked up the paper, pretending to be engrossed in an article, and Carrie afforded herself a sly grin. Fred was no reader and he struggled with words. His look of deep contemplation only served to irritate her until she could bear the silence no longer.

'Tommy Allen was tellin' me 'is wife's pregnant,' she began.

'Oh?' Fred said offhandedly.

'Yeah. She's upset it's 'appened so soon,' Carrie went on. 'Tommy's over the moon. 'E said 'e wants loads o' babies. Mind you, it's all right fer 'im, 'e ain't got ter 'ave 'em.'

Fred closed the paper deliberately and put it down by his feet. 'I wonder what brought 'im inter the cafe. I ain't seen anyfing of 'im fer months,' he said archly.

'Well, if 'e was in the area it's a foregone conclusion 'e'd pop in. We're the best meal place round 'ere, an' after all 'e used ter call in all the time when 'e 'ad that ovver job,' Carrie reminded him.

'Long as it's not you 'e's interested in,' Fred said shortly.

Carrie got up with a deep sigh. 'Yer not startin' that again, are yer, Fred?' she said wearily. 'I've told yer lots o' times me an' Tommy finished long ago. Yer know that well enough. I've got me 'ands full wiv servin' an' lookin' after Rachel – that's besides runnin' the 'ome. I've got no time ter gallivant about.'

'That's all yer want, is it, the time?' Fred said crossly.

Carrie gave him a blinding look and stormed out of the room. It was useless to argue with him while he was in that mood, she told herself. Best to ignore him and let him come around in his own time. He would soon realise he had been acting stupidly and feel sorry for his bad temper. Better though that he simmered for a while, Carrie thought as she stirred the greens and tested the potatoes with a fork. The baby had been very demanding lately, and after trying to divide herself between the shop and the child she felt drained of energy. The thought of her husband fumbling around in bed and urgently attempting to rouse her left her feeling suddenly depressed. It had nothing to do with Tommy's visit that morning, she tried to convince herself. She had got over their love affair before she agreed to marry Fred, although the young man's sudden appearance had stirred a few very pleasant memories for her.

The baby was crying and Carrie sighed resignedly as she quickly replaced the lid of the potato pot and hurried into the back room.

Down in the dark and foggy street a figure stood waiting beneath a lighted gas lamp. The young, broad-shouldered man had the collar of his tattered grey overcoat pulled up around his ears and his cap was drawn down over his forehead. He tightened the red scarf around his neck and blew on his hands, stamping his cold feet on the hard wet cobblestones. The man's pale blue eyes peered into the fog and his ears strained to catch the sound of approaching footsteps. He had waited for over ten minutes and decided that he would give his friend another five minutes before making off home. It had been a hard day and the river could be a severe taskmaster at times. He had moored three laden barges in position midstream and as the tide turned and the fog swept upriver he had finally managed to bring the last of them into its berth below Chamber's Wharf. It had been a long, tiring business and his hands were sore and chafed from the ropes. He should have

11

arranged to meet his friend Billy in the pub instead of in the cold street by the river, but Billy had insisted.

Danny Tanner took out his silver pocket watch and looked at it, an expression of annoyance on his wide, handsome face. Just then he heard footsteps approaching and a figure loomed out of the fog in front of him. The young man walked with a shuffle, his shoulders hunched and his hands stuffed deeply into his coat pockets.

'Sorry, mate,' he said in a husky voice, his grinning face belying his sincerity. 'I got 'eld up wiv one o' the geezers in the Kings Arms. 'E give me an ear'ole bashin' an' I 'ad ter listen, didn't I? The poor ole bleeder's one of us. 'E got a Blighty ticket early on an' 'e ain't bin right since. Talks a lot o' nonsense at times, but what can yer do?'

Danny Tanner shook his head in resignation. He knew Billy Sullivan was never going to change. Always the soft touch, and always so unreliable. He put his arm around his friend's shoulder and grinned widely as they started off.

'I was about ter give up on yer. I knew we should 'ave met in the pub,' he said lightly.

Billy Sullivan stopped in his tracks and turned suddenly to face his friend, his face serious. 'Look, pal, I wanted us ter meet 'ere. I've got somefing ter show yer,' he said, a note of excitement in his gruff voice. With a grand gesture of his arm, he announced, 'Take a look at that.'

'What the bloody 'ell are yer talkin' about?' Danny replied, looking at what Billy was pointing to. 'All I can see is a bloody empty yard wiv a shed in it. What's so excitin' about lookin' at a poxy empty yard on a night that's fair set ter freeze the cobblers orf a brass monkey?'

Billy hunched his shoulders and did a quick shuffle.

'Wasn't I the best prospect Bermondsey 'ad for a long time before I got me wound?' he asked. 'Wasn't I the only bloke who could 'ave give ole Palmer a run fer 'is money? I would 'ave took that title, Danny,' he said passionately, his voice almost breaking with a note of despair.

Danny nodded and slipped his arm around Billy's hunched shoulders once more. 'I know yer could, mate, but what's that got ter do wiv what we're lookin' at right now?'

Billy pulled away from his friend's arm and made towards the empty yard. 'I made a few enquiries an' it's up fer rent,' he called back. 'It's ideal.'

'Ideal fer what, fer Gawdsake?' Danny asked, feeling perplexed.

Billy Sullivan suddenly shaped up to his friend, his clenched fists pawing at the air and his shoulders moving from side to side. 'A gym, that's what,' he said triumphantly. 'A bleedin' gymnasium wiv a ring an' a punch bag, an' lockers, an' a washin' place, an' . . .'

''Ang on a minute,' Danny said quickly. 'Where yer gonna get the money fer all this? If yer ever get the chance o' rentin' the place that is? It'll take a small fortune ter build a gym on this bleedin' dump.'

There was a wide grin on Billy's ring-scarred face. 'Look 'ere, Mister Know-all,' he said in a confident voice, 'I've bin doin' a lot o' finkin' an' I've put meself about. Yer know that our ole boxin' Club's gone down the drain since those new geezers took over. They ain't got a bleedin' idea between the lot of 'em. The young lads at the club ain't very 'appy, an' accordin' ter my information they're all willin' ter lend us an 'and ter knock up a timber buildin'. Farvver Murphy at the church 'as promised us some paint, an' whitewash fer the ceilin's, an' one o' the lads knows where 'e can get all the timber we need, no questions asked o' course.

All we need is the ready money ter lay down ter secure the site an' the weekly rent. Jus' fink of it, mate, me an' you givin' the lads a few lessons an' organisin' a few tournaments. We could make the place pay. It could be a bleedin' goldmine.'

Danny looked into the blazing grey eyes of his friend and felt a sudden urge to throw his arms around him. He had idolised the ex-boxer since they were young children together in Page Street. He had watched Billy Sullivan box at the club tournaments and progress to the professional ranks. He had truly been a contender for the middleweight title until the severe chest wound he sustained during the heavy fighting in France had cut short his promising career. Billy had come home a physical wreck and it was only when Danny himself took up boxing seriously that his friend regained some of his self-esteem by helping and instructing him. Billy had certainly been making some enquiries but he had been misinformed, Danny thought. His best friend was due for a bad let-down, and it was he who would have to spell it out for him.

'Now look, mate, I fink it's a great idea, but yer gotta face facts,' he said kindly. 'The place ain't fer rent. This ole plot, those two derelict 'ouses next ter me sister's dinin' rooms an' that yard's up fer sale. Carrie told me. She said 'er an' Fred only jus' got in wiv their bid before that bastard Galloway bought the land fer 'is business. They scotched 'is little caper an' what was left was too small fer a cartage business so 'e pulled out. I was dead pleased when she told me but yer see, pal, yer'll 'ave ter 'ave anuvver fink. The idea's a good one but yer can't 'ave that place, that's fer sure.'

All the time Danny was talking Billy's wide grin stayed fixed on his face. When his friend drew breath, Billy chuckled. 'It jus' shows yer, yer don't know every-fink, do yer?' he said quietly. 'I know it's foggy, but can

14

yer see a "For Sale" notice on the gaff? O' course yer can't. They took it down, that's why. That site was up for sale but there was no takers. Farvver Murphy told my muvver so only the ovver day. 'E gets ter know all the business round this area. It's all ter do wiv plans ter extend the wharves. Anyway, nuffink's gonna 'appen fer a long while yet so the owners are lettin' the place out fer rent. I can see it now,' he went on, his eyes opening wide. 'Billy Sullivan's Gym. They'll all come 'ere, Danny. Everybody'll know about Billy Sullivan's Gym, you jus' wait.'

Danny felt a wave of admiration for his friend and affectionately put an arm around his shoulders. 'C'mon, mate, let's go an' 'ave a pint at the Waterman's Inn. They've got a nice coke fire in the public bar.'

The two young men walked away from the flickering gas lamp in Cotton Lane, their heavy boots echoing on the wet cobbles.

Chapter Two

Carrie stood behind the counter of the dining rooms with her fair hair pulled up at the back of her head and held in place with a pair of large bone combs. She brushed aside a wisp of hair which had slipped down over her face and smiled placatingly at the florid-faced docker leaning forward over the tea-stained counter. 'Two o' toasted drippin'? Yeah, I've put yer order in, Joe. Give us a chance. Fred's run orf 'is feet back there,' she appealed to him.

'Well, tell 'im ter get a move on, luv. I ain't got all day, yer know,' the docker protested. 'We're goin' barmey at the wharf. Yer know what it's like when we're on bonus.'

Carried smiled and patted his huge gnarled hand. 'Sit down, Joe, I'll bring it to yer in a minute,' she replied.

'Oi, Carrie, where's my ovver mug o' tea?' another docker called out impatiently.

'Jus' comin'.'

'What's that ole man o' yours doin' back there? Kippin', is 'e?'

'Gis anuvver drippin' slice, will yer, luv.'

'Fancy a night at the flicks, Carrie, luv?' another voice called out.

And so it went on. The glass-fronted doors of the dining rooms were constantly opening and shutting and letting in draughts of cold morning air with the busy

17

comings and goings of workers and their loud, raucous banter. The large plate-glass window of the riverside cafe was steamed up and trickles of condensation ran down the yellow-painted walls. The linoleum flooring was muddied and the wooden bench-tables were stained with slops of food and drops of spilt tea and coffee. A steady stream of steam-laden air gushed out from the kitchen and Carrie frequently ran the back of her hand across her hot forehead as she struggled to cope with the customers' demands. It was always the same when trade was booming at the local wharves, and as the convoys of horsecarts and lorries lined up along Cotton Lane so the cafe became even fuller.

Carrie had managed to cope with the twofold demands of the business and motherhood by employing a young woman to look after Rachel during the busy days. Annie McCafferty was a very reliable person who had been recommended to Carrie by the local midwife. She was a shy, retiring girl who had been brought up in a convent school after being abandoned as a baby. A tramp had found her freezing and near to death on the doorstep of a gin palace near the Elephant and Castle and he had carried her to the local Catholic church. There was a crudely written note attached to the child giving her name and saying that the mother was an unmarried Irish girl who had been in service and was going back to Ireland. Annie was nursed back to full health by the kind nuns who adopted her and they were able to give her a good education. When the time came for Annie to leave the convent school she was recommended for training in child welfare. Now twenty-eight, one year younger than Carrie Bradley, the young Irish lady was still single and had no urgent desire to wed, although her pale beauty could turn many a young man's head. She was demure and dark-haired with deep blue eyes, and her full lips were constantly set

18

firmly, giving the impression of sternness, although she was far from from stern when dealing with her charges. She had been denied the company of males during her early life and now found it difficult to talk to members of the opposite sex. She feared the roughness and the roguishness of men and was happy in her work.

Annie led a quiet, uneventful life, living in rooms near the Southwark Park. The building, which was owned by the church, was made up of a dozen self-contained flats rented out to respectable young women who had gone through the children's home and school of St Mary's Convent in Bermondsey. Annie spent her weekends reading, going to church and having tea with other young women in like circumstances. She rarely went out alone, preferring to take her strolls in the company of one or two of her friends. The other women often talked about young men they knew, and one of them had been taking a young man back to her flat during the evenings. Such a practice was frowned on by the church, and instructions were given to the warden of the building that if any young woman allowed a man to stay overnight then she was to be reported to the Mother Superior. All the young women knew the consequences. Should they digress they would be asked to find other accommodation forthwith. Annie felt worried for the young woman who was flaunting the rules and regulations and taking such a risk. She had seen the young man leaving Mary Kelly's rooms and slipping out of the building by the back way on more than one occasion. Other girls had seen him leaving too and Annie felt that it was only a matter of time before her friend was found out.

The young Irish nurse was happy too to be employed by the Bradleys, for the baby's mother was kind and considerate and her husband posed no threat. Fred Bradley stayed very much in the background and his soft, kind eyes helped to put her at ease.

Annie came in at seven-thirty every weekday morning, bathed and fed the child and, weather permitting, took her for an outing in the large black perambulator. She left every day at two o'clock, after the morning rush was over and once the last of the hot midday meals had been served. It was then that Carrie took over, dividing her time between caring for her baby and attending to her customers. She had complete confidence in the young nurse, although she found it very difficult to penetrate her reserve. Carrie's only problem was the other woman who worked in the dining rooms. Bessie Chandler helped Fred in the kitchen, and when business demanded or when Carrie went upstairs to tend Rachel she came out of the kitchen to help behind the counter. Bessie was a fiery character, a large plump woman with a shock of ginger hair, freckles and green eyes. She was talkative and forthright in her opinions, which she gave freely and often without the qualification for doing so. Bessie's opinions on how babies should be cared for were given freely to Carrie and duly ignored by the young mother, who was aware that Bessie had never had children of her own. Annie McCafferty, however, with her training in caring for children, viewed the Bradleys' large and vociferous helper as an ignorant, interfering busybody.

It was Friday morning, cold and clear after the night rain, and Annie brought Rachel down the stairs and settled her in the pram which was kept in the passageway beside the kitchen. Bessie was busy rolling out pastry for the meat pies and she looked up at the young nurse. 'Yer not intendin' ter take the baby out in this weavver, are yer?' she asked in an indignant tone of voice. 'It's bleedin' freezin' out there.'

Annie's lips puckered in irritation. 'It's cold, but as long as the baby's well wrapped up it'll do no harm. In

20

fact, the air will do her good,' she said stiffly.

'Do 'er good?' Bessie snorted. 'Give 'er pneumonia more like it.'

Annie disregarded the remark and as she walked out of the side door pushing the baby carriage Bessie turned to her employer.

'I shouldn't let that young woman take too much on 'erself, Fred, if I was you,' she said quickly. 'Them sort ain't got 'alf the sense they was born wiv.'

Fred was busy cutting meat into small cubes and he ignored his helper's comment.

'I remember what 'appened ter Mrs Orchard's first-born,' Bessie began. 'Baby girl it was. She went cross-eyed. My next-door neighbour Elsie Dobson told me Clara Orchard took the baby out in the fog and the child got a terrible cough. Whoopin' cough it turned out ter be. Nasty that complaint can be, let me tell yer. Anyway it turned the baby's eyes. The child never got better. Yer can still see the poor cow walkin' about wiv both 'er eyes pointin' inwards. She's got two kids of 'er own now an' they're both cross-eyed. No, I tell yer, Fred, yer gotta be so careful where kids are concerned.'

Fred nodded, rolling his eyes in irritation. 'Yes, Bessie,' he growled.

'I was only sayin' ter my ole man last night, this 'ere fog's a killer,' the large woman went on. 'That Mr what's-'is-name who used ter come round 'ere wiv the cockles on Sundays put 'is bad chest down ter the fog. Mind you though, I fink it was the pipe what did it. Never out of 'is mouth that pipe.'

''Ave you ever thought of smokin' a pipe?' Fred asked suddenly, wincing at his own audacity.

Bessie chuckled and waved her hand at him in a dismissing gesture. 'Gawd luv us, no. Mind yer though, there's a lot what do,' she went on, missing the sarcasm in Fred's remark. 'Mrs Dingle always 'ad a clay pipe

21

stuck in 'er gob. She used ter sit in the Kings Arms on the corner o' Page Street shellin' 'er peas in the summer an' puffin' away at that clay pipe of 'ers. She used ter wear a cap stuck on the back of 'er 'ead an' a docker's scarf. Gawd knows what become of 'er. I ain't seen 'er about fer ages. P'raps she's snuffed it.'

Fred cut into the pieces of meat with a vengeance, fighting the urge to shake the chattering Bessie Chandler by the scruff of her neck until she snuffed it. 'P'raps she 'as,' he replied quietly.

Bessie was not finished. 'Like I was sayin' earlier,' she prattled on, 'yer gotta be so careful wiv kids.'

Fred had had enough. He put down the carving knife on the chopping block and wiped his hands on the end of his apron. 'Leave the rollin' out, Bessie. I'll do that. Give Carrie an 'and, will yer?' he almost implored her.

Bessie nodded, glad for the chance of making her views known to the young mother, and she quickly flounced off out of the kitchen. Fred sighed to himself as he looked at the rest of the meat lying on the chopping block and at the pile of dough still to be rolled out. She'll have to go, he told himself, fearful for his sanity while at the mercy of Bessie's constant chatter. He picked up the sharp knife once more with a frown and growled at the meat as he diced it, imagining that it was Bessie he was carving up.

On Friday evenings Carrie was in the habit of visiting her parents in Bacon Buildings. First she bathed Rachel and gave her a feed before settling her down, then she washed and changed, combing out her long fair hair and setting it on top of her head again. Fred watched his young wife go through her weekly ritual thinking how beautiful she looked. Her body had soon regained its youthful shape and he marvelled how trim she looked. Her breasts had become larger since

Rachel was born and the tops of her arms too, he thought. Carrie's bright blue eyes mirrored her good health and she hummed happily to herself as she brushed down her best coat. She was glad to get away from the shop for a short while and she felt confident about leaving the baby in Fred's charge. Normally Rachel slept for a few hours after the feed and Carrie had made sure her husband knew what to do should the baby wake up before she got home. Once ready she turned to Fred and he raised his hands quickly in front of him. 'It's all right, I know what ter do if she wakes up,' he reminded her. 'Pick 'er up an' bring up 'er wind. Check that the pin ain't stickin' in 'er, an' if she don't stop cryin' walk up an' down wiv 'er till she do.'

Carrie kissed her husband lightly on the cheek and made for the stairs. She turned and was about to say something when Fred held up his hands once more. 'I know, get Rachel's next feed ready,' he said quickly.

Carrie smiled at him and hurried down the stairs. As she stepped out into the dark night she thought of the gloomy squalor of Bacon Buildings and the smile left her face. Her parents, William and Nellie Tanner, had been forced out of the terraced house in Page Street, the home they had brought the family up in, when her father's employer George Galloway, who owned the house, decided he was going to make changes. Galloway had now installed a motor mechanic there whom he had hired to look after his new motor vehicles. Carrie's parents and their youngest son Danny had been forced to find alternative accommodation and they ended up in one of the most dilapidated tenement blocks in Bermondsey. Carrie knew how hard it had been for her father, who had spent almost thirty-seven years as a horsekeeper for Galloway, to look for other employment. He had found a job as watchman at the council depot but it had caused him to become morose and ailing. His fortunes had changed, however, when a man who had befriended her father, Joe Maitland, took him on to manage his warehouse in Dockhead. Carrie was very pleased to see the change in her father now that he had settled into his new job, but she still fretted over her parents, and she had not forgotten her vow that one day she would have enough money to buy them a decent house to live in.

The night was clear and the sky full of stars as she walked from the corner shop in Cotton Lane along River Street, then turned left into Bacon Street. The dark tenement block loomed up on her left and through the broken windows she could see the reflection of the naked gas jets that burned on each landing. There were four block entrances and Carrie entered the far one, climbing the rickety wooden stairs to the third floor. Each landing had four flats, two on each side of the landing. The front doors were almost bare of paint and shadows cast by the gas flame took on weird shapes. Carrie shuddered as she walked along the landing to one of the rear front doors. The sour smell from the communal rubbish bins in the alley below drifted up through a broken window and Carrie grimaced as she knocked on the door.

A wind was getting up. It rattled the window frames as Nellie and her daughter sat talking. Despite the difference in their ages, the two women were strikingly alike, with small smooth-skinned faces and high cheekbones.

At fifty Nellie Tanner was still slim and attractive. Her blue eyes were a shade or two deeper than those of her daughter, but her fair hair was exactly the same shade as Carrie's. Life had been kind to her and there were few lines on her face, except in the corners of her eyes and around her swanlike neck just beneath the chin. She looked serious though as she confided in her daughter: 'I dunno, Carrie. I was pleased as punch when yer farvver came 'ome an' told me Joe Maitland 'ad offered 'im that job. Now I'm not so sure. It ain't what 'e's bin used to, but then nor was that watchman's job wiv the council. Yer farvver's never bin one ter talk much about 'is work but 'e clams up whenever I ask 'im what 'e's bin doin'. 'E gets very tired too lately. After 'e 'as 'is tea 'e falls asleep in that chair an' 'e's like that till it's time for bed. 'E's never bin the same since the stables. 'E really loved those 'orses. I get all 'eavy in 'ere when I fink 'ow that ole goat Galloway treated 'im after a lifetime of work fer 'im,' Nellie said, putting her clenched fist up to her chest.

'George Galloway 'urt us all, Mum, but yer gotta try an' put 'im out o' yer mind,' Carrie replied, reaching out and squeezing her mother's hand in hers. 'Yer won't 'ave ter stay in this dump fer ever. One day I'll 'ave enough money ter get yer both a nice place ter live. Danny as well if 'e's still livin' wiv yer.'

Nellie laughed. 'Gawd knows when yer bruvver's gonna get married. I fink 'e jus' loves 'em an' leaves 'em. Still I'm pleased 'e's got that lighterman's job. I was worried 'e was gonna take up boxin' after doin' it in the army. That's all Danny talked about when 'e first come 'ome from France. Mind you though, that Billy Sullivan 'ad a lot ter do wiv it. Yer bruvver worshipped 'im.'

'They still go drinkin' tergevver, don't they, Mum?' Carrie asked.

'They was out tergevver the ovver night,' Nellie replied, nodding. 'Danny met 'im when 'e finished work. 'E come 'ome 'ere drunk as a kite. All I could get out of 'im was this gymnasium Billy was interested in. Danny said Billy Sullivan wants 'im ter 'elp out there. I do 'ope 'e ain't finkin' o' chuckin' that job in. It was 'ard enough gettin' it in the first place. It's a good job

25

too. I know it's 'ard and awkward hours, but at least it's regular money comin' in.'

Carrie was eager to tell her mother how business was picking up at the dining rooms but she was interrupted by footsteps on the stairs outside and a key being inserted in the lock.

'There's the two of 'em now. I warned 'em you was comin' round ternight an' not ter be late,' Nellie said.

William Tanner walked into the flat with Danny following behind him and both men bent over in turn to kiss Carrie on the cheek. William looked frail beside his youngest son although both were the same height. Danny was heavier by at least two stone, and his upright stance made him appear the taller of the two. ''Ow's my little granddaughter doin'?' William asked, a slight slur in his voice.

'She's fine,' Carrie answered with a smile. 'She's sleepin' well an' she's put on two pounds.'

Nellie looked peevishly at her husband and Danny in turn. 'I told yer not ter be late,' she said quickly.

'We got waylaid in the Kings Arms, Muvver,' Danny said smiling. 'Billy was in there wiv 'is family. 'E's dead set on gettin' this gym goin'.'

'I don't know where 'e's gonna get the money from,' Nellie snorted. 'Billy Sullivan ain't done a day's work since 'e got out o' the army. 'E's worryin' the life out of 'is muvver. Sadie was tellin' me 'e's bin 'angin' around wiv a bad crowd from Rovver'ithe.'

'The Tunnel Mob,' Danny explained matter-of-factly. 'They're a bunch o' nuffinks. There ain't one of 'em could punch their way out of a paper bag.'

William was filling his pipe thoughtfully. 'The police come in the yard terday,' he said suddenly. 'They wanted ter 'ave a word wiv Joe. They was wiv 'im in the office fer over an hour. Joe looked worried when they left. 'E told me they was askin' after somebody 'e used

26

ter know. I don't fink it was that though.'

'Oh,' Nellie said, glancing quickly at Carrie as if to signal that her father was being secretive about his work again.

'I fink there's bin some dodgy business goin' on wiv the stuff 'e's bin 'andlin' if yer ask me,' William went on.

'You won't get involved in it, will yer?' Nellie asked in a worried tone of voice.

William laughed. 'I'm just employed as a yard foreman. I jus' stow the stuff, I don't buy it.'

Danny's eyelids were drooping as he sat in front of the warm fire and Nellie gave him a blinding look. 'Yer not gonna fall off ter sleep while yer sister's visitin' us, are yer?' she reproached him.

Danny sat up straight in his chair and grinned at Carrie. 'I 'ad a bad day,' he said. 'There's a lot o' trade comin' in an' the tide was runnin' fast. The barges don't dock themselves, yer know.'

'Yer ain't finkin' o' chuckin' it fer that 'are-brained scheme o' Billy's, are yer, Danny?' his mother asked.

'Course I ain't,' he replied irritably. 'Billy's never gonna raise the money ter open a gym. Yer know Billy, it's all pie in the sky wiv 'im.'

Nellie was not convinced. 'I dunno so much,' she persisted. ''E might be finkin' o' gettin' the money by knockin' around wiv that Rovver'ithe mob.'

'Tunnel Mob,' Danny corrected her.

'All right, Mister Know-all,' Nellie scolded. 'I bet they're up ter no good, whatever they call themselves. Sadie was tellin' me that bloke they 'ung last year fer killin' that shopkeeper over in Stepney used ter be one o' the crowd 'er Billy's gettin' wiv.'

'She's got nuffink ter worry about,' Danny said, rolling his eyes in Carrie's direction. 'Billy wouldn't touch a fing what didn't belong to 'im. Trouble wiv Billy is, 'e don't see no wrong in anybody. All 'e wants ter do is open up a gym club fer the local lads. Yer know 'ow 'e loves boxin'. If it wasn't fer that bullet wound 'e got, Billy would be defendin' the championship by now.'

'Well, the boy's better orf out o' the boxin' business,' Nellie went on. 'An' I'm glad you've seen better sense, Danny. Look at poor ole Solly Green who sells the papers at the top o' Page Street. They took 'im away last week. 'E collapsed as 'e come out the Kings Arms an' they rushed 'im away ter the 'ospital. 'E's in a bad way so Maisie Dingle told me. It's all those punches ter the 'ead 'e's 'ad in 'is time. 'E was boxin' fer years.'

William sighed as he reached for the matches to re-light his pipe. 'Solly was pissed. 'E was drinkin' pints o' porter,' he informed Nellie. ''E was all right this evenin' when I bought the paper off 'im.'

Carrie laughed at her mother's pained expression. 'C'mon, Mum,' she said, 'I'll 'elp yer do the cheese sandwiches. Then I'll 'ave ter be goin', in case Rachel wakes up early.'

William waited until the two women had left the room then he turned to his son. 'Is Carrie all right?' he asked.

'Yeah, I fink so. Why d'yer ask, Dad?'

'She looks a bit pale, an' she seems a bit quiet,' William remarked.

'I s'pose it's the shop,' Danny answered. 'It mus' be a lot fer 'er, what wiv the baby ter care for as well. Yer know what Carrie's like. She ain't one ter complain.'

'I'm wonderin' if 'er an' Fred are all right tergevver,' William went on. 'There's a lot o' difference in their ages, an' Fred don't seem the sort o' bloke who'd be a cheerful soul ter be wiv. P'raps she's findin' it a bit melancholy bein' wiv 'im?'

Danny laughed at his father's misgivings. 'She's 'appy enough,' he reassured him. 'Fred's a diamond,

28

an' 'e finks the world of 'er. As fer the difference in ages, take you an' Muvver. You're quite a bit older than 'er. It ain't made no difference ter you two, 'as it?'

'Of course it ain't,' William said quickly. 'But me an' yer muvver always used ter be goin' out when we were younger, even if it was only up the Kings Arms on Saturday nights. Our Carrie an' 'im never seem ter go anywhere. It's bound ter get a bit miserable fer both of 'em, all work an' no play.'

'I wouldn't worry too much about Carrie, Dad,' Danny assured him. 'She's done wonders wiv that cafe. They're buildin' up the trade an' Carrie's got plans. She was tellin' me the ovver day she wants Fred ter try an' get that empty 'ouse next door ter make the place bigger. They need the room. The place is packed out as it is.'

'That's what I was just on about,' William said with a sigh. 'She don't stop all day. She can't keep goin' on like that fer ever. Yer muvver's worried about 'er as well as me.'

Danny yawned and stretched out his feet towards the fire. 'Well, I'm orf ter bed soon as I've seen Carrie 'ome. I've gotta be up at five in the mornin',' he said, knowing it was useless to discuss it any further.

Carrie came into the room carrying a plate of cheese sandwiches followed by Nellie who was holding the large enamel teapot in both hands. 'C'mon, rouse yer-selves, supper's up,' she grinned.

The late meal was eaten in comparative silence, and then as the clock on the mantelshelf struck ten o'clock Carrie slipped on her coat. 'Yer don't 'ave ter see me 'ome, Bruv,' she said smiling. 'I'm a big gel now.'

Danny waved away her protest. 'There's some funny characters roamin' the streets at this time o' night,' he remarked. 'It won't take long – that's if yer don't stand around 'ere chattin' any more.'

They walked down the dark, creaking stairs to the empty street, and as they turned left and walked towards Cotton Lane Carrie slipped her arm through her brother's, glad of his comforting presence despite her protests. It was a misty night and she could hear the sound of the water lapping against the pilings as they reached the riverside lane. There was no moon showing and the gas lamp opposite the dining rooms flickered and cast frightening shadows down the cobbled lane.

'You sure yer all right, Carrie?' her brother asked with concern.

She nodded with a smile. 'I jus' need a good night's sleep,' she replied. 'It's bin a very busy week. Go on, off yer go, I'm all right now.'

Danny planted a kiss on her cheek and waited until she opened the front door before turning on his heel and walking off. Carrie hurried up the stairs to the sound of Rachel's loud bawling, and with a sigh of resignation she slipped quickly out of her coat and took the baby from a very flustered father.

Chapter Three

Nellie Tanner left the grimy Bacon Buildings on Saturday morning and walked along to Page Street carrying an empty shopping basket. It was quicker to go direct to Jamaica Road and along through the railway arch to Bermondsey Market, but Nellie made the detour purposely. She had spent many years of her adult life in Page Street and most of her old friends still lived there in the row of terraced houses. As she walked briskly along the turning in the cold morning air Nellie spotted Aggie Temple busily whitening her front doorstep and she smiled to herself. Aggie was a spotlessly clean woman who prided herself on her housekeeping. Her modest home sparkled, and her doorstep was the whitest in the street. Even when the lorries coming out of Galloway's yard at the angle of the street splashed mud across the pavement and their exhaust fumes glazed the windows with an oily film Aggie persevered. Her husband Harold was a lamplighter and when he came home from work he was obliged to take off his boots in the passage and place them on a sheet of newspaper before entering the inner sanctum.

Aggie had mice, Nellie recalled, but the woman could not bear the thought of getting a good mouser. 'Cats make the place smell an' they tear yer 'ome ter pieces,' Aggie had told her.

'Get some mousetraps then,' Nellie advised her.

'Oh, no! I couldn't stand seein' the poor fings in those traps,' Aggie groaned.

'Well, it's eivver mousetraps or a good mouser,' Nellie had said.

Aggie got the mousetraps, and the only thing they caught was her Harold's big toe one night when he was hurrying down to the lavatory in the backyard. Aggie still would not contemplate getting a mouser and when Harold raised the roof about the lethal traps she threw them out and blocked up the holes in the flooring and the wooden skirting-boards with old newspapers soaked in lavender water. Far from dissuading the rodents, the smell of lavender positively encouraged them and they soon ate through the paper plugs. Aggie had then sought the services of a good ratcatcher.

'I can put down some poison, missus,' he told her. 'It's gonna smell though.'

Aggie shook her head. 'Oh, no! I can't stand bad smells.'

'Well, get yerself a good mouser,' he advised her.

'No fear. I couldn't stand a smelly cat tearin' me 'ome ter pieces,' she told him.

'Well, there's not much I can do then,' replied the exasperated ratcatcher.

Aggie was at her wits' end. 'What can I do?' she had implored Nellie.

'They sell some good stuff at Goodrich's,' Nellie informed her. 'It's s'posed ter be odourless.'

Aggie went along to Goodrich's, the local ironmonger.

'It ain't exactly odourless,' the helpful Mr Goodrich told her. 'But it ain't a bad smell really. More like turpentine, but it's really effective. I put some down in my place an' I ain't seen any signs of mice since,' he said encouragingly.

Aggie bought a packet of Ransome's Rodent Ridder

from the shopkeeper and was soon back to complain. 'It smelled the place out an' I 'ad ter chuck it away,' she moaned.

'Well, I suggest yer get yerself a good mouser,' Mr Goodrich told her in no uncertain manner.

'Oh, no! I couldn't stand me 'ome gettin' tore ter pieces, an' they're so smelly,' she moaned.

Mr Goodrich laughed. 'Listen, missus. If yer take pride in yer 'ome I'd suggest yer get a mouser. If they're neutered they don't smell. Good cats keep the 'ome free from rodents an' they make good pets. If yer train 'em right they do their business in a tray in the yard, an' they don't take much ter keep.'

Aggie went away thinking about what she had been told and she confided in Nellie Tanner once more. 'I've decided ter get a mouser. It's gotta be neutered though,' she insisted.

Nellie had no idea where her friend Aggie could obtain a neutered tomcat but she had made enquiries. The memory of the outcome brought a smile to her face on that Saturday morning as she walked down towards the crouching figure of Aggie.

She had asked William about getting Aggie a cat but he had no idea where a tomcat could be found on the quick and he shook his head. 'I'll ask George the road-sweeper,' was all he could suggest.

Two days later William had a piece of good news for Nellie. 'I 'ad a word wiv George about that cat,' he told her. 'D'yer remember ole Broom'ead Smith the totter?'

Nellie nodded. 'I ain't seen 'im about fer years. 'E was always up an' down the street.'

'Accordin' ter George, ole Broom'ead is back in circulation,' William went on. ''E went ter live wiv 'is daughter an' 'er 'usband somewhere in Kent. Anyway, Broom'ead caused so many problems there that 'is

33

daughter's 'usband told 'er that eivver 'er farvver went or 'e would. So Broom'ead clouts 'im an' packs 'is bags. 'E's livin' somewhere orf the Tower Bridge Road an' 'e's got 'imself anuvver 'orse-an'-cart.'

'What's that got ter do wiv Aggie's mouser?' Nellie asked him impatiently.

'Well, George said Broom'ead's got a litter o' kittens in the stable where 'e keeps 'is 'orse an' 'e said Aggie can 'ave one of 'em fer two bob.'

Nellie's face had brightened up. 'Good. I'll tell Aggie right away,' she said.

Two days later a horse-and-cart pulled up in Page Street and an elderly man with a shock of ginger hair sticking out from both sides of his battered trilby stepped down and knocked at Aggie's front door. 'I've come about the kitten,' he announced.

'Are yer Mr Broom'ead Smith?' she asked.

'I'm Bill Smith,' the totter replied sharply. 'I don't use that monicker, if yer get me meanin'. I've got yer moggie in a box on the cart. Shall I bring it in?'

Aggie looked horrified as she caught sight of the horse dung on his hobnailed boots. 'There's no need fer that,' she told him. 'I'll come an' get it.'

'Please yerself, missus,' Broomhead replied curtly. 'Keep the fing in the front room near yer fire. I've jus' took it away from its muvver so it'll need the warmth.'

Aggie accompanied the gangling totter to his cart and when she peered into the cardboard box and saw the kitten she shook her head sadly. 'Poor little mite. It don't look very lively. Is it all right?' she asked him.

'Course it's all right. I wouldn't be sellin' it ter yer if it wasn't,' Broomhead said sharply. 'Give it a month or two an' it'll catch all yer mice. Its muvver is a good mouser.'

Aggie paid Broomhead the florin and took the kitten into her spotless home. That night the little creature

34

did not stop crying and its pitiful little squeak tore at Aggie's heartstrings. She took the kitten in its little cardboard box to the bedroom and was constantly getting up all night, peering at the tiny bundle of black fur. Harold was becoming more and more irritable with his wife's bouncing in and out of bed and he declared that if the mice saw the kitten they might well decide to make a meal of it.

Aggie persevered with the kitten and when it was time to get it neutered she went along to the local vet, who informed her that the tomcat was in fact a 'she'. Aggie was mortified. She could not stand the thought of having a she-cat which would one day give birth to a large litter in her nice clean home and she did not wait to find out whether or not she-cats could be neutered. Aggie finally found the cat a good home and from that day onwards she had kept up a running battle with her mice, reverting to paper plugs soaked in vinegar, which seemed to be reasonably effective.

Nellie Tanner had reached Aggie's front door and she stood over the dumpy, dark-haired woman. ''Ow's 'Arold, Aggie?' she asked. 'I 'eard 'e was orf work wiv 'is back.'

'It's a lot better now fanks, Nell. 'E's goin' back Monday,' Aggie told her. 'I've bin rubbin' 'im wiv that liniment ole Doctor Kelly give me, an' I made 'im wear a sheet o' brown paper under 'is vest. 'Ow's your Will keepin'?'

'E's not so bad,' Nellie replied. 'Mind you, 'e's not bin the same since 'e left the yard. I fink 'e still misses those 'orses.'

Aggie got up from her knees and grunted as she placed her hand in the small of her back. 'I still expect ter see 'im come walkin' out o' that yard,' she said, nodding to the Galloway stables on the bend of the street. 'It used ter be nice when there was only 'orses in that yard. 'E's got four lorries in there now an' I did 'ear 'e was lookin' fer anuvver place. Sooner the better, if yer ask me.'

Nellie nodded her agreement. 'I was glad 'e didn't get that site where our Carrie's got 'er cafe,' she remarked.

''Ow is young Carrie?' Aggie asked. 'I ain't seen much of 'er lately. I was surprised at 'er marryin' Fred Bradley. I always reckoned 'er an' young Billy Sullivan was goin' ter get tergevver. I was only sayin' ter my 'Arold the ovver day, I ain't seen nuffink o' Carrie Tanner lately. I always remember 'er walkin' up the turnin' wiv 'er 'ead 'eld up. Such a pretty fing too. 'Ow's 'er Rachel doin'?'

'She's lovely,' Nellie told her. 'Gettin' on very well. Carrie's got a nurse ter look after the baby while she works be'ind the counter. Very nice young woman. Irish she is. I've met 'er a couple o' times.'

The conversation was interrupted by the appearance of Florrie Axford, a tall, lean woman in her early fifties. Florrie was affectionately known as 'Hairpin' Axford through her use of a large hairpin which she had removed from her hair on more than one occasion to 'make a point', as she herself described it.

'Still at it, Aggie,' she said smiling and winking saucily at Nellie.

'Somebody's gotta do it, ain't they?' Aggie replied with a pained expression on her wide face. 'What wiv them lorries up an' down the turnin'. I reckon it should be stopped. One o' these days there's gonna be a bad accident, mark my words.'

Florrie nodded and puckered her lips. 'I told that miserable bloke who looks after the lorries the same fing meself,' she told her friends. 'Mind yer, it's like talkin' ter the brick wall, talkin' ter that silly git. 'Is ole woman's as bad. A right miserable pair they are.

Always arguin' the toss. I could 'ear 'em both the ovver night when I walked past their winder. I could 'ear 'er voice goin' on about somefink or the ovver. She's got a right gate on 'er. Ugly as sin she is too.'

'Well, she can't 'elp 'er looks,' Aggie remarked.

'No, but she could 'ide,' Florrie laughed.

Nellie pulled up the collar of her coat against the wind. 'Well, I'd better be off. I've got me shoppin' ter do before Will gets 'ome,' she said. ''E finishes at twelve on Saturdays.'

'I'm goin' up the market, I'll walk along wiv yer,' Florrie said, straightening the wide lapel of her shabby coat.

The two women bade Aggie goodbye and walked back quickly along the street, turning the corner by Galloway's yard towards Jamaica Road. They nodded to Maggie Jones and Ida Bromsgrove who were chatting together on the doorstep, and to Grace Crossley, the landlady of the Kings Arms which stood on the corner of Page Street. Grace was standing at the door of her pub chatting to Maudie Mycroft.

'I wonder what's goin' on there?' Florrie asked, always keen to keep herself informed about local goings-on.

'I dunno, but Maudie looks a bit worried,' Nellie replied.

'She's gettin' worse,' Florrie said contemptuously. 'It's that new vicar at the church, I'm sure. Yer know 'ow nervous she is. Well, since you've bin away from the street she's bin terrible. Last week she was out on 'er doorstep threatenin' ter chuck a pail o' water over a couple o' Galloway's carmen. They were only 'avin' a chin-wag outside 'er winder an' yer know 'ow they blaspheme. Anyway, they walked orf all sheepish when she started ravin' at 'em, an' then she goes marchin' in the yard would yer believe ter see ole Galloway. 'E

37

wasn't there by all accounts but 'is son Frank was. Well, Maudie 'ands 'im a pile o' leaflets she got from the church an' tells 'im ter 'and 'em out ter the carmen. Now yer know what a cowson that Frank is. 'E told 'er ter piss orf out of it in no uncertain terms an' Maudie told 'im she was gonna send 'er ole man round ter sort 'im out. I felt sorry fer 'er Ernie. 'E come 'ome that night wiv a few drinks inside 'im an' 'im an' Maudie got at it. She come over ter me cryin' 'er eyes out. She said she told Ernie what she told Frank Galloway an' Ernie said 'e wasn't goin' ter get involved, an' she should send the vicar round ter sort Galloway out. What's more, 'e told 'er if she didn't stop 'er silly carryin's on, 'e was gonna leave 'er.'

'P'raps 'e 'as,' Nellie suggested. 'Maybe that's what she was talkin' ter Grace Crossley about.'

Florrie shook her head vigorously. 'Ernie ain't left 'er. The poor sod was only sayin' that ter make 'er act a bit sensible. 'E idolises 'er, despite what the silly mare's doin'. I blame it all on 'im at the church. 'E sounds a right dopey git if yer ask me. I thought the last vicar was a bit dopey, but this one's a sight worse. They should stick ter what they do best, like christenin's, weddin's an' burials, and the Sunday services. When they start runnin' those muvvers' meetin's they put a lot o' nonsense in people's 'eads. I only ever went ter one muvvers' meetin' an' that was years ago. I remember it well.'

The two women were waiting to cross the busy Jamaica Road, and once they had scurried across between the trams Florrie continued her tale.

'It was near Christmas. 'Ninety-eight or 'ninety-nine it would be. Anyway, my ole man 'ad pissed orf an' I was a bit short o' money. I only went 'cos somebody told me they was 'andin' out food parcels. Well, I sat through the service, tryin' not ter fall asleep, an' then the tea an' biscuits came round. I got a right ear'ole bashin' from two o' the ole dears an' then they give out the parcels. I got a jar o' gherkins, a woolly 'at an' a pair o' bedsocks. White ones they was s'posed ter be but they'd bin boiled wiv the colours I should fink. Gawd knows who they come orf of. I give 'em ter ole Granny Pridey who used ter live next door ter me. She was glad of 'em. Come ter fink of it, she 'ad the woolly 'at as well. I kept the gherkins though. I 'ad 'em wiv a bit o' cheese on Christmas night.'

Nellie was chuckling at the story. 'Yer done right, Florrie,' she remarked. 'Some'ow I can't see you in a woolly 'at an' bedsocks.'

'Well, I used ter wear a cotton nightdress when that Joe Maitland lodged wiv me,' she said smiling. 'I reckoned it might tempt 'im, but no such luck. Now 'e's moved out I'm back ter me flannelette.'

They had reached Bermondsey Market and they walked slowly along the line of stalls. Barrows were piled high with fruit and vegetables, and as they passed the fish stall they saw the fishmonger gutting an eel. A little way along there was a young man standing between two stalls with a tray suspended by a strap around his neck. The tray contained buttons, collar studs and various other bits and pieces. The vendor wore campaign medal ribbons and a black patch over one eye, and there was a card pinned to the tray which said, 'Wounded on the Somme'. The two women stopped and each bought a packet of sewing needles and a pair of collar studs.

'Gawd knows who I'm gonna give these to,' Florrie chuckled.

'Keep 'em 'andy, Flo. Yer might get anuvver young lodger soon,' Nellie joked.

The women's kind gesture did not go unthanked.

'Thank yer very kindly, ladies, an' may the Lord

bless yer,' the young man said in a reverent voice.

Charlie Harris was a shrewd street-seller whose appearance and demeanour tugged at the heartstrings of the compassionate. Charlie had never been wounded on the Somme. He had lost his eye when he was a young child, and the nearest he ever got to France was a trip to Brighton. The medal ribbons were borrowed from his elder brother, who really had been wounded on the Somme.

Billy Sullivan had decided that he was going to own his own gymnasium one day and the idea grew in his mind until it became an obsession. He was always talking about it and it caused much worry to his mother Sadie and her husband Daniel.

'I'm sure 'e's goin' out of 'is mind about that gym, Dan,' Sadie fretted. 'We lost two sons in the war an' we're gonna lose 'im if we're not careful. They'll put 'im away, I know they will.'

Daniel put his arm around his large wife and patted her back gently. ''E'll be all right, luv. Billy knows what 'e's doin',' he said encouragingly. 'Besides, it's givin' 'im somefink ter fink about. Surely it's better than the way 'e's bin since 'e got back from France? When I fink of all that time 'e jus' sat at the front door wiv 'is 'ead in 'is 'ands, I shudder. At least 'e's gettin' out an' about now.'

'That's just what I'm worried about,' Sadie told him. 'Billy's runnin' around wiv a nasty crowd of 'ippidy-'oys. 'E'll be gettin' 'imself inter trouble wiv the police if 'e's not careful.'

Daniel patted his wife again and tried to reassure her, although he was worried himself about Billy's well-being. Had he been present at the gathering in the public bar of the Queen Anne pub near the Rother-hithe Tunnel he would have been worried even more.

Billy sat in a far corner of the little pub with Chopper Harris, Frankie Albright and Freddie the Nark, and Freddie was trying hard to sound convincing as he put his plan over to his friends. Billy listened to Freddie the Nark with a growing sense of unease. He had led an exciting life in boxing circles before he went away to the war and he did not consider himself to lack nerve, but the plan the little shifty-eyed character was setting out made Billy want to get up and leave right away. He stayed, however, and as he looked around at the faces of Frankie and Chopper he worried. Frankie was rubbing his hands together and Chopper merely nodded now and then with a silly expression on his face.

Billy picked up his pint of ale and took a large draught. It was how he would have expected Frankie to react. Frankie Albright was nineteeen and just young enough to have missed the war; he had tried to sign up when he was sixteen, only to be informed upon by his mother, who had followed him down to the recruiting office. Frankie's wrath knew no bounds and after subjecting his weeping mother to a tirade of the most vile obscenities he was thrown out of the office by a disgusted recruiting sergeant. Frankie had left home and was now living in lodgings in a little backstreet near the pub they were sitting in. Frankie followed the boxing scene with much interest and it was through boxing that Billy had become involved with the volatile character in the first place.

Chopper Harris, on the other hand, was a dullard who had a big heart where his friends were concerned, and it was he who often stood cups of tea or a pint for his friends. Billy had gone to school with Chopper and knew his background very well. He got his name from an incident when he was a lad. One Saturday night his father came home from the pub the worse for drink and as usual he picked on Chopper's mother. The young lad had also been battered unmercifully many a time and on that particular night he had decided he would put an end to the violence by teaching his drunken father a lesson he would never forget. The young lad took out the large chopper his father used to cleave wood for the fire and chased the bully out of the house and down the street. His mother followed screaming at the boy to stop, but he was too incensed to hear her. At last the father fell down on to the pavement completely exhausted and convinced he was going to meet his maker there and then. The raging young lad raised the chopper above his head and brought it down with tremendous force. Sparks flew up from the pavement only a fraction of an inch from his father's head. He raised the chopper again, but his mother threw herself upon their tormentor screaming for help. Fortunately some of the neighbours intervened, and it was they who invented the sobriquet.

Freddie the Nark had finished setting out his plan and he leaned back in his chair, raising his glass to his lips with a smirk of satisfaction. He could see that Chopper and Frankie were sold on the idea. He noticed, however, that Billy Sullivan was not so smitten with the plan.

'Why d'yer fink we should knock the ole boy around before we tie 'im up?' Billy asked.

Freddie leaned forward. 'Look at it this way, Billy,' he said in a condescending tone of voice. 'If by any chance the police pull us in on suspicion they've got ter 'ave an identification parade, an' if the old watchman recognises any of us we're done for, unless 'e's too frightened ter pick us out, an' 'e will be if 'e knows we're capable o' smackin' 'im around a bit. Anuvver fing is that if we do 'im over 'e won't 'ave the strength ter struggle free too soon after we've gone. It'll give us more time ter get the load stashed. We'll need a couple of hours at least.'

'What about the load?' Billy queried. 'Are yer sure it's what that geezer said it was?'

Freddie grabbed at his glass and took a quick swig of ale then put it down with a bang on the wooden table. 'Joe Wallace 'as worked at Clark's Wharf fer years. 'E knows more about that place than the guv'nor 'imself,' he asserted. 'What's more, Joe Wallace was so pissed that night 'e didn't 'ave an inklin' who 'e was talkin' to or what pub 'e was in for that matter, so there's no come-back from 'im at least. One fing yer can be sure of – drunk or sober, Joe knows what's lyin' in that ware'ouse. Like I said, 'e told me an' Tony McCarthy that there's no end o' silk on the ground floor an' upstairs there's cases o' real ivory ornaments. Them alone are werf a small fortune.

'Now let's go over it once more,' he went on in an encouraging voice. 'Tony's all right about drivin' the lorry as long as we load the stuff ourselves. Two of us should manage the bales an' the ovver two can carry down the crates of ornaments. They're only small crates. We should be able ter manage one each. Tony's gonna bring up the lorry at six o'clock sharp on Saturday night. We've gotta be ready fer 'im. When 'e's backed the lorry in the yard we close the gates like I said. Tony gives us till quarter ter seven then 'e'll come back and drive it out o' the yard. I'll be in the front ter show 'im the way an' it should take us about twenty minutes ter Wappin'. There'll be no trouble the ovver end. They'll be waitin' fer us an' once the load's orf the motor Tony can take it back on 'is own. As I said before, we can stop over the ovver side o' the water fer a celebration drink. I know a few good boozers over there as it 'appens. The only fing we've gotta decide is, who's gonna come wiv me on Sunday evenin' fer the pay out. We can't all go traipsin' over ter see Johnnie Buckram.'

Billy Sullivan was silent for a while, his mind racing. With his share he would be able to get the gymnasium he so badly wanted. The only thing which bothered him was the old night watchman. Supposing something went wrong, he thought anxiously. Supposing one of them got carried away and hit the old boy too hard. No, there had to be no violence to the watchman. He would make that clear, or else he would have no part in the raid. As he stared down at his half-empty glass Billy became aware of Freddie watching him closely and he looked up at the schemer suddenly, fixing him with a cold stare. Freddie the Nark was a shrewd character, he thought, and from what he knew of the man Billy realised that he must tread very carefully. Freddie lived by his wits and he was involved with many shady characters. He had found the fence and he had planned the raid very well. He had a vicious side to his nature and it apparently meant nothing to him that an old man was going to be roughed up during the raid.

Freddie was indeed a shrewd character and he knew that Billy Sullivan was hedging. He was known as the Nark by the local people who placed their bets in Albion Street. Freddie stood on the corner of the turning as lookout for Tommy Green the street book-maker. He knew the local C.I.D. and it was said he could sniff a copper out a mile away. Freddie the Nark also had the reputation of being a womaniser. His long-suffering wife Elsie knew that her man had a mistress tucked away somewhere. What she did not know was that Freddie had two children by his other woman. Elsie kept quiet about his affair and swallowed her pride, however. With six children to feed she felt unable to challenge him about his mistress lest he walked out on her for good.

Billy had made up his mind. He leaned forward, his elbows resting on the table. 'Right, Freddie. I'll go along with the business on one condition,' he said quietly.

'What's that?' Freddie asked.

'We leave the old boy alone. We can throw a sack over 'is 'ead an' warn 'im ter be quiet or else. That should be enough.'

Freddie was quiet for a few moments, then to Billy's surprise he nodded. 'Right. We'll do it your way. But I'm warnin' yer, Billy,' he said with menace. 'If that ole watchman gives us any bovver I'll do 'im meself. Is that understood?'

Billy nodded. 'That suits me,' he said. 'Now let's get a drink in. I'm gonna drink ter Billy Sullivan's gymnasium.'

Chapter Four

Carrie leaned back in her chair and rubbed the tips of her fingers across her forehead as she stared down at the mass of papers on the kitchen table. There were unpaid bills, receipts and invoices, all spread around the large dog-eared ledger that Fred had used for the past few years. 'It's a complete mess,' she groaned aloud.

Fred Bradley was sitting by the kitchen range polishing his best boots and he looked up at her suddenly. 'I've bin usin' that book fer years,' he said defensively. 'Everyfing's in there.'

Carrie shook her head in exasperation. Some of the entries were illegible and others were written across the ruled lines and ran into each other, and they were all in scrawly handwriting, which she found very difficult to decipher.

'Yer should total these, Fred, an' keep yer accounts tidy,' she admonished him. 'We've got ter see 'ow we're doin', 'ow much we're spendin', an' set it against the takin's.'

Fred put down the boot he was polishing and got up from his chair. 'It's all there,' he said, sighing irritably. 'Look, I'll show yer. It's dead simple.'

Carrie folded her arms and stared up at him as he thumbed through the ledger and took out a grease-stained sheet of paper. 'There it is. There's nuffink difficult about it,' he said with a show of impatience, pointing to the two columns of figures with the blacking brush. 'Yer can't 'ave it simpler than that, can yer?'

'Well, I would 'ave thought so,' Carrie answered shortly. 'What does John Percival say when 'e does yer books?'

Fred shrugged his wide shoulders. 'I jus' take everyfing to 'im an' give 'im all those sheets wiv me totals on, an' 'e works it all out. 'E's never complained.'

Carrie had seen the accountant's bill for the previous year's work and she knew why he never complained. 'Well, it's not businesslike ter do it that way, Fred,' she protested. 'We should be able ter look at these books an' see at a glance 'ow we're doin'.'

'But I know 'ow we're doin. We're doin' very good,' Fred replied, sitting down in the chair facing his young wife. 'The place is full most o' the time, an' since the trade's picked up at the docks there's more carmen comin' in all times o' the day while they're waitin' in the rank. You should know that, you're servin' 'em.'

Carrie bit back a sharp reply and instead she leaned forward across the littered table. 'Look, Fred. I asked yer ter let me do these books 'cos I wanted ter sort out the bills an' see where we can make savin's. I fink yer buyin' wrong,' she said quietly.

'What d'yer mean, buyin' wrong?' Fred asked quickly. 'I've got me regular suppliers an' they always come on time. Ole Bert Moseley's 'ere on the dot at nine o'clock every Monday mornin' wiv me stuff, an' Albert Buller comes round every Thursday mornin' ter take me order. I've bin dealin' wiv Johnson's fer years now, an' so was me parents when they 'ad the shop.'

'Well, I reckon we should look at the prices,' Carrie persisted. 'Now we're increasin' the order we should get better quotes. We could get bulk sugar instead o' those silly packs yer bin orderin', an' we should fink o' buyin' tea by the chest. We've bin runnin' out more than once lately. If yer remember, yer 'ad ter send Bessie out fer a couple o' pound last Friday ter tide us over till Monday.'

Fred looked crestfallen. 'Maybe you should talk ter Albert Buller when 'e calls next time,' he suggested.

'An' what about these books? Are yer gonna let me take 'em over?' Carrie asked firmly.

Her husband nodded meekly. 'If yer want to. I bin pretty 'ard put to it in that kitchen lately,' he said, passing his hand through his thick greying hair.

Carrie got up and walked around the table, feeling suddenly sorry for her aggressive attitude towards him. She laid her hands on the top of his shoulders and kneaded the base of his neck with her thumbs. Fred dropped his head and groaned.

'Gawd, that feels good,' he murmured in a low voice. After a pause he added, 'D'yer fink yer can get a discount from Johnson's?'

Carrie walked around to face him and gestured towards the mess of papers. 'I've bin totallin' up the bills fer the past month,' she told him. 'If we could get some discounts an' look at what we're buyin' I fink we could do even better than we're doin' now. There's ovver suppliers who deliver locally. If Johnson's don't give us any satisfaction then we'll take our trade elsewhere. That's business, Fred.'

He looked at her with a smile on his wide, open face. 'D'yer know, Carrie, yer've really changed from the little miss who knocked on my front door that evenin'. Yer was pretty as a picture an' I said ter meself straight away, "Fred", I ses, "this 'ere little lady is gonna be good fer yer business." Little did I know she was gonna be me wife an' 'ave me children.'

'Whoa! 'Old on a minute, Fred Bradley. Children did yer say?' Carrie exclaimed. 'I've got one baby ter look after as well as an 'usband an' the business. That'll do me very well fer the time bein', thanks!'

Fred leaned out and grabbed Carrie around the waist, pulling her to him. She placed her hands against his chest to resist, a serious look appearing on her face.

'We've got no time ter mess about, Fred,' she said quickly. 'I've got Rachel ter wash and settle, an' then I've gotta sort those papers out.'

'The papers can keep,' he replied, his hands tightening around her waist. 'Rachel's quiet. Let's go inter the bedroom.'

'No, Fred,' she demurred, trying to remain calm.

'It's bin a while now, gel,' he said, his voice urgent. 'I've bin missin' yer. All work an' no play ain't good fer anybody.'

She was pushing against his chest but Fred rose to his feet and, moving sideways, suddenly bent down and swept her up in his strong arms. Carrie sighed in resignation as he carried her out on to the small landing and leaned his shoulder against the bedroom door. She could smell the sweat on his body and feel his excited breathing. She closed her eyes and prepared to submit. It was better that way she told herself. Better than enduring his fumbling during the night in the vain hope of satisfaction when the need was strong in her.

The bedroom felt cold and as Fred sank to the bed with her still in his arms Carrie closed her eyes and tried not to let herself focus on the small round damp patch on the ceiling above the foot of the bed. That patch had slowly become an image of despair and frustration over many occasions since she had first shared his bed. Fred was a kind, considerate man, uncomplicated and loving in his way, but she regretted that he had never been able really to arouse her fully and take her to the height of passion. Even when the need in her grew strong in the dead of night and she lay close to his slack body, caressing him and urging him, he was never able to fulfil the need in her.

Carrie's eyes opened reluctantly as he fumbled with her buttoned dress and she saw the small round damp spot on the ceiling. He was removing his thick leather belt with one hand and struggling with one of her buttons. She finished undoing it for him and slipped out of the dress, and as she let him raise her petticoat her eyes strayed again to the patch on the ceiling. Fred's face was flushed a deep red and his breath came fast as he slipped down his trousers and pressed himself on top of her body. He was much heavier than her and Carrie felt breathless as his full weight bore down on her. She bit on her bottom lip as he moved into her roughly, his breath coming faster and changing to a pant. The damp mark above her seemed to take shape. It was like a smiling, mocking face, laughing at her useless attempts to raise her own passion. Fred's trousers were still around his ankles and his movement was hurting her, but by the time she had managed to free one of her legs from beneath him he had finished. He lay prone on top of her for a few moments then he rolled to one side, panting loudly, his breath slowly returning to normal.

'Was it nice?' he said, his dark eyes close to hers.

'Yes, Fred,' she lied. She had tried to imagine Tommy Allen coming into the bedroom and taking Fred's place, but it had made no difference. Just thinking of the dark young man with Romany looks who had taken her virginity, and for a short time had loved her so passionately, did not serve her well enough. She felt frustrated and alone, and a tear glistened in her eye as she lay there on her back with Fred's limp arm lying heavily across her breasts. She had only herself to blame, she knew. After all, it was a marriage of convenience for her. It had been a way of escaping from the poverty into which her family had sunk, and she

51

knew that by working hard for long, tiring hours and helping Fred turn the mediocre business into one that was thriving and profitable she would one day be able to help her parents and her brother too. Why should she feel guilty of deceiving her devoted husband, she asked herself, if it was only in her thoughts?

The Saturday afternoon was drawing in now and Carrie looked out through the partly drawn curtains at the dark, rolling clouds. Rain was threatening and there was a distant roll of thunder. She moved slightly to one side and slipped from under Fred's arm. He grunted and turned over, snoring noisily. Rachel had been quiet but now Carrie could hear her stirring, the growing sounds of protest coming through the open door. It was wrong for her to become obsessed with Fred's inadequacy in the bedroom, Carrie told herself. If she was not careful all that she was working for, all that she had planned and schemed for, would be lost forever.

Bill Smith took off his battered trilby and scratched his fuzzy ginger hair as he sat on his cart and urged the horse forward. The animal took no notice and clopped on at a steady plodding pace through the narrow turning. It had been pulling the small cart through backstreets for years now and seemed to know instinctively that it would probably be required to stop at any moment, so there was no point in hurrying. Broomhead Smith, as the totter was known, thought otherwise. He had been sitting on the cart since early morning and all he had to show for scouring the streets was an old tin bath that he had found on some wasteground, a couple of sacks of rags and one or two pieces of old iron. There was also a badly scratched veneered cabinet which had once housed a gramophone. It was the only piece of junk that Broomhead was optimistic about. The scratches could be filled in with wood-filler and stained to match, and then the veneer cleaned with wire wool and vinegar, he decided. One or two applications of French polish would do the trick. It might even give him a nice profit on his outlay, which was nothing to worry about.

Broomhead had tied the cabinet to the rave of the cart, lest it fall over and become more scratched if by any faint chance the horse decided to show some signs of life. The totter need not have worried. The animal was struggling with a loose shoe and was in no mood to break into a trot. Broomhead Smith had other things on his mind besides the horse. He had been accosted only recently by an irate Aggie Temple when he drove his cart into Page Street, and now he had to steer clear of the little turning until he could fulfil his promise to get the woman a genuine tomcat mouser which had been doctored. The trouble was, the transport yard in Page Street was a good place to pick up bits and pieces of worthwhile scrap. Old horse brasses, damaged wagon wheels and various other items had very often found their way on to the back of his cart in the past without cost. Broomhead had at first considered giving the woman a salutation from his vast treasury of filthy language when she approached him, but he realised that it might damage his rather good reputation. As he prided himself on his fair and honest trading, and the high standards which he always maintained except in extenuating circumstances, the ginger-haired totter had decided he should do the right thing by her.

Broomhead shifted his position on the cart and urged his horse on once more to no effect. They had just turned into Bacon Street when he heard a loud voice calling to him and pulled sharply on the reins. The tired horse stopped dead in its tracks and turned its head around to give him a baleful stare. Broomhead looked up in the direction of the shouting and saw a woman leaning out of a window on the top floor of Bacon Buildings.

'Yer'll 'ave ter come down, missus,' he called out to her, 'I can't climb those stairs wiv me bad leg.'

The window was slammed down and Broomhead waited, taking the opportunity of rolling himself a cigarette. Soon a large woman emerged from the block and walked smartly up to his cart.

''Ere, I've got one o' them there gramophone fings,' she said, looking up at him and slipping her hands into the armholes of her stained flowery apron.

'That's nice,' Broomhead said in his usual sarcastic manner.

'There's nuffink nice about it,' the buxom woman told him. 'My ole man come 'ome pissed last night an' said 'e wanted ter listen ter a bit o' music.'

'I only wanna sleep when I come 'ome pissed,' Broomhead informed her.

'Well, you ain't my ole man,' the woman reminded him. 'Anyway, what 'appened was, 'e puts this record on the fing an' winds up the 'andle, an' guess what?'

'Go on, missus, surprise me,' the totter said unenthusiastically.

'Well, there was this almighty bang an' the bleedin' fing stopped dead right in the middle o' the music. Luvverly song it was an' all. It was fair bringin' tears ter me eyes,' the woman went on.

'Look, missus, I don't wanna be rude, but what the bleedin' 'ell 'as this all gotta do wiv me?' Broomhead asked with a deep sigh.

'My ole man got upset an' 'e told me ter get rid o' the bloody fing before 'e got 'ome from work ternight. 'E works on the trams, yer see,' the woman explained.

'I can't buy busted gramophones, lady,' the totter

said, drawing on his cigarette. "Specially when they go orf bang. When that sort o' fing 'appens it's the spring, yer see. Bloody powerful springs they are as well. I knew one bloke who overwound one o' those gramophones an' the fing busted. Terrible it was.'

'What 'appened?' the large woman asked, her eyes bulging.

'Well, the 'andle spun round an' sent 'im flyin' up ter the ceilin'. Poor bleeder split 'is 'ead wide open,' Broomhead told her. 'Like a bleedin' patchwork quilt 'e was, by the time they finished stitchin' 'im up.'

'Oh my Gawd!'

'I don't fink the Lord 'imself could do anyfing about busted springs, lady. There's nuffink at all yer can do when the spring goes,' Broomhead said, grinning evilly.

The buxom woman's face dropped noticeably. 'Well, I'm in fer a right 'idin' if I ain't got that bleedin' contraption out o' the 'ouse by the time my Joshua comes 'ome, 'specially if 'e's bin on the turps again. What am I gonna do?'

'Why don't yer chuck it down in the dustbin?' he suggested.

'I would if I could,' she said, 'but it's so bleedin' 'eavy. It mus' go 'alf a bleedin' 'undredweight.'

Broomhead's artfulness was working like a treat, and for good effect he rubbed his leg. 'Well, if this war wound stands up ter walkin' up those stairs I might be able ter get it down ter the dustbin for yer,' he said with a grimace. 'Mind yer, I'm not promisin' anyfink, yer understand.'

'Would yer try?' she implored him. 'I'd be ever so grateful.'

'Would yer now?'

The desperate woman's eyes sparkled and she

looked up at the crafty totter with new interest. 'Well, I could make it werf yer while,' she said fluttering her eyelashes at him.

Broomhead heard warning bells starting to ring in his head. It was bad enough having to make a detour around Page Street without some irate husband from Bacon Buildings being out to cut his throat. 'I'm a married man, missus,' he lied. 'I don't mess around wiv ovver women. It's jus' not werf it.'

'Please yerself then,' the woman replied, looking disappointed.

'Tell yer what I'm prepared ter do,' the totter said as he scratched his ear. 'Give us a couple o' bob an' I'll come up the stairs an' carry the bloody fing down, even if it kills me in the process. After all, we can't 'ave a nice lady like you takin' a good 'idin' from that 'usband o' yours, now can we?'

The woman's face brightened up considerably and she gave him a sweet smile. 'I'll get on back up the stairs then an' put the kettle on. I s'pose yer'd like a cuppa fer yer troubles?' she prompted. 'Number 64 it is, on the top floor.'

'Don't remind me what floor it is, lady,' Broomhead said quickly, jumping down and reaching for his horse's nosebag which was strapped beneath the seat.

One hour later, after he had been refreshed and had listened patiently to his grateful client's sad story about the awful life she was leading at the hands of a brutal husband, Broomhead was on his way. The gramophone was sitting next to the cabinet, and the totter thought they paired up admirably. He urged his horse on home, and for the first time that day it responded by breaking into a trot for a few yards, until it decided that it was more comfortable to walk.

Billy Sullivan felt worried as he waited by the Rotherhithe Tunnel entrance for his confederates. It was nearly five-thirty and still they had not arrived. Billy cursed his lack of sense in agreeing to take part in the robbery. It was too late to back out now, he realised. He would have to keep an eagle eye out for Freddie though. He was quite likely to forget the agreement they had made about the night watchman and, given the slightest excuse, batter the old boy.

The large clock over the pawnbroker's in Albion Street was showing the half hour when Billy spotted the trio alighting from a tram. They hurried across to him. Freddie looked agitated. 'There was a bloody 'old-up at Surrey Docks Station,' he moaned. 'A poxy tram broke down.'

The four set off along Brunel Road, following the tunnel wall until they passed the Labour Exchange then they veered left and picked up the road which ran alongside the river. It was quiet on that Saturday night, with all the wharves bolted and barred. Freddie the Nark led the way with Chopper walking beside him, and Billy followed behind with Frankie who was humming tunelessly. It was five-forty when they reached Clark's Wharf.

Freddie turned to the others. 'Now let me do the talkin',' he hissed, 'an' when we get in, follow the plan jus' like we agreed. Don't ferget now, we gotta 'ave the gates ready fer when Tony brings the lorry up at six sharp.'

Jack Price closed the office door behind him, sat down heavily in the large swivel chair and watched the tin kettle popping rings of steam. The Saturday shift always seemed to drag on endlessly for the elderly night watchman and he envied people who did not have to work at the weekends. Beggars can't be choosers though, he thought philosophically as he got up, removed the boiling kettle from the gas ring and emptied it into a small china teapot. Being a night watchman had its compensations, he had to admit. There was no foreman to watch over him and he could please himself when he made his walk around the yard. He knew too that his job was important. Many of the wharves were just padlocked with no one to guard them but Clark's Wharf was different. In the building and the big yard beside it there were cases of very expensive items. The manager had explained to him when he was taken on that the insurance people insisted the wharf was guarded at all times before they would agree to give cover. Jack's only complaint was that the pittance he was paid hardly reflected the responsibility placed upon him.

Jack Price had never married, and he lived with his ageing sister who was also unmarried. He was sixty-four now, but as a young man he had been in the army and seen action on the North-West Frontier. He had been in many tight spots during his life, and guarding a warehouse did not trouble him unduly. He had worked for various firms doing all sorts of jobs, for he was nothing if not adaptable, and recently, just as he was approaching retirement, the firm he worked for in Deptford had become bankrupt. Jack had been worried. Who would employ a sixty-four-year-old man when there were thousands of young men struggling to find work? The ex-serviceman need not have worried. His employer gave him a glowing reference and spoke about him to a friend by the name of Sir Algernon Clark, a fellow businessman who was having problems with insurance brokers over the size of the premium for insuring his wharf and its most valuable contents. Employing a night watchman was the solution to his problem, and so without delay Jack was sent to see the wharf manager, who felt that the sprightly-looking man who had served on the Khyber Pass would suit admirably.

Jack sipped his tea while he read a dog-eared wild west novel. It was a good way of passing the time, he thought. There was a long night ahead of him, and he would not be relieved until eight o'clock the following morning when Ben Thompson arrived. Ben too was an active man in his sixties and had served in the police force for years, rising to the rank of sergeant. The trouble with Ben was, he still thought he was in the police force and was constantly leaving scribbled messages about procedures for patrolling the yard and checking the padlocks and bolts.

Bloody old fool. Who does he think he is, anyway? Jack thought to himself as he poured yet another cup of tea and took it back to his comfortable swivel chair. It's a good job Peggie's not here, he told himself as he sipped the tea. She was always on about the amount of tea he drank. Poor old Peg. Shame she never married. She had never got over that chap who left her in the lurch all those years ago. Nevertheless she had been a good, kind sister and looked after him very well. She was breaking up now, though, Jack reflected sadly. Never mind, he'd buy her a nice bunch of flowers from that stall outside the infirmary on his way home. She'd like that.

A loud knocking on the wicket-gate made Jack start and he muttered to himself as he left the office and walked across the cobbled yard.

Chapter Five

The Kings Arms was a small, homely pub. It stood on the corner of Page Street at the Jamaica Road end, and was the favourite haunt of folk from the surrounding backstreets. The landlord Alec Crossley kept an orderly house and his buxom blonde wife Grace was always jolly and invariably found time to listen to the troubles of her customers, even when she was hard put to it behind the counter. On Saturday evening it was busy as usual, but when Sadie Sullivan walked in the public bar on the arm of her diminutive husband Daniel, Grace soon found herself listening to her troubles.

'That bleeder ain't bin in 'ere, 'as 'e?' Sadie asked.

Grace shook her head. 'No, luv. I ain't seen nuffink of 'im. Anyfing wrong?'

Sadie leant on the counter and looked furtively right and left before putting a hand up to her mouth and whispering, 'I fink 'e's up ter no good.'

Grace smiled reassuringly. 'Billy's a good boy, Sadie. 'E wouldn't do anyfing wrong.'

'I would 'ave agreed wiv yer at one time,' Sadie replied. 'Since 'e's bin in wiv that crowd from the Tunnel, though, 'e's a changed boy. Me an' Daniel's worried sick about 'im, ain't we, Dan?'

Daniel nodded dutifully and sipped his pint, wishing

that Sadie would refrain from airing their private business to all and sundry.

''E went out at four o'clock an' 'e was all nervy. 'E told me 'e might be late an' not ter wait up,' Sadie went on. ''E knows very well I can't sleep till 'e's in. It's that bloody gymnasium. Since Billy's 'ad that gym on 'is mind 'e's bin like a cat on 'ot bricks. 'E said 'e needs a lot o' money ter get it started an' that's what's worryin' me. 'E could be up to anyfink.'

Grace had seen the irritated look on Alec's face and she patted Sadie's hand. 'Don't worry, luv, Billy's all right, mark my words,' she said quickly as she moved away to resume serving.

When William and Nellie Tanner walked into the public bar Sadie found another ready listener, and Daniel breathed a sigh of relief. Now he had the opportunity to stand at the counter with one of his mates and talk about other things.

'It's a good job, an' the money's not bad,' William was saying in answer to Daniel's enquiry. 'Trouble is, I miss workin' wiv those 'orses. I 'ad a long stint wiv Galloway an' I was gutted when I got the push an' we 'ad ter get out o' the 'ouse. Nellie was 'eart-broken. She misses that little 'ouse of ours. That bloody gaff we're livin' in now is gettin' 'er down. Bacon Buildin's should 'ave bin pulled down years ago, if yer ask me.'

Daniel nodded. 'We brought our tribe up in that 'ouse of ours an' I wouldn't change it fer no ovver place,' he declared. 'It's got a lot o' memories too. After our two boys was killed I wanted ter move out but Sadie wouldn't 'ear of it. She was right. I wouldn't move now.'

William knew just how Daniel felt. It had been the same for him and Nellie when James, their eldest son, was killed in France. It was bad enough losing one son, but to lose two must have been almost unbearable. He sipped his pint and thought about his other two boys. Danny the youngest had settled down in his job as a lighterman and seemed to be popular with the local girls. Charles had been wounded in the fighting but had recovered and signed on as a regular at the end of the war. He was now in India, and judging by his last letter he appeared to be enjoying life out there. Charles had always been the quiet one, William recalled. He had always had his head stuck in a book and never allowed anyone to get him flustered. It was losing that young lass of his that made him sign on, William knew full well.

''Ave yer 'eard from young Charlie lately?' Daniel asked suddenly, as though reading his old friend's thoughts.

'We got a letter from 'im only the ovver day,' William replied. ''E seems fine. Nellie worries over 'im though. It broke 'er 'eart when 'e told 'er 'e was orf ter India.'

Daniel nodded sympathetically. 'Mind you though, it was prob'ly the best fing, when yer come ter sum it all up,' he remarked. 'It was a terrible fing losin' that young lass the way 'e did.'

'Poor Charlie never could understand 'ow it come ter 'appen,' William said quietly, staring down at his pint. 'I'll never ferget that night when we got the news she'd bin drowned.'

Daniel slapped down a florin on the counter and caught the landlord's eye. 'C'mon, Will, let's 'ave anuvver pint an' try ter cheer up. Sadie's bin givin' me the bloody 'ump the way she's bin goin' on about our Billy. She's sure 'e's gonna end up in prison the way fings are goin'. It's that crowd 'e's runnin' aroun' wiv. Mind you, they're a nasty bunch, from what I can make out of it.'

*

The three young men stood a few yards apart from their confederate in the quiet empty street by the river and waited. The sound of Freddie the Nark banging on the small iron gate reverberated along the silent turning and Billy Sullivan winced.

Freddie was confident that the watchman would open up. He and Tony McCarthy had plied their unwitting accomplice with drinks that night in the pub and they had gleaned that Clark's Wharf was guarded by a conscientious old-timer who was living with his frail and ailing sister. It had been enough to set Freddie's agile mind working, and he grinned expectantly to himself as he heard the watchman's voice.

'Who's there? What d'yer want?'

'C.I.D. Paradise Street police station,' Freddie called out in his most cultured voice, putting his face up to the closed wicket-gate. 'Mr Price?'

'That's me,' Jack answered.

'I need to come in, Mr Price. It's urgent,' Freddie told him.

The watchman had been schooled in security and he had been told not to open the door under any circumstances. Should there be any emergency he was to phone Dockhead police station, or they would phone him if they had reason to call.

'I ain't 'ad a call from the station,' Jack called out suspiciously. 'Where's yer warrant card? Slide it under the door an' let's 'ave a look at it.'

Freddie gritted his teeth in agitation. The old boy was being difficult, he cursed silently. 'Look, Mr Price, I had no time to collect my warrant card. We were called out to Ship Street an hour ago. It's your sister Peggie.'

'What's 'appened to 'er?' Jack asked fearfully.

Freddie rubbed his hands together and made a sign to his waiting friends. This would do it, he thought.

'I'm afraid she's had an accident,' he went on. 'One of the neighbours called us. They said they heard a scream and the sound of breaking glass. When we got there she was lying in the front room. She's in the Rotherhithe Infirmary, Mr Price. I'm afraid she's been badly cut. She wants to see you. We've got a police car waiting. One of our men will take over until we get you back here. Hurry, Mr Price, it's urgent.'

The watchman stepped back from the wicket-gate. 'All right, I'll get me coat. You wait there,' he called out.

Freddy nodded reassuringly to his friends. After a short time had passed he began to tap his foot on the kerb impatiently. It had gone very quiet. As he waited the young man began to feel the tension knotting his stomach. It was the feeling he got while watching out for the bookies when the police were in the area. 'C'mon, Mr Price. Hurry,' he called out loudly.

There was no answer, and suddenly all Freddie's experience, all his intuition told him to leave, but fast. Panic seized him and with a sudden curse he turned away from the wicket-gate of Clark's Wharf and gestured at the others to get away. He broke into a trot and the three surprised young men did likewise, aware that something must have gone wrong. Freddie felt his fear growing and he was running now through the quiet riverside lane. He did not stop until he was back in Brunel Road, where the warren of local backstreets seemed to offer safety.

Frankie and Chopper were on Freddie's heels, but Billy had not been able to keep up with them. His chest felt as if it was going to burst and he felt sick and dizzy as he settled down to a steady plod. Whatever had gone wrong was not important to him now. He felt suddenly light, as though the burden of the last few days had suddenly lifted from his shoulders. When he finally turned into Brunel Road and stopped to catch his breath the others were nowhere to be seen. Billy pulled up the collar of his coat and rammed his hands deep into his trouser pockets, feeling suddenly cold as he plodded on. It was when he finally reached the end of the turning by the Rotherhithe Tunnel entrance that he saw the three standing together across the street. The pawnbroker's clock showed five minutes to the hour and Billy suddenly remembered that Tony McCarthy was due and his friends must be waiting for him. As he hurried across the street Freddie spotted him. 'Where d'yer get to?' he asked irritably.

Billy looked at him derisively. 'What're you up to then?' he countered.

'It's gone wrong,' Freddie replied. ''E was phonin' the police, that's what 'e was doin'. That's why I said ter scarper.'

Chopper suddenly pulled on Freddie's arm. 'There 'e is!' he said excitedly, pointing.

Billy stifled the urge to laugh out loud. Tony McCarthy was driving a solid-tyred Leyland lorry that had the words 'Salvation Army' emblazoned along its canvas sides and on a board fixed above the cab. Tony had seen the four standing dejectedly on the street corner and he put his foot on the brake pedal, bringing the vehicle to a shuddering halt.

'What's the matter?' he said as he jumped down from the cab.

'The ole bastard twigged it. 'E left me roastin' outside the gates while 'e went an' phoned the police,' Freddie moaned.

''Ow d'yer know?' Tony asked, suspecting that Freddie had lost his nerve at the last minute.

'I could tell,' the Nark replied. 'I get that feelin' in me guts when it's dodgy. It's the same when I'm narkin' out. I can always tell.'

Tony scratched his head and a sour grin appeared on his handsome face. "Ow we gonna get our money back? I've already 'ad ter fork out fer the lorry. Fifty shillin's it cost me,' he growled. 'I 'ad ter spin the geezer a tale that I was usin' it ter move a poor family out o' the buildin's where I live.'

'Yer ain't gotta take it back yet. Let's go fer a ride,' Chopper butted in, his large flat face breaking out into a smile.

'We could go up ter 'Ampstead. I 'eard it's lively up there on Saturday nights,' Frankie said quickly.

''Ampstead's bleedin' miles away. It'll take too long,' Tony replied, shaking his head. 'It'll 'ave ter be somewhere nearer.'

'I know, let's go over the water ter Poplar. That ain't far from 'ere,' Chopper said helpfully. 'It's only the ovver side o' the tunnel.'

'What's so bleedin' good about Poplar?' Freddie chimed in.

'It'll be a ride, an' we can come back over Tower Bridge,' Chopper suggested.

'C'mon then, let's get goin'. I don't feel safe 'angin' around 'ere,' Freddie said, climbing into the cab.

'Where we gonna sit?' Chopper asked.

'You lot can sit on the back,' Freddie said grumpily.

Billy felt a sudden anger towards the shifty-eyed character. 'Move over, I'm gettin' in there alongside you,' he said sharply. 'I ain't climbin' up the back.'

The lorry set off with Chopper Harris and Frankie Albright sitting on the floor of the lorry, their arms resting on the top of the tailboard. Tony was humming to himself as he drove along but Freddie sat silent, sulking over the raid that never was. Billy felt the wind rushing into the cab as the lorry trundled through the tunnel and he felt relieved. It was all so ridiculous, he thought, allowing himself to get involved with these motley characters. It was the chance to get some big money on the quick which had swayed him. The chance to buy the land for the gymnasium had disappeared for the time being, but it was not the end, he told himself. He would raise the money somehow.

The lorry had not long come out of the tunnel when Tony suddenly clicked his tongue and applied the footbrake. A uniformed policeman had stepped out from the kerb up ahead and was waving them into a side road.

'They're on to us,' he groaned, wondering whether he should put his foot down on the accelerator instead. Billy felt his heart sink but Freddie remained calm. 'It's all right. Leave the talkin' ter me,' he said as Tony turned left and stopped the vehicle by the kerb.

'Evenin', lads,' the constable said affably. 'There's a water main burst down by Lime'ouse Church so yer'd be better goin' via Cable Street. I saw the emblem on the front o' the lorry as yer drove up an' I guessed where yer was goin'.'

'That's more than we 'ave,' Freddie mumbled under his breath.

'Strikes me there's a lot o' good bein' done at them meetin's,' the policeman said cheerfully. 'Don't mind a drink meself, but I was never one ter get drunk. Moderation is what I say. That's the trouble, yer see. Too many people can't 'old their drink an' they can't say no. It's the likes o' them should be at those meetin's, an' if your people manages ter convert just a couple o' drunkards each time then they've done a good job. I see a lot of it, as yer would imagine.'

The three young men sat in the cab totally confused by what he was saying, but Freddie smiled benignly at him nevertheless. 'You're perfectly right, constable. I think strong drink is damnation. I think it's worse than fornication in the eyes of the Lord,' he declared, nudging Billy with his elbow.

'Me too,' Billy said quickly.

Chopper Harris had peered around the vehicle, and his mouth fell open as he saw the officer talking to his friends. 'We've bin nabbed!' he gasped out to Frankie. 'It's a bluebottle!'

Frankie Albright put his finger up to his mouth and motioned Chopper to get down. The two slipped quietly over the tailboard and marched off smartly along the Commercial Road, not daring to run in case they attracted the policeman's attention.

'By the way, lads, I'm makin' fer Cable Street. I'd be grateful fer a lift ter the site if yer don't mind,' the constable asked.

Billy made to get out of the cab but the policeman held up his hand. 'Stay there, son. I'll stand on the runnin'-board,' he said.

The lorry pulled away from the kerbside with Tony the driver looking helplessly at his two friends. 'Where we s'pose ter be goin'?' he asked in a whisper.

'It mus' be some sort o' meetin',' Freddie mumbled in reply. 'I fink 'e finks we've got the equipment.'

Billy was too close to the policeman to make any suggestion, though he was at a loss anyway, but Freddie suddenly remembered something he had read in a newspaper about the temperance revivals in the East End of London. ''E finks we've come ter put the tent up!' he hissed.

'Oh, fer Chrissake,' Tony gasped. 'What we gonna do?'

''Ow the bloody 'ell do I know?' Freddie growled. 'Bluff it out, I s'pose.'

The policeman was hanging on to the door and obviously enjoying the ride. 'If yer turn right 'ere then turn first left yer'll come out right by the site,' he shouted helpfully.

Tony did as he was told and finally saw the large area of waste ground ahead. A lorry similar to theirs was parked by the roadside and on the site there was feverish activity. A large marquee was being erected and everywhere men seemed to be pulling and heaving on large ropes.

'I thought you lot 'ad the tent,' the policeman said with a puzzled look on his face.

'No, officer. We've been sent to sort out the finer details,' Freddie said with a flash of inspiration.

'Oh? An' what might that be?' he asked.

'There's lots o' seats to set up and they want a nice big pulpit built,' the Nark continued, beginning to enjoy himself despite the possible danger to their freedom.

'I'd say yer got yer work cut out,' the officer remarked.

'There's anuvver two in the back,' Freddie said smiling.

As the policeman stepped down and walked to the rear of the lorry Billy turned to Freddie and shook his head slowly. 'Yer shouldn't 'ave mentioned those ovver two,' he grated. 'If that rozzer sees Chopper 'e's gonna twig somefing's up. Chopper looks more like 'e's on the run from Dartmoor than a bloody Salvation Army bloke.'

The policeman returned to the front of the vehicle. 'There's no one in the back,' he said. 'There's nuffink in the back. I thought yer said yer was bringin' the seats. Yer did say that, didn't yer?'

Freddie laughed. 'No, officer. I said we was sent to set up the seating and the pulpit.'

'But yer said there was two more of yer in the back,' the policeman persisted.

'No, I said at the back. I meant in the ovver lorry. It's following up. That's a bigger vehicle and it's full o' benches and suchlike, ' he said, a note of desperation beginning to creep into his voice.

The police officer gave the young man a strange look and Billy cut in quickly. 'We'd better give the lads an 'and,' he said, nudging Freddie.

'Well, thanks for all your help, officer,' the Nark said, following Billy and Tony on to the waste ground.

The tent riggers looked surprised and mystified as three strangers started to lend their muscle to the ropes. Freddie groaned as he saw the policeman coming over to him.

'I'll walk up to the main road. Your mates might be stuck in that traffic 'old-up at Lime'ouse,' he said to Freddie.

'I'm much obliged,' the would-be warehouse-breaker replied, shaking the policeman by the hand. 'We'd like to get finished soon as possible.'

The policeman nodded. 'I 'ope so too. We're guardin' this tent all night an' it looks like rain. I'd much sooner guard it from the inside,' he grinned.

Freddie smiled and began pulling on the rope.

'Oi! What yer doin'?' one of the riggers shouted at him. 'If yer pull on that one the 'ole bloody lot'll come down.'

Freddie glanced fearfully in the policeman's direction but he was already walking smartly along the narrow street. 'C'mon, you two. Let's be orf,' he hissed.

'Oi! Give us an 'and wiv this rope,' the foreman rigger called out to them.

'Poke yer poxy rope! I 'ope the 'ole bloody lot falls down,' Freddie snarled at him.

Soon the lorry was rolling once more. Freddie the Nark sat back in the cab, feeling very pleased with

71

himself for the way he had handled such a tricky situation. Both Billy and Tony had praised his coolness, and they were puzzling over the fate of their confederates.

'They might 'ave fell out when we pulled up,' Tony volunteered.

'Nah. They jumped out more like,' Freddie laughed. 'They must 'ave seen the rozzer.'

'Nice bloke, wasn't 'e?' Billy remarked, grinning broadly.

'Chopper an' Frankie's got a long walk 'ome,' Tony said.

'Not if I know Chopper. 'E'll most prob'ly get a cab an' then do anuvver runner,' Freddie laughed.

The three lapsed into silence until the lorry was rumbling over Tower Bridge, then Freddie slipped his hand into his coat pocket and took out a handful of silver. ''Ere, Tony. There's the dosh fer yer pal. Yer'll all 'ave ter 'ave a whip round ter pay yer share. I can't stand the lot.'

Billy nodded. 'I wonder if that ole boy did phone the police,' he said.

'Yer can bet yer life 'e did,' Freddie said positively. 'I could feel it in me water. I can smell trouble o' that sort a mile orf.'

Freddie was right. Jack Price had hurried to the phone and informed Dockhead police station that there was an attempted robbery in progress at the Clark Wharf. Freddie the Nark's impersonation of a police officer had sounded convincing to him, until he said that Peggie had fallen at her home. She had, but it had happened the previous afternoon, and Jack had gone with her to Rotherhithe Infirmary where she had been admitted with a broken hip.

Chapter Six

In the early months of 1920 the little dining rooms in
Cotton Lane prospered. The docks were experiencing a
boom in trade and all day long a steady stream of customers came and went. Carrie and Fred worked hard
all day, aided by the vociferous Bessie Chandler, whose
tales about the trials and tribulations of her friends in
the buildings where she lived became painful ongoing
sagas. Fred suffered the most, for Bessie worked at his
elbow most of the day. She was very efficient though,
and as she went on endlessly about her neighbours she
seemed to race through her chores with increasing
speed. The pastry took a terrible pounding at times,
and Bessie kneaded the dough with a vengeance as she
talked of Kate Kerrigan, one of her sworn enemies.
Fred would listen patiently until he could stand no
more and then depart to the small back yard, where he
sat on an upturned tea-chest and vowed that one day he
would forget how efficient his kitchen hand was and
just do away with her.

Carrie worked unceasingly behind the counter, rushing off upstairs often during the afternoons to tend to
Rachel once Annie McCafferty had left. At such times
Fred Bradley got some respite from Bessie's ever-
wagging tongue. His assistant took over behind the
counter and proceeded to inflict the continuing stories
of her friends and enemies in the buildings on the

dockers and carmen. They took little notice of her, though; the rough, bawdy crowd were more interested in the fortunes of their local football teams, Millwall and West Ham. When Carrie was serving she often became involved in their conversations at the counter. The young woman made a point of following the respective teams' results and their positions in the league tables and she held her own in the sporting discussions and arguments. Bessie knew nothing about football, and her constant harping on one subject caused her to become somewhat of an object of ridicule. The buxom, ginger-haired woman also had a shady past, and it did little to help the poor woman's image when it was resurrected by two regular carmen.

Sharkey Morris and Soapy Symonds had both worked at the Galloway transport firm in Page Street for a number of years. Both had left after arguments with the firm's owner and they now worked for Tommy Hatcher in Long Lane. They liked and respected Carrie's father, who had been their foreman at Galloway's, and it was Sharkey who had told Carrie about Fred wanting a serving-girl for the cafe. He had promised William Tanner he would keep his eye on his daughter and make sure that she was treated right and that none of the customers took advantage of her. Soapy Symonds also minded Carrie's welfare as far as he could, and both men were favourites of the pretty young girl who had now become the joint owner of Bradley's Dining Rooms.

Sharkey and Soapy were both in their fifties. Sharkey was tall and gangling with broad shoulders and a wicked sense of humour, while Soapy was smaller in stature, stooping and with hawklike features. They often came into the dining rooms together and one day they were trying not to listen as Bessie was going on at length about her friend Elsie Dobson.

''Ark at Bessie Bubbles goin' orf again,' Soapy groaned to Sharkey.

'Who?' one of the carmen sitting with the two asked.

'Bessie Bubbles. That's what she was known as when she was on the game,' Soapy informed him.

'Bessie on the game? I don't believe it,' the carman said incredulously.

''S' right. She was a Lisle Street whore,' Soapy said unkindly. 'She was found out by a couple o' the local lads who went over Charin' Cross fer a good time. It's a long story but it's true, sure as I sit 'ere. She used ter wear a blond curly wig. All the street found out eventually. Mind you, there's a lot do it an' never get found out. Poor ole Bessie come unstuck.'

'What about 'er ole man? Didn't 'e ever find out?' the carman asked. 'She's always on about 'im.'

'As far as I know 'e was 'avin' it orf wiv one o' the young gels where 'e worked. They're both as bad as each ovver if yer ask me,' Soapy remarked, biting into his dripping toast.

The enlightened carman managed to resist addressing Bessie by her nickname, but the story was soon common knowledge and she became known as 'Bubbles' to all and sundry behind her back.

The dining rooms were beginning to show a better turnover and the books started to look much more tidy and well kept, thanks to Carrie's efficiency and enterprise. She had gone to the library and borrowed all the books she could find on accountancy, bookkeeping and running a business. A lot of the information was above her head but she had persevered until she learnt how to keep a good set of accounts. Her hard work and determination set her in good stead for the confrontation she had had with the Johnson representative, Albert Buller. He was delivered of an ultimatum and he accepted it with a smile and good grace, although he went away cursing the interference and audacity of Fred's young wife. There was now a discount for orders on a rising scale, and on certain commodities where discounts were not forthcoming Carrie immediately took action by switching her custom elsewhere. The Bradley business now had the benefit of more than one representative calling regularly and Carrie played them off one against the other. Fred often winced when he witnessed his wife's impudence and guile, but he realised she was right. The profits grew and the bank manager began to smile at Carrie whenever she paid in the weekly takings.

There was a cloud on the horizon, however, which worried the Bradleys. Russia and Poland were at war and the Polish army were making gains. The Labour movement supported the Bolsheviks in their struggle and when the freighter *Jolly George* berthed in the London Docks the dockers refused to load a munitions cargo that was destined for Poland. The trade union movement was gathering strength and there was talk of a full dock strike.

'It's likely ter paralyse the country,' Don Jacobs, a dockers' leader, told Carrie. 'If the docks stop, the rest o' the movement's gonna come out in support, yer can take that fer gospel,' he said with severity.

Carrie was in two minds about the situation as she discussed it with Fred one evening in the little sitting-room above the shop. 'I've seen 'ow me own dad was treated by Galloway,' she was saying. 'Me dad was a loyal, conscientious worker an' 'e 'ad no union ter back 'im up. If there'd 'ave bin a union at Galloway's 'e might still be there.'

Fred nodded in agreement, a worried frown showing on his face.

'Trouble is, it's businesses like ours that are gonna suffer,' Carrie went on. 'The men won't come in 'ere if

76

they're on strike, 'specially if it goes on fer any length of time. Will a strike do any good though? The government could always bring in the troops ter load the ships.'

'I dunno 'ow we're gonna pay off the bank if there is a strike,' Fred said with concern in his voice. 'We still owe quite a lot on that money we borrered fer the free'old.'

'I dunno what we'll do,' Carrie replied, feeling that all her hard work and shrewdness in helping to build up the business was going to count for nothing should the threatened strike take place.

'P'raps we shouldn't encourage those dockers' and carmen's union men ter use that back room fer their meetin's,' Fred suggested despondently.

Carrie shook her head decisively. 'If we did that the men would turn on us. We might just as well shut up shop. Besides, I fink they do a good job. It's not only money they argue about. It's the men's welfare an' their rights. Yer know that yerself.'

Fred had to agree, and he smiled at the passion in his pretty young wife's voice. She herself had campaigned for women's rights with the suffragette movement when she was in her teens and he had listened to her tales of the marches and the abuse the women suffered at the hands of many people.

'I s'pose it's all a question o' roots,' he said quietly. 'None of us can sit on the fence. It's eivver the workers or the bosses. Point is, where do I stand? I've bin a worker an' now I'm a boss yer might say. I employ Bessie an' I run a business.'

'We run the business,' Carrie reminded him with a severe look. 'Anyway, we'll jus' 'ave ter see. P'raps it'll all blow over.'

'I 'ope ter Gawd it does,' Fred said with passion.

*

The cool and rainy spring gave way to warm summer days and still the threatened General Strike had not taken place. Things looked more hopeful now that the Poles were in full retreat and an end to the war was in sight. The government had not intervened in the dockers' ban, and although they supported the Poles against the Bolsheviks they were aware of the general feelings amongst the working classes, which were expressed vociferously at workers' meetings throughout the country. 'No More War' was crudely scrawled in white paint on the brick wall of a wharf in Cotton Lane, and further along the narrow riverside turning the message 'Hands off Soviet Russia' appeared overnight. Many local folk who earned their living on or from the river were still worried about what would happen in the end, but one man busy in his small yard behind the bustling Tower Bridge Road market did not give international events a second thought.

Broomhead Smith had managed to get Aggie Temple a tabby tomcat which was the best mouser in the Borough, so he told her. The cat's owner was leaving the area and could not keep the animal, and she wanted it to have a nice home. In fact the woman was fed up with the smell that the tomcat caused about the place and was glad to be shot of it. What was more, there had been a growing number of mice in her house of late and she put it down to the age of the animal. Broomhead did not see fit to let Aggie know this and hoped that a change of abode might revitalise the tomcat's flagging performance.

At the moment the crafty totter had other, more profitable things to think about and he whistled to himself as he gave the cabinet yet another coat of wax. The scratches had been hidden and it now shone like new. It had been in his possession for quite a while and Broomhead felt it was about time he sold the thing. He had originally intended to polish up the wood and sell it for five shillings, but when he was fortunate enough to obtain the gramophone he realised he should repair the machine and install it in the cabinet. He could then expect to get around four pounds ten shillings. When he dismantled the gramophone, however, he saw that the spring had become dislodged from its mounting and needed a new clip. For ages he had been meaning to call in at a place down by the Elephant and Castle where they sold gramophone parts, but it was not until this morning that he had finally got around to it. Now he had managed to install the clip he was not at all sure whether he had done the job correctly. At least the handle turned, and to his surprise the turntable revolved, if rather slowly, when he moved the lever. He tried out a badly scratched recording of Dame Nellie Melba singing an operatic aria from *Pagliacci* which he had found tucked away between a box of rusting tools and a sack of potatoes in the corner of his shed. The recording sounded terrible to his untrained ears, but the horse seemed to enjoy it. It had stopped munching away in its stall, pricked up its ears and jerked its head up and down at the powerful voice of the world-famous soprano.

Broomhead shook his head in resigned disbelief and set about installing the gramophone in its housing. It was a bit small for the wooden supports at the top of the cabinet but the totter got around that problem by nailing a couple of slats of wood on to the supports to act as a base. It did not look very neat, he had to admit, but unless the prospective buyer looked down into the cabinet the bodgery would not be discovered.

Brookhead Smith loaded the cabinet with the gramophone inside it on to the back of his cart, then he looked around the shed to see if there were any more records lying about. He could not find any and he realised that it would be the voice of Dame Melba which rang out in the backstreets as he advertised the fact that he had a gramophone for sale. That horn doesn't look too good though, he thought, scratching his head and glaring at the disinterested horse, which had stepped back on it while it was lying with the rest of the dismantled bits on the floor of the shed. Broomhead had managed partly to knock out the large dent in the horn but he had taken off a fair amount of paint in the process. 'Well, what do they expect for four an' 'alf quid?' he asked the nag.

One hour later the sonorous tones of Dame Melba's singing resonated through a little backstreet near the river. A few windows were flung open, and two little lads pelted Broomhead with rotten apples before they were chased off. An old gent stopped in his tracks and raised his face to the sky, listening intently as he leaned on his walking stick.

'I reco'nise that voice. Who is it?' he asked.

'It's Dame Melba. She used ter sing at the Star in Abbey Street,' Broomhead informed him.

'Wasn't that the one who sung "Some o' These Days"?' the old man asked.

'Nah. That's Sophie Tucker's song,' Broomhead said knowledgeably.

'Well, she sounds like Sophie Tucker.'

'Well, she ain't,' Broomhead told him sharply.

'I know who it is,' the old man said chuckling. 'She's the one who sings that there "Darktown Strutters' Ball".'

'Nah it ain't! That's Sophie Tucker's song as well,' the by now thoroughly irritated totter informed him.

'Are yer figurin' on sellin' that there contraption then?' the ancient character asked.

'Nah. I play the poxy fing ter stop me 'orse fallin' asleep,' Broomhead growled at him.

'Bloody fing looks ready fer the knackers' yard. A good feed wouldn't do it any 'arm,' the old man growled back.

'Look, mate. Ain't yet got any 'ome ter go to?' the totter asked. 'I've got a livin' ter make.'

'I'm sure that's the young woman who sings "Some o' These Days". If it ain't it's the spittin' image of 'er,' the old man persisted.

Broomhead had had enough, realising that the old gent was quite content to stay there all day nattering. He picked up the reins in a temper and slapped them hard across the horse's back. Surprised at being disturbed so roughly the nag jerked forward suddenly, the jolt snapped the rickety bodged-up slatting and the gramophone fell into the bottom of the cabinet. There was a loud clang and Broomhead cursed vehemently, pulling on the reins. The horse was totally confused by now and it eased forward in the shafts not knowing what to do next, until Broomhead reminded it with a few well-chosen obscenities. 'The poxy spring,' he said to himself.

The old man had set off too and as he caught up with the cart he looked up at the fuming totter. 'Yer didn't go far. Wassa matter then?' he asked innocently.

'It's the spring.'

'What yer say?'

'I said the spring's gone.'

The old man nodded. 'Yeah. Still, I like the summer better. Always did. A drop o' sun makes yer feel better in yerself. I can't stan' the winter. Winter's no good fer the ole folk. Gets ter yer bones it does. That's when the likes of us drop orf, yer know. It's yer pneumonia what does it.'

Broomhead had been staring ahead scowling and suddenly he turned to face the old man. 'Look, dad. Why don't yer piss orf 'ome?' he growled. 'They'll be sendin' a search party out fer yer in a minute.'

'Gertcha! Yer saucy young pup! Why don't yer piss orf out of our street? Go on, 'oppit!' the old gent croaked, aiming at Broomhead with his stick and only managing to hit the side of the cart.

The horse got the message and set off once more at a lively gait. This time the aggravated totter did not try to stop it. Instead he sat slumped down in his seat and let the animal have its head, wishing he had thrown the gramophone in the dustbin in the first place.

The docks remained busy throughout the long hot summer months, but as winter drew in there was more trouble brewing as the miners went on strike for better pay. Don Jacobs the dockers' leader spoke of his fears to Carrie one quiet afternoon in the back room of the cafe after his meeting was over.

'I don't wanna frighten yer, gel, but I feel there's a general slump in the makin',' he said resignedly. 'Yer've only gotta read between the lines in the newspapers. World trade is fallin' an' there's a lot of unemployment about. They reckon it's up to a million now.'

Carrie leaned on the table and looked closely at the middle-aged man sitting facing her. He was well read and intelligent, she knew, he was respected by his men, and from what she had gathered he was a natural leader who always dealt firmly but fairly with the employers to get the best deal he could. He had a few enemies amongst the more militant dockers but he had many loyal friends too, and many had told Carrie that they would follow him without question. As she looked into his concerned eyes Carrie saw something else. Don Jacobs looked frightened.

'But why should it be?' she asked.

Don ran his finger along a crack in the table and shook his head slowly. 'I dunno. The whole of Europe's in a turmoil, politically speakin'. There was a lot of expectations o' trade across the continent after the war finished. It's not come about to any large degree an' there's bin a lot o' firms that invested in what's turned out ter be a pipe dream. A lot o' the businesses went bankrupt an' it's made a difference ter the amount of unemployed people around the country. 'Course they're not the only reasons, but those fings 'ave got a lot ter do wiv it. It's times like these when my job is made very difficult. I'm pledged ter get the best fer me men, an' the bosses jus' keep remindin' me about the number out o' collar. I don't need remindin', Carrie. I'm no fool.'

She gave him a warm smile. 'I know yer not by what yer men say. I only 'ope it don't come to a General Strike, Don. D'yer fink it will?'

He shrugged his broad shoulders. 'Well, if it does the first out'll be the dockers and railwaymen. They'll support the miners. Then the transport workers are bound ter foller their lead. The whole country could go ter the wall. Gawd almighty, I 'ope it never comes ter that. We all 'ope that, don't we?'

Carrie got up to bring the union man some more tea and when she returned with two filled mugs she sat down heavily. 'D'yer know, Don,' she said, 'me an' Fred 'ave worked really 'ard ter get this place on its feet. Fred was a bit reluctant ter make changes, but 'e agreed. I want it ter work fer 'is sake as well as mine.'

'Well, yer certainly made changes, gel,' Don assured her. ''Avin' this place fer our meetin's is a boon. It's much better than standin' out on the cobbles like we used ter do. Fred's all right about it, ain't 'e?'

Carrie smiled. 'Fred lets me make the decisions, an' it was my idea ter sort this back room out.'

'Are you an' Fred all right?' Don asked suddenly.

Carrie was taken by surprise at his question and her

first instinct was to give him a sharp reply, but she nodded instead, catching the look of concern in Don's deep brown eyes. 'Fred's a very nice man,' she said quietly. ''E loves Rachel an' 'e'd give me the top brick off the chimney if I asked 'im, but 'e's a worrier. Sometimes I wonder if I'm doin' the right fing by 'im when I suggest we do this or that. I want us ter prosper fer a number o' reasons, Don,' she said with conviction. 'I want it fer me an' Fred, I want it fer Rachel, an' I want it fer me mum an' dad. I wanna get enough be'ind me so I can look after 'em all. Am I bein' greedy?'

The union man laughed and touched her arm fondly. 'Yer not bein' greedy, luv,' he replied smiling. 'Yer doin' it fer all the best reasons. Nobody's gonna give yer anyfing. Yer gotta work fer what yer get. I found that out soon enough. I started out bein' apprenticed ter this firm o' lightermen, jus' like your Danny. I soon found out 'ow dangerous an' uncertain the job was. We used ter fight over work, an' there's still a scramble at times, let me tell yer. Fings are changin' now though, an' it's not come about by the kindness o' the employers. Mind yer there's good an' bad bosses, but it's the solidarity of the workers what's ringin' the changes. It's like what's 'appenin' over in Russia. Workers are risin' against the poverty and 'ardship. They wanna eat square meals an' they wanna 'ave some quality in their lives. They wanna be looked after when they're sick an' 'ave proper education fer their kids. That ain't so bad, is it?'

Carrie was taken by the obvious sincerity of the man and she could only nod.

'Jus' look at what's goin' on wiv the miners,' Don went on. 'They're not only fightin' fer better wages. They want better safety standards an' better facilities at the pit'ead. They 'ave ter walk back 'ome black as the coal they've bin diggin' out. They often work sprawled out on their bellies an' they never know if they're gonna see the light o' day again when they step in that pit cage. At least our blokes work in the open air, though that's prob'ly the only good fing about the work. It's 'ard an' often dangerous, an' everyfing depends on the river. Ole Farvver Thames can be a treacherous ole bleeder at times. Yer can never take 'im fer granted. Sometimes the tides run fast an' sometimes a man gets the feelin' 'e can swim across from shore ter shore with ease when it's runnin' slow. There's dangerous eddies that pull yer under. It's a muddy, filfy river, but it's the lifeblood of London. It always 'as bin, from the early times.'

Carrie had been listening intently, enthralled and hanging on to the union man's every word, but she suddenly caught sight of Fred standing at the counter. He was looking in her direction, apparently ignoring Bessie who was chatting away to him, and there was a look in his eye which Carrie found disconcerting. Her husband's jealous nature made it difficult for her to talk to any of the customers for very long without him questioning her, and it was becoming worse lately.

She got up with a sigh. 'I mus' go, Don,' she said. 'I've gotta start clearin' up fer the day.'

That evening, when Rachel was tucked up in bed sleeping, the moment came when Fred could contain his suspicions no longer, as Carrie had expected.

'I don't mind yer talkin' ter the customers, Carrie, but yer was sittin' wiv that Don Jacobs fer ages,' he said to her, a resentful look on his flushed face. 'Bessie was 'avin' ter do the servin' an' yer know I don't like 'er be'ind the counter more than need be. She's a chatterbox an' it gets on the customers' nerves. I don't wanna lose me trade because of 'er.'

'Well, if that's the way yer feel about Bessie why don't yer sack 'er, or at least 'ave a stiff word wiv 'er?'

Carrie replied with spirit. 'Don's a good bloke an' 'e brings a lot o' trade in 'ere. 'E was jus' tellin' me about the unions, an' 'ow they're all worried about a General Strike. An' as fer Bessie doin' all the servin', there was only a couple o' carmen in the place. I don't fink she was bein' 'ard pressed.'

Fred fidgeted in his chair. 'There's bin times when I was tempted, let me tell yer,' he said. 'The fing is, Bessie's a very good worker, despite the length of 'er tongue. I'd be lucky ter get anybody that could match 'er in the kitchen. I jus' don't want 'er servin' more than need be, that's all.'

'Well, I 'ave ter keep an eye on Rachel when she's 'avin' 'er afternoon nap,' Carrie said sharply. 'I can't be be'ind that counter all the time. If that's what yer want yer'd better ask Annie if she'd consider workin' all day instead o' jus' the mornin's.'

Fred puffed. 'Look, I know yer can't be servin' all the time, but I was a bit narked the way yer was sittin' wiv that Don Jacobs. I didn't know what the two of yer was talkin' about, did I?' he growled.

'I've told yer what Don was talkin' about. There was nuffin' in it,' Carrie retorted.

'What about that Tommy Allen? 'E's bin comin' in quite a lot lately,' Fred remarked, looking surly. ''E always seems to 'ave a lot ter say fer 'imself.'

Carrie felt her anger growing. 'I've told yer plenty of times, me an' Tommy finished a long time ago. 'E only talks about everyday fings. If yer want me to ignore everbody who comes in, jus' say so,' she flared at him. 'I'll tell yer this though. It's no bad fing ter listen ter the customers. It's just as important as the quality o' the food an' drinks we sell. Those carmen are sittin' outside the wharves fer hours on end at times, an' they like ter come in fer a mug o' tea an' a chat. Spendin' a bit o' time listenin' an' bein' pleasant is good fer trade. Yer said that yerself.'

Fred nodded. 'I'm jus' worried yer might be wishin' it was Tommy Allen yer married instead o' me,' he said quietly.

Carrie looked into Fred's eyes and her anger disappeared. She got up from her chair and went over to him. 'Look, Fred. I wasn't pushed inter this marriage,' she said softly. 'I went in wiv me eyes open. I'm quite 'appy, an' I ain't wishin' I was married ter anybody else, so get that stupid thought out o' yer 'ead fer a start.'

Fred reached up and took her hand from his shoulder, squeezing it gently in his. 'I remember that day when yer agreed ter marry me,' he said. 'Yer told me yer liked me a lot, although yer didn't love me. I didn't ask yer why yer suddenly agreed if yer didn't feel love fer me, I didn't 'ave to. I felt it was security yer wanted. That an' the chance ter 'elp me build up the business so yer could get some money be'ind yer. Yer was worried about yer parents an' yer farvver gettin' put orf at Galloways. I knew the pressure yer was under at the time, I'm not stupid, yer know. I am jealous about yer though.' He looked into her deep blue eyes. 'I love yer very much an' I've bin 'opin' an' prayin' that one day yer'd realise that yer've fallen in love wiv me.'

Carrie smiled at him and pulled his head to her chest as she stood over him. 'What is love, Fred?' she said. 'If it means bein' wiv somebody fer the rest of yer life, bein' wiv 'em all of the day an' night, 'avin' their children an' carin' fer 'em, then I've fallen in love wiv yer. But then, I was ready ter do all o' those fings the day I said I'd marry yer. P'raps yer puttin' too much importance ter the word love. Maybe we all do.'

Fred could feel the softness as he rested his head against his young wife's breast, and he could hear her steady heartbeats. 'Maybe we do,' he said.

Chapter Seven

The new year started cold and bleak and many of the wharves in Bermondsey and Rotherhithe were standing half empty as trade slumped. The rivermen were finding it hard; the scramble for work was becoming more and more intense as family debts grew and many valued and treasured items found their way into the local pawnshops. The Bradleys' riverside establishment was still nearly always filled with customers during the day but the takings dropped. Where once dockers and carmen had gone in for breakfast or a midday meal they now sat around drinking mugs of tea and eating slices of toast and dripping. Men who had been unsuccessful in the search for a day's work drifted into the dining rooms to pass the time away and many sat there on the bench seats, grateful for the warmth and a friendly chat.

Carrie and Fred Bradley had come to accept that a drop in their weekly takings was inevitable and there was never any pressure put on the men to leave once they had finished their morning tea or coffee. Most of them looked cold and miserable, and they were the men who had bought meals there when they could afford to do so, men who had helped build up the business. Carrie felt sad when she saw the worried looks on their faces as they sat talking quietly, their hands cupped around mugs of steaming hot tea.

As the cold winter gave way to early spring more shipping sailed up the Thames, bringing some extra work for the struggling rivermen, but there was still much unemployment in the riverside borough. The Bradleys talked about whether or not they could afford to keep the services of Annie McCafferty, and they decided to do so, at least for the time being. Rachel was now in her second year, toddling about and growing sturdy of limb, and she had become very attached to her nurse. Annie herself had grown very fond of the child. Whenever the day was dry and not too cold she would take Rachel into nearby Southwark Park. As the days became warmer they would go to the pond to feed the ducks and then along to the terraced rose gardens before making their way to the nearby swings and roundabouts in the small enclosed area. It was in the rose gardens that Annie McCafferty met the young ex-boxer one fine, crisp morning when the buds were appearing and trees were coming into leaf.

Annie was sitting beside Rachel's pram, talking and laughing with the child, when she noticed the young man walking slowly along the paved path. He had his hands thrust into his coat pockets and his shoulders were hunched. He looked deep in thought as he approached but the thing which intrigued Annie most was the way his mouth moved. He seemed to be talking to himself, and as he drew level he glanced suddenly in her direction. Annie was not used to looking at young men, nor in the habit of attracting their attention deliberately, but on this occasion she met his gaze. He seemed to be troubled but his face suddenly relaxed into a smile and she smiled back. He walked up to the pram and looked down at the young child.

''Ello, young Rachel. Yer lookin' bonny terday,' he said lightly.

Annie's face had flushed up and her natural reticence

caused her to look away from Billy's gaze as he glanced up at her.

'You mus' be Annie,' he said in a friendly tone.

'Yes, that's right,' she replied quickly.

'I'm Billy Sullivan. I'm Danny's best pal. I s'pose 'e's told yer about me,' he said smiling.

'You mean Mrs Bradley's brother?' she asked him.

'That's right. I used ter be in the boxin' game,' Billy told her, still smiling.

'No, I don't recall him mentioning you,' Annie replied rather stiffly. 'I don't know Mrs Bradley's brother very well. I've only met him once.'

The young man sat down beside her and started to pull faces at young Rachel. 'She's a ringer fer 'er muvver,' he remarked. 'I've known Carrie Bradley fer years. We grew up in the same turnin', yer see. Me an' Carrie walked out tergevver once. As a matter o' fact we sat on this very seat, an' if I remember rightly, I stole a kiss. Carrie wasn't very pleased, I might tell yer. She reckoned I was bein' a bit forward. There was no 'arm in it though.'

'I'm sure there wasn't,' Annie said, still avoiding his direct gaze.

'I was doin' boxin', yer see,' he explained. 'That was before the war. The war changed everyfing. Nuffink's ever gonna be the same again, that's fer sure.'

'You don't box now then?' Annie asked, looking briefly into his eyes and reminding herself that she must not prolong the conversation.

'I got wounded in France. It was a chest wound an' I can't do much now wivout gettin' out o' breath,' he told her. 'Still, I s'pose I was lucky. At least I can walk an' see. A lot o' young men wasn't so fortunate. Fousands didn't come back. I lost two bruvvers.'

Annie experienced a sudden feeling of pity for the young man. He seemed perfectly at ease as he faced her on the garden bench, and his wide blue eyes reflected a certain acceptance. Rachel appeared to like him too, she thought, smiling to herself. The child was chuckling as Billy made faces at her and when he looked away Rachel's little face seemed to beg his attention.

'I'm sorry,' Annie said quietly.

He shrugged his broad shoulders and gave her a warm smile. 'Carrie's bruvver Danny was a good boxer,' he went on amiably. ''E used ter box in the army. I taught 'im 'ow ter box at the club. That's the one in Dock'ead. It's closed now though. It's a bloody shame.'

Annie had been brought up and educated within the walls of a convent and she had never become familiar with the more colourful words that people used.

The young man noticed her reaction and pulled a face. 'I'm sorry, I shouldn't 'ave swore, but it is a shame, none the more fer that,' he asserted.

Annie let a smile touch her lips and she passed off her embarrassment by wiping Rachel's mouth with a spotless white handkerchief which she took from her coat pocket. 'It's all right. I suppose I shouldn't be so sensitive,' she said dismissively.

'All the people round 'ere use words like that,' Billy told her with a grin. 'Yer wanna 'ear the gels in the turnin' where I live. They can outdo the men wiv such talk. Still, there's no 'arm in it really. My own muvver swears worse than me farvver when she gets upset, an' 'e's a docker. Yer should 'ear 'er when me farvver comes 'ome pissed – sorry, I mean drunk,' he corrected himself.

Annie laughed aloud as she saw the look on Billy's face. 'Where do you live?' she asked, feeling a little less nervous about talking with the young man.

'Page Street. It's near where Carrie lives,' he told her.

'I know Page Street. That's where the stables are,' she replied.

'That's right. Galloway's yard. Carrie's ole man used ter work there. The Tanners lived next door ter the stables till Will Tanner got the sack. They 'ad ter move out then,' Billy informed her in his easy manner. 'They live in Bacon Buildin's now. Right bloody slum that is.'

Annie laughed once more as Billy put a hand up to his lips in mock horror and then her face suddenly flushed as she realised he was appraising her. For a second or two his eyes seemed to be searching her as he glanced at her dark, tightly fixed hair, her face, her shoulders and her long neck. Annie suddenly felt uncomfortable beneath his gaze. She had never before been in the company of a man, let alone a young, attractive man. He was attractive, she had to admit. His deep blue eyes were expressive, his dark hair was wavy, and his finely shaped mouth and square jaw were pleasing to her eyes. He had an innocent manner about him too, and he had made her feel at ease despite her natural reserve. Now though she was feeling nervous, unsure of herself, and she could feel herself beginning to tremble slightly.

Rachel was getting bored now that Billy had used up all his funny faces. She fidgeted in the pram, straining against the reins which held her secure. It was an excuse for Annie to take her leave. 'I must get back, Rachel's getting hungry,' she said quickly.

Billy got up from the bench and slipped his hands into his coat pockets once more. 'Oh, well, I'd better be orf too. I'm goin' fer an interview,' he said with a grimace.

Annie took off the brake and started to push the

pram along the paved path, feeling decidedly uncomfortable as Billy walked beside her. She felt her face beginning to get hot as two women passed by and gave the two of them a casual glance. 'Er, what job are you going for?' she asked Billy in a voice she hardly recognised.

'Oh, it's only a job at the sawmills,' he replied. 'I gotta get some work. I've got plans, yer see.'

Annie was hoping he would go in the opposite direction when they got to the end of the path leading from the rose gardens but to her dismay he moved into step beside her.

'My ole lady threatened ter chuck me out if I didn't look fer a job,' he said suddenly. 'She's good as gold is my ole mum, but now me farvver's gone on short-time she's feelin' the pinch. Mind yer, I don't s'pose fer one minute I'll get the job. They won't take me on once they know I've got a disability.'

'But you're entitled to a job, aren't you?' Annie said with a frown. 'The way I understand it firms are obliged to take on disabled men from the war.'

Billy laughed bitterly. 'Don't yer believe it,' he said. 'I know loads o' blokes who can't get work through their war wounds. They told us it was gonna be a land fit fer 'eroes when we got back from France, but they soon changed their tune. It's always the same story when yer go fer a job. "Sorry mate, we're full up." Or: "Yer won't be able ter manage the job, pal." What the bloody 'ell do they want us ter do – sell shoelaces an' collar studs in the gutter?'

Annie hardly noticed him swear. She turned to look at him as they reached the park gates. 'Have you tried for many jobs?' she asked.

Billy gave her a sheepish grin. 'Well, ter tell yer the trufe this is me first interview,' he told her. 'I didn't 'ave the guts ter go fer a job before, yer see. I 'eard enough tales from me mates. It was always the same story so I said ter meself, "Billy," I said, "yer wastin' yer time even bovverin' ter fink about it. Yer might as well go an' jump in the river." Mind yer, I never would,' he added with a grin.

'But that's awful,' Annie said with feeling. 'What have you been doing since you got out of the army?'

'Sittin' around mostly,' he replied. 'I used ter sit at me front door when the weavver was good, an' when it was cold I used ter lay in bed till dinner-time. There was no use in gettin' up, I thought ter meself. Anyway, I'm goin' fer a job now, but I tell yer, Annie, if they turn me down that's me lot. I won't try again.'

The young woman felt her stomach flutter as he said her name. It sounded very strange to hear him call her by her Christian name. It was the first time as far as she could remember that any male person had done so since she left the convent school, where the visiting priest would call all the girls by their first names. Mr Bradley called her miss, and even the local doctor called her Miss McCafferty whenever he had reason to talk to her about her charges. Billy had been the first man to call her Annie and she felt strangely pleased.

They were out in the street and making their way back to Cotton Lane, and Billy had obviously decided to walk beside her as far as possible. Annie felt suddenly daring. 'Have you got a young lady friend? I mean, are you walking out steady with anyone?' she asked him.

Billy shook his head. 'Nah. I ain't tried very much,' he said, giving her a shy grin. 'Yer need money ter ask a young lady out. I prob'ly will though. If I get this job, that is.'

They had reached the corner of Bacon Street. 'Well, it's bin nice talkin' ter yer, Annie,' he said, giving her a warm smile. 'Wish me luck.'

'I certainly will,' she said, returning his smile.

He walked off, shuffling along with his hands tucked deep in his coat pockets and his shoulders hunched and swaying as he moved. Annie stood watching him for a few moments. It had been a very unexpected meeting, she thought, and it had made her feel strangely elated. It was the first time she had allowed herself to get into conversation with any man, and it was not the frightening experience she had thought it would be. Billy Sullivan was very polite and proper, if a blasphemer, but he had used the wicked words with passion, unable to express just what he felt in any other way. He knew her name too. Danny Tanner must have told him about her. What had he said? she wondered. Had the two friends discussed her in the way men probably did when they looked at a young woman who passed them in the street? She had noticed men leering at her and whispering to each other with dirty grins on their faces. No, there was nothing lecherous in Billy's conversation. He had been very proper and courteous to her. There was just that brief moment when his eyes seemed to appraise her. But that was the way of men. It was what she had been told by the sisters at the convent. Well, if she ever met Billy Sullivan on the street again she would feel less inhibited about talking with him, as long as he remained proper, she told herself with a smile.

Rachel was crying now and Annie spoke a few comforting words to her as she set off pushing the pram along the shabby street.

In the little turning that ran off Bacon Street Florrie Axford, Aggie Temple and Maisie Dougall were standing together with Nellie Tanner and Sadie Sullivan at Aggie's front door. The Saturday afternoon was fine, with soft clouds drifting in a blue sky. The sun had moved behind the rooftops and it cast shadows halfway up the little houses on the opposite side of the turning.

Florrie dipped down into her apron pocket and pulled out her tiny silver snuffbox. 'I ain't bin a-pictures fer ages now,' she said. 'Last time I went ter the pictures it was up the Grand picture 'ouse in Grange Road. I went wiv ole Mrs Watson who lived next door ter me. Yer remember ole Mrs Watson. She moved away years ago. The Keystone Cops it was, or was it Buster Keaton? I can't remember fer certain. Anyway, I know I walked out 'alfway through the film.'

'Wasn't it any good then, Flo?' Maisie asked.

'Nah, it wasn't the show, it was 'er. Fair gave me the 'ump she did. Goin' on about the seats all the time she was. Mind yer, we only went in the cheapest seats. 'Ave yer ever bin up the Grand?'

Everyone shook their heads with the exception of Aggie.

'My 'Arold took me up there once,' she said. 'We went in the best seats. They was plush ones. Nice an' comfy too. If I remember rightly the cheap seats were wooden ones wiv backrests. I told my 'Arold I wasn't goin' in no wooden seats. Mind yer, 'e likes ter give me the best, does my 'Arold.'

Florrie caught Nellie's eye and pulled a face. 'My first ole man said that ter me once. All I ever got from 'im was the back of 'is 'and.'

Sadie Sullivan folded her arms and leaned back against the doorjamb. 'Well, I'd never let a man knock me about,' she said with passion. 'If my Daniel lifted a finger ter me I'd open 'im. Mind yer, 'e ain't that sort. Soft as butter 'e is. In fact it's me what 'as ter keep my crowd in order. D'yer know that Billy o' mine don't take a blind bit o' notice when Daniel talks to 'im, but 'e soon listens ter me. I'd give 'im the back o' me 'and big as 'e is, an' 'e knows it. It's the same wiv the twins.

They know 'ow far ter go. Pat's a bit lippy at times but I don't get no sauce out o' Terry. 'E's always bin the quiet one. Young Shaun's takin' after Billy though. 'E seems ter be runnin' round wiv a right rough crowd. Joe tried ter put 'im wise an' it nearly come ter blows. I dunno, the older they get the more trouble they seem ter be. Sometimes I wish they was all youngsters again, at least yer could put 'em ter bed an' know where they all were.'

Nellie nodded. 'Your Shaun's got big lately, Sadie,' she remarked. ''Ow old is 'e now?'

'Shaun's twenty, the twins are twenty-one this year, an' Joe's just turned twenty-two. Michael would 'ave bin twenty-four an' John twenty-five,' Sadie told her, suddenly taking out a handkerchief from her apron pocket and dabbing at her eyes.

'My James would 'ave bin twenty-eight this year,' Nellie said sadly.

Florrie took a pinch of snuff and looked up at the sky, waiting for the inevitable sneeze, and Aggie stepped back a pace. She could not abide snuff-taking and was always going on about Florrie Axford's nasty habits. The women of Page Street were very close friends, however, and even Aggie's fastidiousness tended to be overlooked by the rest of the women. She was nearly seventy and still very sprightly for her age. Her hair was grey and well cared for and her apron was invariably spotless. Aggie's husband was five years younger than her and about to retire that year. He had lit and extinguished the lamps of Bermondsey for over thirty years, and now, she confided to her friends in vexation, he was going to be under her feet.

Florrie told her in no uncertain terms that she would have to get used to it. 'Yer lucky, Aggie. At least 'e's a good-un. Yer just 'ave ter ease up on yer tidyin' up, or yer'll drive 'im right roun' the twist. There's nuffink worse than watchin' people workin' around yer.'

Aggie snorted. 'Well, I'll still 'ave ter keep me place clean. It's bad enough wiv that bleedin' cat old Broom'ead the totter got me. It stinks the place out at times, an' I told 'im too. Mind yer, all I got was a load o' lip. Bloody ole goat 'e is. If my 'Arold 'ad 'eard 'im goin' on 'e would 'ave put 'is lights out.'

Maisie Dougall had been listening to her friends going on and she thought it was about time she made a contribution. Maisie was a plump woman in her fifties who always wore her dark hair in a bun at the back of her head. 'I saw Broom'ead goin' in the Galloway yard the ovver day,' she told the gathering. ''E came out loaded up wiv old iron. I fink they've got rid o' that chaff-cutter. I've not 'eard it goin' lately.'

Nellie looked along the turning to the Galloway firm's gates, a hard look in her eye as the bitter memories locked up inside her stirred once more. She thought of the time George Galloway had come to her home while her husband was off work with badly bruised ribs and told them that he was giving William a week's notice. It had been a bitter pill to swallow, and she had made her feelings plain to the man her husband had been friends with since his childhood. The two men had been Bermondsey waifs together, living on their wits and sleeping beneath the damp, infested arches in the dirt and rubbish. Galloway had made his way in life and was now a successful businessman. He owned half the houses in Page Street as well as his flourishing transport concern. William had been his yard foreman, caring for the horses as well as being in charge of the carmen, and yet all the years of friendship and good service had in the end counted for nothing. Nellie had grown to detest the very mention of Galloway and she turned to her friends in disgust. 'I'd like ter see the 'ole bloody place pulled down. Galloway's give our family enough 'eartaches,' she said bitterly.

Florrie had been very friendly with Nellie for many years and she nodded sympathetically. 'Don't I know it,' she said quickly. 'I tell yer what though, Nell. That young Galloway ain't no better than 'is ole man. I reckon 'e's turnin' out worse. Yer wanna 'ear the carmen who work there go on about 'im. There was two of 'em chattin' away outside my winder the ovver day. I could 'ear everyfing they was sayin'. The names they was callin' that Frank Galloway. Apparently 'e's took over there fer good. Yer don't see much o' the ole man these days.'

'I saw ole George Galloway drivin in the yard in that pony-an'-trap of 'is the ovver day,' Aggie said. 'Whippin' that poor 'orse 'e was. 'E looked really fat an' bloated. Mind yer, I fink it's the booze. 'E always liked the drink.'

'Pity 'e don't spend a bit more on these 'ouses,' Florrie remarked acidly. 'My place is lettin' in water again. It's comin' in from the roof. All those roofs want doin'. I've told the rent collector, if there's nuffink done I'm gonna stop payin' me rent.'

'Fat lot o' good that'll do yer,' Nellie said. 'If yer miss payin' 'e'll do the same as 'e did wiv us. Yer'll be out on the street.'

'Well, we'll see about that,' Florrie replied with spirit. 'I'm goin' down the Town 'All an' 'ave a word wiv that medical bloke. They say 'e's all right ter talk to. I'll make that ole goat do the repairs, you see if I don't.'

The discussion was interrupted by the arrival of Maudie Mycroft. She was looking decidedly worried as she put down her shopping bag. 'My Ernie's joined the Communist Party,' she announced gravely.

'Oh my Gawd!' Florrie exclaimed, rolling her eyes in

100

feigned terror. 'We'll all end up bein' murdered in our beds, I'm sure we will.'

'It's no laughin' matter,' Maudie rebuked her. 'I'm worried out o' me life. I said to 'im, "Whatever made yer do it, Ernie?" An' 'e said, "All workers 'ave got ter rise up against the bosses an' seize the means o' production, an' that day's not far orf." I'm worried sick. I mean ter say, Ernie's not bin very interested in those sort o' fings in the past. D'yer know, I 'ad ter nag at 'im ter cast 'is vote before now. It's those men at the docks. There's a lot o' Bolsheviks workin' there, yer know.'

'What the bleedin' 'ell's Bolsheviks?' Maisie asked, scratching the side of her head.

'It's them troublemakers from Russia,' Florrie told her. 'They're out ter overfrow the Government.' With a wry smile she added, 'They'll fink I'm a Bolshevik when I go down that Council on Monday mornin'.'

Maudie had been expecting a better response from her friends, or at the very least a little sympathy, but they seemed not to care. 'D'yer know they're atheists?' she said hopefully.

'What, the Council?' Sadie asked.

'No, the Bolsheviks,' Maudie said impatiently. 'Our vicar was tellin' us about the people who are leadin' the uprisin' in Russia. They don't believe in God, an' 'e knows all about such fings.'

'Who, God?' Sadie asked, hiding a smile.

'No, Reverend Jones. 'E told us on Sunday at the sermon. Gawd knows what I'm gonna go,' Maudie groaned. 'If the people at the church find out Ernie's turned Bolshevik I won't be able ter 'old me 'ead up in there ever again.'

'Sounds like ole Reverend Jones is tryin' ter frighten yer, if yer ask me,' Florrie remarked.

101

Maudie Mycroft could see she was wasting her time seeking sympathy from the women and she picked up her shopping bag. 'Well, I'll best be orf,' she said coldly. 'I've got no time ter stand chattin'.'

The women watched her leave and when she was out of earshot Florrie turned to the others. 'Yer know, I fink she's goin' roun' the twist,' she said, stifling a wicked grin. 'It's that muvvers' meetin' what's doin' it, I'm sure it is. Ole Granny Watson was like 'er. Wouldn't miss a meetin', an' one day she started goin' a bit funny. It's wicked really but I 'ad ter laugh. There she was out in the street in 'er nightshift shoutin' out at the top of 'er voice.'

'I remember that,' Maisie butted in. 'She was on about the end o' the world was nigh. Poor cow was frozen stiff too. Mrs Casey took 'er in an' called fer ole Doctor Kelly. They got 'er took away in the end. That's 'ow she come ter move. They found 'er a place near 'er daughter in Kent somewhere.'

The street was in full shadow by the time the group dispersed. As Nellie Tanner started off Sadie called her to one side.

''Ave yer got a minute, Nell?' she asked.

'What is it, Sadie?'

'It's my Billy. 'E's got 'imself in a bit o' trouble,' she said in a whisper.

'What sort o' trouble?' Nellie asked.

'Come indoors fer a minute an' I'll tell yer. I can't talk out 'ere, Nell,' she said, dabbing at her eyes.

Chapter Eight

On Monday morning the dining rooms in Cotton Lane were full of working rivermen. The regular freighter from Denmark had docked and along the quayside barges were moored, filled with coconuts and spices which had been transshipped from the large Oriental freighters at the Royal group of docks downriver. It was the first day's work in weeks for many of the dockers and all day a steady stream of men passed through the doorway of the little cafe. In the small back room Danny Tanner sat listening to his old friend Billy Sullivan's problems. Carrie's young brother was waiting to tie up a brace of barges to a river tug for their journey back to the Royal Albert Dock and he had taken the opportunity to visit his sister and her husband in the dining rooms. Carrie was hard put to it and she had little time to talk with him, but it was not long before Billy turned up at the cafe eager to see his friend and Carrie directed him into the back room.

Billy was sitting with a mug of tea at his elbow, his flattish face looking serious as he spoke. 'I wouldn't 'ave troubled ter go after the job in the first place, Danny,' he was saying, 'but yer know she worries. That dopey Arnold told 'er there was a job goin' at the saw-mills. Anyway, she told me if I didn't go after it she was goin' ter chuck us out. She said it was about time I started bringin' in some dosh, 'specially now the ole man's on short time. Well, I decided I 'ad ter try. Not that I was worried about 'er chuckin' me out, I know she wouldn't do that, but it was only right after all. Anyway, down I goes. It was that place underneath the arches in Abbey Street. I ferget the name of it – Brindle's I fink it was. Well, there was a silly ole cow workin' in the office an' when I went in there she give me a dirty look an' told me ter take a seat. I must 'ave bin sittin' there fer over an hour an' then this geezer comes out an' beckons me in 'is office. There was nowhere ter sit an' so there was me standin' in front of 'is desk like a bad little boy. 'E said ter me, "What 'ave yer done in the past year?" an' I said, "Nuffink." That didn't go down very well an' then 'e asked me why. I told 'im I was gettin' over me wounds an' 'e said the work was 'ard an' did I fink I could manage it. I said, "'Course I can," an' then 'e starts lookin' at these papers as though I wasn't there. Well, ter cut a long story short 'e ends up tellin' me that the last bloke was put off fer losin' too much time an' I might be a bad time-keeper as well, what wiv me injuries. Anyway, I asked 'im what 'e done in the war an' 'e told me it was no concern o' mine. You know me, Danny, I don't go roun' askin' fer trouble but this geezer got me goin'. I knows I ain't got the job by now so I ups an' tells 'im a few fings.'

'Like what?' Danny asked, guessing the outcome.

'I told 'im 'e was a no-good whoreson an' 'e shouldn't 'ave wasted my time in the first place,' Billy replied, his blue eyes blazing at the memory of it. 'Anyway, 'e told me ter get out an' called me a lazy so-an'-so so I stuck one on 'im. It was only a slap really but it sent 'im sprawlin'.'

Danny winced. He was well aware of Billy's prowess in the ring and knew that although he was far from well he could still punch his weight. 'An 'e called the police?'

"Ow did yer guess?' Billy asked, grinning sheepishly.

'My Carrie told me when I come in 'ere this mornin',' Danny replied.

Billy sipped his tea thoughtfully. 'The ole cow saw me clump 'im frew the office winder an' she phoned fer the police,' he said as he put his mug down on the wooden table. 'I should 'ave 'ad it away smartly but instead I walked inter that little park opposite the firm an' sat down ter fink. The ole cow must 'ave seen me go in there from the winder an' suddenly the law pounces on me. These two coppers takes me ter the office an' the geezer who I whacked told 'em it was me what done it. The coppers asked 'im if 'e wanted ter press charges but 'e said no. Don't ask me why. P'raps 'e knew 'e was in the wrong by provokin' me in the first place. Anyway, they give me a good talkin' to an' one o' the coppers kept givin' me an old-fashioned look. Suddenly, out o' the blue, 'e asked me if I knew the Tunnel Mob. This was out in the street afterwards.'

'What did yer say?' Danny asked.

'I said no, didn't I?' Billy replied quickly. 'This copper said 'e used ter be on the Tunnel beat an' 'e'd seen a bloke who looked like me knockin' around wiv 'em. Mind yer, Danny, I ain't seen nuffink o' Freddie an' 'is pals since that time last year when we was gonna do that job I told yer about. This copper said the Tunnel Mob's bin done fer a ware'ouse job in Wappin'. 'E told me they was still lookin' fer two more blokes who was involved but they don't know who they was.'

'Well if yer wasn't involved yer got nuffink ter worry about,' Danny reassured him.

Billy looked worried. 'Trouble is, Danny, they beat the watchman up an' 'e picked 'em out in an identification parade, so the copper told me. 'E said I might be 'earin' from 'em. S'pose they take me down an' put me in a line-up. S'posin' the ole boy picks me out.'

'Well, if yer wasn't involved 'e won't be able to. I shouldn't worry any more about it,' Danny said dismissively.

Billy was not so sure. 'S'posin' I look like one o' the ovver blokes,' he went on. 'The ole watchman could make a mistake. 'Specially if they was all over 'im when they was doin' 'im over. Anyway, after what I did ter that silly ole goat at the sawmills the coppers might fink I'm a villain an' try ter get the ole boy ter say I was there. It could 'appen.'

Danny grinned. 'Billy, if pigs could fly.'

'What?'

'Never mind. Jus' try ter fink where yer was when they turned the ware'ouse over,' Danny prompted him. 'All yer need is somebody ter back yer up.'

'But I dunno when it 'appened,' Billy said irritably.

'Well, find out. Yer got friends down Rovver'ithe, ain't yer?' Danny reminded him. 'Ask about, or see if there's any ole newspapers lyin' about in yer 'ouse. There might be somefink in there about it. I'll 'ave a look too, an' I'll ask about, some o' my pals on the river might know somefink. Once yer know the date an' time o' the job yer can fink back. It'll all work out right, so don't worry.'

Billy looked gloomy and his friend got up and collected the empty mugs. 'Let's 'ave anuvver mug o' tea. I gotta get back ter work soon,' he said.

It was nearing two o'clock and Annie McCafferty paused as she put on her coat in the back room of the cafe. She had seen Billy enter the dining rooms in front of her as she returned from the park with Rachel, and the sight of him had sent a little shiver through her body.

Annie felt angry with herself for dwelling on thoughts of the young man over the weekend. She had been unable to concentrate on her reading, her mind constantly straying to the conversation she had had with him in the rose gardens. He was obviously not very well educated by the way he spoke, and he seemed very troubled and disgruntled by what had happened to him. She had thought at length over what he had told her and she felt truly sorry for him. There were other, more delicate feelings which Annie realised had been awoken inside her by meeting the handsome young man. He had looked at her in a way that frightened and worried her, but looking back she became excited and stirred by his attention. Often in the past she had listened to other women talking about their young men and she had tried not to dwell on what they said. Marriage was not for her, she told herself. Now though she had met a young man and felt strange feelings which she could not quite understand. It had only been a brief talk and nothing improper was intimated. He had been very careful in the way that he spoke to her and was very apologetic when he swore. He had said he was a very good friend of Danny, Carrie's brother, and it was likely that she would see him sometime in the future. She had not expected to see him so soon, as she returned to the dining rooms.

Carrie came into the back room to take Rachel up for her afternoon nap and smiled at Annie as the young woman was buttoning up her coat. 'Did yer 'ave a nice stroll?' she asked.

Annie nodded. 'We went to the swings and fed the ducks, didn't we, Rachel?'

The young child was more interested in her father who was busy cutting slabs of meat into small portions for the next day's pies.

'I met that young man Billy Sullivan in the park the other day,' Annie said casually, wanting to glean some information about him. 'He said hello to Rachel and introduced himself to me while we were sitting on the bench. He seems a nice young man.'

Carrie smiled. 'Billy Sullivan an' my Danny are like bruvvers,' she said. 'We all grew up tergevver in Page Street. Did 'e tell yer about 'is boxin?'

Annie nodded. 'Yes, he did. He also said he was going for a job that morning. I wonder if he got it.'

Carrie smiled again as she shook her head. 'I wouldn't 'ave thought so. Billy an' work don't get on very well tergevver. In any case, 'e wouldn't be in 'ere terday if 'e'd been lucky.'

Annie tried not to look too concerned. 'Has he not got a young lady?' she asked, trying to sound nonchalant, but she could feel herself almost blushing.

Carrie looked at her child's nurse with renewed interest. Until now she had never thought about Annie being interested in men, she was so reserved and proper, but it seemed to Carrie that Billy might have kindled a spark in the young woman.

'Billy's never been all that interested in women, Annie,' she replied. 'Boxin' was 'is love, but all that's over now. Mind yer, Billy's bin on about openin' up a gymnasium for the young lads around 'ere. I don't know if 'e'll ever do it but yer never can tell wiv Billy.'

'He said you and he walked out once,' Annie mentioned with a shy grin. 'He only said it in passing,' she added quickly.

Carrie laughed aloud. 'Yeah, it was only once. Billy kissed me on the cheek an' I got all silly an' decided 'e was too forward,' she said, not divulging to Annie what happened later, when they were walking home and Billy tried to make love to her.

'Billy told me he kissed you in the rose gardens,' Annie said smiling.

'That's right, 'e did. Billy's one o' the best,' Carrie told her. 'The family are Catholics and 'is farvver's

Irish. They're regular churchgoers an' Sadie, Billy's mum, is very nice. It was a terrible shame about what 'appened to 'im. 'E lost two bruvvers in the war too.'

Annie shook her head sadly. 'It was terrible, the loss of life. Billy got badly wounded, didn't he?'

Carrie nodded. ''E was shot in the chest. It finished 'is boxin'. 'E was goin' ter fight fer a title before 'e went in the army.' She paused for a moment. 'If yer want, I'll tell 'im yer 'ere. P'raps 'e'll walk yer 'ome,' she added.

Annie shook her head quickly. 'No, it's all right. I've to hurry. There's a nurses' meeting at the church this afternoon and I mustn't be late,' she said quickly.

Carrie thought she caught a moment of panic in Annie's eyes and she held up her hands to reassure her. 'It's all right. Maybe you can 'ave anuvver chat wiv 'im when yer've more time,' she said lightly. 'Billy would be pleased, I'm sure.'

Annie McCafferty left the Bradley Dining Rooms and walked home feeling cross with herself. She had wanted to meet the young man again, but now the opportunity had been afforded her she had not been confident enough to accept it. Maybe she was being foolish in placing so much importance on those brief few words she·and Billy had exchanged in the park. Her life was mapped out for her by providence, she told herself firmly. She was going to stay in her profession and concentrate her energies on what she knew best.

She reached the busy Jamaica Road and suddenly felt depressed as she hurried across and turned into a quiet backstreet which led to her home. It had occurred to her that by devoting her life to her work she would never have the chance to look after her own babies, and her thoughts turned once more to the young man with the dark wavy hair and the expressive blue eyes.

*

William Tanner finished tidying up the small warehouse stock and sat down to await the van which was due. He had sorted the boxes of patent medicines and stacked them in one corner away from the cartons of collar studs and bootlaces. He had repaired damaged boxes with sticky brown paper and stacked the large cartons of cleaning cloths and feather dusters up against a back wall, to make room for the consignment of cottons and wools which was due soon. The warehouse looked neat and tidy with all the stock now sorted and listed and as he looked around William sighed to himself. The job was a steady one, and he was left alone to manage the place. Joe Maitland his boss was very often out buying and selling and he rarely interfered with the running of the store. William realised that he should feel contented with his lot, but he was not. Horses were his love and he had spent the best years of his life working at the Galloway stables.

William looked around at the stacks of cartons and bundles and felt that he had been wasting his time tidying the stock. Soon the place would be full of various bits and pieces that Joe Maitland bought in bulk from the manufacturers and sold to outlets and stallholders in the markets. The business seemed to be doing well and all day vans called for items which Joe had listed and William prepared for despatch. It was a never-ending task which offered William little personal satisfaction. He could always get old Benny Robinson, his helper, to sweep the place up and tie up the piles of cardboard, but Benny had already swept up twice that day and he was now busy sorting out bundles of twine which had fallen out of a damaged carton and become unwound. Benny was whistling noisily and he seemed happy in what he was doing so William left him alone. Anyway, the van would be arriving any minute now and Benny would be expected to help in the unloading.

William glanced down at the list of stock he was cataloguing and sighed. He pushed the sheet of paper away and looked around him, his eyes straying up to the dusty rafters. He had been fortunate in getting the job with Joe Maitland, he had to admit. He had been working at the Council depot as an attendant when Joe offered him the job, and he had been very pleased to make the change. William had not been happy at having to work through the night and at weekends and the tasks he had had to perform were not always pleasant. Sometimes he had to push a heavy barrow through the empty streets full of paraffin lamps which had to be placed around holes in the road. On more than one occasion he had had to remove a dead dog from the highway and take it in his barrow to the incinerator, and there were times when he had to take the place of a night watchman who had been taken ill on one of the larger roadworks and stay there until he could be relieved. It had been a very unhappy time for him, especially since he knew that his advancing years prevented him from getting a job as a carman. That would have been something he was very familiar with, having done it in his early years and worked so long with horses since. The job with Maitland had at least given him his weekends off, and the pay was better. He had a good working relationship with Joe too, having known him quite well when the young trader lodged with Florrie Axford.

William looked up at the clock and saw that it was nearing four o'clock. The van was late in coming. Benny usually went home around four-thirty unless the boss offered him some overtime, and Joe Maitland had not arrived back from his buying trip. William realised he would have to handle the unloading alone if the van did not arrive in the next few minutes.

At four-thirty on the dot Benny put on his coat and

cap and bade William goodnight. Ten minutes later there was a loud rat-tat on the heavy iron-fronted door of the warehouse. William got up from his chair at the workbench and went over to open up with a puzzled frown. It wasn't the van arriving for he would have heard the engine, and it couldn't be Joe Maitland. He always used the side door which led into a small office.

As William slid the bolts the doors suddenly swung violently outwards, throwing him off balance, and before he could recover two heavily built men pinned him against the office wall. Their faces snarled at him as he struggled vainly against their far superior strength, and a tall, broad-shouldered man came into the warehouse and walked slowly and deliberately towards him. William saw that he was well dressed with a dark, double-breasted suit and polished shoes. He was wearing a homburg and his face was swarthy, thickly browed and with a thin moustache, which gave him the appearance of a continental.

The man stopped a foot away from him and for a moment or two William stopped struggling. 'Tell Mr Maitland his old friends have paid him a visit,' the man said in a cultured voice. 'And just so you don't forget . . .'

William saw the man lean back, one shoulder dropping slightly, then there was a flash of light which seemed to blind him and a searing pain. William felt the floor move from under him, and then blackness.

Benny Robinson left the warehouse in Herring Street and walked across the road to the tobacconist's opposite. Benny was turned sixty-five and a widower who lived alone in Abbey Street. He had lived in Stepney for most of his life and had come to South London to work for Joe Maitland when the warehouse opened two years ago. Joe had employed Benny when he was buying and selling in the East End of London and found the elderly man to be a conscientious worker who could be relied on to keep his mouth shut. At the time Joe Maitland was involved in some dubious dealing and his buying was not always from legitimate sources. Benny Robinson was content to take his weekly wage and shut his eyes to anything shady, aware that what he didn't know couldn't harm him. Joe had met up with Benny again on one of his rare trips to his old haunts and offered him a job, which Benny was glad to accept. Moving to South London was no hardship for the elderly man. He made friends easily and after his wife died there seemed little to keep him tied to his home area.

Benny had made friends with the local tobacconist and when he walked into the shop at four-thirty-five on Monday he was immediately drawn into conversation. At four-forty-five Benny walked out of the shop and saw smoke coming from Joe's warehouse. It was curling out around the edges of the large double doors and for a moment or two Benny stopped and stared, then with a shout of alarm he ran across the road as fast as he could and pulled on the hanging padlock flap. As the doors swung outwards a cloud of black, evil-smelling smoke gushed out and Benny could see a fire raging in the far corner. What frightened him most was the still figure of William Tanner lying prone beside the office wall, blood already beginning to turn dark on his battered face. Benny knew he had to get William out of the smoke before he did anything else. He bent down, grabbed the inert figure's wrists in his large hands, and pulled.

Carrie had finished cleaning the tables and was busy sweeping the floor when there was a loud knocking on the side door of the dining rooms. Fred was in the kitchen tidying up and putting the freshly washed pots and pans in their proper places. He went to see who was there.

'It's Carrie's farvver. 'E's bin in an accident.'

Carrie's heart was pumping furiously as she dashed through the kitchen to the front door. She found Maisie Dougall standing in the doorway, a serious look on her ruddy face.

'What's 'appened ter me dad?' she cried out in alarm.

'There's nuffink ter worry about,' Maisie reassured her. ''E was in a fire an' they've took 'im ter Guy's 'Ospital as a precaution. 'E'll be all right, luv.'

Carrie reached for her coat, her heart still pounding in her chest and a tightening sensation in her throat causing her to gulp. 'Where's me mum?' she asked quickly.

'She's at the 'ospital wiv 'im, Carrie,' Maisie told her. 'Yer muvver asked me ter come round an' tell yer. Yer dad's in Drake Ward.'

Carrie looked anxiously at her husband. 'Yer'll 'ave ter give Rachel 'er tea, Fred,' she said quickly. 'I'll 'ave ter go right away.'

'Go wiv 'er, Fred,' Maisie urged him. 'Don't worry about the baby. I'll take care of 'er till yer get back.'

Carrie hurried through the evening street and Fred struggled to keep up with her. He had insisted on going with her but Carrie was beginning to wish he had stayed in the shop. As they made their way along the Jamaica Road to the tram stop he tried to reassure her but Carrie's mind was racing. 'I 'ope 'e's not burned bad,' she muttered anxiously.

Fred squeezed her arm. 'Yer dad can't be too badly 'urt, luv,' he said breathlessly. 'Maisie said it's only a precaution.'

They sat together on the rattling tram, Fred holding

her hand and Carrie biting her bottom lip in frustration as the tram stopped at the Tower Bridge Hotel for the conductor to alter the points. 'I do wish 'e'd 'urry up,' she groaned aloud.

Finally the tram got underway and as it started to pull up at the end of the track by the foot of Duke Street Hill Carrie was already out of her seat and waiting on the platform at the rear of the vehicle, with Fred at her side gripping her arm for fear that she would fall off before it actually stopped. They hurried through the long arch, dodging between the workers who were making their way to London Bridge Station, and then quickly crossed St Thomas's Street and hurried through the high, wide gates of Guy's Hospital.

William was propped up against pillows as Carrie and Fred walked up to his bed. He grinned self-consciously at them. His face was discoloured and swollen about the eyes and a plaster was spread across his forehead. Nellie was sitting at the bedside. She nodded to Fred as Carrie leaned over and kissed her father gently on his cheek.

'What 'appened, Dad?' she asked.

'There were some callers,' he replied, a wry smile playing about his lips.

Carrie looked down at him, suddenly aware of how frail and haggard he looked. 'Callers?' she repeated, a puzzled look on her face.

'Some men beat yer farvver up an' then they set the ware'ouse alight,' Nellie said, her voice full of emotion.

'Who were they, Dad?' Carrie asked with anger rising in her voice. 'D'yer know 'em?'

'I've never laid eyes on 'em before,' he replied, 'but I'll never ferget the bloke who laid me out. 'E looked like an Italian but 'e didn't speak like they do. 'E jus' walked up ter me calm as yer like an' ses, "Tell Mr Maitland 'is ole friends 'ave paid 'im a visit." Then 'e ses ter me, "Jus' so's yer don't ferget," then 'e put me lights out.'

Nellie looked very serious as she listened to her battered husband reliving his terrifying experience. She leaned forward and gripped his hand in hers. 'Now listen ter me, Will,' she said firmly, 'yer gotta tell Joe Maitland yer packin' up. Tell 'im soon as yer see 'im. I always knew there was somefink a bit fishy about that bloke when 'e lodged wiv Florrie. She couldn't get ter the bottom of 'im. Then there was that turn-out wiv the boxin' shows. Yer told me yerself 'e put the finger on the goin's on at the Crown. People like Joe Maitland make enemies an' I don't want you gettin' involved wiv somefink what's got nuffink ter do wiv yer, d'yer understand?'

William smiled at his wife and gave her a large wink. 'Righto, Muvver. I'll tell Joe soon as I see 'im,' he replied.

Fred leaned forward in his chair. ''Ave the police talked ter yer yet, Will?' he asked.

'They come in ter see me earlier,' William replied. 'They left jus' before Nellie got 'ere. There wasn't much I could tell 'em except ter give 'em a description o' the Italian-lookin' bloke. I can't remember what the ovver two looked like, it 'appened so quick.'

Carrie sat around the bed with her mother and Fred chatting for a while, and it was not too long before they saw Joe Maitland coming down the ward. He looked very worried and nodded respectfully to the three of them before leaning over the bed, concern evident on his face. ''Ow are yer, Will?' he asked anxiously.

The ward sister came over before William could reply. 'There's only two allowed around the bed,' she said stiffly.

Carrie got up and kissed her father before she left

116

the ward, followed by her husband who was talking to Nellie.

'Yer was sayin' about Joe Maitland blowin' the whistle on the fights at the Crown, Nell. What was that all about?' Fred asked her.

Nellie was holding on to his arm as they walked out into the corridor and he felt her tense. 'It was a couple o' years ago,' she said with a sigh. 'It was just about the time yer was gettin' married. The police raided the Crown in Dock'ead an' stopped the boxin' that was goin' on there, an' they nicked a lot o' street bookies who was there at the time. The same night the lan'lord fell down a flight o' stairs an' broke 'is neck. Joe Maitland used ter go ter the fights, an' apparently 'e was the one who tipped the police off.'

'But why should Joe Maitland do that if 'e went ter the fights 'imself?' Fred asked, a puzzled look on his face.

'Well, accordin' ter Will, Joe's bruvver used ter fight in the pub tournaments over Stepney,' Nellie went on. 'One night 'e got set about over refusin' ter chuck a fight. 'E died in 'ospital a few days later. Rumour 'as it that Maitland only went ter the fights ter get all the evidence 'e could. Mind yer, it's only rumour really. I wouldn't repeat what I said, not to anybody. The people round where we live never talk about it. Yer never know who's listenin'. It was said that George Galloway was one o' the blokes who 'ad Joe's bruvver beaten up, but it was never proved.'

'George Galloway?' Fred queried. 'But I thought yer was sayin' that Joe's bruvver got beaten up over Stepney. That's a bit out the way fer Galloway, ain't it?'

Nellie's face took on a hard look as she walked beside him along the tiled corridor. 'George Galloway is a swine, Fred, believe me,' she said with passion.

117

'Yer know the story about what 'appened ter my Will, but there's a lot yer don't know about the Galloways. That ole goat used ter travel all over London ter the fights. 'E's a man wivout pity an' 'e don't care who 'e steps on ter get what 'e wants. Believe me, I know.'

Nellie's last few words stayed in Fred's mind and later, in the comfort of the cosy front room above the dining rooms, after Maisie had left, he was moved to speak to his young wife about what her mother had said to him.

Carrie leaned back in her chair and stretched out her stockinged feet. 'George Galloway is detested by everybody around 'ere,' she answered him. 'I've told yer before, 'e pays less than any ovver firm in Bermondsey an' 'e sacks 'is workers fer the least fing. 'E wouldn't tolerate the union fer ages an' as soon as any of 'is workers tried ter get the union in they were put off. What's more 'e owns 'alf o' the 'ouses in Page Street an' they're fallin' ter pieces. 'E won't spend a penny on 'em. I jus' loathe and detest 'im. What 'e did ter my dad after 'im workin' fer the man all those years was enough, apart from anyfing else.'

Fred could see her hatred for the man showing plainly on her face, and he thought of Nellie's closing words which kept running around inside his head. Perhaps there was something else, something between the two families which had spawned such detestation. Both Nellie and her daughter wore that same look on their faces at the mention of the name Galloway. Maybe it was better not to dwell on it, he decided. Maybe some things were better left to the natural course of time.

Chapter Nine

Early on Friday morning a tearful Sadie Sullivan woke her son Billy and told him that the police had been. 'Yer gotta go ter Dock'ead police station at ten o'clock an' if yer don't they're comin' for yer,' she sobbed.

Billy climbed out of bed glumly and went down to the scullery where Sadie was stirring porridge over the gas stove. 'Yer'll be the death o' me,' she groaned. 'I bet they're gonna charge yer fer fightin' wiv that guv'nor at the sawmills.'

'No, they're not, Ma,' Billy said irritably. 'They're jus' gonna ask me ter sign the statement.'

'What statement?' Sadie asked as she spooned out the porridge onto a plate.

'You know, the one I made at the sawmills.'

'Well, it seems strange ter me. Why didn't they make yer sign it when they first spoke ter yer?' Sadie asked suspiciously.

''Ow the bleedin' 'ell do I know,' Billy moaned, blowing on the steaming porridge.

'It don't seem right ter me,' Sadie told him. 'I knew the police would mark yer when yer started runnin' around wiv that crowd o' no-gooders. Yer should get yerself a nice Catholic gel an' settle down.'

While his mother was in the back yard pegging out the washing Billy ate the porridge in silence, his thoughts racing. They were going to put him on an identification parade, he was certain. What if the old watchman picked him out? How could he prove he wasn't involved in the robbery? The questions tumbled around in his head and he had no answers. Who would believe him? His mother wouldn't. She was convinced already that he'd been getting into bad ways with the Tunnel Mob. She had told him often enough.

'I'll do yer some bread an' jam. They might keep yer there a long while,' Sadie told him, fighting back the tears.

Billy stood up and wiped the back of his hand across his lips. 'Look, Ma, there's nuffink ter worry about. They jus' wanna get me ter sign that statement, that's all,' he tried to convince her.

'Long as it ain't got nuffink ter do wiv that ovver crowd,' she said, her eyes questioning him.

'Christ! I ain't seen nuffink o' that Tunnel Mob fer ages.'

Sadie's eyes flared and she brought her hand up suddenly and slapped him hard across the face. 'Don't you dare blaspheme!' she cried.

Billy's hand went up to his face in surprise and then Sadie pulled him to her and hugged him tightly. 'I believe yer, but yer shouldn't take the name o' the Lord in vain,' she told him, her voice breaking as tears started.

Billy felt the pain in his chest and he gripped his mother by her shoulders. 'Careful, Muvver. Yer know I'm a bit fragile,' he grinned.

Sadie dried her eyes on her apron and gave him a smile. 'I've boiled a kettle,' she said. 'Get yerself washed an' I'll cut yer some nice bread an' jam. I'll do it up in a bit o' greaseproof so it won't go an' mess up yer pocket. Go on, orf yer go.'

An hour later Billy was presenting himself at the counter inside Dockhead police station.

'Yer'll 'ave ter wait. The inspector ain't arrived yet,' the sergeant told him. 'Take a seat an' we'll call yer.'

Billy sat down and looked around at the posters on the walls. One showed a villainous-looking character who was wanted for murder and another offered a reward of fifty pounds for information. Billy did not get a chance to read on for an elbow suddenly prodded him in the ribs.

''Ere, mate. Got a fag?'

Billy looked at the scruffy individual who had sat down next to him on the hard bench. 'I don't smoke,' he replied.

''Ave yer got the price of a cup o' tea?' the old man asked him.

Billy shook his head. 'Sorry, I'm skint,' he said.

'I ain't 'ad a bite since yesterday mornin' an' I'm bloody starvin',' the man went on, scratching his ribs through a hole in his filthy shirt.

Billy suddenly remembered the jam sandwiches his mother had prepared for him. ''Ere, 'ave one o' these,' he said, feeling sorry for the old gent.

'What are they?'

'Jam sandwiches.'

'Jam sandwiches!' the man repeated, a look of disgust on his stubbled face. 'If there's one fing I can't stand it's jam sandwiches. Are yer sure yer ain't got a fag?'

'I've already told yer, I don't smoke,' Billy replied, his voice rising.

'All right, keep yer shirt on. I fergot,' the old man moaned.

Billy looked around at him, aware that he was constantly scratching himself. Suddenly the man stood up and walked over to the counter.

'Oi, you. Ain't I gonna get any attention 'ere?' he shouted.

121

The desk sergeant looked up at him with a stern expression on his face. 'Now listen 'ere, Winkle. If yer after gettin' yerself locked up, yer barkin' up the wrong tree,' he chided him. 'We're fed up wiv de-lousin' the likes o' you. Now why don't yer piss orf out of 'ere an' go round the local baths. It's only tuppence.'

'I ain't got tuppence,' the man grumbled, reaching out for the sheaf of papers on the desk.

'Now leave those alone or I'll get angry,' the sergeant told him.

Winkle sat down and grinned at Billy. ''E finks 'e's so clever. Jus' wait till that inspector feller walks in. I'm gonna give 'im one. They'll 'ave ter lock me up then.'

Ten minutes later the door opened and a tall, heavily built police inspector entered the station. As he walked towards the counter he stumbled over Winkle's outstretched foot, and before he could recover his balance the old tramp was on his feet dancing around with his fists moving in small circles. 'C'mon, stick 'em up,' he called out.

The inspector glared at him. 'Now get off home or I'll get the lads to dowse you, Winkle,' he growled.

Winkle suddenly shot out a fist which caught the inspector weakly in the chest and then he danced back out of reach. 'C'mon, stick 'em up,' he goaded him.

'Get me a pail of water,' the annoyed policeman called out to his sergeant, whereupon Winkle shot forward and landed a light blow on the inspector's nose.

'All right, lock him up,' the officer shouted, holding a hand up to his face. Winkle was marched smartly away grinning with satisfaction and the inspector disappeared behind the counter. Billy could barely hide his amusement at the tramp's antics, but his face became serious as the sergeant emerged from a back office and called him over.

'William Sullivan?'

Billy nodded and the police officer motioned to the bench. 'Wait there till yer called. Yer bein' taken down ter Rother'ithe nick. Yer goin' on an I.D. parade,' he announced.

Carrie had been hard pressed all morning but she was feeling happy with herself as she scooped fresh tea-leaves into the large enamel teapot and filled it with boiling water from the bubbling urn at the back of the counter. Albert Buller, the catering firm's representative, had called the previous morning and taken a large order, and the discount which Carrie had insisted upon had been confirmed later that day. The weather was holding fine today too and Rachel looked very pretty as Annie McCafferty took her for a walk to the park. Fred was cheerful and humming to himself in the kitchen and Bessie was unusually quiet, which Carrie found out later was due to a toothache. Another reason for Carrie's high spirits was the conversation she had had with Annie earlier that morning.

The young nurse had mentioned seeing Billy Sullivan on her way to the cafe and he had smiled at her and waved from the other side of the road. 'He seems a very nice young man,' she had remarked casually.

Carrie had caught a certain look in the young woman's eye and she decided then to learn something of her feelings towards the young man. 'Do yer like 'im?' she asked outright.

Annie flushed. 'He seems a very nice young man,' she repeated quickly.

Carrie smiled. 'Billy needs a young lady in 'is life,' she remarked pointedly. ''E needs somebody like you ter keep 'im on the straight an' narrow. 'Ave yer got a young man, Annie?'

Annie shook her head. 'I've never considered it,' she said, becoming more embarrassed.

Carrie felt suddenly sorry for the pretty young nurse. 'Well, yer should do,' she said in a firm tone. 'Yer very pretty, yer know, an' it's obvious yer like children. Yer could do a lot worse than walk out wiv Billy Sullivan.'

Annie smiled and averted her eyes, trying to stifle her embarrassment by fiddling with the pram straps which were already fastened around the impatient child. 'I wouldn't dare give Billy the impression I'd like him to ask me to walk out with him,' she replied. 'I just couldn't.'

'Well, 'ow's Billy gonna know yer like 'im unless yer try an' give 'im some indication?' Carrie said laughing.

Annie shrugged her shoulders. 'I don't know. I couldn't be too forward. It wouldn't be right,' she said in a quiet voice.

Carrie decided there and then to take the initiative. 'Look, why don't I talk ter Billy? I could tell 'im yer like 'im an' 'e should ask yer outright ter walk out wiv 'im. All yer 'ave ter do then is say yes. Yer can do that, can't yer?' she asked, smiling broadly.

Annie looked thoughtful. 'If Billy had wanted to ask me, surely he would have done,' she said doubtfully.

'Billy Sullivan is a very nice young man, Annie, but yer gotta remember 'e's bin out o' work fer a long time, an' gettin' wounded ruined 'is future as 'e saw it,' Carrie told her. 'Yer gotta remember too that Billy sees somebody like you as bein' above 'im. Oh 'e'll talk ter yer easy enough, Billy can talk wiv anybody, but askin' a refined young lady like you ter walk out wiv 'im is a different matter. Yer gotta overcome yer shyness. Let 'im know yer like 'im. I can't tell yer 'ow ter do it but yer know what I mean.'

Annie had smiled through her embarrassment and looked Carrie square in the eye. 'Would you ask him?' she suggested in a quiet voice.

Carrie had touched Annie's arm reassuringly. 'Jus'

leave it ter me,' she said boldly.

As Carrie coped with the comings and goings at the dining rooms that morning she was feeling pleased at the progress she had made with Annie McCafferty. This could be the making of Billy, she told herself. The young man needed a woman to steady him and encourage him to get a job. Annie would be just the person. She was a Catholic too, which would make it easy for her to be accepted by Sadie and Daniel Sullivan.

'Am I gonna wait all day fer that two o' toasted drippin', Carrie?' a deep voice shouted out.

Carrie was quickly brought back to matters in hand and she smiled sweetly at the neglected carman. 'Comin' up right away, Bill,' she told him.

In the Rotherhithe police station a motley crowd stood around waiting, and it was not long before they were ushered out into the compound at the rear of the building.

'Right, line up in a straight line if yer will, gentlemen,' the police sergeant requested politely.

There was a mumble of ill humour as the men did what they were told, slowly shuffling into position in the middle of the yard. Billy found himself standing at the end of the line. He stared up at the high barred window in the wall facing him. If this goes wrong that's where I'll end up, he told himself.

'Right, gents, no talking,' the sergeant said loudly.

Billy then saw a slightly built man come out from a far door with a policeman holding on to his arm. The man was led along the line. He stopped and turned to the first man. Slowly he looked him up and down and then moved to the next person. Billy could see the dark patches around his eyes as he drew nearer and he noticed that the man was visibly shaking at the ordeal.

The policeman was still holding him by the arm and he seemed very frail and tottery.

'Take yer time, pop,' the policeman said encouragingly.

Billy looked ahead as the man reached the person next to him and he muttered a prayer to himself. He could see now that the policeman who was escorting the robbery victim was the officer who had warned him that day outside the sawmills.

Finally the man stopped in front of Billy and the policeman tightened his grip on the old man's arm. The young man from Page Street was staring ahead and he missed the silent prompting of the police officer. He could feel the man's eyes on him and he was filled with a desire to run off as fast as his legs would carry him.

'That's 'im!' the man said in a surprised voice.

'Are yer sure?' the policeman said, a satisfied smile breaking out on his flat face as he took Billy's arm in a strong grasp.

Billy felt his heart pounding as the elderly man looked at the policeman. 'Sure I'm sure. That's Billy Sullivan. I'd know 'im anywhere,' he said excitedly.

'That's the man who attacked yer?' the policeman asked him.

'Attacked me? Nah, course not! That's Billy Sullivan the boxer. I seen 'im fight at the Dock'ead Club a few times. I saw 'is last pro fight. 'Ow yer doin', Billy?' he asked, grinning widely.

The young ex-boxer could have hugged the man in his delight. 'I'm all right, pop. 'Ow's yerself?' he grinned back.

The old man pumped Billy's hand enthusiastically while the policeman just stood there, his face a dark mask.

'Right, gents, that'll be all. Thanks for your co-operation,' the station sergeant called out.

Billy stood chatting with the old watchman for a few moments and then as he left the yard the policeman who had escorted the old man beckoned him over.

'I'm gonna be watchin' yer, Sullivan,' he grated. 'Jus' put one foot wrong, an' I'll be down on yer like a ton o' bricks, so yer better remember. I don't like your kind. Give me 'alf a chance an' I'll be on yer, is that clear?'

Billy looked him square in the eye. 'I'm finkin' of openin' a gym soon,' he said coolly. 'When I do yer'll be welcome. P'raps me an' you can put on a demonstration fer the youngsters.'

For a moment the policeman's eyes flashed, then he turned on his heel and walked quickly from the yard.

The Tanners were sitting together in their flat at Bacon Buildings and Carrie had just arrived on her usual Friday evening visit. William was still showing the signs of his encounter with Joe Maitland's enemies as he sat back in his easy chair by the low-burning fire. He looked tired and pale, and his hands shook as he filled his pipe. Danny Tanner was slumped in a battered settee beneath the window, his arms folded and a humorous expression on his handsome face as his mother held court.

'Well, as far as I'm concerned yer can go back ter work fer Joe Maitland, an' if yer get anuvver pastin' don't expect me ter come in the 'ospital ter see yer,' she said with conviction.

William looked fondly at his wife and realised how the years were beginning to take their toll. She was still a very attractive woman, but there were lines now etched around her eyes and her forehead was permanently furrowed. Her figure was as trim as when they first walked out together and the fire in her eyes had not diminished, but he noticed the tiredness in her voice and the way she had of biting the inside of her cheek when she became anxious.

'Look, Nell, Joe's not gonna let that 'appen again,' he reassured her. ''E's rented an arch in Druid Street an' it's a lot better than that scruffy ware'ouse. Besides, I've gotta work. I can't sit around 'ere scratchin' me bleedin' self all day. We gotta get the rent money an' we've gotta live.'

'There's no need ter rush back, Farvver,' Danny told him. 'I've got plenty o' work fer the next few weeks. There's plenty o' trade comin' up river an' I can chip in wiv a few extra bob.'

'There's no need ter worry about food eivver,' Carrie said quickly. 'Me an' Fred won't see yer go 'ungry.'

William puffed on his pipe and then inspected the glowing bowl for a few moments. 'There's no need ter worry on that score,' he told them. 'Joe's payin' me while I'm orf sick an' 'e's told me straight not ter rush back. That's more than ole Galloway ever did. Fing is, I can't expect ter stop out too long. It wouldn't be fair ter the man.'

Nellie snorted. 'That's the trouble wiv you, Will Tanner,' she chided him. 'Yer've always bin fair. Yer should start finkin' o' yerself fer a change, an' if yer can't fink o' yerself, fink o' me. I'm the one who 'as the worry. If it ain't one fing it's anuvver.'

Danny glanced quickly at Carrie and smiled briefly, raising his eyes to the ceiling. Nellie saw him, however, and she gave him a smouldering look.

The young man got up from his seat and put his arm around his mother in a fond gesture. 'We all love yer, Mum, an' we won't let yer worry anymore, so what we're gonna do is start up a business,' he said with a huge wink at Carrie. 'Me an' Sis 'ave decided ter open up a laundry 'ere in the flat. We can 'ang a notice out o' the winder sayin' we take in washin', an' you can do the ironin' if yer like. I'll do the fetchin' an' carryin' an'

Farvver can be the foreman. That way yer can keep yer eye on 'im all day long. Mind yer though, we gotta 'ave time off fer a few drinks at the Kings Arms, ain't we, Farvver?'

'By the way, yer'll 'ave ter mind Rachel as well,' Carrie butted in.

Nellie could not keep up her serious look and she smiled as she slapped Danny around the head playfully. 'Yer might joke about such fings but I remember the time when that poor Mrs Knight took in washin',' she told them. 'She 'ad a tribe ter care for as well. 'Er ole man couldn't work at the time. Terrible shame it was.'

Danny returned to his seat and slumped down with a sigh. 'Those times could come back again,' he reminded them. 'There's a lot o' work on the river at the moment but it don't look too good fer the future, so I've bin told. If it gets too bad I might take up boxin' again.'

'Oh no you don't,' Nellie told him firmly. 'I ain't 'avin' none o' those Billy Sullivan tricks in this 'ouse. Yer know 'ow I feel about boxin'. It's a terrible fing ter see two men punchin' the livin' daylights out of each ovver.'

'They do it every weekend outside the pubs,' William remarked. 'At least in the ring they get paid fer it.'

'I don't care, I'm not 'avin' Danny go boxin' again,' she said, adopting her favourite adamant pose of folded arms and protruding bottom lip.

Carrie gave Danny a look suggesting that he hold his tongue and she got up with a sigh. 'C'mon, Mum. I'll 'elp yer wiv the supper,' she volunteered.

As soon as they were out of the room William turned to his son. 'The police come terday,' he said in a low voice. 'Lucky fer me yer muvver was out shoppin' at the time. They was 'ere fer over an hour. Mind yer, I wasn't worried. When yer muvver goes down the market she always comes 'ome through Page Street, an' there's always one o' the women standin' at their front doors. Yer muvver always stops fer a chin-wag.'

'What did they 'ave ter say?' Danny asked.

'They was pumpin' me about the sort o' stuff Joe 'ad in the ware'ouse. I told 'em about the boxes o' collar studs an' shoelaces, an' about the odd bits an' pieces, but they was on about the ovver stuff Joe stored there.'

'What ovver stuff?' Danny asked, his curiosity aroused.

'Well, there was boxes marked up as patent medicines but I know fer a fact that some o' those boxes were full o' perfumes,' Will told him. 'There was a lot o' fancy leavver gloves too, an' smart shoes, not the sort o' shoes we wear. Joe lost the lot when that ware-'ouse went up in smoke.'

Danny scratched his head, a look of puzzlement on his face. 'The fing I can't understand is, you're in charge o' the ware'ouse an' yet yer don't know what's goin' on there,' he remarked. 'On top o' that, yer get pasted over somefink Joe Maitland's done, an' yet soon as yer feelin' all right yer gonna go back ter that new place 'e's got in Druid Street.'

William tapped his pipe on the edge of the iron fender and picked up a pipe cleaner from the hearth. 'Me an' Joe's got an' understandin',' he said, unscrewing the stem of the pipe. 'I got ter know Joe pretty well when I was at Galloway's an' 'e was lodgin' at Flo Axford's. There's a lot o' good in the man an' it's common knowledge around 'ere that it was 'im that got the boxin' racket stopped at the Crown. There was that time too when the stables caught light. If it 'adn't 'a' bin fer Joe 'alf those 'orses would 'a' perished. 'E 'elped me pull 'em all out. Anyway, when 'e knew I was out o' work 'e offered me a job lookin' after the ware'ouse. There was nuffink 'ard about it. It jus' meant seein' in

130

the stuff an' despatchin' it. Joe told me then that some o' the stuff was pretty valuable an' it wasn't always kosher, yer know what I mean. 'E was honest wiv me at least. 'E said then that 'e could trust me ter do the job an' not ask awkward questions. 'E also said that if ever there was any come-back over the stuff 'e was 'andlin' then 'e would make sure I wasn't involved. That was fine by me, Danny. I told Joe at the time, what I don't know can't 'urt me.'

Danny gave an ironic laugh. 'Well, it did, didn't it, Farvver? Yer got set about fer somefink that didn't concern yer. What's Joe 'ad ter say about that?'

William shrugged his shoulders. 'It was jus' one o' those fings. Joe's still in the dark about it all. 'E told me that as far as 'e knows 'e ain't trod on nobody's toes lately.'

'Didn't the coppers 'ave any ideas who it might 'a' bin?' Danny asked.

'They wouldn't say anyfink ter me even if they did know, would they?' William replied, pulling the pipe cleaner back and forth along the stem of his briar.

'Well, somebody must 'ave 'ad it in fer 'im,' Danny said, shifting his position in the settee.

'There was jus' one fing though,' William said, glancing quickly towards the scullery, from where they could hear Carrie talking to Nellie. 'I've bin puzzlin' about that smart-dressed bloke that clocked me. I knew I'd seen 'im somewhere before. It all 'appened so quick but since then I've give it a lot o' thought. I can still see 'is face clearly in me mind an' it come ter me this mornin' after the coppers 'ad left. That bloke come in the yard once wiv George Galloway. They was in Galloway's trap. I remember it now. It was 'is shoes what jogged me memory. When I got clocked an' fell down the last fing I saw was the bloke's shiny pair o' shoes. Everyfing went black then. I was sittin' 'ere this mornin' turnin' it all over in me mind an' fer some reason I got ter finkin' about the old days at the stables. I thought of ole Jack Oxford an' I wondered 'ow 'e was gettin' on. Yer remember ole Jack the yard sweeper. I 'eard 'e got married recently. Well, anyway, I was finkin' of 'ow 'e used ter dodge off an' I'd 'ave ter look fer 'im ter clean the yard up. Then I suddenly remembered when this bloke got out o' Galloway's trap and stood in some 'orse shit. 'E 'ad shiny patent shoes on an' they was smovvered. George Galloway got the needle an' threatened ter sack old Jack fer lettin' the yard get in a state. It's funny 'ow yer suddenly remember these fings. Anyway I'm certain it was the same bloke.'

'Are yer gonna tell the police?' Danny asked.

William shook his head. 'I'm gonna talk ter Joe Maitland first,' he replied.

Danny stared down at his clenched hands. 'Every time anyfink bad 'appens ter this family of ours it seems Galloway's involved. It's like there's a Galloway curse 'angin' over our 'eads,' he said with feeling.

William nodded in agreement. 'I daren't tell them what I jus' told you,' he said in a low voice, casting his eyes towards the scullery. 'Carrie an' yer muvver feel the same way.'

There was no more time to continue their conversation, for the two women came back into the room at that moment carrying the supper.

Chapter Ten

William Tanner went back to work with Nellie's words ringing in his ears. 'Now don't ferget ter warn Joe Maitland that if there's any sign o' trouble yer'll pack the job in,' she reminded him.

William grinned to himself as he walked down the grimy wooden staircase of Bacon Buildings and out into the cold morning air. He was happy to get away from the dilapidated tenement block and its ever-present stench of rotting garbage in the alley behind. It was no wonder Nellie spent most of her spare time chatting to her old friends in Page Street. Danny did not spend much time in that flat either, he had to admit. He only came home to eat and sleep, preferring to spend most of his spare time in the Kings Arms or hanging around on the street corners with Billy Sullivan and a few other friends from the area. As for Carrie, she was always going on about getting enough money together so that she would be able to help him and Nellie get a better place away from the squalor. The way things were going it looked as though she and Fred were hard pushed to make ends meet, what with the situation at the wharves. She would survive though, William told himself. Carrie was a fighter and she knew what she wanted. She had pushed Fred into action and the changes she had compelled him to make had paid off. They had a regular trade and at least their business was holding its own, when many in the area had been forced to close.

Joe Maitland was waiting for William and he smiled as he called him into the dusty office under the railway arch. 'Nice ter see yer back, Will,' he said, shaking his warehouse manager by the hand. ''Ow d'yer feel?'

'I'm all right,' William replied, looking around the room. 'The law was round ter me last week, Joe. They was interested in the sort o' stock yer 'ad in Dock'ead. I couldn't 'elp 'em much though,' he grinned. 'By the way, is Benny around?'

Joe shook his head. 'Benny said 'e wanted ter go back over the water ter live. I fink the turn-out at Dock'ead frightened 'im off. What about you, Will? Are yer sure yer still wanna work fer me?' he asked.

William sat down in a rickety chair and stretched out his legs. 'Well, Joe, Nellie was against me comin' back ter work 'ere, after what 'appened. She thought I should look fer somefing else. Trouble is I ain't everybody's cup o' tea at my age. I can still work though, an' I'm ready ter start.'

Joe Maitland grinned, exposing white, even teeth. He was a slim, handsome-looking man in his mid-thirties, with dark wavy hair and a square chin. 'I've bin makin' a few enquiries over the water while yer bin off sick, Will,' he said, 'but I've come up against a brick wall. Nobody knows anyfink, or nobody wants ter talk. Ter be 'onest I don't fink the trouble come from over the East End. I fink it's nearer 'ome. I've bin rackin' me brains tryin' ter figure what sparked it but I'm stumped. If I'd 'ave turned anybody over I'd 'ave expected a comeuppance. It's a mystery ter me.'

William shifted his position in the chair and slipped his thumbs into his waistcoat pockets. 'I've remembered where I saw that geezer that clocked me, Joe,' he said quietly.

Maitland's eyes opened wide. 'Where was it, Will?' he asked quickly.

''E come in Galloway's yard once. Some time ago it was. 'E was in the trap wiv George Galloway.'

'Galloway?' Joe repeated.

Will nodded. 'It come ter me yesterday mornin' right out the blue. I'd bin puzzlin' over where I'd seen 'im. 'Ave yer got any reason ter fink Galloway might wanna see yer business go up in smoke?' he asked.

Joe shook his head. 'It might only be a coincidence that geezer bein' wiv Galloway,' he said thoughtfully. 'I can't fink of anyfing I've done that would make George Galloway wanna put me out o' business. I don't fink 'e knows I was involved in that ter-do at the Crown. Anyway, I remember when we 'ad that chat at your Carrie's weddin'. Yer said then that there was a limit to 'ow far Galloway would go ter get what 'e wants.'

William smiled bitterly. 'I mus' confess I under-estimated the man. George Galloway would do a deal wiv the devil 'imself if there was anyfing in it fer 'im. The man's gettin' on in years now, as a matter o' fact 'e's a couple o' years older than me an' I'm sixty-two, but I found out ter me cost that 'e ain't mellowed wiv age. All I'd say is, I wouldn't put anyfing past 'im if I were you, Joe. Even if George 'imself draws a line there's that son of 'is. I reckon Frank Galloway'll turn out every bit as bad as the ole man, if not worse.'

'Is 'e runnin' the firm?' Joe asked.

'Well, accordin' ter the carmen who work there Frank's runnin' the business day ter day, but George Galloway still pulls the strings,' William told him.

'The old fing's a mystery ter me,' Joe said, shaking his head slowly.

'Yer said yer didn't fink that business at the Crown 'ad anyfing ter do wiv what 'appened, Joe. Don't yer fink Galloway could've cottoned on some'ow?' William asked. 'Don't ferget 'e was pretty much involved wiv those tournaments.'

''E wasn't involved in what 'appened ter my bruvver though,' Joe replied. 'That much I do know. No, I fink it's somefing else. I've jus' got ter be careful, an' you too, Will. Don't go openin' those doors unless yer know who it is, an' I shouldn't say anyfing ter the police yet. Let me make a few more enquiries first. By the way, I'm gettin' a young man in ter take Benny's place. 'E's a bit slow upstairs, but there's nobody gonna take liberties wiv 'im, Will. Wait till yer see 'im. 'E's startin' termorrer. Yer'll get on wiv 'im jus' fine. Oh, an' before I ferget it, there's four dozen boxes comin' in later terday by Carter Paterson. Mind 'ow yer treat 'em, they're breakables,' he said grinning.

When Carrie opened the front door to Annie McCafferty on a bright Monday morning she was shocked to see the sad look on the young woman's face. She was saddened too when Annie told her that she was going over to Ireland within the next two weeks and would not be back for some time. Carrie was upset at the news but she could understand and sympathise with Annie's decision. The sisters at St Mary's Convent had finally been able to trace her mother through the sisterhood in the south of Ireland. She was very ill and had been asking the nuns to pray for her that she might see the daughter she had abandoned when the child was only days old. Annie was reduced to tears as she explained to Carrie why she had to make the trip.

'I've always wondered about her, Carrie,' she sobbed. 'What hardships must she have suffered to force her to do what she did? I want to see her before she dies, Carrie. I want to let her know that I always thought about her and always loved her, even though she was only a vision in my mind.'

Carrie hugged her and cried with her. 'You'll find yer won't be disappointed, Annie,' she told her. 'She'll be jus' like yer expect 'er ter be. Be'ind that mask o' pain an' sufferin' she'll still look beautiful, yer'll see.'

Annie hugged Rachel tightly and then took her leave, vowing to come back to Bermondsey as soon as she was able.

Carrie embraced her. 'Always remember, Annie, yer future's 'ere, 'ere in these little backstreets,' she told her. 'We love yer an' want yer ter come back. I'm sure there's a chance fer yer ter find real 'appiness 'ere in Bermondsey.'

Carrie watched her walk away along the windy riverside lane and thought about the conversation she had had with Billy Sullivan only a few days before.

It was in the back room where the young ex-boxer usually met Danny Tanner for a chat during the day. Billy had been expressing his fears about the policeman at the frightening identification parade in Rotherhithe police station and Danny had a few words of advice.

'Yer best bet is ter stay clear of 'im. Keep yer nose clean an' don't give the copper any chance ter nail yer, Billy,' he told him. 'If yer do meet up wiv 'im don't let 'im goad yer inter doin' anyfing yer'll regret. If yer put one on 'im 'e'll get yer. They'll give yer an 'idin' when they get yer down the nick an' then when yer come up in front o' the beak yer'll go down. They don't take kindly ter people who set about coppers. Jus' stay calm an' don't ferget what I said. Do yerself a favour an' try ter get a job. It don't matter what it is, even if yer 'ave ter sweep the streets fer a while. It'll keep yer out o' trouble at least.'

Carrie had heard the last snatch of conversation as she came into the room through the open doorway. 'It's about time yer found somefing else ter do instead o' sittin' around 'ere all day,' she said laughing.

Danny leaned back in his chair. 'Billy was tellin' me about that new bobby on this beat. 'E's got it in fer 'im,' he said.

'Why's that, Billy?' Carrie asked.

'This copper used ter be on the Rovver'ithe beat an' 'e reckons 'e's seen me wiv that Tunnel Mob,' Billy explained. ''E tried ter tie me in wiv that ware'ouse job they done. When the line-up didn't go 'is way 'e got ter threatenin' me. 'E reckons 'e's gonna 'ave me one way or anuvver.'

'Yer know what yer should do. Yer should get yerself a job first,' Carrie told him.

'That's what yer bruvver jus' told me,' Billy groaned.

'Well, 'e's right,' the young woman said firmly. 'An' yer know what else yer should do, yer should get yerself a young lady. Once yer walkin' out steady the copper'll prob'ly leave yer alone.'

Billy laughed. 'Yer sound jus' like my ole lady. She keeps on ter me about gettin' meself a young lady friend. What about you?' he joked with her, turning to wink at Danny.

'I'm spoken for,' Carrie laughed. 'Seriously though, yer should fink about it. It's time a nice-lookin' feller like you was settlin' down wiv a wife an' family.'

'Who'd 'ave me?' Billy asked light-heartedly. 'I ain't got a job an' I ain't got much chance o' gettin one wiv this,' he said, pointing to his chest.

'I know a young lady who would very much like ter walk out wiv yer,' she said slyly.

'Oh, an' who's that then?' Billy asked, raising his eyes.

'Annie McCafferty, that's who,' Carrie told him.

'Annie? She 'ardly said a word when I met 'er in the park,' Billy replied incredulously.

'That's 'cos she's very shy,' Carrie explained. 'Annie's a real nice young woman, an' she's very struck on you. I know 'cos she told me.'

Billy's face had brightened. 'Well, next time I see Annie I'll ask 'er if she'd care ter step out wiv me,' he said boldly.

Well, it will be some time before Billy gets his chance now, Carrie thought sadly as she watched Annie disappear out of sight around the sweep of the narrow turning.

As 1921 drew to a close the weather became bitterly cold. International trade slumped; after the first week in December few freighters steamed into the docks that served London, and on the Bermondsey quaysides berths were empty and the large cranes stood idle. On the streets groups of rivermen waited for a call-on each morning and the majority walked home disappointed. Some hung around the windy streets, hoping for some casual work which never came, and some drifted into the Bradley dining rooms to warm their bellies with mugs of hot sweet tea, knowing that it would be a bleak Christmas for them and their families. Carrie and Fred put up coloured paper chains in their steam-stained cafe and on numerous occasions gave mugs of tea to their regulars who could now no longer find the pennies to pay for them. In the back room Don Jacobs and his union men sought ways of easing the hardship for their members and a special hardship fund was set up from the dwindling money reserves in their branch coffers.

On a cold December night in Bacon Street, the turning around the corner from Page Street, Elsie Wishart sat in front of the dressing-table mirror in the bedroom of flat number 32 and carefully put her greying hair into a bun. When she was satisfied that her hair was all in place she took out her imitation pearl earrings and a matching necklace and put the earrings on. She did up the buttons of her white cotton blouse to the neck and slipped the pearl necklace over the high collar. Carefully she buttoned up the frilly cuffs of her blouse and tucked the waist down into her black satin skirt. She wore no make-up, apart from a trace of powder on her cheeks and a touch of blacking on her eyelashes, which gave her a transparent, doll-like look. She stood up and adjusted the waist of her ankle-length skirt and then walked over to the bed and sat down. For a moment or two she looked at the small, gilt-framed picture on the chair beside her bed, and then with a smile she bent down and retrieved her black patent button-up boots. Lastly, after donning her loosely fitting grey hat which had large, shiny black buttons down one side, she put on her grey coat with its fox-fur collar and surveyed herself in the mirror. Satisfied that all was well, Elsie Wishart picked up her black clutch bag and tucked it under her arm as she let herself out of the flat.

The gas jets flickered on the creaking stairs of Bacon Buildings and cast their frightening shadows on the crumbling plaster walls, but Elsie paid the shifting shapes no attention. Her mind was on other things as she walked purposefully down to the quiet street below. It was cold, with an east wind blowing and flurries of snowflakes dancing in the light of the iron gas lamp. The snow had settled, and an unspoiled carpet of white covered the cobbles and the stone doorsteps of the houses opposite.

Elsie Wishart ran her hand under the fur collar of her grey coat and held her bag tightly against her side as she turned left and walked towards Cotton Lane. The river was running high and the gas lamps on the north shore were plainly visible in the crisp, clear night air, their reflections shining on the cold water. Laden barges bumped and ground together, their thick mooring ropes creaking and straining, and a short distance upriver the looming Tower Bridge stood out plainly against the darkness. Elsie turned into Cotton Lane, walked the short few paces to the steps and stood looking down at the lapping, muddy water. A muffled, urgent voice called out and was answered by a louder, nearer voice. The sound of a rope slapping the water and another shout as the rope was taken up neither disturbed nor interrupted Elsie Wishart. With a deep sigh she walked into the river and let the cold, muddy waters close over her.

Carrie Bradley had settled her young daughter for the night and then sat down by the bright coke fire. Fred was sleeping in his favourite chair facing her and his steady, even snoring was the only sound in the quiet room. Outside the cobbled lane was deserted and Carrie thought about her young brother Danny and his workmates, who would soon be finishing as the tide turned. She stared into the fire. The last month's takings were better than expected, even with the dock trade so poor, and there was reason to feel confident for the future. Other eating-houses in the area were feeling the pinch and some had ceased to operate, she had been told. The accountant had been pleased with her bookkeeping and the figures she had presented him with, and her guarded opinion that the dining rooms could expand further had been received with more enthusiasm than she could have expected. Carrie had already put her ideas to Fred but he had looked shocked.

'But the place is a ruin,' he had almost shouted at her. 'It'll take more money than we've got. No, it's out o' the question. I won't even fink about it.'

Carrie sat back in her comfortable chair watching the tiny spurts of gas flickering briefly among the red hot coke, and she thought about visiting the bank. Fred would be mad at her and he would no doubt rant and rave for a time, but then his natural soft nature and easy way would overcome his anger, and he would at least listen, she told herself. She was sure her idea made sense. The derelict property next door was available and with much work it could be incorporated as an extension of the dining rooms. There would be more space for a bigger, more efficient kitchen, and with some good, sensible planning the seating could be almost doubled.

The heat of the fire and her tiredness caused Carrie's head to droop and her fair hair fell over one eye as she slipped into a doze.

The loud knocking on the front door woke the Bradleys and Fred was first out of the chair, still trying to gather his senses. 'Bloody 'ell!' he cursed. 'It's nearly twelve o'clock.'

The knocking became louder and Carrie turned to Fred, fear in her eyes as she saw him take up the heavy iron poker from the hearth. 'Careful, Fred. They're prob'ly drunken seamen. Don't open the door,' she urged him.

Fred hurried down the stairs with Carrie following him, her hand held up to her mouth in fear. Suddenly she heard her name being called. 'Oh my Gawd! It's Danny!' she shouted.

Fred quickly slid the bolts and as he opened the door Danny fell into his arms. Carrie screamed out and rushed to help.

'Get 'er inside! Quick!' Danny gasped as he slumped down, his clothes sopping wet and his dripping hair hanging down over his forehead.

Fred pulled Danny towards the back room and as he moved away from the open front door Carrie saw the buttoned-up boots sticking up on the doorstep. She looked out and saw the still figure of Elsie Wishart prostrate in the snow, her hair lying bedraggled over her face and her arms outstretched as though for an embrace.

All morning on Christmas Eve the women of the riverside backstreets trudged through the snow to the market and came home with laden shopping baskets, weighing more heavily than normal with the Christmas extras of nuts, oranges, tangerines and dates. Nellie Tanner had started out late after Carrie's unexpected early morning call, and when she arrived back home and finished unpacking her shopping she made herself a cup of tea and sat warming her feet before the fire. Most of her friends in Page Street would have finished their shopping by now, she thought, and Florrie would be sitting with Maisie and Aggie at the Sullivan house drinking tea as they always did on a normal Saturday afternoon. When she had finished her cup Nellie slipped on her coat, made sure that the fire was raked and then let herself out of her flat.

Just as she had anticipated the women were gathered in Sadie Sullivan's cosy front room already sipping tea when Nellie arrived. All the less important gossip of the day was forgotten as she began to tell them about her daughter's unexpected visit early that morning.

'My Carrie come in all excited an' she started ter tell me about this woman who tried ter drown 'erself right opposite the cafe last night,' she said with wide eyes. 'Carrie an' Fred were dozin' in front o' the fire when they 'eard this loud knockin' on their door. Near midnight it was. Carrie didn't want Fred ter open it 'cos she reckoned it could 'ave bin one o' those merchant seamen wiv a skinful, but then she 'eard Danny's voice. When they opened the door there 'e was soaked ter the skin an' just about all in. 'E'd pulled this woman out o' the drink an' she was layin' at 'is feet. Carrie told me she thought the woman was dead at first.'

143

'She would 'ave bin if she'd 'ave bin in that water fer more than a few minutes,' Florrie remarked.

'It was a godsend that my Danny was tyin' up that barge,' Nellie told her eager audience. ''E was moorin' it right by the Cotton Lane steps an' suddenly 'e saw this well-dressed lady walk straight down inter the water. It turns out it was Elsie Wishart.'

'Who?' Sadie asked.

'Wishart, Elsie Wishart,' Nellie repeated, holding a teacup on her lap. 'She lives in Bacon Buildin's in the next block ter me. Mind yer I've never spoken ter the woman, but I've seen 'er walkin' up the street a couple o' times. Yer might 'ave seen 'er walkin' about. She's very smart an' she looks like she's got a few bob. I remember wonderin' 'ow somebody like 'er come ter live in Bacon Buildin's. Anyway, Danny told Carrie that 'e was right at the front o' the barge and saw 'er walk down the steps an' go under. Well, wivout finkin' Danny jumped over the side inter the water an' 'eld on to 'er coat. It was the barge rope what saved 'er. Danny told Carrie that if she'd 'ave gone in anywhere else she'd 'ave gone down in the mud an' that would 'ave been that. As it 'appened she got caught up by the rope an' Danny managed ter pull 'er ter the steps. By the time 'e'd dragged 'er ter my Carrie's place 'e was all in. The woman was unconscious. It must 'ave bin the shock o' goin' in that freezin' water.'

'What made 'er do it fer Gawdsake?' Maisie asked.

'I'm comin' ter that,' Nellie said quickly. 'Anyway they got their wet clothes off an' Fred 'ad some brandy in the cupboard. They warmed 'em by the fire an' all the time the woman was moanin' an' groanin'. She came round all right though. Carrie got 'er ter bed an' 'er an' Fred slept in the armchairs by the fire all night. They wrapped Danny up in blankets an' 'e slept by the fire wiv' 'em. When 'e got up this mornin' 'e was right as ninepence. 'E's a tough lad is my Danny,' Nellie said proudly.

''E's a brave lad if yer ask me,' Sadie remarked. 'Especially the way the currents are. Yer can quite easily get sucked under those barges.'

'I knew somebody who got sucked under a barge once. Used ter live in Poplar she did,' Maisie said.

'Let 'er get on wiv the story, Mais,' Florrie said quickly.

Nellie was enjoying being the centre of attention that Saturday afternoon in Sadie's parlour and she primly tapped the bun on the back of her head with her hand as she went on. 'This mornin' Carrie managed to 'ave a chat with Elsie Wishart an' it turns out that the reason she tried ter kill 'erself was over that bastard Frank Galloway.'

Four pairs of eyes stared at Nellie, and Florrie forgot the pinch of snuff that was lying on the back of her hand.

'Frank Galloway?' they echoed.

Nellie nodded her head slowly for effect. 'My Carrie was livid when she was tellin' me about 'it. Apparently this Elsie Wishart used ter live in Tyburn Square, right opposite where George Galloway lives. 'Er 'usband was a solicitor an' they've got one grown-up daughter. Well, so Carrie was tellin' me, she used ter bump into Frank Galloway a lot when 'e was back an' forwards ter the square seein' the ole man, an' they got talkin'. From what Carrie could gavver, this solicitor feller who Elsie was married to was a bit older than 'er an' a quiet sort o' bloke. Elsie liked a good time so yer can guess what 'appened. She was taken by Frank Galloway's flash ways an' started seein' 'im. They used ter go out tergevver in the evenin's ter places, shows an' the like.'

'What about Galloway's wife? Didn't she get suspicious about 'im not bein' 'ome?' Florrie asked.

Nellie shook her head. 'Accordin' ter what Elsie told my Carrie, Frank Galloway's wife is one o' those actresses on the stage. She was never 'ome 'erself, an' she's got a fancy man. Anyway, one evenin' Elsie an' Frank Galloway was up to a bit of 'anky-panky in 'er place an' Elsie's 'usband comes in unexpected an' catches 'em at it. Elsie told my Carrie that Frank Galloway promised 'er 'e was goin' ter get a divorce an' marry 'er as soon as they was both free. Elsie's ole man 'ad chucked 'er out an' she was livin' wiv' 'er sister in Black'eath fer the time bein'. What made it worse, Elsie's daughter was very close to 'er farvver an' she wouldn't 'ave nuffink more ter do wiv 'er muvver. Well, yer can guess what 'appened next.'

Nellie's friends were enthralled by the tale and they all shook their heads.

'Go on,' Florrie prompted impatiently.

'Frank Galloway found 'imself anuvver fancy piece an' poor Elsie's left 'igh an' dry,' Nellie continued. 'She tried ter patch it up wiv 'er ole man an' one night she went ter the square ter try an' talk 'im round an' found 'im 'angin' from the banisters.'

The women gasped and Maisie shook her head sadly. 'Poor bleeder. What must 'e 'ave bin goin' frew in 'is mind,' she said in a quiet voice.

'That Frank Galloway's got a lot to answer to,' Florrie uttered venomously.

''Ow come she ended up in Bacon Buildin's of all places?' Aggie asked.

'After all what 'ad 'appened, an' then the shock o' findin' 'er ole man 'angin' from the banisters, fings got too much fer 'er an' she 'ad a nervous breakdown,' Nellie told them. 'Elsie was in 'ospital fer some time an' when she come out she couldn't face goin' back ter live wiv 'er sister, so she put 'erself on the mercy o' the Council. They couldn't 'elp an' out o' desperation she did what me an' my Will 'ad ter do. She took a flat in Bacon Buildin's. She was settlin' in there but one day last week she saw 'er daughter in the market an' the gel turned 'er back on 'er as she went ter say 'ello.'

'Ain't that terrible?' Maisie said sadly.

'None of it would 'ave 'appened if Galloway 'adn't come between 'em,' Florrie said, looking at Nellie.

'What's the woman gonna do now, Nell?' Sadie asked.

'Well, she's gonna go back ter live wiv 'er sister fer the time bein',' Nellie replied. 'Carrie's got 'er daughter's address an' she's goin' round ter see 'er. P'raps this might bring 'em tergevver again, please Gawd.'

Chapter Eleven

The new year began with little if any relief for the Bermondsey folk. Rivermen still foraged for work and still hung around the streets hopeful of a call-on. The rows of little houses in Page Street still let in water through the badly maintained roofs and money was shorter than ever.

Carrie had made the trip to see Elsie Wishart's daughter, but when she arrived at the house in Catford she was told by the new tenants that the young woman had left and there was no forwarding address. Carrie had had the sad task of informing Elsie by letter and received a prompt reply from the woman thanking her for all she had done. The letter went on to say that Elsie was settling down once more with her sister, but within a few weeks she had returned to Bacon Buildings after a disagreement.

Throughout the hard year the Bradleys' dining rooms continued to hold on to their customers and Carrie was still hopeful of persuading her husband to extend the business. The bank had been helpful after the manager had pored over the books and Carrie had explained her plan, but Fred was adamant that it was too soon to think of expansion.

Rachel was growing up fast and was now approaching her third birthday. The child had soon got over the departure of Annie McCafferty and the Bradleys decided to get another nurse to look after her while Annie was away.

Carrie did not feel at all sure that Annie would ever return, however. She had received a letter soon after the young nurse arrived in Dublin telling of her joy and sadness on finally meeting up with her mother who had abandoned her as a baby. Annie told Carrie all about the poor woman in the letter. Connie McCafferty was very ill with an obscure blood disorder and the doctors were not very optimistic about her chances of surviving for very long. Annie related that Mrs McCafferty had married in Dublin and her husband was now deceased. The young woman had decided to care for her mother in the family home, and despite all medical predictions to the contrary Connie seemed to be rallying.

Carrie was pleased for Annie but saddened that it was now unlikely the young woman would ever return. Day to day affairs prevented her from dwelling on the past, however, and she pressed on with her plans to make the business more profitable. The interior of the dining rooms had been renovated and now looked fresh and welcoming. The caterering suppliers found her to be a difficult client and Johnson's lost much of their trade with the Bradleys to other more accommodating catering concerns. Carrie had become quite adept at managing the bulk buying and was always looking for ways to keep the costs at a minimum. Sometimes Fred worried unduly as he worked in the hot, steamy kitchen, and often he was driven to distraction by the constant chatter of Bessie Chandler, but he did his best to remain cheerful. He was eager to enlarge their family and it caused a few problems between him and Carrie, who was not yet ready to have another baby. There were other, more pressing things on her mind and she often spurned her husband's advances, fearful of becoming pregnant.

During the summer months Fred and Carrie would walk out to the park or go to the music halls, and occasionally they would visit the local cinema in Grange Road and laugh at the antics of Charlie Chaplin or Buster Keaton. They would often stop on the way home for a drink or two at one of the nicer public houses but Carrie was always wary of her husband having too much to drink. It was after Fred had been drinking that he became careless during his lovemaking and Carrie was filled with dread until her next period. Her feelings for him, however, and her own needs were such that she could not always resist him, and she was painfully aware that becoming pregnant again was only a matter of time.

During the autumn Billy Sullivan finally found a job. He had been desperate to raise some money towards his dream of opening a gymnasium but all his ideas and aspirations had not borne fruit.

'Yer gotta go out an' earn money,' Sadie told him. 'Yer not gonna 'ave any sort o' life givin' me all yer pension ter 'elp feed yer. Jus' look at yerself. Yer only suit is in rags an' those trousers yer got on are so full o' grease if yer slipped over yer'd slide all the way up the street.'

Billy had borne in mind that Carrie Bradley told him about finding himself a nice young lady and he had been upset to learn that Annie McCafferty was no longer in Bermondsey. He despaired of ever finding himself a girl while he was looking like a down-and-out, and one day when he was walking past Peek Freans, the biscuit factory, on one of his strolls he was rudely awakened to his condition by the giggles and taunts of the factory girls. There and then he decided to get a job, and the next morning he joined the long files of men at the Labour Exchange. There was nothing on offer, however, but he refused to get despondent, and the next morning he got up early and spent the last of his coppers on a copy of the *South London Press*.

Billy was feeling optimistic as he shuffled along with his hands deep in his coat pockets. It was a big advertisement and lots of men would have seen it, he realised, but he remembered what his mother had told him when he pointed it out to her. 'Most people won't go after that sort o' job. It's the smell what puts 'em off,' she told him.

Billy could not understand why the smell of soap should put people off and he whistled to himself as he hurried along Bermondsey Street, his mind racing. First he would get himself a new pair of trousers, he decided. Later he could buy a new suit from the tally man when he was getting a regular wage. He might even be able to afford a nice pair of boots to walk out in on Sundays and holidays, and then the local girls would have to watch out. The word would get round that Billy Sullivan was on the loose and looking spruce and they would be falling over themselves to walk out with him.

The smell became noticeable as Billy turned into a narrow alley off Bermondsey Street, and by the time he reached the end of the alley he was almost retching. The smell was like nothing he had ever encountered and his spirits sagged.

'Yes, we have vacancies,' the friendly looking manager told him. 'Now let me see, you haven't been in trouble with the police, have you?' he asked, one eyebrow going up.

Billy shook his head vigorously. 'I go ter church every Sunday,' he said, hoping that would suffice as an answer.

'Very commendable,' the man said. 'Now, just a few questions. Where was your last job?'

'The army,' Billy replied.

'You served in the war?'

'Yes.'

'The war's been over a few years now. What work did you do when you were demobilised?' the man asked.

'I couldn't work, yer see,' Billy told him.

'Oh, and why was that?'

'It was me muvver. She was poorly an' I 'ad ter stay 'ome an' look after 'er,' Billy lied, his fingers crossed behind his back.

'I see. Is your mother better now?' the manager asked him.

'They took 'er away,' Billy said, hoping he was not about to be struck down for his wickedness.

'Oh dear. Where did they take her?'

'Colney 'Atch. She was right off 'er 'ead,' Billy went on. 'Mind yer, she's a lot better now. We're gonna 'ave 'er 'ome soon as me an' me sisters can raise the money ter get a better 'ouse in the country.'

'How many sisters have you got, Mr Sullivan?' the inquisitive manager asked.

'Twelve.'

'Twelve? Well, couldn't one of those sisters have looked after your mother so you could go out to work?'

Billy shook his head, feeling his lips beginning to twitch. 'My muvver wouldn't let any of 'em near 'er. She said I was the only one she wanted round. Mind yer, she was a bit nutty at the time.'

The manager felt a wave of pity for the young man fate had dealt so harshly with. 'Well, you can start tomorrow,' he said smiling. 'We'll supply the aprons and clogs. The hours are from seven till five, with a half-hour break for dinner. I'm sure you'll settle in here nicely. Don't be too concerned about the smell, you'll soon get used to it.'

Billy left the Faraday Soapmakers with mixed

emotions. He was already feeling sick from the putrid smell which was coming from the floor below the office, and he was angry at the man's prying into his personal business. He was also puzzled by what sort of soap they were making there.

Sadie Sullivan was not sure whether to kiss him or kick him when he told her he had got the job. In some respects Billy was very sensible, she reflected, but in others he was so stupid.

'They supply the aprons an' clogs,' he told her as he tucked into a thick slice of bread and jam. 'I s'pose it's a wet job.'

'Greasy more like it,' Sadie replied.

Billy looked puzzled. 'I dunno what was goin' on in that factory but there was this putrid smell. I felt really sick.'

Sadie felt she had to tell Billy what he would be facing, even though he might change his mind about the job. 'Yer'll 'ave ter boil bones, animal bones,' she explained with a sigh. 'That's what they make soap from. Surely yer knew that?'

Billy's face dropped. 'I might 'ave known,' he said bitterly. 'I don't s'pose many people go after those sort o' jobs. Still, never mind. I'll stick it out till I can find somefing better.'

Sadie felt a surge of affection for her son welling up inside her. 'I tell yer what,' she said. 'Yer farvver's left me a shillin' fer the tally man so I s'pose 'e'll be in a good mood. I'll ask 'im if 'e'll let me 'ave a nice pair o' trousers for yer. Now eat yer tea.'

Billy could not stop imagining rotting bones being crushed down in a huge pot and he pushed the plate away from him. 'I'm not very 'ungry, Muvver,' he said.

1922 seemed to pass very quickly for William Tanner. He had settled down at Joe Maitland's new warehouse in Druid Street, and he was feeling less vulnerable now that Sidney Coil was working alongside him. Sidney, or 'The Cruncher' as he was known by the wrestling fraternity, was a young man who had a superbly developed body and a sadly under-developed brain, and he had to be supervised in everything from the time he sauntered in until the time he left. The young wrestler was a very friendly character, however, and a tireless, willing worker. William became attached to the young man and was pleased to have him at his elbow whenever callers came. The attack on him had left William feeling nervous for a while but he had recovered well, and it was now only a bad memory. He felt that whoever had caused his injuries and wrought destruction on the warehouse in Dockhead was now satisfied and that would be the end of it.

The Cruncher was not so convinced though. He had been told by Joe Maitland that somebody was out to cause them trouble and grief and his job was to watch out for the slightest sign. The young wrestler was keen to show his merit, and his intimidating looks and demeanour tended to frighten the carmen and other callers at the warehouse. Sidney's devotion to duty terrified the ratcatcher who Joe Maitland had called in after William told him that rodents had been nibbling at some of the cartons.

Sidney answered the knock on the warehouse door. 'What d'yer want?' he growled.

'I've come ter set a trap,' the ratcatcher said amiably.

Suddenly he found himself pulled through the door and lifted bodily by his coat lapels until he was eye to eye with the powerful young wrestler. His eyes were popping and his breath was restricted by Sidney's grip on him.

'Put me down, yer bloody imbecile,' he gulped.

'Who sent yer?' Sidney snarled.

'I've come ter fix the rats,' the terrified man gasped.

'I'll fix you, yer whoreson,' The Cruncher said in his most menacing voice.

William's prompt intervention saved the ratcatcher from further pain and suffering. 'It's all right, Sid, Joe sent fer 'im,' he shouted in the wrestler's ear.

It was only after the terrified ratcatcher was given a large glass of Scotch whisky from Joe Maitland's private stock and a firm promise that Sidney would be kept out of his way, that the man could be coaxed into laying his traps. Even then he mumbled to himself throughout the whole operation, vowing that it was the last time he would lay traps in that establishment while the wild one worked there.

1923 dawned on a tragic note. Early one Monday morning in January Aggie Temple got up and went about her chores, whitening her doorstep as usual and then dusting through the house. She went to market for bread and potatoes and then stopped at the cat's-meat stall. When she got home she fed the cat, moaned at Harold for getting under her feet and then made herself a cup of tea when he went up to the paper shop. Harold stopped to chat with the newsagent for a while and when he returned he found Aggie dead in her chair, the full cup of tea beside her.

As always the women of Page Street rallied around, and Florrie volunteered to wash and lay out her old friend, while Maisie and Sadie went door-knocking with a collection box.

Early on the morning of the funeral flowers started to arrive. Just before the hearse drove in to the street Broomhead Smith arrived on his cart and laid a wreath at Aggie's front door before driving slowly out of the turning. Aggie was given a nice funeral and everyone in the little turning stood at their front doors to pay their last respects. Harold was a sad figure as he bore up bravely, but he was reduced to tears when he saw Florrie's tribute to her old friend – a wreath in the shape of a broom.

Carrie Tanner had decided that this year she was going to try her hardest to coax Fred into buying the derelict property next door. They had managed to put some money by and she felt that now was the time to expand. Fred still would not be swayed and the atmosphere between them became tense. The uncomfortable situation was not helped by Rachel's nurse putting in her notice. Things had not been altogether easy-going between Carrie and the elderly nurse, who did not seem to have the same rapport with the child as Annie McCafferty. Carrie was not sorry to lose the woman but it meant that she would have to combine her work in the dining rooms with caring for Rachel, now a lively three year old.

Fred decided that Bessie could help out more behind the counter and Carrie should spend more time with the child instead of employing another nurse. 'It'll only be for a year or so. Rachel's gonna be startin' school then,' he told her.

Carrie could understand the thinking behind Fred's decision and she was angry. 'I s'pose yer fink I'll ferget about the plans fer the cafe now,' she grated. 'Well, I won't. Yer just frightened ter take a chance, Fred. If we got that place next door an' spent a few bob renovatin' it we could double our takin's, why can't yer see it?'

'It'll take all the money we've saved,' he barked at her. 'I'm not prepared ter lose it all on a wild idea, so ferget it.'

Carrie could see that there was no way she would get him to change his mind for the present and she reluctantly decided to hold her fire.

The winter months were hard for the Bradleys. Trade along the wharves had diminished and their takings fell. Fred was quick to point out the folly of expanding at such a time but Carrie stuck to her argument.

'It's the same everywhere. We're not the only business that's feelin' the pinch, an' at least we're 'oldin' our own,' she told him. 'If we put in a bid I reckon we could get that place fer next to nuffink, the way fings are. We don't 'ave ter rush in an' do it up all at once. We could do it bit by bit.'

Fred merely shook his head and got on with his cooking to the chagrin of his ambitious young wife, who was determined to succeed with her plans for expansion before the year was out.

During the summer months trouble was brewing along the waterfront as the dock owners tried to cut their overheads by reducing the workforce, and long-standing agreements between them and the union on manning levels were scrapped. Constant bickering between the two sides and frequent stoppages aggravated the situation, and when winter set in and the seasonal trade brought more work the arguments over workforce numbers increased. Don Jacobs held many meetings in the little back room of the Bradleys' cafe during the periods of strife, seeking co-operation from the local cartage firms through their union representatives. Many local firms enjoyed good rapport with the dockers' union but there were some which seemed constantly to hamper the negotiations, and one of these was Galloway Transport Contractors.

In early December 1923 Don Jacobs held an important meeting with all the union shop stewards from his own branch and those of the local transport branch. Carrie and Fred stayed open late that night and the dining rooms were packed with angry union men, who listened intently while Don Jacobs was on his feet.

'Cutting the mannin' levels is like askin' starvin' men ter eat less bread,' he began with passion. 'It's criminal, an' it's downright dangerous as well. We all know very well there's a turn-round time fer those ships, an' unless we can stick ter those times we're not gonna earn a wage. Now I wanna impress on all our bruvvers from the transport branch that when six men 'ave gotta do the work of eight then safety procedures go up the bloody chimney. Yer've only gotta look at the accidents over the past year ter see that. We've 'ad two fatalities an' more than a dozen bad injuries along our stretch o' the water, an' I tell yer, bruvvers, it's not acceptable!'

A roar of approval greeted Don Jacobs' angry words and he held up his hands for silence. 'Now on Monday we're tellin' the employers we've 'ad enough, an' we all know what their next move's gonna be. They're gonna put the screws on us. They'll provoke a stoppage, an' yer all know what that means.'

'Scabs an' blacklegs!' the cry went up.

'That's right. They're gonna take on scab labour,' the union leader concurred. 'But no matter who they take on, they can't put the cart before the 'orse. If the cargoes don't get shifted they can't operate. That's where our transport bruvvers can 'elp us. What we're askin' yer ter do is not ter cross picket lines, it's as simple as that. If we've got a dispute you'll know it, 'cos our pickets are gonna be at the gates. Turn yer carts an' vans round, that's what we're askin', bruvvers.'

'What about us?' one man asked, his voice rising above the din. 'What 'appens when we get the sack fer refusin' ter cross picket lines?'

'I'll tell yer what'll 'appen, bruvver,' Jacobs replied. 'Any employer who sacks a carman fer not crossin' picket lines won't get the time o' day from us dockers. When the stoppage is over an' that cartage firm sends a van down ter the wharves we'll refuse ter touch it. That firm's gonna be blacklisted fer evermore. Any firm that tries it on wiv us is gonna be put out o' business as far as dock deliveries an' collections are concerned.'

The tall figure of Sharkey Morris pushed his way to the front of the gathering. 'Tell that ter George Galloway,' he called out. 'Me an' Soapy Symonds worked fer that no-good whoreson once an' we wouldn't cross picket lines at the London Dock. We ended up gettin' put off. Galloway don't take any notice o' threats, does 'e, Soapy?'

A smaller figure pushed his way to the front beside his friend. 'Galloway got union tickets fer 'is carmen after 'e got rid of us. 'Ow d'yer account fer that then?' he yelled angrily.

One of the transport union officials stepped up alongside Don Jacobs. 'We know what's bin 'appenin' in the past but it's all bin sorted out,' he shouted above the noise. 'What we're tellin' you is from now on no firm's gonna put a few bob in anybody's pocket ter get tickets if they're blacklisted. Yer can rely on it.'

As the men cheered and pushed forward one man slipped quietly out of the dining rooms. No one noticed him leave except Carrie, who was busy laying out mugs on the counter.

When the meeting had adjourned and a few union officials were sitting together with Don Jacobs in the back room, Carrie mentioned what she had seen. 'I bet Galloway knows all about this meetin' already, Don,' she remarked as she put down a tray of tea on the table in front of them.

The union man looked at her with surprise showing on his face. 'What makes yer say that, luv?' he asked.

'When yer meetin' was goin' on I saw one bloke slip out the door,' she told him.

The union group looked at each other. 'Yer can't stop it, I s'pose,' a shop steward said with resignation, shaking his head. 'There's always one in every meetin'.'

'Did yer recognise the man, Carrie?' Don asked her.

She shook her head. ''E's not one o' my customers, as far as I know,' she replied.

As they were leaving one of the men took Don Jacobs to one side. 'I'd watch yer step, pal,' he warned. 'There's a nasty element that's out ter cripple us. One or two o' my men 'ave bin threatened an' ole Bill Gordon got badly duffed up one night as 'e was goin' 'ome from a meetin'. We can't pin it down but it looks like these troublemakers 'ave bin brought in from somewhere, an' yer can bet yer life those monkey firms are be'ind it.'

Don Jacobs shrugged his shoulders dismissively. 'It comes wiv the job,' he said. 'If I'd taken all the threats made against me seriously I wouldn't be doin' what I'm doin' now, Pete, that's fer sure.'

Don Jacobs bade his friend good night and walked off along the foggy lane, feeling unduly troubled by what he had said. Normally he would have taken no notice of the warning, but tonight he felt apprehensive about what might happen.

Chapter Twelve

Billy Sullivan had managed to survive at the soapmakers. Every morning he donned his clogs, rubber apron and rubber gloves and wrapped a meatcloth around his neck, before feeding the rotting, maggoty bones into a boiler. He gritted his teeth and fought back his feelings of nausea, vowing to stick at the job until he was promoted to the other, less nasty tasks of skimming the fats, mixing and filtering. Unfortunately for him he was a good worker and he kept the boilers going at full stretch, much to the delight of the factory foreman who conveniently overlooked him for promotion. During the warm summer when the temperature in the factory rose to an almost unbearable degree and the stench became virtually overpowering Billy stuck at his job, and as the winter set in he felt that he had well and truly served his time and had earned a promotion. One Monday morning in December he had a word with the foreman and told him it was about time he was considered for a better job in the factory.

'It's over a year now since I started an' I ain't complained,' Billy told him. 'I fink it's about time yer put me on somefing else.'

'Well, I ain't got nuffink else for yer, so yer'll 'ave ter get on wiv what yer bin doin',' the foreman said abruptly.

'Now look, mate,' Billy persisted. 'I don't fink I'm

bein' unreasonable but I reckon it's time yer give me a change.'

'Don't yer "mate" me. I ain't your mate. It's Mr Thomas ter you,' the foreman shouted at him. 'Now get ter work, Sullivan, or yer'll be in trouble.'

Billy had felt for a long while that trouble was destined to become his middle name. He slowly and deliberately took off his clogs, his rubber gloves and his apron, unwrapped the meatcloth from around his neck and then grabbed the startled foreman by his lapels and pulled him towards him.

'Now listen 'ere, yer toffee-nosed little git,' he snarled. 'If it wasn't fer yer wife an' kids I'd put yer in the boiler wiv all them maggoty bones an' turn yer inter soap. Now piss orf an' sort me out somefing else, I've 'ad enough o' this job.'

The foreman struggled free and stepped back a pace. 'Yer can't talk ter me like that!' he croaked with disbelief. 'I'll see the guv'nor about yer, see if I don't.'

'Well, yer'd better 'ave somefink werfwhile ter tell 'im then,' Billy said in a menacing tone.

'Keep away from me!' the foreman cried, backing away as the young ex-boxer made towards him.

Billy shot his hand out, grabbed the man by the scruff of his neck and swung him round. He slipped his other hand between the foreman's legs and hoisted him up, and before he could do anything about it the man found himself being carried horizontally towards a large storage container. With a deep growl, Billy lifted him higher and then dropped him into a stinking, rotting mass of animal bones.

All work had stopped on the factory floor by now, and Billy turned and lifted his clenched fists above his head in a sign of triumph, then, smiling broadly, walked away.

*

It was the week before Christmas when Carrie found that she was pregnant again. Her first reaction was one of anger. She had been trying to get Fred to relent and give his blessing to her plans for the dining rooms, and to that end had tried to heal the rift that seemed to be widening between them. Fred had promised to be careful but now what she had been dreading had happened, and she felt he had intended it that way to make her drop her ideas once and for all. He wouldn't succeed, she told herself. One day she was going to see her dream come true.

On Christmas morning when Rachel opened her presents and Carrie saw the look of delight on her pretty face she felt guilty at her own selfishness. Rachel should have a sister or brother to play with instead of growing up to be an only child, she thought, and the anger she had harboured towards her husband left her.

Fred was overjoyed when Carrie told him he was to be a father again, and to her delight he promised that as soon as the child was born he would reconsider her plans for the business.

'We're gonna be a bigger family an' we'll 'ave ter fink about schoolin' and such. Maybe fings'll be better by then,' he told her.

Carrie realised that for a long time she had been ignoring her motherly instincts in her desire for a more profitable business, and now, instead of bank loans and monthly figures, began to dream of whether the baby would be a boy or girl and what he or she would look like. She trusted Fred's promise to her and she found herself growing warmer to him during the Christmas period.

During the week before Christmas a very unseasonal meeting took place at the Galloway yard office in Page Street.

George Galloway sat at a roll-top desk leaning his elbow on the blotting pad, a glass of whisky held in his huge hand. He was heavily built, with a full moustache and thick, grey-streaked hair swept back from his lined and furrowed forehead, and beneath his bushy eyebrows his eyes were dark and brooding. He had on a grey pinstriped double-breasted suit which was unbuttoned, revealing a silver watch chain with a gold medallion hanging from the centre. His black, half-suede boots were highly polished and he had a prosperous look about him.

The younger Galloway was a handsome man of dark complexion and well built. He sat opposite the desk and looked at his father while he spoke at length, ignoring the other person at the meeting.

'Albert Whalley told me last night they're getting themselves organised,' he was saying. 'The meeting went on for over two hours and all the main union people were there, Don Jacobs is the ringleader. He primed them all up with the need to join forces and all that nonsense, and he declared that they'd black the firms which wouldn't play the union game. I tell you, Father, it's nothing to laugh about. You won't be able to bribe these new officials. According to Whalley they were all at the meeting and all for an outright strike. It won't be merely a question of talking to the right man and putting some money his way. From what I can make out they're a bolshie crowd.'

'What about Don Jacobs?' the elder Galloway asked, his fingers toying with the gold medallion. 'What's 'is pedigree?'

Frank Galloway shrugged his shoulders. 'Whalley told me he's a dedicated union man. He's well respected by the rank and file and there's no way you'll be able to get to him with money.'

George Galloway took his arm from the desktop and

sat up straight in his swivel chair, swinging around to face the immaculately dressed figure who sat with his chair tilted back against the far wall. 'What would you suggest then, Gerry?' he asked him.

The man brought his chair away from the wall and uncrossed his arms, dusting an imagined piece of fluff from his coat cuff. 'Well, it seems to me that we're talking personalities here,' he said in a cultured voice. 'When ignorant people like these get behind someone with a little bit of charisma they tend to treat him as though he's some sort of god. Strike at that person and the ranks have got a martyr. Hit out at the small fry around him, though, and it's a different story. It's like pulling the ladder from under him. If there's a loyal following the whole thing becomes futile. What I'm saying is, concentrate on the ordinary man in the street. Get Jacobs' workers worried for their own skins and you're more than halfway there.'

'What d'yer mean, Gerry? We can't take on all the dockers, more than two-thirds o' the people round 'ere work in the docks,' George Galloway said in a gruff voice.

The smartly dressed man studied his hands for a few moments before replying. 'I wasn't thinking of attacking the masses,' he said quietly. 'Where did they hold the meeting last night?'

The elder Galloway shook his head vigorously. 'No, Gerry, that's out o' the question. The meetin' was 'eld at Bradleys' cafe in Cotton Lane an' the bloke that owns it is married ter Will Tanner's daughter. Will Tanner an' me grew up tergevver round 'ere an' 'e worked fer me fer a number o' years. We 'ad our disagreements durin' all that time an' I 'ad ter get rid of 'im, but I don't want 'is family touched.'

The well-dressed man smiled briefly, showing his large yellowing teeth. 'I wasn't thinking of persons, more of property, George,' he replied.

George Galloway shook his head again. 'It's too risky,' he said quickly. 'Somebody could get 'urt.'

Frank Galloway looked from one man to the other and thought about the time Gerry Macedo had intervened on his behalf. Maitland's warehouse had been destroyed and Will Tanner left to perish. Macedo was not one to do things by half. The younger Galloway's only concern was that his own dealings with the man should be kept from his father. The old man had read in the newspaper of the fire at Joe Maitland's Dockhead warehouse, and how William Tanner has been rescued from the blaze in the nick of time. He had said then that Maitland must have crossed someone or other and it was an act of retribution. If he ever found out the true reason behind the arson and the malicious attack on Will Tanner he would be more than a trifle upset to say the least, Frank thought.

Gerry Macedo stood up and reached for his homburg which he twirled around in his hands, studying it for signs of dust. 'Let me know what decision you come to, George,' he said. 'You know where to contact me.'

George stood up and shook hands with Macedo, who then stretched out his hand to the younger Galloway. 'I'll be seeing you soon, Frank,' he said. 'Perhaps you can come over for a few drinks? It's quite a nice place. We tend to dissuade the riff-raff. Bring the wife along, I'm sure she'll enjoy the cabaret.'

Once Gerry Macedo had left the office George Galloway turned to his son. 'I don't want Carrie Tanner or 'er old man touched, d'yer 'ear, Frank?' he said firmly. 'I fink we should stick ter what we agreed. Yer persuaded me ter bring Macedo over this side o' the water ter deal wiv the problem an' that means sortin' out the union, not runnin' riot. I wanna stay in business an' it's werf the money I'm gonna pay 'im, but on my terms. When those union pals o' mine went out of office an' that new lot came in I knew the same as you did that fings were gonna change. I wanted ter put pressure on Ted Marriot an' 'is crowd ter ease off on us. They wouldn't listen as well yer know. What was I s'posed ter do, lay down an' die? No, Frank, I ain't ready ter lose all that I've strived for all these years. I ain't gonna be told where I can trade an' where I can't.'

Frank Galloway leaned back in his chair and sighed deeply. 'Albert Whalley was saying that union leader, Don Jacobs, was priming them all up and he always has his meetings at the Bradleys' cafe. What Gerry was suggesting seems to make good sense. Pull the rug from under him.'

George Galloway snorted. 'Albert Whalley wasn't tellin' me anyfing I didn't know. I've already 'ad a warnin' from those new union scum. It's eivver we allow 'em in wiv a full shop steward ter represent our carmen or I'll never be allowed anywhere near the river again. I ain't bein' dictated to by the likes o' them,' he concluded, his voice rising to a crescendo.

Frank held out his hands in an effort to pacify his ageing father. 'I know the score, Dad. You don't have to remind me,' he said quietly. 'All right, we've got Macedo in to sort the union out, but it's not enough to hit them alone. You've got to put the fear of God into the rank and file. And I'll tell you something else too. If you go about this the wrong way the whole union movement is going to move closer together. It'll be sewn up so tight that even Macedo won't be able to put a foot out of place. Let Gerry sort out the Bradleys. We can tell him that if either of them gets hurt then the deal's off. Gerry's no fool, he knows what side his bread's buttered. He'll be able to go along with that, I'm sure.'

George Galloway slumped back in his chair and

fingered his gold medallion. 'It's risky,' he grumbled, a ponderous look in his eyes. 'But I s'pose there's nuffink else for it,' he stared at his hands. 'All right, let's work out what we want Macedo ter do.'

Carrie had bathed Rachel and put her to bed, the books had been completed and the room tidied up, and the young woman stretched out her feet in front of the hearth. The paper chains were still hung across the room and they moved in the heat of the coke fire, while the cold wind outside rattled the window frames. Fred was sitting opposite Carrie rolling a cigarette with a thoughtful expression on his broad face, and he looked over at her as she sighed sadly.

'What is it?' he asked.

'I was jus' finkin',' she replied in a quiet voice. 'We spend weeks before Christmas plannin', scrapin' an' schemin', then there's shoppin' an' buyin' presents, an' then suddenly it's all over. All that fer a couple o' days. Still I s'pose it's werf it. Christmas seems ter bring people closer, don't yer fink so, Fred?'

He smiled at her, a warm look in his dark eyes. 'Yeah, I do. We've got somefink ter look forward to as well,' he said, looking down at his cigarette and licking the gummed edge of the paper.

Suddenly a frown crossed Carrie's face. 'What was that, Fred?' she asked.

Without saying anything he got up and made for the landing. Carrie could hear the scraping sound clearly now and then suddenly the chilling crack of splitting wood. As Fred reached the bottom of the stairs the door was smashed open and he shouted at Carrie to stay back. Two heavily built men lurched into the passageway and grabbed him by the arms. Fred was a powerful man but he was unable to do anything as they dragged him into the kitchen and bundled him into a chair.

Carrie had ignored Fred's warning and as she rushed down the stairs after him a third man came into the passageway and clutched her, pinning both her arms to her sides. She screamed but a hand came over her mouth and she was carried roughly into the kitchen. She felt sick with fear lest something should happen to Rachel upstairs. Fred was being tied to the chair and he looked helplessly at her as she struggled gamely against the huge man holding her. She was soon trussed beside her husband, and they both had scarves tied around their mouths.

One of the men picked up a rolling pin from the pastry table and began to smash everything in sight. Another took down all the pots and pans and stamped on them with his heavy boots. The third man walked out into the serving area and Carrie winced as she heard the breaking of china. In no time at all the three intruders were reducing the cafe to a ruin. Seats were ripped from their mountings and the marble-topped bench tables were cracked with heavy blows. One of the men took out a large tin of red paint from a sack and proceeded to splash it over the freshly decorated walls. Carrie felt angry tears fill her eyes and she struggled vainly to get free. Fred seemed to be sitting slumped and his eyes were closed tightly, as if he was trying to wish away the act of wanton destruction taking place around him.

Although it seemed an eternity to Carrie it was over very quickly, and with a final gesture one of the men picked up the meat cleaver and brought it down hard on the chopping block, leaving it embedded there.

After the noise it seemed deathly quiet as Carrie struggled against her bonds. Soon she could feel a slackness and she worked on it until she was able to slip one hand free. Fred was still sitting still and not making any effort at all to free himself. Carrie looked at him and called his name but he did not respond. After a while she was able to untie her other hand and within minutes she had freed Fred and they were standing together amongst the shattered crockery and utensils. Carrie was crying tears of anger but Fred merely stared down at the mess, his face ashen.

'Why, Carrie, why?' he finally muttered.

'I know why,' she replied, her teeth gritted and her fists clenched at her sides. 'We've bin singled out, Fred, can't yer see? We've bin warned off.'

Fred looked at her with devastation in his large sad eyes. 'The meetin's. I knew nuffink good was gonna come out o' lettin' the union 'ave their meetin's 'ere. I told yer, didn't I?' he groaned.

Carrie kicked out at a flattened pot in her temper. 'It's not the dock people,' she said firmly. 'There's bin trouble from the very beginnin' between the dockers an' the bosses, but this is the first time anybody's meted out this sort o' punishment. No, Fred, there's somebody else be'ind this, an' I got a good idea who it could be.'

Fred shook his head. 'Galloway wouldn't go this far,' he said incredulously. ''E's a businessman too, yer know. I can't believe 'e'd get involved wiv this.'

Carrie gave him a hard look and bent down to pick up a shattered frying-pan. Suddenly she stiffened as a searing pain shot across the bottom of her stomach. Fred had seen her expression change suddenly and he was at her side.

''Elp me up the stairs, luv,' she said in a hoarse voice. 'I fink I've started bleedin'.'

Paper chains and balloons were still hanging in the

Bargee as Don Jacobs walked in and strolled over to the counter.

"Ello, me ole troublemaker, what'll it be?' Tom Berry the landlord asked him.

Don grinned as he slapped a florin down on the counter. 'I'd like a watertight agreement preferably,' he said jovially, 'but I'll settle for a pint o' bitter instead.'

Tom Berry smiled as he pulled on the beer pump. The two men had been friends for a number of years and it was here that Don Jacobs went to forget union matters for a brief spell. He was not allowed to forget for very long, however, as the landlord had once been a riverman and he liked to engage Don in a discussion about union matters. Tonight was no exception and as he placed the frothing pint of beer down on the counter he pushed the two-shilling piece back towards the union leader.

"Ave this one on me, pal. I 'eard yer done a good job at yer last meetin',' he grinned. 'I was talkin' ter some o' the lads an' they seem ter fink there's progress bein' made between yerselves an' the transport workers. It's about time, I'd say. On yer own yer got a struggle on yer 'ands but tergevver yer've got the bosses by the short an' curlies.'

Don Jacobs smiled as he picked up his pint. 'D'yer know, Tom, there's times when I wanna chuck it all in, times when I fink I'm bangin' me 'ead against a poxy brick wall, but that last meetin' gave me a lot o' satisfaction. The men could see the sense in what we were on about an' the vote went our way fer a change.'

The landlord nodded. 'It looks like we're gonna see some changes on the waterfront, me ole cock,' he joked, raising his hand to acknowledge one of his elderly customers. 'I'll be back in a minute, Don,' he said.

Don Jacobs sipped his pint at the counter and looked

casually around him. There were faces he knew well and one or two dockers waved to him. None of the men ever went over to stand with their union leader when he was drinking alone at the bar, however. It was a habit he had cultivated from the early days when groups of men continued their arguments in the pubs and tempers often became frayed when they were under the influence of drink. Don preferred his own company and his wish was respected. He could feel the cold air rush in as the door directly behind him opened and closed from time to time, but he chose that spot sooner than go to where the fire was burning brightly. He felt it was less likely that he would get involved in arguments and altercations there at the counter.

When Tom Berry returned Don could see there was something wrong. The landlord had a serious look on his normally jovial face and he narrowed his eyes.

'Don, I don't wanna put the wind up yer but there's somefing goin' on 'ere,' he whispered.

The union leader saw the fear in Tom's eyes and immediately felt his stomach tighten. 'What is it, Tom?' he asked quietly.

The landlord leaned down on the counter. 'Jus' before yer came in there was a stranger in 'ere an' 'e asked if yer'd bin in. I didn't take no notice of 'im at the time. There's always somebody askin' fer yer. Funny fing was, I don't know why I didn't twig it, but 'e didn't look like the run o' the mill bloke who'd be lookin' fer yer. I'd say 'e come from over the water. I can tell by the accent.'

'Why should that worry yer, Tom? It could 'ave bin one o' the tally clerks,' Don said casually.

Tom Berry shook his head. 'Before 'e went out 'e got talkin' to a bloke who was sittin' by the door be'ind yer,' he said in a low voice. 'Well, jus' now I saw the geezer who was askin' after yer poke 'is 'ead in the door an' look over at yer. Then the one sittin' by the door 'opped it a bit quick. I don't like it, Don. Yer might be gettin' set up fer a pastin'. It wouldn't be the first time a union steward got duffed up round 'ere, yer know.'

Don shrugged off the landlord's concern. 'There's nuffink ter worry about, mate,' he said easily. 'I'm gonna 'ave one more pint then I'm off ter bed. 'Ave one wiv me,' he suggested.

Tom was called away to serve, and he was in conversation with a few dockers at the far side of the counter when Don finished his pint and waved across to his old friend.

The union man pulled the collar of his coat up around his ears as he walked away from the pub along the cobbled lane, his footsteps echoing and his breath visible in the cold night air. He had gone only a short distance when suddenly two men stepped out from a wharf doorway and blocked his path. They were carrying what looked like lengths of rubber hose and Don Jacobs instinctively clenched his fists. There was another shadowy figure who remained lurking in the doorway as the two men slowly approached him. Don's first thought was to turn and run but something told him to stand his ground. He heard footsteps behind him now and his heart sank. There was no escape.

'C'mon then,' he said in a voice he hardly recognised, his fists held up in front of him.

Suddenly the men closed in and one swung at him with the sand-filled hosepipe. Don ducked and felt the wind of the swipe above his head, straightened up and threw a punch at his assailant. It caught the man full in the face and he staggered back. Don winced as he suffered a heavy blow to his kidney and stumbled to his knees, gasping for breath. The men gathered around him now and the union leader closed his eyes as he waited for the beating.

Suddenly there was a loud roar and running footsteps on the cobblestones. The blows he had prepared himself for never landed. Instead all about him there was a tumble of writhing, twisting bodies, grunts and shouts as the dockers set about his assailants. One of the men fell beneath a flurry of blows and then heavy, steel-tipped boots kicked into his ribs. Another was pinned to the ground with one large docker punching him repeatedly in the face. Don climbed to his feet just in time to see the third assailant aiming a blow at the docker with his back to him. With a shout he jumped at the man and pulled him to the ground. Other men were arriving and soon the cobbled riverside lane was filled with shouting, struggling bodies.

It was soon over and three bloodied and bowed men were sitting on the kerbside with a large group of angry dockers standing over them.

'What we gonna do wiv this lot, Don?' one docker called out.

'String the bastards up!' another shouted, poking one of the sorry-looking assailants with the toe of his boot.

'I know, let's 'ang 'em from the crane,' another suggested.

'Chuck 'em in the river.'

'Why don't we tie 'em up an' parade 'em along the quayside termorrer?' yet another said.

A big docker with blood dripping from his nose pushed his way up to the front and bent down so that his face was inches from one of the bloodied assailants. He took out a pocket knife. 'Now I wanna know who was be'ind this little caper,' he said menacingly. 'If yer don't tell me, I'm gonna slit yer froat.'

The man's eyes widened with terror. 'We was paid a fiver each ter give yer union man a goin'-over by a geezer in the pub we was in. 'E was a stranger to us, honest ter Gawd, pal,' he spluttered.

176

'Don't yer "pal" me,' the big docker snarled, grabbing the terrified man around the windpipe.

Don Jacobs was still rubbing his sore back as he walked up to the three captured men and put his hand on the angry docker's shoulder. 'All right, Charlie, I'll see ter this,' he told him quietly. 'Now listen you lot,' he growled, 'we're gonna let yer go back ter whoever sent yer wiv a message. Jus' say that next time anybody tries a stroke like this we're gonna be ready for 'em, an' when we sort 'em out we're gonna dump 'em in the river tied 'and an' foot. Is that clear an' understood?'

'Well, is it?' the big docker shouted at them.

They all nodded and were then sent off, with a few hard kicks as they went.

Don turned to the angry docker who was wiping the blood away from his nose. 'This is a big turnout, ain't it, Charlie?' he grinned.

'Tom Berry give us the tip, Don,' the docker told him. ''E got the word to a few o' the lads that it looked like yer might be on a pastin'. Jackie Milton run round the Kings 'Ead an' Lofty Weston shot orf ter the Victoria. We wasn't short o' volunteers, as yer can see.'

The battling dockers walked back in high spirits to the Bargee, and at closing time a very inebriated group of rivermen insisted on escorting their union leader to his front door, their singing awakening the whole street.

Chapter Thirteen

In January 1924 the first Labour Government to be elected was one of the subjects of debate amongst the women of Page Street, and they were joined by their old neighbour Nellie Tanner who was still languishing around the corner in the deteriorating Bacon Buildings. Nellie prefered to meet up with her old friends and hardly ever spoke to her own neighbours. The couples who lived on her landing in the Buildings were elderly and tended to stay in their flats for most of the day, and the people in the flats below had large families who could be heard all day and for most of the evenings. Nellie never got into conversation with them other than to pass the time of day, but the one exception was Elsie Wishart who lived in the next block. Nellie had managed to get become quite friendly with her, and the tragic figure was another of the topics for discussion in Sadie Sullivan's parlour one Saturday afternoon.

'Seems ter me it won't make a lot o' difference ter the likes of us,' Maisie was saying.

'I dunno so much,' Florrie interjected. 'It's better than 'avin' those upper-class people in power. After all, what do they know about the workin' classes? At least the Labour people know what it is ter scrounge a livin' an' bring up families on next ter nuffink.'

'Ole Ramsey MacDonald seems a very nice man,'

Maisie decided. 'I remember 'e spoke up against the war. Shouted down 'e was, but 'e stood 'is ground.'

'Well, it might do some good around 'ere,' Nellie said with passion. 'There's bin so much trouble durin' these last few years. Look what 'appened at Christmas. My poor Carrie an' 'er Fred are jus' gettin' straight.'

'Terrible fing that was,' Sadie remarked. 'Ter come in like that an' smash the place up. My Gawd, it was enough ter send the pair of 'em round the twist.'

'It cost Carrie 'er baby,' Nellie said with quiet disgust. 'She was really upset at first, but Fred was a diamond. 'E wouldn't let 'er do a fing. Mind yer, it was early days. She just 'ad a flood an' that was it.'

'It must 'ave bin the shock,' Maisie said, slipping her hands into the armholes of her apron.

Florrie took out her tiny silver snuffbox and tapped the lid with her first two fingers. 'When my second ole man pissed orf I went up the Kings Arms an' got sloshed,' she told the gathering. 'That was shock made me do it. They wasn't gonna let me in there by meself but I jus' told 'em if they refused ter serve me I was gonna chuck a brick frew the winder. Mind yer, I'm talkin' about before they opened that snug bar. Gawdsend that was.'

'I bet that trouble cost your Carrie an' Fred a packet ter put right, didn't it?' Sadie asked.

'The dockers got a collection up an' some of 'em come in an' 'elped clean the place up. Good as gold they was. The union give 'em some money as well,' Nellie replied, sipping her tea.

'I wonder if they'll ever get ter the bottom of it,' Florrie said. 'From what yer've told me I should fink that Galloway family was be'ind it. I reckon it was the same people who done Carrie's place that done the union bloke up.'

Nellie nodded. 'I'm convinced it was the same crowd what set about my Will,' she said with conviction. 'I mean ter say, we've 'ad some ructions round 'ere an' a few street fights but yer always knew what it was about. It's a different fing when yer get yer place smashed up an' people get 'urt by complete strangers. I'm sure there's a link between what 'appened ter my Will an' Carrie's trouble, as well as that Don Jacobs gettin' done up. It could be somebody from over the water. There's some rough blokes over that side.'

Florrie had taken a pinch of snuff and the others waited until the tall, angular woman had had her sneeze before they continued the discussion.

''Ave yer seen anyfing o' that Elsie Wishart?' Sadie asked Nellie.

'As a matter o' fact I bumped inter the woman only the ovver day,' Nellie told them. 'She looks ill. I asked 'er if she was all right an' if there was anyfing I could do fer 'er but she jus' shook 'er 'ead. That daughter of 'ers can't be found. My Carrie went round ter tell 'er about what 'appened to 'er muvver but she'd moved. There was no address so there was nuffink Carrie could do. Elsie was upset when Carrie wrote to 'er. She was livin' wiv 'er sister at the time, by all accounts. Anyway, since the woman's bin back she's bin keepin' 'erself to 'erself. I speak to 'er when I see 'er in the turnin' but I don't fink she's got any friends in the street.'

'D'yer fink 'er daughter would 'ave anyfing ter do wiv 'er after what's 'appened?' Sadie asked.

'Gawd knows,' Nellie replied. 'After all, the gel was very close to 'er farvver an' she's always gonna blame 'er muvver fer what 'appened to 'im, it stan's ter reason. The woman's ter be pitied though. I always say there's two sides ter the story. Yer don't know what prompted 'er ter get friendly wiv that Frank Galloway in the first place. P'raps 'er ole man was never 'ome, or she might 'ave thought 'e 'ad a fancy piece. We'll never know.'

Florrie tapped on her snuffbox again and Sadie's eyes went up to the ceiling as she caught Nellie's look.

'I saw ole Mrs Bromsgrove the ovver day,' Maisie said suddenly. 'I ain't seen 'er about fer ages. Apparently she's bin in Guy's. 'Ad it all taken away,' she said, making a face and pointing to her stomach dramatically.

'I saw Maggie Jones down the market this mornin',' Florrie announced. 'She was tellin' me 'er son Percy's in trouble again. She reckons 'e got sloshed the ovver night an' whacked a copper. Anyway they reckon 'e's goin' away this time.'

''As 'e done it before then?' Sadie asked.

'Every time 'e gets pissed 'e wants ter fight everybody,' Maisie interrupted. 'Mind yer 'e knows who ter pick on. I couldn't see 'im pickin' on your Billy. Or your Danny,' she remarked, turning to Nellie.

Sadie watched Florrie's head go back and her eyes flutter, then she waited for the loud sneeze. 'I started ter tell yer about my Billy before Nellie come,' she said to Florrie. 'Yer know 'e lost 'is job?'

The women nodded their heads and Florrie put her snuffbox away, much to the others' delight.

'Fightin', wasn't it?' Maisie queried.

'Well, it was, sort of, but this time I reckon my Billy was right,' Sadie told her. ''E was workin' at that soapmakers fer over a year an' ter tell yer the trufe I dunno 'ow 'e stuck it. Anyway 'e thought it was time they took 'im orf that bone-boilin' an' 'e asked 'em fer a change. The foreman give 'im a lot o' lip an' Billy shoved 'im in wiv the bones. Tricky git 'e was accordin' ter Billy. Anyway, 'e got 'is comeuppance.'

'What's 'e doin' now then?' Florrie asked.

'Sittin' around the place fer most o' the day,' Sadie replied. ''E's lookin' out fer somefing else though. 'E still goes on about that gymnasium 'e wants to open, but like I told 'im, "Yer don't get somefing fer nuffing, Billy." '

''Ere, I know what I was gonna ask yer. 'Ow's ole 'Arold bearin' up?' Nellie asked the other women.

Florrie shook her head sadly. 'I saw 'im the ovver day walkin' up the street fer 'is paper an' 'e looks terrible,' she remarked. 'They was so close. Mind yer, poor Aggie led 'im a dog's life over that place of 'ers. 'E 'ad ter take 'is boots orf before she'd let 'im in the 'ouse. It's gone ter the dogs since she died. Did yer notice the front step as yer passed, Nell? Never 'ad a bit o' whitenin' on it since the funeral. It stinks o' catshit too. I don't fink 'e bovvers ter tell yer the trufe. I offered ter clean the place fer 'im the ovver day but 'e told me 'e can manage. I can't do any more but offer.'

Sadie got up and collected the empty teacups. 'Well, I'll get us anuvver cup then I must get on wiv the tea,' she told them. 'I'll 'ave Daniel in soon. 'Im an' Billy's gone down Millwall.'

Carrie had recovered from the ordeal she and Fred had endured just after Christmas, but her husband seemed nervous and short-tempered at times. It was unlike him, Carrie thought, but put it down to her losing the baby. It was as though Fred blamed her for causing the raid on the cafe, and there was no denying that it was she who insisted the union meetings should take place there. What had also upset him was her intention to let the union men continue holding their meetings in the little back room.

'We can't let ruffians dictate to us, Fred,' she told him. 'Besides, I fink we owe it ter the customers. They're all in the union, or at least most of 'em are. If

183

we tell Don Jacobs 'e can't use the back room any more what d'yer reckon 'e's gonna feel like? 'E could 'ave chucked it all in after nearly gettin' killed but 'e never. 'E's got the guts still ter be the union leader an' we should let 'im see we're wiv 'im, an' 'is men.'

Fred was still apprehensive but he nodded his agreement, knowing that Carrie was right. The customers had been very generous with the collection and he knew that for most of them money was tight. The union too had given them money to replace the cooking utensils, and now at last things were back to normal. For how long though? Fred asked himself. Was there likely to be a war of attrition along the riverfront, or could there be a settlement of the outstanding disputes between the employers and unions now that a Labour Government was in power? Perhaps it might be worth giving Carrie's ideas some consideration once the winter was over and the river trade improved, he thought. It might cheer her up and help her get over losing the baby.

It was during the early spring of '24 when Nellie Tanner was suddenly roused from her afternoon nap in the front room by voices in the street below. They seemed loud and excited, and when Nellie rubbed her eyes and glanced out of the window she saw groups of women standing by the front doors of their little houses opposite. She opened the window and leaned on the sill, aware that for all those women to be standing there something must have happened. Mrs Jolly who lived below her was walking towards the block and Nellie called down to her: 'What is it, Gert?'

Mrs Jolly waved her hand in front of her and shook her head dramatically. 'She's done it. They've jus' took 'er away,' she called back.

Nellie went to her front door and waited until she

heard Gert Jolly's footsteps on the landing below then leaned over the banisters. 'Is it Elsie?' she asked the elderly woman.

'That's right, luv,' Gert replied. 'She's jus' gassed 'erself. Mrs Corrigan found 'er. She smelt the gas in 'er flat, 'cos she lives right above 'er. She went down wiv 'er old man an' 'e broke the door down but it was too late. She'd put 'er 'ead in the oven. Terrible fing when yer come ter fink about it.'

Nellie shook her head sadly. 'I was only talkin' to 'er the ovver day. She looked ill then. What terrible fings must 'ave bin goin' frew 'er mind ter make 'er do it,' she sighed.

Gert Jolly put down her shopping bag and fished in her purse for her key. 'I'm jus' gonna make a cup o' tea. Pop down if yer like,' she said with a reassuring smile.

Nellie had not spoken to the woman more than once or twice but she felt it would be nice to make her acquaintance. 'All right, luv, I'll jus' get me key,' she called down.

The two women sat by the empty grate and Nellie listened, her eyes straying up to the spray of daffodils standing in a vase on the mantelshelf, while Gert Jolly told her about her family.

'We used ter live over in Jamaica Road,' she was saying, 'right next door ter the pie an' mash shop. My Albert was a saddler, Gawd rest 'is soul. 'E used ter do a lot o' work fer the gentry what lived in Tyburn Square. They used to own 'orse-an'-traps, a lot of 'em did. Elsie come from there, yer know. 'Er ole man was a solicitor.'

'Yeah, I know,' Nellie said. 'It was my Danny that pulled Elsie out o' the river that first time she tried ter do away wiv 'erself. She was lucky then. The way that tide was runnin' she could 'ave bin washed away. As it 'appened my Danny, 'e's a lighterman yer know, 'e saw Elsie walk down those steps inter the water an' 'e jumped in an' caught 'er by 'er coat. The lad could 'ave bin drowned 'imself.'

'I remember the time,' Gert told her. 'Mrs Porter told me all about it. 'Er ole man told 'er, an' 'e got the news from Fred Bradley who owns that cafe jus' round the corner. Mrs Porter's ole man is a carman an' 'e used the cafe a lot, yer see. That's your Carrie's 'usband, ain't it? I was surprised when Mrs Porter told me it was your daughter who was married ter Fred Bradley.'

Nellie sipped her tea. 'My Danny dragged Elsie across the turnin' ter the dinin' rooms an' Carrie managed ter revive 'er,' she continued. 'She sat 'er by the fire an' give 'er some brandy that Fred 'ad in the cupboard. It was a freezin' night an' the poor cow was like a block of ice. Anyway the next day Elsie told Carrie what made 'er do it an' then my gel went ter see Elsie's daughter ter let 'er know what 'ad 'appened.'

'Elsie's daughter?' the woman said incredulously.

'That's right,' Nellie said, puzzled by the woman's tone. 'Elsie gave my gel the address of 'er daughter an' . . .'

'Elsie Wishart's daughter died of diphtheria in 1910. She was only four years old,' Gert Jolly told her.

'But I don't understand,' Nellie said, feeling suddenly thrown. 'When Carrie went ter Catford ter see the gel the people there told 'er that the young woman 'ad left an' didn't leave an address.'

'That would be Elsie's younger sister. 'Er name's Wishart too,' Gert replied.

'I still don't understand,' Nellie said frowning. 'Wishart is Elsie's married name, ain't it?'

Gert Jolly smiled. 'Phyllis Wishart, Elsie's younger sister, married Elsie's 'usband's cousin. Both the women married inter the same family, yer see.'

'So Elsie was makin' that story up about 'er daughter,' Nellie ventured.

'Well, I don't know what the woman told your Carrie, but I can guess,' Gert said, smiling sadly. 'Elsie used ter talk about 'er daughter as though she was still alive, an' she's bin dead fer fourteen years nigh.'

'My Carrie told me Elsie said she see 'er daughter in the market and the gel turned 'er back on 'er,' Nellie recalled. 'Elsie said that the gel wouldn't fergive 'er fer causin' 'er farvver ter take 'is own life.'

'It wasn't Elsie's fault 'er 'usband 'ung 'imself,' Gert said, shaking her head. 'Elsie Wishart was a lovely woman, an' a good wife an' muvver. Me an' my Albert knew the family well. It was a tragedy losin' their only child. Elsie couldn't 'ave any more. 'Er 'usband Lawrence went on the booze after the child died an' 'is business started ter go down the drain. A year later ter the day Lawrence 'ung 'imself from the banisters. Elsie found 'im jus' swingin' there stone cold. I remember the date well. It was March the seventh, 1911. I remember it 'cos that was my Albert's birthday.'

'That's terday's date,' Nellie remarked.

'That's right,' Gert said quietly, pointing to the spray of daffodils. 'I always buy a few flowers ter celebrate Albert's birthday.'

Broomhead Smith was absent from the Bermondsey streets having an enforced rest. The totter had dropped a heavy piece of old iron on his big toe and it swelled up like a balloon. He could not get his boot on and he realised it would be pointless trying to carry on with his totting wearing one boot and one carpet slipper. He decided that he could at least manage to tidy up the shed where he stabled his faithful old horse and also kept his old lumber. The nag seemed to be enjoying the rest and Broomhead swore that the animal had a grin on its face when it looked at him.

The day went well and while he was tidying up Broomhead found bits and pieces which he had mislaid months ago. He discovered what he considered to be quite a few saleable items lying around, and with the thought of earning money on them he struggled to get fit for the road once more. Every night he soaked his foot in salt water and soon the nail of his big toe dropped off. The swelling was going down nicely and the toe was not so painful now, he found, taking a swig of brandy from the hip flask that was his constant companion. It was just as well. The owner of the shed was after his rent, and so was the landlord of his little two-up two-down house around the corner in Weston Street. With a bit of luck he would be riding through the backstreets again on Monday morning, he told himself cheerfully.

Broomhead had not counted on his horse's clumsiness however, and when it stepped back on his tender toe he let out a yell that could be heard in the Tower Bridge Road market.

It was another two weeks before the totter's damaged toe could take his weight and by then his plight was desperate. The landlord was threatening Broomhead with eviction unless the rent was paid forthwith, and the owner of the shed had also issued him with an ultimatum. The totter had thought of selling his nag for horsemeat, but by the look of the animal he would have thought himself lucky to get the price of a packet of Woodbines. Maybe it would be better to sell the business and go into something else, he considered. Broomhead's problem was that he only knew totting, and he had to admit that he wasn't very successful in that profession.

At last Broomhead was back on the streets, and as he vainly urged his tired nag to greater effort he pondered on his future. Perhaps he should find himself a comfortable widow, he thought to himself. There were a few around, although he could not remember any in these parts. He would then be able to get up at a civilised time and stroll up for the morning paper, clean a few windows and maybe brighten up the front doorstep to keep the peace, then saunter off to the pub for his daily constitutional. It seemed a perfect idea, but where was he to find such a catch? All the women around these streets were struggling to make ends meet and they were the hardest people to bargain with he had ever come across.

Broomhead had just coaxed his horse into Page Street when he was hailed by a woman who was cleaning her step. 'D'yer take mangles?' she said.

'I take anyfing within reason, missus,' he told her.

'Well, my ole man brought me a new wringer an' I gotta get rid o' the old one,' she said.

Broomhead climbed down from his cart and followed the woman out to the back yard, where there was a wringer showing clear signs of rust. 'Is this it?' he asked.

'Nah, that's me new one. There's me old one under that sheet,' she told him.

Broomhead lifted his trilby and scratched his head while she fiddled with the strings that secured the cover. 'Tell me somfink, missus. Why keep an old wringer under a sheet an' leave the new one out in the weavver?' he asked her.

The woman put her hands on her hips and surveyed him. 'Well, yer see, I can't bear ter look at it,' she told him. 'Me first ole man bought it fer me, an' 'e's bin gorn fer over twenty years now. Lovely man, 'e was, not like the ole goat I'm married to now.'

'Well, I should fink it ain't much joy lookin' at the new wringer if yer can't stand the man what bought it fer yer,' Broomhead remarked, taking his hat off and scratching his head again.

'Oh, but yer see it's nice ter look at that new one,' she said, smiling crookedly at him. 'That was about the only fing I ever got orf my second ole man that didn't 'urt. A violent man 'e was.'

'Was?'

'Yeah, 'e run orf wiv a barmaid from the Crown. Yer know the Crown?' she asked him.

Broomhead nodded. ''E's still livin' then?' he queried.

'Oh, yeah. Well, I fink so anyway. Last I 'eard 'e was knockin' 'er about, so she ain't won a prize, 'as she?'

Broomhead studied the newly exposed wringer. 'I couldn't give yer anyfing fer this, missus,' he said, shaking his head. 'It's rusted right frew. It'd prob'ly fall ter pieces before I got it on the cart.'

'Well, I really want it out o' the way,' the woman said, her voice taking on a pleading tone. 'Won't yer consider it?'

'I could take it, but it ain't werf nuffink ter me,' Broomhead said in a thoughtful tone of voice. 'It's only good fer the dustmen.'

'The dustmen won't take it. I've already asked 'em,' she replied.

Broomhead studied the woman. She was in her late forties, he guessed. Rather plump, but a nice, kind face, and spotlessly clean. Her dark, greying hair was neat and tidy too. She had dimples in her chubby cheeks, and that was the deciding feature as far as Broomhead was concerned.

'I'll tell yer what I can do, luv,' he said, reverting to the term of endearment he used when he was feeling amiable. 'I'll take it fer two bob. Mind yer, I wouldn't normally do this, but as it's the wringer yer first ole man bought yer I'll make an exception.'

'Well, that's very nice of yer, I mus' say,' the lady declared, giving him a wide smile.

'Righto then, I'll get it on the cart,' Broomhead said, flexing his muscles.

'Would yer like a cuppa?' she asked him.

Broomhead nodded as he struggled with the rusty wringer. This lump of old iron wasn't going to bring much, he knew full well, but the cogs were still full of grease and they could be used to fix up the other wringer he had in his shed. More importantly, though, he had made a good impression on the woman. She might be just the sort he had been thinking about. She was presentable, even if she was a little plump, and it looked like she had a tidy home. He would have to give it some thought while he was having his cup of tea and a chat, he decided.

The tired nag turned its head and stared at Broomhead while he struggled with the wringer, and once it was safely loaded on the cart the totter turned and glared at the horse. 'Who you lookin' at, yer bloody fleabag?' he growled, taking a sack of chaff from under his seat and filling the horse's nosebag.

The woman came out and stood in her doorway watching him fit the nosebag over the animal's head. 'Yer do look after yer 'orse, don't yer?' she remarked with a smile on her face.

Broomhead nuzzled his nag and ruffled its ear fondly. The animal was so surprised at such a show of affection that it jerked its head upwards, blowing into the bag and showering him with chaff. The totter smiled at the woman and dusted himself down carefully, casting a few deadly glances back at the horse as he followed her into her neat and tidy parlour.

Around the walls there were prints in ebony frames and on the mantelshelf Broomhead saw large iron statues of nude maidens holding flaring torches aloft. In the centre of the shelf there was an ormolu clock mounted on a black marble plinth and above it an oval mirror in a silver frame. A gingham tablecloth was spread over the table and in the centre there was a vase containing paper flowers. The two armchairs were shabby but with spotless white linen headcloths and arm covers spread over them, and there was a walnut sideboard against the wall facing the lace-covered window.

Broomhead took off his trilby and placed it on the floor beside him as he settled into an armchair. 'Yer got a nice place, missus,' he told her.

She smiled at him as she went over to the sideboard and picked up a small oval-shaped picture frame. 'That's my first 'usband,' she said, handing him the picture.

Broomhead studied the stern face and looked up at the woman. 'What 'appened to 'im?' he asked.

''E ran orf wiv anuvver woman,' she said without showing any emotion.

'I thought yer said yer second ole man ran orf wiv anuvver woman,' Broomhead queried.

'They both did, but 'e was a lovely man,' she said abstractedly, smiling down at the picture.

The totter scratched his head, realising that he was never going to understand the workings of a woman's mind. 'Ain't yer never thought o' gettin' married again?' he asked her.

'I've never give it much thought, ter tell yer the trufe,' she told him. 'There's nobody round 'ere I fancy. A woman 'as ter be sure before she lets a man put 'is boots under 'er bed.'

'Yer quite right,' Broomhead replied, sipping his tea. 'I'm the same in a manner o' speakin'. I never found a woman I liked enough ter give up me freedom for. I do all me own cookin', yer know, an' me washin'. Sometimes it's 'ard though, luv, but I manage some'ow. I always find time ter read the good book an' look after me 'orse. I reckon that's the best cared for 'orse in Bermondsey, although I'm not one fer braggin'.'

The large woman smiled sweetly at him. 'I fink any woman would be lucky ter find a fish like you,' she told him. 'Any man who 'as ter care fer 'imself an' still finds time ter look after 'is animal an' read a book as well is got ter be a nice man as far as I'm concerned.'

'Not any book, missus,' Broomhead said quickly. 'I'm talkin' about the Bible. Oh, yes, I read it nearly every night. That's if I get me extra chores done in time.'

'Extra chores?'

'Well, the extra washin' an' ironin'.'

'What d'yer mean?' she asked him.

'I live near an old lady who's ate up wiv the rheumatics, yer see,' he lied. 'I take 'er washin' in an' iron it every week. It's the least yer can do fer a poor ole gel who's got nobody in the world except 'er cat.'

'Yer a lovely man, Mr – eh, I don't know yer name,' she faltered.

'It's Bill Smith, at yer service,' he grinned.

'I'm Alice, Alice Johnson, an' I'm pleased ter know yer,' she said, holding out her hand.

Broomhead shook her hand and picked up his teacup, his eyes going around the room. ''Ow d'yer manage, wiv no man ter care fer yer?' he asked slyly.

'Oh, I've got a few bob put away, an' I do a bit o' charrin' in the mornin's,' she replied. 'Then there's me ovver little job.'

'Ovver little job?' Broomhead repeated, hoping he did not sound too interested in the woman's affairs.

'I work be'ind the bar at the Pig an' Whistle four nights a week,' she told him. 'So yer see I ain't got 'ardly any money worries really, Bill. Well, not like most round 'ere.'

193

Broomhead put down his empty teacup. He wanted to stay longer but he had suddenly remembered about his horse. The brake chain was broken and he had forgotten to fix it before he came out that morning. The nag often took it into its head to stroll off on its own and last time it happened he found it four streets away being fed a carrot by a huge woman who slated him for abandoning such a lovely animal.

He got up. 'Well, it's bin lovely talkin' ter yer, Alice,' he said. 'I might jus' come round the Pig an' Whistle one night fer a drink an' a chat.'

'I'm there every Thursday night ter Sunday – saloon bar by the way,' she added quickly.

Broomhead nodded and walked to the front door, feeling slightly disappointed. He had never been in a saloon bar in his life. To him saloon bars of pubs were strictly for the 'hoi polloi', his pet name for the snobs and stuck-up people who didn't want to mix with the likes of him.

When he stepped out into the street Broomhead cursed to himself. The cart had gone! He looked up and down the turning, scratching his head in agitation.

'Oi, you!'

The totter looked over at the tall, stern figure of Florrie Axford standing at her front door, arms akimbo.

'Yer 'orse-an'-cart's jus' pulled inter Galloway's yard,' she informed him. 'Yer wanna keep yer eye on it instead o' leavin' it wivout the chain on.'

Broomhead mumbled an obscenity under his breath and smiled winsomely at her. 'It's broke,' he said.

'You'll be broke if that 'orse does any damage in there,' she retorted sarcastically.

When Broomhead had retrieved his horse-and-cart and threatened the horse biblically he climbed aboard with a swagger, pondering on his good fortune in meeting Alice Johnson as he rode out of Page Street.

Chapter Fourteen

During the late summer Carrie Bradley realised her
ambition at last. Fred finally agreed that they should go
ahead with her plan to purchase number 26 Cotton
Lane, the empty house next door to their dining rooms.
The Bradleys had a meeting with the estate agents, and
then without more ado they went to see their bank
manager and sat serious-faced as he gave them a long
sermon on the practicalities of expanding in business
and the pitfalls to watch out for. Carrie chewed on her
lip in nervous anticipation and Fred sat holding his cap
tightly on his lap while the bank official put on a pair of
gold-rimmed spectacles and proceeded to examine
their yearly accounts. After what seemed like an eternity to Carrie the manager smiled benignly and told
them that he would grant them a loan against the cafe.
The young woman felt she wanted to kiss him but she
resisted the temptation and turned to her husband
instead, elation radiant in her face. Fred responded
with a brief smile, feeling a little overawed by it all. He
was painfully aware that if they failed to repay the loan
then the bank would foreclose on his business.

At the end of October the deal was finally sealed.
Carrie immediately set about making arrangements
with a firm of local builders which agreed to start work
in January, with assurances that their work would cause
the minimum of disruption to the normal running of the

dining rooms. It was all very exciting, and Carrie felt happy at the way things were going. Rachel was now comfortably settled in the infants school just a few streets away and Annie McCafferty had written to her saying that she was well and that her mother was still bravely fighting her illness. Trade was steady along the waterfront and work went on without any disputes of note. Carrie's young brother Danny was now walking out with Iris Brody, a pretty girl from nearby Wilson Street, and the two young people seemed very suited, she thought.

In the surrounding backstreets life went on as usual. Sadie Sullivan hummed to herself as she ran a grubby shirt up and down the scrubbing board in her backyard. Her husband Daniel had had two weeks' solid work on the quay and her family were all doing well, including Billy who had found himself another job at last. Shaun her youngest son was married now, as were the twins Pat and Terry. They all lived nearby and Pat's wife, Dolly, was expecting her first baby any day now. Only Joe, who was twenty-seven, and Billy, coming up to thirty-four now, were still single and living at home. Joe was courting Sara Flannagan, a Catholic girl from Bacon Street, but Sadie's eldest son Billy seemed to be happy leading a bachelor life. Sadie remembered how she had once despaired of him, but now that he had managed to get work she was feeling more optimistic that he would finally settle down. He had found a job with a local builder and there was now some colour in his cheeks. The heavy physical labour of mixing cement and carrying hods full of bricks had been very hard at first and his breathing was often troubled, but Billy persevered and found it less of an ordeal as the days went by.

Sadie heard Maisie Dougall calling to her over the

wall. She went to the front door to let her in.

'I mus' tell yer, Sadie, 'e's bin in there again this mornin'. I'm sure there's somefink goin' on,' she said in a low voice as soon as she came in.

Sadie could not understand why Maisie found it necessary to whisper in the privacy of her parlour but she listened nevertheless.

''E 'ad a tweed jacket wiv a sprig o' lavender pinned on 'is lapel an' 'is trousers looked liked they could do wiv an iron shoved over 'em,' she was going on, 'but it was 'is boots what made me laugh. They was covered in 'orseshit. 'E 'ad that rotten ole trilby on as well. What that Alice Johnson sees in 'im I'll never know.'

'I'm sure there's somefink wrong wiv 'er,' Sadie replied. 'I remember that second ole man runnin' out o' the 'ouse an' 'er chasin' 'im up the road wiv a chopper. The first ole man left 'er as well, by all accounts. I remember 'im. Nice bloke 'e was. Always give yer the time o' day. Smart too. She nagged 'im narrer, accordin' ter Maggie Jones. She used ter live next door to 'er in Conroy Street. Maggie told me Alice was always after the men. It was 'er what used ter 'ave that tally man in fer hours on end while 'er ole man was at work. No wonder 'e pissed orf. My Daniel wouldn't put up wiv what she did. D'yer know, Mais, she'd come out in the street an' shout all the bad language she could lay 'er tongue to as 'e was goin' orf ter work. Bloody shame it was ter see a man put on so.'

'Well, ole Broom'ead's got a shock comin' 'is way,' Maisie chuckled. 'Mind yer, 'e might be 'er match. 'E can get 'is tongue round a few choice words as well.'

''E's a dirty ole goat,' Sadie remarked. 'I remember that time poor ole Aggie Temple 'ad a go at 'im over 'er cat. 'E really let fly at 'er.'

'Well, I'd better get back, I've got the copper

boilin',' Maisie said, making for the door. 'I jus' popped in ter let yer know, Sadie.'

Further along Page Street in the Galloway yard office Gerry Macedo sat toying with a glass of Scotch whisky, while opposite him George Galloway sat looking hard-faced as he listened. Frank Galloway was very quiet.

'You invited me over last year to intervene in your troubles, George,' Macedo said, 'and now you're saying you don't want to join with us on this. I'm sorry but I don't follow your line of reasoning. All right, there was a slip-up in that Don Jacobs affair last Christmas, but we took care of the Bradleys' place like we agreed and no one got hurt.'

Galloway was fingering the small gold medallion on his watch chain. 'Look, Gerry, we've known each ovver fer a while now,' he said slowly. 'I asked yer over last year ter do a job o' work an' yer was well paid fer yer trouble. As it 'appens, fings didn't work out the way I would 'ave liked. They're still 'avin' those meetin's at the cafe an' as far as I can make out they're still well supported. That Jacobs affair only served ter stiffen their resolve. If it 'ad bin done right fings would 'ave bin different. I expected more, Gerry. Yer let me down there.'

Gerry Macedo swallowed the contents of his glass. 'All right, I take your point, George,' he replied, 'but to be fair that was a situation that wasn't really under our control. This is something much bigger. What I'm putting to you now is a chance for you to come in with us and enjoy the mutual benefits. It's a good scheme, and believe me, this has not been put together without first looking at all the pitfalls. There's a consortium in agreement, and there's big money being put up. If we're to succeed we need a one hundred per cent backing from the people who count in this neck of the woods. I'm not joking when I say that if you fall in with us, George, you'll not look back. There's a lot of money in it for you. I tell you now, when you get to meet the rest of the interested parties you'll be very surprised indeed. It can't fail, George. Give it some very serious thought at least, for your own sake.'

George stood up and slipped his thumbs into his waistcoat pockets. 'All right, Gerry, I'll talk it over wiv Frank an' we'll let yer know soon, one way or anuvver,' he replied.

Macedo got up from his chair and glanced briefly at the younger Galloway as he buttoned up his camel-hair overcoat. 'You're either in or out on this one, George. There's no sitting on the fence,' he warned.

The East End gang leader's words sounded like a thinly veiled threat to George Galloway and he blinked as he picked up his glass and swallowed the whisky in one gulp. 'I can't afford ter get mixed up wiv all this business at my age, Gerry,' he said quickly. 'A few years ago maybe, but now I'm gettin' too old. I jus' wanna be allowed ter carry on tradin' until I finally decide ter pass the business over ter Frank.'

'Why don't you do that now, George?' Macedo asked, glancing quickly at the younger Galloway. 'You should sit back and take things easy. Young Frank's a very good manager and he's certainly got your concern running well, as you've already said. We can do business with Frank, providing he's got the reins. Give him the chance. You should be sitting back a little and enjoying the rest.'

'Yer seem ter ferget, Gerry, this is my life,' the elder man answered with spirit. 'I've built this concern up from one bloody van. I tramped the streets lookin' fer work an' it wasn't easy. Now I've got good contracts an' a fleet o' vehicles on order. We're gettin' anuvver yard soon an' then I'm goin' fer the trunkin' jobs furvver afield. It's all beginnin' ter pay orf an' I'm not about ter let it all be destroyed under me very nose. No, my friend, yer can count me out.'

Gerry Macedo donned his homburg and took out a pair of leather gloves from his coat pocket. 'Talk to Frank, George,' he said quietly as he made for the door.

When the gang leader had left, George sat down heavily in his chair and looked over at his son who seemed to be suddenly engrossed in some papers on his desk.

'What did 'e mean, Frank?' he asked.

Frank Galloway shrugged his shoulders. 'I'm sure I don't know,' he said dismissively.

George stared at his son for a few moments, a brooding look on his florid face. There was some deep meaning to Macedo's parting words and Frank knew the answer, he felt sure. He would get to the bottom of it.

'Don't you think we should at least consider the proposition, Father?' Frank said, breaking the awkward silence. 'It makes good sense.'

George Galloway leaned forward, his eyes glaring into his son's. 'You 'ave realised by now the sort o' people we're dealin' wiv, ain't yer?' he said in a loud voice. 'P'raps yer don't understand. Me an' Gerry Macedo used ter take our own fighters ter the tournaments over the East End. That's where I first met 'im. It's goin' back a few years now but I remember Gerry was makin' a name for 'imself then. 'Is family's Italian an' they 'ad a flourishin' greengrocery business in Spitalfields Market. They sent Gerry ter the best schools an' 'e got a good education. They wanted somefing better fer their boy, but 'e got inter gamblin' an' worse. 'E wanted nuffink ter do wiv greengrocery an' when 'e finally got the family business 'e sold it as soon as 'e could. Gerry managed fighters, an' 'alf the local prostitutes who worked the East End. 'E's got 'is fingers in a lot o' pies, Frank. Apart from that nightclub 'e owns up West there's at least a dozen ovver shady concerns that 'e's involved wiv. Gerry's a big man over the water an' now 'e's plannin' on extendin' 'is activities over this side. That's where 'e's gonna come unstuck. All right, I know I agreed ter bring 'em over ter sort our little problem out, but on reflection I know now that it wasn't a good idea. I agreed because I wanted somebody who wasn't known over this side o' the water, somebody who 'ad enough muscle ter get the job done wiv no come-backs. Gerry Macedo owed me a favour an' I was silly enough ter decide I'd collect. Yer don't collect favours orf o' the likes o' Gerry Macedo. Them sort o' people expect all the favours ter be done fer them.'

'But what Macedo's suggesting seems to be a good deal,' Frank cut in. 'It'll put business our way, and we'll need all the regular work we can get for those lorries we're buying. They've got to be paid for.'

George Galloway shook his head sadly. 'Yer don't understand, do yer?' he said in a deflated voice. 'If we go along wiv Macedo an' put money in that Rovver'ithe nightclub 'e's talkin' about we're gonna be part of an exclusive club, granted. It'll mean a few of us are gonna share the best o' the cartage contracts jus' like Gerry said. We're gonna be able ter name our price instead o' cuttin' it ter the bone, but at what cost? Macedo's gonna put 'is prossers in there ter get the bosses o' the big food firms an' sheet metal firms in a position where 'e can blackmail 'em ter give us lucrative contracts, an' 'e'll be creamin' off a tidy bit o' dosh fer 'is trouble. If the law don't get us fer a racket like that, which ain't such a lightweight matter in case yer didn't know, we're always gonna be be'olden ter Macedo. We'll be ferever givin' 'im money, an' 'ow long's it gonna be before 'e starts blackmailin' us?'

The younger Galloway sat forward in his chair. 'I don't think Macedo would cheat us, Father,' he said quickly. 'If we could get regular cartage work for the big firms around here we'd be made, and it'd be no hardship paying Macedo his commission. We'd have no trouble with the dockers' union either. Those ignorant sods might stand up to a handful of bruisers, but if the dock employers had reached an agreement with the rest of the businessmen in the area they'd be starved into submission. What price the union then? They can't expect starving men to form picket lines. The transport and dockers' unions in this area could be broken, Father, not bribed or intimidated but broken for good. We could make an example of them.'

The elder Galloway had been watching his son closely as the younger man said his piece and he felt sick to his stomach. 'Yer talkin' dangerous rubbish, Frank,' he said bitterly.

Frank was staring at his father and he saw only obstinacy in the old man's eyes. 'You're blind to the facts, Father,' he said caustically.

'Now you jus' listen ter me fer a minute,' George countered angrily, banging his fist down heavily on the desktop. 'This borough feeds orf the Thames an' it's lifeblood ter the likes o' you an' me as well as everybody else around 'ere, don't ferget. One way or anuvver it 'as ter supply the bread an' butter an' wivout the river we wouldn't 'ave roofs over our 'eads. Ter talk about starvin' out the dockers is madness. Yer not gonna stop the unions by force. In fact yer gonna make 'em stronger. I've found that out, much ter my regret. An' as fer Gerry Macedo, 'e's gonna learn that soon enough. They're too big fer 'im ter meddle wiv.'

'I'm talking about the power of money, not Gerry Macedo,' Frank cut in. 'If we all act together it'll be more than the unions can cope with. It'll decide the long-term future of this borough, I'm certain.'

George Galloway's eyes narrowed as he faced his son. 'Tell me, Frank, why are yer so anxious fer us ter fall in wiv Macedo's plans?' he asked suddenly. ''E's not puttin' any pressure on yer, is 'e?'

Frank looked away from his father's searching stare. 'Of course not,' he replied quickly.

'I still don't reckon yer give me a straight answer when I asked yer what Macedo meant by that remark 'e made as 'e went out.'

Frank felt nervous under his father's dark gaze and he started to fiddle with the sheaf of papers on his desk. 'He was only hoping I'd get you to see sense, I suppose,' he replied.

'I don't believe yer, Frank,' his father said quietly, with authority. ''E's got somefink on yer, I can tell. Now out wiv it!'

'It's nothing important,' Frank answered, embarrassment showing on his face.

'I wanna know, d'yer 'ear me?' George said angrily, his voice rising.

Frank Galloway took a deep breath. It would have to come out sooner or later, he realised. Gerry Macedo would no doubt tell the old man when it suited him, now that it looked like his scheme had been rejected.

'It was when I was having trouble with Bella,' he began, looking up at his father. 'It was nothing serious, just one of those things that tend to happen. She was always busy at the theatre and I was left much to myself. Anyway, I started to get out and about during the evenings. I went to nightclubs, and one or two gambling houses in the East End. I had a couple of good wins. Then I had a bad spell. I ran up a debt and I was being pressed for payment. Well, I borrowed money, hoping my luck would change, but I got deeper into it. They were tightening the screws and I was desperate. One night as I was strolling home I was bundled into a car and driven around for a while. Then suddenly the car pulled up and this well-dressed man got in. He wanted to know what I was going to do about paying up the debt.'

''Ow much was it, Frank?' his father interrupted.

'A hundred pounds.'

'Yer bloody fool,' George remarked with venom.

Frank shrugged and looked down at his shoes. 'It was put to me that I might be able to cancel out the debt if I did as I was told.'

'An' what was that?' George Galloway asked.

'Well, this man told me that he knew of you and that you used to manage pub fighters. He said that I would be doing you a favour as well as myself if I went along with him in putting Joe Maitland out of business.'

George looked shocked. 'Joe Maitland? Yer mean they got yer ter start that fire at Dock'ead?

Frank looked up at his father. 'I didn't start that fire. Macedo did,' he said simply.

'But why should East End bookies wanna burn Maitland's ware'ouse down?' George asked in a perturbed tone of voice.

Frank took a deep breath and puffed out through his pursed lips. 'Apparently it was Joe Maitland who was behind the police raid on the Crown,' he explained. 'They said it was him and his cronies from Poplar who got their friends put away and they were out for revenge.'

'Why should Joe Maitland interest 'imself in gettin' the tournaments stopped?' George asked, still puzzled.

'Apparently Maitland's brother was a pub fighter and he refused to throw a fight,' Frank replied. 'There was a lot of money going on the other man and after Maitland's brother won he was beaten up. He died a few days later. Joe Maitland went out to find the people responsible and he did a spell in prison for smashing up a pub. Anyway, the vendetta went on after he came out of prison and the last of those responsible for his brother's death met his end the night of the police raid on the Crown at Dockhead.'

'Yer mean Don McBain? But 'e fell down the stairs an' broke 'is neck that night,' George said incredulously.

'That was the verdict, but they seem to think Maitland was behind it. They feel that he killed McBain,' Frank explained.

George was hardly able to believe what he had heard. 'So they used yer ter get at Joe Maitland,' he said in a shocked voice. 'Will Tanner was lucky ter get out o' that fire.'

'I didn't know Macedo was going to harm anyone,' Frank said in a low voice.

'What I wanna know is, 'ow come yer got Gerry Macedo ter do yer biddin'?' George quizzed him. 'An' where did yer get the money ter pay 'im when yer couldn't find enough ter pay yer gamblin' debts?'

'I didn't pay him,' the younger Galloway said quietly. 'He struck a deal with me. Macedo was eager to move south of the river and he saw the opportunity of renewing his ties with you through me. He seemed to think that you had all the right contacts in the transport set-up over this side and he knew you were fighting the unions. It all figured very nicely for him. He pressured me to coax you into calling him in last year. He's been furthering his plans ever since.'

George Galloway sat slumped in his chair for a few moments, his face a black mask, then he looked up at the pathetic figure of his son. 'D'yer know somefink,' he said quietly, 'I fink I lost the wrong son in the war. Geoffrey would never 'ave got inter the mess you got in. 'E was the one I nagged an' pushed inter this business. 'E wanted ter be an engineer. But you – I let yer 'ave yer own way an' become an accountant. What's more, I encouraged yer ter marry that slut Bella. She's got no time fer you or the business. All she cares about is those Fancy-Dans in the music-'all. If she'd 'ave spent more time at 'ome yer might never 'ave got yerself inter this mess. If Geoffrey was alive terday yer'd never 'ave come in the business. I'd 'ave seen ter that.'

Frank sat listening to his father's bitterness in silence. He was right, he could not deny it. Geoffrey had been a good manager and a good brother as well, before his short life was snuffed out in the trenches. The old man was right about Bella too.

George Galloway's hand was shaking as he refilled the glass at his elbow. 'It seems ter me that yer've got us backed against the wall, Frank,' he said in a quiet, controlled voice. 'I should chuck yer out on yer arse fer what yer've done ter me, but I won't. Yer gonna earn yer inheritance, an' yer gonna start right now. I'm tellin' yer straight, boy, I'm not gonna be dictated to by some jumped-up bastard from over the water who finks 'e can tell me 'ow I should conduct me business. I'm gonna fight the scheme an' I'm startin' 'ere an' now, so yer better listen carefully ter what I'm gonna say.'

As the Christmas decorations went up and the market stalls lit up their Tilley lamps for late night trading Maudie Mycroft was feeling very despondent. Her efforts to get Ernest to denounce the Communist Party and pray to the Lord for forgiveness had come to naught, and as she carried her heavy shopping basket home from the market she was determined that none of her husband's friends in the movement were going to set foot in her house. In fact she would make it quite clear to Ernest that unless he listened to her and saw the error of his ways their long-time marriage would be over.

The thought of living alone with only her church friends to support her was not a very nice prospect, but at least she could have peace of mind, Maudie told herself. Ernest had been raving about bringing down the Government and he had been standing on street corners with his dirty literature, as well as going on actual marches to Parliament. He was going to be the death of her if he kept up with this obsession of his, she groaned to herself. She would tell him firmly that he was making her ill with his ranting and raving, but after Christmas. Now wasn't the time. It was the season of joy, peace and goodwill to all men.

"'Ello, Maudie. 'Ow yer doin', gel?'

The preoccupied woman was taken by surprise and she turned to face Florrie Axford who was standing arms folded at her front door. "'Ello, Flo. I didn't see yer standin' there,' she said apologetically. 'I was miles away.'

'I thought yer was ill, not seein' yer about,' Florrie said, taking her snuffbox from her apron pocket.

'I feel ill,' Maudie replied, putting down her shopping basket and rubbing the palm of her hand. 'It's my Ernest. 'E's bin gettin' 'imself more an' more tied up wiv those Communist people an' I'm worried 'e's gonna do somefink terrible one o' these days,' she groaned.

Florrie hid a grin as she tapped on her snuffbox. 'I shouldn't worry, luv,' she told her. 'It'll all fizzle out. My second ole man was like that. 'E used ter get in wiv those anarchists from Whitechapel. They was the same sort o' people. Mind yer, the Government's clampin' down on 'em, so I've bin told. They're gettin' a law out ter shoot 'em as traitors. I saw it in the paper only the ovver day. I know it's drastic. but yer can't 'ave those sort runnin' around loose, can yer?'

Maudie looked frightened. 'Shoot 'em, yer say? Why, that's terrible.'

'Well, yer can understand it, luv,' Florrie went on with her teasing. 'D'yer remember the siege o' Sidney Street? It was a terrible turnout that was.'

Maudie nodded animatedly. 'They shot 'em all there, didn't they?'

Florrie considered herself somewhat of an authority on the Sidney Street siege and shook her head. 'Nah. They never found Peter the Painter. Some say 'e was burnt in the fire afterwards but I reckon 'e got away. 'E's out o' the country now. Russia, I would say.'

'Didn't they shoot a policeman?' Maudie asked with wide eyes.

'Two,' Florrie replied, placing a pinch of snuff on the back of her hand. 'An' the inspector who was in charge. They got the 'Ome Secretary there as well. Winston Churchill it was. 'E called the army in an' they was firin' at the 'ouse where the anarchists were 'idin'. The place caught light an' they found the bodies o' two o' the men. Anuvver o' the anarchists was shot by 'is own people. Worst fing ever bin known in Stepney. Mind yer, Maudie, I can see it 'appenin' again if those Commie people get their way. I can see the soldiers out on the streets, really I can.'

By now Maudie was in a state of panic. 'I can't take no more of it, Flo,' she wailed. 'I'm gonna tell 'im straight after Christmas. It's eivver me or them. 'E's gotta make a choice.'

Florrie felt guilty for her teasing, and after she had sneezed loudly she patted Maudie on the back. 'If yer can't beat 'em yer should fink about joinin' 'em, luv,' she went on. 'Tell Ernest yer wanna go ter their next meetin'. 'E might lose interest if yer tell 'im that.'

''Ow d'yer make that out, Flo?' the worried woman asked.

'Well, yer know men like ter keep those sort o' fings away from us women. Once 'e knows yer wanna go 'e might jus' pack it in.'

'I can't see 'im doin' that,' Maudie said, shaking her head. ''E'd jus' say no. Ernest can be a very determined man when 'e likes.'

'Well, be as firm as 'im, Maudie, an' tell 'im yer goin' ter the next meetin' whatever 'e says. It's better doin' that than seein' 'im shot by the soldiers.'

'It won't come ter that, will it?' Maudie asked tearfully. 'I couldn't bear ter fink o' my poor Ernest layin' there in the gutter bleedin' ter death. I'd jus' die.'

'Well, at least yer'd go tergevver, wouldn't yer,' Florrie said with a wicked glint in her eye.

Maudie picked up her shopping basket and dusted the front of her coat with the palm of her hand. 'I must be orf 'ome, luv,' she said, quickly composing herself. 'I'll take yer advice. The next time Ernest tells me there's a meetin' on I'll insist 'e takes me wiv 'im.'

'Mum's the word though,' Florrie called out to her. 'Don't let anybody know what yer up to. Yer know 'ow some people would put the finger on yer if they got the troops out.'

Maudie hurried home thinking over what Florrie had said, and as she put the key in the door she heard voices.

'I'll canvass this side o' the turnin' an' you can do the ovver side. Now don't ferget it's one of each leaflet,' her husband was saying.

'Shall we all meet back here?' another voice asked.

'No yer bleedin' well don't,' Maudie shouted as she hurried into the parlour. 'I'm not 'avin' my 'ouse burnt down by bloody anarchists. Piss orf out the lot o' yer.'

Ernest looked crestfallen as he watched his comrades

disappointedly trooping out of the house, and he turned to Maudie. 'What's the matter, luv?' he asked quietly.

'Don't yer "luv" me,' she shouted. 'Yer no better than Percy the Painter. I'm warnin' yer, Ern, if yer don't mend yer ways I'm orf after Christmas.'

'If yer seein' ovver men then yer can get orf right now,' Ernest growled at her.

'Ooh! 'Ow could yer be so wicked as ter fink I'd be seein' ovver men,' she wailed.

'Well, who's this Percy the Painter?' he asked.

Chapter Fifteen

In January 1925 Annie McCafferty arrived back in Bermondsey, and without delay she called on Carrie Bradley. The Saturday morning was a busy one at the dining rooms, for there were two Danish freighters docked along the Bermondsey riverside and another ship was waiting to claim a berth. Carrie was busy serving teas and coffees while Fred sweated in the small back kitchen. Bessie Chandler was there too, helping Fred fry bacon and sausages on the wide stove. Annie looked in the steamy window and tapped gingerly on the glass to attract Carrie's attention, and immediately raised a squeal of delight from her.

'I only got in last night,' Annie said smiling as she was shown to the upstairs room. 'I thought I had to come round to see you all as soon as I could. How's Rachel? I really missed her.'

'She's fine,' Carrie replied. 'She's at me mum's this mornin'. You'll be surprised 'ow big she's got. She'll be six this November.'

Carried had left Bessie in charge and she sat back gratefully in the comfortable armchair and studied Annie closely. 'Yer look pale. Was it a tirin' journey?' she asked.

Annie nodded. 'It was a stormy crossing and I was sick most of the time, but it's nice to be back,' she said with a smile.

''Ow's yer mum?' Carrie asked, fearing what Annie was going to say.

'She died before Christmas,' Annie replied, showing little emotion. 'I was with her and she went peacefully, thank God.'

Carrie squeezed the Irish girl's arm in sympathy. 'I'm so sorry. At least yer found each ovver after all that time.'

Annie nodded slowly. 'I had to sort out my mother's things and say my goodbyes but there was nothing, no one, to keep me once I'd taken care of everything,' she said quietly.

'Well, it's lovely ter see yer again, Annie,' Carrie said, smiling fondly. ''Ave yer sorted yerself wiv any work yet?'

'I've been promised a job at the children's clinic they're setting up at the church,' the young woman replied, 'and they've given me my old room back too.'

'That's lovely. I s'pose we'll be seein' yer around 'ere then?' Carrie said keenly.

'Yes, I'll be visiting some of the local mums and their children,' Annie told her. She gazed down at her clasped hands for a few moments and then looked up again. 'How's Billy Sullivan?' she asked.

'Fine the last time I saw 'im,' Carrie answered. 'Billy's workin' now. It's a regular job wiv a builder. Mind yer, yer never know wiv Billy. 'E seems 'appy enough, although it's a bit 'ard fer 'im, what wiv that chest of 'is.'

Annie nodded, trying to appear unconcerned.

''E's always askin' if I've 'eard from yer,' Carrie told her, guessing the young woman's thoughts.

Footsteps on the stairs interrupted their conversation and Bessie Chandler looked into the room. Her face was flushed and she seemed agitated. 'Can yer spare a minute, Carrie?' she said a little breathlessly.

'What is it?' Carrie asked as she followed her out onto the landing.

'There's a woman just come in an' she wants ter know what yer've done wiv 'er bloke,' Bessie said in a low voice.

Carrie excused herself and hurried down the stairs to find the cafe in an uproar. Fred was standing behind the counter remonstrating with a large woman who looked extremely angry.

'Don't try ter cover up fer 'im,' she was ranting. 'Just tell 'im that when I get my 'ands on 'im 'e'll wish 'e'd never bin born.'

'What's the trouble?' Carrie asked.

'I know 'e's 'ere,' the buxom woman shouted at her. 'I saw the cart outside. I'd known that flea-bitten nag anywhere. Look, there it is over there.'

Carrie looked out to where the woman was pointing. 'What, that totter's cart?' she queried.

'That's the one. That's the scruffy whoreson's cart,' the woman raved.

By now everyone in the dining rooms was listening with broad grins on their faces.

'Try the river, missus. 'E might 'ave fell in,' one docker said.

''E ain't asleep in the back o' the cart, is 'e?' another quipped.

'Ain't that Broom'ead Smith's cart?' someone asked.

'I'll give 'im Broom'ead when I get me 'ands on the dirty ole goat,' the woman growled. ''E'll be Pin'ead when I'm finished wiv 'im.'

'Well, yer can see 'e's not 'ere, luv,' Carrie said, waving her hand towards her customers.

'Well, just you tell that scruffy git that I'm waitin' by the cart an' when 'e does show up I'm gonna cut 'is chopper off,' she threatened loudly, banging her fist down on the counter.

'What's yer bloke done, missus?' one of the older dockers asked, trying to look serious.

'What's 'e done? I'll tell yer what 'e's done,' the woman screamed. 'The dirty, no-good cowson's playin' around wiv anuvver woman, that's what 'e's done.'

Carrie tried to keep a straight face as the woman stormed out of the cafe and marched across to the cart which was parked on the other side of the narrow lane.

''Ave any of yer seen Broom'ead?' she asked.

The men were all laughing and pointing to one of the bench seats. Carrie looked over and saw the totter's ginger hair sticking out from under the table. Broomhead looked frightened as he poked his head out.

'Don't tell 'er I'm 'ere, fer Gawdsake,' he pleaded. 'She'll skin me alive!'

Carrie laughed aloud as he ducked down under the table again. 'Well, yer can't stop there fer ever,' she said. 'We close at 'alf past-twelve.'

'Ain't yer got a back door?' the muffled voice said from under the table.

Fred was getting angry. 'No, we ain't. Yer'll 'ave ter go in a minute, whatever,' he told him. 'I don't want this place gettin' a bad name.'

'Blimey, guv, give us a chance,' the muffled voice pleaded. 'Yer don't know the woman. She's as mad as a March 'are. She's got a meat cleaver under that apron. She'll cut me up if she gets at me.'

'Well, that's none o' my concern,' Fred said. 'Yer should be'ave yerself.'

'I ain't done nuffink wrong. She's got the wrong end o' the stick,' Broomhead moaned.

Carrie turned to her husband. 'Can't we do some-fink, Fred?' she appealed to him.

'What about if we dress 'im up as a woman?' one of the dockers suggested.

'I don't care what yer do as long as yer get me away

216

from that bloody maniac,' Broomhead groaned.

Carrie stroked her chin thoughtfully. 'My clothes won't fit 'im,' she remarked.

'What about if I fit 'im up wiv one o' yer old table-cloths?' Bessie suggested. 'We could stick a scarf round 'is 'ead as well.'

Fred just wanted to get the totter out of the cafe despite the man's pleading but Carrie rebuked him. 'C'mon, Fred, where's yer sense o' humour? We can't let that ole cow cut 'im up, can we?'

'I reckon we ought ter call the police. Let them sort it out,' he said offhandedly.

'She'd just as soon put the knife frew the copper by the look of 'er,' Carrie replied. 'All right, Bessie, see what yer can do wiv 'im.'

It was twelve noon when Broomhead Smith reappeared from the back room to the loud laughs of the customers.

'Is she still out there?' he said in a frightened voice.

'Yeah, she's still there. She's bin talkin' ter the 'orse fer the past 'alf hour,' one of the dockers told him.

Broomhead looked resplendent in his flowered table-coth with matching headscarf. His boots were hidden under the makeshift dress which touched the floor and he carried a basket which Carrie had meant to throw out long ago. Bessie had added a little self-raising flour to his stubble and placed a tattered blanket that was used as a draught mat around his broad shoulders.

'Got time fer a kiss, luv?' one man called out.

'Where d'yer get that dress, gel?' another piped in.

'Out yer go, lovely,' the first man said, chuckling at Broomhead's embarrassment.

'I can't. She'll know it's me,' the totter groaned.

Carrie looked at the older docker who was winking saucily at Broomhead. 'Let 'im 'old on ter yer arm, Chas,' she said.

'Bloody 'ell, Carrie, do me a favour,' the man protested.

'Go on, Chas, let 'er 'old yer arm,' the men began to shout in chorus.

As the couple made for the door the men joined together in singing, 'We've bin tergevver now fer forty years, an' it don't seem a day too much . . .'

Carrie and Bessie stood laughing until tears fell down their cheeks and one of the dockers came up to Bessie and patted her on the back. 'Yer done a good job there, Bess,' he said.

Bessie smiled happily. It was not very often that any of the customers said anything complimentary to her and she stuck out her chest as she walked back behind the counter.

Once outside, Chas the docker walked in a very dignified manner along the lane while Broomhead held on to his arm, his fearful eyes darting furtively in the direction of his horse-and-cart.

'Keep lookin' in front of yer, yer soppy git,' the docker muttered, as they strolled along.

The elaborate ploy was doomed to fail, for no one had taken into consideration the totter's faithful horse. It had been standing around for quite a while and when it picked up the scent of the stable from Broomhead's hidden boots it immediately decided to follow on. The totter heard the steady clip-clop behind him and he groaned aloud. 'Stay there, yer bloody flea-bag,' he grunted through clenched teeth.

Alice Johnson had watched the horse set off and she suddenly realised that the strange-looking couple were even stranger than she had first thought. She spotted one of Broomhead's boots showing beneath the dress he was wearing and with a roar she reached under her apron and brought out a large meat cleaver, waving it in the air as she set off after them. Broomhead suddenly saw her giving chase and he broke away from the docker and made off at full speed along the cobbled lane. Chas was grinning as the raving woman ran past him, then he decided perhaps it might be safer in the dining rooms in case she came back to take out her wrath on him.

One hour later a very exhausted totter sat down in his shed and stared at the horse which had nearly caused him to meet an untimely end.

'I warned yer, didn't I?' he told the animal. 'I'm just about fed up wiv yer. I've a good mind ter turn yer inter glue. The only trouble is, the knackers' yard'll take one look at yer an' pay me ter take yer away. Still, it all worked out in the end. It's a good job that copper showed up when 'e did. I don't fink 'e believed me when I told 'im I was bein' chased by a mad woman carryin' a carvin' knife. Alice must 'ave seen the copper an' 'opped it orf 'ome. I wonder why 'e wanted me particulars though. I 'ope I don't 'ear no more from 'im. I must remember not ter go near that cafe again. Alice is sure ter keep 'er eye on the place. I wouldn't mind if I'd done anyfink wrong,' he rambled on. 'She's so jealous. I was only chattin' ter the woman, you know that,' he reminded his horse. 'Trouble wiv Alice is, she wants me ter spend all the bloody day at 'er place. I wouldn't mind if there wasn't much business about an' I could trust yer ter stay put, but I can't, can I? That reminds me, I mus' get that brake chain fixed.'

The horse watched its owner for a while then appeared to lose interest, closing its eyes and leaning against the stall. Broomhead began to tidy up the bits and pieces, whistling tunelessly to himself, when suddenly he looked up and saw Alice Johnson standing in the doorway, and there was a knife in her hand.

The building work started on time at the dining rooms

in Cotton Lane and Carrie made sure that the men were kept supplied with mugs of tea. The builders' first job was to board up the front of the empty house, and when that was done the work began in earnest. The roof was pulled down and the interior knocked out until all that was left was the shell of the house. Soon the new roof timbers were in place and the rafters were covered firstly with slatting and then grey slates. The walls were plastered, the inside was fitted out with a large sink and a place was reserved for a large catering gas stove. Gas lighting was installed, cupboards were fitted, and a new chopping block was added. Then on the last Sunday in February the adjoining wall to the dining rooms was attacked with heavy hammers.

Carrie inspected the work in progress and was pleased by what she saw. When it was finished Fred would have a large kitchen and the counter would be moved back to make room for more seating. There was still much to do but by the end of March the work should be finished, she thought. Fred had been anxious at first but when he saw what had been done and realised just what the new, improved kitchen would mean to him he began to forget his earlier worries.

All through the work the dining rooms remained open and the union men still held their meetings in the back room. Billy Sullivan looked in from time to time, adding his own suggestions and criticisms now that he considered himself to be a professional builder, but there was really another reason for his visits. He had heard from Danny that Annie McCafferty was back in Bermondsey and was eager to meet her once more.

'She pops in now an' again, Billy, but I can't tell yer when,' Carrie told him. 'She's very busy at the clinic. Why don't yer let me talk ter the gel? I could introduce yer formally an' the rest is up ter you.'

Billy shook his head. 'A man's got 'is pride. If I allow

yer ter do that she'll fink I ain't got the nerve to ask 'er out,' he told her.

'But yer might be ages before yer bump inter the gel,' Carrie pointed out.

Billy had decided that merely waiting until he met the young woman by chance was not an ideal prospect and felt that urgent action was necessary. It would mean going to see her, but he realised that a man would never go to the clinic unless he had a very good reason. He had thought of waiting outside the clinic but there again it was difficult. A man would soon be arrested for loitering and there would be some explaining to do. He would talk it over with Danny on Friday night, he decided. There were other things he had to talk about too, now that he was in regular work.

Annie McCafferty had settled down in her new job at the children's clinic and she was grateful for the fact that she was kept very busy. There was little time to think about those last few months of her mother's life when the poor woman suffered so, and that sad time after the funeral when there were lots of papers to go through and many letters to write. Now she could build a future for herself in Bermondsey. What would it hold for her? Annie wondered. Maybe she would meet Billy Sullivan on her travels and he might consider asking her to walk out with him. He was certainly a handsome young man with a very friendly nature. Carrie had said that Billy had a regular job now, and that he had asked after her often. Annie felt her heart beat faster as she thought about the young man. Her life had been very sheltered and devoid of male company. It would be very nice to have a young man of her own, she thought. Maybe Billy would take her to the rose gardens in Southwark Park, and maybe, just maybe, he would steal a kiss and tell her how pretty she was.

But he wouldn't, Annie sighed, staring at herself in the dressing-table mirror. She was too thin, too plain, for the likes of Billy Sullivan. He wouldn't be interested in her, she told herself. He had only asked after her out of good manners. Maybe if she cut her hair or changed it so that she didn't look so severe she just might ask her to walk out with him . . . The way she looked now would probably frighten off any young eligible bachelor, she had to admit.

On Friday evening Billy sat with his long-time friend Danny in the public bar of the Kings Arms, and once again he broached the subject he had held close to his heart for a long time.

'I reckon I'll never get enough money tergevver to even rent a place, Danny, but I've 'ad a word wiv Farver Murphy an' 'e reckons I should write ter the church people. 'E said if I put me ideas down on paper 'e'll send a letter as well an' it jus' might work. What 'ave I got ter lose?'

Danny sipped his pint thoughtfully. 'Carrie was tellin' me that bit o' land next ter the cafe is up fer sale. It was a pity yer never managed ter rent it. That was a good spot fer a gym.'

Billy nodded. 'I tried ter raise the money but nobody would cough up. It was a pity. I 'ad a few lads lined up who were gonna 'elp do the work, as yer know.'

Danny sat watching the comings and goings in the pub as he listened to his old friend expounding his dream and the germ of an idea started to form in his head. He would talk with his father, he decided. He might be able to give him the information he needed.

''Ow's the young lady?' Billy asked as he put down his glass and wiped the froth from his lips with the back of his hand.

'Iris is fine. We're lookin' ter get married next year,' Danny told him.

'I was finkin' o' settlin' down meself soon,' Billy remarked, toying self-consciously with his beer glass.

Danny smiled and shook his head slowly. 'I've 'eard that often enough, Billy,' he replied. 'I reckon you'll be sayin' that when yer walkin' frew the park wiv yer walkin' stick.'

'Don't yer be so sure,' Billy countered quickly. 'I'm finkin' of askin' Annie McCafferty ter walk out wiv me.'

'Yer could 'ave bin doin' that now if yer'd listened ter Carrie. She could 'ave made the right introductions,' Danny remarked.

'I'm serious, Danny. I'm finkin' o' goin' over ter the clinic where Annie works an' askin' 'er.'

'That's gonna be a bit difficult, ain't it?' Danny queried. 'Yer'll 'ave ter tell 'em yer left the baby be'ind an' yer want some advice.'

Billy took another sip from his pint of porter and then suddenly brought his fist down on the table. 'Yer've give me an idea,' he said with a sly glint in his eye.

Danny had listened to Billy's schemes often enough and he felt that more than a few of them had verged on the crazy. 'What yer got in that mind of yours?' he asked grinning.

Billy shook his head, the ghost of a smile showing in the corner of his mouth. 'Just an idea. I gotta fink about it though,' he replied.

The public bar had become packed on that Friday evening and the regular customers chatted together in small groups or sat at the iron tables, one or two drinking alone. Florrie Axford was in the company of Maisie Dougall and Maggie Jones, while Harold Temple sat on his own staring into his full glass of beer, his unlit pipe held in his hand. In one corner a couple sat at a table and chatted together, the man nodding his head often as the woman seemed to be labouring a point.

'Well, it's a good fing yer was talkin' ter yerself that day, Bill, or yer'd be laid out on a slab by now,' Alice Johnson told him. 'I was ready ter swing fer yer. In fact I 'ad that carver all ready ter finish yer. Just remember what I said. If I ever catch yer playin' around, yer'll be done for.'

Broomhead nodded. He had spent his whole life avoiding the very situation he now found himself in and he was not feeling too pleased. It had been very difficult calming her down that day in the shed, he recalled with a shudder. At first she had waved the knife around and made threatening gestures with it, and only after much abject pleading had she finally laid down her weapon. Broomhead had realised that he was very lucky not to end up mutilated, and in his gratitude he had asked Alice to take the next Friday evening off from her bar-maid duties and go to the Kings Arms with him. It had become a regular arrangement for the last couple of months and still he had not managed to worm his way back into her bed. Alice had been very firm about that and she was constantly reminding him that there were certain things he would have to agree to if he was going to become her lover again.

He had complied, and now he called in on her for a cup of tea every evening before returning home, which was difficult for him at times. He had to get his hair cut regularly and keep his boots clean, and he had been required to buy himself a new trilby to replace his old faithful one. He had had to promise Alice too that he would make sure his horse was well fed and always properly groomed. Broomhead had kept his word, and he took exception to her accusing him of starving the nag. He always made sure it got its oats – which was more than could be said for him – but it was a waste of time using the curry-comb and brush on that bag of bones, he grumbled to himself.

All week Broomhead had been agonising over what he should do regarding Alice. Every Friday night he had to listen while she reminded him about how near he had come to a bad end that day in the shed, and he had come to the conclusion that unfortunately the woman he had lost his freedom to was completely mad and had no intention of ever letting him into her bedroom again. Enough was enough, he told himself, and as he sat nodding dutifully to her in the public bar of the Kings Arms his mind was racing. He would get rid of her once and for all, he vowed. He had had to bend to her will after she held the carver over his head but his time would come, surely it must. There could be an accident. He could run her over if he ever saw her in the street, but then his horse would not go fast enough to run anyone over. No, he would have to think of something else. He could rake out his old trilby, forget to clean his boots and let his hair grow long again, but that would only appear as though he wasn't interested in her anymore, which would mean having to watch his back all the time in case she came at him with the cleaver.

'I'll 'ave the same again,' Alice said, interrupting his thoughts as she pushed her empty glass towards him.

Broomhead dutifully walked over to the counter, and as he stood waiting to be served he became aware that he was being stared at.

'I thought I reco'nised yer. Don't yer remember me?'

Broomhead looked down at the diminutive character wearing a red scarf and a check cap and shook his head. 'Nah, I don't,' he replied.

The man gave him a toothless grin and rolled his

225

shoulders. 'I'm Bert Gibson. Yer mus' remember me,' he persisted.

'Sorry, I don't,' the totter said irritably.

'Yer remember. Yer took our ole pianer away. I 'elped yer out wiv it. Bloody glad ter get rid of it, ter tell yer the trufe. Never bin played since our Rene got married. She never comes round now. I don't fink that whoreson of an 'usband likes 'er comin' round ter see us. I dunno what we done ter make 'im keep 'er away, I'm sure I don't.'

Broomhead tried desperately to catch the barman's eye, fearing that he had become fair game for all the mentally unbalanced people in the area.

'Rene's a lovely gel, but she won't stand up fer 'erself,' the little character went on. 'She should tell 'im straight she's entitled ter see 'er family once in a while. After all, it ain't askin' too much, is it?'

'What ain't?' Broomhead asked, wishing the barman would look his way.

The little man rolled his shoulders and poked out his chin as though he was being slowly strangled by the tightly knotted scarf around his scrawny neck. 'Why, 'er tellin' 'im straight,' he said. 'Yer gotta stand up fer yerself or yer'll be put on. That's my motto. Do as yer done by. Stick up fer yerself. Don't let 'em treat yer like a doormat. I wouldn't stan' fer it. That's bloody right.'

Broomhead finally caught the barman's eye and as he gave his order a big woman walked up to the counter and prodded the little man.

'Oi, you, are yer gonna stan' talkin' all night? I'm still waitin' fer me drink. You was 'ere before 'im,' she said in a loud voice, pointing towards Broomhead.

'Sorry, dear. This is the man who took our pianer,' he answered meekly.

'What d'yer want me ter do, ask fer it back?' the

226

woman said sharply, looking the totter up and down.

'Yer should 'ave kept yer pianer an' got rid of 'er,' Broomhead whispered to the little character as he picked up the glasses and walked away from the counter.

In another corner of the public bar Maudie Mycroft sat with her husband Ernest, feeling happier than she had done for some time. He had promised her he would seriously consider leaving the British Communist Party if she would cut down her church commitments. It was a fair bargain, she thought. She had been very busy at the church functions of late, and now that there was another new vicar coming soon she felt it was time to reconsider her position. The Monday meetings were very nice. There was always something going on, and the tea and biscuits afterwards gave her the chance to chat with everyone there. Tuesdays could be cut out though. The sewing circle seemed obsessed with making patchwork quilts and she had four of them already. But then if she cut out Tuesdays she would not get the opportunity to meet Mrs Duckworth and that nice Miss Henshaw from Carter Street. Wednesday could be considered. There was only the church fund committee. The only problem there was that they might think she did not care what happened to the establishment if she didn't go along. What about Thursday? Maudie asked herself. No, she couldn't give up choir practice. Besides, the vicar always came along on Thursday evenings and conducted prayers. Friday was her day off and Sunday was for worship so that left only Saturday. But how could she face the rest of the women if she did not help them with the jumble sales and the other fund-raising events they organised?

Maudie suddenly felt less happy but Ernest was secretly smiling to himself as he sat beside her drinking his pint of ale. There was as much chance of Maudie

227

giving up her church commitments as there was of him getting his old friend Hymie Goldberg to eat a bacon sandwich. No, it was a good bargain, he thought.

Time was called and as the customers trooped out of the pub Broomhead Smith was feeling courageous. The drinks had taken effect and he had been angered by the big woman's nagging at her inoffensive little husband. Alice had been nagging at him all evening too and he had suddenly lost all desire to see her bedroom anyway. He had stood her domineering ways for weeks now and it was time he stood up for himself, he thought as she took his arm outside the pub.

'I was talkin' ter that little feller at the counter, Alice. Did yer see 'im?' he asked.

'Yeah, that was Tommy Blackwell. 'E's a bit of a cowson, by all accounts,' she replied. 'Tommy's ole woman's frightened ter move wivout 'is say-so. Bloody size of 'er an' all. Mind yer though, 'e's bin a bit of a rogue in 'is time. 'E used ter do a bit o' boxin', an' I 'eard 'e done time fer nickin' from the docks. Size ain't everyfing.'

Broomhead grunted his reply as they walked along Page Street. He was preparing himself for a heart-to-heart talk. He would merely say that he was going to end their relationship, such as it was, and if she didn't like it . . . well, she could do her worst. He would have to remind her first though, that the policeman who stopped him when he was running away from her that Saturday had asked him for her name and address, and she should take that into consideration if she decided to come looking for him with a carving knife.

'I was talkin' ter Mrs Knight while yer was up the counter,' Alice said suddenly. 'She was sayin' one of the women in 'er turnin' got 'er froat cut last night. 'Er ole man done it. She said they ain't caught 'im yet, so the local bobby told 'er. Went stark ravin' mad 'e did.

The copper told 'er ter make sure she puts the bolt on 'er door at night in case 'e comes back an' decides ter cut ovver women up.'

Broomhead mumbled a reply, still preoccupied with what he was going to say, and as they reached Alice's door he took a deep breath. 'Look, luv,' he began, 'I know yer not one ter get upset very easy but I'm worried about fings. I fink we should seriously consider what's bin 'appenin' an' try ter sort fings out.'

Alice smiled at him, the first time she had smiled in that fashion for weeks, he noted.

'Bill Smith, yer a very nice man. Fancy yer finkin' about me bein' worried by that maniac at large. C'mon,' she said, taking him by the arm and almost dragging him through the front door.

Broomhead sighed as he allowed himself to be pushed into her cosy parlour. The fire was burning low in the grate and the curtains were tightly drawn against the chilly night. Oh, well. There's another day tomorrow, he told himself.

Chapter Sixteen

Carrie had been preoccupied with the building work going on at the dining rooms, and serving behind the counter, ordering supplies, keeping the books in order and caring for her husband and Rachel left her little time for anything else, but occasionally she would think about Annie McCafferty and wonder how she was getting on at the clinic. Since that one visit Annie had not put in an appearance, and Carrie wondered if the young Irishwoman had met up with Billy Sullivan. She had been interested enough to ask about him and Carrie felt that after the sad time she must have experienced over in Dublin Annie deserved to find some happiness. Billy was a good young man, and he had once shown an interest in Carrie, though that was all in the past. She had considered him forward then and only interested in her body, but she was old enough now to realise that he was probably just like all other young men finding their feet. Billy had only walked out with her on that one occasion and he had tried his luck as they lingered near the river, she remembered, smiling to herself. He had been embarrassed by her angry reaction as they walked back home, but although he had never asked her out again after that they had remained friends.

Carrie's busy life was making her feel tired and jaded, and she found herself snapping at her husband for the least little thing. Fred was turned fifty now and his hair had gone completely grey. He had always been given to nodding off at the fireside for half an hour or so after a busy day but lately he had been sleeping for the best part of the evening and then going to bed early. Carrie was left alone with her thoughts most evenings and after the chores were done she would sit by the fire with a cup of tea and think about where her life was going. She was nearing her thirty-fourth birthday and already she could see the odd line or two showing around her eyes when she studied her face in the mirror. She had given up worrying about becoming pregnant again, however. Fred was very rarely awake when she got into bed and on the odd occasion he did show any interest in her as a woman he would fail to satisfy her needs. She had fretted over her failure to excite and arouse him at first, but all the hard work and the worry of the business had taken their toll and left her feeling tired and empty.

Sometimes she would sit remembering her first lover, Tommy Allen, who had now married and become a father. Sometimes she would sit staring into the glowing coals and fantasise. Don Jacobs, the middle-aged dockers' leader, was always very talkative and forthcoming with her. He was a handsome man with considerable charm, and he had parted from his wife through her infidelity, so word had it. Fred had often become moody and surly through her spending time in Don's company when he came into the cafe, and he suspected that the union leader was eager to get her into his bed. Carrie had rowed with Fred over his jealousy, but on her lonely nights she wondered if there was an element of truth in what he feared, and she wondered what it would be like to have Don Jacobs as a lover.

Billy Sullivan had made up his mind that he was going

to settle down and he told his mother as much over the tea table. 'Ma, I'm gonna get married,' he suddenly announced.

Sadie nodded and carried on re-sealing the margarine. Daniel her husband looked over his evening paper and wondered whether Billy had gone out of his mind, while Billy's younger brother Joe decided that he definitely had. 'Yer gotta get yerself a woman first, yer silly git,' he said quickly.

Sadie picked up the bread knife and pointed it at Joe in a threatening manner. 'What 'ave I told yer about blasphemin' round the food table?' she growled at him.

'Carrie Tanner reckons I should get married,' Billy went on regardless. 'I could 'ave married 'er once. She liked me enough ter marry me but I was too interested in me boxin'.'

'I reckon it was the worst day's work you ever done lettin' 'er go,' Sadie remarked. 'That gel's made that cafe into a really good business. 'Er ole man wasn't doin' all that well before she took it over. Nellie Tanner was tellin' me 'er Carrie's got a good 'ead on 'er shoulders when it comes ter business matters.'

'Well, anyway, I'm gettin' married,' Billy said again.

'Anybody in mind?' Sadie asked.

'It ain't Dirty Dora from Bacon Buildin's, is it?' Joe asked, feigning horror.

'I've warned you,' Sadie hissed.

Joe put up his hands. 'P'raps one of us never explained fings properly ter Billy,' he grinned, looking over at his father.

Daniel was never alive to a conversation when he was reading his evening paper and he jumped when Sadie shouted at him. 'Oi, Dan! Are yer gonna sit there wivout sayin' anyfing?'

'What d'yer want me ter do, book the church 'all?' he growled.

'Well, I'm definitely gettin' married,' Billy said. 'I'm

gonna ask Annie McCafferty out soon as I can.'

'Sounds like a good Irish Catholic name,' his father remarked, feeling he should at least try to show some interest.

'S'posin' she don't want ter go out wiv yer,' Joe said, holding his tea mug up to his lips.

'I'm gonna marry that gel one day,' Billy informed them.

'Well, yer've got a job at least,' Sadie said, beginning to feel that perhaps her eldest son was being serious for a change.

'I'm gonna see 'er termorrer an' I'm gonna ask 'er out,' he said firmly. 'I'm jus' tellin' yer now so yer'll all know.'

''Ow can yer see 'er if yer workin'?' Sadie asked.

'Well, we've got a job on near the church where Annie works an' I'm gonna slip away fer 'alf an hour ter see 'er,' he explained.

'She's not a sister, is she?' Joe asked.

'Annie works in the children's clinic at the church. She's one o' those welfare nurses who look after the kids,' he told them.

'Well, I wish yer luck, son,' Sadie said fondly.

'Yeah, good luck,' Joe repeated, raising his eyes to the ceiling.

'Yeah, good luck,' Daniel mumbled, scanning the winners of the Ascot race meeting.

'Is my ovver shirt ready fer termorrer, Ma?' Billy asked.

'I've gotta put a patch in it,' Sadie replied, and seeing his disappointment added quickly, 'Don't worry, I'll do it before I go ter bed.'

Sadie was as good as her word and next morning Billy went off to work whistling. It was late morning when he slipped away from the site and crossed the road to the church. He found the clinic entrance, and taking a deep breath he walked in to the sound of babies wailing.

'Yes?'

Billy stared at the stern-looking nursing sister. 'I've, er, I've come about me baby,' he said hesitantly.

'Yes?' the sister said again in a deep voice, making Billy feel nervous.

'Well, yer see, it's like this,' he began. 'It's not my baby really, but it belongs to a very good friend o' mine an' she's too scared ter come 'erself.'

'You can tell your friend that there's nothing to be frightened of here, young man,' the sister replied.

'Yeah, but the problem is, if she brought the baby 'ere 'er 'usband would knock 'er about,' Billy told her.

'Oh, I see,' she said, clasping her hands together. 'Is the baby ill?'

'Not really. It's the farvver that's ill,' Billy explained, after the sudden urge to laugh.

'Then he should see his doctor, surely,' the sister replied.

'The trouble is, 'e's a bit sick up 'ere,' Billy said, pointing to his head, 'an' it's the baby that's sufferin'.'

'Are we talking about malnutrition, or is it ill-treatment, or both?' she asked.

'Nah, it's not that. The baby won't stop cryin' an' its ole man keeps sayin' 'e's gonna chuck it out o' the winder one o' these days.'

'I see,' the sister replied, taking up a notepad. 'Give me the address of your very good friend and I'll get one of our nurses to call around.'

'Well, it's a bit tricky, yer see,' Billy said, beginning to feel more confident. 'If my friend's ole man finds out I've come ter see yer it'll be me 'e chucks out o' the winder.'

'This friend of yours seems to be married to a very violent man,' the sister remarked, putting down her pen. 'Look, Mr – er . . .'

'Smedley. Fred Smedley,' he said quickly.

'Well, look, Mr Smedley. Unless you give me your friend's address there's little we can do to help. You'll be fully protected. We never give the source of our information in cases like this.'

Billy scratched his head in a show of uncertainty. 'I understand that,' he said nodding, 'but yer see I'm frightened fer the poor lady that 'as ter go round ter see 'im. The baby's farvver could quite easily attack 'er, an' I'd blame meself.'

The nursing sister was beginning to lose her patience. 'Well, I think you've got to make your mind up what you intend to do if you want to help this friend of yours,' she said sharply. 'You come in here to report a case of neglect and then waste my time by refusing to give me the necessary details. I suggest that either you give us the address or you leave. Am I making myself clear, Mr Smedley?'

Billy nodded sheepishly. 'I was wonderin' if I could 'ave a word wiv the welfare lady who comes round our way. Then I could arrange wiv 'er the best time ter call. I could get the 'usband out the way while she talks ter the baby's muvver. That way nobody would get 'urt.'

'This is most unusual,' the sister replied.

'P'raps it is but it's the best I can do,' Billy told her with an appealing look on his face.

'Well, at least tell me the name of the street,' she urged.

'Page Street,' he replied.

'Wait here a minute and I'll see if the nurse is in the building,' the sister informed him sternly.

Billy looked at the health posters around the cream-coloured room and glanced up at the high window. He could smell disinfectant and it reminded him of the room he was taken to when he received a badly gashed eyebrow while boxing and had to have it stitched.

It was not long before the sister returned and Billy's face dropped as he saw with her a huge woman in a navy blue uniform coat which was buttoned up to the neck. She was carrying a black handbag in her gloved hands and on her head there was a wide hat with a badge at the front.

'This is Nurse Carmody. She'll talk to you,' the sister said, going back to sit at her desk.

'Come along with me, young man,' the nurse ordered him in a booming voice, leading the way into a side room.

There were two chairs beside a small table and Nurse Carmody motioned for him to sit down. 'Sister Jones has put me in the picture. Now let me get this straight,' she said loudly in an official voice. 'You want me to play hide-and-seek while you lure the father out of the house and then I can talk to the baby's mother. Am I right?'

Billy's mind was racing. His little scheme had backfired on him and he had to think of another way to see Annie McCafferty. 'Yeah, that's right, nurse. This bloke's a real violent man,' he told her, his eyes opening wide to make the point. ''E got drunk one night an' it took four coppers ter put 'im in the Black Maria.'

The nurse looked unimpressed. 'I think I should have a word with this animal myself,' she said, cracking her knuckles and glaring at him. 'That sort doesn't intimidate me, young man.'

Billy believed her and he nodded. 'I reckon you'd be able to 'andle 'im, luv, but yer see it's the muvver I'm concerned about,' he said, looking worried. 'After yer'd gone 'e'd set about 'er.'

'Not when I'd finished with him, he wouldn't,' the

huge nurse bellowed at him. 'I'd put the fear of God into the man, and if he laid a finger on that poor wife of his I'd have him arrested and put into prison, you can be sure.'

'All right, nurse. I'll leave it ter you,' Billy said, crossing his fingers under the table. 'The address is 52 Bacon Buildin's, Bacon Street, an' the name is Mrs Brown. By the way, I saw one o' your nurses in Bacon Street the ovver day. I fink she was from 'ere. She was wearin' the same uniform as you, but she was only small. I'm glad it's not 'er that's got ter face Mr Brown.'

'That would be Nurse McCafferty. She's very good, I believe,' the nurse replied.

'Is Nurse McCafferty in 'ere now?' Billy asked casually.

'Why do you ask?'

'Well, ter be honest I was talkin' ter Mrs Green the ovver day about what was goin' on. She lives next door ter Mrs Brown, yer see, an' jus' then Nurse McCafferty walked by and said 'ello, an' she asked 'ow Mrs Green's leg was. Mrs Green told me she was from the church clinic an' that's where I should go. Anyway, when I made me mind up ter come I told Mrs Green an' she said if I see the nurse I was ter tell 'er that 'er leg's much better.'

Nurse Carmody gave him a quizzical look. 'Nurse McCafferty is off today but I'll give her the message. Now if you'll excuse me I must get going. Thank you for calling, and rest assured, Mr Smedley, we'll get this problem sorted out.'

Billy walked out of the welfare centre feeling angry that things had not worked out the way he wanted. He also found himself wondering what the man in number 52 Bacon Buildings was like and what he would do when faced with that mountain of a woman.

*

238

It was nearing five o'clock, and in the small office in Druid Street Joe Maitland sat talking with William Tanner. Joe looked worried.

'I found it 'ard ter believe when I first 'eard o' what was goin' on around 'ere, Will,' he was saying, 'but the word is that fings are gonna get out of 'and unless it's stopped. George Galloway 'as bin talkin' wiv 'is people an' it seems they've all bin approached. There's money bin promised an' from what I can make out Galloway's crowd are dead against it.'

William scratched his head vigorously. 'I don't understand all this, Joe,' he confessed. 'Yer say that the bloke who put my lights out an' burnt yer ware'ouse down was this Gerry Macedo an' 'e was a pal o' Galloway's. Now George is up against 'im an' 'e's tryin' ter get 'is little plan scotched?'

Joe smiled briefly. 'A few o' the lads I do business wiv come from the East End. They know all about Gerry Macedo. The man's got it sewn up over the water an' now 'e's after gettin' established over this side. 'E's got a lot o' villains be'ind 'im an' they're inter gamblin' an' prostitution, as well as the protection business. You name it, they do it. Macedo wasn't above tryin' ter put me out o' business eivver, when the money was put up by a few friends o' the people I 'elped put away. I don't know if they'll be satisfied wiv what 'appened or if they'll 'ave anuvver go at me, that's why we've gotta watch points. From what I can gavver, Macedo put 'is personal stamp on the ware'ouse fire to announce 'is presence. That's the way the man's mind works.'

'It seems strange 'im bein' there 'imself,' William said. 'I could pick 'im out in a line-up if the law pulled 'im.'

'That's why I told yer not ter say anyfing ter the police before I asked around,' Joe told him. 'Your life

239

wouldn't 'ave bin worth a brass farthin' if yer'd agreed ter testify in court. Wivvout your evidence Macedo would walk free. Besides, they left yer there ter die when they set light ter the place, an' it was in the papers about yer lucky escape. So yer not out o' the woods yet, by any means.'

'Fanks fer tellin' me,' William said, smiling mirthlessly.

'I shouldn't worry. I don't fink they'll try ter get at yer as long as yer keep quiet. Anyway, as I was sayin', Gerry Macedo an' 'is crowd can see there's nuffink like their set-up over 'ere. It's just small mobs runnin' their own areas. There's no ambition or drive. Now wiv Macedo we're talkin' about an educated man who can deal wiv the big businessmen on their own level. What 'e's plannin' is a big nightclub in Rovver'ithe. It'll be all glossy an' respectable up front, an' it'll attract people from all over London. Be'ind the scenes though there'll be nuffink but graft an' corruption. Believe me, Will, if Macedo's allowed ter get established over this side o' the water 'e'll be runnin' this area like a king. 'E'll 'ave everybody in 'is pockets, an' that includes the crooked coppers. Jus' fink what that means. Yer'll eivver trade wiv Macedo's people or yer'll go out o' business. All the transport contracts an' dock work'll be controlled by 'is crowd an' the unions are gonna be up against the wall. If they stand out on the cobbles they're gonna get picked orf. The strike leaders'll get seen to an' the men'll starve, or go back wiv their tails between their legs.'

'It seems 'ard ter believe,' William said, shaking his head slowly. 'Surely the businessmen who are backin' Gerry Macedo can see that.'

'They're not all honest traders,' Joe Maitland replied with a cynical grin. 'They see it as a way o' makin' a fortune. I've bin given names an' yer'd be surprised if yer knew who some of 'em were. Fer your safety it's just as well yer don't know. One fing though – George Galloway ain't one of 'em. From what I've bin told 'e's rantin' an' ravin' about anybody tellin' 'im what 'e can do an' can't do, 'specially somebody from over the water.'

William Tanner smiled. 'I've got no time fer the man after what 'appened ter me, but I gotta admire 'is pluck. I only 'ope 'e knows what 'e's doin'.'

'I fink 'e knows what 'e's doin', Will, but I'm not so sure about that son of 'is,' Joe remarked. 'Yer said ter me Frank Galloway could turn out worse than the ole man, an' maybe yer'll be proved right. 'E's bin seen in Macedo's East End club mixin' wiv a lot o' nasty people.'

'So what's the answer?' William asked, taking out his cigarette pouch.

'Well, fer the time bein' there'll be a lot o' chin-waggin' goin' on. Galloway is gonna pull as many people as 'e can be'ind 'im, an' I don't underestimate 'im. The ole boy's bin around fer a few years an' 'e's got a lot o' sway. As fer Gerry Macedo, 'e's gonna do the same, except 'e'll be usin' a different tack. 'E'll put a few frighteners in wherever 'e can get away wiv it. My big fear is that Galloway won't be able ter muster enough support, an' then those waverers are gonna fall in wiv the East End mob.'

William was quiet for a few moments while he rolled a cigarette, then he looked up at Maitland. 'Was that Macedo's crowd who smashed up my Carrie's cafe?' he asked.

Joe nodded. 'Yeah. Word is that Frank Galloway coaxed 'is farvver inter bringin' 'im in when they couldn't bribe the new union men. Galloway 'ad the old lot in 'is pocket by all accounts. Macedo was responsible fer the attack on Don Jacobs as well, but

241

they come unstuck there. I would fink George Galloway is regrettin' ever knowin' that villain. They were
pals once, when they did the fights tergevver.'

William had gone quiet, but Joe could see him clen-
ching his teeth as he stared down at his smouldering
cigarette.

'I wasn't gonna tell yer that much, Will, but there's
nuffink yer can do about it,' he told him. 'Macedo an'
Galloway are both gonna get their comeuppance over
this, you wait an' see.'

William smiled bitterly. 'Galloway's managed to
avoid the reckonin' before,' he said quietly. 'What
about you, are you gonna get involved?'

Joe nodded. 'I've got to. I can't sit on the fence.
Anybody in my position who tries ter stay neutral is
gonna get crushed between the two sides. I'm goin' ter
see a few friends ternight an' then we're meetin' up wiv
Galloway an' some of 'is pals. So yer better wish me
luck, Will,' he said with a smile of resignation.

Billy Sullivan was deep in thought as he walked home
through the backstreets and suddenly he almost col-
lided with a large policeman who had turned the
corner.

'Well, if it ain't young Sullivan,' the policeman said,
leering at him. 'What yer bin up to?'

'I'm jus' goin' 'ome from work,' Billy replied, cursing his luck at finally coming face-to-face with PC
Copeland again.

'Yer mean ter tell me yer got a job? Now who'd be
silly enough ter give a no-good whoreson like you a
job?' the policeman jeered.

Billy took a deep breath. 'I ain't seen yer about
lately,' he said with forced bravado.

'I'm like a bad penny. I keep turnin' up,' the policeman said with a sneering smile. 'I asked fer this beat

again. I like this area, an' I'm familiar wiv all the little toe-rags. Besides, people round 'ere got ter know me, an' they're aware that the rogues don't get any leeway wiv me.'

'I bet they don't,' Billy said sarcastically. 'Well, yer got no worry wiv me, officer. I'm in full-time work now.'

The big policeman slipped his thumbs into his belt and swayed back and forth on his heels. 'All yer pals 'ave bin put away fer a long time, Sullivan,' he announced self-importantly. 'It was lucky fer you yer didn't get picked out on that I.D., but I tell yer now, I know you should 'ave gone down wiv the rest of 'em an' I ain't fergettin', d'yer 'ear?'

Billy felt his neck hairs rising and he struggled to keep calm. 'I wasn't involved in that ware'ouse job an' I ain't bin near Rovver'ithe fer ages,' he said quickly, screwing up his mouth in anger. 'I got a decent job, an' I'm lookin' after it.'

PC Copeland prodded the young man rudely in the chest. 'People like you don't go straight, Sullivan, they only pretend to. If any opportunity comes their way they grab at it. So be warned. I'm back 'ere now an' yer can tell yer little pals ter beware. Give me one chance an' yer nailed.'

Billy stepped back a pace as he felt his anger rising to boiling point. 'Now listen 'ere,' he grated, 'I ain't scared o' threats, an' I certainly ain't scared o' the likes o' you. Yer'd be no better than me inside a ring. It's that uniform that makes all the difference.'

The policeman's face had become dark with anger. ''Ow would yer like ter step round the corner? There's a nice bit o' wasteground there. I'll take me coat orf an' we'll soon see who's the best. Yer don't 'ave ter worry about me uniform, sonny.'

Billy realised that if he did the sensible thing and just

turned and walked away the policeman would consider him a coward, and that was unthinkable. He decided to have it out with him there and then. 'Anywhere yer like,' he said, staring up at his large antagonist.

Just then Billy saw the young woman approaching them. She was smiling at him and as she drew level she looked at the policeman.

'Hello, constable. I hope Mr Sullivan's not in any trouble,' she said sweetly.

The policeman shook his head. 'We're just 'avin' a friendly chat, miss,' he said flatly.

Annie McCafferty looked at Billy. 'I wanted a quick word with you, if you can spare me the time,' she told him.

'I was jus' goin',' Billy said with a grin, and as he turned to the policeman his face changed. 'I'll remember what yer said, officer. Any time I can oblige.'

Annie gave him a quizzical look as he walked along beside her and then a smile lit up her face. 'Mr Smedley seems rather flustered,' she remarked.

Billy winced noticeably. 'Oh. So yer 'eard about me comin' ter the clinic,' he replied.

Annie put on a stern face. 'Nurse Carmody followed up the information you supplied and as it happened the couple she called on were very upset. They were in their sixties. She wanted to inform the police of your visit but luckily she talked to me first. When she described this Mr Smedley I knew it was you. What made you do it, Billy?' she asked him.

'I wanted ter see yer,' he said simply. 'I thought it was you who looked after this area.'

Annie felt her cheeks glowing and she tried to remain serious. 'Well, it's fortunate Nurse Carmody is a good sort,' she told him. 'I told her you were a little backward and imagined a lot of things, and I said I would have a word with you and make sure you never tried anything like that again. Anyway, what was it you wanted to see me about?'

'I wanted to ask yer ter walk out wiv me, Annie,' the young man replied. 'I was 'opin' I'd see yer around the streets but I never did, an' I was gettin' desperate.'

Annie felt her stomach churning and she swallowed hard. 'Well, you could have dropped a letter into the clinic addressed to me, instead of playing such a trick on everybody – and nearly getting yourself arrested,' she told him.

Billy stopped and turned to face her. 'Look, Annie, I know it was stupid, but I really was desperate. Will yer be my girl? Will yer walk out wiv me?'

Annie McCafferty nodded, a smile breaking out on her pretty face. 'I'd be pleased to, Billy,' she said.

Chapter Seventeen

As the year slipped by things were happening in Bermondsey, not all of them apparent to the regular group of women who stood chatting on their front doorsteps in Page Street. The fact that Billy Sullivan and Annie McCafferty were walking out together was apparent to everyone, however, and Sadie Sullivan was very pleased that her eldest son was now keeping company with a nice Catholic girl.

'She's made all the difference ter that boy o' mine,' she remarked to Florrie Axford. 'I was in despair of 'im at one time. Since 'e's bin wiv Annie though I ain't 'eard a peep out of 'im about that bloody gymnasium.'

Florrie reached for her snuffbox and tapped on the lid with her first two fingers. 'She seems a very nice young lady,' she said, 'an' I've noticed 'ow Billy's spruced 'imself right up since 'e's bin courtin' 'er.'

'I see your Danny's goin' steady too,' Sadie remarked to Nellie Tanner, who had just joined them. 'Are we gonna 'ear weddin' bells soon?'

Nellie shrugged her shoulders. 'My Danny don't give much away, Sadie, but I reckon 'e'll be namin' the date soon. She's a nice gel is that Iris. Shame about 'er farvver though.'

'What's wrong wiv 'im?' Maisie Dougall asked.

''E's a bit of a piss artist,' Nellie told her. ''E's as good as gold till 'e gets a skinful, then 'e's very nasty.

247

Mind yer, 'e don't say anyfing ter my Danny, 'cos 'e knows 'e'd come unstuck if 'e did, but 'e's prone ter knockin' 'is ole woman about, none the less. 'E threatened young Iris once but my Danny 'ad a quiet word in 'is ear. 'E told 'im that if 'e laid 'is 'ands on that gel 'e'd 'ave 'im ter deal wiv. Caused a bit o' friction between Danny an' young Iris, but it all worked out all right, I'm glad ter say.'

Florrie sniffed up the snuff and stood swaying gently until the sneeze came, then the tall, gaunt woman wiped her nose on a brown-stained handkerchief and blinked the tears from her eyes. 'Did yer 'ear they've got anuvver yard?' she asked, jerking her thumb in the direction of the Galloway firm.

Nellie nodded. 'My ole man told me it's in Wilson Street. 'E said they've got a new fleet o' lorries an' they've bin doin' grain work fer the brewery as well as machinery an' the like.'

'It's a pity ole Galloway don't spend a bit of 'is money on doin' our places up,' Florrie remarked. 'My bedroom ceilin's soakin' wet every time it rains, an' me copper's leakin'.'

'Trouble is, every time yer get the lan'lords ter do any repairs they put the bloody rents up,' Maisie cut in. 'D'yer know, ole Temple's place is really bad. I don't know 'ow 'e ain't caught pneumonia. I went in there the ovver day ter take 'is clean washin' in an' I could smell the dampness. Mind yer though, yer can't say anyfing to 'im lately. 'E jus' sits in that front room of 'is an' stares out the winder. I'm sure the poor bleeder won't see anuvver winter out.'

Nellie shook her head sadly. 'Aggie would turn in 'er grave if she was alive ter see it.'

''Ow's your Carrie's cafe gettin' on now?' Maisie asked her cheerily.

Nellie's face brightened. 'Since those workmen finished the alterations she's bin doin' very well. The place is always packed an' she said there's a meetin' of one sort or the ovver goin' on nearly every night. I'm pleased for 'er. That gel does work 'ard.'

''Ere, I know what I was gonna ask yer, Nellie,' Florrie said quickly. 'Did yer see that bit in the paper the ovver day about a club or somefing openin' up in Rovver'ithe?'

Nellie nodded. 'It's only talk yet, but apparently there's a group o' the local businessmen puttin' money up ter start a nightclub or somefing. They say it'll be a real posh place. It won't be fer the likes of us, but it'll attract a lot o' moneyed people. My Will said 'e don't fink it'll come orf though.'

'Oh, an' why's that then?' Florrie asked.

'Will wouldn't say too much, but 'e reckons the police might put their oar in,' Nellie told her.

'I wonder if that ole goat Galloway's put money in it?' Maisie asked, looking from one to the other.

'I would reckon so,' Nellie remarked. 'That ole bastard's got 'is finger in everyfing. I 'ear tell 'e's after the rest o' the 'ouses in this street. Gawd 'elp us if 'e gets 'em. We can't get the repairs done as it is, wivout 'im 'avin' more 'ouses ter look after.'

Maisie noticed the tall figure of the local policeman turning into the street. ''Ere 'e comes,' she alerted the other women. 'Lookin' fer 'is 'andout from the bookie no doubt.'

Florrie pulled a face as she looked along the turning. ''E ain't a patch on ole Buller who used ter be on this beat. 'E was a nice man was ole Sid Buller. Always good fer a chat, an' 'e never got smutty like that dirty ole goat comin' along now.'

Sadie nodded. 'That git tried ter get my Billy in trouble. 'E swore 'e was wiv that ware'ouse robbery downtown that time. 'E wouldn't leave 'im alone. 'E fancies 'imself too. One o' these days 'e's gonna pick on the wrong bloke, mark my words. My Billy would 'ave give 'im what for if it wasn't fer the fact that 'e's still got that black mark against 'im down the police station.'

'I wonder what 'appened ter that Sid Buller. 'E left all of a sudden, didn't 'e?' Maisie enquired.

Florrie leaned towards the others as the large policeman approached them. 'Sid got in trouble fer drinkin' on duty,' she whispered. 'The sergeant come roun' the turnin' lookin' fer 'im an' silly Maudie Mycroft told 'im she see Sid goin' in the Kings Arms. 'Im an' Alec Crossley were in the back room drinkin' whisky. Mind yer, Sid wasn't the best copper. The kids was gettin' away wiv blue murder. It's different wiv this one though. 'E's scared the livin' daylights out o' the youngsters. It's all right bein' strict, but I don't 'old in wiv 'im treatin' Billy the way 'e 'as.'

PC Copeland reached the women and nodded briefly to them. 'G'day, ladies,' he said in a loud voice.

'Nice day, ain't it?' Maisie remarked in a quiet voice.

Florrie gave her a stern look and took out her snuffbox once more, while Sadie Sullivan mumbled an obscene remark under her breath and turned her back on him.

Keen to retrieve the situation Maisie Dougall motioned the women to gather round and then looked up the turning as though someone might be watching her. 'Alice Johnson an' that totter bloke are 'avin' it orf again,' she said in a low voice. 'I see 'im come out o' there before nine this mornin'. 'E was in there all night.'

''Ow d'yer know?' Florrie asked.

''Cos I see 'im go in there last night when I was comin' back wiv me faggots an' pease pudden,' Maisie told her. ''E 'ad a couple o' bottles o' stout under 'is arm an' I could 'ave sworn 'e 'ad a bunch o' flowers under that rotten ole coat 'e wears. I reckon there'll be anuvver weddin' down the turnin' before long.'

'The woman' mus' be mad ter fink o' gettin' 'erself 'itched to a bloke like 'im,' Florrie said shaking her head.

'Well, she ain't everybody's cup o' tea 'erself, is she?' Maisie remarked. 'She's chased two ole men away, an' now it looks like Broom'ead's gonna be number three.'

'Nah, she'll 'ang on ter this one,' Florrie said quickly. ''E's got a few bob, 'as Broom'ead.'

The women were soon joined by Maudie Mycroft, who put down her shopping bag and proceeded to rub her shoulder. 'It's me sciatica playin' me up,' she told them with a grimace. 'I've 'ad it fer a week now an' I can't shift it.'

'It's sittin' in that draughty church, that's what's caused that,' Florrie told her. 'Yer wanna get some o' that there 'orse liniment. That's the finest stuff fer aches an' pains.'

''Orse liniment?' Maudie repeated.

'That's right, 'orse liniment,' Florrie told her. 'Ask Nellie if I'm tellin' a lie. 'Er Will used it on 'er when she got that bad back. It was right as rain in no time at all, wasn't it, Nell?'

Maudie looked disbelievingly at Nellie Tanner who nodded her head vigorously.

'That's right,' she said positively. 'Mind yer, it stinks the place out but it's werf it. Get yer ole man ter warm it up an' rub yer shoulder wiv it night an' mornin'.'

Maudie looked unconvinced. 'I do believe it's the worry that brings this on,' she said, raising her painful shoulder and wincing.

'Is it that ole man o' yours?' Maisie asked.

Maudie nodded. ''E's back wiv 'em again,' she replied. 'I did fink 'e'd got fed up wiv it all but I was wrong. The ovver night 'e went over ter that there

251

Speaker's Corner an' 'e come 'ome wiv a black eye. I told 'im then that if 'e didn't give it up I'd leave 'im.'

'What did 'e say ter that?' Florrie asked, hiding a grin.

''E told me 'e wasn't gonna do no such fing an' 'e said 'e'd 'elp me ter pack if I liked,' Maudie said, sniffing tearfully. ''E's not bin the same since 'e joined that evil lot. I told 'im so too.'

'I fink yer makin' too much out of it, if yer ask me,' Florrie remarked. 'Yer need people like your Ernest ter stir fings up a bit, even if they are a bit bolshie.'

Maudie looked worried. 'I don't know what people would say if Ernest got arrested. They're arrestin' Communist people now, yer know. They arrested some over at Speaker's Corner. That's 'ow Ernest got that black eye.'

'What, resistin' arrest?' Florrie asked.

'No. 'E was standin' near the platform listenin' ter this bloke talkin' an' when 'e clapped at the end 'o the speech the man next to 'im punched 'im in the eye.'

'What did 'e do that for?' Florrie asked.

'Gawd knows,' Maudie replied. 'I do wish 'e'd get right out of it an' take up somefing else. I mean ter say, 'e could keep pigeons, or rabbits, or even chickens. We've got plenty o' room in our back yard fer a few 'utches. Ovver men 'ave fings like that fer an 'obby.'

'I don't fink your Ernest joined the Communist Party fer an 'obby, luv,' Florrie told her. 'That's a belief, jus' like goin' ter church. You go ter church. What would yer say if Ernest asked yer ter give it up. I know. Why don't yer pretend yer got a fancy man? That'll keep 'im 'ome. If 'e finks yer playin' about when 'is back's turned 'e won't be too keen ter go on all them there meetin's, it stan's ter reason.'

Maudie shook her head vigorously. 'I couldn't,' she

almost shouted. 'I jus' couldn't.'

'Well, please yerself,' Florrie said offhandedly. 'If yer won't do anyfing about it yer deserve all yer get.'

Maudie picked up her shopping bag and said her goodbyes, and when she had left Florrie turned to the others. 'I got an idea,' she said mysteriously. 'See what yer fink o' this . . .'

For a long time Carrie had been bargaining with the local catering suppliers and comparing their prices, much to her advantage, and when she was talking with her father one Friday evening he let slip that Joe Maitland was dealing in tinned food.

'I've a good mind ter go round an' see 'im,' she said. 'Tinned food would keep an' if the price is right I could buy in bulk.'

William was sorry he had mentioned the cases of foodstuffs he had been stacking for most of the morning. 'I'd be careful wiv Maitland, gel. Yer never know if it's come the ovver way,' he warned her.

Carrie was keen to find out more, however. 'When can I find 'im in?' she asked. 'We've got a phone in now, I could give 'im a ring.'

'Monday mornin's 'e's always there, an' Friday afternoons when 'e pays me an' Sidney Coil our wages,' William told her.

Carrie was quick to phone Joe Maitland and arrange a meeting, but Fred was less than enthusiastic.

'I dunno. Yer said yerself 'e's a bit of a shady dealer. If we buy 'ooky stuff we could be in trouble, Carrie,' he fretted.

'Look, I won't buy unless the price is right an' the goods are straight,' she assured him.

'Why d'yer 'ave ter meet 'im in a pub?' Fred asked. 'Why can't yer go ter the ware'ouse?'

''Cos that's the way ter do business these days,' Carrie told him. 'It's better ter sit in a cosy bar than a draughty ware'ouse.'

'I jus' fink yer gettin' too big fer yer boots sometimes,' he said peevishly.

'We're runnin' a nice business now, Fred,' she countered. 'Since the extension we've almost doubled our trade an' yer know yerself from what the customers say we're the best cafe around – an' our prices are right too.'

Fred could not argue with the facts and he reluctantly went back to the kitchen. It was just after midday when Carrie arrived at the Jolly Compasses, a tiny pub off the Tower Bridge Road frequented by traders. The bar was busy. Joe came up and greeted her warmly.

'What about a drink? I've got a table in the corner,' he smiled.

Carrie hesitated. Whenever she and Fred went out together it was a pint of ale for him and she usually had a shandy. Today, however, she was feeling daring. 'Can I 'ave a port an' lemon?' she asked.

They sat talking over their drinks and while Joe was shuffling a sheaf of papers Carrie watched him over her glass. He had changed very little from the time when he lived near her family in Page Street except that he looked that bit older. His dark wavy hair had one or two strands of grey now and his face was fuller, but he was certainly a handsome man still, of medium build and broad-shouldered, and he knew how to dress. His dark, double-breasted suit was immaculate and he wore a grey tie knotted tightly over a spotless white shirt. His shoes too were quality, and Carrie had noticed that his slender hands were clean.

'I've got a complete list 'ere, Carrie,' he was saying. 'There's the brand names wiv sizes alongside, an' see 'ere, there's the prices in this column. Yer can see the discounts allowed wiv the quantity, an' there, see, that's the storage rate,' he concluded, handing her the sheaf of papers.

Carrie put down her drink and pored over the columns of figures, feeling a little embarrassed as she sensed his eyes on her. 'What's this about storage rates?' she asked him.

Joe laughed. 'When customers buy in bulk, an' I mean bulk, they usually take a part order an' we store the rest until they're ready fer delivery. That way they save space but buy at the maximum discount. Do yer foller?'

Carrie's eyebrows knitted as she studied the figures. 'But the savin's I'd make would be lost if I've gotta pay fer storage,' she told him.

Joe moved his chair around until he was sitting at her shoulder and Carrie could feel his arm against hers. She caught a sudden scent of toilet water and felt her cheeks getting hot.

'Look. Whatever quantity yer buy I'll waive the storage charges an' yer can take delivery at any time,' he said. 'As yer an ole neighbour I'll waive the delivery charges too. 'Ow does that sound?'

Carrie smiled at him, feeling elated with the deal he was proposing. The prices for the canned beans, tomatoes and fruit were better than those of her usual suppliers and she would be saving on delivery charges. The only thing she felt unsure about was the quantity. It would mean an initial outlay far in excess of what she normally paid to her suppliers, though the saving would show at the end of the month.

Carrie could feel his eyes on her as she glanced again down the columns of figures then looked up at him. 'I don't want ter buy the 'ole ware'ouse,' she joked, catching the glint in his eye.

Joe took the sheaf of papers from her and held out

255

his hand, smiling. 'It's a deal. Yer can say 'ow many cases of each yer want an' I'll see what I can do about the discounts,' he said cheerfully.

Carrie sat back in her chair and sighed. 'D'yer know, I could do business wiv you any day of the week,' she laughed.

Joe picked up the two empty glasses and walked to the bar counter, and Carrie watched his confident manner as he eased between customers and smiled at the barmaid. She remembered the time in Page Street when the stables were blazing and her father was in danger of being trampled to death by a terrified horse. She had managed to pull the animal from him and lead it out on to the cobbles, but when she tried to return to the fire it was Joe who had restrained her bodily and dashed into the yard himself to help her father save the other horses. Since that night there had been a camaraderie between Joe and her father, and the young man had later taken William into his business as a warehouse manager when he was unemployed. Joe had always been someone she admired as a young girl and she knew that he had turned a few of the ladies' heads. He had never married, and as far as she knew there was no regular lady in his life. Carrie had heard her father talk about Joe's shady dealings, and she found the aura of secrecy in his life and his easy charm more than a little intriguing.

Joe had returned. He placed two drinks on the marble-topped table. He smiled at her as he seated himself and made no effort to move his chair back away from her. As she sipped her drink Carrie could feel him appraising her. She blinked once or twice to regain her composure.

'My dad was tellin' me you 'ad a job gettin' yerself sorted out after that fire at Dock'ead, Joe,' she remarked.

He nodded. 'It was 'ard at first. I lost a lot o' stock, an' there was a lot I couldn't claim for, if yer know what I mean,' he said with a sly smile. 'I'm all sorted out now though. Yer dad's bin very good managin' the new place an' there's a lot more room there than at Dock'ead. We've got a young man in ter keep 'is eye on our welfare too, but I'm sure yer dad finks 'e's a bit barmy.'

'Dad did mention 'im,' she laughed.

Joe became serious as he looked into her eyes. 'Don't worry about yer farvver, Carrie,' he said quietly. 'It must 'ave bin strange at first, what wiv 'im bein' around 'orses all 'is life, but 'e's 'appy now. We get on very well yer know. That's why I wanted ter give yer a good deal. Yer farvver's bin very loyal. Anuvver man would 'ave bin off like a shot after what 'appened.'

Carrie's face had become grave. 'It won't 'appen again, will it?' she asked with concern.

Joe shook his head. 'I don't know 'ow much yer dad's told yer but it's a bit complicated. I fink it was just a warnin' ter let me know that I'd bin earmarked. As long as I don't get meself involved in their affairs I'm all right.'

'Who exactly are they?' Carrie asked.

Joe sipped his drink and put it down carefully on the table. 'I've told yer farvver as much as I can an' I'll tell you the same. P'raps then it'll 'elp yer understand why yer place got smashed up an' why yer union friend Don Jacobs got attacked that same night. I don't wanna talk 'ere though. 'Ave yer got some time? I'd like ter show yer somefink while we're talkin'.'

Carrie nodded. It was stuffy in the small saloon bar and the two ports she had consumed were making her feel a little light-headed. She knew that Fred would no doubt be anxious until she returned, but Bessie was now quite competent behind the counter, and there were two part-time servers who were good at the job.

'Where are we goin'?' she asked.

Joe smiled and touched his nose with a forefinger.
'Just wait,' he grinned.

The sunny day seemed extra bright as she left the
pub with Joe, and she could hear the calls of the market
traders and the rumble of passing trams from the bustling Tower Bridge Road as she walked beside him
along a narrow sloping alleyway that led out into the
main thoroughfare. She felt the cool breeze on her face
and smelt the strong aroma coming from the jam factory as they walked swiftly towards the Bricklayer's
Arms junction with Joe gently holding on to her arm,
and as they reached the corner he hailed a passing taxi.
Soon they were travelling along the Tower Bridge
Road, past the stalls and shops and then on towards the
high bridge towers, and Carrie felt excited. She had
never in her life been in a taxi before and she sat back
in the leather seat and stared out of the window, feeling
like a newcomer to the city surveying the grimy factories and warehouses as they hurried past.

The taxi swung left at the Tower Bridge Hotel and
pulled up beside the railway arches which faced the
high, busy wharves. Joe paid the driver who thanked
him for the tip and then he took Carrie's arm as he led
her along a narrow side street which ran under a railway arch. They came out into the open facing a plot of
waste ground with a high fence around it and he
stopped and pointed. 'What d'yer fink o' that?' he said
mysteriously.

Carrie was puzzled. 'I don't understand,' she said.

'Billy Sullivan's Gymnasium could be standing there
one day,' he told her, grinning widely. 'I've bin makin'
enquiries ter see if I can get this site on a long-term
lease, an' if I can I'll rent it to our Billy.'

Carrie looked up at him and saw the enthusiasm in his open face.

'I still don't understand,' she said.

Joe took her arm. 'Look, there's a nice little cafe in Bermon'sey Lane jus' roun' the corner. If yer let me buy yer a meal I'll tell yer everyfing. Is that a deal?'

They found themselves a table by the window and Carrie leaned her arms on the chintz tablecloth and stared at the vase of flowers in the centre as Joe explained what the East End villain Gerry Macedo was trying to do. He told her all about how opposition to the gangleader's plans to control the dockside boroughs of Bermondsey and Rotherhithe had thrown enemies together as unlikely allies, and he smiled now and then as if to allay her fears. Carrie listened intently, and when he had finished she smiled ironically.

'Galloway might be doin' all 'e can to oppose this Gerry Macedo but yer can't get away from the fact that it was 'im, or that son of 'is, who brought 'im over this side o' the water in the first place,' she said disdainfully. 'That Galloway family, an' George Galloway in particular, 'as bin linked wiv everyfing that's 'appened ter my family, Joe. It was my dad gettin' the sack that forced 'im an' mum ter live in that slum block. It was what 'appened between the families that made our Charlie go off to India, but that's anuvver story. That family 'as got a lot to answer for.'

Joe nodded as he sipped his coffee. 'The Galloways ain't exactly my favourite people eivver,' he said quietly, his eyes fixed on her.

Carrie looked down at the patterned tablecloth for a few moments, feeling exposed under his gaze. 'Now what about that bit o' land yer showed me,' she prompted, meeting his gaze. 'Yer was sayin' it could be fer Billy Sullivan's gymnasium.'

259

Joe smiled as he toyed with his coffee cup. 'Yer dad gave me the idea,' he told her.

'My dad?'

'That's right. Apparently Billy Sullivan's bin nursin' this idea o' startin' up a boxin' gymnasium fer the young men in the area,' he went on. 'Your Danny knows all about Billy's dreams an' 'e asked yer farvver if 'e'd talk ter me about keepin' me eye open fer a suitable site that wasn't too expensive. The way yer dad put it ter me I couldn't refuse, could I?'

'I fink I know what yer mean,' she replied with a smile.

Joe's face took on a serious expression. 'Yer see, when my bruvver died after bein' beaten up by those bookies' men I swore I'd get even. I did finally, but it don't end there. There's a lot o' young men who could go the way o' my bruvver if ever those pub boxin' tournaments come back. Billy Sullivan's idea is a good one. Young aspirin' boxers could be trained and taught the pitfalls of the profession. They wouldn't go inter the ring unprepared an' 'ave ter fight at the whim o' those money-grabbin' promoters who couldn't care less about the young blokes they profess ter look after. So yer see why I'm tryin' ter get that piece o' wasteground fer Billy. It won't be a gift, mind. 'E'll 'ave ter rent it from me, but I'll make sure it'll be no 'ardship fer the lad. I might be able ter get a few friends o' mine ter chip in wiv money an' materials as well.'

Carrie looked into Joe Maitland's large dark eyes and saw how sincere he was. 'I fink it's a lovely idea of yours, Joe,' she said quietly.

He looked at her for a long time and something passed between them. Carrie felt it. It was as though her insides were tumbling over and over, and Joe felt it too. He sensed a feeling of longing, longing to take the pretty young woman with the flowing fair hair to him in a tight embrace, knowing that it was impossible. He looked away, hardly daring to let her see what was in his eyes.

Carrie broke the pregnant silence. 'D'yer know, I've really enjoyed this little meetin',' she said smiling. 'I dunno what my 'usband's gonna say when I get back 'ome.'

'Well, 'e should be glad yer a smart little operator,' Joe said with a hint of malice creeping into his voice.

Carrie had gathered her handbag and gloves, and as she adjusted the lapels of her light green summer coat Joe closed his hand around the top of her arm.

'I'd like ter see yer again,' he said simply.

Carrie felt her stomach twist again as she looked up at him. 'Well, I'll be sure ter see more of yer now we've got a business arrangement,' she said, trying to keep calm.

When they came outside the little cafe and stood in the busy street Joe took her arm again. 'Yer know what I mean, Carrie,' he said.

'Joe Maitland, I'm a married woman,' she answered with a quick smile, trying to rebuff him gently.

'I don't care,' he told her. 'I want ter see yer again.'

'I couldn't 'urt 'im, Joe. My Fred's a good kind man,' she said with feeling.

They walked under the railway arch in silence. She felt the grip of his arm on hers, and Joe was aware of the softness of her and the clip of her high heels on the hard pavement. He hailed a passing cab and opened the door while Carrie got in, quietly slipping a ten-shilling note into her hand. 'I'll be in touch,' he told her as the taxi pulled away from the kerb.

Carrie sat looking out of the window throughout the short journey along Tooley Street, and as the cab took the bend at Dockhead and drove along the wide Jamaica Road she could not stop thinking of the handsome young man who had wined and dined her, and reawakened certain feelings that were both delicious and dangerous.

Chapter Eighteen

Billy Sullivan had been very careful to avoid PC Copeland since his confrontation with him earlier that year. He had seen the big policeman in the vicinity on a number of occasions but he had so far managed to stay out of his way by crossing the road or by slipping into another turning. Billy was reminded of the danger he faced when one Saturday afternoon Copeland waylaid a drunken young man who had earlier shouted something to him from across the street. The fight on the wasteground nearby was a one-sided affair with the brute strength of the policeman overwhelming the lighter though courageous young man who was the worse for drink. Later that afternoon his friends found him staggering back, his face a terrible mess. His nose was broken and both eyes were almost closed, and he had cracked ribs and a large gash on his cheekbone. As bad as he was the young man would not say how he came by his injuries but there were one or two people who had seen the policeman leading the way on to the wasteground. No one was willing to say anything, however, and PC Copeland walked the beat around Page Street with impunity.

Billy Sullivan was never one to duck a fight but he knew that he would stand little chance against the much heavier and taller man in the weakened condition caused by his war wound. He knew too that he would

263

probably be taken to the police station afterwards, and then he would be in serious trouble. Billy decided that discretion was the better part of valour and began to take the long way home from work each evening. He had recently seen PC Copeland standing on the corner of Page Street outside the little sweetshop and he knew that he would be stopped if he walked into the turning from that end. He decided to walk on the other side of Jamaica Road then cross the thoroughfare opposite Bacon Street and enter Page Street from that end. His ploy worked well for a time until he was noted by the eagle-eyed owner of the sweetshop, Clara Longley, and one evening she remarked on Billy's strange behaviour to none other than PC Copeland when she gave him his regular cup of tea.

Widow Longley sold sticky sweets which were kept in glass-lidded trays and licorice sticks as well as golly bars and scented cachous that gave the shop a smell all of its own. Often the local children would peer into the little establishment when they had no coppers to buy any sweets just to sniff in the aroma. The elderly shop-owner would then glare at them and pull faces until they departed smartly, or, as in the case of older, more adventurous children, stood their ground and leered back at her. Widow Longley knew the business of everyone in Bermondsey, so it was said, and she was not averse to passing that business on to her few close friends. She was a tall, thin woman, with a few long whiskers on her chin and a pair of tortoise-shell glasses which she wore on the end of her long beak-like nose.

For a few evenings Clara Longley had been watching Billy Sullivan from her shop window and she was intrigued by the fact that he seemed to take the long way home. She had found reason to cross swords with his mother Sadie years ago when the Sullivans were regular visitors to her shop, and ever since that time the two women had merely glared at each other. Widow Longley felt that the eldest Sullivan was one day going to find himself in prison, and she had taken to watching his movements with that in mind.

'It's surprising what yer can see from this little shop,' she told PC Copeland. 'I watch fer the little fings too. Take that ole man comin' along wiv the dog. D'yer know every evenin' that man buys the paper at the shop across the road an' then 'e puts it in the dog's mouth an' it carries it 'ome fer 'im. Then there's ole Mrs Cornfield from Bacon Buildin's. I see 'er every mornin' stand by the tram stop fer a while, but she never gets on a tram. She jus' watches 'em come an' go. Then she toddles orf 'ome pleased as punch.'

PC Copeland was grateful for his cup of tea but he did not enjoy the chat very much, until Clara Longley told him about a particular observation she had recently made.

'Now take that Billy Sullivan for instance,' she went on. ''E comes 'ome from work every evenin' at the same time an' fer the past few nights 'e's passed this turnin' on the ovver side o' the road an' crossed over at Bacon Street. What 'e does that for I don't know. It's quicker fer 'im ter walk down this end o' the turnin'.'

PC Copeland's ears pricked up at the last snippet of information and he put down his empty cup with a sly grin breaking out on his ugly face. 'Well p'raps the young feller-me-lad 'as got good reason fer not comin' in this end,' he remarked.

The Widow Longley merely nodded and went about tidying up her shelves, oblivious to what was going on in the policeman's mind.

Danny Tanner finished work early on the morning of the next day. He was due to go back at the turn of the tide to move a couple of empty barges into midstream ready for their journey down to Tilbury. He felt at a loose end and after spending a couple of hours in the Kings Arms and the remainder of the afternoon resting at home, decided to call in to see his friend Billy for a chat before going back on the river. Billy would be home soon he thought, and as he stepped out from the buildings in the evening air and turned towards Page Street he suddenly saw his friend talking with a policeman. The two of them seemed to be arguing and Danny remembered the story going around of the young drunk who was badly beaten up on the wasteground. Billy had told him he was worried about becoming the next target of the sadistic policeman, and young Tanner hurried towards the pair fearing that something bad was going to happen.

As Danny approached he saw the policeman turn and follow Billy towards the wasteground. There was a badly maintained wooden fence running the length of the open land and he saw Billy and the policeman duck under a few broken planks. By the time he reached the fence and followed them in PC Copeland had taken his coat off and was rolling up his shirtsleeves. Billy stood white-faced a few paces away with his hands clenched into fists and his chest heaving as he endeavoured to fill his lungs with air.

'What's the trouble, Billy?' Danny asked as he came up.

'Piss orf out of it,' the policeman growled at him.

'Yer a little bit off yer beat, ain't yer?' Danny said quietly.

'You 'eard me. Piss orf,' Copeland said, glaring menacingly at the young lighterman.

'Are yer out ter make a name fer yerself then?' Danny said, hoping he might deter the policeman from starting the fight.

'If yer don't get out of it I'll make a mess o' your face after I've seen ter young Sullivan,' the policeman snarled at Danny.

'Leave us, Danny. I'll be all right,' Billy called out to him.

Danny shook his head and turned for a moment as he heard a rustling behind him in the tall weeds. 'I reckon yer ought ter try me first,' he said provokingly. 'Billy's bin at work all day an' I've just bin kippin'.'

PC Copeland smiled evilly at the young man. 'Why don't yer both try yer luck tergevver?' he asked. 'Yer'd be no problem.'

Danny shook his head. 'Oh, no. Yer'd like that, wouldn't yer? We'd get done fer attackin' a policeman an' yer'd 'ave us in the nick where yer could give us a goin' over wiv the truncheons. 'Ere'll do us jus' fine, an' one at a time. Yer couldn't nick one of us fer beatin' yer up, mate. Yer'd never live it down on the beat.'

'Right then. I'm gonna do yer over good an' proper,' Copeland told him, turning to face the young man and ignoring Billy.

Danny slipped off his coat and as he rolled up his sleeves a sudden punch in the face felled him. Billy jumped up from his seat on a large mound of bricks. 'That wasn't bloody fair,' he shouted.

The policeman laughed as Danny slowly rose to his feet and shook his head violently. 'That's the first fing yer gotta remember when yer scrap on the street. Defend yerself at all times,' he leered.

Danny had recovered enough to raise his hands in front of his face and Billy winced as he saw the drips of blood running down from the corner of his friend's eye. 'Watch 'im, Danny,' he shouted.

The young lighterman was slowly circling the bigger man and as he feinted with his left hand Copeland charged in. Danny was ready for him and threw a sharp hard punch which landed square on the policeman's mouth.

'Careful, Danny,' Billy called out.

Copeland rushed in once more only to be stopped by a straight left thrown from the shoulder. He staggered back and Danny pummelled him with a volley of lefts and rights which sent him to his knees. The young man stood back sportingly and waited for the policeman to get to his feet but Copeland suddenly sprang forward and butted him hard in the midriff, bowling him over. He sensed he had the young man at his mercy now and he forgot Billy Sullivan who had jumped up from his seat again. Copeland was kicking out at the fallen man when he was sent sprawling himself by a heavy blow to the back of his bull neck.

'Right, that does it!' he shouted, leaving Danny clutching his ribs on the ground as he turned to face Billy. 'Yer nicked! An' 'im too!' he snarled, pointing to Danny as the young man staggered to his feet.

There was a rustling among the high clump of weeds on the edge of the open space and suddenly Florrie Axford appeared.

'From what I can see of it yer in no position ter nick anybody,' she said severely, reaching into her apron pocket and taking out her snuffbox. 'I saw yer attack that boy while 'e was lyin' there on the ground an' as far as I'm concerned yer should be locked up yerself.'

PC Copeland glowered at Florrie and turned his back on her while he wiped his bloodied lips on a handkerchief. Danny had recovered enough to grin sheepishly at Billy, and Florrie motioned silently with her thumb for the two young men to get going.

'I'll be 'avin' a word wiv your sergeant when I see 'im,' she told the angry policeman. 'Yer a bloody disgrace ter yer uniform. There's anuvver young lad who might wanna talk ter yer sergeant too.'

Back in the street Florrie wagged her finger at the two young men. 'Now orf 'ome the two of yer, or I'll talk ter yer muvvers about this,' she said sternly, as though she was talking to young children.

Danny smiled fondly at her. ''Ow come yer interrupted our little bit o' fun?' he joked.

'Fun? Fun?' Florrie yelled at them. 'Maggie Jones was lookin' fer 'er cat on the wasteground an' she saw what was goin' on. She come runnin' over ter me, an' it's a good job she did, or the two of yer would be locked up by now. Take my advice an' stay away from that big git from now on, or I might not be on 'and next time.'

'Yes, Florrie,' Danny said meekly, trying not to laugh.

'Fanks, Florrie,' Billy said, giving her a huge wink.

PC Copeland had left the wasteground dabbing his swollen lips with a bloodied handkerchief and Florrie Axford shook her head sadly as she watched him walk off along Bacon Street. 'I dunno what this area's comin' to,' she sighed. 'It used ter be such a nice quiet place.'

Carrie was feeling nervous as she worked alongside Bessie Chandler in the dining rooms. It was two weeks since her meeting with Joe Maitland and she had not been able to get him out of her mind. He had phoned her on a couple of occasions on the pretext of finalising the deal for the supplies she had ordered but he had quickly brought the conversation around to her meeting him for a lunchtime drink. The second time he had phoned her Carrie had to finish the conversation when she realised that Fred was watching her closely from the kitchen. She had been a little flustered and passed it off as the pressure of work but she was sure her husband suspected her of planning something. She had tried hard to get the young man out of her mind but she found herself thinking of him constantly. Her life with the staid hardworking Fred was a round of unrelieved boredom. Each evening he would sleep in his favourite armchair and Carrie found it depressing that the bubbling young Rachel had to keep quiet until it was time for her to go to bed. Carrie's love life was practically non-existent now, and yet inside she still had an intense longing to be loved passionately and fully.

It was a normal weekday. The cafe was full and the two helpers were kept busy. Lizzie, a petite young woman in her twenties, and Marie, a tall, pleasant girl of nineteen, hurried back and forth with cups of tea and coffee and plates of bacon and eggs as well as slices of toast and dripping and tea cakes, constantly joking with the dockers and carmen. Bessie was her usual chatty self, tripping back to the kitchen now and then to help out with the cooking, and Fred occasionally hummed to himself. It was a normal weekday, but for Carrie it was momentous. She had finally decided she would have to see Joe, even though she knew that she might live to regret it. It was while Fred was in the back yard having a quiet smoke that she picked up the phone. She was prepared to cut the conversation short should he walk back into the kitchen, but he remained outside long enough for her quickly to arrange a meeting for the following day.

Later in the evening Carrie made her excuses to Fred. 'We'll need some more tablecloths and cleanin' powders, an' there's crockery ter replace. I s'pose I could get most o' that from the ware'ouses in Brick Lane,' she said as casually as she could.

Fred glanced up from his paper. 'I don't know why yer 'ave ter go over the water,' he complained, looking at her over his glasses. 'Surely there's places nearer. I used ter buy all the stuff down the market.'

Carrie smiled and shook her head in mild reproof. 'That's why I'm doin' the buyin', Fred. It's a lot cheaper over Brick Lane an' they cater fer businesses like ours. Besides, it makes a change ter get out an' about again.'

Fred nodded. 'I s'pose yer right,' he said grudgingly, going back to the paper.

Carrie felt guilty deceiving him but the excitement she had felt since her meeting with Joe Maitland had been simmering inside her and she had been able to think of little else. The buying could be done very quickly locally, and the firm would deliver. Fred hardly ever took any notice of that side of the business and should he query the source of her supplies she would be able to make up some excuse, she felt sure.

At twelve-thirty Carrie slipped up to her room after making arrangements with Lizzie to collect Rachel from school and quickly got ready. Her face felt hot and her heart was racing as she put her head around the door and smiled at her husband before leaving, hoping that he would not comment on her smart appearance. Fred was busy rolling dough and he mumbled a good-bye, hardly bothering to look up at her.

'Tell Rachel I'll be back at teatime,' Carrie called as she let herself out.

At one-thirty Carrie stepped down from the tram at Long Lane and hurried to the caterers' suppliers. She had arranged to meet Joe at two o'clock, but by the time she had placed her order and made arrangements for delivery and then walked to the Jolly Compasses behind Tower Bridge Road it was ten minutes past.

Joe was waiting for her and he smiled widely as Carrie walked into the little pub. The young woman felt her mouth become dry and her insides tremble as he took her arm and led her to a table.

'I was beginnin' ter get worried,' he told her, 'I

271

thought yer'd changed yer mind.'

Carrie shook her head slowly, her eyes meeting his. 'I 'ad ter come, but it was difficult. I've bin buyin' supplies. Fred finks I've gone over ter Brick Lane.'

'We've got some time tergevver then,' he remarked, his eyes not leaving hers. 'D'yer know, yer look very nice.'

'Well, fank you,' she replied, looking down at his glass of beer.

Joe suddenly laughed. 'I've not asked yer what yer care ter drink. What'll it be?'

Carrie hesitated. The port and lemon she had had on their previous meeting made her feel light-headed, and today she wanted to remain in complete control of her senses. 'I'll just 'ave a small shandy, please,' she replied.

They sat sipping their drinks and making small talk, almost afraid to reveal to each other the burning desire they both felt. It was Joe who finally became impatient with their awkward reserve.

'Look, I'd like yer ter see my place. I've just 'ad it decorated,' he said casually.

'Is it far?' Carrie asked. 'I can't be away too long.'

'It's only at Bermondsey Square. I've got the upstairs flat,' he told her.

They soon reached the crescent of tidy three-storied houses, and when they climbed the few steps leading up to the front door and Joe inserted the key Carrie looked around quickly, as though she was being observed. Inside, the passageway smelt of disinfectant and the stairs creaked as she followed him up to the top floor.

'There's a solicitor lives underneath an' there's a young couple on the ground floor,' Joe told her. 'Most of the day the place is empty. In fact I've rarely seen the solicitor.'

Carrie stood back while he opened the door to his flat and gasped with surprise as they entered. The room overlooking the square was furnished in oak and the draperies at the window were full and frilly. Around the walls there were large framed prints of sporting events, and above the white stone fire-surround there were alabaster statues of Greek maidens in various poses. The high white ceiling was figured in plaster reliefs and in the centre a chandelier hung down over a highly polished table. A large settee stretched along under the wide window and at each side of the empty grate there were brass tongs standing upright in holders above a shining brass fender. The grey- and red-flowered carpet was soft underfoot and Carrie could smell lavender polish. Two doors led off from the room and Joe opened the one facing the window and stood aside while she walked in. The kitchen was like nothing she had seen before. Around the room there were pots and jars containing herbs and spices, while beneath the lace-covered window there was a white porcelain sink and to the left a large Welsh dresser. The gas stove had brass taps and there were cupboards reaching up to the ceiling.

Joe smiled at her surprise and without saying anything he went to her. 'Let me take yer coat fer a while,' he said quietly.

Carrie slowly unbuttoned her coat and Joe came round behind her, reaching his hands up to her collar. With a single movement he had slipped the coat from her shoulders and turned her around to face him. For a second he gazed into her eyes then his lips went down to hers, his arms locking her in a tight embrace. She could feel his hot lips on hers pressing tightly and his arms pulling her to him, closer and closer, until she could feel every inch of his strong body against hers. His mouth was open, moving over her hot lips, and she gave a little groan of pleasure as his hands stroked along her back.

'No, yer mustn't,' she sighed, willing him to go on.

Joe's lips were now searching her neck and she could feel his hot breath as he kissed her throat. With an effort she placed her hands against his chest and held him at bay, but only for an instant. He had slipped to one side and lifted her up into his arms and Carrie closed her eyes fully to savour his lips as he pressed his mouth into her neck. She was being carried from the kitchen into the large front room and then to the closed door in the far corner. Very gently Joe set her down and with one hand he turned the doorknob and eased his weight against the panelling. As the door swung open Carrie could see the bed and the sweep of the heavy curtains which reached down to the floor. She looked around for a few moments as Joe watched her reaction.

'It's beautiful. It's all beautiful,' she sighed, looking at him.

He smiled, his face flushed from the embrace and his eyes burning into hers. Slowly he came to her and his arms reached out and pulled her to him.

'I need yer, Carrie,' he said, his voice husky and full of emotion.

'I want you too,' she replied, hardly recognising her own voice.

He gently unbuttoned her white linen blouse and very deliberately slipped it over her shoulders, letting it drop to the floor. Then he reached his hands around her back and slipped his thumbs under the strap of her brassiere. Soon she was standing before him, not protesting as his lips went down to her small firm breast. She could feel his tongue moving over her nipple and she let her head drop backwards, folding her

274

arms around his neck. Joe's hands were caressing her, stroking her hair, fondling her roused body, moving slowly over her breasts, and then he pulled her tightly to him, his lips smothering hers. They kissed long and passionately and as they parted he buried his head in her loose fair hair, his fingers groping around for the clasp of her long skirt. Carrie could not contain herself and as he slipped her skirt to the floor and reached his fingers into the elastic of her slip she fumbled with his shirt buttons. Soon he was standing before her stripped to the waist, she wearing only her stockings, suspenders and knickers.

Carrie felt unashamed abandonment as she stepped backwards towards the bed and sat down on the soft counterpane to remove her stockings. Joe smiled briefly as he slipped the buckle of his belt, and she smiled back, her tongue moving around her lips, inviting him to love her, take her in a torrent of passion. Everything was forgotten now as he moved towards her, roused to the full. She moved up onto the bed and reclined against the high pillows, her arms spread out to receive him. Two nude, hot bodies met delicately at first but with a growing need, and finally he was above her, his eyes flashing and his hands spread on both sides of her heaving breasts. He lowered himself until his lips were just an inch from hers and she moved slightly, guiding him, urging him to take her. He let his lips brush hers and then as the pressure increased she let out a deep sigh of pleasure. He was one with her now, his body moving over her slowly at first and then faster and faster until she was groaning with the exquisite pleasure, on and on, until his brow was wet with sweat and his arms were shaking. Suddenly a feeling grew from deep inside her, threatening to burst forth and drown her with its intensity. She closed her eyes tightly, letting the feeling grow with no abating, and then she knew for the first time in her life the feeling of true ecstatic fulfilment.

Joe had sunk down on to her. His exhausted body heaved as he pulled himself up on his elbows. 'Darlin',' he groaned, 'you were beautiful.'

'I've never known such love,' she sighed, her face flushed with sated passion.

He slipped to one side of her, his body against hers. 'I wanted yer from the first moment yer walked in the pub, Carrie,' he whispered.

She turned onto her side, letting her head rest against his deep chest. 'It jus' 'ad ter be,' she whispered simply, closing her eyes and losing herself in the magic of the moment.

Chapter Nineteen

The narrow, cobbled Shad Thames would have been an unlikely place for taxicabs to go on a bright summer evening, but in autumn, with the river mist swirling out into the dark, empty lane, it was outlandish. All the warehouses and wharves were bolted and barred with one exception, and the taxi drivers had only agreed to drive through the deserted area to James's Wharf because their fares were well dressed and respectable-looking. Most of them carried a briefcase or a thin leather case, and they paid the taxi drivers adding good tips, but the drivers were glad to get back into the brightly lit main roads nevertheless, and being too well mannered to ask questions they were left wondering why they had been required to go to such a place so late in the evening. The taxi drivers who carried ships' officers and dock officials to and fro in Bermondsey and Rotherhithe knew the riverside area as a rough place of drab streets and large factories and wharves, where the hard life and the often dangerous pubs near the Thames attracted only the most foolhardy and reckless of strangers. If it had not been for the sense of purpose in the faces of their fares the drivers would have recommended Soho in the West End of London, where painted women plied their trade, fortunes were won and lost at the gambling dens, and many a shady deal was struck.

During the late evening the first-floor room of James's Wharf was filling with serious-faced individuals, who took drinks from an array of liquor on a side table then stood around in small groups, looking anxious and occasionally glancing at their pocket watches. A tall, impassive man in a dark suit stood beside the heavy iron door, his hands clasped behind his back, and in the centre of the large emptied warehouse there was a long table covered with a green baize cloth and surrounded with chairs. Ashtrays were set on the table and at each end there was a filled water jug and a tray of glasses.

A short, stocky man in his sixties had hurried in carrying a briefcase. He ushered the waiting group to the table.

'Well, gentlemen,' he began, 'I take it you've all served yourselves? If so we'll get down to business without more ado. For those of you who don't know me, my name is Ronald James and I'm the owner of this wharf. I'd like to begin by saying that after meeting and talking to an old friend of mine, who I regret to say is not here as yet this evening, I decided to make this room available to discuss a matter which is of concern to us all. Now before I go on, is there anyone here who is in any way in the dark as to the business in hand?'

The silence encouraged the wharf owner to continue. 'Most of you I know personally and I see we're fairly well represented. All of you sitting here tonight have been personally invited and I can see wharfingers, transport contractors, factory owners, as well as businessmen in various fields of endeavour. All of us have one thing in common: we trade in this area, and in saying that I include Rotherhithe too. All of us earn our living in one way or another from the River Thames where merchants have settled and worked since Roman times, and it's no coincidence that a thriving trading community has developed in this area over the years. We have a river gateway, ample space for dockage and storage, inland waterways, a growing railway system and a plentiful workforce of craftsmen, rivermen, labourers and factory workers. We can all of us compete, trade together, and help each other along the road to prosperity as long as we're allowed to carry on in our respective professions unhampered by interference, legal or illegal, and I emphasise the latter because it is the reason for the very nature of this meeting here tonight.'

The speaker was interrupted by George Galloway who entered the room puffing loudly from climbing the stairs.

'Sorry I'm late, Ron,' he grunted, going to the far table to pour himself a glass of whisky. 'The bloody taxi driver wouldn't drive down 'ere. I dunno if 'e expected me ter rob 'im.'

There was some laughter at the remark and Ronald James raised his hands for silence. 'To bring us to the point of the meeting,' he went on, 'I'd just like to say that it would appear certain forces are being matched against us, and if we do not assert ourselves and oppose those forces we will find that we are unable to store, shift, buy or sell without first consulting and getting permission from a self-appointed godfather.'

There was a murmur from the gathering and George Galloway banged his fist down hard on the table. 'Why don't yer cut out the fancy talk an' get ter the point, Ron?' he said in a loud voice. 'We all know why we're 'ere. What I wanna know is, 'ow are we gonna deal wiv it?'

Everyone at the table stared at the heavily built man with thick grey hair and a red bloated face and then looked back at the speaker. Ronald James smiled patiently at Galloway.

'That's what we're here for, George.'

'Is there any information available regarding the application for an entertainments licence, and do we know who it might be registered under?' one of the gathering asked.

'As far as we can ascertain no application has yet been made,' the speaker replied. 'What we do know is, there has been a bid put in for the old Town Music Hall by a company calling themselves Eastern Enterprises. The same company own properties throughout the East End of London. That's the first link. The second is that the bid bears the name of the company secretary, a man by the name of Martin Butterfield.'

The vacant stares were noted by George Galloway. 'Butterfield is a company solicitor an' 'e was actin' fer Gerry Macedo over a tax fiddle. I might add that Macedo was acquitted,' he growled.

'Foolproof,' an elderly man with a goatee beard grunted.

'Exactly,' Ronald James replied. 'If the bid is successful there's a double opportunity here. The company can develop the property and apply for an entertainments licence, and if their application is unsuccessful they can demolish the present building and sell the site off as building land when the price warrants it. Eastern Enterprises have subsidiaries as you will have guessed,' James added, looking pleased with himself.

The young man sitting at the end of the table looked along the line of serious faces. 'We can sit 'ere an' agonise over what's takin' place an' what's likely ter be, or we can take one of two actions,' he said quietly.

'What's on yer mind, Joe?' Jack Pickering, a local transport contractor, asked him.

'We can use the local organisations and clubs, such as they are in Rovver'ithe an' Bermon'sey, an' put the information we 'ave in front of 'em,' Joe Maitland suggested. 'The local Labour Party, the men's Labour clubs an' social clubs, an' the Communist Party more than anyone would be dead against Macedo's scheme goin' ahead. They'll make noises ter the papers, an' wiv a bit o' luck one or two o' the councillors may turn out ter be on our side, yer never know. We can get the local groups ter put pressure on the Borough Council, the City o' London an' the L.C.C. ter purchase the land fer blocks o' flats, 'specially when they know what's likely to 'appen ter the neighbour'ood. There's a couple of active charities in the area too, so I understand. They might be able to 'elp out.'

'An' what's the other action you have in mind?' the elderly member with the beard asked.

Joe looked around at the blank faces. 'We could form our own consortium and buy the property ourselves,' he said with conviction.

The speaker looked from one to another of them. 'Well, gentlemen?'

Galloway leaned forward in his chair. 'I say we should turn over everyfing we 'ave ter the police,' he said. 'Let them deal wiv the application fer an entertainments licence. If they know what's goin' on they'll oppose it.'

Joe Maitland looked at the old man. 'It won't work,' he said quickly. 'The company buyin' in is a legitimate company. Licence or not it'll mean Macedo's got 'is foot in the door. 'E'll bide 'is time. There'll be money spread about an' a few charities serviced. Once Macedo's crowd get a foot'old in the area there'll be no stoppin' 'em. You should know that, George.'

Galloway was on his feet. 'What yer sayin', yer young pup?' he snarled.

'Are yer gonna deny you an' Macedo were pals once?' Joe asked in a steady voice.

'I'm not denyin' anyfing,' Galloway shouted. 'I did know Macedo. We did the boxin' circuits tergevver. I've drunk wiv the man in the past, but I was never involved in anyfing illegal wiv 'im, or anybody else fer that matter.'

Joe Maitland waited for the noise to die down. 'My information is that it was Gerry Macedo who burned my ware'ouse down, which nearly took the life o' Will Tanner, your friend an' loyal worker fer a good number o' years, George. Don't fink people's eyes an' ears are shut ter what's takin' place around 'ere . If we go down there'll be nobody ter blame except us.'

The speaker raised his arms for silence, then he looked down at his clasped hands. 'It seems to me that there are three main proposals put forward,' he said quietly, looking up at the gathering. 'Do we have any more forthcoming? Well then, I'll remind you what the options are in case you've forgotten. First we have Maitland's initial proposal that we inform the local clubs and organisations and encourage them to make their voices heard. Is there a seconder?'

The elderly man raised his hand.

'Then we have his other proposal that we form a consortium,' the speaker went on. 'Any seconder to that proposal?'

No one responded and Ronald James looked over his spectacles at the men around him. 'The last proposal is that we turn all our information over to the police. Is there anyone who wishes to second the last proposal?'

Again there was silence and the speaker adjusted his position on his chair before continuing. 'Well, gentlemen, we have one seconded proposal on the table. I think we should take a vote. All those in favour of informing the local groups of our information, raise your hands.'

Only George Galloway and another man sitting near him kept their hands down.

'Those against.'

Galloway raised his hand and the other man sat passive.

'We have ten for, one against and one abstention,' the speaker said, looking pleased with himself. 'I say the vote is carried. I'll need a few of you to remain behind to help me formulate the information. We'll also need a list of known groups in the area who might make use of our information. Can I ask you for one to remain behind, Mr Maitland?'

Galloway had risen to his feet to button up his navy blue overcoat, and as Joe Maitland passed he glowered at him. 'There was no need ter say what yer did,' he said in a dark voice.

Joe looked him in the eye. 'I didn't mention everyfing, George. Yer can fank me fer that at least,' he replied.

Galloway returned his stare and was about to reply, but instead he turned on his heel and left the room.

During the autumn Carrie had managed to meet Joe Maitland on only two occasions, and each time it was at his flat in Bermondsey Square. The time they spent in each other's arms was far too short, she regretted, but the love she felt for him helped to sustain her through the long arduous days and miserable nights. Her husband Fred now seemed to have little interest in her as a woman and for that Carrie was grateful, although she found it disturbing that he could be so jealous of her and suspicious of her movements yet uninterested in making love to her. Perhaps it was her marrying him without ever plainly professing her love which had finally made him lose interest in her, she thought. But there was Rachel, and the baby she had lost so early in her pregnancy. There were times in the past when he had been eager for her body, and it hurt her to remember how she had lain beneath him praying for him to finish loving her. It had become a trial as the months and years slipped by, and now Fred seemed to be ageing fast. He was still only fifty-two but he looked older, and his whole life seemed to be absorbed by the dining rooms now. Even the occasional visit to the pictures or the music-hall on Saturday night was always at Carrie's suggestion, otherwise Fred would not have bothered to make the effort at all.

The only bright thing in her life apart from her rare meetings with Joe was Rachel. She was six years old now and growing into a tall, beautiful young girl with flaxen hair, an oval face with rosebud lips and tiny ears, and pale blue eyes which were always bright and enquiring. Bessie adored her, as did the two helpers Lizzie and Marie who often took her out for walks or collected her from school. She seemed to be the only person Fred lavished his love on, and Carrie came to realise that maybe he was holding on to the one thing he had left in his life as their loveless marriage grew cold.

On the last Saturday before Christmas Danny Tanner was married to Iris Brody and the reception was held at the Brodys' house in Wilson Street, a little backstreet a few turnings along from Page Street. Billy Sullivan acted as Danny's best man and very soon became drunk and decided that he should give a demonstration in the art of fisticuffs to the Brody family, despite Annie McCafferty's pleading with him to behave. Joe Brody pushed him away with a sweep of his huge hand and his eldest son Vic did likewise. Fred the middle son felt he should teach the Sullivan boy a lesson and was promptly knocked to the ground in the back yard. He had had enough and it was left to Paul, the youngest of the Brody tribe, to put the ex-boxer in his place. Billy was in his thirties and past his best but at twenty-eight he considered Paul to be a mere stripling as they good-naturedly shaped up to each other.

'Right then. First one ter go down is the loser,' Billy announced.

'Are yer sure yer wanna fight me?' Paul said.

'Sure as yer got an ugly face,' Billy slurred.

'If I was as ugly as you I'd only go out when it's dark,' Paul told him.

'Well, I fink yer the ugliest bloke in Bermon'sey,' Billy went on, 'an' jus' fer that I'm gonna try an' change the shape of yer face. Yer'll come ter fank me fer it one day.'

The two sparred and circled around each other menacingly, and suddenly Billy dropped his hands to his sides. 'Look, if yer keep on dancin' round me like a fairy yer gonna tire yerself out,' he laughed. 'Why don't yer sling a punch?'

The offer was too good to turn down and Paul immediately threw a straight right hand which felled Billy.

'I reckon that makes me the winner,' he said grinning.

Billy staggered to his feet and shook his head from side to side. 'That don't count. I wasn't ready,' he moaned.

'It was you who told me ter sling a punch,' Paul reminded him.

'C'mon, ugly. Let's see what yer made of,' Billy taunted him, circling around with his fists held high in front of his face.

Paul threw another straight right hand and this time it caught Billy on the nose. Blood trickled down his

285

chin as he stepped back a pace.

'First blood ter you. Now I'm gonna really do yer,' Billy growled.

The impending fight was cut short sharply by Iris's mother Phyllis, who stepped into the back yard with a pail of water and promptly threw it over the two young men.

'Right now, get inside an' be'ave yerselves,' she scolded them. 'Yer upsettin' Iris, an' on 'er weddin' day too.'

Annie was sitting next to Carrie in the small parlour and as her bloodied young man walked into the room she shook her head disapprovingly. 'Billy Sullivan, you ought to be ashamed of yourself,' she told him. 'Just look at your face, and you're soaking wet. Go and get cleaned up this minute.'

Billy grinned with embarrassment and then attempted to look stern. 'I 'ope yer not gonna order me about like that when we're married, Annie,' he said with a sly smile.

'If you behave like that I will,' she replied.

'Yer mean yer will marry me?' he asked, his face lighting up.

Annie saw the amusement on Carrie's face and she struggled to remain serious. 'I don't know,' she said quickly. 'I don't know if I could put up with all this fighting.'

Billy left the room to get cleaned up and Carrie turned to her embarrassed friend. 'If yer ever do marry that feller yer gonna 'ave ter get used ter boxin', Annie,' she laughed. 'An' if yer lucky enough ter be blessed wiv children an' they're boys, yer gonna be 'ard-pressed ter keep 'em out o' the ring.'

Annie's face was anxious. 'I hope not. I wouldn't want children of mine to become interested in boxing, Carrie,' she fretted.

'Tell me, Annie, are yer intendin' ter marry Billy?' Carrie asked her.

Annie looked down at her clasped hands. 'I love him, Carrie, but Billy's got this dream. He wants that gymnasium. I think I'm going to lose him before I've really got him,' she said quietly.

'But yer saw Billy's face when 'e was jokin' wiv yer a minute ago,' Carrie said encouragingly. 'Yer can see 'e wants ter marry yer.'

'Yes, perhaps he does,' Annie said with a sad smile. 'But we'd need a place to live and things to buy for the house. Every penny Billy earns he saves to make that gymnasium of his come true. I don't want him to give up his dreams but he can't have both, Carrie. It's just not possible.'

Carrie squeezed Annie's arm affectionately. 'You'll get married to Billy, an' 'e'll get that gymnasium 'e wants so badly. I just know,' she said.

The small house was crowded to capacity and people were coming in to take a drink with the newly-weds and offer them their good wishes. The food had all been eaten and as darkness closed over the street the celebrations proper got under way. A huge woman sat at the piano pounding out the latest tunes while Fred Brody accompanied her on the banjo and people got up to dance, constantly treading on the toes of everyone around them. Fred and Vic Brody had been to the pub for more bottles of beer and Billy sat in a corner chatting to Paul, their differences forgotten. Iris Brody went around with sandwiches, and in the back kitchen Grandma Brody sat with her arms folded, her face like thunder at being pushed into second place for once.

'I don't know what all the fuss is about,' she moaned to Granny Forester. 'In my day yer said yer vows an' went orf ter the seaside fer the day, if yer was lucky. Kids terday don't know what it is ter want. Take our

Iris. She's got a place ter live, an' they're goin' orf ter Brighton fer a couple o' days.'

'That's nice fer 'em,' Granny Forester said wistfully.

Grandma Brody nodded. 'They've got two rooms next door but one. Mrs Brown let 'em 'ave 'er two upstairs rooms. 'Er lodger won't want 'em any more.'

'Won't 'e?'

'Nah. 'E got two years 'ard labour.'

'What did 'e get that for?' Granny Forester asked.

'A pair o' shoes.'

'A pair o' shoes?'

''S' right,' Grandma Brody said. ''E walked out o' Ringleaders in the Ole Kent Road wiv a new pair o' shoes 'e 'adn't paid for an' left 'is old ones in the box.'

'That's a bit stiff, ain't it, luv?' Granny Forester remarked. 'Two years 'ard labour fer a pair o' shoes.'

'It was a camel-'air overcoat the previous week, an' before that it was a bowler 'at. 'E's bin doin' it at all the shops. Mrs Brown was tellin' me the ovver week 'e walked out of a shop wiv a pair o' stays. Now what does a bloke want wiv a pair o' stays, I ask yer?'

'P'raps 'e's a bit funny,' Granny Forester suggested. 'Mrs Coleman's ole man wore stays.'

'Yeah, but Bertie Coleman wore stays ter keep 'is back straight. 'E was a doorman at the Savoy. Why the silly git should walk out of a shop wiv a pair o' stays I'll never know.'

'I bet those rooms of 'is were stuffed full o' fings,' Granny Forester remarked eagerly.

'Yer couldn't move in there fer stuff,' Grandma Brody told her. 'The police found a load o' clothes, shoes an' ties. They even found women's underwear in there, an' yer know what else they found? A tailor's dummy. One o' them fings yer see in the smart shops wiv dresses on. The copper come out wiv it under 'is arm, would yer mind. I was standin' at the street door

288

at the time an' I didn't know where ter put me face. "Can't yer cover that fing up?" I ses ter the copper. "Why, luv, it ain't all that cold," 'e ses ter me. One o' them there saucy gits 'e was. Anyway they shoved all the stuff in the police van an' carted it orf. That's 'ow Mrs Brown's lodger come ter get two years 'ard labour.'

'Dear, oh dear,' Granny Forester sighed.

On the same day and at the same time that Danny Tanner and Iris Brody were married another wedding took place in Bermondsey, but it was kept secret from the neighbours. Alice Johnson was married to William Nehemiah Smith at the Bermondsey Register office and then the couple departed to Clacton-on-Sea for a week's honeymoon. Broomhead sat next to Alice on the train and worried about his horse, his neglected business, and above all his liberty. He was sixty years old, the same age as Alice, and for all of his adult years Broomhead had enjoyed his freedom. As he watched the fields flash by from the carriage window he recalled how his friends would often say to him that one day he would be captured by a scheming female but he had laughed at them. He had had his chances by the score but he had never believed that at long last he really would marry. Well, there was no sense in crying over spilt milk, he told himself. Alice was a presentable woman who cooked him nice meals and washed his clothes. She was very fond of his horse, and she had a few shillings tucked away. She also had a cosy house which was much better than his grimy, leaking hovel, for which he struggled to find the rent. The only thing he would have to watch out for was her jealousy, he realised. Alice was a very possessive woman who could be dangerous when roused. She had terrorised two husbands and if he was not careful he would find himself in the same boat. Broomhead Smith considered himself to be a shrewd character, however, and he felt that he was going to manage quite well, providing he was very careful.

Alice Johnson leaned back in her carriage seat and sighed contentedly. Bill was a good man, and very active for his age she thought, smiling secretly. He would have to be careful with those boots of his though. She was not going to have horse dung trodden all over her best carpet. He would have to smarten himself up on the rounds too. She was not going to have people talking about how scruffy her husband was. He could be smart, though. He looked smart now in his grey suit, she thought to herself.

'It looks cold out there,' Broomhead said, breaking the silence.

'It does, dear. Never mind, we can snuggle up ter-gevver ternight, can't we?' Alice said with a naughty smile on her face.

He nodded, looking serious, and then after a few moments, 'Alice?'

'Yes, dear?'

'Alice, yer do fink everyfing's gonna be all right, don't yer?'

'Of course, dear.'

'Alice, I'm feelin' a bit worried.'

'Everyfing's gonna be fine, Bill. There's no need ter worry.'

'S'posin' somefing goes wrong?'

'Don't be a silly-billy. Nuffink's gonna go wrong. We're sensible.'

'My pal Smudger ain't though. If 'e gets pissed the 'orse won't get fed.'

Chapter Twenty

In the Bradleys' dining rooms the windows were running with condensation and the floor was wet and muddy from the constant comings and goings. The place was gaily decorated with balloons and paper chains for the festive season, nevertheless, and there was the usual small Christmas tree standing in a tub in the far corner. Bessie was busy in the kitchen alongside Fred while Carrie worked ceaselessly serving the dockers and carmen, and an extra group of labourers who were employed on the new wharf being erected a short way downriver. Lizzie and Marie were very courteous and helpful to the customers, mindful perhaps that the Christmas box had been put up on the counter.

Carrie had no time to think of the shopping trip she was going to make the following day and as she wiped the sweat from her brow Sharkey Morris walked into the cafe accompanied by his old friend Soapy. Sharkey looked cold and miserable as he raised a wan smile and Carrie's heart went out to him. He was now nearing sixty-five and being retired. Even though he had told her only a week or two ago that the job was getting too much for him Carrie knew that he was going to miss his work. He had said that there might be a nightwatchman's job going at the stables where he worked but he was not very hopeful of getting it. Sharkey had formerly worked at the Galloway stables for many years and Carrie remembered all the times he had given her a lift on his cart whenever he saw her in the street on her way home from school. She had never forgotten that it was he who let her father know of the job going at Fred's cafe, and it was he who kept his eye on her at the very beginning. Sharkey was the salt of the earth, she felt. Always cheerful and friendly, always ready to help out in whatever way he could. She remembered how he and Soapy had moved her family to Bacon Buildings with his horse-and-cart. Soapy would miss him too, she knew. The two men were almost inseparable. They always seemed able to meet at the dining rooms for their break and she had never heard a cross word pass between them.

''Ow are yer, boys? Yer look cold, Sharkey,' Carrie remarked.

The long, lean carman shook his head slowly and Soapy put his hand fondly on his friend's shoulder. ''E's a bit upset, Carrie,' he told her. 'This is Sharkey's last day at work. They're puttin' 'im orf termorrer. Sharkey's missus ain't too good eivver. She's laid up in bed wiv shingles.'

'I'm sorry, Sharkey. Give 'er my love, won't yer?' Carrie said sympathetically.

'I'm finishin' up next year,' Soapy informed her. 'Age is catchin' up wiv us all, gel.'

''Ere we are. Two nice mugs o' sweet tea. This is on the 'ouse,' she told them.

The two carmen took their seats and although Carrie was kept busy she could not help stealing glances at the two old friends. She was aware that like many of her regular customers they often made lengthy detours to visit the cafe. It would be nice if she could think of some way to show her appreciation for their loyalty, she thought.

Soapy Symonds had found a paper hat from somewhere and he was sitting quietly in his bench seat sipping his tea with the hat perched askew on his head.

'Look at that silly bleeder,' Bessie remarked as she came out of the kitchen to help at the counter. ''E finks it's a party.'

'That's it! We'll 'ave a party,' Carrie said, smiling at the puzzled woman. She went straight out into the kitchen to see her husband.

'Fred, I wanna 'ave a party.'

'A what?' he asked.

'I wanna 'ave a party 'ere termorrer fer Sharkey,' Carrie told him.

Fred was busy rolling dough and he looked up at her as though she had taken leave of her senses. 'Did I 'ear yer right?' he asked her.

Carrie sat down on the stool beside him and told him how sad she was for the old carman. Fred had known the man for a considerable number of years and his hard look softened as Carrie explained what she intended to do.

'Well, as long as yer can manage it. Remember it's the last openin' day an' there'll be a lot o' customers in an' out,' he reminded her.

Carrie hurried out of the kitchen and caught Soapy's eye. 'Can yer give us an 'and, Soapy?' she asked, winking quickly at him. 'Fred can't lift. 'E's 'urt 'is back.'

'Lazy ole goat,' Soapy joked as he walked around the counter, leaving Sharkey staring balefully at his mug of tea.

When Carrie had finished explaining what she wanted him to do Soapy suddenly leaned forward and kissed her on the cheek. 'Yer a good lass. 'E'll be really touched by yer kindness,' he said. 'Jus' leave it ter me. I'll make sure 'e comes in. They're payin' 'im orf at nine o'clock an' there's no carts out termorrer.'

*

293

At midday on Christmas Eve Billy Sullivan sat facing Danny Tanner in the Kings Arms. He was puzzled by the mysterious attitude of his old friend. 'Yer say yer ole man wants ter see me?' he asked anxiously. 'Why, Danny? I ain't upset 'im 'ave I?'

'Gawd knows,' Danny replied, sipping his beer and struggling to keep a straight face.

'What's 'e wanna see me for? Surely 'e told yer?' Billy asked.

''E didn't say nuffink ter me,' Danny told him. 'P'raps it's about yer makin' a fool of yerself at the weddin'. Joe Brody's a pal o' my ole man an' 'e might 'ave wanted ter pass a message on.'

'Well, why didn't 'e give you the message if that's the case?' Billy queried.

'I s'pose 'e was worried in case I took yer part,' Danny said, 'though I don't know why I should. Yer really upset the apple-cart, didn't yer? Iris thought yer was gonna 'urt 'er bruvvers an' Annie was gettin' all worried in case you got 'urt. Bloody 'ell, Billy, yer gettin' too old fer fightin'. Yer should fink of Annie now. She's a good gel an' yer really lucky ter get somebody like 'er.'

Billy looked down at his glass. 'Yer right, Danny. I don't deserve 'er. I'll make it up to 'er though, you see if I don't. I'm gonna turn over a new leaf. No more fightin' – unless I'm provoked, mind – an' no more gettin' inter trouble. I'm gonna be a changed man from now on – well, after Christmas anyway.'

At that moment William Tanner walked into the public bar and looked around. Danny got up and walked over to him and Billy watched father and son as they stood at the counter waiting to be served. Eventually they came over to the table and Danny placed one of the drinks he was carrying down in front of Billy.

'There's a couple o' my workmates standin' at the

counter an' I'm gonna 'ave a chat wiv 'em while yer sortin' out yer business,' he said, giving Billy a meaningful look as he walked away from the table.

By now Billy Sullivan felt he must have done something terrible to warrant Danny's father coming in the pub especially to see him.

William sat down and sipped his drink, looking as though he was in no hurry to begin a conversation, then he folded his arms and leant forward on the table. 'I was 'avin' a chat ter Joe Maitland about yer, Billy,' he began.

'Was yer?' Billy said.

'I was tellin' 'im all about yer boxin' an' 'ow yer . . .'

'I was only playin', Will,' Billy cut in. 'There was no 'arm intended. I'm sorry Iris got upset about it, but as I explained ter Danny . . .'

'It's nuffink ter do wiv the weddin',' William said with a mischievous smile. 'It don't concern 'im anyway. Nah, I was tellin' Joe some time ago about 'ow yer bin wantin' to open up a gym fer the young boxers round 'ere fer years an' I asked 'im if 'e knew of any spare sites that might be goin' a bit cheap. Maitland's got a lot o' contacts, yer see. Well, 'e's managed ter find a bit o' land an' 'e's been makin' enquiries ter see if 'e can get it on a long-term lease. Anyway, 'e told me yesterday 'e wants ter talk ter yer about it after Christmas.'

Billy's face lit up for an instant, then he sagged back in his chair. 'Well, it's really good of yer ter fink of me, Will,' he replied. 'But yer see, me an' Annie McCafferty are plannin' on gettin' married, soon as I can find a place fer us ter live, an' yer know what it's like when yer get married. There's fings ter buy fer the 'ouse, an' . . .'

Will held up his hands to stop him. 'In the first place it was Danny who asked me if I'd approach Joe Maitland for yer. Joe wants yer ter pop round an' see 'im after Christmas. There's 'is address,' he said, passing Billy a slip of notepaper. 'Go round an' see 'im anyway. Jus' tell 'im why yer can't take up 'is offer. 'E's a nice bloke is Joe.'

Billy smiled appreciatively. 'I will,' he replied. 'I'll tell 'im straight. An' fanks, Will.'

Carrie was feeling excited as she dashed about the dining rooms on Christmas Eve. Bessie and the two young helpers were in a festive mood, and between serving the steady stream of customers that morning they helped out in preparing the back room. Carrie wanted it to be a special event, and occasionally she looked at the wall clock behind the counter and glanced expectantly through the wet window for signs of Sharkey.

'I 'ope Soapy manages ter persuade 'im ter come,' Bessie remarked. 'It'll be a shame if not after all the trouble we've bin to.'

'Soapy won't let us down,' Carrie told her. 'Now go an' get that big box from the stairs an' put it be'ind the counter where 'e can't see it.'

At eleven o'clock precisely Carrie spotted Soapy walking along the lane beside Sharkey and they seemed to be in deep conversation. At the door Sharkey made to turn away but Soapy grabbed his arm and pulled him into the dining rooms.

Sharkey Morris looked puzzled as Carrie came around the counter and took his arm. 'C'mon, Sharkey, we've got a little surprise fer yer,' she said laughing.

The rest of the customers got up and followed as Carrie steered Sharkey into the back room. Small red candles were set around it and the glow lit up Carrie's best china which was set out on a spotless white tablecloth. Sharkey blinked once or twice as he was led to a chair and then Bessie came in proudly carrying two plates of bacon and eggs, fried bread and tomatoes. Lizzie followed holding two mugs of steaming tea and Marie had plates of bread and butter.

'We know that's yer favourite, Sharkey,' Carrie said, smiling broadly. 'We knew yer wouldn't want to eat alone so we've done Soapy a breakfast too. Merry Christmas, luv.'

The elderly carman brought his hand up to his mouth and looked into Carrie's eyes. 'I dunno what ter say,' he murmured, clearly near to tears.

'Well, I reckon we ought ter get on wiv it before it gets cold,' Soapy laughed, winking at Carrie and her team of helpers.

The customers were standing in the doorway and they all called out their good wishes to Sharkey before Carrie ushered them out of the room. Soapy had already begun tucking into the food but Sharkey was too overcome to start eating.

'What a nice gesture,' he remarked, picking up a slice of bread and putting it down again.

Soapy prodded Sharkey on the forearm with his fork. 'Oi, are you gonna eat that or shall I eat it for yer?' he prompted.

Carrie allowed the two men some time to finish their meal then she carried the large cardboard box into the back room and set it down on the floor beside the elderly carman. 'There's a few fings in there fer Christmas,' she said, lifting the lid. 'There's also a present fer Mrs Morris from the staff and customers, Sharkey, an' we all 'ope she gets well very soon.'

'I dunno what ter say,' he mumbled again, blowing his nose hard on a red spotted handkerchief.

'Well, don't say anyfing. We're all gonna miss yer, Sharkey,' Carrie said, going to him and planting a kiss on his forehead.

'Yeah, that goes fer me, ole pal,' Soapy added,

clearly moved by Sharkey's response.

It was a sad collection of people who stood in the doorway and watched Sharkey walking away along Cotton Lane with the cardboard box held under his arm and his old friend Soapy walking beside him.

'It's a shame when a man like Sharkey Morris 'as ter retire,' Bessie said, dabbing at her eyes. ''E was tellin' me 'e's bin drivin' 'orse-an'-carts since 'e was sixteen.'

'They don't come any better,' Carrie remarked, her memories of the kind man stretching back to when she was very small.

'D'yer know,' Bessie began, 'there was a bloke in our buildin's . . .'

'Not now, luv,' Carrie sighed, hurrying away to get ready for her shopping trip.

Joe Maitland had closed down his warehouse the previous evening until after Christmas and he sat alone in his tastefully decorated flat on Christmas Eve with a glass of Scotch whisky at his elbow and a scattering of papers beside him on the settee. There were the letters from various groups in Bermondsey and Rotherhithe which he had opened, some letters of his own which he had written and not yet posted, and sheets of paper containing lists and information. He had received two letters that morning. The first was from the Bermondsey Communist Party who had pledged their support, and it told of the progress being made. The second letter caused him to ponder. It was from an unknown source. It was unsigned, and it warned him that he would need to tread warily because of certain people who knew of his involvement in organising opposition to the Town Music-Hall project, and were concerned about the way things were going. The writing was barely legible and the spelling childlike, but the message was clear enough. Everyone at the Shad Thames meeting had been invited and only he himself and Ronald James had remained behind to discuss which organisations they should contact. The only other person present then was the big man in the dark suit who had stood guard on the door. Ronald James had assured him that the man was a loyal servant who was also as deaf as a post. There had been a leak from some quarter, however, and Joe could only suspect that it was from someone in one of the groups that had been contacted.

Things had been moving fast, and there had been an article in the *Kentish Mercury* about the uncertain future of the old Town Music-Hall. Nothing had been mentioned about a nightclub but the article was important in that it suggested many local people believed the derelict place should be pulled down to make way for workers' flats, and that would have helped to stoke the fire, Joe thought. There had been other developments too. A housing charity which had been set up by a wealthy family who had had business ties with the area was already making waves about the lack of commitment on the part of certain local councillors in getting the slum blocks pulled down and replaced by modern houses with proper sanitary facilities. Another group very much in the news was the Bermondsey branch of the Communist Party. It had already been on the streets demanding the resignation of the Government and asking local people to vote for its candidates at the next election. Things were looking very favourable, Joe felt, but if the letter was to be taken seriously he would have to be careful.

The front doorbell sounded and Joe started nervously. He got up quickly from his chair and took up the heavy iron poker from the hearth before hurrying down the steep stairs. He opened the door quickly and stood back a pace holding the poker behind his back, but when he saw Carrie standing there with her arms full of parcels he breathed a huge sigh of relief.

"Ello, darlin'. Yer look worried. Didn't yer fink I was comin'?' she said, stepping into the passageway and reaching up to kiss him on the lips.

Joe smiled as he helped her up the stairs with the parcels, and when she was comfortably seated in his front room he poured her a glass of whisky with a large measure of ginger ale. 'This'll do yer good,' he said, smiling.

Carrie sipped the drink, watching him closely as he quickly gathered up the papers from the settee and placed them away in the sideboard drawer. 'Was yer expectin' somebody else?' she said suddenly.

Joe shook his head. 'I was jus' bein' careful,' he said, giving her a smile.

'I could see that,' she replied. 'I saw yer try to 'ide that poker. Are yer in trouble, Joe?'

He shook his head dismissively but Carrie could see the look in his eyes. 'It's this Macedo business, ain't it?' she said, her eyes searching him. 'Yer got yerself too involved, Joe. Yer should 'ave let somebody else take the lead. Why you?'

His expression changed. 'I 'ad to,' he said defensively. 'Nobody seemed ter know what ter do, or didn't want ter know. George Galloway wanted ter turn the information over ter the police an' the rest of 'em were sittin' there like a load o' dummies. Besides, I'm committed. I was committed the day my bruvver was murdered.'

'Yeah, but that was an old score. Yer got yer revenge, Joe. The people who killed yer bruvver are eivver dead or locked up, yer said so yerself. This is a different crowd, an' it's a different business. What d'yer wanna do, right all the wrongs?'

Joe picked up his glass of whisky and sat down in the

chair facing her. 'Look, Carrie. Gerry Macedo burned my ware'ouse down an' in doin' so 'e almost killed yer farvver,' he said in a low voice. 'I've already told yer that there's a dangerous crowd be'ind Macedo, the same sort o' people who beat my bruvver's brains out an' ruined our family. My farvver was a fit man who never knew a day's illness, but he only lasted a year after that. Those bookies who were be'ind the killin' are all accounted for, it's true, but their friends an' 'igher-ups are still on the streets, an' they're financin' Gerry Macedo. If enough people stand up an' be counted, an' create merry 'ell wiv those in authority there's a good chance that Macedo's crowd are gonna go down the drain. Local people 'ave gotta be prepared ter fight fer the place they live in. If they don't there's no chance fer any of us.'

Carrie slipped out of her chair and knelt in front of him, her head resting on his lap. 'I couldn't stand it if anyfing 'appened ter you, Joe,' she said in an almost inaudible voice. 'Yer've made me feel a complete woman. I couldn't live wivout yer.'

He stroked her hair gently as she nestled against him. 'I don't know 'ow all this is gonna end,' he told her. 'What we've got is somefing special. Don't let's get ourselves all screwed up. Let's take it a day at a time. We can always meet, 'owever rare the occasions, an' when we do we can make love. The waiting can be good fer us. It makes it that bit special when we are tergevver. Like now, like this minute.'

He leaned forward and slipped out of the chair, sitting down on the thick rug beside her. His arms gently enveloped her and Carrie felt his hot lips pressing against hers as she let herself sink back until he was above her. She sighed to feel how good it was, aware of his hands searching her body, reaching down and gently stimulating her. She felt a delicious sensation as he fervently caressed her, and as her passion mounted she gasped at the intensity of his loving.

It was getting dark outside, and as the swirling mist closed over the busy thoroughfare below the two young people were joined together in a fierce act of love.

In the small office on the top floor of James's Wharf the manager was just finishing clearing away the various papers and invoices when Ronald James walked in.

'I thought you'd gone, Mr James,' he said in surprise.

'I've a few things to finish off,' the wharf owner replied. 'You might as well get off home, Gerald. The weather looks like it's turning for the worse. Don't worry, I'll lock up. I shouldn't be long. Oh, by the way, could you drop this letter in the postbox for me? It won't go out now until after Christmas but I might forget it otherwise. Have a Merry Christmas, Gerald, and give my best regards to your good wife.'

Gerald Simpson hurried down the stairs, anxious to catch the train and glad that he would not have to face another stock sheet until after Christmas. Silly old fool, he thought to himself as he hurried along Tooley Street. He could have been home hours ago instead of fussing around the place. The trouble with Ronald James was, he never gave his staff any credence, never delegated responsibility. The man was always checking the books, countermanding orders and interfering in everybody's work. Trade was down this year, and if James didn't do something about getting enough clients to fill that spare floor space the wharf was going to run into debt. Well, anyway, there was nothing to be done until after Christmas. James would certainly have to pull his socks up in the new year, Gerald thought as he hurried up the steep flight of steps to London Bridge Station.

The subject of Gerald Simpson's angry thoughts was

slumped forward in a swivel chair, his elbows resting on the linoleum-covered desktop. Ronald James glanced up at the large wall clock. It showed ten minutes to five. Bernadene would be entertaining her friends no doubt, he thought with a wry smile. Her stupid friends. They were always calling round and it was always Bernadene who was expected to understand their problems and comfort them. If only she had been able to understand his problems, he thought sadly. If only they had been able to talk to each other more. If he had taken the trouble to find time for her, then maybe he would not be in such a mess now. It was his own fault, though, he knew. He had allowed himself to be drawn in. George Galloway had bullied him into calling the meeting and then that tricky character Maitland had really stirred everything up. Ronald James berated himself for not handling the situation better than he had. Now he was caught with his feet in both camps.

Whatever had possessed him to store that contraband? he asked himself over and over again. The price was good, it was true, but the consequences had proved to be more far-reaching than he would ever have dreamed. One of the wharfingers in the other camp had seen to that. Blackmail. Sheer blackmail. Gerry Macedo would never let him off now, and where would it all end? He had already threatened James, blaming him for not handling the meeting correctly, but what more could he have done without letting the cat out of the bag? He had at least warned Len Bartholomew and Arnold Greenedge, the most influential of the councillors. Surely they could have averted the crisis? Now it seemed all was lost. That bloody Communist demonstration didn't help either, he thought with distaste. What was there left to do? He would be expected to join the rest of the consortium now that they had decided to concentrate their efforts north of the river, but how could he do that without his friends and business associates discovering his terrible, shameful treachery? What was he expected to do, sell off his property and move out? It was impossible. And what was going to happen to Joe Maitland? They had sworn to finish him once and for all. He would no doubt be fished out of the river one day soon, and Ronald James knew that he would have to take his share of the blame. Perhaps he could have averted all of this had he not been so convincing with his speechmaking. But it was too late now. He felt like a fox being cornered, to be torn to pieces between the hounds. There was no escape.

The wharfinger smiled to himself as he leaned to one side and picked up his briefcase. The army had taught him many things, and one of those was to face up to the inevitable. He had seen his men answer his command with blind obedience and clamber out of the safety of trenches at the sound of his whistle to face the murderous fire. He knew what it was to be in a situation where there was no hope and he was not afraid. Poor Bernadene, he thought. She would be so upset.

Ronald James stroked his beard as he pondered for a few moments, then he quickly withdrew the service revolver from the briefcase, put the muzzle into his mouth and blew the back of his head off.

Chapter Twenty-one

A few days after Christmas Billy Sullivan went to see Joe Maitland at his office in Druid Street. When he was shown in he sat down wondering how he was going to reject the kind offer.

'Well, Billy, I'll come straight ter the point,' Joe said. 'I've got the opportunity of takin' out a lease on a bit o' land just off Tooley Street. Now I know yer ambition 'as always bin ter get yerself a gym, so if yer still keen I'd be willin' ter let yer rent the site off me. What d'yer say?'

Billy stared down at the floor for a few moments then looked up at the warehouse owner. 'I fink it's very good of yer, Joe,' he said quietly, 'but I've gotta turn it down. Yer see I'm plannin' on gettin' married soon as I can get a couple o' rooms an' I'll need all me savin's.'

Joe nodded. 'I see. Well, there's a lot o' sense in settlin' down, I s'pose. When did yer decide ter change yer mind? Will Tanner told me yer wasn't gettin' married till yer got the gym.'

Billy shrugged his shoulders and a distant look appeared in his deep blue eyes. 'It was when my Annie told me she was in no 'urry ter get married,' he said quietly. 'She said I should go an' realise my dream. That's when I knew what was important an' what wasn't. I'm sorry, Joe. I appreciate what yer done.'

Joe Maitland stood up and held out his hand. 'Well, I

wish yer luck, Billy,' he said, smiling. 'It seems like yer done the right fing. Annie sounds like a real nice gel.'

'She is,' Billy replied, clasping the warehouse owner's hand. 'I'll see yer about.'

It was a sad-faced Billy Sullivan who walked home through the backstreets. He had come so near to getting his gym, but now there were other things to worry about. It wasn't fair to Annie to keep her waiting. He knew how much she wanted to get married yet was still prepared to wait, maybe for years. Well, she wouldn't have to now, he thought. Joe Maitland was right, she was a real nice girl.

After the ex-boxer had left the office Joe Maitland called Will Tanner in. 'I didn't make much progress wiv young Sullivan, Will,' he remarked, offering his manager a chair.

'Yer mean 'e turned yer offer down?' William said, looking puzzled. 'That's all that young man ever seems ter talk about, accordin' ter my Danny. I wonder what made 'im change 'is mind.'

'It seems 'e's gettin' married,' Joe replied.

'So 'e's finally gonna do it,' William said smiling. 'Well, it must 'ave bin bloody 'ard fer the lad ter turn that offer down, Joe.'

The warehouse owner leaned back in his chair. 'Well, I'll 'ave ter phone up the agent an' cancel the option on that site,' he sighed. 'Never mind, it might all be fer the best.'

Annie McCafferty was feeling upset as she got ready to meet Billy Sullivan. It had been a tiring day and one of the children she was attending to had shown signs of measles and she had had to bring in the doctor. Now as she prepared for an evening walk along the riverside she thought of her stay in Dublin and of the promise she had made to herself that when she got back to

Bermondsey she would experience something of life while she was still young. She wondered if things would ever work out the way she had hoped. Billy was a very nice young man whom she had grown to love. He had kissed her on their first time out together but she had pressed her lips together so firmly she hardly felt it. He had laughed at her and showed her just how a kiss should be given and received. He had been very courteous, however, and he had not made her feel cheap or wanton.

Since that first time out together she had grown more daring, and now she kissed him passionately with her lips open on his. He had at first pressed his body to hers until she felt he was being too forward, but now she wanted him to kiss her, take her in his arms and crush her to him. The natural feelings which had grown in her with his passionate embraces had become so overpowering that she was aching for more. It would be unthinkable to go any further outside of marriage, she knew, but whenever Billy kissed her goodnight she was left with a deep ache that only he could take away. Now there seemed to be no immediate opportunity to get married and to have the family she desired more than anything. It would be hopeless while his dream was unfulfilled.

Annie walked along the tree-lined path from her flat behind Jamaica Road and saw Billy walking towards her. Usually she met him at the main road but tonight he was early. His face was glowing as he came up to her and kissed her unashamedly on the lips in full view of the flats.

'Billy Sullivan,' she reproached him, trying to remain serious. 'Whatever next?'

He smiled as he took her arm. 'There's somefink I've gotta tell yer,' he said excitedly.

They arrived at the junction with Jamaica Road.

'What is it, Billy?' she asked, aware of his impatience.

'I went ter see Joe Maitland terday,' he said. ''E's Carrie's farvver's guv'nor. Well, what d'yer fink? 'E's only offered me a bit o' land fer the gymnasium.'

'Why, that's really good,' Annie replied, trying to hide her disappointment.

'I gotta tell yer somefink though,' he said, taking her arm and propelling her across the main road.

'What is it?' she asked, feeling him almost pulling her along.

They had reached the small public garden beside a little Methodist chapel and Billy led the way in. It was near dusk and the winter sky above was turning from a golden red to a deeper smouldering violet. Seagulls wheeled noisily overhead and a tram rattled by, then all was quiet.

'I told 'im no,' Billy said, grinning widely.

'You what?' Annie said, aghast.

'I told 'im straight, Annie. I told 'im there was somefing much more important at the moment, I told 'im I was gonna get married.'

She felt the tears rising in her eyes. 'Am I hearing you right?' she asked him.

He took her in his arms and squeezed her tightly. 'Will yer marry me, Annie?'

'Yes please, Billy. Oh, yes please,' she whispered, her voice choked with emotion.

He pulled her down on to a wooden bench and she sat upright facing him, her face glowing with happiness. 'I thought you were desperate to get that gym,' she said, still feeling bewildered.

'I want that gymnasium badly, Annie, believe me, but there's somefing I want much more,' he told her tenderly. 'I want you. I want ter marry yer an' 'ave lots o' babies wiv yer. The gym can wait. We can't. If we're gonna 'ave lots o' babies we can't afford ter wait.'

308

She laughed at his serious look and then they were embracing. The feeling of love flowed over her body and through her veins, until she was consumed with her love and desire for him. Without saying anything she got up and took his hand, and he did not resist as she led the way out of the small secluded garden. It was chilly now and the wind was getting up. Her warm flat beckoned them and Annie knew that tonight she was going to experience the fullness of life.

1926 began cold and bleak with the river trade almost at a standstill, and the sight of dockers and rivermen standing around in the cold riverside lanes had long since come to be accepted as inevitable for the time of year. The death of Ronald James was given little space in the local papers save for the mention that his firm was trading at a loss, which was seen by readers as the most likely cause of his taking his own life. Rumours were rife along the riverfront, however, and the word soon spread among the dock workers that he had liked the horses and had run up a large debt with the bookies. The firm continued to trade under his name and very soon the tragedy was almost forgotten in the face of the rivermen's many urgent problems.

In Page Street the venerable women gathered as usual in Sadie's front parlour or in Florrie Axford's home and discussed the crucial topics of the day. Florrie was feeling pleased at the way her little ploy had gone and the saying 'dropping a carrot' never failed to raise secret smiles from her confederates. Maudie Mycroft was excluded from the little secret but it was she who had benefited by Florrie's idea.

It had been common knowledge during the previous year that something was going on between Alice Johnson and Broomhead Smith and it was no surprise to the local women when word got out that they had finally married. Broomhead's cart had been parked outside Alice's front door during the late afternoons and well into the evenings and it had become a standing joke even amongst the men of the street when they gathered at the Kings Arms. Ernest Mycroft had heard the jokes about Broomhead's philandering and had seen the cart parked there for himself but he took little notice of it, what with the affairs of the Bermondsey Communist Party preoccupying his waking hours. He became concerned, however, when one well-meaning lady told him to watch points because Broomhead's cart was now often seen parked outside *his* front door in the evenings. Ernest then suddenly decided that spending his evenings distributing leaflets and tracts about the local communities was not so important as keeping an eye on Maudie. His work suffered and his comrades at the Party office became convinced that Ernest Mycroft's enthusiasm was waning. Maudie however was pleasantly surprised at his sudden desire to stay at home and she responded by cooking him his favourite meals and paying him the little attentions that she had previously neglected.

Ernest was troubled. He suspected that her little kindnesses were an attempt on her part to make amends for leading a double life, and he even thought about challenging the local totter to own up that he was having an affair with Maudie. His pride prevented him, however, and he suffered agonies of uncertainty. She was not that sort of person, he told himself. She was now in her early sixties and too old for that sort of carrying on. Alice Johnson was about the same age as Maudie though and it didn't stop her entertaining the totter, he realised.

Ernest was torn between looking after his own interests and bringing down the Government, and after a lengthy period of staying home and making sure that

Broomhead's cart was firmly parked a few doors away outside Alice Johnson's house he decided that maybe he had been paying too much attention to a rumour-monger. He started attending various meetings once more and delivering Party messages around the back-streets warning of the dire consequences of capitalist overproduction, only to be stopped in the street by another well-wisher who calmly told him that Broomhead's cart was outside his front door again.

Ernest decided angrily that enough was enough. He had once suspected Maudie of a liaison with one Peter the Painter, and now it was Broomhead the totter. Well, the Bermondsey Communist Party would have to find themselves another loyal worker, he told himself. The continuance of his long-term marriage was more important than destroying the Government and Ernest promptly resigned.

Florrie Axford and her friend Maisie Dougall were no longer able to play their little game now, and no more carrots came to be discreetly dropped outside Maudie's front door to entice the scraggy nag along the kerb as soon as Ernest had departed.

The dining rooms in Cotton Lane were the scene of many union meetings during the early months of '26, and when the miners were locked out the mood of conflict intensified. Don Jacobs told his men in no uncertain terms that a General Strike was on the cards.

'The pit owners 'ave locked the men out an' they don't only want more hours out of 'em, they want 'em ter take a drop in wages as well,' he declaimed. 'It's somefing we can't let 'appen. The miners 'ave laid it on the line. "Not a penny off the pay, not a minute on the day." That's what they've told the bosses, an' that's what we've got ter support 'em over. It's the miners terday an' the dockers termorrer.'

Jacobs had found backing from his men but Fred looked glum as he sat with Carrie in the little front room over the cafe that evening.

'We've 'ad strikes before, Carrie, but if it's a General Strike we might as well close down,' he said gloomily 'Nobody's gonna be comin' in 'ere, that's fer sure.'

Carrie tried to sound optimistic. 'I don't fink it'll come to a General Strike,' she said. 'They'll back down when they know everybody's comin' out on strike. There'll be no buses or trams, no trains, an' the ships'll be linin' up in the river.'

'Yeah, that's right,' Fred replied. 'An' what's more there'll be fightin' in the streets once the army get sent in. It nearly 'appened when the Welsh miners come out on strike. The army was gonna open fire on 'em.'

Carrie sighed and stared down into the glowing hearth. Fred was getting worse, she thought sadly. He had never been an optimist, but lately he seemed depressed, and he was not looking himself. In fact he looked ill. There were dark circles around his eyes and his face seemed to have aged. Their love life had ceased to exist and all he seemed to do these days was sleep in the chair until it was time for bed and then he was asleep as soon as his head touched the pillow. He had always been suspicious of her feelings for other men but in the past she had managed to reassure him that there was no one other than him. She could not honestly say that to him now, and she began to feel that his growing silence and his complete lack of physical feeling for her might mean that he had already convinced himself there was now someone else in her life. What was she to do? she wondered. What would be the outcome of her passionate affair with Joe Maitland?

One thing was certain, she told herself, Fred would never know from her. She could never bring herself to hurt him unnecessarily. He was a good, kind man despite everything. He had taken her as a bride even though he knew that his feelings for her would not be reciprocated in the way he might wish. Nevertheless he had provided a home for her and now she had her own independence inasmuch as she held her own bank book. There was just ninety pounds in the account, but it was her savings, the money she was assiduously putting aside to help get her parents out of the slum block in Bacon Street. She had never really denied to herself that it was the reason for her marrying Fred in the first place. Whatever happened in the future that money was going to remain in her account until there was enough for her to achieve her goal.

Fred was already snoring and Carrie picked up the evening paper. There was one item of local interest which caught her eye. Beneath a picture of the Town Music-Hall there was a report which said that the old building was being demolished to make way for a new block of workers' flats. The article contained a brief history of the old music-hall and mentioned that its fate had caused dissent among the local councillors and two of them, Councillors Bartholomew and Greenedge, had resigned. Carrie's thoughts turned immediately to Joe Maitland. He could take pride in the fact that it was his determination which had helped thwart Gerry Macedo's plans to corrupt business in the riverside boroughs for his own criminal ends. The local organisations and clubs had been successful in their agitation, but it seemed very sad that one of the architects of the victorious campaign had seen fit to take his own life.

It had been a busy day at the Druid Street warehouse and during the late afternoon Joe Maitland called his manager into the office. 'Will, I'm takin' a young lad on, an' 'e starts next week. I don't want yer luggin' those cases around, d'yer 'ear?'

'I can manage, Joe. It's no great 'ardship,' William replied firmly, looking his boss in the eye.

'I know that, Will, but those provisions are not like 'andlin' the regular stuff. They're bloody 'eavy. I've seen Cruncher puffin' an' blowin', an' 'e's strong enough. You take it easy, Will, yer not a young man anymore. Let the ovvers do the graft an' you jus' keep yer eye on 'em. Yer'll 'ave enough ter do keepin' tags on all the stock. Besides, I'm buyin' more an' more provisions. They're goin' very well as a matter o' fact an' I'm gonna need more space. As it 'appens I've jus' completed a deal on a site for a new ware'ouse. It's in Wilson Street, along from Galloway's yard.'

'I'm pleased for yer, Joe,' William replied, leaning back in his chair. It was welcome news that there was another young man starting, he thought. Those cases were getting heavy and Joe was right, he wasn't a young man anymore. If Nellie had had her way he would have retired when he was sixty-five, but he had insisted he would remain with Joe Maitland as long as he was wanted. He was now turned sixty-six and the heavy lifting was telling on him. He realised though that he might be forced to stop, along with everyone else.

'There's a lot o' talk about a General Strike,' he remarked after a while. 'D'yer fink it'll mean everybody's gotta come out?'

Joe shrugged his shoulders. 'I fink if it does come off it'll stop the public transport an' the docks o' course. As fer the factories, I should say the large ones'll be affected but the smaller ones will stay open. It's a matter o' conscience. Personally I fink the miners 'ave got a genuine grievance, but as a businessman I shouldn't be sayin' that, should I?'

William stared down at his clasped hands. 'I was never in the union. Galloway wouldn't 'ear of it, as yer

314

know, but even 'e 'ad ter knuckle down. Accordin' ter one of 'is carmen who comes in the Kings Arms the unions are talkin' wiv 'im. Now 'e's got that ovver yard in Wilson Street an' 'e's runnin' lorries 'e's got ter be careful 'ow 'e treats 'em or 'e won't get a look in at the docks an' wharves. Mind yer, there was a time I never thought I'd see the day ole George Galloway 'ad the union in 'is yard.'

Joe settled down to his paperwork as soon as William Tanner left the office. It had been quiet lately, he thought. Too quiet, perhaps. There was little news filtering his way from contacts in East London and he wondered if he had been over-cautious in varying his route home and securing his flat since he received the warning letter. The nights were getting lighter now and as time went on the chances of his coming to harm would diminish. Nevertheless he would still have to be careful, he realised. Gerry Macedo and his cronies were not the sort of people who were likely to forget.

In Page Street the new Mrs Smith had quickly asserted her dominance over Broomhead and she had made him miserable. He was living in her house, she declared, and subject to her rules and regulations. He had been required to smarten himself up, despite his protestations that totters did not usually go out on their carts in pinstripe suits. He had had to be very careful of his footwear too. Alice would not let him into the house if there was a trace of horse dung on his boots, and she also insisted that his horse be smartened up, something which irked Broomhead more than her demands on his person. That scruffy nag had become a laughing stock among his pals, or rather he had, he thought sullenly. Braiding a drayhorse or a thoroughbred was one thing but trying to make that bag of bones look anything other than a cross between a donkey and a mule was like asking him to go to church every Sunday.

Broomhead had not had the worst of it, however. One Saturday evening Alice looked up from her sewing and said, 'I fink we should go ter church termorrer.'

Broomhead shook his head vigorously and shuddered. 'No fear, Alice,' he protested. 'I'd be uneasy in church. Besides, Sunday mornin's I 'ave me lay in.'

'Well, I fink yer better ferget yer lay in, Bill,' she told him. 'I'm goin' ter church, an' if the neighbours see me goin' on me own they'll fink we don't get on anymore.'

'Sod the neighbours,' Broomhead blurted out. 'Why should yer worry about what the neighbours fink? There's that skinny ole cow Florrie Axford. She looks like a good dinner wouldn't do 'er any 'arm. Then there's that dopey mare Maisie Dougall. I reckon she's about as attractive as the back of a number sixty-eight tram. Then there's that Maudie Mycroft woman. Fancy yer bein' worried what the likes o' them fink! Maudie couldn't afford ter criticise the likes o' you. She's a scatty mare too. I don't know who's the worst, 'er or Maisie. As fer the rest of 'em, sod 'em, that's what I say.'

'Well, if yer don't come ter church termorrer there'll be no dinner fer yer, an' that's final,' Alice told him.

'Well I'm not, so there,' the totter replied, thinking already that maybe he had gone too far.

Alice folded her arms and stared into the fire, while Broomhead sighed deeply. Alice was sulking, and if there was one thing he couldn't stand it was Alice sulking. It was better than her attacking him with an axe or a carving knife, but he couldn't stand it. It could go on for days, as he knew from experience.

'All right, I'll go wiv yer,' he said quickly. 'But don't expect me ter sing.'

Broomhead's capitulation cheered Alice up no end

316

and she even condescended to make him a suet pud-
ding for supper.

Next morning Alice and her totter husband left for
church arm-in-arm.

'Good mornin', Mrs Sullivan. We're just orf ter
church,' Alice called out across the street.

'Keep 'im away from the communion wine,' Sadie
mumbled.

'Good mornin', Mrs Axford. Me an' Bill are just orf
ter church,' Alice informed her.

'Don't tell all the bloody street,' Broomhead
muttered.

'Mornin', Mrs Dougall. We're just orf ter church, me
an' Bill.'

'That's nice for yer,' Maisie remarked, mumbling an
oath under her breath.

By the time the couple had left the turning everyone
knew that they were off to church, but Alice was not
finished. 'I must pop in the sweet shop,' she said, pulling on Broomhead's arm. 'Mornin', Mrs Longley. Me
an' Bill are just orf ter church.'

Widow Longley gave Broomhead a frosty stare. She
had had reason to fall out with the totter in the past and
had often remarked to her friends that in her opinion
Alice Johnson was two pennies short of a shilling.
'Mind 'e don't frighten the children,' she said, with a
tilt at humour.

Broomhead was glad that they finally reached St
James's Church without meeting any more neighbours,
but when they took their seats in the pews and the
organist started up Alice dug him hard in the ribs and
pointed to the hymn-book in front of him. The organist
was playing 'Onward Christian Soldiers', a hymn
which Broomhead rather liked, and he realised that
there was nothing else for it. His bass voice resounded
across the rows of pews and Alice's face flushed with

embarrassment as some of the congregation turned to stare at where the noise was coming from. Broomhead was secretly enjoying himself. He was sure that after his little exhibition of hymn-singing Alice would think twice before she ever dragged him off to church again.

He had miscalculated, however. When the sermon was over and his voice once more filled the packed church the vicar was overjoyed. At the end of the service he looked up to the stained-glass window and thanked the Lord for answering his prayer, then he hurried over to the departing couple.

'I really should congratulate you on your fine rendering of "Onward Christian Soldiers",' he said, holding his hands together as though in prayer. 'Absolutely top-hole. I must ask your name.'

Broomhead grinned widely and Alice simply purred with pleasure at being noticed. 'I'm Bill Smith an' this is my good lady, Alice,' he replied.

'Well, Mr Smith, I'd like to invite you to join our choir. Do you know, I prayed to the Lord to send me a bass singer and he's answered my prayer. Say you'll join us, Mr Smith. Please say you'll join us.'

'Well, I'd like to, but . . .'

'But nuffink,' Alice cut in, kicking her husband smartly on his shin. 'Of course you will, won't you, dearest?'

The sight of Alice glaring at him and the vicar fawning over him was too much. 'All right,' Broomhead replied. 'I'll give it a try.'

'That's all we ask,' the vicar said, clapping his hands together like an excited child. 'Monday evening, seven-thirty sharp. We can expect to be through by nine-thirty. I look forward to seeing you then.'

Once outside Alice was already grooming him for the part. 'Now listen, yer'll 'ave ter change yer boots. I don't want yer smellin' the church out wiv horse dung.

Yer can put anuvver shirt on. I don't want yer showin' me up, d'yer 'ear?'

Broomhead nodded dutifully and let his shoulders sag as they walked home to Page Street. It looked as though he might have to find himself suffering a sudden unexplained attack of tonsillitis on Monday morning. Or maybe it should come on suddenly towards the evening, he decided. Sitting around Alice all day Monday would be worse than joining the choir.

Chapter Twenty-two

On the 3rd of May, 1926 a General Strike was declared.
The transport workers and rivermen joined the miners
and the country was plunged into chaos. Trams and
buses stopped, the railways were brought to a standstill, riverside cranes were idle, and hardly a horse cart
or a lorry was to be seen on the roads. On the cobblestones outside the major docks and wharves meetings
took place, and unexpectedly Bradleys' Dining Rooms
in Cotton Lane enjoyed the busiest spell they had had
for a long time.

It did not last, however, and after the first two days
very few customers walked through the doors. Carrie
decided to keep her two helpers on, even though there
was little for them to do. Bessie found it infuriating
having to stand about doing nothing and so she found
a bucket and mop and proceeded to wash down the
paintwork. Her industry was infectious, and Lizzie
scrubbed the floors and the tables while Marie helped
Fred clean out the kitchen. For the first time in ages
Carrie found she had time to herself and took Rachel
for walks to the park and along the deserted riverside.
She had not been able to see Joe Maitland very much
during the past few months. Now she had the time,
but she needed an excuse to get away from the dining
rooms.

Danny called on his friend Billy Sullivan on the

fourth morning of the strike. Billy's firm had been very slack and the only job they were working on was the old tramshed in New Cross. Now that the drivers and conductors were on strike their pickets had confronted the building workers, and after a brief discussion Billy and the other labourers had decided not to cross the picket lines and were all sent home.

'What d'yer fancy doin' then, Danny?' Billy asked.

'Well, we could go up ter Dock'ead an' stand around Shad Thames fer a while. They say there's a load o' blacklegs gonna try an' get inter Butler's Wharf,' Danny suggested.

The two young men sauntered off along the Jamaica Road, Danny upright with his shoulders held back proudly while Billy shuffled along beside him with his distinctive rolling gait, his shoulders hunched forward. When they reached Shad Thames they found dockers and rivermen gathered there in a crowd and their mood was decidedly hostile.

'If they try ter get past us we'll do 'em,' someone shouted.

'If they try it 'ere we'll turn the bloody vans over,' another added.

Soon union officials arrived and told the men to stay within the law but protest verbally if there were any attempts to break the strike with non-union volunteers.

'On yer way,' one irate docker called out. 'If they try it 'ere we'll do 'em in.'

'We'll string the bastards up,' someone cried.

'We'll swing fer the whoresons,' another docker called out.

The union officials pleaded for calm and good sense but soon realised they were wasting their time trying to appeal to the men's better nature.

'It's gettin' nasty. I reckon we should get some of the

local stewards up 'ere,' one of the officials suggested.

'Go on, piss orf,' a large docker shouted out. 'We're stayin' put, an' if there's any attempt ter stop us gettin' ter the blackleg bastards there'll be blood on the pavement, an' yer better believe it.'

The chief union official turned to his deputy. 'See if yer can get Don Jacobs up 'ere, Charlie. 'E's about the only one they'll listen to.'

Danny turned to Billy, his face set seriously. 'I don't like the look o' this, mate. If those blacklegs turn up now there'll be murders.'

'Who are these blacklegs, Danny?' the ex-boxer asked.

Danny shook his head sadly. 'I tell yer, Billy, I saw some tryin' ter get in the docks when we was out once. Lucky fer them Don Jacobs was on 'and ter sort it out an' there was no trouble. The blacklegs went off, but yer never see such a motley crowd in all yer life. They're the dregs. Some 'ave bin out o' work fer so long they'll do murder fer a day's pay. Ovvers are just anti-union, anti-working-class, anti everyfing. There's ovvers too who are paid agitators. They get paid by the shipowners or their agents ter break the strikes. I've never 'eard of 'em succeedin' so far, but yer gotta be careful when they're likely ter show up. They're no pushover, an' a lot of 'em are tooled up. Yer gotta get stuck inter the gits an' let 'em see yer not gonna allow the picket lines ter be broken.'

Billy was getting excited and Danny quickly tried to calm him down. 'Now look 'ere, Billy, I'm not intendin' ter get in any scraps. There's enough blokes 'ere already an' we won't make much difference eivver way. Let's me an' you go an' get ourselves a cup o' tea at Carrie's place. Then we can go up the Old Kent Road an' see if there's any excitement up there. Mind yer,

323

though, I'm not gettin' involved in anyfing. I'm a married man now an' I've got responsibilities, what wiv Iris expectin' an' all.'

'It's all right, Danny,' his friend reassured him. 'I'm gettin' married too, remember. I ain't out ter get me 'ead opened up.'

The two young men were about to walk off when there was a loud cheer. The figure of Don Jacobs could be seen some way in the distance as he clambered up on to a horse cart. His loud voice rang out as he gave the men all the latest news and then there was a silence as he raised his hands.

'Now listen ter me, an' listen carefully,' he began. 'Yer all know me an' yer know that I'm not one ter sell yer down the river. But yer also know that I don't pull me punches. If I fink yer out of order I'll tell yer. Is that right?'

There was silence and he shouted louder: 'Is that right?'

This time there was a roar of assent and he went on. 'Now some of yer 'ave bin in a confrontation wiv blacklegs in the past an' yer know what a load o' scum they can be.'

'What d'yer mean, "can be"?' a docker shouted out.

'What I say,' Jacobs went on in a loud voice. 'Take out the paid agitators an' the anti-union people an' yer left wiv workin'-class men like yerselves but a lot less fortunate 'cos they don't enjoy the protection o' the trade unions. They're the men yer gotta consider.'

'Consider 'em? Kill the bastards, that's what I'd do,' the big docker at the front of the crowd shouted.

Jacobs merely smiled. 'That's the sort o' finkin' the bosses expect. That's why they put their paid men in ter stir up trouble. They want us all ter turn against each over, wiv bruvver fightin' bruvver.'

'What should we do then, Don?' one of the older men shouted out.

'I'll tell yer what we do. First we talk. Then, bruvvers, we defend our lines if we're attacked. But above all we talk ter the blacklegs. If we get a few of 'em ter join the union there an' then we've won the day.'

'That's all very well,' the big docker butted in again, 'but what 'appens when the police escort the scabs inter the wharf?'

'Yer stand back an' do nuffink,' Jacobs said, and was greeted with complete silence while his words sank in. Then there was a mumbling which turned to angry shouts.

'All right, lads. I know what yer finkin',' Jacobs continued. 'We're not breakin' the law, we're just peaceful workers tryin' to assert our rights. But I'll tell yer this – the blacklegs might get past the pickets an' do a good job unloadin' the perishables, but where they gonna move 'em to? Nuffink's gonna leave the riverside while this strike's on, an' if they bring in non-union firms ter try an' shift the stuff then we don't let those firms near the quays, nor ever after. Am I understood?'

A loud roar went up and men were clapping their leader and backslapping him as he stepped down amongst them.

'C'mon, Billy, let's get round ter see Carrie,' Danny said.

The two walked away from the milling crowd and turned into the backstreets. It was quiet after the noise and commotion at Dockhead.

'I fink I've got a place ter live,' Billy said, breaking the silence as they walked out into the quiet Jamaica Road.

'That's good news, Billy,' Danny replied. 'Where at?'

'It's ole Temple's place. Me muvver was sayin' 'e's goin' inter the work'ouse. Poor ole sod's goin' a bit funny. 'E'll be better orf there, at least 'e'll get fed an' looked after.'

'So yer won't be long now then?' Danny asked with a smile.

'Soon as possible. Annie's pleased as punch,' Billy told him, grinning widely.

They turned into Bacon Street and walked briskly along past the row of neat houses on the left and the tall slum blocks to their right. Billy shook his head sadly. 'What a bloody place ter live. I don't know 'ow yer stuck it there, Danny,' he remarked.

'It's the stench that gets yer,' Danny said disgustedly. 'Everybody tips their rubbish roun' the bins at the back an' in the summer it's unbearable. The place is full o' flies an' bluebottles, an' yer can 'ear 'em next door when they turn over in bed. Terrible bloody 'ole. I dunno 'ow the ole man an' the ole lady stand it. One fing's fer sure, they won't be there no longer than need be, not if our Carrie 'as 'er way. She's puttin' money away ter get 'em out. Mind yer, it'll take a time. I know the cafe's doin' well but they've got ter live, an' there's young Rachel ter bring up.'

They reached the cafe and Danny led the way in, strolling up and planting a kiss on his sister's cheek. Billy did likewise and was given a big hug.

'So yer finally gonna tie the knot. Well, congratulations,' Carrie said smiling. 'Yer a lucky feller, I s'pose yer realise that?'

Danny had seated himself at one of the benches and Billy joined him. 'We're gonna slip up ter the old Kent Road, Carrie,' he told his sister as she brought two mugs of tea over.

'Well, don't go gettin' yerself inter trouble,' Carrie

said. 'Lofty Weston came in this mornin' an' said there was murders up at Canal Bridge last night. They've got volunteers ter drive the trams by all accounts, an' police escorts. Lofty told me that one bloke tried ter pull the driver off the tram an' the police tried ter arrest 'im. Everybody started fightin' an' one bloke got 'is 'ead cut open. So jus' you be careful, fer Gawdsake.'

The two young men slipped into the kitchen to say hello to Fred then they left the dining rooms and made their way out on to Jamaica Road and through St James's Road to Canal Bridge. A large group of transport workers were standing around and it was obvious why the strikers had picked that place to stage their protest. The gradient at the bridge meant that the trams would have to slow down at that point, and as it was not very far from the tram terminal at New Cross there would be many vehicles going past. Men were carrying placards and banners, and as policemen continually pushed them back across the pavement voices were raised in protest.

Billy turned to one striker. ''Ow's it goin', mate?' he asked.

'Yer can see fer yerself,' the man answered angrily. 'They won't let us near the trams. We're after gettin' those scabs orf the platforms but we ain't 'ad any luck so far.'

Danny tugged on Billy's arm. 'Let's move on a bit. It looks a bit dangerous 'ere.'

Just then a shout went up. 'There's one comin'!'

Men were pressing forward and the line of police with linked arms were trying their best to hold the throng back. Suddenly the line broke and as one man ran out into the road he was immediately met by two mounted policemen galloping up with their long truncheons swinging. Other men rushed forward and one

327

hung on to a saddle, despite being beaten repeatedly with a truncheon. The tram had clattered up and men were hanging on to the sides, while others fought their way towards the driver's platform. One man made it on to the steps but he was kicked off into the road by the policeman on the footplate. The fighting was becoming very nasty, and men were in danger of getting caught between the iron wheels or having their heads broken by the swinging truncheons.

Billy had surged forward, incensed by one policeman's brutal attack on a cowed striker, but Danny pulled him back. Other men managed to rescue their colleague but the whole situation was getting out of control. Suddenly a group of police reinforcements arrived from behind and the whole area seemed to be turning into a battleground. Everyone was getting drawn into the fray and Billy Sullivan slipped inside a swinging truncheon and floored his attacker with a well-aimed punch to the jaw. He had been spotted and immediately was attacked by a number of other policemen as Danny fought to get to his side along with a bunch of strikers. Violent scuffles and fighting were breaking out everywhere, and when the two opposing groups were finally parted Billy was grinning widely despite a cut eye and Danny had blood seeping from a head wound.

'C'mon, we've outlived our welcome,' he said, grabbing Billy's arm.

At that moment there was a police charge on the small group beside them. They struggled and fought back gamely but were outnumbered and gradually, one by one, were all bundled roughly into waiting police vans and driven away.

When Danny caught his breath he looked around in the gloom at the miserable faces of the strikers and saw Billy grinning at him.

'This is a nice mess ter get ourselves in, I mus' say,' the young ex-boxer remarked.

Danny felt the tender spot on the top of his head and grinned back ruefully. 'Carrie did warn us.'

A man sitting next to Danny on the floor of the van groaned as he felt his bruised ribs. 'I wish I'd 'ave got me 'ands on those volunteer tram drivers,' he growled. 'They want 'orsewhippin'. What makes 'em do it?'

''Cos they're the Midianites o' Bermon'sey, that's why,' remarked a bearded man with a bloodied nose.

'They're what?' the man next to him asked.

'Midianites. They were a lousy tribe o' bastards in the Old Testament. Don't yer ever read yer Bible?'

'Nah. I prefer the *News o' the World*.'

'Well, the Lord told Moses ter smite the Midianites, an' that's what we should 'ave done,' the bearded man growled.

The van pulled up at Tower Bridge Police Station where the men were all bundled out and made to line up beside the high counter.

'Right, yer all bein' charged wiv disorderly conduct,' the station sergeant said wearily. 'Jus' fink yerselves lucky it ain't more serious, like obstructin' the course o' justice an' assaultin' police officers.'

'That's a turn-up fer the book,' one man said. 'I expected ter get the lot chucked at us.'

'They're playin' it down,' another said. 'It suits 'em this way, what wiv the newspapers. I bet 'alf these coppers wish they could strike.'

'Quiet!' the sergeant shouted. 'Right now, let's get started.'

At about the same time back at the cafe Carrie heard the bad news. Tubby Wright the local coalman jumped down from his cart and hurried into the dining rooms.

'There's all 'ell broke out up at the Canal Bridge,' he said excitedly. 'I was up there ter see if the gasworks was open fer me coke an' I saw it all start up. I see young Billy Sullivan get bundled inter the police van. 'E 'ad a nasty eye.'

'Did yer see my Danny there?' Carrie asked quickly.

Tubby took off his cap and scratched his head. 'Nah, only Billy.'

'Where would they take 'em?' Carrie asked him, trying to stay calm.

'Tower Bridge nick, I should fink,' he replied, 'They'll be charged there, 'cos that's where the court is.'

Carrie rushed in to Fred to give him the news and then dashed out of the shop. She was hurrying towards Dockhead when she saw Billy and her younger brother walking along towards her, grinning broadly.

'I s'pose yer fink that's clever, don' yer?' she said angrily. 'What did I tell yer? Didn't I tell yer ter keep out o' trouble? It's your fault, Billy. Yer can't keep out of a fight, can yer?'

Danny slipped his arm around his sister's shoulders. 'It's all right, Carrie. It wasn't Billy's fault. We all got roped in. We was only watchin'.'

"Ave they charged yer?' she asked.

'We're up termorrer. Disorderly conduct,' Danny told her.

'Well, yer better stay roun' the street from now on,' Carrie admonished them. 'I've got some business ter take care of now an' yer makin' me feel like I should be lookin' after you two instead. Yer like a couple o' kids.'

Despite their injuries Carrie felt quite relieved as she walked on towards Tower Bridge and turned into the backstreets, and could not help smiling to herself at their cheeky mood. Ahead of her she saw the Druid Street arches and her heart beat a little faster. The excuse she had invented for Fred was feeble but she had to see Joe.

Her father was in the office and when he saw her peering through the window he hurried to let her in.

'What's wrong, gel?' he asked in a worried voice.

'There's nuffink wrong, Dad, unless yer call gettin' nicked wrong.'

'Who's bin nicked?'

'Danny an' that mad-brain Billy Sullivan,' she told him. 'They got involved in some pushin' an' shovin' up at Canal Bridge an' they got charged wiv disorderly conduct.'

William shook his head slowly. 'What the bloody 'ell was the pair of 'em doin' up there?' he asked her.

'Lookin' for a bit of excitement if the trufe's known,' Carrie said, smiling. 'Anyway, I thought I'd drop in while I was up this way. I wanted ter get Joe to 'old back on that next delivery fer a couple o' weeks. There was 'ardly anybody in the cafe terday, an' it won't get any better while the strike lasts.'

William sat down heavily in his chair. ''E's not in terday, Carrie,' he told her.

The young woman sat talking with her father for a few minutes then she looked up at the clock. 'I'd better be making a move, Dad,' she said, 'there's still work ter be done.'

Once out in the street she hurried towards Joe's flat, eager to have him hold her in his arms once more. Their meetings had been all too infrequent lately and she could hardly wait to be with him again and cherish the fleeting time they would have together.

Tower Bridge Road seemed very quiet without the usual noise of the buses and trams, and here and there small groups of workers were standing around talking quietly. Carrie could not get rid of the guilty feeling that persisted inside her. Normally she would have shrugged such feelings off, but today was different. Fred had looked far from well and he appeared to be worrying about something. He had hardly spoken to her all morning and even Bessie had remarked that he looked queer.

Carrie reached the tin factory just aross from Bermondsey Square but hesitated to cross the road when she spotted the smart black car parked outside Joe's front door. A chauffeur was standing by it with his hands clasped behind his back and glancing up at Joe's window. She had a terrible feeling something was wrong, and walked on a few paces, stopping at a dressmaker's shop opposite the square. She could see the reflection of the car in the window and suddenly Joe appeared, accompanied by two men who seemed to be holding his arms. Carrie turned to see her lover being bundled into the car, then it pulled away quickly and sped off in the direction of Tower Bridge.

Her heart sank and she suddenly felt physically sick. Joe had always laughed away her fears for his safety but she had known all along that he felt himself to be in danger. The men who had taken him looked evil, and the way he was bundled into the car left her in no doubt that he was in mortal danger. For a few moments Carrie stood outside the dressmaker's shop feeling helpless, not knowing what to do, then she quickly turned and set off in the direction of the tram stop.

It was nearly three o'clock by the time she got back to the cafe and as soon as she entered the door she knew there was something wrong by the look on Bessie's pale face.

'Fred's bin took bad, Carrie,' she said. ''E's in the Rovver'ithe Infirmary.'

'What's wrong wiv 'im?' Carrie asked nervously, trying to steel herself for another awful shock.

''E jus' collapsed in the kitchen. It was terrible,' Bessie blurted out, her voice breaking as she reached for a handkerchief. 'I 'eard a bang an' when I looked round there 'e was lyin' on 'is back. 'E was frothin' at the mouth an' I didn't know what ter do. Lucky fer us there was a couple o' carmen sittin' outside an' they come in an' put a coat under 'is 'ead an' made 'im comfortable. I phoned for the ambulance an' the driver said 'e reckons it could be a stroke.'

'Oh my Gawd!' Carrie gasped. 'I must go to 'im. Can yer see ter fings 'ere, Bessie?'

'Of course I can. Off yer go now, luv. I do 'ope 'e'll be all right.'

Carrie hurried along the Jamaica Road feeling as though the day had gone mad. Danny and Billy arrested, Joe was in serious trouble, and now her husband was in hospital. Her head was thumping painfully as she quickly walked through the infirmary gates and went up to the reception desk. The elderly woman was infuriatingly slow in looking through the records and when Carrie finally reached the ward she was met by the ward sister.

'Fred Bradley,' she said, dreading what she might hear.

'The doctor's with your husband now, Mrs Bradley,' the sister said. 'Can I get you a cup of tea? You look all in.'

Before Carrie had finished her tea the doctor peered into the sister's office. 'Mrs Bradley?' he enquired.

Carrie stood up quickly but the doctor motioned her back into her chair. 'Your husband's a very sick man, Mrs Bradley,' he told her gravely.

'Was it a stroke, Doctor?' she asked.

'Yes, I'm afraid it was,' he said.

'Will 'e be all right?' Carrie blurted out, close to tears.

'It's too early to say,' the doctor told her, stroking his chin thoughtfully. 'We don't know how much of the brain is affected as yet, but I think we can say that it's

333

unlikely he'll work again, at least not for a long time, and then only in a very limited capacity.'

Carrie realised with a terrible pang of guilt that she should never have left Fred that morning, and reproached herself bitterly. She had been selfish, thinking only of herself, while Fred was ill. If she had been with him it might have been different. Well, she would never leave him again, she told herself. She would spend her time caring for him and nursing him back to health. He would need her much more than Joe Maitland would. Joe was a fit young man who could look after himself. He would be all right. Nothing was going to happen to him. Poor Fred was helpless though. He would need all the love and attention she had to offer. He wouldn't have to work again, she would see to that. She would see to everything. It was the least she could do for him. He was a good man who deserved someone better, but she would make it up to him.

The pain and guilt weighed like a stone inside her and she suddenly dropped her head in her hands and cried helplessly.

Chapter Twenty-Three

As the fast car approached Tower Bridge Joe Maitland looked out of the window from the back seat at the small groups of people standing around on the pavements. No trams or buses were running and there was only an occasional horse cart to be seen. The driver swung the steering wheel over and sent the car speeding into Cable Street. Along the narrow turning the scene was the same, with groups of men standing together idly and no dock traffic anywhere.

The men sitting on either side of Joe did not speak. They had hardly said anything since knocking on his door and telling him that he must accompany them to the car. It had seemed pointless to object, considering the size of them, and in fact he felt some measure of relief that now the uncertainty which had been hanging over him was to be resolved once and for all. Behind the relief, however, fear was gnawing at him. The men he had upset were not like the wheelers and dealers he had come to know through his business. They were merciless and capable of anything towards those they saw as their enemies.

The car had left Cable Street and entered a narrow turning that looked very run-down. The man on Joe's left leaned forward and whispered something to the chauffeur as the car pulled up outside a factory yard. Then he got out, holding the door open for Joe to follow. As the men grabbed his arms the young trader took a deep breath, trying to remain calm as they propelled him across the cobbled area and through an iron door to a flight of stairs. When they reached the second floor Joe was led into an office, sat down in a chair and told to wait. He looked around at the grimy walls and the shabby office furniture, his mind racing. Why had they brought him here? he wondered. If it was merely to do away with him it could have been done more easily in Bermondsey. Perhaps they wanted to force some information out of him beforehand. He must try to stay calm and let them see that he was holding a trump card. One thing was certain: if he played his hand wrong it was unlikely that he would ever see Bermondsey again.

One of the men from the car suddenly looked out of an inner office and beckoned Joe to come in. The room was well furnished, with a deep-pile carpet and gilt-framed paintings around the walls. The window behind the large oaken desk was hung with velvet curtains, pulled back to allow as much light as possible into the office, and to one side there was a large bookcase reaching almost to the ceiling. The man sitting behind the desk waved Joe into a chair in front of him and then motioned with his head for the other man to leave. Joe guessed him to be in his forties. He had long sideburns and dark hair brushed down sideways above his high forehead, and was smartly dressed in a dark suit, starched collar and spotted tie. It was his grey eyes which disturbed Joe. They were heavy-lidded and unblinking, and they looked cold, almost lifeless.

'I'm glad you could come,' the man said in a slightly mocking tone. 'I hope you've not been too inconvenienced?'

'I wasn't very busy at the time,' Joe said casually, forcing a smile.

His host nodded his head slightly. 'My name is Martin Butterfield and I represent Eastern Enterprises. I understand you've been active in opposing our attempts to buy a certain property in Rotherhithe. Would that be right?'

Joe sat up in the chair and leaned forward, clasping his hands on the edge of the desk. 'I don't see why I should answer questions,' he said icily.

'Oh dear,' Butterfield sighed. 'I was hoping you'd agree to co-operate, Mr Maitland. It would make things so much easier.'

'Well, I might do, if I knew what yer wanted,' Joe replied, sitting back in his chair again.

Butterfield toyed with a silver paper-knife for a few seconds before looking up. 'We know what you've been doing and the reasons behind it,' he said quietly. 'What we'd like to know is, how well did you know the late Ronald James?'

'I got ter know 'im fairly well over a short period o' time,' Joe answered. 'Why d'yer ask?'

The company solicitor pushed the paper-knife away from him and leaned back in his chair with his arms folded. 'Let's be frank with each other, Mr Maitland,' he said. 'We have reason to believe you know why James decided to do away with himself.'

Joe decided to play his card. 'Yeah, I know,' he replied, looking hard at his host. 'Ronald James made the mistake o' usin' 'is ware'ouse ter store a contraband cargo an' when your crowd used that knowledge as a lever ter force 'im inter doin' yer biddin' 'e realised 'e couldn't live wiv it. The papers said it was suicide while 'e was unbalanced. I'd say it was murder, as good as.'

Butterfield smiled mirthlessly. 'Rumours on the riverside are still rife, Maitland. I wouldn't pay any attention to rumours, if I were you.'

'No, not rumours. Fact,' Joe replied. 'James told me

'imself, in a letter 'e wrote ter me jus' before 'e killed 'imself. It was all there. Names, places, even the agent who arranged the cargo storage. It made interestin' readin', an' my solicitor thought so too. 'E's mindin' the letter, by the way. It's my little piece of insurance.'

Martin Butterfield pulled the paper-knife towards him again and spun it on the polished desk surface. 'We expected that James might have written to you,' he said quietly. 'He indicated as much when he left our meeting early on Christmas Eve to go to his wharf. He'd already decided his own fate, Mr Maitland. He was merely worried about yours, for his own sentimental reasons. As it happens I don't think that letter is as valuable as you seem to believe. The cargo has long gone, and any illegal goods wouldn't be entered on the manifest as you can imagine. There would be no record. Let's go a bit further. Names and places, you say? *I* say they were innocent company meetings attended by members of Eastern Enterprises, which is a bona fide company. We can supply minutes to cover all of our meetings.'

'Can yer supply minutes fer the meetin' at the Bargee public 'ouse wiv James an' Gerry Macedo?' Joe asked in a low voice.

For a brief moment Butterfield lost a little of his composure. 'I know of no such meeting,' he said quickly.

'Well, I can assure yer there was such a meetin',' Joe told him. 'It was described at length in the letter I got from James, 'cos it was at that meetin' that Gerry Macedo left him wiv no option but ter join yer company in gettin' that Rovver'ithe deal through.'

'Hearsay,' Butterfield declared. 'Macedo would not discuss business of any sort other than in privacy. There'd be no witnesses to the meeting.'

'Oh, but there was,' Joe replied, smiling. 'Somebody

who Macedo wasn't aware of because 'e was sittin' the ovver side o' the bar.'

'I don't follow you.'

Joe leaned back in his chair. 'James was a very shrewd man who made one big error,' he went on. 'At the end o' the day it cost 'im 'is life. 'E knew 'e was compromised badly an' 'e'd 'ave ter do as 'e was told, but 'e wanted a witness who could be relied upon should 'e ever feel that 'is life was in danger once 'e was no longer useful. It was 'is insurance, the same as it's mine now. I've instructed my solicitor ter pass that letter on ter the police should anyfing 'appen ter me. I've also got the name an' location o' the witness. This man is as deaf as a post, but 'e's got a talent. 'E can lip read. I bet 'e could give a good demonstration in court.'

'I'm sure he could,' Butterfield remarked. 'What we'd like to know now is, what are your future plans? In a few words, is the little war between yourself and Eastern Enterprises over?'

Joe nodded. 'As long as I'm left alone ter get on wiv my business the war's over an' the letter collects dust.'

Butterfield looked satisfied. 'I'm sure that my people will be pleased with the outcome of our little chat,' he said. 'Our company is moving with the times and sadly some of us outlive our usefulness. A fact of life, Mr Maitland, and something you'll no doubt read about in the papers very shortly. I wish you good luck with your ventures. I'll get Marks to run you home,' he concluded as he stood up and held out his hand.

Joe felt the soft clammy grasp as he took Butterfield's hand and matched his steady gaze. He was determined not to let the man see how happy he felt. He knew that the letter he had received from Ronald James and placed into safe keeping was almost certainly the only reason he was being allowed to leave the East End factory alive, and as he walked out of the office and crossed the yard he breathed a huge sigh of relief.

Martin Butterfield was feeling anything but happy as he stood at the gate watching the car pull away, and his face became serious as he went directly back to his office. Maitland might have been bluffing, he thought, but it was unlikely. The man was too cool. He knew he held a trump card. Fortunately he did not hold the whole suit, Butterfield reflected as he picked up the telephone.

Carrie Bradley held a meeting with the staff as soon as she got back from the hospital and it was agreed that Bessie Chandler should take over Fred's role in the kitchen for the time being. Lizzie and Marie were both efficient workers and established favourites with the customers and they were taken on full-time, which pleased the young women. The arrangement suited Carrie, who knew that all of her time would be taken up with caring for Fred as well as their daughter. She would have to get an experienced cook as soon as possible, she realised, but for now the dining rooms could function almost as normal. There was a breathing space at the moment, while the General Strike was on and trade had slumped considerably at the cafe.

As soon as she had made the necessary arrangements Carrie hurried off to Joe's flat. He had been on her mind constantly, and even while she sat at Fred's bedside full of guilt Carrie had not been able to stop herself worrying over his safety. Her heart was thumping in her chest as she climbed the front steps and rang the bell. The footsteps on the stairs made her almost jump for joy and when Joe opened the front door she threw herself into his arms.

'I thought I'd never see yer again,' she cried, burying her head in his chest.

340

'It's all right,' he said quietly, gently patting her back. 'There was nuffink ter worry about.'

Carrie looked up into his face, her eyes clouded with tears. 'I saw those men wiv yer an' I expected the worst,' she sobbed.

Joe took her hand in his and led the way up to his flat, and when they closed the door behind them she was in his arms, her lips pressing on his urgently and her body curled against him. After all the distress the moment was especially precious. With the future so uncertain Carrie did not know how much longer they could enjoy such time together.

The late afternoon was quiet outside and in the top-floor flat Carrie sat talking to Joe, struggling to contain her sadness.

'I can't leave 'im, 'e needs me more than ever, Joe. Yer mus' understand,' she implored him.

Joe nodded sadly. 'I understand, but we can still meet whenever yer get the time, 'owever brief,' he replied, reaching out and taking her hands in his. 'I know yer can't leave 'im, an' I wouldn't want yer to. Jus' say yer'll try ter come ter me whenever yer can.'

'I will, I will,' she said, choking back her tears. 'I love yer, Joe. I'd die if I lost yer.'

He stood up and gently pulled her to her feet. 'Fings are gonna work out jus' fine, you'll see,' he said softly, stroking her back. 'I don't fink I'll be bovvered by Macedo an' 'is villains again, an' we'll find time ter be tergevver.'

Carrie felt the warmth of his body against her and she lifted her face to his. 'I want yer ter love me, Joe,' she whispered. 'Love me now.'

On Tuesday, 11 May the General Strike was over, and on the following Saturday Billy Sullivan and Annie McCafferty were married in St Joseph's Church. Billy intended to have lots of babies with Annie but he had to admit to himself that it might have been a little more proper to have waited at least until the ring had been placed on Annie's finger. The young bride looked radiant as she was escorted down the aisle by William Tanner and her happiness was overflowing. It mattered little to her that she had gone to the altar unchaste. She welcomed the baby growing inside her with all her heart. There had been too much sorrow and loneliness in her life for her to feel anything but joy on this special day.

Sadie Sullivan cried throughout the service. She had despaired of the day she would see her eldest son take the vows. Annie looked a picture, she thought. Her radiant smile said it all, and Sadie had noticed her eyes. There was a certain sparkle to them, and Sadie remembered well the last time Daniel had told her that her eyes were sparkling. She had been a few weeks pregnant with Shaun at the time.

Danny Tanner was the best man and he had been instructed by Sadie to steer Billy away from any likelihood of trouble. ''E's gonna be the same as you, Danny,' she told him. 'Yer've both got responsibilities now, an' besides, yer gettin' too old ter fight. There's Billy wheezin' like a concertina an' still finkin' 'e's the best around 'ere.'

''E was once, Sadie,' Danny said.

'I know that, son,' she replied, 'but the war's took its toll on 'im like the rest of us. Tell 'im ter save 'is strength. I've a feelin' 'e's gonna need it ter push the pram.'

'She ain't, is she?' Danny laughed.

'Who knows? Yer better ask Billy,' Sadie said mysteriously.

The following Saturday Joe Maitland was visited by the

police and subsequently charged with receiving stolen property. The warehouse at Druid Street was full of canned provisions and tinned meat when the police arrived and Joe could not help but laugh at the irony of it all. He had built his business up from shady wheeling and dealing, being prepared to take the risks involved, but this last consignment had been bought in good faith. The price had been right and the import certificates looked to be in order, but the shipping agent could not be traced and the police told him that the large number of cases in his warehouse were part of a stolen consignment.

The awful truth dawned on Joe that same day when he read in the newspaper that Gerry Macedo, a well-known figure in the East End of London, had met his death in mysterious circumstances. His body, bound hand and foot, had been recovered from the River Thames at Wapping Basin. Joe remembered how Martin Butterfield had told him to watch the newspapers. It seemed that Gerry Macedo had finally reached the end of his usefulness to Eastern Enterprises. It also looked very much like he had been set up too. Well, there was one more card to play, Joe thought.

Frank Fuller had been waiting patiently at his lodgings for a visit and as he shaved in front of the smoky mirror he whistled tunelessly. He could feel the vibration on his lips and judge the length of the notes by the shape of his mouth, but what the whistling sounded like was lost to the bulky figure as he pulled the razor down his stubbled face.

Frank Fuller had heard the last sound he would ever hear during the Mons retreat, and as always when he faced a situation that required fortitude and determination he recalled the events of that fatal day in his mind. Lance Corporal Fuller of the 1st Royal West Kents, batman to Major Ronald James, had stood at the officer's side in the trench and waited for the whistle to sound. The shelling had been relentless since just after dawn and the casualties were high. Now the remnants of A company were poised to counter-attack, and as the major sounded his whistle the men clambered up out of the trench and dashed forward across the devastated field in the bright August sunlight.

Shells were still coming over and men fell to the left and right as explosions deafened the splutter of machine-gun fire. Corporal Fuller stayed close to the major who was waving his revolver in the direction of the German trenches to urge his men on, and saw him fall. Fuller could have gone on to the relative safety of the first abandoned enemy trench but instead he ran to his officer. Major James had lost his steel helmet and was bleeding from a head wound, but he was alive. Corporal Fuller pulled the lighter man up on to his shoulder and staggered the hundred yards to the safety of the trench through withering fire. It was only after the major had been handed over to the medical team that Fuller left the trench, and was immediately blown back into it by a shell exploding a few feet away. Apart from one or two minor splinter wounds he was unhurt, but his hearing had gone. For his heroic action in saving the major's life Fuller earned the Military Medal, and Ronald James's eternal gratitude. When both men were invalided out of the army and James returned to his business he had taken Frank Fuller on as his valet and general man.

Ronald James's suicide had shocked the devoted man and he knew that one day he would be called upon to bear witness, just as the major had warned. He had been present at the meeting in Shad Thames as well as the pub meeting the major had had with Macedo, and he had seen the suicide verdict declared and nothing happen, but now things seemed to be moving. After reading of the East End villain's death in the newspapers and receiving the letter from Joe Maitland, he realised that now was the time, and he was ready.

Frank Fuller finished shaving and then put on his coat and hat to take his usual morning walk from his lodgings in a quiet Peckham Street. The sun was shining as he stepped out of the house and glanced along the turning before crossing the road. He saw the motor car parked outside the doctor's house but he could not hear the engine roar into life, nor the sound of the car drawing quickly away from the kerb.

A few seconds later the car roared out of the turning leaving Frank Fuller lying dead in the gutter.

The dining rooms in Cotton Lane were continuing to flourish despite Fred's absence from the kitchen. Carrie ran the business with fortitude, dividing her time between caring for her husband and supervising her willing staff. Fred's stroke had left him paralysed down one side and he could only move about with great difficulty. His speech was slurred and he had become prone to bouts of deep depression. Carrie had to wash him, feed him, and in effect make herself responsible for his survival. Fred's condition had caused Rachel to become a very grown-up seven year old, however. She had learned to feed him, help her mother tend to his daily needs, and make herself generally useful about the house.

Carrie's trying days were filled with worries. Joe's business had been forced to close and her father was now out of work and living on his meagre old-age pension. Joe's case was to be heard at the Old Bailey and the strain of waiting had affected him badly. He had lost his devil-may-care attitude, and only on the very rare occasions that he and Carrie found time to be together could the two of them briefly forget the trouble and torment in both their lives. The need for a cook to replace Fred in the kitchen was another big worry for Carrie. The effervescent Bessie was coping well but she was not afraid to admit that being a kitchen helper was more to her liking than being solely responsible for the cooking. The dock trade was booming again now and as customers continued to fill the popular dining rooms in Cotton Lane Bessie sweated away in the hot kitchen and Lizzie and Marie shared the serving and waiting on tables. Carrie was hard pushed with the ordering of supplies, maintaining the books and caring for Fred, and it was a great relief to her when Danny walked in the cafe one morning and brightly declared that he had found the ideal replacement for Fred.

Whenever Danny was working downriver he invariably visited a riverside coffee stall in Wapping which was run by an effeminate character known to everyone as Corned Beef Sam. The stall itself was a ramshackle monstrosity of galvanised sheeting, pieces of timber and weather-board nailed together to produce what many of the locals described as 'a bloody disgrace to the neighbourhood'. The stall had wheels, and in the distant past it had been hauled to its present site as a temporary measure. The council objected, the locals objected, and efforts were made to get rid of the eyesore, but to the customers of Corned Beef Sam the stall was a godsend. Sam sold the best and cheapest sandwiches for miles around and his tea was always hot and strong. The Gas Board threatened to cut off his gas, the Water Board threatened to cut off the water and the newly appointed food inspector tried his hardest to catch Sam out, but the resilient character prevailed.

Sam was now in his mid-thirties and was finding it difficult not to become disillusioned. The rates were going up, his old copper boiler was playing up, and to add to his troubles the local Council had informed him that his contraption would have to be removed while they did major repairs to the road.

'I'm bleedin' upset, really I am,' he moaned in his effeminate voice to his docker customers one morning. 'I've a good mind ter chuck the bleedin' lot in. I sweat 'ere fer nine hours every day, an' fer what? What's me fanks? I gotta listen ter you lot moanin' about the bleedin' tea an' the state o' the corned beef. I mean ter say, what d'yer expect fer tuppence?'

The customers grinned at Sam's tantrum and one young docker flapped a limp wrist and shook his head. 'Never mind, Sam, give us a kiss an' ferget yer troubles,' he joked.

'Don't yer be so rude, yer great lummock,' Sam shouted at him. 'Yer not gettin' on an' orf me fer tuppence.'

The roar of laughter helped to force a coy smile out of the hard-pushed stall owner. 'Bleedin' sauce! As if I ain't got enough ter do, what wiv sawin' up the bread, makin' tea an' coffee an' keepin' the food inspector orf me back, I've gotta put up wiv your bleedin' cheek. Why don't yer go 'ome an' nag yer missus?'

'C'mon, Sam, where's me cheese sandwich?' a carman called out.

'Give us two more teas, Sam.'

'Gis a large tea on the quick, I'm due fer a call,' another carman urged him.

'Why don't yer wait yer turn, I've only got one bleedin' pair of 'ands,' Sam replied, raising his eyes and tutting.

Danny was standing at the stall and he grinned at the harassed man. 'Don't let 'em upset yer, Sam,' he told

347

him. 'We all know yer do the best food around 'ere.'

Sam gave Danny a rueful smile. 'I've bin finkin' o' shuttin' up fer good, really I 'ave,' he said, holding a hand to his side and wincing. 'It's jus' not werf the trouble. I tell yer, Danny, if I could get a decent job I'd close termorrer.'

When Danny left the stall he wrote the address of Carrie's dining rooms on a piece of paper and handed it to him. 'That's me sister's place. She's lookin' fer a good cook. Yer'd be all right there, provided yer can do the job,' he grinned. 'Why don't yer look 'er up?'

'I'm a bleedin' first-rate cook,' Sam replied indignantly. 'There's nuffink I can't cook.'

'No, that's right,' a docker remarked. 'Yer cooked this bloody tea by the look of it.'

'Shut yer ugly trap,' Sam shouted at him, and as Danny left he called out, 'I'll look yer sister up on Saturday, luv.'

During the last week in August when the women of Page Street gathered in Sadie Sullivan's parlour there was much to talk about.

'Alice was tellin' me 'er bloke's in the church choir,' Maisie informed the others.

'Whatever next?' Florrie said. 'They'll 'ave ter watch everyfing that ain't screwed down. 'E'd nick the collection plate if it was werf anyfing.'

'My Carrie's took on a new cook,' Nellie told her friends. 'Funny sort o' bloke by all accounts. 'E comes ter work wiv a shoppin' bag over 'is arm. Carrie's pleased wiv 'im though. She said 'e's a good cook an' really 'ard-workin'.'

'What's the latest about Joe Maitland?' Florrie asked.

'The case comes up next week,' Nellie told her.

'I 'ope 'e gets orf,' Florrie remarked. ''E's a nice fella

is Joe. Good as gold ter me when 'e was lodgin' at my place. I mean ter say, it ain't as if 'e's 'urt anybody.'

The women nodded sympathetically and Florrie got out her snuffbox.

''Ere, I know what I was gonna tell yer,' Maisie said quickly. 'Yer remember that ugly git Jack Oxford who used ter work at the stables? Well, I saw 'im at the market the ovver mornin'. Arm in arm wiv a big woman 'e was. 'E 'ad a nice suit on, an' a collar an' tie. 'E did look smart.'

The first round of snippets over, Florrie took a pinch of snuff and Sadie went out to make the tea. There was still much to discuss, but Sadie had decided earlier she would not mention the fact that her daughter-in-law was pregnant. She was well aware that all her friends were rather good at simple arithmetic.

Joe Maitland stood trial at the Old Bailey. The case dragged on for two days and when he was found guilty his previous conviction was read out. Carrie was sitting in the public gallery and she covered her face with her hands as she heard the judge sentence him to seven years' imprisonment.

1931

Chapter Twenty-four

Carrie slipped the bolts on the front door and looked in on Rachel who was finishing wiping down the tables. 'C'mon, luv, let's get some tea,' she said, wiping the back of her hand across her forehead. 'I want ter get fings sorted out wiv yer farvver.'

Rachel took off the apron which reached down almost to the floor and looked closely at her mother. 'S'posin' Dad won't agree, Mum? Yer know 'e's not gonna like the idea,' she replied.

Carrie took her daughter's hands and pulled her down into one of the bench seats with her. 'Now listen ter me, Rachel,' she began, looking into the eleven-year-old's deep blue eyes. 'I've 'ad ter run this place fer the past five years since yer dad 'ad the stroke. It's not bin easy but I've made it pay. We've built up an established trade an' a lot o' goodwill. I've got what I fink is a fair price an' I can't let it pass.'

The young girl looked down at her clasped hands and studied her thumb-nails for a few moments. 'It's bin Dad's life. This cafe is all 'e knows,' she said quietly. 'I can't see 'im bein' 'appy about it.'

Carrie looked at her pretty, flaxen-haired daughter with a warm light in her eyes. 'Fer five years yer farv-ver's sat in that room upstairs 'ardly ever movin' out of it, unless it was when I took 'im fer a walk along the riverside. 'E's gettin' slowly worse, Rachel. I can't let 'im die in that room. Besides, there's space in the new place fer yer gran an' gran'farvver. It's gettin' 'ard fer 'em ter climb all those stairs in the Buildin's. Yer gotta remember, yer gran'farvver's seventy-two this year.'

'I know, Mum, an' 'e'll be really 'appy bein' around 'orses again, won't 'e?'

Carrie nodded. 'When I told 'im me plans 'e was so excited. Yer gran was a bit worried in case it don't work out, but Gran'farvver soon talked 'er round.'

'It will, Mum. I know it will,' Rachel said, her young face lighting up.

Carrie slipped out of her seat and together with Rachel she climbed the stairs to the front room over the shop. Fred was sitting back in his chair beside the empty grate, staring towards the window, and when the two women entered the room he looked up slowly, as though the movement was painful.

'Is the shop closed?' he said in his slow voice.

Carrie nodded and sat down facing him. ''Ow yer feelin', luv?' she asked with concern.

He nodded in reply, his head moving slowly. 'Well, are yer gonna tell me all about yer plans?' he said, forcing a crooked smile that left the right side of his face unchanged.

Carrie was taken aback, but she reached out and laid her hands on his. 'Sam's made us an offer fer the cafe an' there's a cartage business goin' in Salmon Lane we can afford, Fred,' she said encouragingly. 'There's a nice 'ouse included an' yer'll be able ter spend the day on the ground floor. There's room fer me mum an' dad too.'

Fred looked into the empty grate for a few moments then his eyes came up to meet hers. 'I might be infirm, but I've still got me 'earin', Carrie,' he reminded her, 'an' some o' the time when I've bin sittin' 'ere wiv me eyes closed I wasn't asleep. I've 'eard yer talkin' about yer plans fer the future.'

'Well, don't yer fink it's a good idea, Fred?' she asked.

His eyes seemed to cloud as he looked at the excited expression on his wife's face. 'Yer've cared fer me as well as 'avin' the business ter run an' it couldn't 'ave bin easy by any means. If it 'adn't 'ave bin fer yer the place would 'ave gone ter the wall. I reckon yer've got a right ter wanna sell it. I'm only worried in case yer takin' on too much wiv the cartage business. After all, it ain't a woman's sort o' work.'

'Yer ferget I was brought up wiv 'orses,' she said quickly, playfully tapping his hand. 'Besides, me dad's still pretty sprightly an' 'e can give us all the advice we need. There's a lot o' carmen who'd be glad of a job wiv us as well.'

'Yer keep sayin' "us", Carrie,' he muttered sadly. 'I'm not gonna be able to 'elp yer the way I am.'

She smiled at him. 'Look, luv. The business is yours as much as mine. All right, I'm managin' it, but I never make any moves until I've got yer approval, yer know that. Besides, I've done all right by us so far, an' I jus' know we'll do well in the cartage business, I jus' know it.'

'What about the contracts? Can we get enough work ter make a go of it?' he asked. 'Yer said yerself there's more an' more firms changin' ter motor vans. Even Galloway's got rid of all 'is 'orses.'

Carrie leaned forward, eager to reassure him. 'Galloway could 'ave got regular dock collections an' deliveries if 'e'd 'ave unionised earlier. Instead 'e went fer the long-distance work wiv lorries. There's a lot o' local work goin' beggin' an' we can undercut the motorised firms. Our carmen would all be in the union too, an' they'll 'ave no trouble wiv the dockers. Also there's two good contracts goin' wiv the business. If we can be relied on we'll keep the work wiv the leavver-buyers an' also the rum merchants. Galloway lost those contracts 'cos o' the way 'e 'andled 'em. I won't make that mistake, believe me.'

Fred forced a wan smile. 'No, I don't believe yer would.'

'Well, what d'yer say, luv? Can I start the ball rollin'?' Carrie asked him excitedly.

Fred nodded. 'Yer might as well. Yer wouldn't take no fer an answer anyway, would yer?' he said.

Carrie stood over him and slipped her hands around his neck. 'I'll make it work fer us, Fred. Fer the three of us,' she told him, touching her lips to his forehead in a gentle kiss.

Billy Sullivan stepped out of his house in Page Street and walked proudly beside Annie who was carrying their new baby in her arms. It was a bright Sunday morning and they were off to the christening at St Joseph's Church. Billy was holding on to four-year-old Patrick and two-year-old Brendan who yawned widely as he toddled along the turning. Sadie was waiting at her front door. She called out to her husband Daniel and the Sullivan tribe increased as they walked towards Jamaica Road. Sadie stepped out of her house holding on to Daniel's arm and Shaun followed on with his wife Teresa who was carrying the baby. Behind them came the twins Pat and Terry with their wives Dolly and Frances, each holding the hands of their two children. Joe brought up the rear holding the arm of his wife Sara, who was carrying their new baby.

Florrie Axford stood at her front door talking to Maisie Dougall. Now turned seventy-two, Florrie was still upright and alert, and she nodded to the Sullivan family as they passed. 'It looks like they're after startin' a football team,' she joked. 'Billy seems ter be makin' up fer lost time too.'

Maisie was now in her mid-sixties and had become even more plump over the past few years. 'They'll be runnin' out o' names soon,' she laughed.

The two women watched the Sullivan tribe leave the narrow turning then they got back down to serious matters. ''Ere, Flo, 'ave yer 'eard about that Ellie Roffey who's bin creatin' merry 'ell up at the market?'

Florrie shook her head. 'Who's she?'

'Red Ellie they call 'er,' Maisie went on. 'Apparently she's one o' those Communists, so they say. Anyway, there's bin a bit o' trouble wiv the stall 'olders an' the Council over the pitches by all accounts, an' this Ellie's bin fightin' fer the stall 'olders. She 'ad a stall 'erself once an' everybody knows 'er. Apparently she's bin a widow since she was twenty-three an' she was left wiv two young children. I was talkin' ter that Tommy Allnut – you know 'im, 'im who's got the fruit stall outside the ironmonger's. Well, 'e was tellin' me that this Ellie got chucked out of 'er 'ouse when 'er kids were jus' babies an' she got some 'elp from the Communists. That's why she joined 'em, so Tommy Allnut reckons. 'E said she's bin fightin' fer people's rights ever since.'

'We could do wiv somebody like 'er ter fight ole Galloway about our places,' Florrie replied. 'It's a bloody disgrace the way 'e's let these 'ouses go. D'yer know, I've told that rent collector a dozen times about my roof but nuffink's bin done.'

'I know,' Maisie said. 'My place is the same. I've got the water comin' in my upstairs rooms an' I'm sure the ceilin's gonna come down before long. P'raps we could see 'er about it.'

'Would she be able ter do anyfing fer us?' Florrie asked.

'We can but try,' Maisie said. 'From what I

understand this Red Ellie 'olds meetin's every Friday night at the school in Fair Street. I'll find out more about it an' maybe we could get a few of the neighbours ter come wiv us. After all, everybody's complainin'. What we got ter lose?'

'Quite right,' Florrie agreed. 'I'll 'ave a word wiv Sadie Sullivan when I go in there ternight. She's invited me ter the christenin' party. Are you goin?'

Maisie nodded. 'I fink all the street's goin'. Maudie said she's bin invited, an' that Alice Johnson too. I do 'ope 'er ole man won't be there.'

Florrie reached into her apron for her snuffbox. 'I don't fink so. Sadie ain't got no time fer 'im. She only invited Alice 'cos she borrered 'er pianer. I see it goin' in early this mornin'.'

'Is Alice gonna play it?' Maisie asked.

'I expect so. She can knock out a tune, so I've bin told.'

''Ere, is 'er ole man still in the choir?'

'Nah. There was some trouble wiv the vicar, by all accounts,' Florrie explained. 'Apparently Broom'ead went in ter choir practice one night the worse fer drink an' then annuver time 'e trod 'orse shit all up the aisle. What finished 'im was when 'e 'ad an argument wiv the vicar about gettin' paid. 'E reckoned they should 'ave a collection fer the choir every Sunday. Mind yer, it was Maudie who told me, an' yer can't believe a word she ses. She gets everyfing arse-up'ards.'

Maisie watched and waited while Florrie went through her usual ritual, and after the loud sneeze she pointed along the turning. 'That's gonna cause a bit o' trouble as well,' she remarked.

Florrie nodded in agreement. It was common knowledge amongst the people of Page Street that George Galloway had decided to move all his lorries to the Wilson Street depot which had been enlarged. The new owner of the yard was going to be a rag-sorter and the news had upset everyone in the turning.

'I thought it was bad enough wiv the stench an' fumes o' that petrol but now we're gonna be plagued wiv rats an' mice, mark my words,' Florrie said disgustedly. 'I remember that rag sorter's in Bermondsey Lane. Yer used ter see the rats runnin' across the road like a bleedin' army. One of 'em run in ole Mrs Coffey's passage one night an' got in 'er bedroom. Up under the springs of 'er bed it went. 'Er ole man was scared out of 'is life but ole Elsie Coffey wasn't. She killed it wiv a yard broom.'

'Good Gawd,' Maisie exclaimed. 'I 'ope we're not gonna 'ave the same trouble round 'ere. My ole man can't stan' rats eivver.'

The winkle stall had opened at the end of the turning and Florrie went inside her house to get her purse. 'C'mon, Mais, let's walk up the top,' she suggested. 'I've gotta get me tea, an' I fancy a nice milk stout.'

The two women strolled down to Arnold's seafood stall, where Florrie bought her usual half pint of winkles, then they sauntered into the Kings Arms, observed by Alice Johnson, who had been peering through her lace curtains for the past half hour, worrying in case it was her the two ladies were talking about.

Nellie Tanner sat with William in their drab flat in Bacon Buildings discussing the coming move. 'If it all goes frew I don't want yer gettin' too involved wiv the 'orses, Will,' she told him. 'Yer not a young man any more an' besides, yer done enough. Carrie wouldn't expect yer ter do anyfing anyway. She'd be grateful fer yer advice.'

'All right, Muvver, don't go on so,' William urged her. 'Anybody'd fink I was a dodderin' ole fool to 'ear yer talk. I can still get about, fank Gawd, an' I've still got me faculties. I'll be able ter look the 'orses over an' make sure they don't get ill treated by any o' the carmen. Some o' the bleeders don't value their 'orses. I've always said an 'orse'll work till it drops, so yer gotta make sure they get their food an' water. It's very important, yer see.'

Nellie puffed loudly. 'Yeah, all right, Will. I know what 'as ter be done, yer bin tellin' me that fer the past thirty-odd years.'

William smiled at his wife. She was now in her sixty-second year and still a striking woman, he thought. Her hair was streaked with grey but her body was trim and upright. Her eyes were still bright too, he often noted, and she had lost none of her fiery nature. Things had been hard for her. Losing their son James in the war and then Charlie going off to India had been very sad occasions for both of them but Nellie seemed to have grieved longer than he. He knew that the memories of both the lads would always remain with him until his dying day, but Nellie seemed never to have quite come to terms with the double loss. It was as if Charlie had died too, William felt. He had never returned since he left early in 1919. All they had to remember him by was the bundle of letters from India which Nellie kept in a cardboard box under the bed. They were happy letters in the main. Charlie was now a regimental sergeant-major in the Indian Army and had married an Assam tea-planter's daughter. They had two sons, William who was now seven years old and named after his grandfather, and Lawrence who was five. Often he had gone into the bedroom and seen Nellie reading through the letters, tears falling down her cheeks. It was the same when a new letter arrived every six months or so. She would read it through over and over again and then say that she lived in hope of seeing her Charlie and his family before she died. William hoped so too, but he thought that it would be a few more years before Charlie retired from the army, and he wondered with a sinking feeling whether seeing him again might not be like meeting a stranger.

'D'yer fink she'll make a go of it, Will?' Nellie asked, interrupting his thoughts.

''Course she will,' he replied, puffing on his pipe. 'Our Carrie's got a good start. Those 'orses of Buckman's are well looked after. 'E was always strict about the way 'is carmen 'andled 'em. There's four teams an' they've all got a few years' work left in 'em yet. Besides, yer know our Carrie. She won't tolerate no nonsense wiv the carmen. They'll get a fair deal an' be lucky they're workin' fer 'er an' not that ole goat Galloway.'

'Yer right, Will,' Nellie concurred. 'We should fink ourselves lucky we're gettin' out o' this bloody 'ovel. She always said she'd get us out one day an' she's done it.'

'Not yet she ain't,' William reminded her. 'There's a lot ter do yet. She's got ter make sure the bank loan's all right, then there's the cafe ter be sold. I wouldn't count yer chickens just yet. Fings could go wrong.'

'Nuffink's gonna go wrong,' Nellie said firmly. 'Carrie won't let nuffink stand in 'er way now.'

William tapped his pipe on the edge of the grate and reached for his tobacco pouch. 'I bin finkin' about young Joe Maitland,' he said suddenly. 'Carrie told me 'e's bin shifted ter Dartmoor.'

''Ow did Carrie come ter find that out?' Nellie asked him.

''E wrote 'er a letter by all accounts,' William replied.

''Ow comes 'e wrote ter Carrie?' Nellie asked, looking puzzled.

'Well, they was friends,' William said, averting his

361

eyes. 'Carrie used ter buy stuff at the ware'ouse, remember?'

'So did a lot o' people,' Nellie retorted.

'Well, p'raps Joe wrote ter them as well,' William said offhandedly.

'Yer don't fink there's bin anyfing goin' on between 'em, do yer, Will?' Nellie asked.

'I dunno. Joe always liked our Carrie, an' she seemed ter like 'im too. She's bin ter the ware'ouse a few times an' they was always laughin' an' jokin' ter-gevver. It was nice ter see. Carrie ain't 'ad much of a life wiv Fred. I know 'e's a good man an' 'e's good to 'er an' young Rachel, but they never seemed to 'ave much fun tergevver. Now she's got that business ter run on 'er own. Poor ole Fred's gettin' worse by all accounts.'

'I 'ope there's nuffink goin' on, Will. When yer take the vows it's fer better or worse, sickness an' 'ealth,' Nellie reminded him. 'I wouldn't like ter see 'er playin' around wiv ovver fellers.'

'Well, it's 'er life, Muvver. We can't interfere,' William replied. 'As long as she knows what she's doin'.'

'Shall we take all this furniture wiv us?' Nellie asked, deliberately changing the subject.

'What furniture?' William laughed. 'The bloody lot's only fit fer the bonfire. I reckon we should try an' get 'old of a couple o' sticks o' new stuff an' leave this lot 'ere.'

'At our time o' life?' Nellie said. 'These bits an' pieces 'ave bin wiv us since we tied the knot. I ain't leavin' 'em an' that's final.'

'All right, Muvver,' William replied, smiling fondly at her. 'Anyway, I'm orf ter the Kings Arms. Comin'?'

On Friday evening Florrie Axford, Maisie Dougall, Sadie Sullivan, Alice Johnson and Nellie Tanner set off for the school in Fair Street accompanied by Maudie

Mycroft and Maggie Jones, who was now in her eighti-eth year. Maggie slowed them down, as she had to stop frequently to rest her bad leg, and when they arrived the meeting had already started.

'Get some chairs fer the ladies,' the speaker bawled out to the school porter who was standing at the rear of the hall.

Maisie turned to Florrie. 'That's Red Ellie,' she whispered.

Maudie looked around the walls and saw the posters of women carrying picks and shovels, and uniformed men marching in long columns. She pulled a face. 'I stopped my Ernest goin' ter these sort o' meetin's,' she muttered to Nellie.

Florrie overheard her. 'That was down ter the car-rots,' she said, grinning at Sadie.

Red Ellie was on her feet. 'The world's workers are bein' exploited,' she shouted out to her subdued audi-ence. 'While we get crusts o' stale bread the bour-geoisie lap up the cream. Fings are never gonna alter until the workers rise up an' shake off their shackles o' servitude. Arise one an' all! Down wiv the capitalists!'

'This is a bit much,' Florrie remarked to Sadie. 'We ain't seekin' ter change the world, only our 'ouses.'

Nellie yawned. 'I knew I shouldn't 'ave come,' she said to Maisie. 'I can't keep me eyes open.'

Another speaker was on his feet. 'The workers of the world have seen the light. Beacons are burning around this globe of ours,' he ranted. 'Now the capitalists of the world are on the retreat everywhere. Long live the revolution!'

His outpourings were greeted with silence and Florrie turned to Maisie. 'That's the last time I let yer talk me inter goin' anywhere,' she grumbled, climbing to her feet.

Maisie followed her example and the rest of the

363

women got up as well. Nellie was just slipping off to sleep. She jerked awake as Sadie nudged her.

'C'mon, luv. This is a bloody loony 'atch,' she remarked loudly.

The women of Page Street walked out of the hall and gathered at the head of the stairs.

'I reckon we should 'ave gone ter the Kings Arms instead,' Florrie said, giving Maisie a wicked look.

Just then Red Ellie stepped out of the hall on to the landing. 'What's upset you, ladies?' she asked in a formidable voice.

'Why, that bloody nonsense,' Florrie retorted, unflustered. 'We come 'ere fer a bit o' 'elp wiv our 'ouses an' instead we've 'ad ter listen ter that load o' twaddle.'

Ellie stared at her for a few moments, then an indulgent smile appeared on her face. 'I know we sometimes get carried away,' she said magnanimously, 'but there's a lot o' sense in the argument if yer really fink about it.'

'That's as it may be,' Florrie answered, 'but yer can't expect *us* ter rise up an' change the world. Jus' look at us. There ain't one of us fit enough ter walk fer more than a few yards wivout puffin' an' blowin', let alone carry a bleedin' banner on a march. Poor ole Maggie's eighty, an' I'm plagued wiv corns. Then there's Maisie. She ain't bin right fer ages wiv 'er back.'

Red Ellie nodded sympathetically. 'Right, ladies, yer made yer point. Now 'ow can the Party 'elp yer?'

'It's our 'ouses, yer see,' Florrie began.

Billy Sullivan sat in his cosy parlour facing Annie who was breast-feeding Connie Elizabeth. He was beaming. 'I can't believe it,' he said, shaking his head. 'When I saw that letter from the prison I didn't know what ter fink.'

Annie smiled at him and moved the baby up over her

364

shoulder, gently patting its back. 'I think it's wonderful,' she said quietly.

'I feel like it's me birfday an' Christmas all rolled inter one, Annie.'

'Well, don't get too carried away, Billy,' she told him. 'It's a beginning, but there's a lot to do, and you have to get backing.'

'Farvver Murphy said 'e'd always be willin' to 'elp. Then there's the lads around 'ere. I'm sure they'll muck in if they can see fings movin'. It'll work out, I know it will.'

Annie put the baby to her other breast and settled down, her gaze full of happiness as she saw the excitement in Billy's deep blue eyes. 'Just be patient,' she warned him. 'I know it's what you've always dreamed about and I've prayed to God for it to come true, really I have, but you must be careful. Don't do anything silly. You know what I mean.'

Billy got up from his chair and bent over Annie, kissing her on her forehead. 'D'yer know, I'm the 'appiest man in the world right now. I've got a job, an' a new baby, an' now this,' he said, sighing contentedly.

'Is there nothing else that made you so happy, Billy?' she asked him.

He shook his head, watching her closely, and as her face dropped he grinned widely. 'Of course there is. Bein' married ter you is the best fing that could 'ave 'appened ter me. Yer've given me lovely kids an' more love than I ever felt was possible. I do love yer, Annie,' he said earnestly, lowering his lips to meet hers.

Annie pushed him away playfully. 'There's a time and place for everything. Right now I'm trying to feed your daughter. Do you want the milk to curdle?'

Billy walked over to the door and took down his coat. 'I won't be late, Annie,' he told her. 'I'm gonna tell Danny the good news.'

'Don't get drunk tonight, Billy,' she said quietly.

'I promise,' he told her, making a criss-cross movement over his heart with a forefinger.

In the gloomy house in Tyburn Square George Galloway sat with his son in the gaslit front room. The curtains were pulled against the night and the room smelt of stale tobacco smoke. George was slumped in his chair looking all of his seventy-four years, his face lined and his hair now completely white. His eyes were rheumy and heavy-lidded, but his mind was as alert as ever.

'We gotta push fer it, d'yer 'ear me, Frank?' he growled. 'Yer know very well I went after that piece o' land five years ago, jus' before Maitland went away in fact, but 'e beat us to it.'

Frank sipped his Scotch. 'I've told you what Streetley advised us to do,' he replied. 'There's an application lodged at the Council for a gymnasium to be built on that site and the planning committee is voting on it soon. If there are any objections lodged then they'll discuss them beforehand. Streetley seems to think he can carry the vote, providing the case is a good one.'

George gulped his drink and pulled a face as the strong liquor burned his throat. 'I know what yer said,' he replied cantankerously in his gruff voice. 'What I'm sayin' is, there's no need ter go down that road. My information comes from a reliable source, somebody who's more reliable than that gin-swillin' excuse for a councillor. Maitland bought that land as an industrial site, not fer leisure or anyfing else. There's a bid of ours still lodged wiv the land agents fer that piece o' land ter be used as an extension fer our yard.'

'Well, we can be sure that Streetley would put that fact to the Council committee,' Frank said, twirling the Scotch around in his glass.

'I'm not gonna grease that pissy git's palm,' George growled.

'Well, what do you suggest we do then?' Frank asked impatiently.

'D'yer know, Frank, I sometimes wonder why I ever bovvered ter spend all that money givin' yer a college education,' the old man complained. 'All right, let's assume that Streetley wins the day, which I'm not too sure of, knowin' 'im. Maitland won't be able ter lease off the land fer a gymnasium. What's 'e gonna do? Well, I'll tell yer. 'E'll be out o' the nick soon an' 'is business 'as gone down the drain. 'E might keep the land, but it's more likely 'e'll sell it orf fer industrial use ter raise money, an' if 'e does sell it certainly won't be to us. No, Frank, my way is better. We'll get our solicitor ter stick an injuction on the improper sale. The proof is the application fer leisure use at the Council. I'm pretty certain it'll stick, an' then the land reverts back ter the agents wiv Maitland only gettin' 'is original stake back. That leaves the site free fer our outstandin' bid ter be accepted. I've bin told we'll 'ave no trouble.'

Frank drained his glass, irritation building up inside him. The old man's getting past it, he thought. He's paying too much attention to those drinking cronies of his, and the booze is getting to him. It wouldn't be the first time he had let drink cloud his judgement, Frank recalled. There was a prime piece of land which had been going begging at Cotton Lane years ago and if he had acted swiftly he could have got it for a song. Well, he had better listen this time.

'It won't work,' Frank said calmly.

'What d'yer mean, it won't work?' George growled, reaching for the bottle of Scotch.

Frank leaned forward in his chair. 'I've been trying to tell you. The application Maitland lodged at the Council is in effect an application to change the land's

367

usage from industrial to leisure. There was no improper sale, so where does that leave your argument?' he asked. 'Going down your road we would be involved in an expensive exercise we wouldn't have a chance of winning. No, Dad, we've only one chance of getting that land. We lodge a protest at the Council opposing the building of the gymnasium, basing our case on the fact that our bid was more suitable and if it had been successful it would have contributed more to the area. We'll also use the argument that, due to the shortage of industrial land in Bermondsey, none should be made available for any other use.'

George Galloway poured a large measure of whisky into his empty glass and took a swig. 'All right, I take yer point,' he grumbled, 'but like I've jus' said, if Joe Maitland is forced ter get rid of the site, 'e ain't gonna sell it to us is 'e? Not after we've blocked 'is little scheme.'

Frank smiled slyly. 'We'll renew our bid at the original price, and we'll use our own agent to negotiate for us with an improved offer from a limited company that he'll register. Maitland will have no way of knowing it's coming from us. All that's needed then is a resale. It'll be a little more expensive, but by no means as expensive as going through the courts.'

George Galloway stared at his glass for a few moments then he drained it in one go and grimaced. 'All right. Do it your way, but I want Streetley ter know the score. No result, no money. Is that clear?'

Frank nodded. 'Leave it to me, Father. I'm seeing him this evening. We'll draw up a document that'll discredit Maitland's scheme. There should be no trouble.'

Chapter Twenty-five

When Carrie first thought about selling the cafe she had been prepared for some hard bargaining with the new buyer, ready to insist adamantly that in recognition of their hard work and loyalty Bessie and the other two helpers must be allowed to keep their jobs, but she need never have worried. One morning Corned Beef Sam had strolled in blithely and told her that he would buy the business. He had saved up a large sum of money over the years working at his decrepit stall, which he had kept in big white five-pound notes under the floorboards beneath his bed ever since the man in the bank had upset him one day.

Sam had struck up a rapport with the ebullient Bessie Chandler after a hesitant start and they spent much time discussing Bessie's strange neighbours and Sam's strange friends, and Carrie often heard the big ginger-haired woman roaring with laughter at the stories of Mutton-eye Jack and Vaseline Vic. Sam was also a shrewd businessman and he saw the value of having someone like Bessie employed in the cafe. He was quite content to keep the two helpers on as well. Both Lizzie and Marie were by now firm favourites with the dockers and carmen who frequented the dining rooms and Sam felt that he should be able to get on with the cooking without getting disturbed by all the chatter and cheekiness at the counter.

Carrie had a trying meeting with the bank manager, who pored over the books, looked at the trading figures for the Buckman Cartage Contractors and gave her much professional advice before agreeing to a renegotiated bank loan against the new business. There were legal matters to take care of and the change-over had to be arranged, and Carrie had the sometimes tiring duty of explaining to Fred all the intricacies involved. He questioned every move, every step along the way, feeling that he was being helpful with his criticisms, but they only served to make Carrie have misgivings and begin to doubt her own confidence. The transactions seemed to drag on endlessly and Carrie was left exhausted, but finally, in the spring of '31, she and Fred became the owners of Bradleys' Cartage Contractors.

The transport yard was located in Salmon Lane, a turning which led down to the riverside in Dockhead. On the right-hand side of the street a row of little houses ended at a large warehouse that stretched down to the end of the road and the river walkway. The transport yard was sited in the middle of the turning on the left-hand side between another shorter row of houses and a pickle factory that faced the warehouse. The yard was compact, with an office just inside the gate to the left. Next to the office there was a ground-level stable for twelve horses, and across the cobbled yard there was a house which was in fairly good condition. Adjacent to the house was a large shed for storing the carts, and at the end of the yard a high brick wall enclosed the area.

Carrie said her goodbyes to the tearful Bessie and the sad-faced Lizzie and Marie, and when Corned Beef Sam gave her a departing kiss on the cheek he had some advice for her. 'Don't stand no bleedin' nonsense from those carmen, luv. Show 'em who's the boss, an' if yer get any ole sauce from 'em do what I do, 'it 'em wiv yer 'andbag!'

Carrie watched with emotion as her parents' meagre belongings were carried down from Bacon Buildings and placed on a horse cart. It had taken her quite some time to realise her dream of moving them from the slum block, but when the day finally arrived she found it hard to force back a tear.

Nellie and William Tanner installed themselves in the upstairs of the house and Carrie arranged the downstairs to suit her husband's needs. Fred was now more mobile since there were no stairs to climb, and he was able to sit in a comfortable chair beside the window and watch the comings and goings. Rachel was happy, feeling very excited at the prospect of being around horses. She had listened to her mother's endless stories about when she was a little girl at the Galloway stables.

There were two carmen who had been retained for the existing contracts. Jack Simpson, a tall, gangling character in his forties, was employed on the leather contract. He had a habit of stretching the corner of his mouth and rolling his head whenever he got agitated, which was very often. He had a toothless smile and a shaven head, and he reminded Carrie of Sharkey Morris. Paddy Byrne, the other carman, was the exact opposite. He was employed on the rum contract and he handled his team of horses expertly. He was a pleasant character, short and stocky with a mop of dark, wavy hair and large brown eyes, and he was given to expressing himself in song, whenever he had sampled an extra tot of rum. He was also in his forties, and had worked for John Buckman more than twenty years.

William Tanner had taken an early opportunity to look over the horses and he was pleased with what he saw. The pair of black Clydesdales used on the rum contract were in prime condition, as were the pair of Irish draughts that Jack Simpson drove. There were four other horses in the stable, a pair of grey Percherons and two Welsh cobs. All had been well cared for and William told his daughter that the Percherons would be ideally suited for heavy work, something that Carrie had already noted. The carts were in reasonable repair, although there were one or two that had worn wheels and wood rot along the raves. William stressed the need for a good yard man who could be relied upon to look after the carts and harnesses, keep the yard clean and muck out the stables.

'Yer need somebody reliable, Carrie,' he told her. 'The right man could 'ave this yard lookin' ship-shape in no time. 'E could fix those carts too an' keep the 'arness well dubbined an' the brasses clean an' shiny.'

''Ave yer got anybody in mind?' Carrie asked him.

William made a pretence of thinking for a moment. 'I know. What about ole Sharkey Morris?' he said suddenly. ''E's still active. 'E's a year or two younger than I am. 'E'd be yer man.'

Billy Sullivan had taken the opportunity to visit Father Murphy at St Joseph's Church, and when the ageing priest had finished reading the letter Billy handed over he had some sound advice to offer. 'You've got to think this thing through carefully, Billy me lad,' he told him. 'It was a fine gesture on the part of Joe Maitland to give you that piece of land, especially as he'll be coming home soon and could have realised some capital on it, but I'm sure the Lord will bless him. It leaves you with a lot of work to do, though. You'll need to give the project a name and it'll need to be registered as a charity. That way we can ask for donations.'

'I wonder why Joe did it, Farvver?' Billy asked. 'Like yer say, 'e could 'ave made good use of it 'imself.'

'I think it's God's work. The Lord moves in mysterious ways, my son,' the priest told him, his eyes going up to the stained-glass window high in the wall facing him. 'We should leave it at that, I think.'

'Would yer consider takin' charge o' the project, Farvver?' Billy asked him forthrightly.

'I'd be delighted,' the priest replied. 'Now let's see. According to the letter there's an application already lodged at the Council offices for permission to build a gym. I hope that doesn't pose a problem, but we must be positive. As soon as the application is granted we'll get our heads together and look at ways to raise the money. In the meantime go home and think about it. Oh, and Billy, don't forget to pray. And while you're at it, you might say a short prayer for your benefactor. I'm sure Joe Maitland could do with a few prayers said on his behalf.'

'I'll do that, Farvver,' Billy promised. 'I'll go roun' wiv the beggin'-bowl too. I've already bin promised a load o' timber.'

'You'll need bricks and mortar as well,' the priest informed him.

'Bricks an' mortar?'

'Why yes. You weren't thinking of knocking up some ramshackle shed, were you?' Father Murphy asked him, one eyebrow raised incredulously.

'Well, yes, but it wouldn't be ramshackle,' Billy replied.

'Nonsense! A fine, solid building, equipped with a changing room, showers and a full-size, raised ring – that's what you should be thinking about, Billy,' the priest told him, using his hands to elaborate. 'A place for the young lads to practise the noble art of fisticuffs, and learn Christian virtues at the same time.'

Billy had gone to see Father Murphy expecting to be given a small donation or at least the promise of a helping hand from some of his younger parishioners, but instead he had been made to see the huge problems he was facing. Well, the gym was going to be built now, come what may, he vowed, and nothing would ever dent his enthusiasm and determination. It would just mean going around with a larger begging-bowl.

Red Ellie Roffey called round to Page Street and was taken on an inspection tour of the houses. Florrie showed Ellie her leaking roof and Maisie took her up to her bedroom where the ceiling was bulging dangerously. Maudie too was moved to invite Ellie into her house, although she had already warned her husband Ernest not to engage the woman in a political discussion.

'We've bin all frew it before, Ernest,' she reminded him. 'I ain't standin' fer yer goin' out at all hours again wiv those silly leaflets. Besides, yer gettin' too old ter go round in all weavvers knockin' on people's doors. Yer could catch pneumonia or pleurisy. Yer know 'ow yer chest is.'

'All right, Maudie, I'll keep me mouth shut,' he promised her. 'But don't ferget ter show 'er the bedroom. If nuffink's done about that ceilin' pretty soon there'll be a tragedy in Page Street.'

Red Ellie saw all the signs of wilful neglect and decay, and when she had finished going round the dilapidated dwellings she sat down with the women in Sadie Sullivan's parlour and set out a course of action.

'Now look, ladies,' she began, 'first fings first. I'll draw up a list of repairs needed an' a demand that they be carried out wivout fail. I want yer all ter sign it, an' then I'll go over ter see Galloway wiv two of yer as representatives of the Page Street Women's Committee. Then, if the repairs are not carried out by the set time, we'll take further action.'

'It won't mean violence, will it?' Maudie asked fearfully.

'It might come to violence, my dear,' Ellie replied. 'Sometimes there's no alternative.'

Maudie was feeling decidedly uneasy. 'I couldn't bear gettin' involved in violence,' she told the meeting.

'Yer'd be involved in violence if that bleedin' ceilin' o' yours fell down on yer,' Florrie told her. 'Yer'd 'ave a bloody violent 'eadache.'

Red Ellie sipped her tea and studied the women closely. She had learned their names and was making mental appraisals. Sadie was a tough woman, she decided. Florrie too. They could both be relied upon to lead the campaign. Maisie was less of a leader but very enthusiastic. Maggie appeared to be half-hearted, but Maudie seemed to be afraid of her own shadow. That one was the weak link and would have to be coaxed along.

'Would one of yer like ter sit down wiv me an' 'elp get the demands sorted out?' Ellie asked. 'What about you, Maudie?'

'Oh, I couldn't,' Maudie replied, bringing her hand up to her mouth.

'Well, one of yer should be involved,' Ellie told them.

Florrie was secretly revelling in Maudie's discomfort. 'Why don't yer, Maudie?' she prompted. 'Yer'd be pretty good at that sort o' fing. After all, yer get involved wiv loads o' different fings at the muvvers' meetin'.'

The nervous woman looked around at the smiling faces of her friends and felt a little confused, for it was not often that they complimented her on anything.

'Well, I s'pose I could 'elp,' she said hesitantly. 'Nobody would 'ave ter know it was me though, would they? Outside o' this meetin', I mean.'

'Don't worry, gel,' Florrie reassured her. 'We won't tell a soul. We don't wanna see yer get victimised fer us.'

Maudie wished she had bit on her tongue. If this ever got out she'd be thrown out on the street, she was sure she would. What would Ernest say, after all the nagging she had done to make him resign from the Communist Party?

The women were leaving now and Florrie turned to Maudie in the doorway. 'Good luck, gel, an' don't worry, we're right be'ind yer,' she said, hiding a smile.

That's just what I'm worried about, Maudie thought.

Carrie had soon settled into the new routine. She realised that she would have to try for new contracts right away if the business was to get on a good footing, and to that end she telephoned around the local factories and sent out a tariff of charges worked out from the previous owner's records and books. She was fired by the challenge to make the enterprise work. Fred was of little help in his present condition and she realised that it was up to her alone to establish her name in the competitive cartage business. Being a woman was not to her advantage, she knew, but she was determined that before very much time had passed the name Bradley would stand for something with the companies in the area.

With all that had been taking place recently Carrie had had little time to dwell on thoughts of Joe Maitland, but as the months slowly slipped by she thought about his coming release and how it would affect her life. She knew that she had to see him again. It had been three years now since he had been transferred to Dartmoor and there had been no opportunity to see him there. In fact she had only managed to visit him before on two occasions, and seeing him looking so pale and drawn had made her feel depressed for days afterwards. Nevertheless Joe seemed to be taking his incarceration very well, considering, and his regular letters were cheerful. There was little in them of an intimate nature and Carrie had realised early on that he was deliberately avoiding upsetting her. It had been impossible not to get upset, however, and Carrie tried to console herself by looking forward to his release when she would let him see how much he meant to her.

Fred suddenly took a turn for the worse. He had been poorly during the first few weeks in the new house and one night as he was getting into bed he suddenly collapsed and fell on to his back, his face contorted. Carrie felt sick with fear and guilt and her shout of distress brought young Rachel hurrying into the room. 'Is Daddy gonna die, Mum?' she cried, tears soaking her pretty face.

''Elp me get 'im on the bed,' Carrie said quickly, taking him by the shoulders.

Between the two of them they managed to settle Fred on the bed and then Carrie rushed to telephone the doctor. The elderly Doctor Kelly seemed unsteady on his feet when he called and Carrie could smell whisky on his breath, but he quickly realised how serious the situation was. After he had carried out a full examination he slipped his stethoscope into his black bag and motioned Carrie out of the room with him.

'The man's very sick,' he said in his usual brusque tone. 'I think we should get him admitted to hospital right away. If I'm not mistaken he could be due for another stroke.'

Towards the end of May George Galloway was informed by his solicitor that the planning committee would sit the following week and it would be an open meeting. Joe Maitland had earlier received details of the date and time of the meeting, with notification that objections to the proposed building of a gymnasium would be raised. He immediately wrote to Billy Sullivan who informed Father Murphy, and following a frantic flurry of preparations the session at Bermondsey Borough Council took place.

The meeting started promptly at eight o'clock in the evening and it was well attended by interested parties and merely curious members of the public. It was held in a large, oak-panelled committee room and for the first hour various other items on the agenda were discussed. The room became filled with smoke as the chairman puffed importantly on his large cigar. The announcing of item number ten on the agenda caused a ripple of murmuring throughout the room and the chairman called for order.

'We have an application before us concerning the land adjacent to Smithson's warehouse in Wilson Street, Dockhead. It's for permission to erect a gymnasium on the site,' he opened.

'I understand from the information provided that the land was designated for industrial use,' Councillor Edith Squires remarked, looking up over her gold-rimmed spectacles.

'That is so,' replied the chairman.

'Was the land bought for industrial use originally?' Councillor George Smith asked.

'Yes.'

'Does the application refer to the site as being industrial land?' Councillor Thompson interjected.

'Yes.'

'Hence the application,' Councillor Squires remarked with a smug grin.

The chairman puffed on his cigar and sent a jet of smoke ceilingward. 'I have an objection on the table. It's from Messrs George Galloway and Sons, Cartage

Contractors of Wilson Street, Dockhead. Have we a representative present to speak on their behalf?'

A tall, thin man in thick spectacles stood up and raised his hand. 'Yes. I'm Bernard Duffin of Duffin and Skellen. I'm empowered to speak on behalf of Galloway and Sons,' he said in a reedy voice.

'Go ahead, Mr Duffin,' the chairman said, studying the ash on his cigar.

'The main objection of my client is one of limitation through deceit,' the solicitor began. 'Limitation of scarce industrial sites in the borough, in this case aggravated by deception.'

'Would you be more precise, Mr Duffin,' the chairman said impatiently.

Duffin coughed nervously and adjusted his spectacles. 'My client contends that the present owner of the site, a Mr Joseph Maitland, obtained the site with the intention of leasing it off for the development of a boxing gymnasium knowing full well that the land was designated for industrial use only. Further, my client contends that the application should be refused due to the fact that he had already put in a bid for the land to develop his transport business.'

Heads nodded in sympathy and one councillor was heard to remark that business rates were higher than private rates anyway.

'Is there anyone present to represent the applicant?' the chairman asked, brushing the cigar ash off the arm of his blue serge suit.

A rotund man stood up and waved to the chairman. 'My name is Theodore Winkless of Benchley and Company,' he began. 'My client is unable to attend in person as he is at present a guest in one of His Majesty's prisons. He wished me to point this fact out before someone else did.'

There was another outbreak of murmuring around

the room and Councillor Squires was heard to click her tongue noisily.

'My client wishes it to be made clear that he did not set out to deceive,' Winkless went on. 'The land was originally purchased for the express purpose of adding floor space to his expanding business but another, more suitable site was then found. Mr Maitland subsequently intended to dispose of the site, but then decided to lease it off at a greatly reduced rent for the benefit of the local youth whose welfare he is greatly concerned about.'

Councillor Edith Squires was seen to roll her eyes and jerk her head in disgust, and Councillor Smith turned to Councillor Thompson and pulled a face. It was then that Councillor Bernard Streetley got up and raised his hands in a theatrical manner.

'Do we have to prolong this charade indefinitely, members of the committee?' he said in a lofty tone. 'We have here a site owner who has the temerity to waste the time of this committee with an application of gross effrontery. Industrial land, may I point out, is land for the nurturing and development of industry, and our industriousness is something of which we in this ancient borough can be justly proud. No, gentlemen and good lady, the answer must be no.'

Councillor Squires led the applause and Councillor Streetley sat down smiling smugly.

'Are there any other points of view before we take the vote?' the chairman asked.

Someone shouted from the public section at the back of the hall, but all eyes were on the ageing priest who had risen to his feet and held up his hand to the chairman.

'I wish to say something,' he said quietly.

'Feel free, Father,' the chairman said in a smooth voice.

Father Murphy cleared his throat. 'I've been the parish priest in this riverside community of ours for more years than I care to remember,' he began in a measured voice. 'I've seen some of you toddling into my church and I've watched you grow into upright, Godfearing members of the populace. I've seen the young men go off to war and I've comforted my flock when their sons fell in battle. I've watched the survivors come home, some wearing their medals for valour proudly, but by far the majoritory broken in body and spirit. Not so many years ago, it seems to an old man like me, I had the sad task of comforting the Sullivan family.

'Now Mr and Mrs Sullivan gave four of their seven sons to the war. Two fell in battle and two came home, one of them broken in body but not in spirit. Billy Sullivan was the eldest of the seven boys and he took a bullet through his chest during the heavy fighting on the Somme. It was particularly cruel for the young man because he was at the time a leading contender for the middleweight boxing championship of Great Britain. Tragically, Billy was forced to spend the next few years sitting at his front door, when weather permitted, doubled up like an old man. But I'm pleased to tell this committee, and I do beg your indulgence for a few minutes more, that Billy Sullivan has now recovered from his wounds although he will never fight in the ring again, and has now married a young woman whom many of you knew as Sister McCafferty, the local welfare nurse. The Sullivans have three children, and I might add that I baptised them all.

'Billy Sullivan still nurtures his dream, and he nurtured that dream all through the long weeks and months when he sat doubled in two on his rickety chair in Page Street. He hoped more than anything that one day he would be able to open a boxing gymnasium for the benefit of the youth in this riverside parish of ours. That dream is still strong in Billy Sullivan's heart, and he was overjoyed when another of our young men, who unfortunately has fallen by the wayside, decided to atone for his sins by donating a valuable piece of land that he owned so that Billy's gymnasium could be built. Billy came to see me a short time ago with his heart bursting with happiness. I told the young man I would help him fulfil his dream and I will, if you, ladies and gentlemen of this committee, vote for Billy.

'I thank you for your patience in listening to my plea, and I would like to say just a little more before I resume my place. Industrial land is very scarce in this borough, I agree, but so are facilities for our young people. Industrial development is all very well but it counts for nothing without the quality and endeavour of our future adults who will work the lathes, drive the transport and toil on our waterfront and in our factories. We owe it to them to provide them with leisure facilities which will strengthen and embolden their hearts and enrich their spirits. We owe it to the youth, countless thousands of whom went out to fight for this country and laid down their lives for us. A vote for the gymnasium is a vote for Billy, a vote for all the youth of our borough, and a vote for Jesus Christ.'

Councillor Edith Squires dabbed at her eyes and Councillors Thompson and Smith swallowed hard. Councillor Streetley sat impassive, while the chairman fiddled with the nameband of a new cigar. Billy Sullivan sat with his head lowered, unable to look up lest people should see the tears in his eyes. He did not hear the call for a vote but he heard the loud cheering which broke out around him and finally he lifted his head. There in the doorway he saw Annie, with the baby in her arms and his two sons holding on to their mother's skirts. She was smiling broadly and he got up and rushed over to her, his arms going around her and the baby.

'You've won, Billy!' she said proudly.

He opened his mouth to speak but the words would not come. Instead he lowered his face on to Annie's soft shoulder and wept.

Chapter Twenty-six

Carrie walked back from the Rotherhithe Infirmary through the cool of the evening, saddened by Fred's condition. He had been in good spirits when she sat with him in the long white-painted ward, but he was very weak. His face had become drawn and grey, and his arms resting over the bedclothes looked thin and drained of blood. He seemed much older than his fifty-six years and his speech was slow and faltering. The doctors said that he had suffered another stroke, and although it was a mild one in the light of his previous condition it had had a bad effect on him. His heart was weak and they said that it was quite likely he would now remain bed-ridden.

It was going to be hard, Carrie thought, what with the problems of running the new business and going out to find contracts, apart from the day-to-day tasks of seeing to the horses and keeping the carts in good condition. She was glad that Sharkey Morris had agreed to put in a few hours every day. He was turned seventy but still active and alert, and he had worked wonders with the harness leathers and brasses. The horses looked very well turned-out and the carts were clean too. Sharkey had seen to the axles, working grease around the moving parts and along the shafts. He had explained to Carrie the importance of always keeping the cart axles well greased.

'I remember when I was workin' fer ole Galloway an' one o' the axles seized up,' he said with a serious expression on his face. 'I lost the full load o' wet skins. Stinking ter the 'igh 'eavens they was. They shot orf the cart right outside the pub in Long Lane. Nobody could get in or out. Mind yer, it was all right fer those ins'de. They all come out pissed as 'and-carts.'

Sharkey kept the yard well washed down too and the horses' stalls were always mucked out and fresh straw provided daily. He never appeared to hurry in his work but he was efficient, and he seemed to have taken on a new lease of life in the short time he had been at the stable. He had always been on good terms with William Tanner and the two men spent much time talking about the old days when they both worked at Galloway's yard.

Carrie had managed to secure a year-long contract with a wine merchants in Bermondsey, which entailed collecting casks of sherry and pipes of port from the wharves in Tooley Street and making an occasional journey to the coopers in Stepney. She had taken on another carman who was experienced in handling the heavy, dangerous barrels, and the wine merchants seemed to be happy with the arrangement. The new carman, Percy Harmer, was a short, powerfully built man in his mid-thirties who handled the casks with ease. He was good with the team of Percherons, which could be difficult to handle at times, and Carrie felt pleased that she had at least made a start with the new contract towards building up the business.

The sun was dropping behind the rooftops as she crossed Jamaica Road on that Saturday evening and walked along to Salmon Lane. Her parents had gone to Greenwich for the day and taken Rachel with them, and as she opened the wicket-gate and stepped into the yard she heard someone call out to her.

Don Jacobs was crossing the street holding an envelope in his hands. 'I've got the men's union cards, Carrie,' he said smiling, 'I was on me way ter the pub so I thought I'd drop 'em in.'

She beckoned him into the yard. 'C'mon in, Don,' she said, fumbling in her handbag for the front door key. 'I'm dyin' fer a cup o' tea. D'yer fancy one or will it spoil yer pint?'

Don laughed. 'I'd sooner 'ave a cup o' tea wiv you than a pint wiv that crowd at the Crown,' he said, stepping into the yard.

Carrie let herself into the quiet house and waved Don into the front room while she went into the scullery and lit a gas jet under the kettle. 'It won't take long,' she shouted out.

'Where's Fred?' he called out to her.

Carrie walked back into the parlour. ''E's in 'ospital,' she told him. 'It's anuvver stroke.'

Don's face dropped. 'I'm sorry, luv. When did it 'appen?'

'Last week,' she replied. ''E collapsed by the bed an' we 'ad ter get 'im away.'

''E's gonna be all right, ain't 'e?' the union man asked.

Carrie shrugged her shoulders. 'They say 'e's not gonna get out o' bed this time,' she said quietly.

Don got up and walked over to her, taking her by the shoulders. 'If there's anyfing I can do, don't ferget, yer know where ter find me,' he said with concern in his voice.

Carrie gripped his forearms. 'Fanks, Don. I won't ferget,' she said, giving him a friendly smile.

For a moment or two they stayed together, looking into each other's eyes, then Carrie dropped her gaze and moved away, suddenly feeling disturbed. 'I'll see about the tea,' she said quickly.

Don sat down again beside the table and opened the envelope, laying the contents on the white tablecloth, and when Carrie came back into the room carrying the tea on a tray he looked up at her and smiled. 'I've got three cards 'ere. All they need ter do is sign the forms,' he explained. 'We 'old the monthly branch meetin's every last Friday evenin' at the Sultan in Bermondsey Lane. If there's anyfing they wanna know, tell 'em ter call in.'

Carrie handed him his tea. 'I thought it best ter get the carmen ter join,' she said, sitting down in the chair opposite him. 'Paddy Byrne was tellin' me Buckman wasn't too keen on 'em bein' in the union.'

Don nodded. 'The trouble wiv Buckman was, 'e was one o' the old school, but fings are changin', as yer know,' he said, sipping his tea. 'Yer best chance ter win contracts now is ter see yer men keep their union tickets. They're tightenin' up at the quaysides since the General Strike. There was too many blackleg firms jumpin' on the bandwagon. Every now an' again they'll 'ave a purge. No tickets, no loadin'. There's one or two firms who won't get a look in now, Carrie, an' I should fink there'll be a few more contracts in the offin'.'

Carrie watched the union man while he sipped his tea. She recalled the times he had sat talking to her in the back room at the dining rooms while Fred eyed them both with a dark look on his face.

'Penny fer yer thoughts,' he said suddenly, smiling widely at her.

'Oh, I was jus' finkin',' she told him. 'Remember that back room at the cafe?'

He nodded. 'What about when Fred used ter fink I was chattin' yer up?' he grinned.

'Poor ole Fred used ter grill me after yer'd gone.'

Don put his cup down and leaned forward, resting his elbows on the table. 'D'yer know, Carrie, I used ter love those talks we 'ad,' he told her, his face becoming serious. 'I used ter fink yer was a bit special.'

''Ave I changed much then?' she said, smiling.

Don shook his head slowly. 'I still fink yer somefink special, Carrie,' he said with deliberation. 'Yer remind me o' the way Margie used ter be, before she got ill.'

'D'yer still see 'er?' Carrie asked, resting her elbow on the table and cupping her chin.

'Nah,' he replied. 'It's two years or so now since I clapped eyes on 'er. She's courtin' again, by all accounts. 'E's not a union official though,' he added quickly with a wry smile.

Carrie gazed at the fine line of his face, now showing the strain from years of union work and hard bargaining. He was still a handsome man, she thought. His hair was greying and his grey eyes looked tired and sad but his mouth had a humorous twist, which made him look as though he was enjoying even the most arduous union meetings when in fact he was battling hard to unite his men against the odds. His mannerisms intrigued her too, the way he had of rolling his cigarette and the way he would smile patiently from the corner of his mouth when angry dockers were shouting and raving. He had excited her at those meetings in the cafe, she admitted to herself. There were times when Fred had been sleeping soundly next to her and she had lain awake, needing love and wondering what it would be like to lie next to Don Jacobs and have him turn towards her and wrap his arms around her.

'Is there a new woman in yer life, Don?' she asked him, suddenly feeling embarrassed at what she had said.

Don looked down at his empty cup and swirled the tea-leaves, then his eyes met hers. 'I spend a lot o' time on union business an' it's usually in men's company. Besides, I couldn't go frew all that again,' he said quietly. 'I couldn't expect a woman ter suffer the hours o' loneliness the way Margie did.'

Carrie leaned forward and touched his hand. 'Yer'll find anuvver woman, I'm sure,' she told him.

He looked intently at her, his eyes unblinking. 'I wish I'd met yer before Fred,' he said in a low, husky voice. 'I've always thought yer was a cut above the rest.'

Carrie felt her face grow hot and she stood up. 'Would yer like anuvver cuppa?' she asked, averting her eyes.

'Yeah, I would,' he replied, watching her as she picked up the cups.

Carrie walked out into the scullery with her heart suddenly pounding. It had been a long time since anyone had aroused her so. Only Joe had made her feel this way and she had almost forgotten how nice it was with him. She could feel her hands shaking and her stomach tighten at the thought of making love.

Carrie's back was to the door and as she heard his footsteps she turned around. Don stood there for a moment, his eyes fixed on hers, and then slowly walked up close to her. She felt as if her whole mind were laid bare to him though not a word was spoken. She was in his arms, her body pressed hard against his. She could feel his chest rising and falling and his strong arms enfolding her and moving slowly across her back, and as delicious feelings of love filled her she joined her lips to his in a long and sensuous kiss, her breath coming in gasps as his hands fondled her body. The long months, years, of being without a man holding her, caressing her, had left her feeling empty, and suddenly long-forgotten sensations were once more flowing through her. Nothing mattered now, only her passionate desire. She slipped her hand in his as she broke away from his ardent caress. He followed her as she pulled on his hand, leading him to her bedroom, and as they passed through the doorway she was in his arms again. He slipped his hands around her back and down to the small rounded bottom, and her arms went around his neck as her lips found his in a kiss that seemed to send her head spinning. He had moved backwards to the bed and pulled her down to him. Two bodies writhed together, each needing the love which had for so long passed them by. Don groaned in her ear as he struggled with the buttons of her dress and her hands went to his belt, slipping the clasp. 'I need yer, Don,' she moaned.

He kissed her ears and her neck as she struggled out of her dress and then reached down to her long, slender thighs and they kissed wildly, struggling and twisting together, their lips exploring each other's secret places, their naked bodies hot and expectant. He sought her lips and kissed her hard and long as she enfolded him in a passionate embrace. No longer able to delay their consuming desire, at last they were one.

Outside the office in the Galloway yard at Wilson Street a group of women stood together while their leader Red Ellie was inside talking to a young man, who appeared to be nodding his head vigorously. Florrie Axford reached inside her coat pocket for her snuffbox and turned to Maisie Dougall. 'She's givin' 'im what for by the look of it,' she remarked.

Maisie chuckled. 'I wouldn't like ter be in that young man's shoes,' she replied.

Maggie Jones touched the bun on the back of her head as she peered in through the window. 'Poor little sod looks terrified of 'er. Mind yer, though, she is a bit of an 'andful.'

Jamie Robins had been with the Galloway company for only a short time and he had never before had to deal with anything other than ledgers and bills. Now he felt completely out of his depth as he faced the determined woman.

'But I can't tell you when Mr Galloway will arrive. I'm afraid he doesn't take me into his confidence,' he said plaintively.

'Don't yer get shirty wiv me, young man,' Ellie told him. 'I wanna know when I can get ter see one o' the Galloways. I don't care if it's senior or junior, they're both owners.'

'Well, I can certainly take the petition,' Jamie said helpfully, 'but I can't promise when either of the owners will see it.'

Ellie put her hands on her hips and glared at the young man. 'Now look, my son,' she said in a low, menacing voice, 'if yer don't try an' locate one o' the Galloways an' get 'em ter come ter the yard right away, us ladies are gonna sit down in the doorway an' stop any o' your vans comin' in or goin' out, d'yer understand?'

Jamie Robins scratched his carroty hair anxiously. 'Someone could get killed if you attempt to block the gateway,' he warned her.

'Listen ter me,' Ellie said, waving her forefinger at him. 'If any o' my ladies get 'urt frew carmen drivin' in the yard, we'll pull 'em out o' those seats an' lynch 'em. Yer know what lynchin' is, don't yer?'

The young clerk nodded and held out his hands to Ellie placatingly. 'What can I do?' he implored her.

'Phone around. Tell Galloway the yard's on fire or somefink,' the women's leader shouted at him. 'I don't care what yer say but get 'em round 'ere sharp.'

Jamie sighed as he picked up the telephone, knowing he was going to be for it, and Ellie Roffey marched back into the yard.

''E give me a bit of ole lip at first,' she told the women, 'but I soon showed 'im the light. 'E's phonin'

392

around ter try an' find 'em. We'll 'ave ter stay 'ere until one of 'em gets 'ere.'

Maudie looked around the yard, remembering the last time she and the women had been involved in a protest against Galloway in Page Street. 'I wonder if 'e's phonin' fer the police?' she asked Florrie. 'We could be locked up fer trespassin'.'

'Don't be so melodramatic, Maudie,' Florrie told her. 'We've come ter see Galloway, not ter trespass. All we wanna do is present the petition.'

'But surely yer could 'ave give it ter the young man,' she said to Ellie.

The leader smiled patiently at Maudie. 'Now look, luv. If that young man takes the petition 'e'll only pass it on ter Galloway an' 'e'll no doubt put it in the bin. Then when we come round again 'e'll say 'e didn't get no petition, an' where's that leave us?'

'Up the Swanee wivout a paddle if yer ask me,' Florrie remarked.

Maggie Jones peered into the office window and turned to Sadie. ''E's on the phone. Poor little sod looks scared ter death,' she told her.

''E'll be more scared when Galloway comes marchin' in 'ere,' Sadie growled. ''E'll most likely tell 'im 'e should 'ave chucked us out the yard.'

'I don't s'pose ole Galloway'll take any notice o' the petition anyway,' Maggie remarked.

'Well, 'e better,' Sadie said in a loud voice, 'or somebody's likely ter start anuvver fire in the Galloway stables.'

Maudie looked at the big woman with fear in her eyes. She had for a long time been of the opinion that Sadie Sullivan was unstable. She had seen her fight like a man when she was younger, and her sons too had been involved in many scuffles, several amongst themselves. Her advancing years had done little to curb the woman's violent leanings, Maudie thought. They would have to be careful or Sadie was going to get them all locked up.

Suddenly the young man appeared in the office doorway and beckoned Ellie who was talking to Maisie and Maggie. 'I've located Mr Frank Galloway. He's on his way,' he said, relieved that the woman's wrath would now be directed at someone else.

Ellie motioned for the women to gather around. 'Now, look. It only wants one of us ter do the talkin'. D'yer want me ter speak on your be'alf, or will one of you ladies deal wiv it?'

Florrie shook her head. 'You'd better do it, luv,' she told her. 'A strange face might 'elp. Galloway knows all of us.'

It was nearly one hour later when Frank Galloway walked into the yard with a face like thunder, and when he saw the women gathered together he turned his head and stormed into the office.

Maggie crept up and peered in through the office window. 'Ole Galloway ain't 'alf tellin' that poor lad orf,' she said, turning to her friends.

Ellie left the group and walked boldly into the office. 'Mr Galloway?' she asked loudly.

'Wait outside,' Frank said, pointing to the door.

'Don't you take that tone wiv me,' Ellie told him in a threatening voice. 'I'm not one of yer workers, an' while yer at it, don't tell 'im orf. What else could 'e do but get yer round 'ere? We 'ad no intention o' movin' till yer showed yer face.'

Frank Galloway nodded to the young clerk, who went back to his books with a red face, then motioned for Ellie to follow him.

'What is all this about a petition?' he asked as soon as they were in the inner office.

'My name is Ellie Roffey an' I'm a member of the

British Communist Party,' she informed him. 'I've bin asked by the women ter represent 'em in their campaign ter get somefing done about the shockin' state o' their 'ouses, 'ouses that are owned by the Galloway company.'

'So they've all gone Bolshie, have they?' he remarked, grinning scornfully.

'I'd say they were makin' a stand against the capitalist exploitation of workers,' Ellie said coldly. 'Anyway, I'm not 'ere to argue the toss wiv yer. There's the petition signed by everybody in Page Street who rents an 'ouse owned by your company. There's also a list of outstandin' repairs that need ter be done right away,' she added, throwing the papers down on the desk in front of him. 'Now yer can please yerself what yer do about this petition, but I tell yer straight, Mr Galloway, if nuffink's done ter put fings right yer gonna be sorry.'

'Oh, I see. Threats, is it?' he mocked her.

Ellie put her hands on her hips and leaned forward over the desk. 'Yer got a chance ter put fings right in a civilised manner,' she said quietly, 'but if yer don't, every time you or yer lorries move out o' this yard yer'll run a gauntlet. Every time one o' yer vans parks anywhere fer more than five minutes there'll be posters stuck all over it. I jus' wonder what the firms yer contract to are gonna fink when they realise they're tied up wiv a slum lan'lord. They might even consider changin' their cartage contractor.'

Frank Galloway had become furious. 'Get out of this office before I call the police!' he shouted. 'I'm not prepared to sit here and listen to wild threats from a Bolshie cow like you. Go on, get out!'

Ellie walked slowly to the door and then turned to face him. 'I understand yer ole man lives in Tyburn Square,' she said quietly. 'Funny fing, we're 'avin' a workers' march on Sunday next. P'raps we could make

395

a little detour. I might even get on to our bruvvers in Ilford. Yer do live in Ilford, don't yer, Mr Galloway?'

'Get out!' he screamed.

'Don't ferget ter read the papers I've left yer,' Ellie told him as she walked out of the office, giving the young clerk a big wink as she passed.

''Ow d'yer get on?' the women asked, gathering around her.

'Well, 'e looked like 'e was gonna 'ave a seizure at first,' she told them, 'an' then I thought 'e really was 'avin' one, but I fink 'e's got the message at any rate.'

'Did 'e threaten ter chuck us all out?' Maudie asked.

'If 'e'd 'ave said that I'd 'ave burnt the place down,' Ellie declared with venom. 'Now c'mon, gels, let's march out of 'ere like we've won already.'

Billy Sullivan was sitting in the white-painted room staring up at the crucifix above the row of dusty books while Father Murphy finished off the letter. The scratching of the pen was loud in the otherwise silent room and Billy turned his gaze to the shiny pate of the ageing priest.

Suddenly Father Murphy looked up and sighed deeply. 'Well, that's taken care of that,' he said smiling. 'Now let me see. We've got quite a few donations in this week and there's one in from Councillor Squires' ladies' sewing group. There's five pounds from the T and G branch fund and another five pounds from the police fund. Things are looking good, Billy. We'll soon be able to get the footings done. We'll need much more before we can start the actual construction but at least we're not short of volunteers for the digging. A good foundation, that's very important.'

Billy nodded. 'The Kings Arms 'as got a tin box fer a collection an' my guv'nor's promised me 'e'll lend us

396

the picks an' shovels, provided we replace any that get broke,' he said helpfully.

Father Murphy rested his elbows on the desk and placed the tips of his fingers together. 'Billy,' he said, in a tone that made the young man fear what was coming next.

'Yes, Farvver?'

'Billy, I'm not altogether sure how to begin, but I s'pose I must ask.'

'Ask what, Farvver?'

'Would you consider yourself to be a violent man, Billy?'

'Certainly not, Farvver.'

'Have you been to confession lately, Billy?'

'No, Farvver.'

'Wally Walburton thinks you should.'

'What's it got ter do wiv 'im, Farvver?'

'Wally's suffering, Billy.'

'Did 'e tell yer, Farvver?'

'Wally Warburton is in no state to say anything at the moment, Billy. His mouth is swollen and he's lost two teeth.'

Billy fidgeted in his chair. 'Well, Farvver, it was like this. Wally was cuttin' up rough in the Kings Arms the ovver night. 'E saw the collection box on the counter an' 'e started goin' on about how the idea of a gymnasium was a load o' cobblers – I mean, rubbish. Anyway I ignored 'im at first. Everybody knows 'ow Wally goes off at times, but when 'e started gettin' personal an' sayin' that my Annie must be mad ter put up wiv me I smacked 'im in the mouth – I mean, I punched 'im.'

Father Murphy hid a grin. 'We can't have an upstanding member of our little community going around smacking people in the – I mean, punching people for merely shouting off, and certainly not in front of everyone in the Kings Arms,' he lectured him.

'Nobody saw me do it, Farvver, except Wally's mate, Tubby Abrahms. 'E was 'oldin' Wally's coat,' Billy explained. 'We was out in the yard, yer see.'

'Oh, well, that's different. But you're still at fault, Billy. You're not a twenty year old anymore and you've a wife and family to consider,' the old priest reminded him. 'Turn the other cheek, and try not to rise to the bait in future.'

'I'll try,' Billy replied, 'unless Wally mentions my Annie again.'

Father Murphy shook his head slowly, feeling that he was wasting his time trying to reform Billy Sullivan. 'Well, I've got a parish meeting to attend so we'd better get back to business,' he said, picking up a sheaf of papers. 'Now let's see about those footings.'

The last of the horse carts had left the Bradleys' firm in Salmon Lane and Sharkey was busy hosing down the yard. The morning sun was streaming through the office window and Carrie could hear the noise of the traffic outside the gates as it passed back and forth to the factory and the warehouse. She could not put her mind to the task of entering the tonnage and hours worked into the large bound ledger. She sighed deeply and leaned back in her chair, stretching her legs out in front of her. It had been madness allowing herself to get carried away with Don, she rebuked herself. It had been truly wonderful and he had tried hard afterwards to reassure her that it was the loneliness they both felt which had made it happen, but she could not help feeling terribly guilty that she had not stopped herself before it was too late. They had both been embarrassed afterwards and had spoken no endearments or made no promises to each other. They had lain there on the bed together, her head on Don's chest with his arms around her, both seeming to sense that it was a very brief interlude in their organised, predictable lives. Don had taken her hands in his and kissed her gently on the cheek before he left, and he had not turned back as he let himself out of the yard.

Carrie looked down at the ledger and closed it. There was much to do, phone calls to make and people to see, but for the moment she could only stare out at the blue sky and the fleecy clouds, wondering what the future would hold for her. Fred was very ill and it was almost certain that he would never get better. Joe was coming home very soon and it was likely that the long period in prison had changed him considerably. He would be bitter, unsure of himself, and probably unable to pick up the threads of his life without a lot of help. Would there be the same feeling between them? she asked herself. Perhaps Joe would decide to start afresh somewhere else, and even if he did not it would be hard to continue with their relationship now that Fred needed her more than ever. Carrie was beset by conflicting thoughts and feelings of guilt and she closed her eyes tightly, trying to shut out all the worries and doubts.

She jumped as the phone rang loudly, and as she reached for the receiver she felt afraid.

The voice at the other end of the line sounded cold and matter-of-fact. 'Can you come to the hospital right away? Your husband has taken a turn for the worse.'

Chapter Twenty-seven

Joe Maitland stared out of the carriage window and watched the bleak countryside flash past. Snow lay on the fields and the distant hills, and up above a January sun hung in the changing sky like a red globe. The other occupants of the carriage stared fixedly ahead, lost in their own thoughts, the two old ladies sitting upright with large black handbags resting on their laps and sucking noisily on mints, and the young, ginger-haired man occasionally crossing and uncrossing his legs. None of them had spoken and Joe felt relieved that he could keep his own counsel, hopefully until the train arrived at Paddington Station.

As the train pulled out of Swindon Station the ticket collector slid back the compartment door and entered, a pair of small clippers held in his hand. The two ladies fumbled in their handbags for their tickets but could not find them, and the young man searched all his trouser pockets and his luggage before producing his from the top pocket of his coat. Joe handed his ticket to the collector and the man rewarded him with a grateful smile. Both the ladies had finally discovered their tickets and they passed them over to the man without looking at him. He left the carriage humming to himself in a deep voice, while the young ginger-haired man recrossed his legs and the ladies resumed their noisy sucking of mints.

Joe cast his eye out of the window again and watched the changing landscape as the train sped towards London. He was dressed in a grey double-breasted suit, once his best but now looking creased, and a pale blue shirt, the top button undone and the collar held close with the small knot of a royal blue tie, which was also creased. Above him on the luggage rack were his belongings, wrapped in a brown paper parcel and tied up with string. The parcel had been noted by the two elderly sisters, who had made the trip to London regularly. They usually engaged the fellow occupants of their carriage in conversation during the tiring journey but they had long since come to know that released prisoners from Dartmoor usually carried such parcels, and they considered it more prudent to suck on their mints and ponder.

Joe thought about the letter he had received from Carrie in the autumn of last year, the one he had now in his coat pocket. It was the only one he had saved and as the train clattered on he thought of the pretty woman with the long fair hair and the pale blue eyes that he remembered so well. He had been shocked to hear of Fred's death, and the selling of the cafe. The fact that Carrie had gone into the cartage business did not surprise him very much, however. She had always loved horses, and her father would be a great help in looking after them and putting her straight on many aspects of the business. Inside the letter Joe had found a photo of Carrie and Rachel standing together beside a team of horses, and he had been taken by how much alike the two were. Rachel had her mother's long fair hair and finely moulded features and she was almost as tall as Carrie. They were both smiling, and Joe remembered the first time Carrie smiled at him when they met in the little pub off the Tower Bridge Road. It had been the first of several meetings and the first day that they had made love. What would the future hold for him now? he thought anxiously. His business had closed down and all he had to show for his endeavours, now that he had given Billy Sullivan the piece of land, were two hundred pounds in the bank. He was forty-five, foot-loose, and he had spent a number of years in prison.

The train rattled on and Joe closed his eyes, feigning sleep as he tried to concentrate his mind on his future plans. He would have to bury a lot of the past first, he realised. He had become obsessed with seeking revenge for his family and had made many enemies along the way. He had traded dishonestly and become involved with unscrupulous people, and when his guard was down his enemies had exacted their own revenge. He had gone in over his head trying to fight powerful people and they had seen to it that their interests were protected. Gerry Macedo had been their envoy, and he had met a violent end. Frank Fuller had been prepared to stand up in court and testify to their involvement with Ronald James and the pressure they had exerted on him, which had ultimately caused the wharfinger to take his own life, and Fuller too had met a violent end. Those same powerful people had set Joe up and he had been unable to do anything to prevent himself going to prison. He had not known of Fuller's demise before the trial, and when he asked for the ex-soldier to be brought to the stand it was terrible to be told that, even if the man had been able to attend, there was no evidence available, no documents, no collaborated testimony which would implicate Eastern Enterprises in any way. The case against him was one of receiving, and the only person who could have testified that the produce in question had been obtained in good faith seemed to have vanished. Joe felt certain that the agent had most likely been in the pay of Eastern Enterprises and had met the same fate as Macedo and Fuller. He would never know. Perhaps Martin Butterfield, the lawyer who looked after the company's interests, did not know either. Only the shadowy, faceless people whose names appeared on company letter headings would know, and they were beyond the reach of the law.

The train pulled into Paddington Station on time and Joe Maitland walked from the platform with the brown paper bundle tucked under his arm. His first desire was to see Carrie once more before looking for lodgings, though he needed a bath too, and a change of clothing. The hustle and bustle of the station made him feel jumpy and he hurried from the concourse and hailed a cab. The journey across London after the long train journey left him jaded, and when the cab pulled up on the south side of Tower Bridge he was glad to get out and stretch his legs. He wanted to walk the short distance to Carrie's yard to get the feel once more of the area he knew so well.

Carrie had just finished making up the carmen's pay packets when Joe walked into the yard and tapped on the office window. Her eyes lit up and as he stepped into the office she threw herself into his arms. 'I knew yer was comin' terday but I didn't know what time!' she said excitedly, looking him over closely. 'Yer look a bit pale, an' yer've lost some weight.'

'They didn't set out ter fatten me up,' he said smiling. 'I'm feelin' all right though, but I could do wiv a bath an' I need anuvver suit. This one's a bit moth-eaten.'

'Come an' say 'ello ter Dad, Joe,' she told him, taking his arm. ''E'll be so pleased ter see yer.'

Joe's face became serious. 'I was very sorry to 'ear about Fred,' he said, turning to her. 'I was shocked when I got yer letter.'

Carrie looked into his large brown eyes. 'It was

sudden,' she said quietly. 'I got to the 'ospital just in time. 'E was in no pain. 'E went off in 'is sleep at the end.'

As Joe crossed the yard with Carrie, William came to the door and beamed widely. 'Yer look well, Joe, considerin',' he said, pumping the younger man's hand in a strong grasp.

'Yer look very well yerself. 'Ow's Nellie?' Joe asked.

'She's fine. Come an' see 'er, she's boilin' a kettle.'

The Tanners and their daughter Carrie sat with Joe in the little parlour sipping tea. 'Danny's two boys are gettin' big an' Billy Sullivan's married wiv three kids now,' Nellie told him eagerly.

'Yeah, I know,' he laughed. 'Carrie kept me supplied wiv all the news.'

'Galloway left Page Street. 'E's got a big yard now in Wilson Street,' Nellie went on, to Joe's amusement and William's irritation.

'Joe's jus' told yer that Carrie's bin keepin' 'im up wiv the news, Nellie. Go an' put the kettle on again,' William urged her.

Nellie had noticed the way Carrie looked at Joe and she felt sure that there had been something going on between them. 'What's yer plans, Joe?' she asked, ignoring her husband.

Joe looked quickly at Carrie and then he stared down at his empty cup for a few moments. 'I gotta get some lodgin's an' then I'll decide what I'm gonna do,' he told her. 'I might go back ter Stepney. It's bin a long while but I've still got a few good mates over the water.'

Nellie saw the glance Carrie had given Joe and the disappointment on her face, and she knew then that she had been right. 'I'll put the kettle on,' she said quickly.

'There's no need ter rush orf, Joe,' William remarked, glancing quickly at his daughter. 'Carrie can fix yer up in 'er spare room. Yer can 'ave a bath in front o' the fire an' I've got a shirt yer can borrer fer the time bein'.'

Carrie felt that she could have kissed her father. 'P'raps Joe would sooner not,' she cut in, hoping she had said the right thing.

'As long as Carrie don't mind,' Joe replied.

'Of course I don't,' she said, trying not to sound too enthusiastic.

'Right, that settles it then. I'll go an' light the copper. It'll take a good couple of hours,' William said, giving Carrie a glance which spoke volumes.

Billy Sullivan sat in the Kings Arms with Danny Tanner, his face grimy from the day's toil. 'I'm worried, Danny,' he said, sipping his pint. 'They've told us when this job's finished there's no more work. If it don't pick up we'll all be laid orf.'

'Fings are bad on the river too,' Danny replied, looking gloomily around at the few customers standing at the bar. 'There's no new ships in. I've only 'ad two days' work this week.'

Billy leaned back in his chair and followed Danny's gaze. 'I've seen this pub a lot more busy than this, Danny boy. I reckon everybody round 'ere's on short time.'

.''Ow's the site goin'?' Danny asked, picking up his pint again.

Billy's face brightened. 'We've got the foundations down an' the bricks are comin' next week,' he said. 'I've gotta get some volunteers ter get 'em stacked. Farvver Murphy's gonna see what 'e can do but we'll need plenty of 'ands.'

Danny had noticed Wally Walburton walk in accompanied by his long-time friend Tubby Abrahms. The two had gone up to the bar and they glanced over at Billy, who had not seen them.

406

'When's the bricks comin'?' Danny asked, trying to keep his friend's attention.

'Next Tuesday,' Billy replied. 'Farvver Murphy persuaded 'em ter leave it till as late as possible. We can get more volunteers that way. Mind yer though, the way fings are goin' we'll 'ave no trouble. 'Alf the people round 'ere'll be 'angin' around on the street corners the way the work's goin'.'

Wally Walburton sidled over with Tubby Abrahms following behind. 'I see the foundations are down,' he said, slipping his thumbs into his braces. 'Tubby was tellin' me yer bin recruitin' volunteers.'

Billy did not look at him. 'That's right,' he said abruptly.

'Who yer got, the church choir?' Wally said sarcastically.

Billy looked up at the bulky young man. 'Well, they'd be a sight better than you two,' he growled. 'I would 'ave asked yer both ter give us an 'and but yer wouldn't last five minutes. It's 'ard work unloadin' bricks.'

'I'd stan' the pace better than anybody you could put up,' Tubby cut in.

'I doubt it,' Billy replied, grinning at Danny.

'I tell yer what we'll do,' Wally said quickly. 'Me an' Tubby against any two you can put up. Loser stands a round o' drinks.'

'Righto, Wally, yer on,' Billy said, holding out his hand.

Once the yard had been bolted up for the night Carrie placed the large tin bath in front of the banked-up fire. Joe passed back and forth from the scullery with pails of steaming hot water, and at last the bath was ready. He glanced at Carrie as he unbuttoned his shirt and she averted her eyes. 'While yer 'avin' yer bath I'll cook

407

some eggs an' bacon,' she said quickly. 'I've put a clean towel on the chair wiv the soap. I'll give yer a shout when the tea's ready.'

'Will yer scrub me back?' he asked.

'Call me when yer've got in,' she said, feeling her face getting hot under his gaze.

Joe smiled as he peeled off his shirt and when Carrie had left the room he stripped and climbed into the bath. The water was soothingly hot and after a few minutes soaking he stood up and soaped himself all over with Lifebuoy, revelling in the luxury of an unhurried bath. When he had sat down in the water once more he called out to Carrie, and as she came into the room he could see that she was aroused. Her face was flushed and she had let her long fair hair down and tied it with a black ribbon. He could see quite clearly too that she had removed her bodice and he noticed that her small firm breasts were taut, with her nipples standing out against the fabric. She came over to him and without saying a word took the soap from his hand and gently rubbed it over his back. He could hear her breathing and he felt the gentle rubbing becoming more like a caress. He turned his head towards her and she suddenly leaned over him and put her lips against his. He reached his arm round and pulled her down to him and she slipped sideways into the bath, her dress riding up around her thighs. Their kiss was long and sensuous, her tongue searching his, her breath coming fast, and he could feel her hands seeking him beneath the soapy water.

Suddenly she brought her legs down on the floor and pulled herself from the bath, still holding on to one of his hands, urging him up. Joe rose from the water and stepped out of the bath, grasping her and pulling her to him. Carrie felt his kisses on her neck and throat, her face and open lips. She moved away from him, deliberately pressing his hands against the front of her sopping blouse. He slowly undid each button, his eyes never leaving hers, and then he reached down to her long, slender skirt. As it dropped to the floor Joe saw she was completely naked. Carrie closed her eyes as she lowered herself backwards across the table, her feet still resting on the floor. He leaned over her, his mouth going down to her nipples, and then she sighed deeply and gave a little groan as she felt him enter her. All the waiting, all the long, lonely and empty nights were forgotten as she moved with him, together in a fantasy of love.

Father Murphy had been very busy organising the charity committee and to the whole family's delight the charity came to be known simply as 'Sullivans'. The ageing priest had contacted the brick company in Bedford and on Tuesday at four o'clock the first supply of bricks arrived in Wilson Street. Billy had been put off work that Monday and on Tuesday Danny had finished early. Both men had stood waiting on the corner of Wilson Street since early afternoon and later they were joined by two hefty young men whom Father Murphy had conscripted. It was not long before Wally and his friend Tubby turned up. When the lorry drove into the site and squealed to a halt Wally took off his coat despite the cold and rolled up his shirt sleeves, exposing his muscular arms. Tubby took off his coat too and stood shivering beside the lorry while the driver lowered the sides of the vehicle.

'Right then,' Billy said, spitting on his hands. 'We work in three teams. We've gotta pack the bricks in piles around the site so as ter make it easier fer the bricklayers. No chucking the bricks, they've got ter be stacked neatly. Right, when yer ready.'

Tubby and Wally started off carrying eight bricks at a

time as they ran from the lorry to place the first of them at the far end of the concrete base, and soon they were gasping for breath. Billy and Danny worked at a steady pace each carrying six bricks, and soon their twins piles had grown. The other two volunteers had clambered on to the lorry and were placing the bricks ready for the two teams. The cold afternoon was forgotten as sweat soaked the competitors' faces and necks, and by the time two equal stacks had been completed the four men were panting hard. Tubby was finding it difficult to keep up with the much stronger and fitter Wally and he was being subjected to a string of abuse by his friend, who could see the chance of a free pint and the acclaim that would go with it disappearing. The driver was beginning to feel that the volunteers had been recruited from the local lunatic asylum but he was pleased that the load was disappearing quickly off his vehicle.

Danny was feeling the strain on his arms and Billy was fighting for his breath but they were outstripping Wally and Tubby. Their second stack of bricks was almost completed and they had taken a clear lead. Tubby had by now come to the end of his tether. He slumped down on the kerbside and fought for his breath, unable to rise despite Wally's coaxing. He watched as his friend ran back and forth across the wide concrete base carrying the bricks, his face red with exertion and his breath coming in gasps. Suddenly Billy dropped the bricks he was carrying and held up his hands to their lone opponent. 'Wally, I gotta 'and it ter yer,' he said, rubbing his sore and bleeding palms. 'Yer'd kill yerself before yer gave up the chance of a free pint. Well, as far as I'm concerned yer've earned it. Now let's take it easy. What d'yer say?'

Wally spat on his sore hands and rubbed them together, then with a huge grin he held out his hand to the young Sullivan. Danny meanwhile had slumped down on the kerbside next to Tubby. 'C'mon, mate, on yer feet,' he said. 'Let's get the rest o' the load off the lorry an' we'll go fer a pint.'

One hour later six tired and aching volunteers walked wearily to the Kings Arms and slumped down over the bar counter. Without asking for the orders Alec Crossley pulled on the beer pump and filled six pint glasses with his best ale, placing them down in front of the exhausted men. Billy reached into his pocket but Alec waved the money away. 'It's all right, lad,' he said cheerily. 'Farvver Murphy's bin in. The drinks are on 'im.'

George Galloway leaned forward in his office chair and rested the palms of his hands on the silver handle of his cane walking stick. His face was furious and his eyes bulged as he glared at his son.

'Yer could 'ave told me,' he raged. 'First fing I 'eard on Sunday mornin' was that rabble passin' under me winder. Ole Jackley 'ad ter call the police. Then I come in 'ere an' see bloody great posters stuck on the walls outside.'

Frank was equally irate. 'I had a protest group camp under my window!' he shouted. 'They were carrying banners saying "Down with slum landlords". How do you think I felt?'

'Well, why didn't yer try ter talk ter the Bolshie mares?' George growled. 'Yer could 'ave stopped it if yer'd called the police. They 'ad no right ter come in this yard wiv their petition.'

'Well, I don't know what you propose to do about it, but unless something's done we're going to be plagued with them,' Frank replied, pacing the office.

The first of the lorries drove in and Frank Galloway looked through the office window. 'God God! Look at that!' he exclaimed.

411

The older man got up and walked to the window, then he banged his walking stick down with temper. 'Get the driver ter wash that orf!' he raved.

The driver had jumped down from his cab and was crossing the yard. His hair was matted and there was a gluey mess down the front of his boiler suit. 'I've never seen anyfing like it, Mr Galloway,' he said agitatedly. 'There was I parked outside Mark Brown's Wharf when I spotted this crowd o' lunatics. One of 'em started ter paste the side o' the lorry while I was sittin' there. Well, I went ter jump down, but I couldn't open the door. The gits 'ad tied the door 'andles tergevver. I see this big woman pastin' that poster on the side an' I shouted out, an' she give me a load of abuse a docker wouldn't use. All I could do was try ter get through the winder but as I lowered it she chucked the pail o' gum all over me. I'll never get this out o' me 'air.'

Frank Galloway shook his head slowly. 'All right, Tom, scrape that poster off then get off home,' he said. 'I'd better phone the police.'

George Galloway was searching through his desk drawer when Frank walked back into the office. 'Where's that bloody repair book got to?' he moaned.

Frank sat down and sighed loudly. 'I've been through the list of repairs needed. Ten ceilings, four sinks, two coppers, and God knows how many roof slates. It'll cost a small fortune.'

'Not if I find that bloody book,' George Galloway scowled.

'What do you need that for?' Frank asked irritably.

''Cos it's got Alf Comber's address in it,' George replied. 'I got 'im ter do the last lot o' repairs. 'E's a bit of a bodger but 'e's the cheapest by far.'

The younger Galloway shook his head in despair. 'You're not getting that drunken old sot to do those repairs, are you?' he asked, staring at his father. 'I remember the last time you got him in. We had the tenants over complaining that he'd caused more damage than he'd repaired. If you're going to spend money on those Page Street houses why don't you get a reputable firm in? If the work's done properly we can put a couple of shillings on the rent.'

George had found the repair book and was flipping through the pages. ''Ere we are. Forty-five Eagle Street,' he said suddenly, ignoring Frank's argument. 'I'll call roun' ter see 'im soon as I can. In the meantime, Frank, you go roun' an' see that ole witch Axford. Tell 'er I'm gettin' the repair man in, but only when 'er Bolshie friends stop their bloody caper. Don't take no ole lip orf 'er neivver. Put the fear o' Gawd inter the ole cow if she starts. Tell 'er she can be evicted fer causin' trouble.'

Frank Galloway gave his father a wicked look. It's about time he retired, he thought. Every time the silly old fool comes into the yard he causes disruption. Now he wants me to tidy up his dirty work. I don't know why he doesn't call round to the tenants himself.

George was staring thoughtfully at the papers on his desk, his fingers caressing the gold medallion hanging from the chain on his waistcoat, then suddenly he took out his pocket watch and glanced at it. 'It's early yet. Why don't yer pop roun' an' see that Axford woman right now?' he said.

Frank got up from his chair just as the phone rang. He picked up the receiver. George watched his son's reaction as he tried to get a word in. It was obvious that the caller was angry.

'Yes, yes, all right. I'll take care of it. Yes, of course. Leave it to me, and thank you. Goodbye, Mr Blackmore,' Frank said angrily.

'What's wrong?' George asked.

'That was Brockway's,' Frank replied, slumping

down in his chair. 'Our lorry's unloading there, and the managing director's walked in and created merry hell. There are posters stuck all over the vehicle. He's threatened to cancel the contract if we send another lorry there in that state.'

George banged his fist down on the desk. 'Get round an' see Axford right away,' he shouted. 'I'll go an' see Peter Brockway meself.'

After Frank had left, the elder Galloway reached into the drawer and took out a bottle of Scotch. Once fortified, he walked out to his trap which was standing just inside the gate. He climbed into the contraption and picked up the reins, pulling on them to force the pony around towards the entrance, and as the trap drew out of the yard into the street the poster could be seen clearly on the rear of the coachwork: 'Down with Slum Landlords'.

Chapter Twenty-eight

1932 dawned with little prospect of work for the many folk in the riverside borough who had been made redundant before Christmas. Many more were on short time as the factories' orders fell and money became scarce. The river trade was experiencing its worst spell for many years and hungry workers hung about the streets or travelled to other boroughs seeking work. Carrie Bradley, however, had been fortunate in winning another contract, and it was one which gave her much satisfaction. Brockway Leather Factors had decided that the cartage rates they were paying to the Galloway firm were too high, considering that on two occasions the vehicles supplied to them appeared to be advertising for the British Communist Party. Most of Brockway's output was destined for the local railway freight depots and the management felt that it would be prudent to hire the less expensive horse transport. With dropping orders for their goods and the prospects for any improvement looking very grim, the firm of leather factors decided to cut their costs and obtain the services of Bradleys' Cartage Contractors, whose hire rates were very reasonable.

Carrie now had four regular contracts and frequent daily hire work in the borough, much of the latter needed by various firms whenever trade picked up and orders trickled in. The extra work meant that Carrie had to hire casual labour when required and she also took on another regular carman, Lofty Bamford. He was one of Galloway's old casuals and William knew him well. He had told his daughter that the man was an experienced carman and reliable. Carrie was gratified to see that the business was holding its own in the first year, considering the way things were. She had already thought about the possibility of buying a lorry in the not too distant future and trying for some of the more lucrative contracts, but she refrained from talking to her father about her plans for the time being.

Life became a little complicated in the Tanner household as the year progressed. Joe Maitland stayed on at the house as a lodger and his being there caused some friction between William and Nellie Tanner, who was not afraid to make her point.

'It's not right, Will,' she said. 'I know Carrie's a widow an' she's got nobody to answer to, but people will talk.'

'Sod the people,' was William's abrupt reply.

Nellie had known from the first day of his arrival that Joe Maitland and her daughter were more than just friends. 'It mus' be obvious to everyone whenever they're tergevver,' she remarked. 'I saw Carrie wiv 'im when I come in wiv the shoppin' the ovver mornin' an' 'e 'ad 'is arm round 'er.'

'So what?' William replied.

''Ow long 'as it bin goin' on? That's what worries me,' Nellie said.

'Look, Nellie, our Carrie's not 'ad an easy time,' William reminded her. 'I know Fred was a good man an' 'e would 'ave given 'er the top brick orf the chimney but 'e was a good bit older than 'er an' not the sort o' bloke who liked ter take 'er out an' about. I don't fink they ever went ter the music-'all more than a couple o'

416

times, nor the pictures. All it seemed ter be fer 'er was drudgery.'

Nellie would not be swayed. 'Fred was 'er 'usband, Will,' she said firmly. 'If Carrie an' Joe were carryin' on while 'e was alive then she was wrong, an' yer won't make me see it any ovver way.'

'Well, as far as I'm concerned she ain't done no wrong,' William persisted. 'I'm sure she thought a lot o' Fred but I fink she married 'im mainly so she could 'ave the chance o' lookin' after us, an' that's what the gel's done.'

Nellie was staring into the fire, pinching her lip. 'We've bin over this time an' time again,' she said irritably. 'I know she worries about us but I fink she married Fred fer security. After all, most o' the gels round 'ere of 'er age were already married.'

'Well, whatever the reason was, she wasn't 'ead over 'eels in love wiv 'im,' William remarked. 'I fink it was on the cards that one day some young man would come along.'

Joe had taken Carrie's breath away, and for the first few weeks after his release from prison when he was staying at the house life for her was idyllic. He helped her with the books and busied himself about the stables, repaired broken planking, re-hung stable doors and generally made himself useful. They spent their evenings together taking long walks along the riverside, or sometimes they would catch a tram to Greenwich or the Embankment where they would get off and stroll leisurely through the brightly lit streets. At night Carrie lay awake, awaiting him, and when the house was quiet he would come to her bed and make gentle and passionate love to her.

Joe had quickly become a favourite of Rachel's and he spent time talking with her and taking her for walks

417

along the river or to the park while Carrie was busy. Rachel took to calling him Joebo, clinging to him like a limpet, and Carrie felt very happy for her daughter. Fred had adored her but he had never seemed to have enough time to spend with her and he had tended to lecture her during their spare moments together. Rachel had loved him too but she had never been able to confide in him the way she felt she could with Joe. He made her laugh and chased away her fears and anxieties, and she grew to love him.

Gradually, as the weeks passed, Carrie began to sense a change in Joe, although at first it was hardly noticeable. He started to become edgy and began to make the odd trip to Stepney, telling her that he wanted to set up a business which this time would be perfectly legal. He would speak about various ideas he had, and then relapse into a period of moodiness. His interest in her as a desirable woman was still as strong, however, and Carrie felt that, whatever thoughts and worries he harboured during the day, she could make him forget when he came to her room in the quiet of night.

Carrie could sense, however, that Joe's long incarceration had changed him inside. He was bitter and less confident, although he tried hard to hide it from her. He had been in business of some sort since he was very young and his idleness now was getting to him. She could understand to some degree how he must be feeling. There were few opportunities for starting up in business again, the way things were. Thousands of young men were being thrown out of their jobs, to hang about the streets between long hours of standing in line at the labour exchanges, and the growing poverty and degradation could be seen on every street corner and in every labour queue.

Joe was becoming more and more edgy and

depressed as the days passed and Carrie worried lest he should decide to resume his old life of wheeling and dealing. One day when he told her he would have to make a trip to Stepney she confronted him.

'Yer wouldn't go back ter what yer was doin', would yer, Joe?' she asked in an anxious voice.

'Look, Carrie,' he said irritably. 'What I decide ter do is my concern. I can't stay 'ere fer ever. All right, I pay me keep, but the money's runnin' out. I don't want charity, an' besides, yer parents wouldn't take kindly ter me spongin' on yer, now would they?'

Carrie took him by the arms as though she was scolding a child. 'Now listen, Joe,' she said firmly. 'It's nuffink ter do wiv my parents. Besides, I love yer. I'll worry terrible if yer put yerself at any risk. If yer get caught doin' anyfing wrong they'll lock yer up an' chuck away the key next time.'

Joe's face was set hard. 'I won't make the same mistakes next time, Carrie,' he said obstinately. 'I've 'ad a lot o' time ter fink. Look around yer. There's men standin' on every street corner an' they've all got that same look o' despair. Then on the ovver 'and yer've got rich and powerful people like them who run Eastern Enterprises. They can pick up a phone an' then some poor sod gets done in. They can set people up, just like they did wiv me. They can manipulate an' wangle, an' control people's lives at their leisure, an' all the time they live like lords, eat the best food, drink the best booze, while those poor sods on the street corners are goin' 'ome ter mutton stew or bread an' drippin', if they're lucky. I'm not prepared to end up in the gutter, Carrie.'

Joe went across the river to Stepney and returned later that evening looking a little less depressed, but he made other trips, more and more frequently, and Carrie began to feel that he was slowly slipping away

419

from her. She often smelt drink on his breath when he came home from a trip, and his visits to her bedroom were becoming less frequent.

The business was taking up more of Carrie's time now, and she began to devote her energies to building up her cartage firm. Often she would call into her old cafe in Cotton Lane to talk to Sam. He had become a favourite with the local dockers and carmen, and his effeminate behaviour and quick wit served to ensure his popularity and success. Sam was able to give Carrie plenty of advice and information, and whenever there were problems or strife amongst the cartage firms in the area he was the first to know.

'I was gettin' a right old ear'ole bashin' yesterday, Carrie,' he told her one day. 'I was bleedin' sick of it, really I was. I 'ad this carman tellin' me all about 'ow 'is firm was goin' down the drain, an' then ter top it all Bessie wanted ter know all about what 'e was sayin'. I tell yer, luv, Bessie Chandler wants ter know the ins an' outs of a nag's arse.'

'What firm was this carman talkin' about, Sam?' Carrie asked him, her business sense aroused.

'Taylor's,' he replied. 'They do all the cartin' fer the clothes firms in Bermon'sey Lane an' Tooley Street. From what I can make out they 'ad a lot o' trouble wiv their 'orses a little while ago an' they lost contracts over it. I don't know much about 'orses but Taylor's poor fings look like they're 'alf starved, an' I'm sure their bleedin' carmen are tuppence short of a shillin', really I am.'

Carrie was enjoying his impudent chatter. ''Ow's the cafe doin', Sam?' she asked smiling.

'Don't ask,' he replied, waving his hand at her limp-wristedly. 'There's no money about. The poor boys are on short time at the wharves an' I'm doin' 'ardly any meals these days. Tea an' toast, an' slices o' bread an' drippin' are all I seem ter be doin'. I tell 'em they can't make love on bread an' drippin' but I might as well talk ter meself. Still, not ter worry, I'm sure fings are gonna pick up before long. I 'ope so anyway, or I'll 'ave ter pack up an' go out on the game.'

Carrie took her leave of the beguiling character and decided to try her luck by visiting the clothes firms Sam had spoken about. She took a batch of cartage tariffs with her and by the end of the day she had managed to talk to most of the managers at the factories. Very soon her efforts began to pay off and one or two firms began to hire her transport on a daily basis. It was a trying situation, having to find casual carmen and keep to varying daily schedules, but it paid off when one of the largest clothing contractors called Carrie in to discuss a regular contract. Things were beginning to take an upward turn, and she sat down one evening to talk to her father about her plans.

'I'm goin' ter buy some more 'orses, Dad, an' a couple o' new wagons,' she told him.

William felt a surge of pride as he saw the determined look on his daughter's face but he urged caution. 'Don't run before yer can walk,' he warned her. 'Yer gotta make sure there'll be work fer 'em. Yer can't afford to 'ave too many stuck in the stalls all day.'

Carrie brushed aside his concern. 'Look, Dad, I've got new contracts an' there's more where they come from. My rates are as good if not better than any o' the ovver firms around 'ere an' I'm gettin' more an' more dock work now the firms know my men are all in the union. They know that I don't 'ave any trouble wiv the dockers.'

'What about the room? Yer've got no spare space in the yard,' he reminded her.

Carrie smiled as she took out a piece of paper from the hip pocket of her dress. 'I was workin' it out,' she said, spreading the sheet of paper on the table in front of him. 'I can get a weavverboard stable put up across the back wall. It'll mean less space fer the carts if I use a bit o' the shed but we can manage. I can stable anuvver few 'orses there.'

William looked at his daughter with a smile on his lined face. 'Yer never stop, do yer?' he said fondly. 'It was the same when yer 'ad that cafe. Always lookin' fer ways to improve the business. I dunno where yer get it from. It certainly don't come from me. I've never bin one fer business.'

Carrie grinned at him and prodded the sheet of paper lying between them. 'Well, what d'yer fink?' she asked.

He nodded. 'I can see ole Sharkey gettin' the 'ump wiv the extra work 'e'll 'ave ter do,' he told her.

'Leave Sharkey ter me, I can 'andle 'im,' Carrie said with a laugh.

William leaned back in his chair and watched his daughter as she folded up the piece of paper. She still looked as pretty as ever, he thought, but there seemed to be a hardness about her now. It was as though she was forcing herself to succeed above all else and it worried him. He had seen the ruthless streak in George Galloway develop and take possession of the man over the years and he hoped it wouldn't happen to Carrie. Maybe there was something that was driving her on, he reflected, making her use up all her time and energy to avoid facing it.

'Is everyfing all right wiv Joe?' he said suddenly.

'Why d'yer ask, Dad?'

'Jus' wonderin'.'

'Why?'

William could see that he would have to make a clean breast of his concern. 'Look, luv, yer don't 'ave to 'ide yer feelin's fer Joe in front o' me. I've known fer a long time yer care a lot fer 'im, it was obvious. Are you an' 'im plannin' ter get married one day?'

'We've never discussed it, Dad,' she replied. 'But, yes, I do care fer 'im an' 'e cares fer me, I know 'e does. The trouble wiv Joe is 'e can't abide 'avin' time on 'is 'ands. That's the reason fer those trips over the water. 'E's got friends over there an' 'e's tryin' ter get started up in business again.'

William shook his head sadly. 'I'd 'ave thought 'e'd learnt 'is lesson after the last turn out. 'E played too near the edge when 'e 'ad that ware'ouse an' I was in a position ter know. It worried the life out o' yer muvver. She told me dozens o' times ter leave the job. She reckoned I'd get roped in if 'e got caught wiv that dodgy stuff 'e was 'andlin'.'

Carrie ran her finger along the pattern in the table-cloth, her face becoming sad. 'It's not only the busi-ness, it's the drink,' she said quietly. 'Joe's started drinkin' 'eavy an' it's affectin' us.'

''E's not started knockin' yer about, 'as 'e?' William said, his face hardening.

'Of course not,' Carrie replied quickly. 'Joe's kind an' gentle, but I can see what the drink's doin' to 'im. Yer must 'ave seen the way 'e's bin lately?'

William nodded. 'That's why I asked 'ow 'e was,' he replied. ''Eavy boozin' shows in a man's face. I've seen the way ole George Galloway used ter look when 'e was on the bottle. It clouds yer judgement too, an' in Joe's case it could be dangerous, what wiv 'is record.'

Carrie looked pained. 'I've tried ter tell 'im, Dad, but 'e jus' laughs it off. I'm worried fer 'im.'

William got up from his chair and bent over to kiss Carrie's forehead. 'Don't worry, luv,' he said quietly. 'It'll all work out all right. After bein' in prison fer a long time Joe's prob'ly got a lot o' fings inside 'imself 'e needs ter sort out. Give 'im time. An' don't you push yerself too 'ard eivver, luv. Let the business build up steadily. Don't want too much too soon. It can become an obsession that can ruin yer life.'

She got up and hugged him. 'I know, Dad,' she said gratefully. 'I won't ferget what yer said.'

As the year wore on Billy Sullivan was constantly on short time and struggling to provide for his family. Annie told him that she was pregnant again and his heart sank. The builders he worked for had just finished a contract and there was no work available until September when they were due to start renovating an old factory in Rotherhithe. Billy took comfort from the fact that the job would see him over Christmas, but for the time being there was only dole money coming into the home. Annie was her usual cheerful self, however, and she did her best to make him feel less worried. 'We can manage,' she told him. 'We're luckier than most. I've still got a few coppers put away and the children are all well. We won't starve, Billy.'

The long days of idleness were made easier for Billy by the progress of the gymnasium building. Every day he would go to the site in Wilson Street and watch the brickwork growing. It was to be a two-storeyed building with the upper floor devoted to changing rooms, wash-rooms and showers, as well as store rooms and office space, leaving the lower floor solely for the ring and training area. The roof was to be of grey slate with a large board beneath the front gable announcing 'Sullivan's Gymnasium'. Billy wanted it to be called after Father Murphy but the ageing priest would not agree. 'See the building as a tribute to you, Billy, for your Christian thought,' he told him, 'and equally as a tribute to the memory of your two brothers, John and Michael, and all the young men of this parish who fell in the war.'

The bricklayers were working on the site thanks to

Father Murphy. He had managed to recruit the tradesmen from among his parishioners and the men were glad to work for a daily meal and a few items of food and clothing for their families, provided from the church fund and from well-wishers who had answered the priest's appeal. The men worked under the supervision of Benjamin Corrigan, a retired master builder who was the architect of the new building. Like the Sullivans Ben had lost two sons in the war and he answered the call after Father Murphy explained to him the proposed plan for a gymnasium which would be a practical memorial to the fallen. The priest promised Ben that there would be a plaque erected in the hall to his two sons, and it gave him great comfort.

Billy stood at the site beside the old priest one morning, watching the scaffolding going up.

'It's looking very good, Billy,' Father Murphy said, slipping his hands in the sleeves of his cassock. 'When the upper floor is bricked, however, we'll be faced with a problem.'

Billy looked at the priest quizzically.

'The roof, Billy, the roof,' Father Murphy said loudly. 'We'll need timbers, lots of timbers and slates.'

'Is there any money left in the fund, Farvver?' Billy asked fearfully.

'It's like old Mother Hubbard's cupboard, young man,' the priest informed him. 'It's depleted.'

'What can we do about it, Farvver?' Billy asked.

'Other than praying for a miracle to happen there's not a lot we can do, I'm afraid,' Father Murphy told him.

During the late summer months there was a sudden frenzy of anticipation in Page Street. Florrie Axford knocked on Maisie's door and told her the news. The two women then went to Sadie's house and told her

425

too. Maggie Jones was quickly enlightened, as were Alice Johnson and all the rest of the tenants concerned.

'Don't be too eager ter let 'im in,' Florrie warned them. 'The last time Alf Comber done a job o' work on my 'ouse 'e was puttin' a few slates on the roof an' 'e put 'is foot right frew me winder on 'is way up. The man's nuffink but a bodger.'

'I remember the time 'e mended me copper,' Sadie piped in. ''E was pissed at the time an' it took 'im two days ter do it. The bloody fing's never bin right since. I dunno what 'e done to it but it takes hours ter boil.'

'Well, if we get any trouble we'll see Red Ellie. She'll sort 'im out,' Maisie said confidently.

Maudie Mycroft had not yet heard the news. When she got home from the mothers' meeting at the church Maisie was standing at her front door.

'Guess what, Maudie? We're gettin' our repairs done at long last!' Maisie told her. 'Yer'll 'ave ter be careful an' watch 'im though. 'E's put 'is foot frew Florrie's winder an' 'e's buggered up Sadie's boiler.'

Maudie brought a hand up to her mouth. 'I won't let 'im in my place,' she said firmly. 'I'd sooner put up wiv the leaky roof.'

'Yer won't 'ave no say in it,' Maisie replied. ''E'll go up the outside on a ladder.'

'Well, we'll see about that,' Maudie said with a passion that surprised Maisie.

Alf Comber was a once-respected builder and decorator who had fallen on hard times. His heavy drinking had ruined his marriage – although some people said it was his marriage that had ruined his drinking. The man had become a bodger, although he had once been a good craftsman. He had lost pride in his workmanship and now he rushed his jobs and hurried off to the pub to drink himself into a stupor. The men who had been working for him had left after he spent all the money

426

put aside for their wages in an orgy of drinking. Alf then returned home to discover that his wife had walked out on him and the poor inebriate went on to sell his ladders and trestles, his tools, and finally his motor van to pay for his constant drunkenness. It was not long before he reached rock bottom. Slowly Alf had realised that he had to pull himself together. He borrowed the money for some rickety ladders and a hand barrow and started touting for business. The problem was, everyone in the area had come to know of Alf Comber's reputation for heavy drinking by now and they shunned him. The unfortunate builder had finally got some work repairing properties belonging to the Galloway company, and apart from a few minor disasters managed to fulfil what was required of him, broadly speaking. Alf struggled on, hardly making enough money to satisfy his huge thirst, until he got another visit from George Galloway.

'There's the list of properties I want repaired,' George told him. 'Yer can see from the list what's ter be done so get on wiv it, an' 'ere's a few quid on account. Now I'm warnin' yer, Alf, if yer don't do a proper job I ain't payin' yer, understood?'

Alf nodded, grateful for his drinking stake. 'Leave it ter me, Mr Galloway,' he said dutifully. 'I'll do a good job, don't worry.'

'I ain't worryin'. You're the one who's got ter worry. No results, no money,' George warned him.

Alf Comber pushed his dilapidated barrow into Page Street one bright morning in September and set it down outside Maudie Mycroft's front door. He then took out a sheet of paper from his pocket and studied it for a few minutes. Roof slates on number 16, he read out aloud.

Maudie was peeping through her curtains and saw Alf take the rickety ladder off his barrow and lean it against the house. She wished Ernest was there to stop the man and began to fret, wondering what she should do. Outside Alf was singing to himself as he extended his ladder, and after narrowly missing smashing the upstairs windows he decided that all was ready. He went to his barrow and picked up a few slates, and when he turned round saw Maudie standing at her front door with a worried look on her face.

'Yer can't go on my roof, young man,' she told him.

'Why's that then?' he asked.

''Cos I said so,' she replied sharply. 'I don't want yer puttin' yer foot frew my winder like yer did ter Florrie Axford's.'

Alf Comber had never heard of Florrie Axford and any recollection he may have had of smashing some-body's window had long since been boozed from his mind. 'Now look, luv, I gotta mend yer roof an' there's no way I'm gonna be able ter do it from down 'ere, now is there?' he said, making for the ladder.

'I don't care, I don't want yer treadin' all over my roof in case yer do some damage,' Maudie replied, feeling as though she wanted to burst into tears.

Alf put the slates down on his barrow and faced the agitated woman. 'Listen, luv,' he began. 'I've bin repairin' 'ouses fer donkeys' years an' I know what I'm doin'. D'yer realise it's a skilled job roofin' an' tilin'? Yer gotta know what yer doin' goin' up ladders onter roofs. Just yer leave it ter me, I know what I'm doin'.'

'Yer will be careful then, won't yer?' she pleaded with him.

Alf nodded and licked his lips as the craving for a drink overtook him. 'It's a very dry job puttin' roof slates on,' he informed her. 'I don't s'pose yer got a drop o' drink in the place, 'ave yer?'

'I'll make yer a cup o' tea if yer like,' Maudie said, beginning to feel a little better.

'No fanks, missus,' Alf replied, feeling a big giddy at

the mention of tea. 'I meant, 'ave yer got a drop o' beer in?'

Maudie shook her head, feelin uneasy again as the man seemed to stagger slightly. 'I don't keep any beer in the 'ouse,' she said, going back inside.

Alf picked up the slates, his stepped plank and his tiler's hammer, and proceeded to climb the ladder. The roof felt hot as he placed the plank across the slates, and when he had inched along it to the damaged section he decided to take a rest. Climbing ladders always made Alf feel tired so he lay back and spread himself out in the warm sun.

Nellie Tanner had thought to pay her friends in Page Street a visit. As she walked along the turning she saw Maudie Mycroft standing on the edge of the kerb beside a barrow with her hand up to her mouth, peering up at her roof.

'What's wrong, luv?' Nellie asked her.

'I'm 'avin' me roof mended an' the bloke's bin up there fer a long time,' Maudie replied. 'I'm wonderin' if 'e's all right.'

Alf had had a nice nap and was beginning to set to work as Nellie came up. He had removed the first of the broken slates and let it slither down into the guttering. Nellie heard the noise and turned to Maudie. 'Yer'd better get inside in case one o' them slates comes down,' she warned.

Maudie decided it was good advice and Nellie walked on to Sadie's house. Meanwhile Alf Comber was getting on well. His first task of tidying up the damaged area was completed and he was about to replace the first of the slates when he lost his footing on the stepped plank and fell feet first through the hole in the roof.

Maudie was making herself a cup of tea to steady her nerves when she heard the loud crash and then a shout.

She hurried up to her bedroom, fearing the worst, and when she entered the room she nearly fainted. She had never believed that anything as bad as this could happen. The bed was covered in plaster and laths, and there was a leg sticking down from the hole in the ceiling. Alf was groaning. She climbed on to the bed and touched his leg. 'Are yer all right?' she called up to him.

'Get me out of 'ere, I can't move!' Alf shouted.

Maudie took hold of his foot and pulled.

'Stop! Yer'll ruin me!' he screamed out.

'Wait there, I'll get 'elp,' she called up.

'I'll be 'ere,' he groaned.

Maudie ran to Sadie's house in a state of shock. 'Quick, Sadie! That builder's fell frew me ceilin'!' she cried.

The women all hurried from the house and Maudie led the way up into her bedroom. Sadie looked up at the leg and at the mess on the bed. 'I dunno what we can do,' she said.

'P'raps we could all pull on it,' Nellie offered.

'I reckon we should send fer the police,' Maisie suggested.

Florrie took out her snuffbox and tapped on the lid thoughtfully. 'Why don't we send fer Galloway? 'E's ter blame,' she remarked.

'Get me down, fer Gawdsake,' Alf called out.

'Shut yer trap, we're tryin' ter fink,' Sadie shouted to him.

Maggie Jones stared up at the leg. 'Let's just all take 'old an' pull,' she cut in.

Sadie scratched the back of her head. 'Where's yer ovver leg?' she called out.

'It's fixed round the rafter,' Alf told her.

Sadie shook her head. 'We can't do it from inside. 'E'll 'ave ter be pulled out from the roof,' she declared.

'Jus' get me out,' the voice pleaded.

There were footsteps on the stairs and Ernest looked in. 'Aw, no,' he said dejectedly.

'Oh, Ernie, what are we gonna do?' Maudie cried out.

Ernest took off his coat. 'Get me the poker,' he said, rolling up his sleeves.

Maudie did as she was told and all the women watched while Ernest set to work making the hole bigger, knocking down more pieces of lath and plaster on to the bed. When he was satisfied with his handiwork he looked up into the gap he had made. 'Can yer fiddle yer ovver leg free?' he called out.

There was a groaning and grunting, and the occasional obscenity, then Alf called out, 'It's free.'

Ernest spat on his hands and grabbed Alf's ankle. 'Get ready,' he shouted up.

The women backed away from the bed as Ernest took the strain, and as he lifted his feet off the ground and hung suspended from Alf's leg there was a loud yell followed by the crash of falling bodies and a cloud of dust which rose to fill the room.

Alf Comber slowly got up from the bed and tried out his leg. 'Bloody 'ell, mate, yer nearly pulled me in 'alf,' he gasped.

Florrie prodded him in the chest. 'Yer can tell Galloway that Flo Axford said 'e's got anuvver repair on the list now,' she grated.

Alf took out a sheet of paper from the breast pocket of his overalls. 'Mrs Axford? I've got a repair ter do at your place,' he told her.

'Over my dead body,' she growled.

'It might well be, if yer let 'im in,' Sadie remarked.

Alf Comber put his ladder and his various bits and pieces on to his barrow and limped out of the street, wishing that he had never agreed to Galloway's

431

request, while the women helped Maudie clear the rubble from her bedroom.

When the task was finished Florrie took out her snuffbox once more. 'Right, ladies,' she said with a flourish. 'I fink we should contact Red Ellie again, don't you? She said ter fetch 'er if we wasn't satisfied.'

Chapter Twenty-nine

On a very cold morning early in October Ellie Roffey called around to see the women of Page Street and together with Florrie and Maisie went to visit George Galloway. Unlike the last time the three women were shown into the office and given chairs. George Galloway sat down facing them, and away in the corner, trying to make himself as inconspicuous as possible, was the young clerk.

'Get the ladies some tea, laddie,' Galloway ordered, leaning back in his chair. 'Now let me see, you're Ellie Roffey,' he said, fingering his gold medallion. 'I understand yer representin' these good ladies?'

'That's right, Mr Galloway,' Ellie answered. 'Yer repair man should be locked up fer the damage 'e done ter poor Mrs Mycroft's 'ouse. I . . .'

'The repair man ain't got paid,' George butted in. 'In fact I'm chargin' 'im fer the ceilin' ter be fixed. Now I tell yer what I'm gonna do. I'm sendin' a firm o' builders round in the next fortnight ter fix the places up. All the repairs are gonna get done, yer can take my word fer it.'

Florrie felt that her ears were playing her tricks. 'All of 'em?' she asked.

'All of 'em,' Galloway repeated.

'What about the rents? Yer ain't puttin' 'em up soon as yer done the work, are yer?' Ellie asked.

George Galloway shook his head. 'No. In fact I'm 'avin' a look ter see if we can lower the rents in some cases,' he said, beaming at the ladies.

Florrie decided it must be her ears, or else George Galloway had received a visit from the ghost of Christmas past. 'Is that right?' she queried.

George Galloway nodded and picked up a sheet of paper lying on the desk in front of him. 'I've bin lookin' at the list o'tenants,' he said cheerily. 'I see yer live alone, Mrs Axford. And you, Mrs Dougall, you're livin' wiv yer 'usband an' one son.'

Maisie shook her head. 'My boy's married. 'E don't live wiv us any more,' she corrected him.

'I see,' George mumbled, making an alteration to the list. 'Right then. Now this is what I propose ter do.'

The young clerk came into the office carrying a tray of tea. When the women were served George went on. 'We'll start wiv you, Mrs Axford. I see yer pay ten shillin's an' sixpence rent fer the 'ouse. I'm finkin' o' puttin' yer rent down ter nine shillin's a week an' yer can take yer pick, top or bottom.'

'What d'yer mean?' Florrie asked, glaring at him.

'What I say,' Galloway said quietly. 'Put yer stuff up or down an' when yer've made up yer mind I'll rent the ovver 'alf o' the 'ouse out.'

'Yer can't do that,' Ellie butted in. 'What about the use o' the gas stove? Yer can't 'ave two families usin' one gas stove.'

George smiled. 'That won't be a problem,' he said. 'I'll get anuvver gas stove put in on the landin'.'

'What about the closet an' the copper?' Florrie asked angrily.

'Lots o' families share closets an' coppers,' George replied.

'S'posin' we refuse?' Maisie asked.

'Well, yer could always stay the way you are, but in

the new year the rent fer the 'ouse is goin' up one an' sixpence,' he told them.

As Christmas approached Carrie found herself stretched to the limit. Her four carmen were working regularly on the existing contracts, she had bought four horses, young Welsh cobs, which were suitable for the light vans, and she was employing on average four casual carmen daily. Other contracts were promised for the new year, and she had talked to the local building firm which had carried out the extension to her dining rooms about erecting the new stable. Her mother and father had both gone down with bronchitis and Rachel had to spend most of her time after school acting as nurse and housekeeper.

She had grown into a tall, beautiful girl with long flaxen hair and eyes that matched her mother's. Her temperament was much like Carrie's when she was the same age, except that Rachel did not have the same fascination with horses. Seeing her mother stretched almost to breaking point, she got on with her chores without complaining and was a great comfort to Carrie.

Rachel had seen the change in Joe during the past few months and she felt sad that he did not give her much of his time now he was drinking heavily. Joe himself had realised that he could not go on lodging with Carrie unless he stopped drinking, or at least attempted to curb it. He had tried hard, but the week before Christmas he learned that the money he was trying to raise for his share in a business venture with four friends would not be forthcoming. The news came after a series of disappointments and he forgot about the promise he had made to himself and walked into a pub in Limehouse to drown his sorrows. The place was noisy, and the clientele were speaking in foreign tongues for the most part. There were women frequenting the bar who were obviously looking for easy pickings amongst the foreign seamen and river workers who ventured there. One woman with heavy make-up and a tatty fur coat accosted him almost as soon as he went in the bar but Joe shrugged his shoulders and ignored her as he sought to blot out the bad feelings inside him.

The evening was wearing on and Joe had become drunk. The woman with the fur coat had left the pub with a Dutch seaman but she was back now, still showing an interest in the good-looking man who was lolling against the bar, moodily contemplating his near-empty glass. He had looked over at her a few times, trying to focus his eyes on her, and she decided he was ready. She ambled over and with a big smile took his arm.

'I fink yer need a little company, dearie,' she said in a low voice.

Joe smiled crookedly. 'I – I jus' wanna be, I wanna be . . .'

The street woman pulled on his arm, half dragging him to the door, and as she struggled out of the pub still holding on to him a hefty young man in a cap swigged the remains of his drink and followed her out.

'C'mon, luvvy, roun' the corner. We can do it roun' the corner,' she said, glancing behind her to see if her accomplice was there.

Joe suddenly felt sick, his only concern at that moment to break free from the woman and her over-powering perfume. He pulled against her arm but then suddenly his other arm was taken and he found himself being almost carried into an alley. His instinct told him he was in mortal danger and he let his body go limp, for a moment catching the two off balance. The woman stumbled and fell to her knees cursing loudly but the man swung him round and hit him hard in the pit of his stomach. The excruciating pain sent Joe falling in a huddle with his legs drawn up tightly over his stomach. Suddenly he was lying there untouched as his assailant fell beside him and received a kick full in his face. The woman screamed as she was slapped hard across the face and thrown out of the alley. Her accomplice was bundled to his feet and whacked with a barrage of blows to his face and body, pummelling him into a crumpled heap. The two rescuers picked Joe up and pushed him against the wall while they brushed him down and straightened his tie. 'There yer are, me ole mate, yer look nearly presentable,' one said, laughing loudly.

Joe had been in a drunken haze but now he was cold sober, though still unsteady on his legs and feeling sick from the blow to his stomach. He had been vaguely aware of the attentions being paid to him and suddenly pushed the men away and staggered out of the alley, hearing their loud laughter behind him. He walked on until he was in the main thoroughfare and then he stopped beneath a gaslamp to gather himself.

His watch had gone, and his signet ring. So had his wallet. Joe smiled ruefully to himself. He had been the victim of the bundlers, hard, ruthless young men who frequented the dock area of East London and preyed on the sort of situation he had found himself in. The bundlers not only robbed the prostitutes and their pimps but also the women's customers too, usually by pretending to aid and assist the unfortunate.

Joe looked around him to make sure he was not being observed then reached beneath his waistcoat and felt the small bulge in his money belt. Well, they were going to be disappointed when they opened the wallet, he thought, smiling to himself. Knowledge of the area and an awareness of just those sort of incidents had made him very careful. He never had more than the price of a few pints in his wallet, but wearing the ring and the watch had been a mistake. He would be more careful next time, he vowed as he walked off towards the welcoming lights of a pub he knew well.

Late that night Joe arrived home and staggered through the wicket-gate into the yard. Carrie had left the gate open until he arrived home and as she met him in the passage he fell into her arms, totally inebriated. She looked at him with disgust as she dragged him bodily into an easychair and proceeded to loosen his tie and undo his shirt buttons. When she had taken off his shoes and placed his feet up on a chair, she threw a blanket over him and turned out the gaslight.

The week before Christmas Billy and his old friend sat together in the Kings Arms. 'I've managed the kids' presents an' I've got a shawl fer Annie,' he said, sipping his pint.

'Yeah, I've got my two their presents but I ain't got nuffink fer Iris yet,' Danny replied. 'I've got the large amount of tuppence in me pocket an' that's gotta do till pay day.'

'Well, that's tuppence more than I've got,' Billy chuckled. 'These two pints cleaned me out.'

The two men sat sipping their pints slowly, trying to make them last while they continued their chat. Each had bought a round and they both knew that it was the last time they would be able to go into the pub before Christmas. There was still much to buy and little money forthcoming.

'I see the brickwork's all finished,' Danny remarked cheerfully.

Billy smiled. 'Yeah, it looks good, don't yer fink?'

'What about the roof?' Danny asked.

'That'll 'ave ter wait,' Billy told him. 'There's no more money in the kitty an' it'll cost a pretty penny. It seems a shame now it's comin' on so well, but it can't be 'elped.'

'Maybe yer should talk ter the Borough Council or the big firms,' Danny suggested. 'They might chip in a few bob.'

Billy shook his head. 'Farvver Murphy's already bin aroun' wiv the beggin'-bowl. Some o' the firms put in an' the Council gave 'im a grant terwards it but the foundations an' pipes an' the bricks took all the money.'

'Never mind, the collections might start comin' in again once Christmas is over,' Danny remarked hopefully.

'I s'pose so,' Billy said, looking at his near-empty glass of ale. 'We gotta be fankful fer small mercies. Farvver Murphy's done all 'e could. 'E's bin a diamond.'

Danny finished his pint. 'Well I'd better get orf 'ome,' he said. 'Iris wants me ter keep an eye on the kids ternight. She's 'elpin' out at the church wiv the Christmas parcels fer the old folk.'

'Yeah, they're doin' the same at our church,' Billy said. 'Annie was gonna go but I put me foot down. She ain't bin too good carryin' this one. The doctor's already told 'er she's gotta take it easy.'

The two friends left the pub and Billy turned towards Jamaica Road. 'I'll see yer termorrer, Danny. I jus' wanna take anuvver look at the gym,' he said grinning.

Father Murphy put down his pen and grimaced as he rubbed his clenched fist up and down his chest. For a few moments he sat staring at the row of dusty books on the wall facing him then he reached into his desk drawer and took out a bottle of brandy and a tumbler. The old priest afforded himself a smile as he poured a

439

liberal measure of the spirit into the glass and downed it in one swig, then he dropped his head into his hands to rest his tired eyes. All of the new batch of letters had been finished and the weekly report to the Sullivans Charity Committee was compiled and signed. The notes for the morning service had been completed and there was just one other task to take care of. For a time the old priest sat with his face buried in his hands, and then with a sigh he raised his head, blinked a few times to clear his eyes and picked up the pen again.

Father Murphy wrote in a clear, concise hand and for a time the pen moved briskly back and forth across the paper. Occasionally he stopped and studied what he had written, then he carried on to the bottom of the sheet. With his head held askew the priest signed the letter with a flourish, and after reading the whole page through he folded the sheet and sealed it in an envelope. The pain was coming again, and this time he did not go to his desk drawer.

Christmas was a very quiet time for the Tanners. Both Nellie and William were still feeling the effects of their bad bout of bronchitis and Carrie felt exhausted after her hectic few weeks. Joe was very subdued, and after returning from the pub on Christmas morning and sitting down to the festive meal with the Tanner family he went to his room and slept. He had given Carrie money to buy presents for everyone and she had wrapped them up herself and placed them under the small Christmas tree in the parlour. Nellie and William both had slippers and Rachel had a beautiful dress of emerald green which she insisted upon wearing on Christmas night. The dress was high in the neck with ruched sleeves, trimmed with white lace at the cuffs and bodice, and it reached down to just above her ankles and swished as she spun around. Carrie had taken care

440

in choosing it and it complemented the child's natural beauty.

Joe had given Carrie a small package and when she opened it her face lit up. It was a gold locket which had a tiny ruby set in the centre of the chasing. It was secured to a thin gold chain and on the back of the locket an inscription read, 'To Carrie from Joe with love'.

'I was gonna ask 'em ter put "sorry" instead,' Joe said, smiling humbly.

Carrie kissed him on the cheek and asked him to put it on for her, and as he did so she could feel his hands shaking.

Rachel was pleased that Joe was around during Christmas and she hung around him as much as possible, holding on to his every word and giggling whenever he joked with her or paid her any sort of attention. Carrie had noticed the love Rachel had for him and it caused her pain. She could not help thinking that the rift between herself and Joe was widening and that Christmas would prove to be merely a time for hiding true feelings. Joe would leave their home soon, she felt sure, and Rachel would miss him desperately. He had given her fatherly love in a way that Fred had never been able to. Joe had joked with her, listened patiently to her childish chatter and become her good friend. With her father it had been different. Fred had seemed incapable of demonstrating his feelings of love for his daughter, though his adoration for her could clearly be seen in his eyes. Rachel needed to be held close and hugged and kissed. She had so much love to give, and with her father she had never really been able to express the tender feelings inside her. With Joe the child could be her natural self, but she never overwhelmed him with her affection. It was the little things that Carrie noticed: their little hug after the goodnight kiss, and the tender moments during their light-hearted chats together when Rachel would sit at his feet and lean her head against his leg while he gently stroked her hair.

Carrie hoped Joe would pay her some attention and come to her room when the house was quiet. She lay awake until the early hours, tossing and turning, desperately needing his arms around her. She heard the sound of late revellers as they passed by and then the wind rattling the windows. She heard Joe cough once or twice, the sound of her parents turning over in bed upstairs, and twisted on to her back and stared up at the dark ceiling. For a time Carrie lay there, trying to let her body settle down to sleep, but the release from her worries and need would not come, and finally she climbed out of her bed and slipped on her warm dressing robe. Gently she tiptoed from the room into the passage and carefully opened the door to Joe's room. She could hear his heavy breathing and the grunt as he suddenly twisted over. There beside his bed was a half-empty bottle of whisky. She could smell the fumes from the doorway, and with a deep sigh of resignation she slipped quietly back to her own room and buried her head in the pillow.

Christmas was a solemn time at St Joseph's Church. On Christmas Eve Father Murphy died in his sleep. On the mantelshelf in his study there was a sealed letter addressed to Billy Sullivan and on Christmas morning the young Father Kerrigan came to the Sullivan home to break the sorrowful news, bringing the letter with him. St Joseph's Church was packed to capacity for the Christmas morning mass as everyone who knew the old priest came to pay their respects. Billy was greatly saddened by the passing of Father Murphy but he took comfort from the letter he had received, and when he arrived back from the service with his family he went to the bedroom and sat reading it once more.

Dear Billy,

Time runs out for all of us and the day must come when each of us has to pay our dues for living. For me I feel the time is near, but I have no fear or grief. I'm sure I'm going to a far better place, and I look forward to meeting many old friends. Grief and pain are not for us, only for those we must leave behind. I will say a prayer for you and your family, Billy, and I shall pray for all the folk I know and have grown to love.

I see that the fire has burned low and the hour is late so I will leave you with certain instructions and a little advice. Firstly, I am not a wealthy man, for the priesthood is not compatible with wealth, but I have one or two life policies which, after the necessary expenses have been deducted, will amount to around a hundred pounds or thereabouts. This sum of money will be for the committee to use as required, and we do require a roof for the gymnasium. Use the money wisely, Billy, and when the day of opening comes and the doors swing back for the young men of our parish, just remember that I'll be there with you.

Lastly, a few words of advice. Learn forbearance, Billy. It is a virtue to be prized.

Goodnight, and may God bless you.

Seamus P. Murphy

Billy sat on his bed, fond thoughts and memories of the old priest filling his mind. He could hear his excited children playing noisily in the parlour and the sound of Connie crying. Annie came into the room and stood beside him, putting her hands on his shoulders.

'He was a good priest, Billy, and a good man,' she said quietly.

He nodded and picked up the letter from the bed. 'What does forbearance mean, Annie?' he asked.

She leaned over and kissed him on the cheek. 'Patience, Billy. Patience.'

Chapter Thirty

During the whole of January 1933 it was bitterly cold and snow fell on the cobbled streets. It lay deep, with little sign of a thaw, and it claimed a victim in Page Street. Maggie Jones fell and broke her hip as she struggled to the market one day, and a week later she died in hospital. Her old friends in the little riverside turning stood silently at their front doors as the hearse departed, the horses straining to keep their feet as they were led away from Maggie's front door. The old lady's son Ernest and his wife were accompanied by Florrie Axford and Sadie Sullivan in the following coach, and as the cortege disappeared into Jamaica Road Maisie Dougall turned to Maudie Mycroft and dabbed at her eyes. 'Maggie was ever so proud of young Ernie,' she said, trying to raise a smile. 'When 'e won that medal she couldn't stop talkin' about 'im. She was pissed fer a solid week.'

''Ave a bit o' respect, Mais,' Maudie reproached her.

Maisie gave Maudie a dark look. 'Well, it's true,' she told her. 'Ole Maggie 'ad ter be carried 'ome from the Kings Arms one night. Me an' Florrie was sittin' in the snug bar an' Maggie come in wiv 'er bonnet all lop-sided an' she could 'ardly stand up. Florrie reckoned she'd bin doin' all the pubs in Dock'ead that night. She give 'er a pinch of snuff ter try an' steady 'er but it only made the poor cow sick. Gawd, what a night that was.'

Maudie made her excuses and went back inside the house, fearful of being party to what she thought were wicked words, while Maisie moved along to another door to continue her observations.

Although the cold wind was blowing through the backwater folk stayed at their front doors to discuss the funeral and the abundance of flowers which draped the hearse. Eventually their conversations returned to the plight they found themselves in. Work was hard to find and many of the women had their husbands and sons sitting around the house doing nothing. Factories were on short time and the docks and wharves provided very little work. Men trudged through the snow to join the ever-lengthening dole queues and returned home with their shoulders bowed and their shabby coat collars turned up against the cold wind. Women struggled to feed their families and searched through cupboards and drawers to find items to pawn. Stew pots simmered over fires which were kept going with bits of wood and tarry logs, and watery soup was thickened by adding bacon bones, potato peelings and flour. Folk in desperate need knocked on their neighbour's door and cups of sugar and flour were passed out along with a few slices of bread and a smile. Pats of margarine and a smear of jam made up the meal for many families, and in many cases the woman of the house went hungry as she lied about already having eaten, watching with a heavy heart as her man and her children ate a frugal meal.

The houses in Page Street did not let in the weather, however, and the gas coppers were now all working. Maudie's bedroom ceiling had been fixed and Florrie wondered how she was going to find the extra rent George Galloway had threatened her with if she did not comply with his new scheme. Each Monday morning the rent man called and Florrie along with the rest of her neighbours awaited the bad news, unaware that their landlord had shelved his plans to install more tenants in the old houses. Galloway had other, more pressing matters to take care of, and as he sat in the yard office talking with his son Frank he was a very worried man.

'Five years we've 'ad that contract an' now the whoresons are not renewin' it,' he moaned. 'We're bein' underbid, an' what's more we're losin' out on the day work. I told yer we should 'ave kept a few 'orses. Those bloody lorries are useless this weavver. If it goes on like this fer much longer we'll be in the poor-'ouse.'

Frank Galloway stared moodily at his ageing father. He had seen trouble ahead when the old man refused to move with the times. He had wanted his father to go for the more profitable transport work with the larger food factories in the area and instead had seen the business lose out because the old man insisted on sticking with the smaller firms which were now hit hardest of all by the depression that seemed to be sweeping the country. Other transport firms in the area had changed from horse transport to lorries and had picked up work that until then had been transported by rail to cities and towns up and down the land. They were riding the storm while the Galloway business was suffering badly. The old fool will end up going bankrupt if he's not careful, Frank groaned to himself. It's a pity he doesn't retire and be done with it.

George Galloway reached down into a drawer of his desk and took out a bottle of Scotch whisky and a glass. 'I see they've started work on the gymnasium again,' he said, pouring himself a large measure. 'They're puttin' the roof on now.'

Frank nodded and watched as his father downed the whisky. It's a wonder the silly old fool hasn't pickled his liver before now, he thought to himself. 'It amazes me where all the money's coming from,' he remarked.

'I 'eard that Farvver Murphy left a large sum in 'is will,' George replied. 'If it wasn't fer 'im we might 'ave got that site. It would 'ave bin ideal. We could 'ave moved all the lorries there an' brought a few 'orses back in this yard.'

Frank sighed irritably. 'That's just going backwards,' he argued. 'What we should have been doing is going for the journey work.'

'Goin' backwards?' George repeated, raising his voice. 'Look at Will Tanner's kid. She's got more work wiv 'er 'orses than she can 'andle.'

Frank gave his father a hard look. 'I expect Will Tanner's holding the reins,' he replied. 'It was a mistake to get rid of Tanner. I thought so at the time.'

'Well, I didn't 'ear you arguin' very much ter keep 'im on,' George told him. 'Anyway, it's water under the bridge now. Yer'd better get on ter some o' the ovver transport firms an' see if they've got any work they want us ter cover.'

Frank set about the task with distaste. Any work gained in that way was sure to be the dregs, he thought as he picked up the phone. Maybe he should listen to Bella. She was always suggesting ways of persuading his father to hand over the business. He would have to be very careful if ever that day came, he told himself. Bella was a scheming bitch whose fascination with expensive clothes had already proved very costly. She had also started to rig out their daughter Caroline with elaborate dresses and at fifteen she looked more like a twenty year old, which worried Frank. Caroline was spoilt and getting to be more like her mother every day. Soon she would be introduced to Bella's theatrical friends and quite possibly seduced by someone like that idiot Hubert who had made a thorough nuisance of himself before he was finally and firmly ejected from the family home.

The phone calls proved to be a waste of time and Frank leaned back in his chair and studied the grimy ceiling. George had left the office and the only other person there was the young clerk who had his head bent over a large ledger. Frank found it all very depressing. At work he was constantly being blamed for the state of the business and at home he was constantly being reminded that he should be more assertive in the office. Bella had become a vixen since she had been replaced in the show by a younger and more vivacious woman, he thought disdainfully. She had not worked for some time now and was forever on the phone to her agent pleading for him to find her a role. The trouble was, he told himself, Bella would not come to terms with the fact that time had taken its toll on her as it had on everyone else. She lived with high hopes of landing a leading role in a musical and to that end engaged in endless partygoing, sometimes coming home in the early hours with her expectations raised. At least she had been coming home alone and always at a respectable hour since the days of Hubert the nancy boy, he reassured himself.

Frank's understanding of Bella's behaviour was only partly accurate. Bella did come home alone and at a respectable hour, but what Frank did not know was that his wife was once again prostituting herself at the parties she went to in the hope of turning the head of some important impresario. On these occasions, however, Bella was careful not to give her husband any reason to suspect that she was not behaving in a dutiful manner. Her trysts were now taking place during the day, often in the cluttered office of a fat, balding man whom Bella felt could help in furthering her career.

Myer Wilchevski belonged to a circus family which had come to England from the Ukraine at the time of the pogroms. He had been a middling to good juggler and clown, and after years of travelling throughout the country had changed his name to Bernard Payne and set up an agency for circus performers. He prospered, and before many years had passed he branched out into the wider field of theatrical promotions. Bella saw the potential in Bernard Payne and she turned a blind eye to his shortness, lack of hair and abundant girth in her desire to get back to the top in her field of entertainment.

Myer, or Bernard as he was now called, had a wife called Delia, who also came from a circus family. Delia had a correspondingly wide girth, and a wide pair of shoulders too. She had bent iron bars and lifted anvils above her head during her circus career and had earned the name of the strongest woman alive. She was putty in the hands of Bernard, however, until she found a pair of silk stockings in his coat pocket one morning and then she almost tied the poker into a knot in her anguish. She caught the next train from Barking where they had a comfortable house and made her way through the cold streets of London to Bernard's offices in Shaftesbury Avenue. It was her first visit to her husband's place of work and as she climbed the long flight of stairs Delia vowed that if she found the owner of the stockings she would rip her legs off with her bare hands.

'I'm sorry but Mr Payne has a full diary today. I'll try and fit you in tomorrow,' the pretty receptionist told her.

'I'll wait. Maybe he'll have a cancellation this morning,' Delia replied, giving the young woman a look which told her she should not attempt to argue.

There were quite a lot of comings and goings but Delia had not been able to fit any of the visitors to the silk stockings and she sighed sadly as she leaned back in the uncomfortable armchair and scanned through a variety paper yet again. At first she had thought it might be the young receptionist who had left her stockings in Bernard's possession but she soon ruled her out. The girl wore lisle stockings and her legs were the wrong size. The next major suspect came into the office near midday, rolling her hips and swinging her handbag, and Delia noticed that her legs were long and slender. There was something uncannily familiar about those legs, she thought, racking her brains to work out what it was, and when the woman came out of Bernard's office looking decidedly unhappy Delia smiled to herself and hid her face behind the paper. Barney Preston was up to his tricks again, she chuckled. Barney had been a female impersonator for years.

At ten minutes after midday a youngish woman walked into the waiting room and Delia's stomach muscles contracted. She was wearing a strong perfume and it was the same smell that was on the stockings in Delia's handbag. The woman was told to go straight into the inner office and then Bernard appeared, his face flushed, and told the receptionist to cancel the rest of his appointments for the day.

'So this is what you do behind my back!' Delia shouted, throwing down the paper and moving towards him.

'What in heaven's name are you doing here?' Bernard spluttered, moving around the desk.

'Where is that trollop?' Delia roared. 'Let me get at her!'

As Bernard tried to calm his raging wife, all the while staying out of reach of her flailing arms, Bella Galloway slipped out from the inner office and attempted to reach the outer door. With a mighty shove Delia despatched Bernard across the room. He came to rest against a filing cabinet. Then the huge woman turned

451

towards Bella who was at the door. As she made a grab for her she tripped over the magazine table and was left holding a handbag by its broken strap as Bella tore down the stairs making her getaway. Inside the handbag Delia found a name and address. She grinned evilly at her terrified husband. 'There'll be no more engagements today for Mr Payne,' she growled to the receptionist, who had been peering from below desk-level at the goings-on. 'Get your coat and hat. You're taking me to lunch,' she told Bernard.

Two days later a parcel arrived at the Galloway house in Ilford. It was addressed to Mr Galloway and it contained one damaged handbag and an accompanying note which, amongst other things, said that Mrs Galloway was nothing more than a common tart who had been very fortunate to escape from the premises of Bernard Payne, Theatrical Agent, in one piece.

Frank Galloway had already left for work when the parcel was delivered and Bella breathed a huge sigh of relief when she opened it as she had been expecting a visit from the mad woman herself at any time. Nevertheless she still felt the need to keep a lookout from her upstairs window that day, lest Bernard's enraged wife should decide to make a personal call as well.

As the icy weather continued into February work proceeded on the gymnasium in Wilson Street, and soon the roof was finished. Billy Sullivan stood in the cold air one morning and admired the grey slates which seemed to shine in the watery sun. Banging came from inside the red-brick building as workmen fitted doors and floorboards. Billy sighed deeply. This was the realisation of his dream, he marvelled, a dream he had nurtured alone for years until he talked that first time with Father Murphy. How proud and delighted the old man would be if he was standing here today, he thought sadly.

'It's a sight for sore eyes to be sure,' a voice said to him.

Billy turned to see Father Kerrigan standing beside him. 'It sure is, Farvver,' he replied, rolling his shoulders against the cold. 'I was jus' finkin' 'ow proud Farvver Murphy would be if 'e could only see this buildin' now.'

'Oh, he can see it sure enough,' Father Kerrigan answered with a smile. 'In fact, I'm certain of it.'

Billy nodded his head slowly and then looked up at the hardwood sign high up on the wall in front of them. 'I want that taken down, Farvver,' he said to the priest.

'Why, Billy? It was your idea in the first place. What better name to call the gym than Sullivan's?'

Billy shook his head. 'Look, Farvver. It was my idea fer sure, but Farvver Murphy made it 'appen. I want 'is name ter go up there. Wivout Farvver Murphy there'd still be weeds growin' on that bit o' land.'

The priest smiled and put his hand on Billy's shoulder. 'All right, if that's what you want I'll talk to the committee,' he replied. 'I don't think they'll raise any objections, do you?'

Billy Sullivan bade the priest goodbye and turned for home. The wind had got up and as he walked towards Page Street he plunged his frozen hands deeper into his tattered overcoat. Seeing the gymnasium had cheered him but the nagging worry still remained that all his money had been spent and there was little food in the house. The meagre dole money hardly went round and Annie was desperately in need of a warm coat. She was having a hard time carrying this baby, and as the end of her pregnancy drew near she was looking pale and drawn and her usual cheerful nature was noticeably

453

absent. Both Patrick and Brendan had been ill with whooping cough and baby Connie had started sleeping badly at night. Maybe things will change when the weather gets a little warmer, Billy thought hopefully as he turned into Page Street.

As he walked along the turning Florrie appeared at her front door. 'I see yer comin' down the street from me winder,' she told him with a concerned look in her eyes. 'Yer better get 'ome quickly. The baby's comin'.'

Billy broke into a run and slithered on the ice as he reached his front door and pulled on the latch string. The sound of a thin wail greeted him and as he hurried to the bedroom door his mother came out looking serious-faced.

'Yer can't go in yet, son. The doctor's still wiv 'er,' Sadie said, taking him by the arm.

'Is she gonna be all right, Ma?' Billy asked in a shocked voice. 'The baby wasn't due till next month.'

'Annie's gonna be all right, please Gawd, but it was a bad delivery. They 'ad ter turn the baby,' she told him in a quiet voice.

'Is the baby all right?' Billy asked, finding his mouth dry with anxiety.

'The baby's fine. It's anuvver gel,' Sadie said smiling.

Billy felt tears rising and he swallowed hard. 'I wanna see Annie, Ma,' he pleaded.

'Soon, Billy, soon,' Sadie said, leading him into the cold scullery. 'I'll make yer a nice cuppa.'

'There's no tea left, Ma,' he told her, leaning against the copper.

'I brought some round, and Florrie's bin in wiv a slab o' fruit cake. Maudie called too wiv a cup o' sugar an' Maisie left a nice apple pie. It takes times like these ter really appreciate yer neighbours,' Sadie said quietly.

Billy was sipping his tea when Doctor Kelly finally

454

came out of the bedroom carrying his black bag. 'I've given her something to make her sleep. She needs a lot of rest,' he remarked in a stern tone.

'Is she gonna be all right, doc?' Billy asked.

Doctor Kelly nodded. 'It was a difficult birth and your wife is exhausted,' he said. 'She'll be fine after she's rested. I must stress that she's not to get up too soon. You can get help with the children, I take it?'

Sadie nodded. 'I'll be 'ere, doctor,' she replied quickly. 'That young lady's gonna get all the rest she needs.'

'Can I go in now?' Billy asked.

'Yes, but don't be too long. I want her to sleep,' the doctor told him.

Billy eased open the bedroom door and stepped into the tiny room almost fearful of what he might find. When he saw Annie smiling through her pain his heart melted. She was holding the tiny bundle in the crook of her arm and Billy gently leaned over the bed and planted a soft kiss on her clammy forehead. 'Yer look beautiful, Annie,' he said softly, his eyes filling with tears.

'You look pretty good yourself,' Annie replied in little more than a whisper.

Billy stared down at the screwed-up face of his new daughter and very gently eased back the coverlet. 'She's a Sullivan right enough,' he said grinning.

Annie closed her eyes and sighed deeply as Billy stroked her forehead. 'Did yer see the gym?' she mumbled.

'Yeah, I saw it,' he replied, running his knuckles very gently along her pale cheek. 'Now get ter sleep. The doctor said yer gotta rest.'

While Billy was with Annie Sadie answered a knock at the door and found Nellie Tanner standing on the doorstep, her face full of concern.

'I 'eard it from Florrie,' she said. 'Are they both all right?'

Sadie reassured her that everything was under control and invited her in. 'There's some tea in the pot. Would yer like a cuppa?' she asked.

The two women stood talking in the scullery. 'I ain't said anyfing ter Billy yet but it was touch an' go,' Sadie told Nellie in a low voice. 'The cord was twisted. She nearly lost the baby an' 'er own life too. It's a good job it was Doctor Kelly who called round. 'E's delivered more babies than ole Granny Johnson. I was in there wiv 'im an' 'e 'ad a fight on 'is 'ands. I don't know what damage 'as bin done but 'e said it could be dangerous fer 'er ter fink of 'avin' any more kids.'

Nellie shook her head sadly and reached into the carrier bag at her feet. 'I've brought some fings Annie might make use of,' she said. 'There's some bootees my Carrie bought at Abrahms, they're white ones, an' there's some dolly mixtures fer the kids ter keep 'em quiet.'

Sadie smiled gratefully as she accepted the small gifts and Nellie dived down into her bag once more. 'I've got some tea an' sugar in case yer've run out, an' 'ere's a bonnet my Rachel bought. Carrie sent this round too,' she went on, fishing into her purse and taking out a pound note.

Sadie gasped. 'I can't take that, Nell,' she told her.

'Don't be silly,' Nellie said firmly. 'It seems ter me Billy's gonna need money now there's anuvver mouth ter feed. Go on, take it. Carrie wants yer to 'ave it. She can spare it.'

Sadie's eyes filled with tears and she hugged her friend. 'I dunno what any of us would do wivout our neighbours,' she said, her voice charged with emotion. 'Maisie's bin round wiv a few fings an' Maudie as well. I won't ferget the kindness o' the people round 'ere.'

Nellie slapped her arm playfully. 'Ain't it all right? Yer come round ter see people an' they only give yer one cup o' tea,' she said indignantly.

Sadie reached for the teapot. 'I'll 'ave ter get my Daniel to 'ave a word wiv young Billy,' she said in a serious voice. 'That boy o' mine 'as only got ter slip 'is braces orf an' Annie gets pregnant. 'E'll 'ave ter tie a knot in it from now on.'

The two women chatted together for a while and when it was time to leave Nellie looked appealingly at her friend. 'Can I just 'ave a peep?' she asked.

When she was making her way back to Salmon Lane Nellie dwelt on Sadie's words. 'Yer can see it's a Sullivan,' she had said. The years seemed to roll back and Nellie could see her son Charles as he stood in the doorway, looking handsome in his uniform. She remembered clinging to him and the terrible pain of parting as he hurried down the wooden stairs of Bacon Buildings to leave for India. It was the last time she had seen him, and she said a silent prayer that she would see her son once more before she died.

During the cold January business had been very quiet for Carrie, but one or two firms which normally used motor transport contracted her to move their goods when they were let down by vehicles failing to start in the icy conditions. The business had started to pick up by the middle of February, and Carrie found herself stretched to the limit as she struggled with the books and wages as well as managing the well-being of the horses and keeping her eye on the condition of the wagons. Sharkey had long since proved to be an asset and took pride in keeping the yard spotless. He had also made himself responsible for the harness and brasses and whenever the horse-and-carts left the

Salmon Lane yard they were in first-class condition. Will Tanner was invaluable too. Even though he was now becoming frail and unsteady on his feet he regularly made an evening inspection of the animals and gave his advice on how to deal with their minor ailments.

Rachel was now in her fourteenth year and already showing the signs of womanhood. Her back was straight and she walked proudly, her flaxen hair reached down to her waist and her blue eyes seemed to shine with the joy of living. Her nature was very much like her mother's had been at the same age, except that Carrie felt her daughter was much more confident and knowledgeable than she had been as a fourteen year old. Rachel helped her mother around the house and was beginning to show an interest in the running of the business, a thing that pleased Carrie considerably.

The dark cloud on Carrie's horizon, however, was Joe Maitland's deterioration. He had remained lodging at the house despite Carrie's belief that he would leave as soon as Christmas was over. He had insisted on paying for his board and lodging and every day he left for the Poplar market where he ran a stall for an old friend of his. Carrie began to wonder how long he would be able to maintain his punishing lifestyle. Each evening he would return home late and looking the worse for drink. He would eat his meal and nod off to sleep in front of the fire, hardly ever staying awake long enough to have a sensible conversation. There was no contact between the two of them now, other than a few mumbled words before he went to bed. Only Rachel managed to get him talking, but she had been aware for some time of the change in the man she had grown so close to.

It was late February as the last of the snow was disappearing and Joe came home looking haggard and bleary-eyed. He fell asleep over his tea and went to bed early, causing Carrie to become irritable. She cleared the meal table in a noisy manner, watched by William and Nellie who exchanged worried looks. Rachel followed her into the scullery with a headful of questions.

'Why does Joebo always come 'ome drunk, Mum?' she asked, picking up a tea towel.

Carrie was feeling jaded and near to tears as she washed the dinner things but she was conscious of the need to protect Rachel's feelings. 'Yer gotta remember that Joe's tired when 'e gets 'ome,' she said vaguely.

'But why does 'e always come in drunk, Mum?' Rachel persisted. 'Joebo never 'ardly talks ter me like 'e used to. Is 'e ill?'

Carrie put down the plate she was washing and turned to face her daughter. 'Look, luv, yer growin' up fast an' soon yer'll be a woman. When the time comes fer yer ter leave school an' go out ter work yer'll realise that life's not a bed o' roses. We 'ave ter do fings we don't like doin' an' there's times when yer'll wonder what it's all for. We all 'ave ter do it ter survive, it's as simple as that. Wiv Joe 'e's survivin' fer the time bein' by drownin' 'is sorrows in drink.'

Rachel sat down on an upright chair, a frown creasing her forehead. 'I can see Joebo's sad, Mum, but what is it that makes 'im so sad?' she asked.

Carrie walked behind the chair and rested her hands on Rachel's shoulders, feeling that she might start crying if she had to look directly into her daughter's enquiring eyes. 'Yer remember when I said that Joe 'ad ter go away, Rachel? Well, 'e went ter prison,' she said quietly.

'Well, that's no secret,' Rachel replied.

Carrie was taken aback. ''Ow did you find out?' she asked, bending over her.

'I 'eard you an' Gran'farvver talkin' once,' she said,

459

looking down at her fingernails.

'Did yer know why Joe went ter prison?' Carrie asked her.

Rachel shook her head. 'I wanted to ask but I was scared. I couldn't bear ter know if it was somefing real bad,' she replied.

'Joe used to 'ave a business,' Carrie told her. ''E used ter buy an' sell all sorts o' stuff an' one day the police called round an' saw a lot o' cases that they said were stolen.'

'Did Joebo steal 'em, Mum?' Rachel cut in.

Carrie shook her head. 'Joe told me that 'e bought the stuff in good faith. The trouble was they couldn't find the man who sold 'im the cases an' because Joe couldn't prove 'e was innocent they sent 'im ter prison fer seven years. 'E managed ter get out after five years on good be'aviour but 'e'd lost the business an' 'e 'ad very little money left. There was a bit o' land in Wilson Street that Joe bought a long while ago ter build a bigger ware'ouse on an' 'e could 'ave sold it, but 'e didn't. Instead 'e gave it ter the charity so that Billy's gymnasium could be built there. Yer see, Joe's bruvver died after boxin' fer money at a pub over where Joe used ter live an' 'e didn't want any o' the young boys round 'ere ter fight in those pubs an' get knocked silly, or even worse. That's why, when 'e found out that Billy Sullivan wanted ter get a gym built, 'e gave 'im the land. Joe's a good man, Rachel. The trouble is though, 'e's got a lot o' pride. 'E can't abide 'avin' ter work fer somebody else, an' 'e drinks a lot ter ferget the pain 'e feels.'

Rachel slipped out of the chair and turned to face her mother. 'D'yer love Joebo?' she asked, her eyes searching Carrie's.

'Yes, I do, Rachel. I love 'im dearly,' she replied, her voice faltering.

'I love 'im too, Mum,' Rachel said, suddenly burying her head in Carrie's chest.

Chapter Thirty-one

During the bad weather of January Broomhead Smith felt very low. He found it impossible to motivate his old horse and whenever he ventured out on to the streets the nag would clop very gingerly over the icy cobbles and often stop for no apparent reason, leaving Broomhead wondering why he had bothered to harness up the flea-bag in the first place. There was no trade to speak of and the ageing totter came to the conclusion that most of his regular customers had either run out of bits and pieces they wanted to get rid of or were too cold to venture away from their warm hearths. Sitting around in a cosy armchair before a roaring fire was all very well for the likes of them, he thought, but it was no joy for him, not with that nagging bitch he was married to.

Alice seemed to think that it was a piece of cake going out in bad weather and having to shout at the top of his voice to urge everyone to bring out their old lumber. She didn't know what it was like to sit in that dicky seat half frozen to death arguing with a bloody nag that was getting too lazy to pull the cart when it was empty, let alone when he was lucky enough to get a few scraps of old iron. Alice should have the sense to realise that he wasn't a young man anymore. Most men of his age had retired and were sitting in front of their fires with the newspaper and a cup of tea whenever they wanted one. The trouble with Alice was, she expected him to get out from under her feet regardless of what it was like outside. She couldn't see that a man needed to rest at times, he grumbled to himself as he harnessed up the horse. All she was interested in was keeping the place spick and span in case anyone called. Who the bloody hell was going to call in this weather? he asked himself.

It wouldn't be the vicar, that was for sure. Not after the turnout at the church when he asked to be paid for singing in the choir. Bloody old fool had been taking liberties anyway. Rehearsing twice a week was bad enough, but to suggest that the choir should practise on Saturday afternoons as well was too much. Alice had not been very pleased when he told her that he had decided enough was enough and had put his notice in. In fact she had ranted and raved about the disgrace and how she wouldn't be able to show her face at the services any more. Silly old cow. It wasn't as if it was the only church in the neighbourhood.

Broomhead finished harnessing up the horse and after he had filled the nosebag with chaff he took a long look at the cart. It was in need of a coat of paint and the wheels didn't look all that good, he told himself. Never mind, he would spruce the contraption up when the weather improved. Not much could be done with the nag though. One more season and it would have to be put out to graze. 'Yer gettin' past it, old son,' Broomhead said, tweaking the horse's ear.

The nag seemed to be in agreement, dourly turning its head and watching as the totter scrambled up into the seat. A flick of the reins did not make any difference and it was only after Broomhead cursed loudly that the animal lackadaisically began to strain on the shaft chains to set the cart in motion.

Broomhead Smith set off for Page Street. It was a cold morning and he huddled down in the dicky seat, his coat collar up around his neck and his battered trilby pulled down around his ears. Alice would be horrified if she knew he still had the trilby, he thought with a grin. She had put it in the dustbin long ago and he had had to retrieve it and hide it away from her. That trilby had seen service for donkeys' years and he was not going to let her have all her own way.

Broomhead's destination was the rag sorters, who had taken over the Galloway yard. He had found a buyer for the larger sacks, a bacon curers in Tooley Street. They used the sacking to wrap up their greenbacks before the smoking process began. A bundle earned him a few pennies and it was less of a chore than humping old wringers down flights of stairs, he thought. The only problem was the itching. Twice now he had gone to the yard and loaded a few bundles of the torn sacking which was of no use to the sorters, and each time he had itched terribly. The foreman there said it was his imagination but Broomhead knew differently. It was lice, he was sure of it. They lived in sacking just like they did in the old mattresses he had often carted away. The problem was that he couldn't use lice powder on the sacking as he had on the bedding. 'Well, me ole son, beggars can't be choosers,' he told his tired horse as he encouraged it to keep moving.

Florrie Axford was talking to Maisie at her front door and the two women greeted Broomhead with a dirty look as he passed by. He gave them a crooked smile and then glanced fearfully at his own front door. If Alice saw him in that old trilby she would start another row, he thought anxiously. All was well, however. His front door remained shut and he whistled tunelessly as he drove into the yard and jumped down from the cart.

'There's only two bundles terday,' the foreman told him curtly.

465

The totter loaded the sacking on to his cart and immediately his neck started to itch. The horse seemed uncomfortable too. Its tail started twitching and it swished from side to side as the animal tried to get rid of an irritation.

'Don't you start,' Broomhead growled at the animal as he scratched the back of his hand. 'C'mon, let's get out o' this flea pit.'

The journey to the bacon curers in Tooley Street seemed to take a long time and when he finally got there Broomhead was feeling in need of a cup of tea. He parked the cart outside a coffee shop and walked in, taking off his greasy hat and scratching his spiky ginger hair as he stood at the counter.

'Oi! Don't do that in 'ere,' the proprietor said, giving Broomhead a hard look.

'It's that poxy sackin',' the totter replied, putting his trilby back on and scratching the back of his hand.

'I don't care what it is, I don't want it all over my customers, so yer'd better leave,' the angry man said sharply.

'Sod yer then,' Broomhead told him, storming out of the shop.

The horse turned its head and watched as the red-faced totter climbed back into the seat and then it started off reluctantly.

The bacon curers was only a short way along the busy Tooley Street but when Broomhead arrived he began to wish he had never got up that morning.

'Those bundles are no good ter me,' the manager said sharply. 'I 'ad ter chuck the last lot away. They were full o' lice.'

'Two bob the lot,' Broomhead said hopefully.

'I wouldn't take 'em if yer paid me,' the man replied, turning his back on the totter.

Broomhead made the journey back to the rag sorters in Page Street blaming Alice for nagging him into going out. 'Let 'er start on me when I get back,' he told his horse. 'I'll give 'er the back o' me 'and, that's what I'll do,' not believing it for a minute.

It was certainly not one of Broomhead's better days, for when he drove into the yard once more the foreman came out of a shed and waved him away. 'I told yer that was the lot,' he growled.

'I don't want any more,' Broomhead replied. 'I've come back ter dump these. I can't get rid of 'em. The bloody bundles are covered in lice.'

'There's nuffink wrong wiv those sacks,' the angry foreman told him. 'There's more fleas on that nag than on those sacks.'

'Well, I'm dumpin' 'em in the yard,' Broomhead said, making to get down from the cart.

'Oh no yer don't,' the foreman shouted. 'If yer try an' dump 'em 'ere I'll put the dog on yer. Now go on an' piss orf out of it.'

Broomhead Smith swore under his breath as he flicked at the reins and set his tired horse moving again. There was only one thing to do now, he decided. He would have to dump the sacking in the river, but first he would stop off at the dining rooms in Cotton Lane. They served a nice sweet cup of tea, and their dripping toast was a tempting thought.

Corned Beef Sam was engaged in an argument with one of his regulars when Broomhead walked in. ''Ello, luv. I ain't seen yer around fer ages. I 'eard yer was dead,' he said, giving the totter a limp-wristed greeting.

Broomhead scratched the back of his neck and rolled his shoulders as he sought relief from the itching. 'I will be if yer don't 'urry up an' pour me a cup o' tea,' he replied.

'Anyfink wiv it?' Sam asked, a little piqued.

'Two o' drippin' toast, an' don't burn the toast,' Broomhead told him.

''Ere, don't get saucy,' Sam retorted, his eyes going up to the ceiling. 'I've got enough ter put up wiv in 'ere wivout you comin' the ole soldier. What d'yer expect fer fourpence?'

'Who's upset you?' Broomhead asked as he fished into his pocket for his money.

'Well, it makes yer sick. I've 'ad the bleedin' food inspector round,' Sam replied in his lilting voice. 'Mind yer, though, 'e couldn't find anyfing wrong wiv this place. I'm very careful about the food, an' I keep the kitchen spotless. In fact the young man said it was the cleanest place 'e's bin in fer a long time. Still it makes yer sick the way they come in lookin' all mean an' 'orrible.'

Broomhead felt too uncomfortable to get into a lengthy discussion and he puffed loudly as he stared at the large teapot standing on top of the steaming urn. Sam gave the restless totter a choice look and proceeded to pour the tea while Broomhead got to grips with the itch that seemed to be moving under his chin and towards his left ear.

'I 'ope yer've not brought anyfing in 'ere,' Sam remarked, watching Broomhead with concern.

'Nah, it's me blood. It's got over'eated, I s'pose,' the totter replied, taking up the mug of steaming tea and making for one of the bench seats.

Sam was not convinced and he turned to Bessie Chandler who had just walked out from the kitchen. ''Ere, luv, look at that scruffy git over there,' he said under his breath. 'I'm sure 'e's cootie.'

Bessie took one look at Broomhead and leaned over to whisper in Sam's ear. 'They're all the same those totters. It comes from 'andlin' those ole mattresses,' she informed him. 'I remember ole Mrs Stanway who used ter live in our buildin's. She 'ad a pissy mattress she wanted ter get rid of an' when the rag-an'-bone man come round 'e took one look at it an' refused point blank ter touch it. Yer could see the state of it jus' by lookin'.'

Broomhead was continuing to scratch himself, much to the consternation of the docker sitting opposite.

'Oi, mister. 'Ave yer got visitors?' he said to him.

'Nah, it's me blood,' Broomhead replied.

'Well, yer should get somefink done about it,' the docker retorted. 'It could be catchin'.'

Broomhead swallowed his tea in gulps and when Bessie came up with the dripping toast he had started to scratch his right ear. As the big woman walked back behind the counter she was scratching the back of her hand. 'I dunno what that bloke's bin 'andlin' but 'e stinks to 'igh heaven,' she remarked to Sam.

The docker opposite the totter had started scratching now and Sam felt his back itching. With a flourish he almost threw the heavy teapot back on top of the urn and hurried around the counter. 'Look, Mr What's-yer-name. I can't 'ave yer sittin' there scratchin' all the time,' he said firmly. 'Yer got us all doin' it now. I'm afraid yer'll 'ave ter leave.'

Broomhead took one look at the docker who was leaning towards him in a menacing manner and grabbed up his toast. 'All right, I'm goin',' he growled.

Bessie watched from the window as Broomhead made his way across the lane to his cart and she turned to Sam. 'It's those ole mattresses 'e's got on the back o' that cart,' she said. 'Look, yer can see they're mattresses. 'E's got 'em tied up in sackin'.'

Later that afternoon Sam had another visitor, who stood eyeing the cafe proprietor with guarded suspicion. 'D'yer know it's an offence ter block the footpath wiv goods?' he said sternly, scratching the back of his hand.

'I'm sure it is, officer,' Sam replied, licking a finger and brushing it over his eyebrow.

'Well, yer'd better get those two bales o' sackin' removed from under yer winder before I 'ave ter take action,' the policeman told him.

'Oh my good Gawd!' Sam sighed in disbelief as he hurried out of his shop.

The weather had become less cold, although the skies were overcast and leaden. Men stood around on street corners and women walked back home from the markets with their shopping baskets half empty as firms in the area continued to operate short-time working and the wharves along the riverside were ghostly quiet throughout the working week. Young children pushed battered prams to the gasworks for coke and young lads scoured the streets for tarry logs to burn. The dole queues became longer and folk who owned a presentable Sunday suit soon found it missing from the house. Only the pawnbrokers flourished, though there were not so many goods being offered for pledge now. Mrs Harrowcot and Mrs Becket from Bacon Buildings went into the workhouse, and one young man from Dockhead took his two children along to the market in Southwark Park Road and offered them for sale. He stood with a notice around his neck saying, '£1 the pair. Well behaved and tidy.' Soon an angry crowd had gathered and he told them that: 'Anything was better than seeing the kids starve to death.' The ploy worked, for the children were taken to the local church hall where they were fed before being handed over to the welfare officers. The father was shown pity and offered a temporary job clearing the church gardens of weeds and leaves, but his wife was unimpressed. ''E boozes most of 'is wages away when 'e is in work,' she said scornfully.

For Carrie, the depression meant that she was having to rely on day work as opposed to more profitable long-term contracts. Work was coming in, however, and she felt that compared with most of the other cartage contractors in the area she was doing well. Her main concern was Joe's drinking. He was getting worse. Every evening when he came home his breath smelt strongly of liquor and he hardly touched his food. Carrie knew that the money he earned working on a market stall would not keep him in drink and she suspected that he must have slipped back into his former devious business of buying and selling. She knew that there were always stolen goods on offer, especially from the dock areas, and Joe would not be able to resist the temptation to make some quick money. Carrie worried that with his previous convictions he would be punished heavily if he got caught.

One rainy evening Joe walked into the house in a bad way. He could hardly stand and when Carrie remarked on his condition he pushed her against the passage wall and glared into her eyes. 'Just leave me alone. D'yer 'ear?' he shouted.

Carrie's eyes filled with tears as she struggled to free herself from his strong grasp. 'Can't yer see what yer doin' ter yerself?' she cried. 'Can't yer see what yer doin' ter me, an' Rachel? That kid adores yer, an' what d'yer do in return? Yer frighten the life out of 'er wiv yer drunken ways.'

Joe dropped his hands and staggered backwards against the wall. 'I don't need yer. I don't need any-body,' he slurred.

'Yer just a drunken no-gooder,' Carrie yelled at him. 'Yer'll never be any good till yer finish wiv the booze. Can't yer see it's killin' yer?'

Joe's eyes flared and he jerked himself upright. 'Jus' leave me alone,' he said, rocking back and forth.

'No I won't!' Carrie screamed. 'Not while yer comin' 'ome in that state. Yer ruinin' yer own life, don't ruin mine an' Rachel's.'

Joe stood erect and his hand came up to strike her but suddenly Will Tanner had grabbed him and forced him against the passage wall. 'If yer touch that girl o' mine I'll kill yer meself!' he shouted.

Joe's face drained of colour and he closed his eyes tightly as though trying to shut out what had happened from his mind, then he bowed his head and went limp in Will's grasp. Carrie stood looking at the two men in disbelief, fighting back her tears.

Will's face was white as he glanced at his distressed daughter. 'I'll get 'im ter bed,' he muttered. 'Yer'll 'ave ter make yer mind up about 'im. I'm not standin' by an' seein' yer get 'urt. 'E's jus' not werf it.'

Carrie watched while William took Joe Maitland by the arm and led him away, then she walked into the darkened parlour and slumped down heavily into a chair. Her father was right, she knew. It would be an impossible situation if she allowed Joe to stay any longer. As much as she loved him he would have to go. There was no future with him now, not since the drink had taken a hold of him. Carrie wiped her eyes on her apron and thought how lucky it was that Rachel was out of the house when Joe came home. She would be back from visiting her friend soon and would see there had been an upset. Carrie went to the scullery and splashed cold water over her face and then dabbed at it with a towel. Her cartage business seemed to mean little to her at that moment. Only Joe mattered, but she knew that tonight had spelled the end for him and her together.

*

As March winds gusted along Wilson Street a group of people gathered outside the new building. A flagstone path led from a wrought-iron gate to the lighted entrance and over the heavy wooden door a sign read, 'Murphy's Gymnasium'. Amongst the crowd was Billy Sullivan, looking happy in his tight-fitting, navy blue suit and grey cap. He wore a starched collar and a tie with a pin fastening it to his shirt. Beside him stood Annie, looking pale but cheerful as they waited for the guest of honour to arrive. She was wearing a brown, fur-collared coat done up with large grey buttons and a fur-decked hat, which made her look older than her young years.

'I hope they're not too long, Billy,' she said in a worried voice. 'I can't expect old Mrs Foggarty to stay with the children for too long.'

He looked along the street. 'There they come,' he said pointing.

Mayor Robertson was accompanied by the mayoress and other members of the Council along with Father Kerrigan, and he seemed in no hurry to get to his destination. When they drew near some women who were standing beside the entrance hurried forward to present flowers to the mayoress and Billy recognised them as members of the charity committee. He watched while they engaged the mayor in conversation, and it seemed a long while before the pleasantries were over. Finally the mayor came to the gate and marched quickly to the entrance. There was a red silk ribbon stretched across the doorway and without more ado he took the pair of scissors offered to him and turned to face the crowd. 'I name this building Murphy's Gym,' he said in a loud voice as he snipped the ribbon.

Once inside there was a round of speeches. The mayor was first, limiting his address to praising the committee for their hard work in raising the necessary funds and thanking the ruling members of the Borough Council for their support of the project. Then there was a thank you address by one of the committee members, who praised the mayor for showing interest in the project. Last of all came Father Kerrigan. He stood in front of the gathering, his eyes glancing down at the highly polished floorboards and around at the cream-painted walls. He looked at the roped ring in the centre of the floor and the equipment scattered around, the table set out with food and drink, and finally he turned to the assembly.

'You all know me as Father Kerrigan,' he began. 'My position has been as a subordinate to Father Murphy and I would like you all to know that I am proud to have known him. Father Murphy was the parish priest in this neighbourhood for many years, longer than most of us can remember. He gave of himself tirelessly in the service of God and in the service of his fellows, and his last wish was for the money coming from his estate to be used solely for finishing and equipping this fine building. Well, now we can see a dream fulfilled, and I'm sure that our reverend priest can see it too, although he has left the tribulations of this world behind. Now will you please step forward, Billy Sullivan.'

The young man walked out from the crowd and the priest stepped forward and took his arm. 'We all know that Billy worked very hard to get his idea for a gymnasium taken seriously,' Father Kerrigan continued, looking around at the gathering.'This building is a tribute to him and to all the members of the charity committee who worked so tirelessly in raising the money needed. It is also a memorial to Father Murphy and it is fitting that this gymnasium will be known simply as ''Murphy's''.'

When the applause had died down Father Kerrigan

turned to the far wall where a short purple curtain was hanging. 'Over there my friends is another memorial,' he said, his voice lowering in reverence. 'It's to all the young men of this parish who died in the Great War. There you will see the names of two of Billy's brothers, so I'm going to ask him to unveil the plaque.'

Billy walked beside the priest and when he reached the spot below the curtain he glanced at him a little uncertainly.

'Pull the cord, Billy,' Father Kerrigan said quietly.

The plaque was of marble carved in the shape of an open book. Billy looked up at the list of names and felt a sadness growing deep down inside him. He saw the names of his brothers John and Michael, and also those of James Tanner, Ronald Dougall, Geoffrey Galloway, and many more of the young men he had known and grown up with in the backstreets of Bermondsey. For some time Billy stood looking up at the plaque until he felt the pressure of Annie's hand on his arm. The gathering had started to move away but he remained, images and memories forming in his mind.

Father Kerrigan put his arm around his shoulder. 'Come on, let's get a bite to eat before those clothes-horses eat it all,' he said smiling.

'I 'ope there'll never be the need for more plaques like this, Farvver,' Billy said quietly.

'We can only pray, Billy. We can only pray,' the priest replied, aware of the rumblings that were already coming from the mainland of Europe.

Chapter Thirty-two

The summer morning promised another hot day as the early clouds drifted away, and as Carrie crossed the yard to slip the bolt on the wicket-gate she could hear Sharkey's heavy footsteps coming along the cobbled turning. Her heart was heavy as she went to the office and checked the work sheets she had laid out the previous evening. She sat down heavily in the office chair, unable to stop thinking about Joe. Every morning since he had left it was the same. She had woken up with him on her mind and she wondered how he was getting on. Was he in trouble with the police again? she worried. Was he ill? Did he ever think of her? As time went on it became no easier. She found herself dwelling on thoughts of him at odd moments during her busy day and she knew that he would always be close to her no matter where he was and who he was with. The thought of someone else taking her place caused her much heartache. To ease the pain of their separation Carrie busied herself with her work, hardly drawing breath as she flitted from one task to another. She had become yard manager, wages clerk, bookkeeper and stable hand all rolled into one, and there were still the household chores which she handled after the busy day was over.

Sharkey walked into the yard with a gruff 'good morning'. It was always some time before the elderly character felt awake enough to have any kind of conversation and Carrie totally ignored him for that first hour. She watched from the office as he unbolted the gates and swung them back on their hinges before giving the yard a quick sweep through. The men would be arriving soon and there were two casuals to hire for the week. There was a wagon which needed work done on it and one or two wheels that needed replacing. The sacks of chaff were running low and one of the horses was showing signs of lameness. Carrie sighed deeply as she thought about Joe. Why did he have to walk out on her the way he did? Why couldn't he at least have said goodbye instead of leaving that short note which broke her heart, and Rachel's too? The young woman reached down into her desk drawer and took out the leather-bound diary. She removed the folded piece of paper from the middle pages and spread it out on the desk.

Dear Carrie,
    There is nothing I can say that will put right the wrong I have done to you and young Rachel. I love you both and I always will. Please don't think too badly of me. I did try, believe me I did. I wish you well. Ask your parents to forgive what has happened and give Rachel a big kiss from me.
All my love,
Joe

Carrie quickly folded the piece of paper and replaced it in the diary as she heard Sharkey's footsteps, brushing a tear away as he put his head around the door. 'D'yer want me ter take those wheels ter the wheelwright terday, Carrie?' he enquired.
    'If yer will, Sharkey, an' will yer tell me 'ow many bags o' chaff I've got left?'

Will Tanner brought Carrie a hot cup of tea and as she leaned back in the chair sipping it she heard the first of the carmen arrive. She heard Paddy Byrne's cheery voice as he greeted Sharkey and then the rest of the carmen as they came into the yard together. Normally there would be a general clamour as the wagons were pulled rattling out from the shed and the horses' hooves clattered on the cobbled yard, but this morning it was strangely quiet. Carrie thought she heard voices raised in anger and when she looked out of the window she saw the men standing in a group.

William came into the office just then and his face looked serious. 'Yer got trouble, luv. I don't fink the men are goin' out this mornin',' he said, slumping down in a chair beside her.

Carrie's expression grew determined as she jumped up and walked swiftly out into the yard. 'Are you lot gonna stand around chatting all day?' she said sharply.

The men looked embarrassed and they turned to Percy Harmer who nodded briefly to them and then walked over to Carrie. 'I'm sorry, Mrs Bradley, but we're not gonna work wiv Lofty Bamford,' he said quickly. 'The man's a scab an' we're all union men 'ere.'

Carrie put her hands on her hips as she glared at the powerfully built character. 'Now listen 'ere, Percy, I'm runnin' this firm, not you,' she replied sharply. 'I'll decide who's employed 'ere. Now get yerselves out on the job, yer late already.'

Percy shook his head. 'Sorry but we can't. Not till yer sort out the problem. Yer got Lofty booked out ter the rum quay along wi' me an' there's bin a lot o' card checks there lately,' he said, slipping his thumbs through his braces. 'I just asked 'im jokin'ly if 'e 'ad 'is union card wiv 'im an' 'e told me 'e wasn't in the union.'

'Well, if there is a card check there this mornin' an' they turn Lofty away that'll be my problem,' Carrie told him irritably. 'They won't stop you goin' in.'

Percy looked down at his feet for a few moments then his eyes came up to focus on Carrie's. 'Bamford used ter work fer George Galloway, Mrs Bradley,' he said. 'They was a non-union firm as yer know. We all thought Bamford joined the union when 'e came 'ere ter work. We didn't know yer'd take on scabs.'

Carrie could see that she was faced with a difficult situation and she beckoned Percy into the office and motioned him into a seat. 'Now look,' she said quietly, sitting down at her desk, 'I don't know if you lot are aware that my farvver worked fer Galloway fer more than thirty years. I grew up next door ter the stables when they were in Page Street. I know all about what sort o' firm that was. That was the main reason why I wanted all my carmen ter be in the union, but I can't force any of yer ter join. It's your decision. Now I'll tell yer what I'm prepared ter do. I'll change the work around. Jack Simpson can go wiv yer ter the docks an' I'll stick Bamford on the tannery job fer terday. Before I send 'im out I'll 'ave a talk wiv 'im an' see if 'e'll agree ter join the union. That's the best I can do.'

Percy scratched the side of his head for a second or two, then he nodded. 'All right, we'll leave it fer terday, but if yer don't persuade 'im ter join there's gonna be trouble,' he said a little apologetically.

When the changes had been made and the rest of the carmen had left the yard Carrie walked over to the doleful-looking Lofty who was standing beside his hitched-up wagon. 'Now look, Lofty, yer've given me a problem,' she said with a quick smile. 'I'm tryin' ter run a union-reco'nised firm, an' it suits me ter do so. Carmen need cards fer the dock work an' I can't afford ter get my carmen sent back fer bein' non-union. It's time an' money ter me. Is there any reason why yer won't join?'

Lofty looked uncomfortable as he fiddled with the shaft chain. 'Mr Galloway used ter give us cards whenever we went ter the docks,' he replied. 'We never 'ad ter join ourselves.'

Carrie looked at the tall, thin carman with some sympathy. 'Well, it won't work like that anymore,' she told him firmly. 'George Galloway was bribin' the union officials, but times 'ave changed. Everybody needs their own card now.'

The embarrassed man shook his head vigorously. 'I couldn't stand up in front of all those men at the union meetin' an' ask fer a card,' he told her. 'Besides, I ain't got no money ter pay fer one.'

Carrie lowered her head in dismay. 'Did Galloway tell yer that's what yer 'ad ter do?' she asked him incredulously.

Lofty Bamford nodded. 'We all wanted ter join the union an' Mr Galloway told us what we'd 'ave ter do. 'E said there'd be no trouble if we left it fer 'im ter sort out.'

Carrie felt her old detestation for George Galloway welling up inside her again. Lofty was a simple, hardworking man, and his good nature like that of many others had been manipulated by the crooked carter. One day Galloway would reap a sour crop, she hoped, but she had no time now to waste on thoughts of revenge. There was her business to take care of and a worried carman to be reassured.

'Look, Lofty, you get out on the job, an' when yer come in ternight I'll 'ave a union application form ready fer yer signature,' she told him. ''Ow's that?'

Lofty looked down at his feet. 'I can't write, Mrs

Bradley,' he said in a low voice.

Carrie smiled at him. 'Don't worry, Lofty, we'll sort it out.'

A happy carman sent his team of cobs trotting out from the yard and Carrie breathed a huge sigh of relief as she set about the work in hand.

The gymnasium in Wilson Street was open from Monday to Friday and staffed by priests from the two Catholic churches in the area. Billy Sullivan and Danny Tanner both worked at the gym two evenings a week for which they were paid a nominal sum of one pound. The money was a godsend, especially for Billy, who was on short time and had been laid off twice already since Christmas. Both Billy and Danny had been good boxers during their younger days and their experience in the ring benefited the young lads who had joined the club. Soon there were youngsters who had progressed enough to be entered for contests and the two trainers talked about organising an inter-club competition.

'I reckon we should challenge St Michael's in Deptford,' Billy remarked one evening. 'They've got a good reputation.'

Danny was less enthusiastic. 'I dunno,' he replied. 'I don't fink our lads are ready fer the likes o' them yet.'

'Young Ginger Smith's a match fer anybody 'is weight, an' Shaun's comin' on nicely,' Billy persisted. 'I fink we should 'ave a word wiv Farvver Kerrigan an' see if 'e can get the ball rollin'.'

Danny grinned at his old friend's zeal. 'I bet yer'd be in there yerself, given 'alf a chance,' he said, nodding towards the roped square.

'That I would,' Billy replied, returning the grin. 'Still, my own two boys are shapin' up nicely. I'll be enrollin' 'em in a few years' time.'

Danny was now the proud father of two young boys,

Jamie and William, and he too was looking forward to the day when he could enrol them in the boxing club, although his pretty wife Iris was totally opposed to the idea and had told him so in no uncertain terms.

'I reckon we should be able ter raise one champion between us,' he joked.

Unknown to the two trainers, a cloud was looming on their horizon in the shape of one Mrs Hettie Donaldson who had been campaigning to ban the sport of boxing. Mrs Donaldson was a local councillor and she had made it known to all and sundry that if it were at all possible she would get a bye-law passed forbidding the sport within the borough. Most of the other councillors ignored Hettie's stand against boxing but they were aware that she was beginning to enlist some support from other parts of the country. Hettie had heard of Murphy's Gym and decided to see for herself just what was going on there. She invited a few loyal supporters to join her and a letter was sent off to Father Kerrigan asking for permission to visit the club one evening. Mrs Donaldson did not state her reasons for the visit, and the Council notepaper on which the letter was written led the priest to believe that it was merely to observe how well the club was doing.

On a Thursday evening Hettie Donaldson, accompanied by a Mrs Entwhistle from Lancashire and a Mrs Springall from Shropshire, descended upon the unsuspecting club just as two of the members were lacing up their gloves for a contest. Danny Tanner was acting as referee between the two lads who had fallen out with each other and decided to settle their differences in the ring.

By the time the introductions were over and Father Kerrigan had delegated Billy to show the women around, the contest had started and the two young lads were battering each other. One immediately received a bloodied nose, which caused Mrs Entwhistle to gasp and Mrs Donaldson to tut-tut noisily. Mrs Springall peered through her gold-rimmed spectacles, her eyes blinking like an owl's as she tried to see what was amiss.

'They're killing each other. Why don't you stop it?' Mrs Entwhistle said quickly.

'Stop it?' Billy laughed. 'Why? They've only just started. Wait till Frankie gets 'is second wind, 'e'll murder the ovver lad.'

'Oh my good God!' Mrs Springall gasped, only just spotting the blood on Frankie's face.

Hettie turned to Billy, her face dark with anger. 'It's barbaric. If I had my way I'd stop it,' she said in a loud voice.

'Nah, yer gotta give Frankie a chance ter get 'is own back,' Billy remarked, grinning evilly at the women. 'The ovver lad's tirin'. Frankie should finish 'im in the next round.'

Mrs Entwhistle leaned into the ring and tugged at Danny's trouser bottoms. 'Stop them!' she shouted.

Danny could not hear what the woman was saying above the shouts of encouragement coming from the young club members and he leaned over the ropes. 'What d'yer say?' he asked.

Frankie took advantage of having the referee's back to him and promptly bit his opponent's ear, provoking a roar of protest from the other lad.

'Oi, Danny, 'e bit me!'

'Oh no I never!'

'Oh yes yer did!'

'It was your fault. Yer tried ter put yer 'ead in me mouth.'

'Well, yer shouldn't 'ave busted me nose.'

'Good Lord, they're trying to eat each other!' Mrs Springall cried out.

Danny waved the two lads back to their respective corners. 'Right, you two, that's enough. Get the gloves off and shake 'ands,' he ordered.

Frankie walked over to his opponent and slipped his arm around the bigger lad's shoulders. 'It was a good fight, wasn't it?' he said grinning, blood still dripping from his nose.

'Yeah. Yer nearly beat me, Frankie, but yer shouldn't 'ave bit me ear.'

'It was your fault.'

'Oh no it wasn't.'

'Oh yes it was.'

Danny quickly stepped in before hostilities broke out again. 'Now go an' get cleaned up, you two, an' if I 'ear any more arguin' I'll bash the pair o' yer, understood?'

The two lads went off to the washroom, with their arms around each other, and Danny stepped from the ring to be properly introduced to the three women.

'Tell me, Mr Tanner, what possible good can come from two young lads punching each other silly?' Hettie Donaldson asked him.

Danny looked at the three women carefully before he answered. 'In the first place those gloves are so well padded they're 'ardly likely ter cause any lastin' damage,' he began. 'An' secondly I fink it's better fer young lads ter settle their differences in the ring rather than clobberin' each ovver over the 'ead wiv 'ouse bricks. Besides it's a great sport, it teaches the kids discipline and sportsmanship.'

'Well, I should make it clear that we are totally opposed to boys boxing,' Hettie said in a loud voice. 'We've come along here this evening to see for ourselves, and I must say we're disgusted that you should stand by and see two little boys punching each other and drawing blood.'

'Bloody 'ell, missus, it was a boxin' match,' Billy

said quickly. 'What d'yer expect 'em ter do, kiss each ovver?'

'Well, I can tell you now that we're going to do our very best to get this vile sport banned,' Mrs Entwhistle chimed in.

'Ter be honest, missus, I fink yer got about as much chance o' gettin' a pork chop out of a synagogue,' Billy said, grinning at Danny.

Mrs Springall was incensed. 'See these?' she shouted at Billy. 'They're petition papers. My friends and I are petitioning the people around here to get something done. I'm sure the parents of these children should know just what is going on in this club.'

Billy's face remained blank as he nodded. 'Some people round 'ere are against boxin' I must admit,' he remarked. 'P'raps I shouldn't tell yer this, but if yer dead serious yer should start yer petition in Page Street. It's only a few streets away. The woman at number thirty-seven might sign.'

The three outraged women took their leave rather abruptly and when the door had closed behind them Father Kerrigan appeared from the washroom where he had been hiding.

'Number thirty-seven?' he queried. 'Isn't that your mother's house, Billy?'

Red Ellie Roffey was making a name for herself championing various causes in the neighbourhood while she was campaigning for a seat on the Borough Council. She had been helping a family in Dockhead who had fallen on hard times after the man of the house was badly injured in an accident. Alf Robins had lost three fingers in a press at the tin factory where he worked and his employers had denied responsibility, which prompted the Communist candidate for the borough to advise them that a substantial out-of-court settlement would be the most sensible attitude for them to take. Ellie was not getting through to them, however, and she had been a constant visitor to the Robins family during the last few days. It was during one of her visits that she learned that Jamie Robins, the eldest son, was working as a clerk for the Galloway cartage firm in nearby Wilson Street.

'My Jamie's a good boy,' Mrs Robins said. ''E 'ands every penny over, an' if it wasn't fer 'im I don't know 'ow we'd manage. Mind yer, though, I wish 'e 'ad a better job. That Galloway firm treats their workers very badly an' I know my boy's not very 'appy there.'

Ellie Roffey had no reason to like the Galloways after her recent confrontation with them and she suggested to Mrs Robins that maybe it would be better if young Jamie tried to find work with a more appreciative employer.

'I've told 'im that,' Mrs Robins replied. 'Trouble is, my Jamie's such a quiet boy. 'E's not one ter push 'imself.'

The following day Red Ellie was out canvassing in the neighbourhood and as she strolled along Salmon Lane she spotted Carrie talking to Sharkey in the stable yard. The women in Page Street had told her about the Tanner family's involvement with Galloway and how Carrie was working hard in building up her cartage business, and Ellie was curious to see for herself just what sort of a woman Carrie was. She realised that the Tanner girl would probably have little sympathy with a campaigning Communist whose main aim was the overthrow of the capitalist system, but her curiosity overcame her reluctance and she walked smartly into the yard.

'I'm Ellie Roffey an' I've 'eard about yer from Florrie Axford,' she said.

Carrie knew of Red Ellie's efforts on behalf of the

487

Page Street women and she held out her hand. 'Yer bin creatin' quite a stir around 'ere, so I understand,' she replied, a smile playing on her face.

For a few moments the women looked hard at each other as they stood together in the cobbled yard, each wary of the other's strength of character. Ellie was the same height as Carrie though heavier, and like the Tanner girl she was in her early forties and carried herself proud and upright. She was as dark as Carrie was fair, with large, piercing brown eyes and black hair that was pulled back and tied with a ribbon at the nape of her neck.

'I fink I've caused certain people a few sleepless nights,' she said, suddenly grinning.

Carrie nodded towards the office. 'Let's go in there,' she said.

Once she was seated Ellie leaned towards Carrie. 'Look, I expect yer know that I'm campaignin' fer a seat on the Council next month,' she said, her eyes searching for some reaction in Carrie's face. 'I don't expect yer ter be sympathetic ter what I stand for, you bein' a business woman, but . . .'

'Yer might be wrong,' Carrie cut in, a smile hovering about her lips.

Ellie feared that Carrie might be mocking her and her eyes hardened. 'I believe that workers are exploited by the capitalist plutocracy an' they should fight fer a socialist government that takes care o' them instead o' panderin' ter the moneyed minority,' she said with conviction.

Carrie was looking down at her clasped hands, and her smile was wry as she raised her eyes to meet her visitor's stare. 'I know what yer mean about exploitation,' she said with bitterness creeping into her voice. 'My farvver knew better than most.'

Ellie nodded quickly. 'Florrie Axford told me about

yer farvver workin' fer Galloway all those years an' 'ow yer got chucked out o' yer 'ome in the end. Is that what made yer go in business fer yerself?' she asked a little accusingly.

'Yeah, it was,' Carrie replied. 'When we lost our 'ome the only place we could find was Bacon Buildin's. I didn't want my mum an' dad ter spend the rest o' their lives in a slum that's not fit fer pigs ter live in, so I 'ad ter do somefing. I've managed ter get 'em out o' that 'ovel, fank Gawd. They live 'ere wiv me now. I'm glad ter say I run a business that's doin' fairly well, an' I look after my carmen. We're a union firm an' there's no exploitation 'ere.'

Ellie saw a certain look in Carrie's eyes and she glanced quickly around the room. 'D'yer do all the office work yerself or 'ave yer got a clerk?' she asked.

Carrie shook her head. 'I've bin finkin' about takin' somebody on. In fact I'll 'ave to very shortly. I'm gonna need more time ter go out an' win contracts, but I can't while I'm tied ter the office an' all this paperwork.'

Ellie smiled. 'I know just the bloke fer you,' she said with a wise look in her eye. 'What's more, I fink 'e'll more than earn 'is pay.'

Carrie looked at her visitor with a puzzled frown. 'What d'yer mean?' she asked her.

Ellie sat forward in her chair. 'I've bin 'elpin' a family called Robins whose breadwinner 'as been injured at work, an' in the process I found out that their lad Jamie does clerkin' fer the Galloway firm. Jamie's not very 'appy workin' there an' I'm sure that if yer offered 'im a job 'ere 'e'd jump at it. I should fink 'e'll know all about the Galloway contracts and charges. Jus' fink about the possibilities.' She winked.

Carrie's sharp mind was already working overtime. 'Will yer be seein' the Robins family in the near future?' she asked.

Ellie grinned. 'This evenin', if there's any reason to.'

Carrie grinned back at her. ''Ow about comin' over ter the 'ouse an' meetin' me mum an' dad? We can 'ave a nice cup o' tea while we talk.'

'Well, I don't usually spend my time socialising wiv the bourgeoisie, but in this case I'll make an exception,' Ellie replied.

Chapter Thirty-three

Throughout the rest of 1933 and into the new year things did not improve for the Bermondsey folk as factories continued on short-time working and trade at the docks and wharves slumped still further. Men fought to get a day's work and many ended up spending long hours in the depressing and soul-destroying dole queues. The women had been struggling to make ends meet for a long time but now it had become a battle to provide the bare necessities of life for their families. They found it almost impossible to pay for a doctor and treated illnesses with potions, herbs and home-made poultices. Cupboards were stripped bare and most of the spare bed linen joined the rings and trinkets in the pawnshops. Often pledges could not be redeemed and many people had the heartbreak of seeing their treasured items of jewellery put up for sale in the pawnbrokers' windows.

For the two friends who ran boxing classes at Murphy's Gymnasium things were very hard. Billy had been out of work off and on for the last two years and Danny was suffering too with the slump along the waterfront. However, to Billy's great relief his wife Annie had regained her strength after the last difficult pregnancy and the baby, Mary Jane, was doing well. As much as Annie wanted a large brood she dreaded the thought of bearing any more children while her husband was unable to bring home a regular wage, and Billy shared her concern. Danny had a new son who was named Charlie and his wife Iris had now decided that three young mouths to feed were quite enough.

Murphy's Gym had become a well-known club throughout South London and boxing tournaments were regular occurrences there. It was often used for political meetings too, and the payments for the hire of the hall helped in the upkeep of the building. The campaign to get boxing banned in the riverside borough had failed completely and the champion of the proposed new bye-law had resigned from the council. Hettie Donaldson had had little success with her petition and had encountered open hostility on her visit to Page Street. One woman had dowsed her with a bucket of cold water and another woman, at number 37, had told her in no uncertain terms that if she ever showed her face in the street again everyone would think that she had been in the ring herself.

For Carrie Bradley the passing months were a time of mixed fortunes. She had engaged Jamie Robins as a clerk and was very pleased at the way he had settled down with the firm. Jamie felt much happier working in the calmer and friendlier atmosphere of the Salmon Lane yard and he got on well with his new employer. His contribution to the success of Carrie Bradley's cartage firm was evidenced by the new contracts which had been prised away from the greedy grasp of George Galloway. Jamie knew at first hand the fees and charges of the Galloway company and with the knowledge he imparted Carrie was able to undercut on two lucrative contracts when they came up for renewal. One was with a food company which distributed to hotels in London's West End, and the other was with a Tooley Street manufacturing clothier who supplied the military with uniforms. Carrie found that her transport was now being stretched to the limit and she realised that the day would soon come when she would have to consider using motor vehicles if she wanted to compete with the bigger, more established transport firms.

Carrie still thought about Joe constantly. She had heard nothing from him and she wondered and worried about his well-being. Her personal life had become mundane, an endless round of work and sleep. Every day was spent running the firm and working alongside Jamie Robins on the accounts and wages, but when the long hours were over she nearly always managed to find a little time to sit with her ageing parents and young Rachel, who was growing into a very beautiful woman. Like herself, Rachel missed having Joe around and she was always asking after him. Carrie knew in her heart that she would always love the roguish character, and she had grown to realise that there could be no other man in her life. Rachel was aware how much her mother missed Joe, and she had lain awake some nights willing him to return and praying for his safety as she heard the stifled sobs coming from her mother's room.

William Tanner was finding it more difficult to get about now and he sat around the house for most of the day, his mind drifting and his thoughts returning to the days and nights he had spent caring for the horses at Galloway's stables. Occasionally, when the weather was mild, he had been in the habit of taking a short walk to the main thoroughfare and meeting with some of the old men he had known for many years. The group had always met under the giant plane tree in Jamaica Road and had sat together on an iron bench watching the traffic hurry by and folk passing to and fro. There had been Albert Swain and Charlie Smedley, Bob Maycock and George Chislet, as well as Peter Foster, who had sometimes brought his harmonica along and played a few of the old songs. William had enjoyed meeting them on summer afternoons when they sat in the shade of the tree while Peter blew on his musical instrument, the haunting tones carrying the men's thoughts back through their happier, younger days. Now though the men did not go there. Instead they walked into St James's Church gardens and sat in the shade of a sycamore tree. The giant plane tree which shaded the iron bench was nearer and there was no busy road to cross but after what George Chislet referred to as the 'Bank Holiday Affair' the men all shunned their original meeting-place.

It had happened on the Monday afternoon of the August bank holiday the previous year when the old friends gathered in the shade around the iron bench. Charlie Smedley was there early and some time later he was joined by Albert Swain. The two men sat talking about their army days during the Great War, smoking their clay pipes and occasionally spitting tobacco juice on to the already well-stained pavement. Later they were joined by Will Tanner and Bob Maycock and then by George Chislet who got about with the aid of a pair of walking sticks. The five men squeezed on to the bench together and when Peter Foster arrived a little while later he had to sit on the arm.

'She went out terday,' George said suddenly.

'Who did?' Albert asked.

'Why, the *Baltic Star*,' George told him.

'What d'yer say?' Bob asked, his hearing seriously impaired since his accident in the gasworks.

'She went out terday,' Albert shouted in Bob's ear.

'Where she go?' Bob Maycock asked.

''Ow the bleedin' 'ell do I know?' Albert said irritably. 'Back ter the Baltic, I s'pose.'

'Lovely ship that is,' Charlie Smedley cut in. 'Bin comin' up the river fer as long as I can remember.'

'There's no such fing as 'olidays when yer a seaman,'

Albert remarked. 'It's yer tides, yer see. Yer gotta stick ter the tides or yer can't get away.'

'There's not much traffic on the river these days,' Will said, rolling a cigarette.

George tapped his clay pipe on one of his walking sticks and blew down the stem. 'I remember back in the early twenties when they was linin' up ter get a berth,' he said with authority. 'Bit different now though. If it goes on like this fer much longer we'll all be in the work'ouse.'

'Who's gone in the work'ouse?' Bob asked.

The men exchanged grins and Albert leaned towards the dull-eared Bob Maycock. 'Dirty Doris from Dock'ead,' he shouted.

Bob nodded and stared out at the passing traffic for a few moments then he folded his arms. 'She was always 'angin' round the Crown at one time,' he remarked. 'She used ter pick up the seamen.'

'Who, Dirty Doris?'

''Alf a crown she charged by all accounts,' Bob rambled on. 'Bert Shanks 'ad 'alf a crown's worth. 'E told me 'e'd sooner 'ave gone up the Star Music-'All wiv 'is 'alf crown. In an' out in five minutes 'e was. 'E said the bed was rotten an' there was fish-an'-chip leavin's in a newspaper on the washstand. Bert said 'e wouldn't get on the bed. Frightened 'e'd pick somefing up. 'E 'ad it be'ind the door, 'e did, then 'e asked fer change. Bert said it was only worth two bob.'

'I bet Dirty Doris give 'im a piece of 'er tongue,' Albert shouted in Bob's ear.

'Who's talkin' about Dirty Doris?' Bob replied indignantly. 'I'm on about Peggy Macklin from Rovver'ithe.'

Charlie Smedley cut off a piece of plug tobacco and proceeded to chew on it, occasionally spitting out a jet of juice. 'I remember the time when somebody stuck a red lamp outside Dirty Doris's 'ouse,' he said presently. 'She kicked up merry 'ell the next mornin'. She swore it was ole Broom'ead Smith what done it. Mind yer, I wouldn't put it past 'im. Broom'ead was a character in those days. Changed now 'e 'as though, since 'e's bin married ter that Alice Johnson. Poor ole sod's frightened ter move wivout 'er knowin'. I'd give 'er the back 'o me 'and if she was married ter me.'

The other men grinned at each other, and Peter got out his harmonica.

'Give us that there one about the miner's dream, Pete,' Albert asked him.

Peter spread his elbows as he cupped the instrument to his mouth and the melancholy strains of 'The Miner's Dream of Home' drifted out on to the summer breeze. The men sat listening quietly, with the exception of Bob Maycock who started on about Peggy Macklin again.

'Shut yer row, we're listenin' ter the music,' Albert shouted in Bob's ear.

Bob went quiet and it was not long before he drifted off to sleep. The rest of the men sat thinking and remembering as Peter went through his repertoire, and then when the breeze was getting up and the dust started to swirl around their feet Peter lowered the harmonica from his mouth and rubbed it along the sleeve of his coat. 'There's a storm brewin',' he remarked.

William Tanner stood up and banged his foot down hard on the pavement to restore the circulation. 'I'd better be orf 'ome ter me tea or my Nellie's gonna wonder where I've got to,' he said.

Peter Foster waved goodbye to the group and walked off, while George Chislet stood up and leaned heavily on his sticks. 'I fink Peter should 'ave bin on the stage the way 'e plays that there mouth organ,' he remarked.

Albert Swain did up his bootlace and glanced at Bob

Maycock who had not moved. 'Look at that lazy git,' he said grinning. ''E's bin asleep fer the past hour.'

'Give 'im a nudge,' Will said. ''E'll be there till mornin'.'

Albert shook Bob by the shoulder and the man's head rolled to one side, his mouth open wide. 'Gawd blimey, I believe 'e's gorn!' Albert exclaimed. 'Look at 'is face.'

William Tanner put his hand on Bob's neck then slipped it inside the man's shirt. 'Yer right, Albert. The poor sod's dead,' he said quietly.

'We'd better get a copper. Yer not s'posed ter move 'em,' Charlie said fearfully.

'Ain't yer s'posed ter stretch 'em out before that there rigid mortis sets in?' George queried.

'Leave 'im alone,' William said. 'I'll slip over the paper shop an' phone the police.'

When the body of Bob Maycock was finally removed from the seat the friends started off for their homes, unable to get the policeman's words out of their minds. 'Bloody dangerous that seat,' he had said. 'That's the second body I've pulled off o' there. Two years ago ole Granny Applegate sat down there wiv 'er shoppin' an' passed away just like that. If it was down ter me I'd take the bloody seat away an' chuck it in the furnace.'

From that day on the group of men gave the bench seat a wide berth, and whenever they sat together in the pleasant gardens of the church Albert Swain felt obliged to say, 'If ever I fall asleep on this bench, wake me up straight away, fer Gawdsake.'

It was during the hot summer of '34 that Broomhead Smith made the biggest decision of his life. He felt that it was even more momentous than agreeing to give up his independence and marry Alice, and that was saying something. Broomhead had decided to retire once and for all. He sat alone in the public bar of the Kings Arms late one morning, a pint of porter at his elbow, and suddenly all the reasons why he should not retire crowded into his mind. They made the idea of taking up his pipe and slippers seem a lot less attractive and the Bermondsey totter felt depressed. Retiring was not for the likes of him, he reflected. Every morning he would have to get up and face Alice, curlers and all, without the comforting thought that he would soon be on his rounds. Every day he would get under Alice's feet and before long she would no doubt get him to do the dusting, or put the washing through the wringer. Then there were the windows. Alice always kept them clean and with him around she would most certainly delegate the job of doing them. Then there was the front doorstep.

'Oh my Gawd!' Broomhead said, addressing his glass of porter: Broomhead Smith, a local businessman and a well-respected member of the community, on his hands and knees whitening the doorstep. No, there was a limit to what he could be expected to do, however much it upset Alice.

Broomhead took a large draught of his beer and wiped his mouth with the back of his hand. He knew that he had to face the facts. He was now seventy-four and almost ten years beyond the normal retiring age. Getting up into the seat of his cart was becoming more and more difficult and carrying pieces of lumber down flights of stairs was now an agonising task. He did not have the strength to manhandle those wringers out of the houses and on to his cart anymore, nor the inclination to haggle over the price of things. His eyesight was not too good now either, he had to admit. Many a time he had urged his nag out into the main roads when there was traffic coming and if it hadn't been for the good sense of the animal the pair of them would have been maimed or even worse. Well, there it was, he told himself. It was going to be the pipe and slippers, Alice's sharp tongue and the prospect of becoming a doddering old fool in next to no time at all. Still it had been a good innings, and he had made a good number of friends over the years, and a few enemies too.

Broomhead finished his pint of porter and ordered another. The thing that upset him the most was Alice's change of heart when he told her he was thinking of retiring. At one time she had insisted that he look after the horse and make sure it was properly fed, even demanding that he plait the animal's mane and tail and add a few extra brasses to the harness. Now she had become callous and insensitive, and the elderly totter growled to himself as he sipped his beer. 'Yer can't be soft,' she had told him in no uncertain terms. 'It'll be better if yer take it ter the knackers' yard. Yer should get a few bob on it, an' the cart should raise a shillin' or two. Clear out the stable an' sort out that pile o' rubbish as well before yer pack up. Burn the lot, it's not werf anyfing.'

Selling the cart was all right, he thought, but there were a lot of sentimental items that he had hoarded over the years. Parting with them all would be a sad thing to do. As for taking the horse to the knackers' yard – that was the most terrible thing Alice had ever said. All right, the nag wasn't up to it anymore, but it was only feeling its years, the same as him. It had pulled that cart around the streets for quite a few years now and it didn't cost much to feed. Alice had been adamant though. The horse must be turned into glue.

Broomhead sat back in his chair and shook his head slowly. Alice had become a hard bitch, he thought distastefully. She had listened while he told her about the cost of transporting a horse to the knackers' yard and then she had suggested that he pole-axe the animal himself and sell the carcase to the local cat's-meat man. Well, one thing was for sure, he told himself, the nag was not going to suffer. It had a right to a dignified end the same as humans did. Maybe he should have pole-axed Alice there and then and sold *her* to the glue factory.

When he had finished his beer Broomhead left the pub and walked to the tram stop.

'Ain't yer workin' terday?' a voice greeted him.

Broomhead looked at the big woman and shook his head. 'Nah, I'm retired,' he replied.

'It must be nice ter sit around the 'ouse instead of 'avin' ter go out in all weavvers,' she remarked.

'Yeah, it is,' he said without any enthusiasm in his voice.

'I bet Alice is pleased,' the woman said, grinning at him.

'Yeah, I s'pose she is,' the totter growled.

The arrival of the tram prevented Broomhead from upsetting the woman with the rest of his reply, and as he climbed aboard he made sure that he sat down as far away from her as he could.

When he finally arrived at the small stable behind the Tower Bridge Road after first making a call to the cat's-meat man Broomhead fed and watered the horse and mucked out the stall. The nag looked at him with its baleful eyes and Broomhead gave it a little tweak on its ear. 'Yer not goin' ter suffer, ole mate,' he said. 'Yer bin a good pal ter me over the years even though yer just a lazy, scruffy, flea-bitten ole nag.'

The horse stamped its hoof and got on with munching into its nosebag while Broomhead took off his coat and trilby and searched amongst the bits and pieces in one corner of the stable. He pulled the old horse collar out and tossed it to one side, then he dragged out the heavy padlocked box and bent down to pick up the thick, heavy pole that was lying against the wall. It had once served as a shoemaker's last, with a socket at the narrow end to accommodate the different shoe irons, and it was banded with iron along its length. 'This'll do nicely,' he said aloud as he tested the weight of the pole.

The nag blew into its nosebag and tossed its head in the air as Broomhead prepared himself. 'Yer know, I'm gonna miss yer, ole pal,' he said, glancing at the animal as he spat on his hands and then clasped the pole firmly, raising it high above his head.

One hour later a van pulled up outside the stable and the driver alighted from the cab wearing a leather apron. He walked into the stable and nodded to Broomhead. 'Are yer ready?' he said.

The totter blew into his red-spotted handkerchief and put it back into his trouser pocket. 'It was a good 'orse. I couldn't see it suffer,' he said sadly.

Money changed hands and then the driver glanced at Broomhead. 'Let's get it loaded then,' he said.

'I'll do it,' the totter said, sighing.

'Please yerself.'

Broomhead removed the nosebag and led the animal out to the van. 'Yer'll be 'appy on the farm, ole pal,' he said aloud as the van pulled away.

Before he left the stable for the last time Broomhead kicked the splintered box into the corner. It had held the money he had saved over the years, money that Alice did not know about, which had provided for the horse's retirement. The key to the padlock had been lost years ago but he had slipped a regular amount of money through a gap in the lid every week.

'Cat's-meat indeed,' Broomhead said with distaste,

as he closed the stable door and walked to the Horse-shoe public house to drink to his horse's happy retirement.

Chapter Thirty-four

Red Ellie Roffey had been unsuccessful in her attempt to get a seat on the Bermondsey Borough Council but she was still very active in campaigning for the maligned and hard done by in the riverside community. Everyone knew her, or of her, and Ellie's fame and infamy grew. Tales abounded, and her exploits became topics of conversation in the pubs and around family dinner tables and firesides. Ellie had seven children, someone reported. Ellie had been in and out of Holloway Prison in her younger days, another story-teller related. The woman had known Peter the Painter and was one of the plotters who escaped from Sidney Street during the siege, yet another far-fetched tale would have it. In fact, Ellie Roffey was much more maligned than she deserved, and it served to affect the progress of her campaigning. Some folk simply saw her as evil, a wicked woman whose sole aim was to bring down the government and send the workers out on to the streets in an orgy of terror and destruction.

In reality Ellie was the mother of two grown-up children whose father had died when the youngest was born. Ellie had scrubbed floors, worked on stalls in the markets around Bermondsey and slaved in factories to provide for her children. She had drifted into the Communist Party after listening to a series of speeches in Hyde Park one summer which condemned the ruling classes and urged the workers to take their rightful place in modern society. To Ellie it seemed a sensible argument, although she could not agree with the more outrageous calls for violent confrontation between the classes. Ellie was a warm-hearted woman beneath her abrasive front and she had made good friends amongst the women in Page Street. Her efforts in getting repairs done to the houses in the riverside turning had not been forgotten, and when next Florrie and her friends asked Ellie to mediate on their behalf no one could have possibly forecast what would happen, while for Ellie the outcome was something she would remember vividly for the rest of her life.

In the spring of '35 things had come to a head between the rag sorters in Page Street and the families who lived in the turning. During the mild April rats were seen coming from the sorters' yard, and one or two of them found their way into the little houses. Florrie killed one with her broom in her back yard and Sadie's husband Daniel killed another in the street outside his house. The council sent ratcatchers and poison was spread about the sorters' yard but still the rats remained. Maudie Mycroft was reduced to a nervous wreck and Florrie Axford raved that she was going to get the rag sorters' premises burned down if nothing was done to get rid of the rodents.

When one of the children in Page Street was taken to hospital with a fever Florrie called a meeting. 'All right, I'm not sayin' that the rats caused the poor little mite's illness, but yer never can be too careful where children are concerned,' she declared.

Sadie Sullivan was vociferous. 'If any o' my Billy's kids get ill I'm gonna burn the place down meself,' she told the gathering in no uncertain terms.

'Well, I fink we should get somefing done about this,

gels,' Florrie said, taking out her snuffbox and tapping the lid.

'What can we do?' someone asked.

'There don't seem a lot we can do,' another woman said, stroking her chin.

'Oh yes there is,' Florrie told her. 'I reckon we should get Red Ellie ter see if she can stop it. After all she did get that ole goat Galloway ter do somefing about our 'ouses.'

There was a silence while Florrie went through her ritual, and after she had sneezed loudly Maisie Dougall leaned her forearms on the parlour table. 'We can't keep expectin' Red Ellie ter fight our battles, Flo,' she said. 'I reckon we ought ter go over an' see the guv'nor again. All of us tergevver.'

'What's the good o' that, Mais?' Florrie replied. 'Me an' you went over there a few weeks ago, an' what 'appened? We got a lot o' promises an' nuffink's bin done. Mrs Allen saw a rat comin' out the yard the ovver mornin' when she was goin' ter work an' ole Marie What's-'er-name reckoned she saw a line of 'em in the kerb outside 'er 'ouse. Mind yer, though, yer can't always take what Marie ses as gospel. She is inclined ter put a bit on it.'

Maudie was sitting huddled up at Florrie's table, her eyes darting around the room as though she expected an army of rats to march in at any minute. 'I'm scared ter death of 'em,' she said in a low voice. 'I'd die if one of 'em came inter my place, I know I would.'

'Shut up, fer Gawdsake,' Florrie said contemptuously.

'Well, it's all right fer you, Flo, you can kill 'em. I can't,' Maudie moaned.

Sadie Sullivan banged her fist down on the table sharply. 'I say we get Ellie Roffey in ter see what she can do.'

Florrie tapped her silver snuffbox again. 'Right, gels, leave it ter me,' she said. 'I'll give 'em a message at the fruit stall. Ellie said I could always leave a message there.'

It was late summer when Carrie heard news of Joe. She had just finished going over the wages with Jamie Robins when the phone rang. The woman's voice on the other end of the line sounded hesitant. 'Am I speaking to Mrs Carrie Bradley?'

'This is Mrs Bradley.'

'This is the almoner speaking, Poplar Hospital. I'm phoning about a Mr Maitland. He was admitted this morning.'

'What 'appened? What's wrong wiv 'im?' Carrie asked, her heart racing.

'I'm afraid he collapsed in the street,' the woman answered. 'Mr Maitland had just checked out of his lodgings. We found your name and address in his belongings.'

'What's wrong wiv 'im?' Carrie asked again, fearing the worst.

'The doctor's seeing him this afternoon,' the almoner replied. 'Mr Maitland is comfortable, that's all I can tell you, I'm afraid.'

Carrie put the phone down and bit on her knuckles as she stared at the desk.

Jamie looked up from his work, concern showing on his face. 'Is anything wrong, Mrs Bradley?' he asked.

'It's a friend o' mine,' Carrie told him. ''E's bin taken ill.'

'I'm sorry,' Jamie said, looking down at the ledger again.

Early that evening Carrie left the yard with her father's words ringing in her ears. 'Be prepared, luv.

506

Yer might not like what yer see.'

She boarded the number 42 bus and stared distractedly out of the window at the quiet wharves and factories. The river looked peaceful and the dockside cranes seemed to glow in the light of the setting sun. She saw seagulls wheeling and diving, and up ahead were the white stone walls of the Tower of London. At the Minories she got off and boarded a trolley bus to Poplar, thoughts beginning to crowd in on her mind as she neared the hospital. She began to fear that her father might be right. Perhaps Joe had changed more than she could imagine. Was she acting sensibly in going to see him, she wondered, or should she just remember him for the good times that they had together? Well, it was too late to turn back now, she told herself. Better she should face him rather than spend the rest of her life in regret.

The man at the reception desk seemed to take an eternity as he pored over the entries in the large book, then he looked up, his face blank. 'I'm afraid Mr Maitland discharged himself this afternoon,' he said.

In the late summer the rag sorters' premises in Page Street burned down. Maudie Mycroft saw the smoke coming from the yard as she returned from a mothers' meeting at the church. It was nearing six o'clock, and by the time her husband had run to the Kings Arms to raise the alarm the yard was ablaze. The following morning Red Ellie Roffey was arrested and charged with arson. Word spread fast and that afternoon the ageing Florrie Axford sat down in her parlour with Maisie and Sadie to discuss the affair.

'They wouldn't let me see 'er,' she told her friends. 'The copper told me they're tryin' ter raise bail.'

'Who is?' Maisie asked.

'Ellie's party people, o' course,' Florrie said sharply, feeling tired after her trek to and from the Tower Bridge police station.

'What a silly cow. Fancy 'er burnin' the place down,' Maisie remarked.

'We don't know if she did do it,' Sadie replied angrily, giving Maisie a hard look.

'Well, we all 'eard 'er threaten that ole goat when 'e told us all ter get out of 'is yard,' Maisie said.

Florrie stared into the empty grate. It was true, she couldn't deny it. The owner of the yard had not exactly been very helpful from the start, and when Ellie asked him what he was doing to get rid of the rats he had become abusive and told her to stop pestering him and mind her own business. Ellie had held her temper though, until he called her a Bolshie cow. That always seemed to enrage her. That was when she had threatened to burn the place down herself.

Sadie had been quiet for some time. 'Was there anybody there apart from the guv'nor when Ellie threatened 'im?' she asked.

'We were all there,' Maudie cut in.

Florrie and Sadie exchanged exasperated glances. 'Apart from us,' Sadie said irritably.

Florrie stroked her chin with her thumb and forefinger. 'Not as far as I can remember. Wait a minute though. There was that bloke what looked in the office wiv some papers in 'is 'and. The ole goat went out 'an spoke wiv 'im fer a few minutes, don't yer remember?'

Sadie nodded. 'Yeah, that's right. I remember now. 'E might 'ave 'eard what Ellie said. Mind yer, it's not enough fer the police ter nick 'er for. Yer threatened ter burn the place down yerself, Flo, an' they ain't nicked you.'

'They must 'ave got the evidence,' Maudie chipped in. 'They must 'ave found fingerprints an' suchlike.'

'Listen ter Mrs Sherlock Holmes,' Sadie scoffed.

'She's right,' Florrie said quietly. 'They must 'ave somefing on 'er.'

More tea was passed around and the Page Street women sat deliberating the fate of their friend and ally. 'Arson's a serious charge,' Sadie said. 'She could go away for a long time.'

'Can't we do anyfing?' Maisie asked. 'I feel so 'elpless sittin' 'ere. Poor Ellie come up trumps fer us an' we ain't doin' anyfing for 'er.'

'I tell yer what I will do,' Florrie said suddenly. 'Termorrer I'll go round ter that place where Ellie used to 'old 'er meetin's. I'll find out if there's anyfing we can do fer 'er. They might want a petition got up or somefing.'

'Good idea, Flo. I'll come wiv yer,' Maisie said.

In the Tanner household another problem predominated as the family sat around in the parlour talking together. 'Well, I can't see that it's much ter worry about,' Nellie was saying. 'If 'e was fit enough ter walk out o' the 'orspital there can't be much wrong wiv 'im.'

'I'm not so sure,' Will said, reaching for his pipe. 'A man don't collapse in the street fer nuffink.'

Danny was paying his family a visit and he glanced at Carrie with concern in his eyes, aware of the feelings she had for Joe Maitland. 'It could 'ave bin 'e needed a good meal inside 'im,' he said quickly. 'I've felt like faintin' more than once when I've gone out wivout a breakfast inside me.'

'Yer gotta eat a breakfast, son,' Nellie cut in. ''Specially workin' on those barges. If yer fell in the water it'd be all over.'

Danny wished he had not made the remark in front of his mother and he fidgeted in the armchair. 'Ain't there no clues as ter where Joe could be?' he asked.

Rachel was sitting on her haunches near the fireplace. 'We could go over Poplar and look fer 'im,' she said. 'Somebody must know 'im. We could go ter the market in Poplar where Joe worked.'

'Joe left that market ages ago,' Carrie told her. ''E said ter me jus' before 'e left that 'e was workin' in a market in North London. It could be anywhere.'

'Well, it seems ter me that if Joe was lodgin' in Poplar 'e'd be workin' in the area,' Rachel persisted.

Carrie smiled at her daughter. 'Look, luv,' she said kindly, 'Joe 'ad 'is suitcase wiv 'im when 'e collapsed. We don't know 'ow far 'e'd travelled before it 'appened. Goin' lookin' fer 'im would be like lookin' fer a needle in an 'aystack.'

'I'll ask about,' Danny said, stroking Rachel's hair fondly. 'Some o' my mates live over the water. Yer never know. Joe was well known to a lot o' people.'

Danny's remark made Carrie's insides grow suddenly cold. Joe was well known, it was true. He had made enemies too, how could she ever forget, and there were people who might want to harm him.

Will was puffing on his pipe. 'I could take a ride over the water if the weavver's all right termorrer,' he volunteered. 'I could ask around.'

'Oh no yer don't,' Nellie said quickly. 'Not wiv that chest o' yours, an' those legs. I don't want the police knockin' 'ere an' tellin' me *you've* collapsed.'

When the supper was over Danny got up to go, clutching the small parcel of food Carrie had prepared for him. 'I'll let yer know as soon as I 'ear anyfing, Sis,' he said smiling.

Carrie walked across the yard with him. Above, the night sky was filled with stars and a full moon lit up the few scurrying clouds. The air was sweet with the smell of hay and they could hear the sounds of the horses moving in their stalls.

'D'yer know, Danny, I've always loved the smell o' stables. It reminds me o' when I used ter go wiv Dad ter the stable in Page Street,' Carrie said, taking her brother's arm.

Danny smiled. 'Yer love Joe, don't yer, Sis?' he said suddenly.

They had reached the gate and Carrie nodded. ''E's the only one fer me, Bruv,' she replied, squeezing his arm.

'You'll find 'im, Carrie. It'll turn out all right in the end, you'll see,' he said, planting a kiss on her forehead.

When she had bolted the wicket-gate Carrie stood for a few moments looking up at the velvet sky. 'God, where are yer, Joe?' she said aloud, tears clouding her eyes.

Ellie Roffey was brought before Tower Bridge Magistrates' Court and remanded on bail for trial at the Bermondsey Crown Court in November. On advice Ellie stayed away from the Page Street area, and until her trial she went to lodge with her married daughter in Kent. During her absence from the riverside community the fire at the rag sorters was a main topic of discussion in the pubs. Many people were convinced that Ellie had started it and when Florrie walked into the snug bar of the Kings Arms one evening with her jug and ordered a pint of mild and bitter she became embroiled in an argument.

'She's as guilty as the day's long,' a big woman was saying to her friend in the adjoining bar. 'They're all the same those Bolsheviks. 'E was a Bolshevik, that there Peter the Painter, an' look what 'e got up to.'

'Yer talkin' out o' yer arse,' Florrie told her in a loud voice, leaning on the counter and peering around the partition.

'I'm not talkin' ter you,' the woman said, glaring at Florrie.

'Well, I'm talkin' ter you, yer silly big mare,' she replied, clutching her purse tightly and jutting out her chin.

'Who's chucked 'er a bun?' the big woman asked her friend.

'You mind I don't come round there an' smack yer in the gob,' Florrie told her.

'You an' whose army?' the woman growled.

Alec Crossley came over and raised his hands in the air. 'Now look, I'm fed up wiv 'earin' about the fire an' who done it,' he shouted. 'Now drink yer beer an' shut yer trap, Polly. And as fer you, Florrie Axford, if yer don't stop threatenin' my customers I'm gonna bar yer. Yer gettin' as bad as Sadie Sullivan. I nearly 'ad ter bar 'er once.'

Grace Crossley had filled Florrie's jug and she put it down on the counter by her elbow.

'Good job 'e only nearly barred 'er,' Florrie said to the landlady. 'Sadie would 'ave pulled the bloody place down.'

Grace had known Florrie for many years and she had grown very fond of her. 'Mind 'ow yer go 'ome, luv,' she said kindly. 'Ellie's gonna be all right, yer'll see, an' if it's any consolation ter yer, I don't fink she did it.'

Frank Galloway locked the wicket-gate and walked along Wilson Street. His mind was troubled. Bella had been acting strangely of late and he sensed that something was going on. She had been very attentive to his everyday needs, and that was not like her. He was aware that the last time she had shown any decent amount of consideration for him was when she had that little toad Hubert in tow. Frank had been duped for a while, until he saw her kissing Hubert by the taxi cab when the two of them arrived home from a show and she thought he would be fast asleep. He had pretended to be sleeping when she came in and Bella had been unaware that he knew what was going on, until the little toad showed his face at the flat. Frank had shown him what was what then and since that time Bella had behaved herself, it seemed, apart from her spasmodic forays to the dress shops where she usually ran up a considerable bill. Caroline was becoming secretive too now and it seemed as though he was being played for a fool. It had been a mistake allowing Bella to talk him into sending the child to that exclusive school. Caroline was becoming more like her mother by the day.

Well, things were going to change, Frank vowed. They would have to. The business was going through a bad spell and a couple of lucrative contracts had been lost to that Tanner woman. She was proving to be a thorn in his side and it was causing him problems with the old man. Lowering the contract rates was the only answer if they were to stay in business but his father would not hear of it. He seemed to think they could ride the storm but he was wrong. Their rates had remained static while most of the other transport firms in the area had lowered theirs and competed for contracts with a considerable advantage. The trouble was, the old boy was living in the past. The silly old fool would be the undoing of them all, Frank thought, sighing deeply as he pushed open the door of the Crown saloon bar.

'Evening, Frank. What's it to be?'

Frank smiled briefly at the thick-set man at the counter. 'I'll have a large brandy, Theo,' he replied, leaning languidly against the bar rail.

Theobald Harrison collected the drinks and nodded towards the far corner of the bar. 'Let's take a seat, Frank,' he said.

The two men sat together in the comfortably furnished bar talking in low voices, occasionally casting furtive glances around the room.

'Well, it all seems to be under control,' Frank said, taking a swig from his glass and looking with sly amusement at Theo's prominent, staring eyes. There's something wrong with that man's brain, he thought to himself. 'How did it go with the assessors?'

'Fine. They queried a few figures and haggled about that old stitcher, but they could see it was beyond repair,' Theo replied, a smile lurking at the corner of his mouth. 'They didn't query the stocks though. I should come out all right, though it'll be some time before they pay out. We've got to get the trial over first.'

'I don't see there's anything to worry about,' Frank said, toying with his glass. 'That bitch is going to see the inside of Holloway, I'm certain of it.'

The owner of the rag sorters took a swig from his glass and pulled a face as the spirit burned his throat. 'She's brought it on herself,' he growled, a glint of hideous glee growing in his big glassy eyes. 'Her sort deserve all they get.'

'Well, I'll be glad to see the back of her,' Frank said vehemently. 'She's caused us more trouble than enough, and she's cost us money too. I wouldn't mind betting it was that Bolshie bitch who enticed young Robins away. The little rat's working for Will Tanner's girl now. As a matter of fact one of my carmen has seen Roffey going into Bradleys' yard on a couple of occasions. It doesn't need much working out, Theo.'

The two businessmen sat talking together for another hour, then Theo made to leave. 'Now are you sure that stitcher of mine won't be in your way?' he asked. 'I can't take it back until everything's settled and you know it might take some time.'

'There's no urgency and it'll be quite safe, I've got it stored away,' Frank replied.

After Theo had left Frank Galloway ordered another drink. There was still an hour to go before Peggy arrived, he thought. Better not talk to her here though. Theo might have a few friends who used the Crown.

Chapter Thirty-five

The trial of Ellie Roffey began on a foggy November morning, and amongst the people sitting in the public gallery were some of her friends from Page Street. Carrie and her ageing father were there and sat solemn-faced beside Florrie Axford and Maisie Dougall as the defendant entered the dock looking pale and drawn. Ellie wore a loose-fitting grey coat, which seemed to accentuate her wan complexion, and her black hair was curled and set in a quiff over one eye. Beneath the coat she was wearing a royal blue blouse, buttoned high in the neck, and a grey skirt and high-heeled shoes to match.

Carrie looked down on the members of the jury and glanced over at the bewigged judge, then her eyes fixed on Ellie Roffey. 'Doesn't she look ill?' she whispered to Florrie.

The old lady nodded and wondered whether or not she should get out her snuffbox. 'D'yer fink it'll be all right if I 'ave a pinch?' she asked.

'I should fink so,' Carrie answered, hoping the elderly woman would be able to contain her usual loud sneeze.

The prosecuting counsel was addressing the jury. He was a huge man and he held on to the lapel of his black gown and looked over his wire-rimmed spectacles as he sought to impress upon the twelve the severity of the charge. Ellie looked impassive, occasionally glancing up at the high bench then looking down at her hands which gripped the brass rail in front of her. The first witness was called and there was a murmur from the gallery as a well-built young man with dark wavy hair and a tight-fitting, check suit entered the witness box.

After taking the oath in a loud voice he shrugged his shoulders confidently as the prosecutor approached him.

'You are Derek John Talbot, and you lodge at number twelve Corporation Street?'

The witness nodded and the judge immediately grunted loudly. 'Will you please answer yes or no?' he commanded.

'Yes, that's right,' Talbot replied.

The prosecutor looked over his spectacles. 'Will you please tell the jury what you were doing at seven o' clock on the evening of the fifth of July this year?'

Talbot shrugged his shoulders and glanced towards the jury. 'I was walkin' down Page Street.'

'And why were you walking down Page Street?'

'I was comin' from the pub an' I was gonna see me pal in Bacon Buildin's,' he replied.

'And did you see your, eh, pal?' the prosecutor asked.

'Nah. 'E'd moved.'

The counsel for the prosecution leaned forward and picked up a sheaf of papers from the table, studying them briefly before throwing them down again. 'Will you tell the jury what you did see that evening, Mr Talbot?' he requested.

Talbot looked a little uneasy as he glanced from the staring jurymen to the judge and back to the prosecutor. 'I saw Ellie Roffey unlockin' the gate of the rag sorters an' I saw 'er go in,' he said.

Ellie's eyes went up to the high ceiling briefly and

then she dropped her gaze once more. There was mumbling among members of the public and the judge turned his stern gaze to the gallery. The large hall became silent except for a muffled coughing and then a sudden loud sneeze.

'I want you to take a look at the defendant, Mr Talbot,' the prosecutor told him. 'Is that the woman you saw letting herself in the rag sorters?'

'Yes.'

'Tell us what happened next, Mr Talbot.'

'Well, like I say, my pal wasn't in the Buildin's, so I stood on the corner o' Page Street fer a while finkin',' Talbot went on. 'Then I see Ellie Roffey walkin' up the street, quickly like.'

'Coming towards you?'

'Yeah, that's right.'

'Which direction did she take then?'

'She turned right an' walked up Bacon Street ter the main road.'

The prosecutor studied the notes briefly and then rocked back on his heels with both hands clasping the front of his robe. 'What did you do next, Mr Talbot?' he asked in a loud voice.

The young man shrugged again. 'I strolled back towards the pub an' . . .'

'The Kings Arms on the corner of Page Street, you mean?' the counsel queried.

'Yeah, that's right.'

'What then?'

'Well, I saw the smoke comin' from the rag sorters,' Talbot replied.

'What did you do then?'

'I jus' walked off.'

'I see,' the prosecutor said, nodding and then glancing quickly at the jury as he asked, 'You did not attempt to call the fire brigade?'

'I would 'ave done, but I 'eard an ole lady say one o' the men 'ad already run up ter the pub ter phone fer the fire engines,' Talbot answered.

'Thank you, Mr Talbot,' the prosecuting consel said, glancing to the bench.

'Do you wish to cross-examine?' the judge asked, eyeing the defence counsel.

A short, stocky figure stood up and cleared his throat as he made his way to the witness box. 'Mr Talbot, I understand that you know Mrs Ellie Roffey. Is that correct?' he asked in a quiet voice.

Talbot nodded and was again addressed firmly by the judge. 'You must answer yes or no,' he said in a tired voice.

'Yes.'

'Will you tell the jury how you came to be acquainted with the defendant, Mr Talbot?' the counsel asked.

'She used to 'ave a veg stall in Albion Market near Dock'ead,' Talbot replied.

'And you also had a stall in that market, Mr Talbot?'

'Nah, it wasn't mine. I only 'elped out on it,' he replied.

'I see. And were you friendly with the defendant, Mr Talbot?'

'Objection, your honour!' the prosecutor interrupted. 'My learned friend is attempting to lead the witness.'

'Overruled,' the judge replied.

The defending counsel brought his clasped hands up in front of his chest. 'Were you friendly with the defendant?' he asked in a louder voicer.

'Nah. She was a troublemaker,' Talbot replied. 'She was always goin' on about the 'igh rents fer the stalls.'

'And you felt that Mrs Roffey was unreasonable in challenging the rents, in your enlightened opinion of course?'

'Objection!'

The judge looked irritably at the prosecutor. 'The line of questioning seems to me to be quite in order. Overruled,' he growled.

The defending counsel smiled at the jury then turned to the witness. 'Did you feel in your opinion that Mrs Roffey was unreasonable in complaining about the excessively high rents?' he asked.

'She was always complainin' about somefink or the ovver,' Talbot replied, glancing at the jury. 'She was known as a Bolshie troublemaker an' all the ovver stall'olders was sick of 'er.'

The defending counsel took a hold of his lapel and cleared his throat once more. 'All of the other stallholders?'

'Yeah, that's right.'

'That will be all, Mr Talbot.'

The next witness to be called was Theo Harrison, and when he stepped into the witness box to take the oath he looked flushed. In answer to the prosecutor's prompting he described how he had spent the late afternoon supervising the blocking-up of suspect holes in the yard following complaints about rats coming from his premises and then at six o' clock that evening he had locked up the yard and gone home, after first stopping off at the Horseshoe public house in Jamaica Road where he stayed until seven-thirty.

The counsel then asked about the visit to the yard by the women of Page Street. 'The defendant was putting forward the women's complaints about the rats, I take it?' he asked.

'Yes.'

'And where did this meeting take place?'

'In the yard office.'

'Did you leave the women alone in the office at all during the meeting?'

'Yes. I was called out during the meeting to sort out a problem.'

'For how long were the women left alone in the office?'

'About five minutes.'

'Five minutes?'

'It might have been a little longer.'

'I see. And at any time during that meeting were there threats made to burn down your property?'

'Yes.'

'Will you enlighten us, Mr Harrison?' the prosecutor asked.

'Mrs Roffey said that if we didn't get rid of the rats she was going to burn the place down herself,' Harrison replied.

'Did you tell her that you were doing your best to sort out the problem, Mr Harrison?'

'Yes. I assured her, and the women, that I was doing all I could to get rid of the rodents,' he replied.

'Was that the last time you had any communication with the accused?'

'Yes.'

'Then you did not send a note around to Mrs Roffey's house requesting her to meet you at the yard that evening?'

'No, I did not.'

The prosecutor then handed him a sheet of paper. 'This is the note Mrs Roffey received. Is this your handwriting?'

'No.'

'Then you did not send this note?'

'No, I did not.'

'Thank you, Mr Harrison.'

The defending counsel then took up his questioning. 'You stated that threats were made to you during the meeting with the Page Street women and the accused?'

'Yes.'

'Apart from the women and yourself, were there any other persons present in the office at the time?'

'No, but . . .'

'Thank you, Mr Harrison, that will be all.'

The next witness was an employee of the rag sorters'. He was a tall, bespectacled man in his late fifties, and he stated on oath that he had heard Ellie Roffey threaten to set fire to the yard.

As he gave his evidence Florrie shook her head sadly. 'The poor cow don't stand a chance,' she told Carrie. 'She'll go away fer sure.'

'It's not over yet,' Carrie replied, though she felt that it looked very bad for the woman.

Worse was to come. A fire officer took the stand and identified an exhibit, a black and twisted paraffin lamp which he stated was the object he had retrieved from the end shed after the blaze had been brought under control.

The last of the prosecution witnesses took the stand as the clock neared twelve noon. Detective Sergeant Bolton was shown an exhibit which he identified as the object he had discovered while making a detailed search of Ellie Roffey's home.

'What exactly is this item?' the prosecutor asked him.

'It's cuttle-bone.'

'And what is its use?'

'Under normal circumstances it would be placed in a bird cage to assist in sharpening a bird's beak,' the officer replied.

'Under normal circumstances?' the counsel queried.

The officer looked bored as he went on. 'Yes, but in this instance there was no sign of a bird cage in the premises we searched,' he said.

The murmur in the public gallery increased to a noisy

chatter and the judge banged his gavel down hard. 'Silence in the court!' he ordered.

The prosecutor smiled briefly at the jury and then turned his attention to the witness. 'In the light of your experience as a police officer, would you hazard a guess as to what other use this piece of cuttle-bone might be put to?' he asked.

The detective looked up at the bench. 'Cuttle-bone is often used by criminals to obtain the impression of a key, your honour,' he replied.

Once again the judge was compelled to call for order and this time he threatened to clear the court if there was any further noise.

When the court went into the lunchtime recess Florrie took Carrie's arm, and with Will Tanner following them down the long flight of stairs holding on to Maisie's arm they made their way out into the swirling fog. A short distance along the wide Borough Road they found a little public house and when they were settled comfortably William started the conversation. 'Well, I wouldn't give much fer Ellie's chances now,' he said, staring down at his pint of ale.

'We ain't 'eard the ovver side of it yet,' Florrie said quickly. 'As fer that cuttle-bone, she could 'ave 'ad a bird once. Anyway, what did they 'ave ter search 'er place for?'

'I s'pose they 'ad ter do a search,' William replied. 'After all, it's a serious crime is arson.'

'Well, yer never gonna convince me that Ellie Roffey burned that place down,' Florrie said, taking out her snuffbox from beneath the folds of her shabby coat. 'Not in a fousand years yer not.'

Maisie was looking thoughtful. 'I wish I could fink where I've seen that young bloke before,' she said.

'What bloke?' Florrie asked.

'Why, that one who said about 'em all bein' fed up

524

wiv Ellie at the market,' Maisie replied.

'That whoreson,' Florrie growled. 'The likes of 'im wants 'orsewhippin'. It's the Ellie Roffeys o' this world what stand up fer people's rights, an' what's their fanks? Gits like 'im stickin' their oar in an' blackin' their name. I tell yer now, if I see the bleeder in the street I'll smack 'im right roun' the jaw, see if I don't.'

Carrie had been sitting quietly, thinking about Ellie Roffey's plight. They had become friends since Ellie first contacted her about employing Jamie Robins and Carrie could not bring herself to believe that the campaigning woman would go to such lengths to achieve her aims. Ellie had said herself on more than one occasion that she was opposed to any form of violence and that a lasting change for working people would only come about through everyone using their vote in the proper way. She had a wicked tongue sometimes but she never really meant her threats seriously. Ellie was a good, caring person who had inadvertently fallen foul of a scheming businessman, it was obvious to Carrie, and unless the trial took a dramatic turn the poor woman was going to be locked up for a considerable length of time.

William was looking pensive. 'I wonder what Ellie's gonna say about that cuttle-bone?' he remarked. 'That's enough ter put 'er away, let alone everyfing else that's bin said.'

Maisie stood up and buttoned her thin coat. 'Well, we'll soon find out,' she said, helping Florrie struggle up from her seat.

The trial continued into the afternoon and when the defending counsel called Ellie Roffey into the witness box there was complete silence.

'Could you please tell the court whether or not you were in Page Street on the evening of the fifth of July?' the defending counsel asked her.

'Yes, I was.'

'And what was the purpose of your visit, may I ask?'

'I went to the rag sorters there.'

'Mrs Roffey, I ask you to tell the truth. Did you let yourself into the yard via the wicket-gate and with a key?'

'No.'

'Did you enter the yard?'

'Yes.'

'Then how did you obtain entry to the yard?'

'The gate was unlocked.'

'About what time in the evening would this be, Mrs Roffey?'

'About seven o' clock.'

'So it is possible that the witness Mr Talbot could have seen you at that time?'

'Yes.'

'Did you see him?'

'No.'

The counsel for the defence turned briefly to the jury once more before asking the next question, as though signalling for them to take special note. 'Mrs Roffey, did you intend to go to the rag sorters' yard to commit the crime of arson?'

'No,' Ellie said in a voice that was loud and clear.

'Will you tell the jury why you went to the yard that evening?' the barrister asked her.

Ellie Roffey took a deep breath. 'At twenty past five that evening there was a note slipped frew the letter box,' she replied. 'It said I was to phone the sorters' yard an' ask for Mr 'Arrison. By the time I got ter the phone it must 'ave bin about 'alf five. Anyway, Mr 'Arrison answered the phone 'imself.'

'And what did Mr Harrison say to you over the phone?' the defending counsel asked.

Ellie looked at the bench and then back to the barrister. 'Mr 'Arrison told me that 'e'd managed ter find out where the rats were comin' from an' if I'd pop round straight away 'e'd show me 'imself, so that I could report ter the women that everyfing 'ad bin taken care of once an' fer all.'

'Did you not think that was a strange request?' the counsel asked.

'Yes, I did,' Ellie replied. 'The last time I was at the yard Mr 'Arrison wasn't very 'elpful.'

'And did he abuse you?'

'Yes, 'e called me a Bolshie cow.'

'What was your reply, Mrs Roffey?'

'I was very angry an' I threatened ter burn the place down.'

'And was that ever your intention?'

'Most definitely not,' Ellie replied. 'I only said it because I was mad at 'im.'

'Let us get back to the evening of the fire,' the counsel said. 'Tell us exactly, step by step, what you did on reaching the wicket-gate of the rag sorters in Page Street.'

Ellie looked down at her clenched hands for a few moments then she turned her eyes to the jury. 'I pushed open the gate and stepped into the yard,' she began. 'The yard was quiet an' I suddenly thought about those rats. I felt meself goin' all shivery and I called out Mr 'Arrison's name. There was no answer and for a few moments I stood in the yard wonderin' what was wrong.'

'Carry on, Mrs Roffey.'

'Well, I crossed the yard an' saw that the office door was ajar. I pushed it open an' looked in the office. There was no one there. I turned back an' it was then I 'eard a scrapin' sound.'

'A scraping sound?'

'Yes. It frightened me,' Ellie said, shuddering

527

noticeably. 'I thought it might be one o' those rats an' I run ter the wicket-gate an' out inter the street as quick as I could.'

'Did you, or did you not, speak with or see anyone during your time in the yard that evening?' the counsel asked.

'I didn't see anybody an' I didn't speak to anybody at all while I was in the yard. There was nobody there,' Ellie replied in a firm voice.

'What did you think when you stepped out into the street again, Mrs Roffey?'

'I didn't know what ter fink. I couldn't understand it,' Ellie answered.

The counsel leaned on the rail of the witness box, his face turned to the jury. 'Did you use a key to let yourself into the yard?' he asked slowly and deliberately.

'No. The gate was open, like I said.'

'Mrs Roffey, can you account for the cuttle-bone that the police found in your flat?'

'No, I can't.'

'Have you any ideas as to how the cuttle-bone got there?'

'All I can say is that somebody must 'ave planted it there so the police would find it,' she replied hesitantly.

'Would it be easy for someone to enter your flat, Mrs Roffey?'

'Yes. I live on the groun' floor an' the winder catch doesn't fasten prop'ly.'

The defending counsel had finished his questioning and Florrie turned to Carrie as the prosecutor got up on his feet. 'I don't like that whoreson,' she said in a loud voice. ''E's a shifty git.'

'Mrs Roffey, let us recapitulate,' the counsel said in a quiet voice. 'You say on oath that you did threaten to burn the sorters' yard down when you visited there with the women from Page Street. Correct?'

'Yes, but it was . . .'

'Yes will be sufficient,' the prosecutor said quickly. 'Mrs Roffey, have you ever owned a caged bird?'

'No.'

'You also stated on oath that you did not know how the cuttle-bone came to be in your flat and that it must have been planted there. Correct?'

'Yes.'

'Let us turn our thoughts to the evening of the fire, Mrs Roffey. You say that you were asked to go to the yard at seven o'clock to meet with Mr Harrison and that the wicket-gate was left open, presumably for you to enter.'

'Yes.'

'Yet Mr Harrison states that he left the yard earlier and after locking the wicket-gate he went to the Horse-shoe public house where he stayed until seven-thirty that evening. What are your thoughts on that?'

'Objection!' the defence counsel shouted, rising to his feet in anger. 'The onus on my learned friend is proof, not supposition, Your Honour.'

'Sustained,' the judge said in a tired voice, leaning forward. 'Kindly stick to a direct line of questioning, if you please.'

The prosecutor seemed unperturbed as he glanced down at the papers in his hand and removed a sheet, approaching the bench with it. 'I have here a deposition, Your Honour, taken on oath from a Mr Terris, landlord of the Horseshoe public house in Jamaica Road. Mr Terris is at present in Guy's Hospital where he is recovering from an appendectomy. You will note that Mr Terris states that Mr Harrison was a customer in his establishment between the times Mr Harrison indicated earlier.'

Ellie bowed her head and gripped the brass rail of the dock until her knuckles showed white. Above her in the public gallery Florrie shook her head sadly, feeling that the tragic figure was surely going to be found guilty. 'I need a pinch,' she whispered to Maisie.

The prosecutor walked back to the witness stand. 'I'm almost finished,' he said, glancing back to the bench. 'Mrs Roffey, are you a member of the Communist Party of Great Britain?'

'Objection, Your Honour!' the defence counsel shouted, jumping to his feet angrily. 'Mrs Roffey's political persuasion is of no interest to this court.'

'Oh but it is, in this case,' the prosecutor insisted.

The judge turned to the accused. 'You do not need to answer the last question, Mrs Roffey,' he said in a quiet voice.

'It's all right, Yer Honour,' Ellie said, turning her head and fixing the prosecutor with a hard stare. 'I am a member of the Communist Party and I'm committed to working for a socialist government peaceably and through the ballot box.'

The prosecutor nodded briefly and then studied his notes again. Suddenly he swung around to face Ellie. 'It is my contention, Mrs Roffey, that you went to the sorters' yard in Page Street, not as an invited guest of the owner, but to commit arson. I submit that you obtained a key by criminal means and used it to enter the premises of Mr Harrison with the express purpose of burning the place down. Am I or am I not right, Mrs Roffey?'

For the first time that day Ellie looked confused as she faced the sudden attack. 'I, I . . .'

'Answer the question, Mrs Roffey. Answer the question!'

'Objection! The prosecution is attempting to browbeat my client,' the defence counsel shouted, banging the desk with his clenched fist.

'Sustained,' the judge decreed. 'Will the learned

gentleman please allow the accused time to answer the question?'

As the prosecutor turned to face Ellie once more she swayed slightly in the dock, her hands sliding along the polished rail. Her eyes shut tightly as though she was fighting to regain control of herself, then she slipped down in a dead faint. The public gallery was in an uproar as court ushers went to the accused's assistance, and two young women had jumped to their feet and were screaming obscenities down into the well of the court. Policemen hurried over to them and with a struggle they were escorted out.

'They're Ellie's two daughters,' Florrie said, nudging Maisie.

'Bloody shame the way that nasty git shouted at 'er,' Maisie replied. 'It must be a terrible ordeal.'

Ellie Roffey had recovered somewhat and as she sipped a glass of water which had been provided for her the judge announced that the court would adjourn until the following day.

The fog had persisted throughout the day and as the court emptied it was thickening. A cold, damp feeling made Florrie shiver as she took Carrie's and Maisie's arms and walked slowly between them. Will Tanner walked behind, his coat collar turned up against the chill and his laboured breath clouding out in front of him as he tried to get his cramped legs working properly. Traffic was still running and the sounds of unseen trams rattling along reached their ears as the party walked slowly into the Borough Road. Will glanced at the placard by the newspaper stand and read, 'Mussolini gasses Ethiopians'. Another placard displayed the words, 'League of Nations fails', and as he saw it he suddenly felt sick to his stomach. It was all moving towards another war, he thought. All the signs were there, just as they had been a little more than twenty years ago. What horrors and destruction were destined to happen? he wondered fearfully. How many young lives would a world war claim next time?

The fog spread its sulphurous fumes through the Bermondsey backstreets and along the river. All night it hung like a thick, poisonous blanket, and when folk rose from their beds to face another day it was still there, though thinning gradually as a blood-red sun climbed up over the rooftops. The morning traffic moved at a crawl, and when the Bermondsey Crown Court went into session at ten o' clock the air was still laden with fog.

Ellie Roffey looked composed as she stepped into the dock. There was an air of expectancy in the large courtroom as the trial got under way, and in the public gallery the number of police had been increased. Florrie Axford looked around at the blank faces surrounding her. Carrie sat to her left and on her right Maisie sat impassive, her arms folded. William Tanner was not present, however. He had felt ill when he arrived home the previous night and was confined to bed with a bout of bronchitis. Carrie had left Jamie Robins in charge of the yard and had given the ever-present Sharkey instructions to keep his eye on things. The old man was still sprightly and could be relied upon in case of an emergency.

The last of the witnesses had been heard and the prosecuting counsel rose to his feet to address the jury. The huge man, looking even more gross as he puffed out his silks, began by making the jury aware of the longstanding trading record and integrity of the owner, then he suddenly raised his voice for effect.

'We have here a threat,' he began, 'a dire threat of which this heinous crime perpetuated against Mr Harrison is but one manifestation. Mr Harrison's thriving business has now been destroyed, even though he was doing his best to solve the problem of the rats, and even after he had willingly met with the women of Page Street to try to reassure them. The defending counsel would have us believe that Mr Harrison is a devious person who has schemed to bring an innocent party to trial. An innocent party? The accused threatened openly to burn down Mr Harrison's business. You heard the witness state on oath that he saw the accused using a key to enter the yard, and minutes after she was seen hurrying away the fire broke out. Further, the defence wishes you to believe that the piece of cuttle-bone found at the home of the accused was planted there. What else could they say? I ask you, members of the jury, is this trial to become a sinister precedent, casting aside the standards of moderate decency and good sense so that the forces of chaos may enter in, wreaking havoc and destruction where they will? Or shall it be a vindication of the sane and democratic British judicial system? You have to decide, and I submit to you that the only possible verdict you can return in this case is one of guilty.'

Murmuring and muttering in the public gallery died away as the defending counsel rose. 'You have to remember that Ellie Roffey did not attempt to deny her presence at the yard on the evening of the fire,' he explained, addressing the jury. 'In fact she went there in answer to a request. Now you have seen the note, which my client assumed to have come from the owner of the rag sorters. Mr Harrison stated that he did not send the note, but someone did. Someone sent that note. I submit to you, members of the jury, that who-ever originated that note wanted Mrs Roffey to be seen at the yard immediately before the fire started. I also submit that the same person was hiding in that yard at the time, and as soon as my client left he started the blaze which destroyed the premises. Mrs Roffey, because of her campaigning on behalf of the women of Page Street, had become a nuisance.

'Are we to believe, as the prosecution would have us, that when my client first went to the yard to confront the owner about the problem with the rats, she suddenly took advantage of Mr Harrison's absence from the office by making an impression of the key which would open the wicket-gate, using a piece of cuttle-bone which she happened to have in her pocket? I say categorically that this is supposition, pure supposition based on the discovery of a piece of the aforesaid cuttle-bone in my client's home. You have heard my client deny all knowledge of it. Well, it was found there, so how did it get there? I submit to you, ladies and gentlemen of the jury, that it was put there, in the knowledge that a subsequent search of the house would uncover it. I say here and now that it was part of the monstrous, meticulously worked-out plan to bring my client here before you today. Well, ladies and gentle-men of the jury, are we to believe that this melodram-atic concoction of barefaced lies and shameless collusion, this callous victimisation of my client, consti-tutes the truth of the matter? Were the consequences for my client not so grave it would be laughable, the stuff of fantasy one finds between the dog-eared covers of a penny dreadful. I therefore ask you to ensure that justice is upheld by bringing in the only just verdict, one of not guilty.'

After the lunch adjournment the judge began his summing-up. Ellie Roffey stood passive in the dock throughout, her head bowed slightly and her hands clasped in front of her. Her dark hair was pulled tightly behind her head and secured by a thin black ribbon and she looked wan and hollow-eyed, her face clearly reflecting the ordeal she was going through. Above her in the public gallery her two adult children sat together, clasping each other's hands, their eyes staring down at the stern figure of the judge. A few feet away Florrie Axford sat beside Maisie Dougall and Carrie Bradley, all three listening intently to the solemn voice which echoed around the lofty court room.

Finally the jury left to deliberate and Florrie turned to Maisie. 'I could do wiv a nice cuppa, Mais,' she said. 'I'm fair parched.'

The tea room in the basement of the building was packed, and for an hour the three women sat sipping cups of tea, talking quietly and watching the comings and goings.

'D'yer fink they'll be out long?' Maisie asked.

'Well, I 'eard once that the longer juries are out the better the chances fer a not guilty verdict,' Carrie told her.

'In that case I don't mind stoppin' 'ere all night,' Florrie said, taking out her snuffbox and giving the inquisitive woman sitting near her a hard look.

Suddenly the word passed around that the jury were returning, and by the time Florrie had negotiated the many stairs to the gallery the jury were taking their places.

'Foreman of the jury, have you reached your verdict?' the judge demanded.

'We have, your honour.'

'How find you the accused? Guilty or not guilty?'

'We the jury find the defendant guilty as charged.'

A loud anguished cry rang out from the gallery and down in the dock Ellie Roffey lowered her head. Florrie took out her handkerchief and dabbed at her eyes while Maisie remained impassive, hardly believing what she had heard. Carrie looked down at her clasped hands feeling pain for Ellie's two daughters who were sobbing loudly, while Ellie's many supporters gave vent to their angry feelings shouting obscenities down into the well of the court.

After order had finally been restored the judge pronounced sentence. 'Arson is a serious crime, and apart from the destruction of property it very often happens that in the perpetration of the crime of arson innocent lives are lost. Mercifully in this instance no deaths occurred, but the crime is not made any less dire by circumstance. The lives of those dwelling nearby and the firemen who were required to fight the fire were put at great risk. Ellie Roffey, you will go to prison for five years.'

Chapter Thirty-six

In January as the hard winter took a grip Carrie was finding it increasingly difficult to keep the business running smoothly. Icy roads and lame horses stretched her resources to the limit, and when one of her customers phoned her to say he was forced to cancel their contract she slumped down at her desk and dropped her head in her hands. It had been a miserable Christmas with her father ill in bed, and two lame horses for which she had made poultices day and night. There had been no news of Joe and Carrie had thought about him constantly. Rachel too had seemed very subdued, spending much of the time alone in her room, when she was not helping her mother with the household chores. Only once had she mentioned Joe, and that had been on Christmas Day when the two of them were alone in the cosy parlour.

'Do yer still wish Joe was 'ere, Mum?' Rachel had said as she sat in front of the roaring fire, her head resting on the edge of Carrie's armchair.

'Of course I do,' she answered, stroking her daughter's hair.

'Yer still love 'im, Mum, don't yer?'

'Yeah, I do.'

'I wish we could find 'im,' Rachel sighed.

'P'raps Joe don't want to be found, luv,' Carrie replied.

'If I 'ad one wish I'd wish for Joe ter come back, Mum. I can't stand ter see yer so miserable an' lonely,' Rachel said, taking her mother's hand in hers.

Carrie sighed sadly as she gazed into the glowing coals. Her daughter was growing into a beautiful young woman and life for her should now be exciting, happy and carefree. Instead she had been lending a hand in the business and tending the home as well as helping to care for her sick grandfather ever since she had left school at fourteen. She never seemed to complain, but there were times when Carrie noticed a sad, tired expression on her daughter's face and she worried for her. One day the business would be hers, and if it prospered Rachel would be able to enjoy a good future and a good life. Would it all be worth the price she was having to pay now?

The bleak winter days were long, tiring and empty for Carrie, with the constant worry of the business and her father's failing health taking its toll. Her mother seemed to have accepted that William was not going to get better and she sat around for most of the day, hardly ever venturing far from the house in case something happened to him. Carrie's only relief from the endless grind was when Don Jacobs visited the yard. She always looked forward to his visits. What had happened between them before Joe came home from prison seemed to have sealed their friendship in a strange way and their short passionate encounter was never mentioned. They both understood that their loneliness and need for human warmth had thrown them together for a brief moment in time, and in the future they were destined to go their separate ways, remaining just good friends. Don was now courting again and he was well aware of Carrie's yearning for Joe, for whenever he visited the yard the conversation invariably turned to the absent man.

During the cold, bleak January folk were still talking about the Roffey trial and Ellie's subsequent imprisonment, which had shocked and saddened the little riverside community. Everyone felt that Ellie had been unjustly imprisoned and there was talk of an appeal being made as soon as possible. In the meantime the burnt-out premises in Page Street remained closed, and rumours abounded that the owner of the rag sorters had done very nicely by way of insurance.

The women of the little riverside street blamed themselves for involving Ellie in their troubles and whenever they gathered together they always ended up discussing the affair.

'Yer know, I can't get that bleedin' young bloke out o' me mind,' Maisie said as she sat with Sadie and Florrie one day in Sadie's parlour. 'I'm sure I've seen 'im somewhere.'

'It was that git who 'elped put 'er away,' Florrie growled. 'I'd take a bet it was 'im what put that bloody cuttle-bone in Ellie's 'ouse.'

"E looked a shifty git, didn't 'e?' Maisie remarked with distaste.

Sadie had been ill with pleurisy during the trial but she had been kept informed of what happened. 'What must that poor cow be goin' frew?' she said sadly. 'Fancy bein' stuck away in that 'orrible 'ole. They say 'Olloway's worse than the men's prisons. There's all sorts in there. Mind yer, though, I reckon our Ellie's converted a few of 'em already.'

Florrie took out her snuffbox and tapped her two fingers on the lid. 'I saw Ellie's younger daughter at the market the day before yesterday,' she told them. 'The poor cow looks done in wiv the worry.'

'I wish there was somefink we could do,' Maisie said, sipping her tea.

'Well, there's not a fing we can do, so it's no good

keep goin' on about it, Mais,' Florrie replied sharply.

'I wish I could fink where I've seen that bloke before,' Maisie went on.

Florrie raised her eyes to the ceiling and put down her teacup. 'Yer'd better be careful, Mais, or yer'll be talkin' about 'im in yer sleep. Your Fred'll end up givin' yer a back-'ander.'

During the wintry January William Tanner took a turn for the worse. His breathing became increasingly difficult, and when the doctor was called he diagnosed pneumonia. William was rushed away to hospital and for two days he hovered between waking and unconsciousness, then on the third day he sank into a peaceful sleep from which he never awakened. The funeral was attended only by William's immediate family but as the cortege passed along Page Street everyone seemed to be at their front doors, the women holding handkerchiefs to their eyes and the men standing erect and bare-headed. As the funeral carriages swung around the turning Nellie glanced from the carriage window at the deserted yard where William had spent so much of his working life. 'At least yer farvver never suffered at the end,' she said, her voice betraying little emotion.

Danny sat with his head bowed. He had become very close to his father during the latter years of his life and he knew that he was going to miss him badly. Carrie glanced at her grieving brother and then her mother as though fearing that they might see how hollow she felt inside. There was no tearful emotion, no despair, only an emptiness that frightened her. All the memories of her childhood days helping her father in the Galloway stable came crowding back as she sat in the carriage following after his coffin, but she could not bring herself to cry. It was as though all her emotion, all her feelings had been drawn away from her. The only comfort she had was knowing that before her father died she had managed to fulfil her vow, taking him and her mother away from the slum dwellings that had been their home for so long. At least her father had known some comfort and happiness in his final years, helping in the yard and being amongst the horses that he loved so much.

In February 1936 Carrie realised her long-time ambition when she bought two Leyland lorries and openly competed for the longer-distance haulage work. Bradley Cartage Contractors was now firmly established and the contracts started to come in. In March she bid against the Galloway firm for a regular contract with a large food-processing company in Bermondsey and her tender was accepted. For a time everything ran smoothly. The two drivers she had employed proved reliable and there was still regular contract work for her horse transport. Carrie's business had weathered the quiet winter months better than most of the cartage firms and she now looked forward to a busy spring.

Towards the end of March, however, things began to go wrong. One of the lorries broke down at the food factory one Monday morning and it was later discovered that there was sand in the fuel-lines. The following week one of the wagons was almost run off the road by a speeding lorry and the cheerful carman Paddy Byrne just escaped being thrown under the wheels. Another incident occurred soon after and almost proved fatal for the lorry driver.

Tom Armfield had spent the early morning loading cases of canned foods at the factory and by eleven o'clock he was on his way to make a delivery to the Royal Navy depot at Chatham. Tom was feeling happy and whistled to himself as he drove up the steep hill to Blackheath. The vehicle was a new one and it handled well. The sun was shining and the day promised to remain fine as he slipped into top gear and motored across the empty heath. He could see the little village church away to his right, and beyond, Blackheath village. Way in front he saw the long steep rise of Shooter's Hill. The engine sounded sweet, with a comforting reserve of power beneath his feet. As he caught up with a slow-moving horse cart in front of him it slowed almost to a standstill and swung round tightly into a narrow side turning. Tom was forced to brake. It was then that he felt the excess movement of the brake pedal and had to press down harder than normal to ease back his vehicle.

The road ahead was clear now and he pressed down on the accelerator. The responding roar was strong and he felt the power as the lorry took the steep hill at a good rate. Twice down through the gears and he was at the brow of the hill. Below him in the early spring air he saw the countryside spread out and the distant township. The weight of the five-ton load was thrusting forward as he headed down the hill in third gear and applied the footbrake. Again the pedal travelled too far for comfort, and then suddenly it went straight down to the floorboards. There was nothing there! Tom pumped hard on the pedal as the speed of the vehicle increased and a sickening feeling gripped his stomach as he realised that the brakes were useless. There was nothing he could do except try to steer tight to the kerbside in an effort to slow the lorry down. It bumped and jolted with a shudder and he could feel the momentum and hear the screeching of the tyres against the kerbstones. It was holding for the moment he thought and with a quick action he managed to change down a gear. He gritted his teeth at the grating noise, dreading he would strip the gear, but it worked. The vehicle was holding a constant speed and Tom was anxious to throw on the handbrake, but he knew that it would be no good if he applied it too soon.

'Oh my Gawd!' he cried aloud as he saw the motor car pull out from a side road at the bottom of the hill and pressed hard on the horn as he drew closer and closer. The car pulled in towards the kerb and by swinging hard on the wheel Tom managed to miss it by inches as he passed. It was now or never, he thought, and with all the strength he could muster he pulled back the handbrake, letting the nearside wheels rub against the kerb at the same time. The lorry jarred horribly but he managed to hold it steady and it pulled up abruptly with a shudder. Tom dropped his head over the wheel, his breath coming fast.

'Bloody maniac!' the car driver shouted at him as he drove by.

Tom Armfield forced a grin and then retched out of his cab window.

On Friday evening all of Carrie's workers were assembled in the yard office, Carrie stood with her back to the door, her face grim as she addressed them. 'I don't know what's goin' on, but yer can be sure I'm gonna find out,' she said in a determined voice.

Paddy Byrne looked up from rolling a cigarette. 'It's lucky me an' Tom wasn't killed, Mrs Bradley,' he remarked. 'Somebody's be'ind all what's 'appened, right enough.'

Carrie nodded. 'Now look, all of yer. I'm givin' yer the chance ter leave now. There'll be a full week's wages fer anybody who wants ter leave right away. I can't ask yer ter take chances fer my sake.'

Big Jack Simpson rubbed his hand over his shaven head. 'We ain't finkin' o' leavin', Mrs Bradley. We jus' want yer ter get it sorted out, that's all.'

'All right, Jack. I promise yer I'll get ter the bottom

of it,' Carrie told him. 'What yer mus' remember though is not ter leave yer wagons or lorries unattended. When yer use the coffee shops make sure yer pull up where yer can see 'em. If possible use the coffee stall so yer can keep a better eye out. I know it's gonna be 'ard fer a time but I'll do me best ter get it sorted out, that's all I can say.'

''Ave yer got any ideas who might be at the back of it, Mrs Bradley?' Tom asked.

'Well, whoever it is they've got some knowledge o' lorries,' Carrie replied. 'First there was sand in the fuel-pipes of Tubby's lorry, then your lorry 'ad the brake-cables loosened. Fings like that don't 'appen by accident.'

Tubby Walsh rubbed his stubbled chin thoughtfully. 'Don't yer fink it's about time yer called in the police?' he asked.

Carrie folded her arms and arched her back against the door. 'I've given it a lot o' thought, Tubby, but the police'll only take statements an' advise us ter be careful. They can't foller us about all over the place. Besides, whoever's doin' it will jus' lie low till the coast is clear. No, it's gotta be 'andled anuvver way. I tell yer this though. Stick wiv me frew this an' I'll make sure yer'll all benefit. I'm workin' out a bonus scheme over the weekend. When I earn, you'll earn.'

Paddy Byrne took a puff of his cigarette. 'That sounds all right as far as I'm concerned,' he said, looking round the room.

Voices were raised in support and Carrie smiled with relief. 'Right, men, get off 'ome now, an' fanks fer yer support.'

Frank Galloway slipped out of the Crown and made his way past the quiet wharves to London Bridge Station. He carried a small attaché case and a light mackintosh over his arm, and as he reached the long flight of steps which led up to the station forecourt he smiled smugly. Bella had taken the story hook, line and sinker, he told himself. But then she would, if she thought there was money involved. Going up to Yorkshire to look into the possibility of buying a fleet of lorries from an ailing transport concern seemed a tall story but he had been convincing. He had made sure he looked peeved when he told her he would have to spend Friday and Saturday nights in a grotty boarding-house in some dull provincial town, but pound notes worked with Bella, and the gift of a new coat had helped to put her into a happy frame of mind. The bloody woman was clothes mad, he grumbled to himself. She would soon need another wardrobe to hang the stuff.

Never mind, the weekend he had planned would be worth the cost of that new coat. Peggy Harrison was the sort of lady who could make anyone forget their troubles. Two whole nights in a discreet hotel on the Sussex coast with Peggy for company was going to be something to remember, Frank thought with relish. She was some woman, and her story to her husband Theo Harrison had been even more bizarre than his to Bella. Theo was desperate for children and Peggy had no intentions of supplying him with any, but as far as Theo was concerned his dutiful wife was as sad as he was about her inability to become pregnant by him. A private clinic in Bournemouth had been doing tests on women desperate to conceive, and the results had been staggering, according to Peggy's make-believe friend. It would mean two whole days and nights bed rest, and some pretty horrible tests, Peggy told Theo, but anything was worth trying if she could give him what his heart most desired. Theo had been very pleased at the hopeful news, and he had even offered to book himself into a nearby hotel while his wife suffered on his behalf, just to be near her, but Peggy had dissuaded him. She had told him she couldn't bear to think he was suffering too. Better he had a pleasant weekend at the golf links with his drinking friends and did not worry unduly. All would be well.

Frank hid a smile as he boarded the seven-fifteen to Rye. Peggy was a very shrewd lady, and Theo's increased fortune, thanks to the insurance pay-out, made her tread very warily. There would be no poison added to his soup. Peggy already had a very substantial allowance and access to Theo's bank account. It was all looking very rosy, Frank thought, unaware of the heavily built character in a dirty raincoat and trilby hat who boarded the same train, and who had been following him since he left the Crown.

On Monday morning after the last of the transport had left the Bradley yard Don Jacobs called round. Carrie gave him her usual peck on the cheek and took his arm as she led him to the house. 'It's bin a long time, Don,' she said, looking at him closely. 'Yer've lost weight.'

'It's the long meetin's an' short sleeps,' he replied grinning. 'I understand there's bin trouble in the camp.'

Carrie's face became serious, and while she brewed the tea she told him about the recent acts of sabotage to her fleet. 'I'm worried, Don. Tom Armfield was nearly killed, an' Paddy Byrne too,' she said, handing him his tea.

Don stared down at the brimming teacup for a few moments then looked up with a frown. ''Ave yer any ideas who's responsible, Carrie?'

'I'll give yer two guesses,' she said.

'Yer fink it's Galloway?'

'I'm positive,' she replied. 'I beat 'im ter the Mason contract an' then I got anuvver contract ter cart Bedwall's machinery by undercuttin' 'im. I've become

546

a thorn in 'is side an' 'e's feelin' bad about it.'

Don shook his head. 'I dunno, Carrie, Galloway's bin in business a long time. All right I know yer got no time fer the man, an' I know yer always suspected 'im o' bein' be'ind those troubles we 'ad durin' the General Strike, but it was never proved. I know what a cantankerous ole goat Galloway is, especially from the union point o' view, but would 'e resort ter those kind o' tactics?'

'Maybe George Galloway wouldn't, but I don't trust that son of 'is, an' after all, it is Frank Galloway who's runnin' the business now.'

'Is that a fact?' Don said, looking surprised.

'It's common knowledge,' Carrie told him. 'When I went after that food factory contract I was told by their transport manager that it was the younger Galloway who 'andled their tender. It would 'ave bin the ole man 'imself a few years ago. George Galloway must be near eighty now. Dad told me once that Galloway was two years older than 'im, an' Dad was nearly seventy-six when 'e died.'

Don sipped his tea. 'What about the police?' he asked.

'I dunno,' she replied, toying with a teaspoon. 'I got the men tergevver last Friday evenin' an' they felt I should get the police in, but yer know yerself there's not much they can do wiv so little ter go on. No, I told the men I was gonna 'andle it meself.'

Don looked closely at her, a smile growing on his wide face. 'Yer never give up, do yer, Carrie?' he said, shaking his head. 'What yer gonna do, go round an' front Frank Galloway?'

'That's exactly what I am gonna do,' she told him.

Don Jacobs looked at her with concern. 'D'yer know what yer takin' on? If yer openly accuse 'im 'e'll just laugh at yer. Yer gotta 'ave proof, an' what proof 'ave yer got? For all yer know it might be one o' the ovver contractors whose nose yer've put out o' joint.'

Carrie shook her head slowly. 'I'm sorry, Don, but I'm convinced I'm right. I'd be willin' ter bet everyfing I own that whoever's gettin' at me is in the pay o' the Galloways. That family 'ave caused us enough grief over the years an' I'll never be satisfied until I see that firm go out o' business. Whenever the Galloway firm tender fer contracts I'll bid against 'em. I'll cut my tenders ter the bone an' I'll even cover a short-term loss if I 'ave to.'

Don Jacobs put down his teacup and leaned back in his chair. 'Yer know, Carrie, when yer first bought Buckman's out I gave yer six months,' he said, smiling at her, 'I couldn't see yer lastin' in this cut-froat game, but I know now that I was wrong. Yer've not only lasted, yer've now got about the best transport set-up in the area. I'm very pleased fer yer, but yer beginnin' ter scare me, I don't mind admittin'.'

'What d'yer mean, Don?' Carrie asked with a puzzled look.

'I've bin a union convenor fer a number of years,' he said, 'an' I've 'ad ter deal wiv some 'ard-faced gov'nors. I can always spot 'em before they open their mouths, an' yer know why? 'Cos they've all got that certain look in their eye. Don't ask me what it is. It's just a hardness, like the cold shine on a piece o' flintstone. I can see that look in your eye, Carrie, an' it wasn't always there. I never noticed it when you an' Fred run the dinin' rooms, an' that's what troubles me.'

'Listen, Don, my men get a fair deal, an' . . .'

'I know they do. I'm not talkin' about that,' he cut in. 'I'm on about that look I saw jus' then – when yer mentioned Galloway. Don't let yer 'atred fer the Galloways destroy yer, Carrie, 'cos it will if yer not careful, mark my words. Concentrate on buildin' up yer own business an' let the future take care o' the Galloways. If they can't compete against the rest then they'll go under.'

'So in the meantime I sit back an' let their hired scruffs injure my men an' ruin my transport,' Carrie snorted. 'No chance, Don. I'm gonna arrange a meetin' wiv our precious Mr Frank Galloway. I might be a woman but 'e doesn't scare me.'

Don got up to leave, feeling that he was wasting his time trying to dissuade Carrie from acting rashly. 'Look, gel, I can see yer mind's made up, so let me give yer a bit of advice,' he said, taking her by the arms. 'Don't go ter see Galloway on yer own. Take yer bruvver Danny along. Frank Galloway won't try 'is arm while Danny's there wiv yer.'

Carrie nodded and then gave the union man a peck on the cheek. 'Take care, Don, an' fanks fer listenin'.'

As soon as Don Jacobs had left Carrie crossed the yard and walked quickly into the office. Jamie Robins looked up from his desk, a questioning look on his thin features as he saw the hard set of Carrie's face. 'Anyfing wrong, Mrs Bradley?' he asked.

Carrie ignored his concern. 'Jamie, get me Galloway's number right away,' she barked at him.

Chapter Thirty-seven

Frank Galloway arrived home from Sussex early on Sunday afternoon to find a note awaiting him.

> Darling,
> Good news! Desmond Prescott phoned.
> Thinks he has a backer for his new play,
> and guess what? There's a part for me! Am
> at 'The Firs' to meet the rest of the
> cast. Caroline is with the Mortons for
> the weekend. I may be late so don't wait
> up. Wish me luck, darling.
> Ever yours,
> Bella.

Frank scowled as he threw the note down on the sofa. Desmond Prescott had been trying to get a backer for that idiotic play of his for years and now at the drop of a hat Bella had dashed off to that house of fornication. The only part she was going to land was in one of Prescott's private bedroom farces. Well, she can do what she likes from now on, he thought as he poured himself a stiff Scotch. It had been a very exciting time with Peggy and he wasn't going to let Bella's carryings on upset him. The future looked decidedly rosy, as long as Peggy played her cards right in milking that stupid husband of hers.

Three Scotches later the phone rang and Frank suddenly sat upright on the sofa as he heard the tearful voice crackling down the line. 'No, it's all right, I'm alone,' he said. 'What's wrong? . . . Good lord, he hasn't, has he?'

The voice became more distressed and then Frank was on his feet and striding into the middle of the lounge, the telephone cord stretched to its limit. 'Oh my God! No, I can't get away tonight,' he answered irritably. 'Bella's due back soon . . . No, I can't . . . But, Peggy . . . Oh, all right. Meet me at London Bridge Station . . . Yes, at the buffet. I'll be as quick as I can.'

Frank slipped on his mackintosh and fedora, grabbed up his door keys and left the house in a fluster, suddenly aware that he was getting hopelessly caught up in his own web of intrigue.

Carrie was feeling nervous on Monday evening as she watched the two lorries being shunted into the yard. It was the nightly ritual, after the last of the horses had been stabled and the carts stowed away in the shed. The lorries took all the yard space and there was barely enough room to close the gates, but Tom Armfield had packed them perfectly and he called out a goodnight as he ducked through the wicket-gate, leaving Carrie to slip the heavy padlock through the hasp.

It was quiet, with only the distant sound of a tug whistle carrying on the cool evening air, and as she slid the wicket-gate bolt the young woman thought about the phone call she had made that morning. Frank Galloway had obviously been surprised that she was contacting him and there had been a lengthy pause when she told him she wanted a meeting with him. He had not asked why she should want to see him, but he had dithered about the time and place. He had been adamant that they could not meet at the Galloway yard, and when he said he would ring her back later it had seemed to her that he was trying to put her off. It had been early afternoon when he finally rang, and the venue he suggested had taken her completely by surprise. The Anchor and Hope was a riverside pub with its own particular character. It was situated near Blackfriar's Bridge and was known as the 'courting couples' pub'. Its three small bars were sectioned off into cubicles and alcoves where lovers sat in the dim light, undisturbed and unobserved as they pursued their courting. Carrie remembered going there once with Fred on a summer evening. They had sat out on the veranda overlooking the Thames with a fine view of St Paul's Cathedral. Why should Frank Galloway pick that particular pub when they could meet at any local establishment? she wondered.

Carrie hurried into the house to get ready. She had thought about Don Jacob's advice to take Danny along but decided against it. With her brother present Galloway might feel threatened and not disposed to talk openly. Besides, she did not consider herself to be in any physical danger from the man. Although the Anchor and Hope was a secluded pub it was still a public place, and she would be careful not to put herself in any danger by going off anywhere with him.

'Who exactly is it yer seein' ternight, Mum?' Rachel asked as she stood watching her mother brush out her long blonde hair.

'Oh it's only a business meetin', luv,' Carrie replied, avoiding her daughter's quizzical stare.

'It's a funny time fer a meetin',' Rachel remarked. 'Is it a beau?'

'No, it's not a beau,' Carrie replied quickly, glaring at her. 'Now don't yer be so inquisitive. As a matter o' fact it's about a contract I've bin after, but it's gotta be kept secret fer the time bein'. Now are yer satisfied?'

Rachel looked unconvinced but she left her mother to finish getting ready, and at eight o'clock when the taxi arrived at the gate she stood at the front door and gave her a kiss on the cheek. 'I 'ope it goes all right, Mum,' she said.

The taxi drove along the quiet Tooley Street and turned under the Stainer Street arch to St Thomas's Street. It continued on past Guy's Hospital and Borough High Street before turning into Southwark Street, skirting the empty Borough Market and the hop warehouses, and soon it was winding its way through the little backstreets by the river. Carrie could not shake off the feeling of nervousness. How was she going to open the conversation without venting her hostility towards him? she wondered. What would be his reaction? She had gone over what she was going to say to him again and again in her mind, but when the taxi pulled up beside the little pub Carrie felt at a loss.

The place was quiet, with a few couples sitting close together and one or two men standing at the bar talking to the landlord. Carrie stood by the door feeling uncomfortable, and suddenly she spotted Frank Galloway coming towards her. It had been a long time since she had seen him and she was surprised at how old he looked. He was a heavily built man with dark wavy hair that had streaks of grey in it and his face looked flushed, as though he had been drinking heavily.

'I've got a seat over there,' he said nodding his head. 'Can I get you a drink while we talk?'

The matter-of-fact tone gave Carrie confidence. If Galloway had shown any sign of fake friendliness towards her she would have found it harder to confront him calmly, but as it was he seemed in a hurry to get the meeting over and done with. She took a seat in the far alcove and watched as he strode to the counter. It seemed unreal to her that she was actually alone in the company of a Galloway, and in a pub at that. Her mother would have been horrified if she had known of the meeting, but as it was she was still in deep mourning and not really aware of her daughter's business dealings. Carrie clenched her hands under the table as Frank Galloway came back with a Scotch for himself and a large port for her.

'You said it was urgent we talk,' he said when he was seated, glancing at her briefly then staring down at his drink.

Carrie took a sip of her port and fixed him with a hard look. 'Yes, it is urgent we talk,' she replied quietly. 'Because if I don't talk wiv you I talk wiv the police.'

'The police?'

'I'm not gonna beat about the bush,' she said, her voice rising. 'Somebody's gettin' at my transport. Two o' my drivers were lucky they wasn't killed, an' if it carries on like this one of 'em will be.'

Frank spread his hands out in front of him and glanced around furtively. 'All right, keep your voice down,' he said quickly. 'Now am I to understand that you feel I'm responsible for whatever's happened to cause these accidents?'

Carrie leaned forward in her seat, her clasped hands resting on the table. 'One of my lorries 'ad sand in the fuel-pipes, an' the ovver 'ad brake failure, which nearly cost the driver 'is life,' she said in a voice seething with anger. 'An' that's not all. One of my carmen was bumped by a speedin' lorry which swerved inter the side of 'is cart an' 'e was almost knocked under its wheels. Now I don't call them occurrences accidents. They were caused on purpose. The firm that repaired the lorry's brakes told me that the brake-cables 'ad bin tampered wiv.'

555

'All right so they weren't accidents, but what the hell's that got to do with me?' Frank said in a low voice.

'I fink it's got a lot ter do wiv you,' Carrie replied, her eyes boring into his. 'It's my belief that whoever's be'hind what's bin 'appenin' ter my transport is actin' on your orders.'

Frank Galloway leaned back in his chair, a mirthless smile creasing his heavy, flushed features. 'And what put that ridiculous idea into your head?' he asked sarcastically.

'Ridiculous, is it?' Carrie said scornfully. 'I've beat yer fair an' square wiv the food factory tender, an' then I won the machinery contract from under yer nose. I've taken yer clerk Jamie Robins as well, an' yer don't like it. The way I see it I've become a danger ter yer. Yer can't win fair an' square so yer resortin' ter gettin' at my transport in the 'ope o' puttin' me out o' business.'

The smile was still there on Galloway's face as he leaned forward, but his eyes held a menacing look. 'That's not the way we conduct our business,' he said coldly. 'All right, so you've beaten us to a couple of lucrative contracts, but that doesn't mean you've got the monopoly. There'll be others, and we'll be right there with our tenders.'

'Well, I'm warnin' yer now,' Carrie said through clenched teeth, 'keep yer villains away from my transport, or I will go ter the police. There's a lot I could tell 'em about the upright Galloway family. It won't 'urt us any more than it 'as already, an' it won't 'urt my farvver now.'

'What do you mean by that?' Galloway asked, frowning.

'Well, if yer don't know yer'd better ask yer farvver,' Carrie told him, her eyes wide with anger. 'P'raps yer didn't know it was my bruvver Charlie yer sister Caroline was sweet on. They were plannin' ter get married an' yer farvver broke that poor gel's 'eart, an' my Charlie's too. 'E might just as well 'ave pushed that poor cow in the river 'imself. An' while I'm at it there's somefing else yer should know too. When yer farvver sacked my dad after all the years' loyal service 'e'd put in, I swore ter meself that one day I'd get even. I'm gonna fight yer every step o' the way. Every contract yer go for I'm gonna be there too. We'll see who weavvers the storm best.'

Frank Galloway swallowed his drink in one gulp, taken aback by the ferocity of the young woman's words. He remembered clearly his young sister running from the house in a distressed state after their father had forbidden her to see Charlie again and he sighed deeply. 'I did know about Caroline and Charlie, and if it means anything I did try to persuade the old man not to sack your father,' he said quietly. 'There was nothing I could do though. His mind was made up. As for you fighting us every step of the way, so be it. There's another way though,' he added, his eyes suddenly narrowing as he twirled his empty glass.

Carrie had been about to leave but the intonation in his voice made her hesitate. 'An' what d'yer mean by that?' she asked.

Frank Galloway stood up. 'I won't be a minute, I'm going to get a refill,' he said, allowing her to dwell for a few moments on what he had said.

Carrie let her tensed body sag in the chair, realising that she was trembling with emotion. She looked around her at the smoke-stained ceiling, the wooden partition and the flickering gaslamps over the bar counter, and her mind was racing. She knew that she would have to be careful. Frank Galloway had not reacted to her accusations in the way she expected but she was still certain that he was behind the sabotage of her transport. His sudden offer of a solution to their feud

557

worried her greatly and she breathed hard in an attempt to compose herself as he returned towards her with drinks in his hand.

He sat down and looked at her for a moment. 'Look, I know there's never going to be any love lost between our families, but there's no reason for us to let our dislike for each other destroy our businesses,' he said, toying with his filled glass. 'Now let's take this step by step. You've accused me of trying to ruin your business and I'm denying it. Supposing, however, that I exert pressure in certain quarters to get this villainry stopped, and what if I also give you certain information which will be of great benefit to you? Will you bend a little?'

'What yer askin'?' Carrie said curtly.

'I know you're aware that in a few weeks there's a big contract up for tender,' Galloway replied. 'We both know that the hop contract with the brewers is the largest one of its kind and I've been told by a reliable source with inside information that you intend to bid for it.'

Carrie did not let him see her surprise and dismay. She had already met with the transport representatives from the brewery and had plans to increase her fleet of lorries if she were successful in winning the contract, which was to begin towards the end of the year. She had felt that she had a head start and could outbid the Galloway concern, as well as the other two transport firms which she had been told were showing some interest.

'S'posin' I am goin' in wiv a bid?' she said, her eyes narrowing.

'I'm asking you to step aside on this one,' Galloway said quietly, his eyes fixed on her.

'Yer mean let yer win the best contract yet wivout a fight just ter get yer 'ired villains off me back?' Carrie snarled at him. 'Yer must be mad ter fink I'd even consider it. What yer proposin' is nuffink less than blackmail.'

Galloway shook his head slowly, a smile playing on his lips. 'I don't consider it to be blackmail,' he replied. 'It's a trade, and after all, we are all traders of sorts. Besides, the information I'm in a position to pass on to you should be worth one contract, however lucrative it is.'

'All right, s'posin' the information is worth it,' Carrie countered. 'What's ter stop me gettin' the information an' then biddin' against yer anyway?'

Galloway smiled slyly. 'I'm not exactly stupid, Mrs Bradley,' he said. 'I'd want a written agreement from you in which you'd state you were not going to compete against my firm with regard to the brewery contract, and as a token of good faith I'd do the same for the tin makers' contract that's in the offing. That way if either of us goes back on the deal then the other makes public the conspiracy. I think you'll agree that a disclosure of that sort would put both of us out of business. I can't see any company offering us cartage if they're aware we work a cartel. There are other, independent firms they could go to.'

Carrie studied her drink for a few moments, thinking frantically. Suddenly she looked up at Galloway. 'I'd need to 'ave some indication of what the information was,' she said.

'Let's say it concerns the imprisonment of Ellie Roffey,' he said in a low voice.

Carrie felt her heart leap but she struggled to remain calm. 'Why should that sort of information concern me?' she asked him casually.

Galloway took a sip from his glass. 'I happen to know Ellie Roffey visited your yard a few times,' he replied smiling, 'and I understand it was she who persuaded you to filch Jamie Robins from my employ. Carmen do talk amongst themselves as I'm sure you know, and a lot of their chatter comes back to me. It's common knowledge too that Ellie Roffey is highly regarded by the local women, and I think that includes you. Let me just say this – the information I have could well get her freed, if it's acted upon sensibly, and I'm sure you'll know what has to be done.'

Carrie fought back the excitement she felt. 'Why don't yer pass the information on ter the police?' she asked. 'Why offer it ter me?'

'Because it's all part of the package,' Galloway replied, his face becoming serious. 'Besides, I realise that the process of law would grind on and on in its own inevitable way, and all the time the Roffey woman is languishing in prison. With what I make available to you steps could be taken which would give the police all the evidence they'd need. Think about it.'

Carrie already knew that there was only one answer she could give him, and as she looked at his smug expression she realised that he knew it too. The man was contemptible, she thought. He should have taken the information he had directly to the police. His professed concern for Ellie while all the time he was bartering for his own advantage was sickening.

'All right, I'll go along wiv yer, but I'm not puttin' my name to anyfing unless the information yer've got is valid,' she told him.

'Right then, we'll get together tomorrow first thing,' Galloway said brightly. 'I'll get the papers drawn up and we can both put our signatures to them. As soon as that's taken care of you'll have the information you need, and if it's not valid then you'll have the opportunity of tearing up the agreement there and then: I warn you though, Mrs Bradley, if you go back on the agreement I swear I'll pull you down with me.'

560

Carrie slipped out from the alcove and stood looking down at Frank Galloway contemptuously. 'Yer don't need ter worry about me,' she said icily. 'The Tanner family don't go back on their word. What yer see is what yer get wiv us, but then you Galloways should know that already. Yer farvver saw that wiv my dad fer all those years since they were lads tergevver.'

Carrie turned on her heel and Galloway's eyes followed her as she walked quickly from the bar. He was put out by her offhandedness, but he felt a grudging admiration for her as a woman who had made it in the hard, competitive transport business. What endless possibilities there would be if they were to amalgamate, he thought.

On Tuesday evening Florrie Axford hurried to the corner shop for her snuff and then knocked at Maisie Dougall's front door. Maudie Mycroft had already called round to Maisie and the two women were sitting in the parlour with their coats on ready.

'Where's Sadie?' Florrie asked.

'We're gonna knock fer 'er on the way,' Maisie told her, giving her husband Fred a nudge in the ribs which woke him from his nap. 'Oi, sleepy 'ead, don't let that fire go out while I'm gone,' she told him firmly. 'It gets cold these evenin's.'

Fred grunted and sat up straight in his comfortable armchair, staring at Maudie as she dusted an imaginary piece of fluff from the front of her coat. 'Does your Ernest know yer out on the town ternight?' he asked grinning mischievously.

'I'm not out gallivantin',' Maudie replied, looking aggrieved. 'This is important business.'

Maisie gave Fred a hard look. 'You just keep that fire in,' she said, following her friends out into the quiet street.

Sadie was standing by her front door and the four women set off for Salmon Lane.

'Nellie was all mysterious when she called round,' Florrie said. 'I couldn't get anyfing out of 'er at all. It must be important.'

'P'raps she's 'eard somefink about the rents,' Maisie volunteered. 'That ole git Galloway might be gonna do what 'e threatened ter do about bringin' in more tenants.'

'Nah, I don't fink so,' Florrie replied. 'I fink Ellie frightened 'im orf wiv the Council people. 'E knows it wouldn't 'ave worked anyway, what wiv two families sharin' one closet. I reckon it's somefink much more important if yer ask me. Nellie ain't one to invite people round.'

When the women arrived at the Salmon Lane yard Nellie was waiting for them at the gate. She had a serious expression on her face and with a brief greeting she led them into the front parlour. Soon they were seated comfortably with cups of tea which Carrie had passed round, still wondering why they had all been summoned. They were soon to be enlightened, however. Nellie sat down on the one remaining seat and looked at Carrie. 'Go on then, gel, tell 'em what yer found out,' she urged her.

Carrie glanced around at their eager faces as she stood with her back to the door. 'Ellie Roffey didn't start that fire, ladies,' she said, waiting for their reaction.

'Well, we all know that, luv,' Florrie said, taking out her snuffbox.

'But there was no way she could convince 'em at 'er trial,' Carrie replied. 'Now I fink we can prove it.'

The women looked at her wide-eyed.

'C'mon, luv, out wiv it then,' Florrie said as they sat there in suspense.

Carrie looked from one to another of them. 'Yer remember that young bloke Talbot who told the court 'e saw Ellie go in the yard? Well, 'e was in the pay of 'Arrison, the guv'nor o' the rag sorters. It was 'im who planted that piece o' cuttle-bone in Ellie's 'ouse.'

'I knew it!' Florrie exclaimed. 'I 'ad 'im pegged fer a no-gooder right from the start. Didn't I tell yer, Mais?'

'I said the same meself,' she replied. 'I only wish I could remember where I'd seen 'im before. I know it wasn't at the market. It was somewhere else.'

'There was two of 'em bein' paid by 'Arrison,' Carrie added quickly. 'The ovver bloke's name is Bennett. 'E was in the yard that evenin', an' it was 'im who actually set the place alight as soon as Ellie left.'

''Ow did yer find all this out?' Florrie asked.

'I can't tell yer yet,' Carrie replied. 'It's gospel though.'

'Yer'll 'ave ter go ter the police right away,' Maisie said excitely.

Sadie had been quiet so far but suddenly she banged her teacup down on the table. 'I wish my Billy could get 'is 'ands on those whoresons. 'E'd soon get the trufe out of 'em,' she growled.

'My Danny too,' Nellie added.

'Well, what do we do wiv the information? Do I take it ter the police, or do we sort it out ourselves?' Carrie asked, looking at each of the women in turn.

Maudie fiddled with her bag straps. 'I fink yer should let the police deal wiv it,' she said meekly.

'Well, I don't,' Sadie cut in. 'They won't go on 'earsay. Yer gotta give 'em somefink concrete ter go on. 'Ave yer got any proof, Carrie?'

Carrie shook her head. 'That's just it, I 'aven't,' she replied. 'All I can say is that I'm certain the information's genuine.'

'What d'yer fink we ought ter do?' Maisie asked her.

Carrie studied their faces for a moment. 'I fink we should try ter find that Talbot bloke an' lure 'im 'ere on some pretext,' she said. 'Then maybe we can get the trufe out of 'im.'

'I'm not tryin' ter pour cold water on yer scheme, Carrie, but 'ow are we expected ter do that?' Maisie asked.

'We won't 'ave to,' Carrie told her. 'My Danny said 'e'll do what's needed.'

'My Billy won't let 'im be on 'is own,' Sadie added quickly. 'Them two fellas are good pals. My Billy won't take long ter get ter the trufe, mark my words.'

Carrie held her hands up as the women became excited. 'Look, ladies, what we mustn't ferget is that Ellie's still stuck in that prison. We can't waste no time findin' this Talbot bloke. I fink we should give it one week an' then if we still 'aven't found 'im, I'll go ter the police. What d'yer say?'

The women nodded their approval and Sadie leaned forward in her chair. 'Right then. Where do we start?'

'If she could fink where the bloody 'ell she'd seen 'im it'd 'elp,' Florrie said, jerking her thumb in Maisie's direction.

'It's no good,' Maisie sighed anxiously. 'I've puzzled me brains out an' fer the life o' me I can't remember where it was.'

Nellie Tanner stood up and brushed down her apron. 'Right, ladies,' she said, 'while yer workin' fings out I'm gonna put the kettle on.'

Chapter Thirty-eight

On Friday evening after Carrie paid the men and then locked up the yard she went into her quiet parlour and sat down heavily in a chair feeling utterly depressed. The women were doing all they could in their limited way but with no results. Nellie had recalled that Talbot's address was read out at the trial, which made them all feel foolish, but try as they might no one could remember it. Florrie had made enquiries at the markets and Maudie had asked the women at the church club if any of them knew of a Talbot family, while Sadie had talked to all her sons and her husband Daniel who was in his last few weeks at the docks before retirement, but none of them had had any success. There had been one or two leads, but they all came to nothing. Florrie had learnt of a Talbot family in Bermondsey but they had no sons. Another Talbot family did have a son, Maudie learned, but she discovered that he was currently doing five years for robbery. Daniel Sullivan learned of a family who had four sons, all of whom worked in the Surrey Docks, and for a while the women's hopes were raised. Florrie and Maisie visited the pub where the men drank every Friday evening after work, and when the landlord pointed out the brothers to them the two women groaned with disappointment.

It seemed to Carrie that she had made a big mistake in not going straight to the police. She had herself asked all her men if they knew of a Talbot family and urged them to keep their ears open but it was of no use. She was worried for Danny and Billy too. If Talbot could eventually be located and lured to the yard then the men would have to use force to get the truth from him. What if Danny or Billy got hurt in the process? she thought anxiously. And what if Frank Galloway was lying and Talbot was a bona fide witness? Carrie dismissed that worry almost immediately. Galloway had too much to lose by giving her false information, and knowing him to be devious she felt that he had his own sinister reasons for wanting the truth to out. What still concerned her most though, often forcing its way to the front of her mind and causing her to toss and turn in her bed at night, was the worry of Joe. She imagined him lying in a hospital bed ill, or injured somewhere in the street, and had frequent visions of him consorting with other women.

Rachel came into the parlour, her long blonde hair tied loosely behind her head with a black ribbon, and Carrie could not help but notice how beautiful her daughter had become. Her large eyes shone radiantly and she seemed to move with a natural elegance.

'Yer look tired, Mum. 'Ave yer bin finkin' o' Joe again?' she asked with concern.

Carrie smiled wanly. 'No, luv, I've not,' she lied. 'It's this Talbot business.'

'Still no luck?' Rachel asked, sitting down facing her mother.

Carrie shook her head. 'I'm givin' it till Monday then I'm goin' ter the police,' she replied. 'I can't leave it no longer.'

'What would Frank Galloway say?' Rachel asked.

''E told me that if I went ter the police an' told 'em where I'd got the information 'e'd jus' tell 'em 'e over'eard it in a pub. The police'll most likely discount it as gossip anyway,' Carrie told her, leaning back in her chair and staring up at the smoke-stained ceiling.

'I wish Joe was 'ere, Mum. I bet 'e'd find that Talbot fella. Joe could do anyfing,' she sighed.

'I wish 'e was 'ere too, darlin',' Carrie said softly.

Maisie Dougall had been feeling depressed all week. She had moped about the house, constantly sitting around deep in thought, until on Friday evening her husband finally decided that something had to be done.

'Look, luv, yer can't spend all yer time rackin' yer brains about that Talbot bloke. If yer can't remember that's the end of it,' he told her sharply.

'But if I could jus' remember where I'd seen 'im we might be able ter go there an' find 'im,' she replied, sighing deeply as she stared into the low-burning fire.

'Look, gel, yer bin like that since yer come back from the Tanner place. Go an' get yerself ready an' we'll go up the Rovver'ithe 'Ippodrome. There's a good review up there,' he told her. 'Go on, it'll do yer good ter get out o' the 'ouse fer a couple of hours.'

Maisie did not feel like going anywhere but Fred was persistent and she finally relented. She did her hair, put on her best brown coat and her matching high-heeled shoes, picked up her handbag and then stood gloomily in the parlour watching while Fred raked out the ashes from the fire.

'Yer do look a picture o' misery,' he remarked, smiling fondly at her. 'It's the music-'all we're goin' to, not a funeral.'

Maisie did her best to brighten up and when they stepped down from the tram at Rotherhithe Tunnel she was feeling slightly better. Folk were passing to and fro and a line of people was forming by the entrance to the theatre.

'Fancy a drink before we go in, gel?' Fred asked.

'That'd be nice,' Maisie replied, feeling better than she had done all week. 'Could we go in that pub we went in last time we come down 'ere?'

'Yer mean the Albert. Yeah, if yer like,' Fred said, taking her arm as they crossed the main road. 'It's nice an' comfortable in there an' yer can always get a seat.'

They had spent a happy half hour chatting together when the door suddenly opened and a little old man walked in and made his way to the bar. He was bent and walked with the aid of a stick, but what caught Maisie's eyes was the row of medals pinned to his coat lapel. The ribbons looked discoloured and the metal tarnished, and they were all secured with a huge safety-pin. Suddenly Maisie gasped and tugged on Fred's arm. 'It's the ole boy!' she exclaimed.

Fred picked up his drink. 'What ole boy?' he asked.

'That's it! That's where I seen 'im!' she shouted excitedly.

'What yer goin' on about?' Fred asked irritably.

'What 'appened last time we was in 'ere?' Maisie quizzed him.

'We 'ad a drink,' he said, smiling at her.

'I know we 'ad a drink, but don't yer remember what else 'appened?' she went on excitedly.

Fred pulled on his chin. 'I remember now,' he said. 'That ole boy at the counter was gettin' a bit upset over those two yobs what was takin' the rise out of 'im.'

'That's right,' Maisie said triumphantly. 'Yer was gonna get up an' stick one on 'em over 'em takin' it out of 'is medals, but I stopped yer.'

Fred grinned. 'Yeah, I remember. The guv'nor told the two blokes ter get out and' they give 'im a lot o' sauce.'

'One o' the blokes was Talbot,' Maisie said with emphasis. 'I'm dead certain of it.'

Fred took another gulp from his pint of ale. 'Well,

p'raps we can get a bit o' peace now,' he remarked.

Maisie eased herself from the chair and Fred held on to the table. 'Where the bloody 'ell yer goin'? he growled.

'I'm gonna 'ave a word wiv the lan'lord,' she told him.

Fred shook his head slowly as he watched her hurry to the bar. When she finally returned he could see the disappointment written on her face.

'No luck, gel?' he asked.

She shook her head. 'The silly git don't remember chuckin' those two out,' she replied. ''E told me 'e chucks so many people out 'e can't remember 'em all.'

'Didn't yer tell 'im the bloke's name?' Fred asked her.

'Yeah, but 'e said 'e didn't know anybody called Talbot,' Maisie replied disconsolately.

'Well, never mind, at least yer tried,' Fred said kindly.

At twenty minutes past seven the two of them walked from the pub and made their way to the box office to purchase their tickets. Throughout the show Maisie felt unable to relax completely, her mind going back to Ellie Roffey's trial. She could picture the young man's face clearly as he stepped into the witness box to give his evidence but she could not for the life of her remember the address he gave. Nevertheless she knew for certain that he was one of the two men who had harassed the old soldier. He might not be a local man, she thought. He might have travelled there to meet someone and in that case he could have come from anywhere.

Fred was enjoying the show. Occasionally he turned his head and saw that Maisie was preoccupied.

'Are yer still finkin' o' that Talbot bloke?' he asked her during the interval.

Maisie nodded. 'I'm sorry, Fred, but we gotta find 'im if we're gonna get Ellie out o' that 'orrible prison.'

'Well, I fink the information should 'ave bin 'anded over ter the police in the first place,' he told her. 'It's bloody stupid you lot playin' detectives. The bobbies could find that bloke in no time whatsoever. Besides, yer not s'posed ter take the law inter yer own 'ands. What 'appens if young Billy an' Danny knock 'im about too much an' the bloke lands up in 'orspital? They'll get nicked fer sure.'

'They'll only frighten 'im,' Maisie said defensively.

'Yeah, I know all about that,' Fred snorted. 'Those two lads won't mess about, an' Billy Sullivan's a mad sod if ever there was one.'

'Well, it looks like Carrie'll be goin' ter the police now anyway,' Maisie said ruefully as the band began to return to the orchestra pit.

When the show was over the two stepped aboard the number 68 tram with Maisie still brooding. Fred was in a happy frame of mind, however, and he turned to her and said, 'D'yer know, luv, we ought ter do this more often. It makes a nice change ter get away from the street fer a few hours.'

Maisie nodded. 'Yeah, I s'pose yer right,' she replied in a vacant tone.

'Must 'ave bin a good six months since the last time we see a show,' Fred remarked.

'All o' that.'

'Might 'ave bin longer.'

'About May, I fink,' Maisie said, glancing out of the window.

'Come ter fink of it, it was the middle o' July,' Fred said. 'I remember 'cos it was the night o' the fire. Don't yer remember when we walked down the turnin' an' saw the fire engine? The firemen were still dousin' the smoulderin' sacks.'

570

Suddenly Maisie gripped Fred's arm tightly. 'What time was we in that pub last time we went out?' she asked urgently.

'I dunno. The show started at 'alf-seven,' Fred replied. 'We left there about twenty past. Why?'

'Don't yer see?' Maisie said quickly. 'If that Talbot bloke got chucked out o' the pub before we left at twenty past seven, 'ow the bloody 'ell could 'e see Ellie Roffey comin' from the yard just after seven?'

'Yer right,' Fred said smiling. 'That's somefing ter tell the coppers about.'

On Sunday evening the Page Street women were gathered together once more in Carrie's parlour. 'Well, we tried our best,' Florrie said sadly.

'I'm only sorry my Billy didn't get 'is 'ands on that whoreson,' Sadie remarked.

Carrie tried not to be downhearted as she sat with the women. 'Anyway, at least we've got somefink ter give ter the police now,' she said hopefully. 'If the publican identifies Talbot then it'll prove 'e was lyin' on oath. That should be enough ter get Ellie out o' prison.'

'When yer gonna see 'em?' Sadie asked.

'I'll go soon as I can termorrer mornin',' Carrie replied, sipping her tea thoughtfully.

Maisie looked pleased with herself, but she was soon deflated by Florrie's cutting remark. 'Pity yer didn't remember where yer'd seen 'im a bit sooner,' she said.

'Well, if the rest of us 'ad paid attention at the trial an' remembered 'is address we wouldn't 'ave 'ad this trouble, would we?' Maisie replied sharply.

Carrie raised her hands. 'Look, it's no good talkin' about what could 'ave bin,' she said quickly. 'We've just gotta pray she gets out quickly.'

'S'posin' the police can't find this Talbot man?' Maudie said.

'Gawd a'mighty, Maudie, why don't yer look on the bright side fer once?' Sadie admonished her.

Florrie took a pinch of snuff and when she had sneezed loudly into a discoloured handkerchief she looked around at the others. 'I fink we should be considerin' what sort of 'omecomin' we're gonna put on fer Ellie,' she remarked.

'Why don't we get the church ter let us use Murphy's?' Sadie suggested. 'We could 'ave a good ole knees-up there.'

'We'd 'ave ter borrer a pianer from somewhere,' Maisie said.

'What about Alice Johnson? She's got a pianer,' Maudie chipped in.

''Ow the bleedin' 'ell are we gonna get it round ter Wilson Street?' Sadie asked her.

'That's no trouble. I'll get one o' the men ter cart it round there,' Carrie said.

Fresh tea was passed round and the women sat making plans for Ellie's release, while above, in the small back bedroom, Rachel was busy with her own plans.

Frank Galloway had purposely stayed away from the yard all week with the excuse that he was suffering with his stomach. The business was being looked after by the yard foreman, who was aided by the new clerk and overseen by the aged George Galloway who looked in now and then, walking slowly with the aid of a silver-tipped walking stick. On two occasions Theo Harrison had called around to ask Frank Galloway's whereabouts, only to be told by the harassed clerk that he was off sick. Harrison's remark that he was going to be a lot worse very shortly was passed on to the older Galloway who in turn contacted his son by phone to ask just what was going on.

Frank Galloway wished he had given Carrie Talbot's address. He began to despair over the women's delay in locating him, which meant that Theo Harrison would be at liberty for longer, and was not encouraged by Peggy's depressing information that Theo had taken to carrying an axe tucked down his belt and was threatening to bury it in Frank's head. Peggy herself was now temporarily installed at her sister's home in Surrey and had told Frank that he should stay away from her for the time being. She had also added that her personal account had been stopped by Theo and that her aggrieved husband was intending to seek a divorce, naming Frank as the co-respondent.

Frank Galloway began to look over his shoulder as he left the house for his morning papers, believing that Theo Harrison would no doubt be using his private investigator to discover his whereabouts. Bella would soon find out about his infidelity, and she would get wild and insist he leave the place. It was all so worrying, he thought anxiously, picking up the telephone and consulting a small address book. He had originally passed on the addresses of Talbot and his cohort Bennett to Theo with the information that the two were reliable scoundrels and would do anything for a price. Now there was no time to lose, and he just hoped that his involvement in the affair would not be uncovered.

Billy Sullivan and Danny Tanner walked through the maze of backstreets behind the Elephant and Castle late on Monday evening. When they turned into Corporation Street and glanced up at the house numbers Danny took Billy by the arm. 'There's number twelve,' he said, pointing across the turning. 'Now look, Billy. We gotta do this right. We don't mention money, remember? All we do is be friendly an' look like we're a bit green.'

Billy grinned as he reached up for the knocker. 'I 'ope they fall fer it,' he said quietly.

The loud knock brought no response from inside and Billy began to look disappointed. ''Ave we got the right address?' he asked.

Danny nodded. 'I'd jus' popped in the office ter see Carrie when she picked up the phone. I saw 'er write it down.'

Billy brought the doorknocker down hard once more and then they heard someone moving about inside. The door finally opened and they were confronted by a heavily built man with a stubbled face and bleary eyes. 'What d'yer want?' he asked brusquely.

'Are yer Mr Talbot?' Danny asked amiably.

'Nah.'

'Are yer Mr Bennett then?'

'What d'yer want wiv 'im?'

'We've come about the stuff,' Danny said.

'Yer better come in,' the man said gruffly, leading the way up the flight of steep stairs to a room at the back of the house.

Danny and Billy were left standing alone in the dingy room for a few minutes, then their unwilling host walked back into the room accompanied by a taller man with dark wavy hair and narrow-set eyes. 'I'm Talbot,' he announced. 'I got the message yer was comin'. Sit down an' we'll talk.'

Billy sat down alongside Danny on a dilapidated settee which had springs poking out from the upholstery, while Talbot pulled up a chair and motioned to Bennett. 'Get us some glasses an' the bottle,' he told him.

When the slouching figure left the room Talbot pulled out a packet of Woodbines and handed them around. ''Ow much yer got?' he asked.

'There's two 'undred cases,' Danny replied quickly. 'Fifty salmon, seventy corned beef and the rest are peaches. They're all sixteen ounce an' two dozen ter the case.'

Talbot stroked his chin, eyeing the two thoughtfully. 'What yer askin' fer 'em?' he enquired.

Danny shrugged his shoulders, trying to look unsure of himself. 'I dunno really,' he replied. 'They're straight off the barge an' we can't 'ave 'em stored at our gaff too long. If we knocked 'em out separately we could get a decent price, but we'd sooner drop the price a bit an' get rid of 'em in one go.'

'Well, yer'd 'ave ter drop it quite a bit in that case,' Talbot said. 'There's always a risk in 'andlin' bulk stuff an' we'd 'ave ter get transport.'

'No fear o' that,' Danny cut in. 'I can get yer transport, providin' yer take the lot.'

Bennett walked into the room carrying glasses and a bottle of whisky and when Talbot had passed the drinks round he leaned back in his chair and eyed the two visitors. 'Give us some idea of what yer askin',' he pressed.

'I dunno really,' Danny said, glancing at Billy for inspiration.

'I dunno neivver,' Billy added, looking even more puzzled than his friend. 'What d'yer reckon?'

Talbot drained his glass in one gulp. 'Look, I gotta 'ave some idea,' he said impatiently.

'P'raps yer could come round an' see the stuff,' Danny said hopefully. 'If yer make us a decent offer we could get an 'orse-an'-cart right away an' we'd 'elp yer load it. We can't leave it at our place too long, yer see.'

Talbot tried to contain his enthusiasm as he poured himself another drink. They were obviously two idiots who did not have a clue and were worried about the amount of stuff they had filched. 'All right then, I'll come round,' he said after a moment or two. 'What time?'

'Can yer make it termorrer night? About seven if yer can,' Danny replied.

'Right then, let's drink ter that,' Talbot said, reaching for the bottle.

'Fanks, but it's all right,' Danny said, holding up his hands. 'That's very strong stuff.'

Talbot gave the two a condescending look as they got up from the settee. 'Give us the directions then an' me an' Kenny'll pop round,' he said.

When they had left the house and were walking along the narrow turning Billy turned to his friend. 'Yer could 'ave took that ovver drink,' he said.

Danny grinned. 'I wanted us ter look a right couple o' dopes,' he replied.

'Well, yer certainly done that,' Billy said, returning the grin. 'I bet that Talbot finks 'e's on a winner wiv us two. I 'ope 'e don't smell a rat.'

Danny shook his head. ''E'll be there termorrer. I could see the pound notes flashin' in 'is eyes.'

Chapter Thirty-nine

Frank Galloway was feeling decidedly nervous and glanced around behind him as he walked into the Wilson Street yard on Tuesday morning. George Galloway was sitting in the office chair, and his face grew dark as he eyed his son.

'Now what the 'ell's goin' on, Frank?' he growled. 'There's two lorries orf the road an' the yard foreman tells me yer've not left 'im wiv any instructions. Then I've 'ad Adams whinin' about this bloke who keeps comin' in 'ere askin' fer yer. What yer bin up to?'

Frank sat down in the chair facing him. 'Surely Jackman can handle a breakdown or two without everything having to be spelt out to him,' he replied irritably.

'I'm not so concerned about Jackman,' George growled. 'I'm more concerned about this bloke who keeps on comin' in 'ere askin' fer yer. 'E won't give 'is name or anyfing. Phelps told me 'e's a nasty bit o' goods. Yer better tell me, Frank, I can't do anyfing if I don't know the score.'

Frank sighed deeply. There was nothing the old man could do to help him. No one could. This was one mess he would have to sort out for himself, and if that Bradley woman had acted on his last phone call to her then everything might be all right. She had been less difficult than he had expected, and although she was now going to take the information he had given her to the police she had said she wouldn't divulge the source. She had also told him that she had proof of Talbot's whereabouts on the night of the fire and that would help speed things up. The sooner Theo was behind bars the better for him, and Peggy. She was becoming a nervous wreck.

'This character who keeps asking for me is deranged,' Frank told his father. 'He's labouring under the misapprehension that I had something to do with luring his wife away. Good Lord, I've only met the woman once, and that was on business.'

'Well, yer wanna chuck 'im out the yard next time 'e calls,' the old man said sharply. 'Tell 'im that if 'e shows 'is face 'ere again yer'll phone the police. If I see 'im 'e'll feel the weight o' me stick over 'is 'ead.'

Frank prayed that Theo would not make an appearance while his father was in the yard. 'Don't get yourself upset, Dad,' he replied. 'Let the yard man handle him. Now what about a drink? I've got some good news. I think we'll get that brewery contract. My contact tells me our tender was the best.'

George Galloway looked relieved as he took the glass of Scotch from Frank and sat fingering the gold medallion on his watch chain. 'So we bettered that Bradley woman?'

Frank nodded. 'She won't get this contract, and you can take that as definite,' he said, smiling smugly.

George Galloway stood up wearily and took hold of his stick. 'I'm orf ter see somebody,' he said in a tired voice. 'I take it yer gonna be in fer the day?'

Frank nodded, but as soon as the old man had left he went out to talk to Jackman the yard man. Ten minutes later he left the yard, glancing about to left and right as though expecting to be followed. When he reached the end of the turning he glanced behind him quickly, and after reassuring himself that there was no one dogging his footsteps he crossed the road and hurried along to London Bridge Station.

Harold Simpson was no novice when it came to the intricacies of following people around. He had spent many years in the police force and the last four years with a firm of enquiry agents who specialised in obtaining evidence in divorce cases, and as he stepped from a doorway and watched Frank Galloway cross Jamaica Road Harold smiled to himself craftily.

Danny sat together with Billy Sullivan in the changing room at Murphy's Gym, eyeing the wall clock anxiously. Both men wore heavy woollen jumpers and their fists were strapped with bandages.

'The kids won't be arrivin' till eight so we've got an hour, providin' Talbot an' that ovver dopey git arrive on time,' Danny said, looking up at the wall clock once more.

Billy grinned evilly. 'Yer sure we ought ter deal wiv Bennett first?' he asked.

Danny Tanner nodded. 'I fink Bennett's the best bet. Besides, 'e was the one who actually set fire ter the place. Once we get 'im babblin' we're 'alf-way there wiv Talbot. That one won't be so easy. 'E looks 'ard, an' 'e won't panic too quickly. After all, 'e did front it out in the witness box.'

At five minutes past seven Talbot and Bennett walked up the path and knocked on the oaken front door. Billy slipped the bolts and pulled the heavy door open. 'Come in, gents, we've bin waitin' fer yer,' he said, hiding a grin.

The two men walked into the hallway, looking around curiously as Billy led the way into the main hall. 'In 'ere,' he said, pointing to the changing room.

Danny got up and held out his hand. 'Glad yer could come,' he said cheerfully. 'I've got a list o' some prices 'ere.'

Talbot ignored the outstretched hand. 'Right now, I've . . .'

'Look, while we're talkin' my pal's gonna take the covers off the stuff. Can yer mate give 'im an 'and?' Danny interrupted him.

Talbot glanced down at the sheaf of papers in Danny's hand. 'Yeah, all right,' he replied.

Billy led the way out of the changing room, closing the door behind him, and led Bennett towards the centre of the gymnasium, stopping beside the ringed area. 'Ever bin in a ring?' he asked, grinning wickedly.

'Where's the stuff?' Bennett asked, looking around.

Suddenly Billy swung a hard punch into Bennett's stomach and the man doubled up, gasping for breath with his eyes popping. Billy followed with a downward punch to the side of his head that flattened the bulky man. He rolled on to his side, pain and shock showing on his flushed face as he tried to stagger to his feet. Billy brought his knee up sharply and caught him full in the face, throwing him backwards. Blood ran from his nose and he was gasping for breath

'What d'yer start that fire for?' Billy asked, his clenched fist poised in front of Bennett's bruised face.

'What fire?' Bennett spluttered.

Billy hit him full in the face and the man's head jerked back.

'Now look, I can go on like this all night,' he growled. 'I'm gonna ask yer once more. Why d'yer start the fire at the sorters' yard?'

Bennett shook his head and suddenly made a dive for Billy's legs. Billy's kick landed on his ear and he fell sideways clasping his head.

'I don't know nuffink about a fire,' he groaned.

Billy took him by the coat collar and dragged him towards the wall. Bennett lay in a heap, fearfully watching while his tormentor took down a stretching spring from a hook and unclipped one of the handgrips.

'Now I'm gonna give yer one last chance,' Billy snarled, holding the remaining handgrip tightly in his clenched fist. 'This spring's gonna strip the flesh from yer back an' I'm gonna take no notice o' yer screams.'

'It was Talbot, not me!' Bennett whined.

Billy brought the steel spring down hard and drew a scream of agony as the back of the man's coat ripped. He lifted the spring again and Bennett rolled over on to his side.

'It was Talbot! 'E told me ter do it,' he groaned. 'Ask 'im, can't yer?'

When Billy had left the changing room Danny threw down the papers and stood between Talbot and the door. 'Right, now you an' me 'ave gotta 'ave a little talk,' he said between clenched teeth.

Talbot saw the look in Danny's eyes and stepped back a pace. 'What d'yer mean?' he asked, surprise showing on his face.

'There's a good friend o' the people round 'ere who's rottin' in 'Olloway because you told a pack o' lies at 'er trial,' Danny snarled. 'Right now my pal Danny's sortin' out yer mate. What I'm gonna do is knock the livin' daylights out o' yer unless yer come up wiv the trufe.'

Talbot backed away from him, realising that he had been lured into a trap. 'Yer not gonna touch me,' he said, his voice shaking.

'Oh, is that so?' Danny growled, moving forward.

Suddenly Talbot produced a long, thin-bladed knife from the back of his belt and held it menacingly in front of him. 'Come any nearer an' I'll put this in yer,' he snarled.

A scream sounded from outside and Talbot backed against the wall. 'Yer not touchin' me,' he said in a dry voice.

Danny moved forward slowly, his eyes never leaving the knife. 'Put that down, Talbot, or I'll take it off yer an' cut yer froat wiv it,' he growled.

For a few minutes the two glared at each other, like two animals about to lock into a fight to the death. Suddenly there was a scuffling sound outside the room and then the door burst open. Billy had the terrified Bennett by the coat collar and when he saw Talbot holding the knife he pulled Bennett in front of him and held him with his arm curled around the man's throat.

'Stand back, Danny,' he said urgently, slowly advancing on the snarling Talbot.

'Mind 'im,' Danny warned, but at that moment Billy pushed his human shield straight at the knife-wielding thug.

Bennett fell forward, then with a groan reeled back and collapsed, holding his midriff. Blood oozed from between his fingers as he lay groaning and for a second or two no one moved. Then Talbot was on his knees, the knife forgotten as he cradled the injured man's head in his arms.

'It was an accident, Kenny, I swear! I wouldn't 'urt yer, yer know I wouldn't,' he groaned.

Billy picked up the knife while Danny bent over the ashen-faced Bennett. 'It's bad. We'll 'ave ter get 'im ter the 'ospital,' he muttered to Billy. 'Lock Talbot in the cupboard an' then phone fer an ambulance. I'll see what I can do ter stop the bleedin'.'

Chief Inspector Green sat at his desk studying a pile of papers while the two young men sat in front of him, solemn-faced and silent. Presently he looked up and eyed the two in turn.

'Well, it seems that Kenneth Bennett is making a good recovery,' he said, a smile breaking out on his wide face. 'The wound was serious enough, but he'll live. Bennett's given us a full statement which implicates Talbot and in which he says that the injury was purely accidental. For that you can thank your lucky stars, both of you.'

'Even if it wasn't accidental, we didn't do it,' Billy said quickly.

The inspector locked his fingers together and rested his elbows on the desk. 'Supposing Talbot had said you stabbed Bennett and Bennett himself had corroborated his testimony?' he said. 'Where would that leave you two? In the mire, I should think. You see, that's the danger of playing coppers. What you two should have done was to hand them both over to us after apprehending them with the minimum of force. As it happens, Bennett looks like he walked out in front of a train. As for Talbot, he's so remorseful for injuring his pal that he made a statement without any form of pressure on our part. Now with those statements and the information about Talbot's whereabouts on the night of the fire I should think we can start to set the ball rolling to get Mrs Roffey released from prison.'

'Billy won't get charged fer beltin' Bennett, will 'e?' Danny asked.

'Belting? Is that what you call it?' the inspector said sarcastically. 'I would have thought hammering would have been a more apt description. But no, to answer your question, he won't. Bennett made no complaint, and by the time his stomach wound is healed there won't be any facial marks left to influence a judge, other than a slightly crooked nose.'

'What about the factory owner?' Danny asked.

'Ah, yes, our Mr Harrison,' the inspector replied, looking down at his notes for a few moments. 'Well, I can tell you that we are looking for him. We will be able to cope by the way, thank you very much. Harrison will be charged, of course. The rest is up to the court. However, there is one thing I'd like to ask before you gentlemen leave. You stated that it was you who apprehended Bennett, Mr Sullivan?'

'That's right,' Billy replied, frowning.

'Well, I got some dirty looks from the surgeon. I believe he felt that we inflicted the injuries. What exactly did you hit him with, a girder?'

'Nah, 'e slipped over,' Billy replied, a smile playing around his mouth. ''E must 'ave caught 'imself on somefing or the ovver.'

Harold Simpson had done his job well, and after reporting back to his client was rewarded with a fat bonus. Theo now felt ready to exact his revenge on the man who had stolen his wife's affections. He shut up the house and went to his garden shed before he departed, taking up a sharp axe which he tucked into the back of his belt. Ilford was unfamiliar territory to him but he was certain that he would soon find the man and deal with him, once and for all. Later there would be time to deal with his fickle, lying cheat of a wife, he vowed.

Theo boarded the train at Broad Street and as he leaned back in his seat he could feel the comforting pressure of the sharpened axe against his back. What pleasure it would give him to sink it into the skull of that no-good cheat he had once thought was his friend. It would be in all the papers but no one would suspect him, except maybe the investigator, but then he would respect a client's confidence, Theo thought. No doubt the police would be baffled, and they would most probably seek a local maniac. It would be exciting reading the account of the Ilford axe murder in the Sunday papers. He would have to remember not to leave the axe in Galloway's head though. Better to yank it out and throw it in the river.

The train jerked to a halt at Ilford Station and Theo stepped down, walking swiftly to the exit. There was no time to lose if he was going to do the deed properly. He had to find Primrose Gardens and then return via the river before it got too late.

'Primrose Gardens? Yessir. Take the road ter yer left an' after about a mile or so you'll see it. There's a church on the corner.'

Theo thanked the porter and suddenly felt a little uneasy. It wasn't a good omen to have a church nearby, he thought, but never mind, it couldn't be helped.

Primrose Gardens was a quiet suburban avenue with well-tended front gardens before gabled houses. Theo held his head low as he passed the church and walked into the leafy turning. Towards the end of the avenue he counted the numbers along to a smart house a little way ahead, and when he drew near consulted a slip of paper which he took from his top pocket. Yes, number 20. Mustn't make a mistake, he thought. Wouldn't be very nice if some old gentleman opened the door and got chopped up. That fornicating excuse for a man was going to get his comeuppance though.

Theo was about to step on to the path when a police officer seemed to appear from nowhere behind him. 'Evenin', sir. Lookin' fer somebody, are we?'

Theo cursed his luck. 'It's that church,' he muttered.

'I beg yer pardon, sir?'

Theo looked at the police officer. He looked a kindly soul. I bet he never had any trouble with his wife, he thought. 'I'm visiting a Mr Galloway,' he said, feeling the axe against his spine.

'Are yer, sir? And what is your name, may I ask?'

'Theodore P. Harrison.'

'And what is the purpose of your visit?' the constable asked, swaying back and forth on his heels.

'I've come to kill him,' Theo said quietly.

The police officer eyed him suspiciously. 'And 'ow d'yer propose ter kill 'im?' he asked a little patronisingly.

'With this,' Theo replied, taking out the sharp axe from his belt.

The policeman stepped back a pace. 'Now let me have that instrument, if yer please, sir.'

'Why? Would you like to kill him for me?' Theo asked.

'I don't think so, sir. Now come along,' the policeman said, holding his hands out to placate him. 'We'll take yer down ter the station. Yer'll get a nice bed fer the night, an' if we 'urry there'll be some supper too, I've no doubt.'

Theo slowly handed over the axe and allowed himself to be taken by the arm. 'Tell me, officer. Is your wife true to you?' he asked.

'I'm not married, sir,' the constable replied, feeling suddenly sad for the strange character with wide, staring eyes.

'I'm married,' Theo told him. 'My wife's been seeing another man. I was on my way to kill him when you stopped me. Are you sure you wouldn't like to do it for me? I could pay you well.'

'No, I'd sooner not, if yer don't mind.'

They reached the police station in time for supper, and one hour later Theo Harrison was sleeping like a baby in a police cell.

On a mild evening during the first week in April a car drove into Wilson Street and pulled up outside Murphy's Gym. Ellie Roffey looked pale and drawn as she stepped out to loud cheering and was embraced by the aged Florrie, who handed her a large bouquet of roses. Inside the hall more people had gathered and when Ellie walked in she was mobbed by many well-wishers, all eager to shake her hand. The boxing ring had been taken down and high on the far wall a bunting read, 'Welcome Home, Ellie'.

The piano was playing and Maisie got up to dance the jig with Broomhead Smith, much to the annoyance of Alice Johnson who sat biting the inside of her cheek. Florrie was feeling tired. She sat for a while talking to Ellie about the campaigner's time in Holloway, while Maudie sat with Sadie and some of the street women sipping beer and munching cheese sandwiches, all of which had been supplied by Father Kerrigan.

Billy Sullivan had been in regular work for the past few weeks and he had managed to buy himself a new shirt to go to the party. His wife Annie looked radiant as she walked with him into the hall wearing her new dress, her four children toddling along at her side. Danny and Iris Tanner followed them in, Danny holding his two older sons by the hand and Iris carrying the youngest. Danny and Billy both went over to speak with Ellie who had been told of their part in her release, and she embraced them warmly.

'Well, I 'ope yer gonna take it a bit easier from now on,' Danny remarked with a big grin. 'An' don't let anybody see yer next time yer burn somebody's yard down.'

'Bloody cheek!' Ellie replied laughing. 'Anyway, I don't fink I'll be doin' much around 'ere from now on,' she said, winking slyly at Florrie.

'I don't fink yer gonna 'ave time fer anyfink,' Florrie said to her as soon as the men had left. 'What wiv all that prison reform work yer said yer gonna take up.'

The piano player was getting into his stride, and as he banged out his repertoire of popular tunes

Broomhead's voice rang out loudly.

'Yer know, that man o' mine's got a lovely voice, even if I say so meself,' Alice said to Sadie Sullivan.

'Yeah, it is a bit strong,' Sadie replied. 'I 'ope 'e don't want payin'.'

Carrie arrived with her mother and her daughter Rachel, who looked stunning in her pale green dress with her long flaxen hair arranged on top of her head. Nellie took Ellie's hand and planted a kiss on her cheek and then after chatting for a short while she sought her friends from Page Street. Carrie stayed talking with Ellie while Rachel slipped away as soon as she spotted Danny.

'Uncle Danny, 'ow d'yer get ter the Isle o' Dogs?' she asked him.

'What d'yer wanna go there for?' Danny enquired, grinning.

'Oh, it's not me, it's a friend o' mine,' Rachel replied.

'Well, it's a long way by bus,' he said. 'Yer gotta change twice. Besides it's not the sort o' place fer young ladies ter be goin' on their own. Tell 'er from me.'

The evening was going well and one or two of the young lads asked Rachel for a dance. Carrie was sitting with Annie and Danny on a wooden bench and she smiled to see the happiness reflected on her daughter's face. Danny saw the look in his sister's eyes and he touched her arm. 'I remember you lookin' like that when you were 'er age,' he remarked. 'I used ter fink yer was the most pretty gel in the street, even if yer were me big sister.'

Carrie grinned and kissed his cheek fondly. 'Yer know, Danny, I worry fer that one,' she said quietly. 'Rachel's missed out on a lot, what wiv 'er farvver dyin' the way 'e did, an' 'er 'avin' ter work at the yard. I sometimes wonder if I've done right by 'er.'

Danny slipped his arm around Carrie and gave her a big hug. 'Look, Sis, it couldn't 'ave bin easy fer yer but yer've done right. Yer've done right by all of us, an' one day it's all gonna be Rachel's. She's 'appy enough, jus' look at 'er.'

Rachel was laughing as a young lad twirled her around in the centre of the floor and Carrie nodded. 'I 'ope she is, Danny. She's bin very secretive lately though. She spends a lot o' time in 'er room.'

'It was the same wiv you if I remember rightly,' Danny told her. 'Mum used ter say you were a dreamer. She despaired fer yer at times, so Dad told me not long before 'e died.'

Carrie looked down at her feet for a few moments. 'I wish Dad could 'ave seen our Charlie once more before 'e died. 'E was always talkin' about 'im towards the end.'

Danny nodded. 'I don't know if any of us will ever see Charlie again,' he said sadly. ''E may decide ter come back 'ome one day, who knows?'

'Charlie's built a new life fer 'imself,' Carrie replied. ''E's got a wife an' kids. Can yer expect 'im ter bring 'em 'alf-way round the world jus' fer us, 'specially now that Dad's dead? 'E'll be faced wiv all the bad memories too.'

'But we're 'is family, Carrie. It's got ter count fer somefink,' Danny said quietly.

'Charlie said goodbye fer ever when 'e boarded that train at Waterloo, Danny. 'E knew we'd never ferget 'im,' Carrie almost whispered, feeling the sadness gathering in her chest.

'It would be lovely fer Muvver ter see 'im once more though,' Danny said.

'Mum said 'er goodbyes too,' she told him, remembering so vividly the day that Charlie left. No one would ever know what was in their mother's heart that morning, and perhaps it was just as well, Carrie thought.

Chapter Forty

In her small bedroom at the top of the stairs Rachel leaned back on her pillow and sighed deeply. She had been writing another of her many letters and her eyes felt tired. Below in the bright cobbled yard it was quiet. Occasionally she heard the stamping of horses and their blowing into the troughs but on these Sunday mornings there was little to disturb the quietness of the house. Carrie had gone with Nellie to church, something that the old lady had become accustomed to doing during the last year. Rachel knew that they would probably be away from the house for at least two hours and it gave her the chance to make some progress with her letter.

It was the early spring of '37 and almost a year now since she had made that first journey to the East End in search of Joe Maitland. It had been difficult to arrange, she recalled. Her mother would have forbidden her to go to that citadel on the Isle of Dogs had she known, and Rachel had had to make excuses for her day's absence from home. The Salvation Army people there were very nice though and they had been honest with her about the limited possibilities of tracing Joe. She had given them all the information she could and explained the reasons for wanting to find him. They had been very understanding, and since that one visit she had kept in touch with them by writing letters secretly in the seclusion of her tiny bedroom, with the replies sent to her friend Amy Brody, Danny's young sister-in-law who had been sworn to secrecy.

The last letter she had received was very hopeful. A man of the right age had visited a soup kitchen only a week ago and had been called Joe by one or two of his acquaintances. When the Salvationist who was on duty at the time tried to question him he became evasive and left soon after, so the letter said. There was no more, however. The men who called him Joe had said on prompting that he was a 'will-o'-the-wisp' character who appeared and disappeared like the wind. He never seemed to stay in one place for very long, but his friends did say that he told them once he often earned a few coppers doing 'penny-up-the-hill'. The letter had gone on to explain that the expression referred to men who helped the fish porters push their laden barrows up the steep cobbled lanes from the fish market in Billingsgate to the waiting vehicles in Eastcheap, which ran parallel.

Rachel closed her eyes and recalled the cold, silent morning a few days before when she had sneaked out of the house and let herself out of the yard as dawn was breaking. She had caught the early tram to London Bridge and walked over the windy Thames to the fish market, where she had wandered around for an hour, hoping against hope that she would spot Joe. It had been in vain, and when she returned at eight o'clock her mother was frantic with worry. The excuse she made that she couldn't sleep and wanted to get some early morning air had sounded feeble, and she knew that her mother was beginning to worry about her secretive ways.

Rachel stared at the recollections she had just put down on paper to her confidante at the Salvation Army citadel and ended by saying she would try again to visit the fish market as soon as possible. This time though she would try another way, although she did not include her intentions in the letter.

The day dragged on interminably and when the Sunday evening meal was over Rachel stretched wearily and said that she needed an early night. Carrie and Nellie exchanged glances, and when Rachel had kissed them goodnight and gone to bed Carrie turned to her mother with a frown.

'Yer know, Mum, that child is worrying me,' she declared. 'She shouldn't be so tired this early. She's become so secretive too. I don't know what's the matter wiv 'er, I'm sure I don't.'

Nellie put down her piece of embroidery and peered at Carrie over the top of her metal-rimmed glasses. 'There's nuffink wrong wiv that gel that won't right itself before long,' she said. 'It's 'er age. It was the same wiv you. She's growin' up, Carrie, be patient.'

Up in the tiny front bedroom Rachel was making her plans, and when Carrie looked in before she retired for the night she heard her daughter's even breathing and decided that she was fast asleep. Rachel waited until she heard the door click shut and then she sat up in bed. She knew that she would have to be patient. It would take some time for her mother to settle, and if her acquaintance at the cafe in Eastcheap had explained things properly there was no desperate hurry anyway.

'Those "penny-up-the-'ill" men are always in 'ere,' he had told her in answer to her persistent questions. 'They earn all right – well, some of 'em do. They spend most o' their earnin's on cups o' tea but they keep a few pennies fer their cider. They sleep rough down at the market an' the stench o' their fires fair makes yer sick. They use ole fish boxes, yer see.'

The thought of tramping around that fish market did not worry Rachel. She had learned that lorries and horse carts started to arrive a little after midnight and in the early hours it was a bustling place as the fish merchants opened for business. She intended to arrive there as soon after twelve as possible and maybe look for Joe at the camp fires.

At ten minutes past midnight she slipped into her long coat and wrapped a woollen scarf loosely around her neck. With extreme care she crept down the stairs, holding her breath in case the creaking disturbed her mother or her grandmother, and then crossed the yard and unlocked the wicket-gate. The harsh grating of the hinges sounded extra loud in the stillness of the night, and it was not until she had locked the gate after her and set off along the empty Salmon Lane that she began to breathe easier. There was no going back now, she knew, and her heart fluttered excitedly at the task ahead. Joe was out there somewhere. He would come back with her, she told herself. He just had to. Surely he could be made to understand what his long absence was doing to her mother, to both of them.

Jamaica Road was empty except for one or two people who hurried along, coming or going from their night shifts. The all-night tram trundled past but Rachel let it go. There was a full moon lighting her way and the air was surprisingly mild. As she reached the foot of Tower Bridge she glanced towards the tall stone towers bleached white in the moonlight. It would be just as quick to travel over the bridge, she thought, but she knew that the City policemen patrolled it throughout the night. One of them might ask her what a young girl was doing out on her own at that hour and he might get someone to take her home. Better to cross the Thames at London Bridge, she decided. As she quickly walked along Tooley Street the deserted wharves looked eerie in the moonlight and she was glad when she finally reached the foot of London Bridge. With a silent prayer she set off over the dark, swift water of the river, her hurrying footsteps echoing on the flintstone walkway.

The market was lined with lorries and horse carts when Rachel turned into Monument Street and walked beneath the tall fire memorial topped with its gilded iron cap of flame. The pungent smell and the increasing noise as shutters went up and traders shouted cheered her and she set off along the brightly lit lower stretch which backed on to the river. Alleyways were piled high with empty boxes and here and there a group of carmen stood talking together. Rachel tried to disregard the bawdy remarks as she passed one group but felt her face flushing hot. A drunken man lurched towards her and as she halted in her tracks he staggered back into a doorway and mumbled some unintelligible remark. A scruffy cat was picking at a fishhead in a passageway, and a little deeper into the shadows two men were arguing and struggling with each other over a bottle of cider which they both had hold of.

Rachel purposely crossed the greasy cobbled lane to avoid passing by a coffee stall and as she did so saw a group of men sitting around on boxes just inside an alleyway. There was a lighted brazier giving off clouds of smoke and as she stood trying to catch a glimpse of the men's faces one of them saw her. He staggered to his feet and came out of the alley, swaying and tottering with a leer on his smoke-blackened face. ''Ave a drink, girlie,' he slurred. 'C'mon an' 'ave a drink wiv yer ole friend Jim.'

Rachel hurried off, looking over her shoulder fearfully in case the man was following her. Further along the lane a fish merchant was lifting a huge shutter. He noticed her as she drew near. 'Careful, young lady, it's slippery just 'ere,' he said, smiling at her.

Rachel returned a faint smile and he looked closely at her. 'This is a bit off the beaten track fer a pretty gel like you, ain't it?' he asked.

The man was tall, with a wide girth partly hidden under his clean white smock. He wore a flat-topped fish porter's hat with a wide brim. His face was ruddy, and his pleasant smile seemed to reassure Rachel.

'I'm lookin' fer somebody,' she told him.

'Well, there's many a lost soul frequents this market,' he said.

'The man I'm lookin' for is called Joe Maitland,' she informed him.

'They're all called Joes an' Jims in the market, luv,' he told her. 'Nobody gets called by their full moniker. Now yer see them lads over there? Them what are waitin' fer a few shekels?'

Rachel followed his gaze to the other side of the road and saw a group of scruffily dressed men standing beneath a canopy.

'There's a few Joes over there,' he said grinning. 'But I don't s'pose any o' them would be your Joe.'

Rachel smiled and made to walk on but the fish merchant planted himself directly in front of her. 'Tell me, luv, is the Joe you're lookin' for a kinsman? Is 'e family?'

She nodded. 'Sort of.'

'Is 'e your beau?'

Rachel felt her face flush. 'My mum's,' she said quietly.

The man gave her a huge grin and beckoned her to follow him. Rachel hesitated but he was persistent. 'C'mon, luv, yer quite safe,' he said. 'I want yer ter meet my ole china.'

She followed him into the open-fronted warehouse and he suddenly whistled loudly through his teeth. 'Oi! Come 'ere, Lofty. I wanna ask yer somefink fer a friend o' mine.'

A tall, gangling fish porter strolled up and eyed Rachel warily. 'Yeah?'

'Lofty knows all the "penny-up-the-'ill" men, don't yer, Lofty?'

The tall man nodded. 'I know most of 'em, yeah,' he said in a tired voice.

'What about a Joe Maitland?'

'I know a couple o' Joes, but we don't get ter know their full monikers,' he answered.

'That's what I told 'er,' the big man said. 'What's 'e look like, luv?'

'Well, 'e's tall an' pretty broad, an' 'e's got black wavy 'air. 'E speaks quietly an' 'e . . .'

'That could fit anybody,' the tall one cut in. 'I tell yer what, though, it could be Big Joe. What d'yer reckon, Solly?'

'Yeah, I s'pose it could fit 'im,' Solly replied, stroking his chin. 'Now I tell yer what yer do. Carry on along 'ere till yer come ter the coffee stall. Big Joe usually uses that stall. Failin' that, try the flea-pit.'

'I beg yer pardon?' Rachel said, frowning.

'Sorry, luv. It's an alleyway jus' past the coffee stall on the same side. Most o' the "up-the-'ill" lads kip down there.'

Rachel smiled her thanks to both men and hurried away, hoping against hope that this would be the end of her long quest.

Solly watched her go and then turned to his friend. 'It's what I've always said, Lofty. There's a tragic story be'ind most o' them dregs o' 'umanity what pitch their weight be'ind our barrers,' he remarked with feeling.

There were only two old men standing at the coffee stall and Rachel walked on past. She spotted the alleyway, and when she glanced along its dark, filthy length she saw a few men sitting hunched together beside a smouldering brazier. Without thinking she slowly passed between the dank brick walls into the shadows, stepping quietly along the stinking cobbles of the alley

597

to look at them. There were four men sitting with their heads bowed and they hardly seemed to notice her presence. One looked up vaguely and Rachel saw that he was an old man. 'I'm lookin' fer a bloke called Joe Maitland,' she said in a voice she hardly recognised.

'Maitland, yer say? Never 'eard of 'im, miss,' the man croaked.

'They call 'im Big Joe,' Rachel said, blinking against the pungent smoke.

'Oi, Big Joe. Somebody wants yer,' the man growled, prodding the man next to him.

When the sleepy-eyed tramp looked up at Rachel she felt her heart would break. It was Joe Maitland, but she could barely recognise him. He had a thick stubble on his grubby face and his eyes were bloodshot and bleary. His clothes were in tatters and his clasped hands were black and scarred from work. His previously well-brushed wavy hair was matted and filthy, and as he struggled to focus his eyes his mouth dropped open.

'Joe, it's Rachel. Don't yer remember me?' the young woman said in a shaking voice.

'It's Rachel!' Joe exclaimed to his companion, his eyes widening with surprise as he struggled to find his feet.

She took his arm and helped him stagger up. 'Yer gotta come back, Joe. Mum needs yer, we both need yer,' she said, her voice breaking as tears filled her deep blue eyes.

Joe took her by the arm and tried to lead her from the alley, his feet moving unsteadily over the cobbles. He turned his head towards her every few steps, as though not believing it was really her. 'Yer look like an angel from 'eaven,' he said in a husky voice. 'I thought I'd died when I looked up an' saw yer.'

Rachel gritted her teeth. She had found him at last and now she was going to take him home, whatever it took, regardless of what he said. 'C'mon, Joebo, let's get yer a cuppa an' somefing to eat,' she said, pulling on his arm.

Joe shied away but she held on to him tightly. 'C'mon, don't argue,' she said sharply.

They walked slowly up the steep cobbled lane which led out to Eastcheap and Rachel steered him towards the little cafe that she had visited on her earlier search. The moon had dropped down lower in the early morning sky and the air felt damp as they approached the brightly lit establishment. Rachel could see that Joe was beginning to tremble as she pushed open the door and stepped inside.

''Ello, Big Joe,' the owner called out in greeting, giving Rachel a strange look when he saw her holding on to his arm.

Joe nodded and started to fish down into his coat but Rachel had already taken a ten-shilling note from her pocket and laid it down on the counter. 'We want two mugs o' sweet tea, an' eggs an' bacon, please. Oh, an' fried bread,' she said quickly, aware that that particular breakfast was Joe's favourite.

'Will that be twice?' the cafe owner said, eyeing Rachel closely.

'Yes, an' two slices o' bread each,' she added.

They had found an end table and Rachel ignored the strange looks she was receiving from the other customers as she tucked into her early breakfast. The night air and the excitement had given her a ravenous appetite but Joe seemed to be struggling with his food.

'Is Carrie – I mean, is yer mum keepin' well?' he asked, avoiding her gaze.

'She's not stopped talkin' about yer, Joebo, an' I know she worries terrible in case yer not well.'

Joe breathed deeply and pushed away his plate. 'Look, luv, I know yer mean well an' I love yer for it,

599

but what's done's done,' he told her in a husky voice. 'I can't just walk back inter yer muvver's life now. Take a good look at me. Would she want somebody like me ter show up on 'er doorstep? Look at my 'ands,' he said, holding them out in front of him. 'D'yer know what that is? It's called the boozer's twitch. Take a look at these clothes. I've not 'ad 'em off me back fer weeks. Go 'ome, Rachel. Go 'ome an' find a nice young man who'll make yer 'appy instead o' spendin' yer time tryin' to act as Cupid. I'm not werf the time an' trouble.'

Rachel felt the anger rising inside her and she glared at him. 'Now just you wait a minute,' she almost hissed. 'Yer show me 'ow sick you are by 'oldin' out yer 'ands. That ain't somefing I've never seen before. Yer was like that before yer left us. Yes you are a boozer, but yer can stop. Yer can do it easy, an' I'll tell yer 'ow. Yer can fink what misery it's put on my mum every time yer take a drink. As fer yer clothes, Mum told me more than once that yer was the smartest man in the street at one time. Yer could be again. But that's not the bit that's made me angry – an' I am angry wiv yer, Joebo. It's what yer jus' said about me goin' 'ome an' findin' 'appiness. 'Ow can I ever be 'appy when I can see my mum fadin' a little bit every day? She misses yer terrible an' yer never out of 'er mind. I've seen the sadness on 'er face every livin' day, an' I've 'eard 'er cryin' in 'er room late at night. I know yer love 'er too, I just know. It's just yer stupid pride. Well, where's yer pride now? Big Joe, that's what they call yer over 'ere. Yer not Big Joe ter me anymore. Yer just a little Joe. I wish I'd never come ter find yer.'

Joe had seen the tears welling in Rachel's eyes as she berated him and when she suddenly pushed back her chair and ran from the cafe he staggered to his feet. The room seemed to spin around and he knocked into a table and then fell against the counter in his hurry to reach her. He stumbled and pushed his way anxiously towards the door and almost tripped out into the street, desperate to get to her before she ran away for ever.

Rachel was standing a few feet away, a handkerchief held up to her face, and with a heavy heart he slowly walked over to her side.

'Look, luv, I need a bath an' a shave first,' he said quietly, laying his hand on her arm.

'Does that mean yer comin' back?' Rachel said, her wet eyes wide as she bit the corner of her handkerchief.

'Go 'ome, darlin', before yer missed. I'll be over the water as soon as I straighten a few fings up.'

'Terday?'

'Yer can bet on it,' he replied, smiling at her.

'Promise me, Joebo.'

Joe took her by both arms and looked directly into her eyes. 'Big Joe's got a little pride left,' he said, a light appearing in his eyes. 'I promise, an' I never break promises.'

The lorries went out of the yard on time and then the horses were led from the stable and harnessed into the carts, while the aged but sprightly Sharkey leaned on his broom and waited patiently to begin his morning ritual. Carrie had overseen the daily operation, and when she was satisfied that everything was in order she went back into the house to take her usual cup of tea.

'Mum, I've got a feelin' about terday,' Rachel said casually, trying to keep her excitement under control.

'Yeah, I 'ave too,' Carrie said sarcastically as she sipped her tea. 'I 'ave that feelin' every day. The lorries might break down, the 'orses might go lame, an' I might get an angry customer ringin' me up about one o' my carmen.'

Rachel put down her teacup and got on with the cleaning. 'Terday could be a good day, Mum,' she said, glancing at her mother over the large ornament she was polishing.

Carrie puffed and shook her head slowly. 'Yer know, I worry about you, Rachel. I fink yer go about sometimes wiv yer 'ead stuck in the clouds.'

The knock on the door was ignored by Carrie and Rachel held her breath in anxiety.

'Well, go an' answer the door then,' Carrie said sharply.

Rachel shook her head as the doorknocker fell again, louder this time.

'God, yer gettin' impossible!' Carrie stormed as she hurried out to the door.

Rachel stood up with her hands clasped tightly together and she closed her eyes in a silent prayer. She heard the door open then for a few moments all was quiet. 'Oh God, please let it be 'im,' she whispered aloud, wringing her hands.

The sudden squeal of surprise brought Rachel rushing into the passage. It was Joe, and her mother was in his arms, her feet off the ground as he hugged her to him. Rachel rushed forward and Joe reached out for her, hugging her tightly to him as their tears wet the shabby collar of his coat.

'Joe, Joe! I thought I'd never see yer again,' Carrie cried, burying her head against his heaving chest.

Joe finally managed to free himself from the two tearful women. He held his shoulders back in an exaggerated display of indignation. 'Well then, am I allowed ter come in?' he said, before suddenly relaxing into a beaming smile.

'I told yer I 'ad a feelin' about terday, Mum, didn't I?' Rachel said, grinning widely.

'Remind me to 'ave a word wiv yer about that,' Carrie said, wiping her eyes.